GP 2/24 Fic £3.50

Three Novels

DAVID LODGE

Three Novels

Ginger, You're Barmy

The British Museum is Falling Down

How Far Can You Go?

Secker & Warburg LONDON

Ginger, You're Barmy first published in Great Britain
in 1962 by MacGibbon & Kee
The British Museum is Falling Down first published
in Great Britain in 1965 by MacGibbon & Kee;
this edition first published in Great Britain in 1981
by Martin Secker & Warburg Limited
How Far Can You Go? first published in Great Britain
in 1980 by Martin Secker & Warburg Limited

This collection first published in Great Britain in 1994
by Martin Secker & Warburg Limited,
an imprint of Reed Consumer Books Limited,
Michelin House, 81 Fulham Road, London SW3 6RB
and Auckland, Melbourne, Singapore and Toronto

A CIP catalogue record for this book
is available from the British Library
ISBN 0 436 20217 4

Phototypeset by Intype, London
First printed in Australia 1994
by Griffin Paperbacks

Contents

Ginger, You're Barmy

For Mary

Author's Note

The coarseness of soldiers' speech and behaviour is a well-known fact, the representation of which I found necessary to my purpose in this novel. Readers likely to find such representation disturbing or distasteful are warned.

I am very grateful for the assistance, on points of information, of Dr G. Billington, Arthur Harris, John Jordan, Marcus Lefebure, and a Regular Army officer who would, I am sure, prefer to remain nameless. None of these gentlemen is responsible for any errors or improbabilities which remain in the book.

The characters (including the narrator) and the action of the story are fictitious; but in the reference to the Lane Bequest picture I have associated my fictitious characters with an actual event, the true details of which are unknown to me.

D.L.

Ginger, you're barmy,
You'll never join the Army,
You'll never be a scout,
With your shirt hanging out,
Ginger, you're barmy.

Prologue

It is strange to read what I wrote three years ago. It is like reading another man's writing. Things have certainly not worked out as I expected. Or did I deliberately prevent them from so working out? I suppose my present circumstances derive, ultimately, from that visit to the w.c. on the train to London; but I am still not sure what I meant by it. I only remember that I felt I had to do something. At any rate, I take no credit for the action, for I regretted it bitterly later. If I take any credit at all, if I think any better of myself now, than I now think of myself *then*, – as I portray myself in these pages, – it is because I think I have realized that a deterministic conception of character and individual destiny is the subtlest of temptations that dissuade a man conscious of his own defects and others' needs from doing anything about them. I don't think I am a better person, or even a happier one; but perhaps there has been a small advance. I could never again write so unflattering an account of myself as the following, because it would open up so many awful possibilities of amendment. The whole story reeks of a curiously inverted, inviolable conceit.

It reeks too, for me, of the sweet, sickly smell of seaweed which hung about the Mediterranean resort where, in its original, shorter, unpolished version, it was written. Written in a confessional outpouring, at every moment that could be spared, – and at many that could not be spared without impoliteness. Written on beaches where the sun curled the paper and dried the ink as it flowed from the nib; written in the stifling bedroom of the *pension* while the rest of the world slumbered through the

9

siesta; written far into the night by the erratic light of a naked bulb that swung from the impact of bulky moths.

I say 'confessional' because, though there was little contrition about it, the impulse that drove me on to write, which welded the pen to my aching fingers for so many hours, was not a literary one. It was only when I returned to England, and re-read the sweat-stained, sand-dusted pages, that the demon Form began to whisper in my ear about certain alterations and revisions, particularly the aesthetic advantages of concentrating my time at Badmore into a few days, and recounting my weeks at Catterick in a series of flash-backs. And so, what had started out as an attempt to record and confront my own experience subtly changed into an agreeable exercise in the manipulation of bits of observed life. I became a *voyeur* spying on my own experience.

Even now, it seems, I am not immune from the insinuations of Form. It occurs to me that these notes, which I am jotting down on this momentous morning, might usefully form a prologue and epilogue to the main story. . . .

ONE

'I feel worn out. I think I'll get ready for bed,' said Pauline.

'O.K.'

This was the ritual. Ostensibly it meant that she could go to bed as soon as I left to catch the 12.15 coach back to Badmore. In fact it lent an added intimacy and excitement to our regular necking sessions last thing on Sunday nights. She took her night-clothes into the kitchenette, and I heard the taps running and the flare of the gas jet under the kettle. Pauline was very hygienic. Because there was only one bathroom to the whole house she could only have two baths a week. But on the other nights she washed herself from the waist up at the kitchen sink. I knew the extent of her ablutions because, a few weeks before, I had squinted into the kitchen through the narrow aperture between the door and the upright.

I got up from the divan and wandered over to the door. But I did not peer through the aperture. It had been too disturbing last time. I had only seen her bare back, but that was enough to set the mechanism of desire lurching into motion. It was only a back; but a nice, shapely back. And I had never seen her back completely bare before. Even the narrow straps of a bathing-suit top made all the difference, I discovered. If I looked now I might see more. But I did not want to see more, unless I could touch more.

'What are you doing, Jonathan?' said Pauline, her voice slightly muffled by a towel. 'Not peeping I hope?'

'Just looking for a match.'

'My lighter's in your jewellery box.'

I had given her the green tooled-leather jewellery case for her last birthday. Rummaging amongst the ceramic earrings and glass beads I found the little heart-shaped lighter. Then my eyes fell on an imprinted metal tab, at the bottom of the case, of the kind that you get from machines on railway stations. I took it out and read the inscription. It said: 'M.B. LUVS P.V.' A door in my mind I usually kept bolted suddenly gave way, and a wind of memories howled through me.

I was still holding the tab, mentally dazed and breathless, when Pauline came back into the bed-sitting room in her dressing-gown, brushing her hair. 'Would you like some coffee?' she was saying. Then, as I did not reply, she stopped brushing and looked at me.

'What on earth have you got there?'

I showed her, and she flushed slightly.

'I didn't know I still had it. Michael gave it to me as a joke once.'

'I know, I was there.'

'Were you? I don't remember.'

'I was watching from the train. And I didn't think it was a joke.'

Pauline was silent, a little sulky. 'Well it's all over now, anyway.'

'Is it?'

'Of course it is.'

'I wonder where he is now?'

'Who, Michael? I expect he's all right. He usually managed to fall on his feet.'

'That's just about the last thing you could say about him. He usually fell on his head.'

'Well, don't let's make ourselves miserable thinking about him now, just before you've got to leave. Come and sit down on the divan.'

This was usually my suggestion, and 'sit down' was a euphemism for 'lie down'. But I obeyed the summons sluggishly, and retained an upright posture. Pauline said:

'Darling, I believe you're jealous.'

'Not jealous. The opposite really. What's the word for feeling you don't deserve to be better off than somebody else? I don't think there is one.'

'Why should you feel like that?' asked Pauline, resuming her hair-brushing.

'I mean I've got you, and he hasn't, for one thing.'

'But darling, we suit each other so much better. Michael and I were never really suited. I was very fond of him – he was my first regular boy-friend. But I never had a moment free from worry. And with us . . . it's been so much fun. I mean, for instance, Michael never took me to a single serious play.'

'And I've never taken you to a dance.'

'Well I agree with you that going to the theatre is more worth while.'

Yes, I had indoctrinated Pauline very successfully. I had not only made her do what I wanted: I had persuaded her to like it. I was silent, and Pauline put down her hairbrush.

'You know, you *are* jealous, whether you admit it or not. I suppose you think I've kept that bit of tin for a souvenir. Well I haven't, and to prove it,' – she rose to her feet – 'I'll throw it away.'

She looked round the room, with somewhat comic puzzlement, for some way of disposing of the tab in a sufficiently decisive fashion. The fire, which would have been the obvious place, was a gas-fire. Finally she dropped the tab into a wastepaper basket.

'How do I know you won't ferret it out when I've gone?' I teased her.

'All right.' Her lips pursed in vexation, she retrieved the tab from the basket, opened the window above the divan, and flung the strip of metal into the garden.

'You could still look for it tomorrow morning,' I observed.

'Well, I don't intend to,' she replied crossly.

I laughed, and pulled her down on to the divan. After a token struggle she first submitted, and then responded to my caresses.

She always seemed to get more out of it than I did. At the first touch of my hand, which I slipped under her dressing-gown and pyjama-top, on her stomach, she lapsed into a kind of sensual trance. I enjoyed it all right, and my flesh signalled its response in the usual way, but I never stopped *thinking*, as she seemed to. Perhaps when it came to the real thing I too would stop thinking. Meanwhile my chief pleasure was in a sense of power over her body. There was also a certain academic curiosity in seeing how far I could go.

This time I seemed to be climbing higher up her rib-cage than usual, until my fingers met the soft protuberance of her breast. I held my breath like a thief who has trodden on a creaking floorboard, and then my hand closed over her breast. It felt good, but almost at once I was a little sad. This established a precedent, and yet no subsequent contact would be as exquisite as this. Pauline moaned faintly, 'Better not, darling,' and I withdrew my hand. But I continued to kiss her, guiding her back to the ground.

We lay together and smoked in silence for a while. Pauline yawned and stretched happily.

'Darling, it doesn't seem possible that you're going back to camp for the last time.'

'No, it doesn't.'

For nearly two years, the same hundred miles between Badmore and London covered in each direction, every week-end. Well, nearly every week-end. I had only missed two: once before the General Inspection, and once when I was inevitably kept back with the Rear Party at last Easter's Block Leave (having wangled my way out of every previous Rear Party). It annoyed me slightly that I had missed those two week-ends, but even so it must have been something of a record. It was fortunate of course that at Badmore week-end guard duties were done by visiting N.C.O.s who were on courses. Before I was made up I had paid impecunious troopers to do my week-end guards for me. Expensive, at fifteen shillings a time, but worth it.

'It certainly doesn't,' I repeated. 'I'm sure that next Sunday I'll board the coach to Badmore out of sheer habit.'

'No you won't, darling,' said Pauline gleefully, 'because we'll be in Majorca!'

'So we shall! I'd forgotten that delightful fact for a moment. What time is it again?'

'Six-fifteen in the morning at the terminus.'

'It's a good job they let us out a day early at Badmore.'

The following Thursday morning, the day after I was released from the Army, we were flying to Palma, on a cheap charter-flight, for a holiday. The prospect gave me great pleasure. To throw off my khaki and fly into the sun: it seemed a symbol and a celebration of my release from two years' curtailment of liberty. It would also eliminate that treacherous feeling of faint regret and nostalgia with which we part from any familiar environment, however uncongenial it has been. I had already planned to send to the 'A' Squadron staff from Majorca some glossy, glamorous picture-postcard with a gloating, jubilant message on the back. Perhaps not after all. It would only be a gesture towards that arbitrary, illusory 'comradeship' people talked about so glibly. Better cut off all connections with the Army at once. Except perhaps – for memory is like a sieve that lets the unhappy bits through – to set aside an occasional few minutes for meditation on how boring and tedious and exasperating it all was. And at times really miserable. The first few weeks at Catterick particularly. Catterick. That brought back Mike.

'What about that coffee?' I said.

My friendship with Mike Brady began on a platform of Darlington station on a Thursday late in August in the mid-fifties. I have forgotten what day of August it was, but I know it was a Thursday because all new intakes of National Servicemen were required to report to their training regiments on Thursdays, at fortnightly intervals. All over England that morning trains had drawn out of stations, out of great termini, out of village halts, with their cargoes of callow youths in varying moods of confidence, apprehension and fear: public schoolboys wondering if they would get a commission in father's old regiment (they needn't have worried, father had written to the Colonel); grammar school boys making resolutions to keep studying in preparation for the university (they scarcely opened a book for the next two years); office boys and factory workers and young fellows of every kind wondering how they could keep their girls or pay the H.P. on their motorbikes or generally enjoy the prosperity the newspapers accused them of (they soon found they couldn't).

I had come up to Darlington from King's Cross with a pretty fair cross-section. There was the ex-public schoolboy (a minor public school I guessed) who took command of the situation, and of the conversation once it started. He had flat, blond hair and a handsome face, and I took an instant dislike to him. He had been, we swiftly learned, a sergeant in his school O.T.C., and he remarked that he had brought his brasses with him. The significance of this observation escaped me at the time, but I envied him later. After he had succeeded in undermining the morale of the two West Country lads who sat opposite him, grinning awkwardly and twisting their hands, he turned to me and addressed me through my newspaper.

'Are you going to Catterick, too?'

He was a born officer; I was forced to lower my paper, and to reply.

'Yes. Isn't everybody on this train?'

'Not necessarily,' he said humourlessly. 'Which unit?'

'Eh?'

'Which regiment are you going to?'

I fished in my pocket, under his disapproving gaze, for my draft notice. 'Twenty-first Royal Tank Regiment,' I read.

'So am I. Did you apply for the R.A.C.?'

'R.A.C.?'

'The Royal Armoured Corps,' he explained testily. 'The R.T.R. is part of the R.A.C.'

'All these initials make me dizzy. No, I applied for the Education Corps. I'm hoping that this is just preliminary training.'

'Want a cushy time, eh? Well it's not a bad idea if you don't mind giving up the chance of a commission. You get made up to Sergeant automatically in the Education Corps. But I don't think you'll get in. Education Corps chaps usually do their Basic Training with the Infantry.'

I cursed his air of knowledgeability, the more heartily because I thought he might be right. What the hell would I do in the Armoured Corps for two years?

'Got your G.C.E.?' he asked.

'I've just taken my B.A.,' I said, hoping this would deflate him.

'Oh! Where?'

'London.'

He nodded, reassured. 'I'm going up to Oxford myself after the Army.'

Yes, you would, I thought. P.P.E. and hockey Blue. I flipped my paper up to my face. He turned to the remaining member of our little group, a rather slovenly, oafish sort of person, who had got into our compartment at Grantham.

'Are you going to Catterick?'

'Me? Naw.' He guffawed. 'Naw. Ah've 'ad Catterick.' He guffawed again. 'Ah've 'ad the Army.'

'You've done your National Service, have you?' I asked.

'Aye! T'day!'

We all laughed, a trifle edgily. Even the public schoolboy was a little taken aback, displeased to find himself a tenderfoot after all. Actually it wasn't such an ironical coincidence as we all imagined, for, as I afterwards discovered, intake day was also, officially, release day. One of us was taking the place vacated by this released soldier. I looked at him with curiosity. He didn't look very soldierly. His hair was long and his clothes were cheaply flashy – that North of England flashiness that is always about two years behind the South. His pimply brows were creased in some kind of mental effort. Finally his forehead cleared, and he said with a grin:

'Well, you've only got seven hundred and thirty days t' push!'

The train was slowing as it drew into Doncaster. He stood up and looked eagerly out of the window, took his bag from the rack and disappeared into the corridor.

'*His* unit must have been a shower,' said the public schoolboy, re-asserting himself.

I refused to make any further contribution to the conversation. The jubilation of the released soldier had disturbed me slightly. I realized how little thought I had given to the Army. It had been merely an irritating idea which I had brushed aside in the intensive study for Finals, and the anxiety of waiting for results. I realized that I knew nothing about the thing that I was to be for the next two years. I was glad when we reached Darlington, where I was able to shake off the public schoolboy. I was quite delighted when I saw Mike fiddling with an automatic machine on the platform.

'Mike!' I cried, 'Fancy seeing you here!'

'Hallo, Jon,' he replied, more calmly. 'Don't tell me what you're doing here. I can guess.'

'Catterick?'

He nodded.

'Which unit?'

'Eh?'

'Which regiment?'

'Oh . . . Twenty-first something or other.'

'So am I.' I was delighted. 'Come and have something to eat. We've got half an hour.'

He turned back to the automatic machine, and gave it a kick. 'This thing's got my last sixpence and it won't even give me a bar of chocolate.'

'Oh, have something on me.'

We went into the buffet, and I bought a couple of glossy pork pies and two cups of tea.

'Well, this is a coincidence,' I said. As with the released soldier, however, I was wrong. It wasn't really a coincidence. The number of forms you filled in might have led you to believe that some thought and discrimination went into the allocation of National Servicemen to particular branches of the Services. In fact it became quite clear that nobody paid the slightest attention to the forms, bundles of which were pushed into whatever pigeonhole happened to be empty. Mike and I had both come down from the same college of the same university at the same time, and it was not really surprising that we were destined for the same training regiment. However we were both pleased to find a friend amid the alien crowd of bewildered and unhappy youths shambling about Darlington station.

Our greeting was warmer under these circumstances than it might otherwise have been. For though Mike and I had both studied the same subject, English, and had both been in the same year, we had had very little contact with each other at college. Neither of us had been very typical undergraduates. I had lived at home, and devoted myself almost exclusively to study. But even had I participated more fully in 'Union activities' I doubt whether I would have been any more intimate with Mike, who had taken as little interest in the extra-curricular activities of the college as he had taken in the curriculum itself. I knew him mainly as a curiously aimless individual who could be seen at most hours of the day in the Union Bar, drinking beer and playing darts with a group of cronies who seemed hell-bent on occupying their time at the university as unprofitably as possible. He contributed some violent and obscure poems to the college literary magazine from time to time, and on one occasion had delivered in a debate what was said to be a striking speech against birth control. ('Mr Brady said that the people who advocated birth control always waited until they were born before doing so,' the college newspaper had reported.) That was the sum total of Mike's contribution to university life, as far as I knew.

I looked across the marble-topped table at Mike, and speculated, with some amusement, as to what the Army would make of him. In his soiled and neglected clothing he had always stood out from the calculated and self-conscious bohemianism of college like an authentic cowboy on a dude ranch. He wore now a dirty sports shirt open to the lower chest for want of buttons, and revealing the absence of a vest; an old brown sports jacket frayed at the cuffs and button-holes; a pair of shapeless, stained corduroy trousers; and black shoes that had never been polished since he walked out of the shop in them, leaving their disintegrating predecessors, no doubt, in the hands of a scandalized salesman. His vivid ginger hair was longer than I had ever seen it, hanging shaggily down over his white, freckled forehead and neck.

'Hanging on to your hair till the last minute?' I joked.

'Is it very long?' he asked innocently. 'I meant to have it cut, but I couldn't afford it.'

A topic of some embarrassment hung between us, and I was relieved when he acknowledged it.

'Congratulations on your First.'

'Thanks,' I replied. 'It was bad luck for you.' Mike had failed. I didn't really mean what I said. Mike hadn't been unlucky. He hadn't done a stroke of work, and the only surprise was that the Department had let him carry on at college after his first year.

'Yes,' he said, 'It was a nuisance. My mother got rather worked up.' He shook his head like a horse in summer, as if to rid himself of unpleasant memories. I was sorry for purely selfish reasons that Mike had failed. My First was still recent enough to give me a pleasant glow whenever I thought of it, and I would have welcomed the chance to gossip about the papers and other people's results. But this would have been tactless in the circumstances.

'Couldn't you have stayed on to do research?' he asked.

'I'm going back afterwards. I wanted to get this thing over first.'

'I'd have kept out of it, if I were you; they might abolish it soon.'

'Yes, that *would* be rather sickening. But I didn't want to start studying again so soon. I think it might do me good to have a break.'

God knows where I had got this idea from, that the Army might 'do me good', that two years of tedious serfdom would be 'a break'. I suppose I had concocted it as some kind of reassurance.

'Our train goes in a few minutes,' I said, glancing at the clock above us. 'We'd better move.'

Darlington was never for me anything more than a railway station, a junction on the route to London, a frontier post. One could almost trace the line of the frontier through the station. Where the London expresses pulled in the platforms were wide and spacious, with buffets, bookstalls, prosperous-looking travellers and smart girls. Mike and I now left this sector and crossed over to the smaller, bleaker, dirtier part which was the terminus for the branch line to Richmond. We got into a compartment of a train full of conscripts. The air was thick with Woodbine smoke and confused accents from every quarter of the British Isles. There was a constant restless activity in and about the train: doors were opened and slammed shut, faces were thrust in at the window, and abruptly withdrawn. People changed seats and sometimes compartments, charged past at a gallop, and rushed back again, leaned out of the windows, shouted gutturally to each other. There was a strange nervous hilarity in the air, as if a Clacton Excursion had got mixed up with the Siberian Special, and no one quite knew whether they would end up at Butlin's or a concentration camp.

Our first weeks in the Army were to lean towards the latter.

23

We had an indication of this as soon as our train, after wheezing and creaking through the soggy Yorkshire countryside for three-quarters of an hour, reached Richmond. In the station yard were several lorries drawn up to take us to our various units, each lorry with an N.C.O., and each N.C.O. with a mill-board.

'Twenty-first R.T.R. over here,' called out a tall, tense corporal with a thin, fair moustache. Mike and I clambered into the back of the awkwardly high vehicle. Finding the interior dark and dank, we stayed near the tailboard. Other conscripts scrambled in. One lit a cigarette.

'Put that cigarette out!' rapped the corporal sternly. There was a nervous tittering from the rest of the passengers as the offender hurriedly dropped his cigarette on to the floor, and stamped on it.

'And we don't want your dog-ends in the truck,' continued the corporal. The dog-end was duly picked up and ejected from the truck. The episode seemed such a naïve act of military assertiveness that Mike and I instinctively looked at each other and grinned.

'What are you two grinning at?' the corporal barked at us. 'The first thing you nigs can learn is that you don't smoke in army vehicles.'

We learned more than that from this brief episode: a new word, 'nig', meaning new conscript, an item in the weird philological tangle of army slang; and the realization that for the first time since childhood we were to be subjected to abuse and criticism without any appeal to the written and unwritten laws which control conduct in civilized life.

'Well, you're in the Army now,' I said to Mike, as the corporal called 'Roll it', and the truck jerked into motion.

'A rather unpleasant individual,' he remarked. 'I hope they're not all like that.'

Richmond is a lovely town blighted by the Army. Through it, in it and round it, Catterick Camp has spread like a pox, defacing the antique beauty of the town and the fine contours of the Yorkshire hills with its squalid architectural improvisation. The size of the camp is appalling. Our truck ground and whined through a seemingly endless expanse of squat huts huddled together round bleak parade grounds, forbidding barrack blocks, dejected rows of married quarters, and everywhere obtrusive military notice boards, with their strident colours and barbaric language of abbreviations.

Amiens Camp (the name was pronounced phonetically), the home of the Twenty-first Royal Tank Regiment, lay on the outskirts of Catterick. In one sense this was a disadvantage since one was at some distance from such amenities as Richmond offered, and in particular from the railway station. On the other hand, one looked from the slopes of Amiens Camp on to a noble landscape as yet unspoiled by the Army. There was something peculiarly oppressive about the older, inner part of the camp, where a military slum had grown up with the haphazard ugliness of an industrial town in the nineteenth century. Not that Amiens Camp was by any means new. Most of the huts had been condemned in 1939. But it suggested rural rather than urban decay: grass grew thick and rank around derelict huts, and a few sheep were allowed to graze on various parts of the camp to keep the vegetation under control.

We jumped down from the truck and were fed into the machine that dealt with new intakes. Clerks behind trestle tables took down details we had already given on various forms to various officials before being called up: name, address, occupation, education, sports, religion.

'Catholic,' said Mike, who was just beside me.

'R.C.,' muttered the clerk, penning the letters laboriously. 'Hobbies or special interests?'

'Red Indians,' replied Mike. The clerk looked up, startled.

'Now don't be funny . . .' he began.

'I'm perfectly serious. I'm very interested in Red Indians. My great-grandmother was raped by one. She was a pioneer in the Wild West. *I* may have Red Indian——'

'All right, all right.'

I was so absorbed by this exchange that I missed the question my own clerk was asking me.

'Religion?' he repeated.

'Eh? Oh, Agnostic.'

'What's that?'

'I don't subscribe to any religion.'

'Atheist,' he said.

'No, Agnostic. They're quite different.'

'You've got to be C. of E., R.C., O.D. or Atheist.'

'What's O.D.?' I asked, interested.

'Other denominations.'

'Put down Agnostic. I'll explain if necessary.'

He hesitated.

'How d'you spell it?'

Next we had a medical examination. We sat round the walls of a warm, stuffy room which smelled of perspiration, wearing only jackets and trousers, waiting to be called in to the Medical Officer. Three soldiers in denims were making some adjustments to the lights. We sat, quiet and depressed, hoping perhaps that the medical might result in a last-minute reprieve, while the three soldiers conducted at the tops of their voices, as if oblivious of our presence, the most obscene conversation I had ever heard in my life. It might almost have been laid on by the authorities as an introduction course in Army language. It was obscene not only in its liberal and often ingenious use of the standard expletive that lingers like a persistent echo throughout any conversation in the Army, but also in its use of words whose obscenity, at that stage, I could only guess at, and in its content: sexual encounters experienced at the last week-end, or anticipated at the next, the merits and demerits ('too messy') of virgins as sexual prey, the dangers of intercourse with menstruating women ('my mate said 'is bollocks turned blue') *et cetera*.

I listened with a kind of furtive fascination, furtive because I thought Mike might disapprove. But he seemed lost in thought.

'Very select company,' I said at last.

'Hmm? Oh, them. Yes they are rather tiresome. But you'll get used to it.'

Meditating on this remark, I realized that Mike had had far more acquaintance with this kind of thing than I. At school and at college I had lived a protected life. Unlike most students I had never worked during my vacations, but had prudently conserved my grant to be able to study. Mike, on the other hand, had taken all kinds of temporary jobs, in factories, on building sites, often, unknown to the college authorities, during term. He had, therefore, already a broad experimental knowledge of the manners and conversation of the vast, uncouth British proletariat which were to me, in my first weeks in the Army, a revelation.

One of the things I shall always associate with Basic Training is the exertion and indignity of carrying large, heavy objects. We always seemed to be moving our belongings at Catterick from one part of the camp to another. It started on that first afternoon when, after the cursory medical, we were issued with knife, fork, spoon, mug and bedding. A mattress, I found, was a peculiarly awkward thing to carry, since it was impossible to get one's arms round it in any way. Eventually, after dropping the mattress once, and smashing my mug in the process, I stumbled into a hut and flung my burden down on a vacant bed. I quickly tossed my blankets on to the next bed to keep it for Mike.

I sat on the bed and inspected the inhospitable interior of the hut. The floor was of uncovered stone flags. Several panes were missing from the windows. There was a low, battered tin locker beside each bed. Two deal tables and a few chairs made up the rest of the furniture. In the middle of the hut, at some distance from my bed, was a small, ineffective-looking stove. I was glad it was still August.

The hut was already partly occupied by new Regular recruits. It was the practice to train these with the National Servicemen, but to receive them a few days earlier. If this was intended to give the Regulars a certain superiority of status, it was partially successful. For in Basic Training one lost one's sense of proportion, as regards time. A fortnight later I looked upon a newly arrived intake, long-haired and civilian-clothed, with the jaundiced relish of an old lag seeing the prison gates open to admit some bewildered new detainee. So it was that we felt somewhat ill at ease before these Regulars of three days' seniority, who lay on their beds with an air of composure and familiarity, directing rhetorical questions at us and exchanging jokes with each other in coarse, harsh voices.

But their supremacy was not to last long. When training started in earnest we were all on equal terms, and soon the National Servicemen had the upper hand. The Army blundered, in fact, in training Regulars with National Servicemen. In any argument or exchange of abuse every National Serviceman could rely on the unanswerable riposte of 'Well, at least I haven't got three [or six, or twenty-two] years to push.' Ironically the Regular soldiers, who had voluntarily enlisted, were quickly infected by the National Serviceman's habit of 'counting the days'.

When Mike came in and deposited his bedding, we followed a bunch of Regulars to the cookhouse, a dark, high-roofed cavern, echoing with the clash of cutlery and the noisy mastication of sausages, mashed potatoes and gravy. It was a meal I found peculiarly repulsive at that hour, particularly the gravy, which I was too slow to intercept as it was splashed on to my plate. Mike ate his food mechanically, without discernible pleasure or distaste.

'Did you put down for the R.A.C.?' I asked him.

'No. I didn't put down for anything.'

'I put down for the Education Corps. I said that it was the only Corps in which I thought I could be of any use. Do you think they sent me here out of spite?'

'I doubt if they have the intelligence,' replied Mike. 'I doubt if they see anything inappropriate about putting you in the Armoured Corps. I expect they think they're honouring you.'

'I hope to hell I can get transferred,' I said, looking round at the dismal scene.

An officer in a black dress uniform, with highly polished belt and buckles, moved among the weary conscripts as they sat shovelling sausages and mash down their gullets. A sergeant with a black sash paced watchfully at his heels, as if he were conducting the officer through some zoo of cowed but potentially dangerous animals.

'Any complaints?' inquired the officer briskly as he came up to us.

The others at our table muttered 'No, sir'. I couldn't find the courage to complain, but Mike said in his soft, distinct voice:

'The potatoes are watery.'

The officer checked himself in the act of turning away. One could almost see the mechanism of his training grinding laboriously into motion. He appropriated my spoon and tasted a morsel of the potato with a rigid control of his facial muscles. Swallowing hard, he said:

'Nothing wrong with that.'

The sergeant lingered behind after the officer had walked off.

'Just arrived?' he asked, in a tone of ironically affected doubt.

'Yes,' replied Mike.

'Uhuh. . . . You'd better change your attitude quick, sonny, or you'll be in trouble. And just remember to address an officer as "Sir" and a sergeant as "Sergeant".'

The others at our table regarded Mike curiously.

'Pom,' said one of them, digging his fork into the potato.

'Eh?' said Mike.

'Pom. That's why it's watery.'

'Oh. Yes, I see.'

'What's Pom?' I asked Mike.

'Dehydrated potatoes. They mix it with water.'

I pushed my plate back in disgust.

'No wonder it's so vile. What's the object? Potatoes are cheap enough.'

'They're probably still using up stocks from the last war.'

We rose from the table and went over to the waste-food bin, into which I scraped most of my meal. I learned to avert my eyes while performing this task in future. As we moved towards the door I saw a face which I seemed to recognize.

'Just a minute, Mike, who's that over there? My God, surely it isn't——'

But it was: Gordon Kemp, another member of our department who had graduated that summer. My surprise was due partly to the fact that all three of us should be in the same place, but more to the change in his appearance, which had caused me to falter in recognizing him. His clumsily-cropped hair stuck up in tufts above a white, haggard face; his neck, always rather long and thin, sprouted like a sickly stalk from the gaping collar of his drab denims, which seemed to contact no part of his anatomy between his shoulders and ankles. He was eating greedily, and spluttered when we clapped him on the back.

'Oh hello,' he said finally. Then, with a grin, observing our civilian clothes, 'Just arrived?'

'Yes,' answered Mike. 'How's life?'

'Pretty grim at the moment. Bags of bull. But we pass out on Thursday, thank God.'

'Bull, what's that?' I asked him.

He grinned again. 'You'll soon find out.' He looked up at me as he sluiced down the last of his gravy-sodden potato with a gulp of the sweet amber-coloured tea. 'Congratulations,' he said, laying down his mug.

'Thanks,' I replied, taking the reference to my First with more alacrity than was perhaps consistent with modesty. 'You were unlucky not to get a First yourself.' Gordon had plodded his way to a deserved Upper Second.

'No, I was quite satisfied. I'd never have got a First in a thousand years. Mike here would have, if he'd done a stroke of work.'

Mike shrugged his shoulders. It was true, and the honesty of the remark was typical of Gordon. But it seemed to disqualify Gordon from membership of the small cell of cultured resistance to the Army which I was already subconsciously forming with Mike. Despite his gaunt appearance Gordon seemed to be almost enjoying the rigours of Basic Training; or at least applying himself to mastering them with the same dogged persistence he had brought to the study of Anglo-Saxon sound-changes and textual variants in *Love's Labour's Lost*.

'Must dash now,' he said, scrambling to his feet. 'Full kit layout tomorrow.'

'We're just going too.'

We followed him out to the tank of murky, lukewarm water in which we rinsed our plates and cutlery. Gordon's hut was in the same direction as ours, and we accompanied him for a while. We learned the reason for his zeal: he was set on getting a commission.

'Why d'you want one?' asked Mike.

30

He seemed somewhat taken aback by the question.

'Don't *you* want one?'

'I don't know. I haven't thought about it.'

'Well you get better living conditions for one thing. And it's always useful for getting jobs afterwards.'

'What sort of jobs?'

'Oh, industry, Civil Service, that sort of thing.'

We parted from him, and wandered back to our hut, which was chill and damp in the evening air. Mike threw himself down on his bed and smoked a cigarette. We exchanged a few desultory remarks about Gordon as I dusted the inside of my locker and unpacked my grip. I took out the Pelican translation of the *Inferno* by Dorothy Sayers, but found it difficult to concentrate. A few National Servicemen sat glumly on their beds, writing letters or watching the boisterous pranks of the Regulars. The dominant personality among the latter was an individual called Norman, squat and powerfully built, with short legs and a great pear-shaped head ravaged by what I took to be the legacies of venereal disease: he had what the Elizabethans called a 'French crown'. He spoke a thick, harsh dialect of the East Midlands. His favourite exclamation was 'a French letter wi' a patch in it', and his favourite threat 'I'll ride ya'. This last, when carried into action, consisted in his throwing himself on one of his mates who was lying on his bed and pretending to rape his victim by bouncing violently up and down on top of him. This had evidently become quite a sport among the group, and often half a dozen of them would pile on top of one man and pound the breath out of him, shouting and laughing. After the third such demonstration I closed my book in despair.

'Isn't there somewhere else we can go?' I asked Mike.

'I think there's a Naafi somewhere,' he replied, sitting up.

'Let's go and look for it.'

'Our friend Norman is rather like Caliban, don't you think,' he observed as we walked through the dusk. ' "A very land-fish".'

'That's Ajax, in *Troilus and Cressida*, actually,' I said. '*He's grown a very land-fish, languageless, a monster.* Thersites, Act

31

Three scene three, I think.' Catching the flicker of a grimace on his face I added hastily: 'But it fits him all right. So does Caliban.'

The Naafi canteen was a large, high room with round Formica-topped tables screwed to the floor at regular intervals and a long bar which supported two urns, some wizened doughnuts under a plastic cover and the breasts of a pasty-faced girl who surveyed us listlessly as we approached her. The canteen was almost empty except for a group of seasoned-looking veterans who were sitting round a table littered with beer bottles. Mike's eyes brightened as he saw the latter.

'Can you lend me a pound, Jon?'

'Sure.'

'I feel like a drink. In fact I feel like a whisky.' He asked the girl for a whisky.

'What d'you think this is, the Officer's Mess?' she replied, without lifting her breasts from the counter.

'Oh all right, I'll have a beer. What have you got on draught?'

'Only bottled.'

Mike sighed. 'Bass?'

'Yes.'

'Red Triangle then.'

I was glad to see that there was a better selection of food behind the bar than on it. I bought a ham roll and a cup of coffee. We occupied one of the corner tables. Mike swallowed a third of his beer and lit a cigarette.

'Penny for your thoughts,' I said.

'Not worth it. I've just taken a pound off you.' He added: 'I must write off for some money.'

'Don't worry, I've plenty.'

After a pause Mike said:

'Actually, I was thinking that if I had had any sense I wouldn't be in this place.'

I was pleased to hear this. I had been trying to disguise from Mike my own increasing dismay at the prospects opening up on all sides, fearing that he might consider me rather weak.

'Where would you be then?'

'In Ireland.'

'*Are* you Irish, Mike?'

I had been wondering about this. His name and physical appearance seemed to suggest that he was Irish, but his speech was distinguishable from standard Southern English only by a certain melodic softness of the vowels.

'No, unfortunately. Otherwise I wouldn't be here. My parents are Irish, but I was born in England.'

He told me something about his family background, which was a vivid miniature of recent Irish political history. The Bradys were a politically conscious clan, fervently nationalist and anticlerical. Mike's great-uncle had been a friend of Parnell. His father, a medical student at the time, had been closely associated with the Easter Rising of 1916. He still treasured a piece of rusty thread with which he had stitched a flesh-wound of Pearse's. Mr Brady had escaped the reprisals after the failure of the Rising, but he had continued to support the Nationalist movement until, disgusted by the betrayal of Partition, he had emigrated with his wife, paradoxically to England, in 1924. He re-qualified as a doctor and set up practice in Hastings. Mike had been born there in 1934.

'Has your father ever been back to Ireland?'

'Never.'

'Have you?'

'Oh yes. I go there nearly every summer. I was in Dublin this summer, actually. I got my call-up papers there. I burned them, and took a job as a guide to American tourists.'

'Why did you come back?'

'My mother sent me a telegram saying my father was seriously ill.'

'Oh, I'm sorry Mike. Is he all right now?'

He smiled wryly. 'It was only a cold. The telegram was a trick, to get me back to England. My mother didn't want the disgrace of having a deserter in the family.'

I groped unsuccessfully for a reply. Mike's laconic words opened a door on a violent, dramatic family life quite beyond my experience or comprehension. Ever since I had won my scholarship to a grammar school I had never encountered or expected any objection to my conduct from my parents. They were both over forty when I, their only child, was born, and they still seemed somewhat dazed by surprise. Sometimes I wondered if they had stumbled on the trick of procreation by accident; at other times I wondered if I were their child at all. They behaved towards me like an honest peasant couple in an old myth, entrusted with the care of some divine changeling. My by no means exceptional academic success had awed them into a timid submission to my will. Since my own temperament leaned naturally towards a tranquil, prudent, industrious existence, our relationship was an untroubled one.

I was beginning to feel tired, and had heard that we would be woken at some impossible hour the next morning, so I suggested that we should return to the hut. Most of the occupants were in bed, some sitting up reading or writing letters, some asleep, despite the noise and chatter of the Regulars, some just staring vacantly at the ceiling, dreaming perhaps of the girls, suits and record-players they had left behind them. One – a married man with a family, as I later discovered – was reading a child's comic, *Beano* I think it was.

I changed into the pyjamas my mother had packed for me, and got into bed. Mike, like most of the others, slept in his underpants, and, like most of the others, continued to do so after pyjamas had been issued. This curious distaste for pyjamas among a large section of the male population of Great Britain, was another of those small, interesting discoveries I was constantly making in the first weeks of National Service.

Just as the hut was settling down for the night, a lance-corporal came in, followed by a young fellow entirely hidden behind a mattress. The lance-corporal dropped a bag on a vacant bed, and guided the new recruit towards it.

'Here you are,' he said.

A muffled 'Thank you' was heard from behind the mattress, which dropped on to the bed to reveal the latest and unhappiest addition to our ranks. He was a slender, willowy boy whose physical appearance suggested that he was a product of aristocratic inbreeding. The refinement implied in his fine, white skin and delicate bony fingers was qualified by a certain foolishness and even decadence suggested by his weak mouth, receding chin and pale, alarmed eyes. And even in those first few minutes I noticed that all his limbs were just perceptibly out of control. He fumbled awkwardly with the straps of his bag, dropped several objects several times, and his rather large feet were constantly getting entangled with the legs of his bed. At the time I put this down to nervousness. For he was unfortunate in that the only vacant bed was in the midst of the Regular camp at the far end of the hut. The Regulars welcomed the diversion afforded by his late arrival.

'Miss yer train mate?' asked one of them.

'Yes, I did actually,' replied the newcomer, blushing. There was a general laugh. Someone echoed the 'actually'.

'Yer wanner watch it mate. Yer'll be in the guardroom before yer've got yer uniform on.' More laughs and cat-calls.

'Don't listen to them, youth,' said Norman, with mock sympathy. 'They're as thick as a cow's c——t.'

'I beg your pardon?' said the young boy, plainly uncomprehending, but hoping that this misshapen creature might be friendly.

''E don't understand you, Norman,' someone shouted. 'You're too ignorant.'

'Shut up or I'll ride ya.'

'Why don't you ride 'm. 'E's got a nice arse.'

The young boy flushed violently.

'What's your name, youth?' inquired Norman.

'Higgins.'

'No, your first name.'

'Percy.'

Norman turned his head away, grinning with triumph at the information he had extracted. His pals crowed with delight, tossing the name to each other on gales of laughter. Percy's name gave them a kind of purchase on him, and he was assailed with questions from all sides. If he had had any sense he would have remained silent and got into bed as quickly as possible. But he took a painfully long time over his unpacking, and answered all the questions he understood with instinctive politeness. Those he didn't understand were answered for him.

'Where d'you come from, Percy?'

'I was born in Lincoln, but I've been at school in Hampshire.'

'Was it a girls' school, Percy?'

'No, it was a boys' school.'

'Percy, 'ave you ever shagged a girl?'

'No, Percy shagged the other boys.'

When Percy asked where the w.c. was there was a cry of 'Norman, take Percy to the shit-'ouse, 'e wants a piss.' And when the unfortunate boy took off his trousers preparatory to going to bed, the noise grew to a crescendo. One Regular writhed in his bed, vividly simulating uncontrollable sexual excitement. We National Servicemen at the other end of the hut sympathized with Percy, but made no protest. There was in fact nothing really malicious about the ragging; the pain was all in Percy's acute sensitivity, the tenderness of which none of us appreciated until he began to go very red in the face, and puffy around the eyes.

'Christ, I think the poor fellow's going to cry,' Mike said to me.

The poor fellow was evidently a glutton for punishment, because he proceeded to kneel down and say his prayers. This took his tormentors by surprise. A certain atavistic respect for religion enforced a lull, but they soon recovered themselves. Since he no longer answered their questions they were obliged to use him as a kind of reflector for their own exchange of insults. Norman was begged not to take advantage of Percy's posture. This inspired one of his pals to get out of bed and stand in an obscene attitude behind Percy. At this, Mike tossed back his blankets and stepped over to the Regular, tip-toeing on the cold stone flags. His white, muscular body was covered with fine, red hair.

'Why don't you leave the poor fellow alone,' he said quietly. There was a sudden, expectant hush. Percy remained kneeling, but looked up wonderingly at his rescuer.

'It's only a joke, mate.'

'Well, the joke's over. I should get back into bed if I were you.'

36

'Who are you ordering about? I'll do what I fugging well like,' blustered the other.

This tense situation was resolved by the re-entrance of the lance-corporal who had originally escorted Percy to the hut.

'What the fugging hell's going on in here,' he roared. 'I could hear the row half a mile away.' His eye took in the little tableau around Percy's bed. 'Get back into bed you three,' he said sharply. Percy crossed himself and got between the blankets. The other two returned to their beds in silence. The lance-corporal stood at the door with his hand on the light-switch.

'If I hear another squeak out of this hut tonight I'll have you all on fatigues every night for the next five weeks,' he said. Then he put out the light.

TWO

I left Pauline's flat at the usual time, 11.35. It was my practice to propose leaving at 11.20, so that I could enjoy her pleas to stay a little longer without worrying about missing the coach. Even if I did miss it there was the 1.30 milk-train from Waterloo, but it was a slow journey and meant a long, cold walk from the station. I took the tube to Waterloo, changing at Leicester Square almost unconsciously: I had done it so often.

The car park opposite the Old Vic was full of coaches, though already several were leaving, packed with soldiers, sailors and airmen. The hot-dog stall and the coffee-stall were doing a good trade. A lot of people are going to be sorry to see the end of National Service, I reflected. Ben Hardy for instance. I caught sight of him beside his big grey Bedford Duple, talking to another driver. Ben nodded as I came up to the coach door.

'Nice week-end, Corporal?'

'Fine thanks. Last time you'll be seeing me, Ben.'

'What! Getting demobbed?'

'Next Wednesday.'

'Bet you're sorry.'

'Oh sure! I'm going to sign on.'

'Get out!' said a voice from behind. 'There's only one thing worse than a Regular and that's a National Serviceman what signs on.'

I looked round and saw Chalky White, who worked in the Q.M.'s Stores. He was a curious creature, by turns witty, naïve, boastful and timid. His long chin, hunched shoulders and the limping, hopping movement of his spindly legs always put me in mind of a wounded heron. We climbed into the coach.

'After you,' I said, motioning him into the inside of the seat. My action was prompted not by politeness but by self-interest: it was easier to sleep sitting on the outside, with one's feet in the aisle.

'Nice week-end, Chalky?'

'Fair. Very fair. We played at this pub see. Got thirty bob each. Not bad eh? *Oh I never felt more like singin' the blues . . .*' Chalky drummed on the window ledge with his finger-tips. He played the washboard in a skiffle-group.

'How about you, Jon? Good week-end?'

'Very pleasant. I completed my plans for my holiday.'

'What, after your release?'

'That's right.'

'When's that then?'

'Next Wednesday.'

'Next *Wednesday*!' His voice rose several octaves. 'I thought it wasn't for three or four weeks yet.'

'Wednesday's the day, Chalky. On Tuesday I'll be handing you my boots and uniform and the rest of the junk with the greatest of pleasure.'

It was difficult to refrain from this ceremony of rubbing your imminent release into everyone you spoke to, when for two years you had suffered the same thing from others.

'How long have you got to push, Chalky?'

'Nine bloody months,' he replied gloomily.

'Get some service in, youth,' said a flat Midland voice. Lance-Corporal Boon, Orderly Room clerk, carefully placed his grip on the luggage rack, and sat down beside me on the other side of the aisle, spreading his hands over his fat khaki-clad thighs. Since being made up he wore uniform on leave – in order to show off his stripe at home, according to Chalky. As Chalky said, 'It must be a pretty crummy place if they get worked up over a lousy stripe.'

'I see they've got you down for a guard tomorrow night,' observed Boon, looking at me.

'Bollocks! First I've heard of it,' I exclaimed.

'It was on Squadron Orders on Friday,' said Boon smugly. 'But I suppose you didn't see it, seeing you scived off at lunch-time.'

I had wangled permission from my superior, Captain Pirie, to leave early on Friday, on the pretext that I had to see the Prof. at college about my research. I had gone up by train and booked a coach ticket for the return journey only.

'That bastard Fotherby, I bet,' I said venomously. 'I'll fix that tomorrow morning.'

'You're due for a guard, aren't you?' said Boon. He took a proprietary interest in Squadron Orders, which he rolled off on a duplicator. He always enjoyed telling people that they were down for a duty, before they read it for themselves. 'I noticed you haven't done one for some time.'

'Christ, Boon,' I said. 'Do you memorize every bloody guard anybody does? Haven't you got something better to think about?'

'Keep your hair on. I thought you'd like to know.'

'That's 'ard, that is,' interposed Chalky, 'Doin' a guard in your last week.'

'Hard?' I muttered. 'It's bloody ridiculous. I know who it is. Sergeant-Major Fotherby, the new-broom boy. I'll soon settle *him*.'

But inwardly I was not so confident. My whole strategy at Badmore had been directed towards securing my own comfort and convenience by ingratiating myself with key figures of author-ity. To my immediate superior, Captain Pirie, I was indispensable, and there was a tacit agreement between myself and the senior officers of the unit that I would contain Pirie's innate tendency to commit acts of disastrous folly. But Captain Pirie, besides being President of the Regimental Institutes (that is, in charge of the welfare and recreational side of unit life) was also the Officer Commanding 'A' Squadron. And while I held sovereign sway over his activities as P.R.I., being myself the P.R.I. clerk, in his capacity as O.C. 'A' Squadron he was under the influence of the Squadron Sergeant-Major. For most of my time at Badmore this post had been filled by a bored veteran of the North African war, whose goodwill I had experienced no difficulty in enlisting, since I was able to get him sports equipment for his son at a considerable discount. A month before, however, he had departed, to be replaced by Sergeant-Major Fotherby, a sour, sardonic individual, whose most eloquent comment on Badmore was a harsh, contemptous laugh. I had lacked the time and – as my release was imminent – the inclination to win him over. And although Captain Pirie was in some ways frightened of me, he was even more frightened of Sergeant-Major Fotherby. I began, therefore, unwillingly to resign myself to doing the guard the following evening.

The coach was now full. Ben climbed into his seat and started the motor. We lurched into motion, and I settled back into my seat. The long, familiar journey was beginning, – for the last time in this direction.

As we passed London Airport a plane roared over our heads, lights winking from tail and wing-tips. Usually I felt a pang of envy at this sight. It always seemed a kind of travelling – exciting, adventurous, purposeful – essentially different from my wasteful shuttling backwards and forwards between London and Badmore. I nudged Chalky and remarked:

'That's me in four days' time.' But he was asleep.

Chalky slept until we swung off the A30 into the car park of the 'Alnite Kaff'. We climbed out of the coach and walked stiffly into the hot, smoky café, blinking in the light. Chalky moved like a homing pigeon to the gaudy juke-box and selected a tune.

> Bye bye love
> Bye bye happiness
> Hello loneliness
> I think I'm gonna die
> Bye bye my love bye bye.

I got two cups of tea and took them back to a table. The café, as always at this time, was full of soldiers returning to camp by car, motor-cycle or coach. They sat at the greasy tables, staring vacantly, exchanging few words, tapping their feet gratefully to the music, nourishing the memory of the leave just spent, plan-

44

ning the next one. There was an atmosphere of defeat in the air, the dejection of a retreating army. But for once it did not touch me. I was leaving the battle shortly. This was the last time I should visit the 'Alnite'. I looked round me with a new attentiveness. Recently I had found myself registering the dull repetitive actions of my service life with this detached precision. It was a strange interior ritual, a litany to which the constant response was 'This is the last time.'

As the coach drew away from the café Ben extinguished the lights inside. This was illegal, but was a welcome aid to sleep. At the back of the coach a quartet of Regulars were trying to prolong the beery euphoria of their week-end's leave by singing bawdy songs.

> *We are from Green Street, good girls are we,*
> *We take a pride in our virginitee.*

But the majority of the passengers were, like myself, respectable week-end commuters, who preferred to pass the journey in a decent silence and, if possible, sleep. After several remonstrations the singers quietened down, and I dozed uneasily. Chalky's head, the hair of which was almost solidified with Brylcreem and dirt, fell on to my shoulder. I shrugged it off, but it kept lolling back. I stood up on the pretext of getting something from the rack, and Chalky overbalanced. He woke up and swore at me.

'You shouldn't put your head on my shoulder,' I explained. 'I'm not your tart you know.'

'Nah,' he replied, 'She's got bigger tits for one thing.'

'How d'you know they're real, Chalky?' asked a voice from the darkness. A little ripple of laughter spread round us.

'Wouldn't you like to know,' said Chalky sourly, settling himself to sleep again, this time inclining his head towards the window.

But I found it difficult to sleep. The little exchange about Chalky's girl brought back the moment on Pauline's divan a few hours before. Our relationship was approaching a critical point. There was a ratchet on love-making: you couldn't go back, you could only go on, or stay put. And there was a time-limit on

45

staying put. Looking back over the last few weeks it seemed to me that the ratchet had been clicking over faster than usual lately. At Palma, anything might happen. I forced myself to be more exact: what might happen was that Pauline would be ready for me, would want me to take her. It was essential to decide in advance what course of action I would adopt in such a situation. Otherwise it might be awkward and embarrassing and spoil our holiday.

I considered the matter coolly. I had more or less decided that I would marry Pauline, – I couldn't think of anyone who would be more suitable, – and I was slightly hesitant about applying the have-now-pay-later principle to her virginity. If I did deflower her it would not affect my intention to marry her, but it might blunt the edge of pleasurable anticipation. I have always tried to avoid occasion for regret, the most lingering of all the unpleasant emotions, by prudent foresight. This, then, was a consideration to be weighed carefully. On the other hand I had no intention of marrying till I had completed my research and obtained a satisfactory post. That would be at least two years from now. It seemed unlikely that our self-control would stretch over such a long period: and if it had to give way, would not our holiday in Palma be an appropriate time and place? And at the same time I could propose that we get engaged. Such a sizeable deposit would go a long way towards overcoming my reservations about the hire-purchase system.

The remaining problem was how to provide myself with contraceptives. I regretted the fact that I had not considered these matters before. For it was one of my duties as P.R.I. clerk to indent, from time to time, for contraceptive sheaths (10 per cent discount) which were distributed by the regimental barber. They arrived regularly at the office, wrapped in plain brown paper parcels with a slip enclosed trusting that the goods would meet our requirements for planned parenthood. With a little more time at my disposal I could have obtained what I wanted through the comfortable anonymity of the post. But delivery usually took four or five days, and I couldn't risk not having them when I left Badmore. I had little enough time to play with between leaving the camp and boarding the plane; and I couldn't have a potentially embarrassing brown paper package following me around in the post. I would have to get them from Henry the barber.

At this point I must have dozed off. The next minute, as it seemed, I was woken by the lights which came on in the coach. We were back. I gave Chalky, hunched up against the window, a rough shake. He swore, and opened his eyes, blinking in the light. We stepped down from the coach, and stood for a moment buttoning our coats as Ben drove away to drop the rest of the passengers at another part of the camp.

The shape of a gutted tank of the First World War, which stood outside the camp on a grass mound, loomed up above us. Chalky cast a nervous glance at it as we moved away. The story went that it was haunted by a German soldier who had been burned alive inside it. The tank had been captured by the Germans and used by them, until a British patrol had recaptured it by setting fire to it. Two of the crew had escaped, but one had been trapped inside. I had never met anyone who had seen the ghost, but the story was widely believed, and many soldiers would make a long detour rather than enter the camp by this entrance when alone, late at night. Guards responsible for this part of the camp studiously avoided even getting the tank in sight.

As we turned the corner of one of the hangars a guard came towards us, his pick-shaft tapping on the ground like a wooden leg. He was a friend of Chalky's, and asked him for a cigarette. Chalky gave him a bent Woodbine. At the Q.M.'s Stores Chalky and I separated.

I pushed open the door of number 4 hut and inhaled the familiar sweet-sour odour of dust, bad breath and perspiration. I switched on the light to plot a course across the hut which would avoid chairs and tables. Huts were not inspected on Sundays, and there was the usual squalid disorder. Tattered Sunday newspapers littered the floor: the pin-ups leered up at me with a jaded, ravished air. Mugs half-full of stagnant tea stood on tables marked with sticky rings. The windows were all shut. I opened two. Someone groaned and cursed. I switched off the light and felt my way across the floor to the far end of the hut where I had a small, partitioned-off cubicle known as a 'bunk'. I switched on my bedside lamp, which illuminated a shelf of books, and the Toulouse-Lautrec poster I had pinned to the wall. Slipping gratefully into bed, I glanced at my watch. Three-thirty. Ben had done quite good time. Soon the autumn fogs would be holding him up. But not me.

As I waited for sleep I thought about Pauline, Palma, and my errand at the barber's. A fragment of a poem by Mike, printed in the college magazine (the editor of which was subsequently forced to resign), floated into my mind. Something about *The rubber-gloves of lechery*. No, *The rubber-gloves of* prudent *lechery*, that was it. And there was an echo of Blake. After about ten minutes' strenuous effort I had assembled seven lines:

> *It's not the harlot's cry,*
> *But the contraceptive sheath*
> *From street to street*
> *Will weave old England's winding sheet;*
> *The rubber-gloves of prudent lechery*
> *Leave no traces*
> *Rifling the virgin's bottom drawer . . .*

The lines didn't scan or rhyme very well, but, recalling the general nature of Mike's poetry, this was not necessarily an indication that my memory was at fault. Pleased with my success, I relaxed and fell swiftly asleep.

'Stand up, Brady, Browne, Fallowfield, Higgins, Peterson.'

Mike and I, the first two named, stood up with the others. On the Monday after our arrival at Catterick, 'C' Squad was addressed by its N.C.O. – Corporal Baker, the tall, moustached corporal who had greeted us at the station. Corporal Baker was not, unfortunately for us, typical of the R.T.R. soldier. The Tanks (as distinct from the cavalry, who were burdened with an older tradition), tended to produce a particular type of trooper and N.C.O.: squat, stooped and grimy, with a healthy contempt for the wilder excesses of 'bull'. Corporal Baker had somewhere acquired that fanatical reverence for meticulous turn-out and drill which made him, in the Army's eyes, so admirably suited to the training of raw recruits. He was tall, thin and wiry; his skin was stretched tightly over the bones of his cheeks and jaw, and shone from the closeness of his shaves. His uniform was impeccably pressed and pleated, and his belt bit cruelly into his narrow waist. Every ounce of surplus flesh seemed to have been burned away by his energy and bad temper.

He looked at the six of us who were standing. The other members of the squad, National Servicemen and Regulars, also regarded us curiously.

'The Personnel Officer,' he began, with a faint sneer, 'has seen fit to class you lot as Potential Officers. I want to get a few things straight before we start. You've been called Potential Officers because you're supposed to be educated. Though Christ knows why, seeing that one of you failed his degree and another couldn't even pass his School Certificate.' He looked at Mike and Percy.

'But even if some of you *are* supposed to be educated, even if you have degrees in every subject under the bleeding sun, that doesn't mean you're any better as soldiers. In my experience it makes you worse. You needn't think that because you're Potential Officers you've got a cushy time in front of you. You haven't. Even if you manage to pass Uzbee and Wozbee, which I very much doubt, you've got several months of training at Mons which will make the next five weeks seem like a kindergarten. And they won't be a kindergarten, I'll see to that. As Potential Officers I shall expect your conduct and turnout to be outstanding. And if they aren't, I'll want to know the reason why.'

He surveyed us with a thin-lipped, malicious smile, displaying two rows of regular, sharply-pointed teeth. His cold blue eyes rested on each of us in turn. First me.

'Name?'

'Browne.'

'Browne, *Corporal*.'

'Browne, Corporal.'

His eyes flickered to the papers in front of him. 'You've been writing a lot of letters to the Army, Browne.' (I had written once, as requested, to inform the authorities of my Finals result, and had taken the opportunity to reiterate my desire to go into the Education Corps. Evidently the letter had been forwarded to the 21st R.T.R.)

'Only one.'

'*Corporal!*'

'Corporal.'

'Wanted to go in the Education Corps, eh? That's where all the scivers want to go. Sitting on your arse all day teaching a lot of nigs their ABC. Well you're unlucky this time.' His eyes wandered to Mike.

'Name?'

'Brady, Corporal.'

'Well it's nice to see you now you've had your hair cut. When you arrived I thought we'd called up a ginger rug.' He waited for, and got his laugh. Mike presented a very altered appearance; deciding to go the whole hog he had directed the regimental barber to give him a crew-cut, which conformed to regulations, but enabled him to retain a certain grotesque individuality.

Baker dealt cursorily with Fallowfield and Peterson. Fallowfield was the blond ex-public schoolboy I had come up with in the train. Fortunately he was not in our hut. Peterson was also from a public school, but was separated from Fallowfield if not by a social abyss, at least by a pretty sizeable trench. Peterson was an Etonian, and carried about with him an almost tangible aura of nonchalant charm and confidence. His father had been in the Greys, and there was little doubt that if he conducted himself with a mere token show of enthusiasm he would get his commission. Fallowfield's school, on the other hand, had only just crept into the Headmasters' Conference. Although he might easily obtain a commission in one of the less exclusive infantry regiments, or in the Service Corps, it would not be easy for him to become an officer in the R.A.C., which still, as regards its officers, retained something of the traditional and entirely unjust-ified sense of superiority of the old cavalry. And it was such a commission that Fallowfield desired. He knew what efforts it would require, and in contrast to Peterson he was tense, anxious, and deadly serious. One could be sure that if the unthinkable happened, and neither got his commission, Peterson would adapt himself with cheerful amusement to life in the ranks, while Fal-lowfield would fret and pine.

Finally Baker turned on Percy.

'Higgins?'

'Yes, sir?'

'You don't call me sir, you fool. My name's Corporal Baker.'

'I beg your pardon, Corporal.'

'Why in Christ's name did they make you a P.O.?'

'I don't know, Corporal. The officer said he'd give me a chance.'

'How old are you?'

'Eighteen, Corporal.'

'Eighteen, and you haven't passed your School Certificate?'

'I was rather backward in Latin and Greek, Corporal.'

There was a general laugh. Baker closed the proceeding by saying, 'Thank Christ we've got a Navy.' We rose to our feet with a clatter of boots and capsized benches, and lined up outside the hut for our first drill instruction.

That Fallowfield and Peterson were P.O.s was of course in the nature of things. Mike, Percy and myself had drifted into this category without premeditation. On the second day in Amiens Camp my already enfeebled hopes of eventually getting into the Education Corps had been crushed. Between being issued with boots and having my hair cut I had a brief, unprofitable interview with an irritable and overworked Personnel Officer. My immediate resentment of his manner was evidently reciprocated, for later I had the opportunity of reading the comments he made that day on my training record sheet: *Educated up to university level: thinks too much of himself.* What I read later only confirmed the impression I received during the interview itself. It was then that I first began to realize how uncongenial the Army was going to be.

I dimly perceived that I had been wrenched out of a meritocracy, for success in which I was well qualified, and thrust into a small archaic world of privilege, for success in which I was singularly ill-endowed. I was brusquely told to forget about the Education Corps. Even if there were a vacancy in the latter I could not be transferred because the R.A.C. was senior in the line to the Education Corps, and a man could not be transferred from a corps of greater seniority to one of lesser. All my arguments broke on this granite wall of irrationality. Because I had been arbitrarily allocated, contrary to my wish, to the R.A.C., which aroused in me neither loyalty nor interest, I was to be barred, by a meaningless convention, from the one occupation in which I might have been of some use to the Army and to myself, and to be retained in a position which promised to be equally unprofitable to us both. I put this, as politely as I could, to the Personnel Officer. He flushed and made a visible effort to control himself.

'Look . . .' (he glanced at his papers to remind himself of my name) 'Browne. You've only been in the Army for two days, so I'll make allowances. I'll just tell you that you could be put in the guard-house for what you've just said. Forget about the university. Forget about the Education Corps. You're in the R.A.C. for two years, and you might as well make the best of it.

'Let me make the situation quite clear to you. On Monday you begin your Basic Training, which lasts for five weeks. You will then receive trade-training, unless you are a Potential Officer. The four trades open to you are: Signaller/Gunner, Gunner/Driver, Driver, or Clerk. If you wish I can put you down as a Potential Officer, since your educational qualifications warrant it. In that case you will have a short P.O. Course here, at the end of which you will go before Uzbee, or Unit Selection Board. If you pass that you will go to Wozbee, or War Office Selection Board. If you pass that you will go to Cadet School, and if you are successful there you should receive a commission in about ten months' time, though it is extremely doubtful whether you would get a commission in the R.A.C. Probably an infantry regiment, or the Service Corps.'

'Excuse me, sir, but you just said that I couldn't be transferred from the R.A.C.'

He reddened and looked at me sharply. 'The situation is different for officers. There aren't enough places for all the cadets who would like commissions in the R.A.C. Now do I put you down as a P.O. or not?'

Disheartened and demoralized, I pondered dully.

'Come on, Browne, I haven't all day.'

I told him to put me down as a P.O.

Mike was interviewed immediately after me. While the Personnel Officer was committing his unfavourable impressions of me to paper, we had a moment in which I told Mike the unsatisfactory result of my interview. Then his name was called, and I sat and sulked in the ante-room while I waited for him.

It was depressing to find myself in a situation in which all the possibilities were equally unpalatable. I did not want to be an officer. I did not want to be a Signaller/Gunner. I did not want to be a soldier, period. However I thought in my innocence that a P.O. might have an easier time, and I had therefore elected to be one. Even then I felt a certain uneasiness at having entered for a competition I did not particularly want to win. But my main anxiety was that Mike should make a similar choice, and so bear me company. I was relieved to find my hopes fulfilled. His interview had gone more easily than mine, perhaps because he seemed utterly indifferent to what might happen to him. Or perhaps the Personnel Officer was disarmed by his failure to pass his Finals. At any rate the officer had at once suggested that he should try for a commission.

It was immediately obvious from that first drill-instruction that Percy was in for a bad time. We did only simple marching and the halt, but Percy was always out of step, always colliding with the man in front of him on the halt. As, in the succeeding weeks, the drill became more complex, Percy's blunders became more outrageous. At the turn or about-turn, he was sure to go stumbling off at a tangent to the rest of the squad. In arms drill he frequently dropped his rifle, and was a menace to himself and anyone within two yards radius. In his hand the weapon had more offensive possibilities than Lee-Enfield ever dreamed of.

Actually I myself was surprised and somewhat vexed to find that drill was quite difficult, and that it extended my concentration and mental alertness to the full. Arms drill I found particularly irksome, for the rifle was heavy to my meagre muscles, and bruised my collar-bone painfully. Most of us felt the spiteful edge of Baker's tongue at one time or another, but Percy rapidly established himself as Baker's chief butt. Watching Percy inevitably bungling the simplest order and agonizing under Baker's coarse sarcasm, was a painful experience, an army farce in bad taste. Of course there was plenty of laughter from the squad, which Baker made only a token effort to suppress. Sometimes he would stand the rest of us at ease and make Percy perform solo for the general diversion. Once he stopped a fellow instructor who was passing, and showed off Percy's paces like a circus animal's. The other N.C.O. grinned uncomfortably, and I suspected that he didn't really approve. Perhaps the cruellest thing Baker inflicted on Percy was to punish the whole squad because of his ineptitude. Often we would be left pounding the vast, arid barrack square after the other squads had been dismissed, because Percy couldn't master the about-turn on the march, while the precious minutes of Naafi-break or lunch-hour ticked away. Even I, a friend of Percy's in a way, found myself cursing him under my breath at such times; while the resentment of the others, needless to say, was more vocal.

But I was not really a friend of Percy's. I found him pathetic, touching, but dull. However, since Mike's heroic defence of Percy on the first evening, their relationship had followed an archetypal school-yarn pattern and a curious friendship had sprung up between them. I therefore saw more of Percy than I might otherwise have done.

Gradually I filled in his background – partly by what he told me himself, but mainly from what Mike passed on to me, for Percy was far less reticent when he was alone with Mike. He came from down-at-heel gentlefolk in Lincolnshire, but his parents had died when he was young, and he had been brought up by an uncle and aunt. His family were 'Old Catholics' which, Mike explained to me, meant that they belonged to the small minority of English Catholics who had kept their Faith through the Penal days. I gathered that they were a tightly-knit, conservative, clannish group, who regarded Irish and convert Catholics with rather more suspicion than they did Protestants. Percy's guardian had sent him to a seminary school in Hampshire, a boarding school which was attached to a seminary. The education there had a decidedly ecclesiastical slant, and likely boys were groomed for the priesthood from an early age. This was thought to be an appropriate destiny for Percy, and one that his parents would have approved of. Percy, with his usual obligingness, had happily accepted the idea. When he failed to pass his 'O' level G.C.E. at the third attempt, however, his masters regretfully informed his guardian that there was no point in encouraging him to study for the priesthood any more. This slightly surprised me. The life of a priest seemed so unattractive and uncomfortable that I thought the ecclesiastical authorities would have hung on to anybody who was foolish enough to put himself into their hands.

'Agnostic be damned!' snorted Mike, when I expressed this

opinion. 'Maria Monk dies hard. I bet you think the Inquisition carries on in dark cellars under presbyteries in Basingstoke and Camden Town. Seriously, I agree with you that it's surprising how difficult it is to become a priest when you consider the shortage of vocations. It's good policy though. In Spain and Italy, where it's much easier, you find the worst ecclesiastical scandals.'

This conversation took place on the Saturday at the end of our first week of Basic Training. That morning we had received a lethal three-in-one injection against tetanus, typhoid and some other scourge whose name I forget, plus vaccination against smallpox. The effects were highly unpleasant, and we had been put on 'light duties' for the week-end. Some of the lads had violent fever, and lay shivering and sweating under blankets. I had a headache, but the main effect of the injections on me was an indescribable mental depression. Mike and I lay prone on our beds, too wretched and ill to move.

'Was Percy disappointed when he was turned down?' I asked.

'I don't think so. Except that he didn't like his guardians to be disappointed. They sound rather grim. But the Army must be a nasty shock to him.'

'He's not the only one,' I replied with feeling.

'Yes, but it's different for us, Jon. In some ways Percy led a more Spartan life in the seminary school than this. He's used to lousy food, sleeping in dormitories, getting up early for mass, the lack of freedom and so on. That doesn't worry him as it worries us. What worries him is the way people shout and swear at him, no matter how hard he tries to please. Seminarians can be pretty bloody, but at least they keep up the appearances of decency. There's a respect for peace and privacy. It's bad enough leaving a seminary and going out into the world, – my brother did it. But to go straight out of the seminary into the Army – it must be like taking a wrong turning in Paradise and plunging down into the Pit.'

I didn't admit it to Mike, but his simile fitted my feelings as well. Paradise: London, the dull suburb where I lived; college, the cramped lecture-rooms in the converted warehouse block, the dingy, stale-smelling lounge. That was Paradise. And the Army,

– yes, I thought, as I looked down the cheerless hut, at its iron beds on which the grey-faced youths writhed and groaned in the grip of their ague, yes, this was the Pit. I closed my eyes.

One thing everyone acquires in the Army is a gluttonous appetite for sleep. To normal young people sleep is just an irritating demand of nature's, confiscating hours of possible enjoyment and study. Sleep is the opium of the soldier, the cheap universal drug, the anaesthetic against boredom and homesickness. The experience of missing sleep, – on guard or on the journey back to camp after leave, – teaches him the value of sleep, makes him greedy for sleep, so that he begins to sleep even when he is not tired. When he hasn't got a leave pass or money, the soldier will customarily spend Sunday in bed, even after a lazy and idle week. But during Basic Training we slept at every opportunity because we were exhausted after square-bashing all day and cleaning equipment half the night.

The day began at 5.30. Groaning and cursing we wrenched ourselves from sleep's narcotic embrace as the orderly corporal slammed in and out of the hut leaving his harsh summons lingering on the air. We reacted in different ways: some hopped straight out of bed; some twisted under the blankets, trying futilely to corkscrew their way back into oblivion; some sat up in bed, yawning, scratching, farting. Mike reached out automatically for the half-smoked cigarette he had extinguished the night before. I lay as I had woken, motionless, as if with practice I might be able to will the world into immobility for a few extra minutes. When Mike had finished his dog-end he swung his legs to the ground, and I followed suit as if our limbs were connected by invisible wires. The more wretched I felt, the less I liked to let him out of my sight. We pulled on our boots and denims, and shuffled out, speechless, to the wash-house, shivering slightly in the chill morning air. If we were lucky there was still hot water in the taps; if not, there was the rasping agony of a cold-water shave and the sting of styptic pencil on ghastly wounds along the jaw bone.

Then, articulate at last, to breakfast: flaccid bacon and tinned tomatoes in a pool of red juice on a cold plate, like the leftovers of a nasty operation, served by surly, white-faced cooks who had already been up for two hours. Back to the huts. We emptied our bowels as quickly as possible: the lavatories never flushed, and each one could be used exactly once without offence. But often there was not time. There were the various jobs to be done in and around the hut: sweeping the floor, polishing the windows, and, if one were unlucky, 'ablutions'. This last meant hurling buckets of water down the clogged pans so that the inspecting officer wouldn't be reminded that the plumbing didn't work. In the hut there was feverish activity as the time of first parade approached. We made up our beds, folding up the blankets to regulation measurements; laid out whatever pieces of equipment were required for inspection; struggled into our webbing and polished our boots.

At five to eight Corporal Baker arrived on his bicycle, dismounting by numbers, to goad us out of the hut with his carefully chosen insults. He marched us off to the barrack square to parade with the rest of the Intake. Then commenced the solemn pantomime of inspection: standing to attention in the brisk air, bowels uncomfortably heavy if one had not had time to visit the lavatory, while the leathery-faced Sergeant Box moved slowly along the line, Baker a pace behind, his needle-sharp pencil poised to inscribe the sergeant's inevitable condemnation of our turnout. Box pored over our brasses like an archaeologist examining some rare bronze medallion. 'What's all this shit?' he would inquire, pointing at a minute smear on a buckle.

It was the special delight of the N.C.O.s to ask questions which could only be answered to one's disadvantage within the framework of military discipline. In the following illustration the words in italics represent possible truthful replies which had to be suppressed for obvious reasons.

'What's all this shit?'

I don't see any shit.

'I don't know, Sergeant.'

'Well, I'm telling you, it's shit. See?'

No.

'Yes, Sergeant.'

'Did you clean your kit last night?'

Of course I did as you very well know.

'Yes, Sergeant.'

'Well you didn't clean it properly, did you?'

Yes.

'No, Sergeant.'

'Why not?'

Firstly, I don't accept that my equipment isn't properly cleaned. Secondly, if it isn't cleaned to your satisfaction, that's because you are not to be satisfied. Thirdly, you know and I know that it's a question of no importance, that you have to pick on something to establish your authority, and that we are going through an elaborate and meaningless ritual to create the illusion that I am being made a soldier of.

'I don't know, Sergeant.'

'You don't know! Well you'd better find out before tomorrow morning. Your trouble is that you're idle. What are you?'

A bloody sight more intelligent than you, for a start.

'Idle, Sergeant.'

Actually Mike developed quite a successful technique for dealing with the 'You're-idle-what-are-you?' formula. He would innocently reply: 'What you said, Sergeant.' Then the N.C.O. would ask with a smirk, sure of getting the admission he wanted: 'And what was that?'

'You said I was idle.'

This would usually satisfy the bone-headed interrogator, but even he would be dimly aware that 'you said I was idle' was not the same thing as '[*I'm*] idle'. I regret that I never had the nerve to imitate Mike.

The inspection was a farce of course, but it was depressing to find how quickly one came to treat it seriously, to observe the approach of Sergeant Box almost with anxiety. A least *I* did, and Percy could be seen visibly trembling. I'm sure Mike never treated the business with anything other than contempt.

After the inspection there was a brief drill period followed by P.T., – the most hateful hour of the day as far as I was concerned.

We changed into singlets and shorts, and trotted to the gymnasium in boots, carrying our plimsolls. We made a grotesque spectacle, with our baggy shorts, knobbly knees, hairy legs, all terminating in clumsy black boots. But then the whole object of the exercise was to destroy one's dignity. At the gym we were handed over to the tender mercies of the P.T. instructors, who were typical of their tribe: lounging bullies in soiled white sweaters, who kept up an appearance of muscular fitness and agility thinly disguising a profound laziness and perceptible homosexual proclivities. Everything was done relentlessly at the double. 'Last one into the gym is on fatigues.' And so there was always a stupid scramble to get off one's boots, with one of the instructors playfully wielding a rubber slipper. 'If he tries any of *le vice anglais* on me he's looking for trouble,' Mike muttered to me one day. But the instructors were wary with the older conscripts, and made up for it by being particularly vindictive in the gym. This was the usual hygienic torture chamber with wall bars for racking limbs, horses for rupturing abdomens, ropes for skinning hands, and bristly mats laughably supposed to soften one's falls. Having been to a school equipped with a gym, I was able to acquit myself just well enough to avoid censure. Some of the other lads, however, were obviously experiencing it all for the first time. Percy was in pure misery.

I had quickly developed a bruised heel from marching which made P.T. very painful, and I debated inwardly whether to go sick and get excused P.T. But this would also mean being excused all training, and if that went on for more than a few days I would be 'back-squadded', the most dreaded sentence of all: it meant joining a fresh Intake, and starting Basic Training all over again. It was worth any pain to avoid that, and very few of us went sick during Basic Training.

After P.T. the day was occupied mainly by drill, relieved by the odd lecture on fire-arms or V.D. We squatted on the grass in a circle round an oily-fingered N.C.O., who took a Sten gun to pieces with the dexterity of a magician, and sneered at our attempts to reassemble it. 'The object of war,' he said, 'is to kill the enemy.' He paused to let the words sink in. 'Don't aim at his head: you may miss. Don't aim at his legs: you may not kill him. Aim at his body.' A little tremor of blood–lust rippled through his audience. A young medical officer stared at a point on the wall at the back of the lecture-room and said: 'The best way to avoid getting V.D. is to refrain from sexual intercourse.' There was more interest in his description of other ways. On camps overseas, contraceptives and carbolic soap could be obtained at the guard-room, we learned.

These lectures were welcome opportunities for resting aching muscles, but Mike and I most looked forward to the Education periods, when those of us who were P.O.s were left in the library. We were supposed to study Current Affairs. Mike and I sat around chatting and reading the Arts pages of the weekly reviews, – the latter an almost painfully nostalgic occupation. News of the latest books and plays seemed to come from a great distance, from a bright, unattainable world thousands of miles away. Sometimes its controversies and talking-points seemed trivial and frivolous compared to the more concrete world of our present discontents; but I longed to return to those trivialities and frivolities.

Mail was distributed after lunch. I received few letters, and those few from my parents. Regular food parcels from my mother, exquisitely selected and packed in fond memory of my special tastes, were very welcome, but did not appease my hunger for letters, for communion with the outside world. For the first time in my life I realized how few friends I had, and for the first time I regretted the fact. One felt a great need for the kind of sympathy parents could not supply, – particularly my parents, since I could never bring myself to tell them how miserable I was. I had no girl-friend, and found myself almost coveting the letters the other lads received, their contents flamboyantly advertised by lipstick imprints and cryptograms like SWALK (Sealed With A Loving Kiss) over the seals. To receive a letter, however, could be more unpleasant than not receiving one. Letters from girl-friends 'breaking it off' were common. Usually the girl had found another admirer, or was tired of being tied to a soldier who was absent most of the time, and penniless when he was at home.

I was curious about the letters in long, pale mauve envelopes which Mike received every other day. They looked feminine in origin, but I had never seen him with a girl at college, and he never mentioned one. He rarely wrote letters himself. For some reason I refrained from questioning him on this point. If Mike proved to have a girl, I felt obscurely, she would come between us in some way.

There was no such thing as 'free' time in Basic Training. The evenings and week-ends were fully occupied, mainly by cleaning and polishing equipment, or in army jargon 'bull'. Someone had obviously given considerable thought to this part of our training. First of all we were issued with brasses that were green and deeply corroded, and therefore had to be rubbed for hours with emery paper before the application of 'Brasso' produced any effect. Our boots had a dull, orange-peel surface, which is of course a characteristic feature of good waterproof foot-wear, but we had to eradicate the dimples and produce a patent-leather shine. The approved method was to heat a spoon handle over a candle and to rub the boots with it, squeezing out the oil and smoothing out the surface. This process naturally ruined the boots *qua* boots, but such functional considerations were irrelevant within the mystique of 'bull'. Some of the lads used more drastic methods, such as rubbing a hot iron over the boots, or even covering them with polish and setting fire to them. In addition to brasses and boots, there was webbing to be blancoed and clothing to be pressed. When we were first issued with webbing Baker ordered us to scrub off the existing, deeply ingrained khaki blanco. 'I want them white,' he said. Four hours' scrubbing with cold water produced a dirty grey. The next day we were instructed to blanco the webbing again in exactly the same colour as that in which it had been issued. The 21st tanks themselves, like all battalions of the R.T.R., wore black webbing, which gave them a peculiarly brutal and sombre appearance. Until we were allocated to particular regiments at the end of our

62

training we wore khaki webbing. 'I hope I'm not put in the Tanks,' Mike observed to me once, 'I'd feel like a bloody Black-and-Tan.' But the black webbing, which was treated with shoe-polish, seemed to me to be much easier to keep clean.

Pressing was somewhat difficult for me at first, because I had never pressed a single garment in my life before I was called up. The usual pressing technique was to use the iron over a sheet of brown paper which had been wetted with a shaving brush. The hiss of steam and the pungent odour of scorched brown paper are still inextricably connected with the Army in my mind, like the whine of shells and the smell of cordite in the memories of war-veterans. I minimized the pressing by using my own pyjamas and underpants. I pressed the Army's issue once, according to the regulation measurements, and kept them undisturbed for kit layouts throughout my service, carrying them carefully from place to place in polythene bags.

The amount of equipment that was required to be laid out for inspection in the mornings was subtly increased during the period of Basic Training, starting with a few items and culminating in a series of full kit-layouts which kept us working late into the night. An additional vexation was the occasional 'Fire Picquet', a quaintly-named duty which consisted in parading with the guard in steel helmets and peeling potatoes for two hours in a small annexe to the cookhouse, awash with freezing water and potato peel. One had heard of this sort of thing of course, – peeling potatoes was more or less a cartoonist's cliché for depicting the Army – but it came as a shock, to me at least, to find myself doing it. I had supposed that it was some kind of punishment, and probably obsolete, like flogging. I felt the same, only more strongly, about cookhouse fatigues.

One Sunday we had a Church parade. I presumed that even the Army would not compel me to attend church, and said so to Baker, with a certain challenging note in my voice which was probably my undoing.

'You can presume what you fugging well like,' he replied. 'You'll parade with the rest of the squad. After the inspection,

fall out and report to me. We'll find you something to do while
the others are saying their prayers.'

When I reported to him he sent me over to the cookhouse. If
there is a God, and if, as some say, He whiles away the long
light evenings of eternity devising choice punishments for His
creatures, He need not hesitate over selecting my particular hell.
It would be an everlasting cookhouse fatigue. By the end of that
Sunday I was almost weeping with misery and a sense of injustice.
Whereas those on the Church parade were free (relatively
speaking) by noon, I slaved all day in that stinking, greasy cookhouse. It was an old building, irremediably dirty: platoons of
soldiers could not have scrubbed it clean, though the Cook
Sergeant nearly drove me and my companions into the tiled floor
in the attempt. I remember kicking a hot water pipe in sheer
wretchedness and frustration, and the shudder of disgust that
shook me as a swarm of cockroaches scuttled out over the wall.
I kicked and kicked at the pipes in a masochistic frenzy until the
wall was alive with the repulsive vermin. Then I retched into a
nearby sink. I went over to the Cook Sergeant and said pleadingly:
'I've just been sick. I feel ill. Can I leave?' He looked at my white
face and gave permission with a contemptuous jerk of his head.
Blessing him, I staggered weakly back to the hut, and collapsed
on to my bed. Mike was less sympathetic than I had expected.
'You can now count yourself one of the glorious martyrs for
Agnosticism,' he said. Percy, sitting on the same bed, laughed.
Their visit to church seemed to have put them in good spirits.

'At the moment I'd cheerfully become a Jehovah's Witness, if
it would get me out of cookhouse fatigues,' I said savagely.

'A very good idea,' he replied. 'Being a Jehovah's Witness
would get you out of the Army altogether. They're conscientious
objectors.'

'That's the religion for me,' I said.

'My brother-in-law was a Jehovah's Witness, but it didn't get
him out of the Army,' observed the soldier on the bed opposite
to mine. He was an odd, though pleasant little chap called Barnes,
with a quaint Leicestershire accent. He had seen me reading the
Inferno one evening. 'What you reading? Po'try? Here's some

good po'try.' And he had thrust a tattered second-hand copy of *The Lady Of The Lake* into my hand. Encouraged by this evidence of literacy, though by no means sympathetic to his tastes, I had attempted to extend the discussion. 'Do you like Scott?' I had asked him. But he hadn't seemed to realize that the poem was by Scott. 'That's good po'try' was all he would say; and taking the volume from me, he had returned it carefully to his locker.

'What happened to your brother-in-law then?' inquired Mike.

'Well, it was in the war, like. And they wouldn't let our Ernie be a conscious objector. But Ernie said he weren't going to put on a bloody uniform no matter what they did. So they sent him to this training depot, and he wouldn't put on his uniform. So they put him in this cell in his underclothes, and threw in his uniform. It were winter, like, and they reckoned he'd be so cold he'd have to put the uniform on.' Barnes paused.

'And did he?'

'Did he fugg. When they opened the cell next morning our Ernie were still in his underclothes; and on the table were his uniform, – all in pieces.'

'What d'you mean, all in pieces?'

'He'd spent the whole night taking his uniform to pieces. He never tore nothing mind you. He bit through the seams with his teeth. His socks were two balls of wool. He said with a bit more time he could have taken his boots to pieces. He could've too. He was in the boot trade.'

The story pleased us immensely.

'They should put up a statue to that man,' said Mike reverently.

'What happened to him eventually?' I asked.

'A few days after they came and told him his ma had been killed by a Jerry bomb. Went fuggin mad he did. Couldn't get his uniform on quick enough. Joined the paratroops and finished the war with thirteen medals.'

We laughed ruefully.

'The traitor,' said Mike.

'God, is there no way of getting out of this Army?' I wailed.

'Roberts told me he's going to buy himself out,' said Percy. 'Is that possible?'

'Christ!' I exclaimed. 'How much does it cost? I'd sell my birthright to get out of the Army.'

'Calm down, Trooper,' said Mike. 'Only Regulars can buy themselves out. Anyway, he'll only be called up again to do National Service.'

'He says he won't,' answered Percy. 'Because he works in the mines. He said he joined the Army to get out of the mines, but now he can't wait to get back.'

'Well, Jon,' said Mike, 'there's only one thing you can do now. Shoot your trigger finger off, like they used to do in the Great War.'

'My bulling-finger you mean,' I replied, inspecting my forefinger, red and sore from rubbing brasses and boots.

THREE

'Wakey-wakey!'

The call of the Orderly Corporal scratched the surface of my sleep without penetrating it. I turned over and dozed, until the sound of someone whistling off-key woke me at seven. Leaning from my bed I pulled back the curtain over the door of my cubicle and held out a mug to the nearest soldier.

'Get me a cup of tea when you go to breakfast, Scouse,' I said. 'Send it back with one of the other lads.'

'Right, Corporal,' he replied, taking the mug from my hand. He was a new arrival to Badmore, who treated me with flattering deference. He added: 'Ah'm a Geordie, not a Scouse.'

'Oh well, I never know the difference between those little villages up north,' I countered mechanically. One must never let slip an opportunity of teasing the next man about his geographical origins. Geordie, Scouse, Taff, Paddy, Jock. Shakespeare knew what he was doing when he made the comedy in his army play, *Henry V,* a comedy of dialects.

At 7.30, refreshed by the tea, I got up, washed and shaved. I then supervised the cleaning of the hut. There was a Monday-morning gloom in the air, but I felt cheerful. My last Monday. Dust-motes glittered prettily in the bright sunlight.

'Come on! come on! Get that shit swept up,' I said briskly to a group leaning on their broom handles.

'Don't be like that, Corp. You've not got long to push. Why worry?'

'See they've got you on guard tonight, Corporal,' said Jock Gordonstone. 'Will you want me to do your boots for you?'

My mood darkened. 'Fuggit, yes. I'd forgotten about that.' I pondered. 'Yes, do them for me will you, Jock, unless I tell you not to at Naafi-break.'

Jock was always broke, because every month he took a forty-eight home to Paisley. Deducting the time he spent travelling, he only had about twelve hours at home, and his fares cost him nearly four pounds, but he always took the forty-eight. When I was on guard I usually gave him half a crown to clean my boots.

Morning parade was at 8.15. I called the roster for my troop, and handed the sheet to Sergeant-Major Fotherby. His predecessor had rarely bothered to take the morning parade, but Sergeant-Major Fotherby was keen. Or, rather, he had been keen: already there were signs that he was realizing the impossibility of mending the ways of Badmore. On his first morning parade he had taken an hour over his inspection. Now he surveyed my troop with pained resignation, and broke his silence only once, to observe to Jock Gordonstone that his hair was long enough for him to wipe his arse with it.

Badmore was, and always would be, the despair of any sergeant-major, because the sergeant-major is a man who works in the medium of outward appearance. His object is to make every man look identical, because if all men look alike, they will act alike, and eventually think, or, rather, not-think alike. But the sergeant-major must have a basic structure of uniformity to work on. Without this he is like a theologian without dogma. The analogy is not inapposite. A regiment is like a religion. Its dogma governs the way its members wear their lanyards, the angle they wear their berets, the manner in which they perform the movements of drill. As in Newman's theory of religious doctrine, developments may occur. It is the responsibility of the sergeant-major, as of the theologian, to control and rationalize such developments, to distinguish genuine developments from heresies, and ruthlessly to suppress the latter. In fact, in the Guards, the regimental sergeant-majors of each battalion have an annual conference, a sort of General Council, in which such matters are discussed and regularized.

Badmore, however, was not a regiment. Known officially as the

R.A.C. Special Training Establishment, its function was to train officers and N.C.O.s in the use of new technical developments in armoured vehicles. Its courses were attended by personnel from all the regiments of the R.A.C., and it was staffed with soldiers from as many regiments. When the entire unit paraded for the Queen's Birthday Parade it looked as if remnants of a whole defeated army had met up and banded together. There were cap-badges of every description: the antique tank of the R.T.R., the skull and crossbones of the Dragoon Guards, the wreath of the Bays, the harp of the Irish Guards, the crossed lances of the Lancers. The R.T.R. wore black berets and black webbing; the cavalry wore navy-blue berets and khaki webbing. The R.T.R. wore plain black lanyards; the cavalry wore white or yellow plaited lanyards. Insignia on shoulder tabs and lapels varied similarly. Even from a long distance the 11th Hussars or 'Cherry Pickers' disturbed any impression of uniformity with their curious brown, badgeless berets ringed with a band of crimson, the stigma of some ancient disgrace, when the regiment had stopped to pick cherries on the way to a battle. Soldiers belonging to R.E.M.E., the Signals, the Catering Corps and the Royal Artillery, only added to the confusion. It was enough to break a sergeant-major's heart.

Beneath the surface Badmore resembled a regiment even less. It was more like a sort of military Narkover. The ranks were composed largely of National Servicemen under twenty; the N.C.O.s of aged and decrepit Regulars. The former had been sent to Badmore because they had flat feet, or compassionate reasons for a home posting, or were unemployable elsewhere; the latter because they had varicose veins, or had been involved in some scandal in their regiments, or were unemployable elsewhere. The relationship between the two groups resembled that between the boys and masters of Narkover. National Service N.C.O.s like myself occupied the position of prefects. It was impossible to think of the ranks as anything but boys. Once, Captain Pirie, searching for something to say to Fotherby before a big parade, had asked him: 'Are the men in good heart, Sergeant-Major?' The inquiry was kindly meant, and not without relevance: 'A'

Squadron was sufficiently apprehensive about being inspected by a visiting Brigadier. But the contrast between the image summoned up by the words, of grim Tommies with blackened faces, waiting to go 'over the top', and the reality – an irregular file of pimply youths fidgeting in their best uniforms, – was richly comic.

I snorted at the recollection. Fotherby eyed me suspiciously before bringing us to attention.

' "A" Squadron, dis . . . miss!'

We dispersed to our various tasks in offices, stores, messes, stables. The unit was divided into two squadrons: 'B' Squadron was responsible for the cleaning and maintenance of vehicles used in training. The rest of the unit's activities were controlled by 'A' Squadron, which included the Orderly Room staff. In fact the 'A' Squadron offices were in the same low, rambling building as the Orderly Room.

Captain Pirie's office had three doors: one connected with my office, another with Fotherby's office, and the third with a corridor. Captain Pirie usually sat cowering in a corner of his room waiting for one of the doors to open: Fotherby urging him to inspect the huts, the Second-in-Command or the Adjutant complaining about sports equipment, or me, with ledgers to be balanced. He was usually least worried to see me, since I pencilled in all the figures, and he had only to ink them over.

I shared my office with Mr Fry, a civilian. He was responsible for the pay and insurance of the civilians who worked on the camp, mainly as gardeners, groundsmen and storekeepers. There were quite a lot of them, but one rarely saw them except on Wednesday afternoons, when they crept out of their holes and crannies, and shuffled into the office to receive their pay, grinning and coughing and touching their forelocks like a gang of Hardy's rustics. Mr Fry was a conscientious man, but, however slowly and meticulously he did his work, he could not stretch it over a forty-two-hour week. As usual, therefore, he had the *Daily Express* spread out over his desk when I entered.

'Good morning, Corporal Browne.'

'Good morning, Mr Fry.'

'Did you have a pleasant week-end?'

'Yes thank you. Very pleasant. And you?'

'Quiet you know, quiet.' It would be sensational when Mr Fry had a noisy week-end. 'Got some weeding done in the garden. Lovely weather.'

'Lovely.' I went to the window, and looked out over the playing-fields. A mechanical mower droned and circled in the middle distance, throwing up a fine spray of cut grass. I opened the window and the smell floated in.

'Won't be long now, eh, Corporal Browne?'

'No, Mr Fry.'

'Wednesday, isn't it?'

'That's right.'

'I'll be sorry to see you go, Corporal Browne.'

'It's very nice of you to say so, Mr Fry. I can't honestly say *I* shall be sorry to go.'

'Of course not. Of course not. The Army's a waste of time for a young man like you. You'll be going back to the university then?'

'Not at once. I'm taking a holiday first.'

'Ah yes, of course. Stupid of me to forget. Spain, isn't it?'

'Majorca. An island off the coast of Spain.'

'You'll send us a post-card I hope?'

'I'll send *you* one, Mr Fry.'

In the distance a door banged, and a pair of boots clumped thunderously up the corridor to the accompaniment of a pop-song, piercingly whistled. Mr Fry winced. The chief reason why he would be sorry to see me go was that he did not find my replacement, Trooper Ludlow, congenial. The door crashed open and Ludlow lurched into the room.

'Ullo, Jonny-boy! Ullo, Mr Fry,' he cried boisterously in the accent of Brum. ''Ave a good week-end?' he asked me, and without waiting for an answer jerked his head in my direction and observed to Mr Fry: 'Bloody 'ard man i'n 'e? Takin' a forty-eight just before 'e's released.'

Mr Fry forced a smile, but offered no comment.

'How about you, Roy? Nice week-end?' I inquired.

'Fair. Got pissed on Saturday night,' he replied. 'Got a fag?'

'Only cork-tipped.' Filtered cigarettes were not popular, and I had adopted them as a partial protection against cadging. 'Ask Boon, I heard him just come in.'

'That bastard? 'E's as tight as a crab's arse-'ole. Give us one of your tipped ones then.' He broke off the tip, lit the mutilated cigarette, and strode across to the window to throw out the match. To a soldier who was passing he called out 'Git yer 'air cut, Connolly,' imitating the grating timbre of Fotherby's voice with considerable success. Connolly looked round apprehensively, grinned and made a V-sign. At that moment one of the typists from the Orderly Room passed with her nose in the air. Connolly hastily converted the gesture into a scratch behind his ear. Ludlow responded to this pantomime with ear-splitting laughter. Recovering his breath, he observed that the typist would make a good grind. 'Maybe I can knock 'er off when I've got a stripe, eh, Jonny? When d'you think the Major'll make me up?'

'After the next audit I should think. If the books balance you'll get your stripe. If they don't you'll probably both be court-martialled.'

'Don't you worry, Jonny-boy. I could do them books with me 'ands tied behind me back.'

To do Ludlow justice, he was better at figures than I was, having been a bookie's clerk in civilian life.

'Here comes the Captain,' said Mr Fry, folding up his newspaper. We gathered at the window. It was always worth watching Captain Pirie's arrival, on the off-chance of his hitting something expensive. The green vintage Bentley swept into the camp in a fast four-wheel drift, passed behind a long row of buildings, and, after a strangely long interval, emerged at the other end going slowly, and disconcertingly, backwards.

'Must've 'it an oil-patch,' observed Ludlow knowledgeably.

After much audible wrestling with the gears Captain Pirie pointed the car in our direction and drove furiously towards us, clinging to the great, string-bound steering wheel, and peering myopically through the yellowing windscreen. He swung into the parking bay outside the office, and drew up, missing the Adjutant's Jaguar by inches. The great car seemed to go on shuddering and panting for several seconds after he had switched off the ignition. Captain Pirie prised his great bulk out of the cockpit and climbed down. Two cocker spaniels leapt out, and followed him as he puffed his way towards the office, apparently connected to his heels by invisible elastic threads which plucked them back whenever they roamed more than three yards from him. We heard the dogs snuffling in the corridor as he passed the door and entered his office. I gathered up a sheaf of bills and, knocking perfunctorily at the door, entered the office.

'Good morning, sir,' I said, saluting.

Captain Pirie was filling his pipe. ''Morning, Corporal Browne.' He sketched a vague gesture in the air which was his approximation to a salute. Unfortunately he was still holding his tobacco pouch in his right hand, and some of the contents fell on to the floor. One of the spaniels sprawling under the desk instantly retrieved the tobacco, and offered it to his master, who took the soggy tangle from the dog's mouth with a proud smile. Shreds of tobacco still adhered to the mouth of the animal, who licked his chops meditatively.

'A few bills to be paid, sir,' I said firmly, putting them on his desk.

'Oh. Ah. Hmm,' he muttered. 'Couldn't they wait? I think Sergeant-Major Fotherby . . .'

'Two of them are over-due already, sir.'

'Are they? *Are* they? Hmm. Oh well, we'd better pay them then, eh?'

'Yes, sir.'

'Now where's that damned cheque-book?'

'Top left-hand drawer, sir.'

'What? Oh yes. Thank you.'

As he was writing out the cheques, a knock sounded at the door leading to the Sergeant-Major's office. Captain Pirie pretended not to have heard it, but Fotherby came in uninvited. He thudded over the lino in his heavy boots and saluted with precision.

'Can I see you for a moment, sir?'

'Got some urgent P.R.I. business on hand here, I'm afraid, Sergeant-Major. Haven't we, Corporal?' He gave me a sly, conspiratorial glance from under his bushy eye-brows.

'Yes, sir,' I replied, but added to Fotherby: 'It won't take very long, sir.' I was trying to soften up Fotherby, but he wasn't responsive.

'There are two men for orders, sir.'

'Oh. Hmm. Remand to C.O.?' asked the Captain hopefully.

'I think you can deal with it yourself, sir.'

The Captain looked glum. He was a kind-hearted man, and disliked administering punishments. No doubt this was one reason why, at forty-five, he had not yet been promoted to Major, and had few prospects of such promotion.

'I'll get the charge-sheets,' said Fotherby, and left the room.

'It should be ten shillings, sir, instead of ten pounds,' I observed, pointing to the cheque the Captain was signing.

'Oh. Ah. Yes.' He panicked a little, and made a blot as he crossed out the figures.

'What shall I do?'

'Put in the ten shillings and initial the correction, sir.'

He put away the cheque-book with a sigh of relief.

'Well, Corporal Browne, it won't be long before you leave us.'

'No, sir.'

'When do you go?'

'Wednesday, sir.'

'*Wednesday*. Is it really? Will Ludlow be all right? Have you shown him the ropes?'

'He'll be all right, sir. You needn't worry. I'm handing over the inventory and the petty cash to him today.'

'Good, good.'

He rummaged through the paper slum that covered his desk, and produced a pink booklet. It was my release book.

'I've written your testimonial, Corporal Browne,' he said, handing me the document with a shy smile. 'I hope it's all right.'

He seemed to want me to read it, so I did.

'An honest, Trustworthy and efficient N.C.O. who is very much above the Average in Intelligence. He is a good Organizer and very thorough at Clerking and accounts. He likes Games, plays a good game of Hockey and gets on well with Others in the Squadron.'

Captain Pirie's weakness for capitals gave his writing an oddly archaic air. It was nevertheless the most coherent piece of prose he had ever composed, and it must have cost him a great effort. I was touched. I hadn't the heart to tell him that I loathed games and had never played hockey in my life.

'Thank you, sir. That's very nice . . .' As I gave the booklet back to him, Fotherby re-entered the office. I saluted and left.

While orders were in progress I handed over the contents of the cupboard behind my desk to Ludlow: 137 jars of blanco. 23 assorted regimental lapel-badges. 961 Badmore Christmas cards (tank and holly motif). 8 paper hats. 1 Father Christmas beard. 1 camera (broken). 15 books of cloakroom tickets. 1 egg-poacher. . . .

'One *what?*' exclaimed Ludlow.

'One egg-poacher.'

'What the fugg's that for?'

'For poaching eggs.'

'I *know* its for poaching eggs you funny bastard. What's it doing in the P.R.I. cupboard?'

'Look, if you're going to start asking why things are in the P.R.I. cupboard I'm not going to get out on Wednesday. If you look at the inventory you'll see that that egg-poacher has been handed on to P.R.I. clerk after P.R.I. clerk. Surely you don't want to break a splendid old tradition like that?'

'I dunno what the fugg you're talking about. All right, let's get on.'

After we had finished I went into Fotherby's office. He was writing out Squadron Orders.

'Excuse me, sir.'

'Well.'

'I see that I'm down for a guard tonight.'

He looked up for the first time. 'That's right.'

'Well, sir, you may remember that on Friday I got the Captain's permission to leave early because——'

'You scived off at twelve. I know that much. Well?'

'Well, sir, I didn't see Orders. So I didn't know I was on guard till this morning.'

'Well?'

'I was wondering whether in view of the circumstances I could be excused guard.'

'You've got a bleeding nerve, Corporal Browne. What bleeding circumstances?'

'Well, sir, I haven't had time to get my kit ready.'

'You've got the lunch hour.' He added with heavy sarcasm: 'And if you're so worried about the state of your kit, I'll ask the Captain if you can dismiss early this afternoon.' There was a brief silence.

'Anything else, Corporal?'

'No, sir.'

I left the room seething with rage. It was a defeat, such as I had rarely received at Badmore. Tubby Hughes from the Pay Office was chatting with Ludlow when I returned to my office.

'Another guard to push then?' he greeted me.

'Oh fugg off.'

Ludlow chortled. 'You didn't get out of it then?'

'No I didn't,' I snapped sourly.

'Corporal Browne!'

Captain Pirie's voice was muffled by the door, but there was a note of urgency in it. I didn't feel like coping with him.

'You go,' I said to Ludlow. 'Get some practice. Tell him I'm not here.'

Ludlow came back looking red and baffled.

'His bloody dog has been sick. He wants me to wipe it up.'

Now Hughes and I laughed together at Ludlow's expense. Unsympathetic laughter was always circulating in this way, making new alliances and dissolving the old ones.

'It must be the tobacco,' I gasped.

'What bloody tobacco?'

'The dog was eating his tobacco.'

'Then he can clean up the shit himself.'

'You'll have to do it, Roy, if you want that stripe,' I said, taking my beret off a hook. 'Coming over to the Naafi, Tubby?'

Roy's misfortune, and a belated breakfast of hot sausage rolls and coffee, made it easier to resign myself to the guard. I saw Jock Gordonstone in the canteen and told him to go ahead and bull my boots.

'Only a few more days to push then?' said Tubby, stirring his coffee.

'Yes. I hope you're working on my demob pay.'

'It'll be ready lad, don't worry. What does it feel like?'

'What? Only having a few days to push? Sort of an anti-climax.'

That wasn't true, but how could you answer such a question, without telling the questioner the story of your life?

'What the fugg's that?'

'You know, when you feel let down. I've waited too long.'

'You're an educated bastard, aren't you, Jonny. Why didn't they make you an officer?'

'Because I didn't want to be one, Tubby. Would *you* want to be one?'

'I wouldn't mind. I wouldn't mind getting pissed in the Officers' Mess instead of pushing the stags.'

'That reminds me. Who's Orderly Officer tonight?'

'The Adjutant.'

'Christ,' I groaned. 'Just my luck.' The Adjutant was a keen young careerist who could be relied upon to be a nuisance on guard. He occasionally came round in the middle of the night to see that everything was in order. Such conduct was considered rather unsporting at Badmore.

I lingered on in the canteen after Tubby had gone, smoking and musing contentedly. I reflected with satisfaction that I had no reason to regret not having been made an officer.

The Army, it soon became clear to Mike and myself at Catterick, was the last surviving relic of feudalism in English society. The Sovereign was the nominal head of a hierarchy which descended in carefully differentiated grades of privilege to the serf, – the ordinary private soldier. Lip-service was paid to the Divine Right of the Sovereign (on the Queen's birthday we lifted our hats by numbers and gave three compulsory cheers in the general direction of a Union Jack fluttering above the barrack square). The upper ranks of the hierarchy were riddled with jealous intrigue and administrative inefficiency, though corporately they regarded their right to authority and power as natural and unchallengeable. They preserved their position by a farcically unjust system of discipline which they called Military Law. The serfs had no rights and did all the work.

Mike and I were now among the serfs, and agreed in finding it unpleasant. But the opportunity offered to us, as Potential Officers, of rising in the hierarchy, did not arouse our enthusiasm. There were advantages in being a P.O. during Basic Training in that we were occasionally released from drill to attend some special lecture or interview. But these activities, though welcome as a relief from square-bashing, produced in us a growing uneasiness.

In my own case this uneasiness was compounded of several different intuitions and responses. I did not like the officers I encountered at Catterick, and my subsequent experience did little to modify my opinion that the officer class was on the whole arrogant, stupid and snobbish, with a grotesquely inflated sense of its own importance. To get a Regular commission in the R.A.C. was no great personal achievement, – any mediocrity with the right background could do it. Yet the officers strutting about Catterick, with their noses fastidiously averted from the more noisome aspects of serf-life, plainly regarded themselves as an élite.

Somehow this superstition, that to be an officer was to belong to an élite, was conveyed to the majority of the P.O.s, amongst whom an oppressive competitiveness developed, as to who could manifest the most keenness and enthusiasm. When we went over to the P.O. Wing they pestered the N.C.O.s there with questions about their prospective training as officers. The descriptions of the latter filled me with gloom. It sounded like a more prolonged and intensive version of Basic Training. Was it worth it? I began to ask myself. Even if one succeeded, one would be at the very bottom of a higher section of the hierarchy: a Second Lieutenant with a National Service Commission. And would I succeed in any case?

This was the crucial question. All through my life I had succeeded in every competition for which I had chosen to enter, because I had restricted my entries to the field of academic study, in which I had some ability. I did not want to experience failure, and I did not want to give the Army the satisfaction of failing me. This competition was one for which I was ill-equipped: intelligence, critical judgment, culture – all the benefits of a liberal education, were of course liabilities rather than assets in applying for a commission. What exactly *was* required in order to pass the successive hurdles of Uzbee, Wozbee and Mons (the cadet school) I never really discovered. It seemed to be enshrined in the mystique of 'leadership'. 'You don't have to be particularly brainy to be an officer,' the Captain in charge of the P.O. Wing would tell us proudly. 'We don't need long-haired geniuses in the Army. (Ha! ha!) But there's one thing you must have. And that's *leadership*.' Whatever this mysterious quality might be, I was fairly certain that I did not possess it. At Wozbee it was apparently assessed by one's ability to handle a knife and fork and to cross a seven-foot ditch with two three-foot planks. I did not see myself excelling in either of these tests.

My growing uneasiness about my status as P.O. was exacerbated by Corporal Baker's continual taunts. We had discovered the reason for his particular spite towards P.O.s: he himself had tried and failed to get a commission. In a way, much as I disliked him, I understood his grievance. He was a cruel, foul-mouthed individual, but he was considerably more intelligent than most N.C.O.s, and by the Army's standards a 'good soldier'. He had been rejected after getting as far as Mons. I could imagine him at Mons, a very different Baker, subdued, anxious, insecure, mixing uncomfortably with the other cadets, speaking as little as possible, and then very deliberately, to disguise his plebeian accent; excelling at drill, initiative tests and map-reading, but fluffing his five-minute talk, and using the wrong spoon for soup. I could understand why he resented us P.O.s who, by benefit of class or education, might soon obtain the commission that had eluded him. But, as I smarted under his insults, powerless to reply, I hated him. And I think that of all the P.O.s, he hated me most. Fallowfield and Peterson he treated with a kind of grudging deference, like the boxing pro. at a public school licking the young gentlemen into shape. His hostility to Mike was tempered by a certain respect for Mike's physical and mental ruggedness. Percy he tormented as a cruel child torments a helpless animal. But in me he found a victim worthy of his spleen. I was from the same class as him, but boosted by educational advantages he had missed. I was bumptious and cocksure. I was physically unimpressive. I exerted myself in all departments of Basic Training to the bare minimum necessary to avoid serious trouble. I did not disguise my personal dislike of him, and I did not laugh at his jokes. And so he reserved his most spiteful abuse for me, usually centring on my pretensions to be a P.O.

All these considerations were accumulating throughout the first weeks of Basic Training, but they did not reach critical proportions until the fourth week when Mike compelled me into a decision. One afternoon that week, all the P.O.s were interviewed by the officer in charge of the Intake, Second Lieutenant Booth-

Henderson. He was himself the worst possible advertisement for the desirability of a commission. He was pudgy, flabby, pimply, stupid, nervous and pompous. We discovered his history – how I'm not quite sure, but I think Baker, who shared our contempt for him, had leaked it to a few of his toadies in the squad. Booth-Henderson had tried unsuccessfully three times to get a National Service commission, and since he belonged to a social class where such failure was a slur, had in desperation signed on for a third year and had been rewarded with a Regular commission. When I marched into Booth-Henderson's office I found that I simply could not make the effort to create the right impression.

'Well, Browne,' he began, 'I suppose you think it's going to be easy to become an officer?'

'No, sir,' I replied.

'Well I can tell you it isn't,' he continued, undeterred. 'It's jolly difficult. Now I have Corporal Baker's report on you here. I must tell you that it's very unsatisfactory. Have you any explanation?'

'The only one I can think of is that Corporal Baker happens to dislike me.' His jaw sagged slightly.

'You can't say that, Browne. I mean, it's ridiculous. It's Corporal Baker's job to, er, to . . . to knock you into shape' (he fell upon the phrase with obvious relief), 'to knock you into shape. There's nothing personal about it. It's all a part of, er, knocking you into shape. Now he says here that your brasses are usually dirty. Now that's not good enough, Browne. It really isn't. You must improve.'

'It's not just me, sir. It's all the P.O.s. He seemed to have a grudge against us. He's always trying to make us look fools in front of the other lads.'

'Now that's enough, Browne! I'm not here to discuss Corporal Baker. I'm here to . . . Now what about these brasses?'

'They're as clean as anyone else's,' I replied.

'Ah!' he cried triumphantly. 'That's just the point, Browne. As a P.O. we expect a higher standard of turn-out from you than from the others. Now next week you'll be going before the C.O. for interview before you move over to the P.O. Wing at the end of your Basic Training. I advise you to pull your socks up and get your finger out if you want to have a chance of passing Uzbee. Now have you got any questions you would like to ask me?'

'Yes, sir. Is it true that P.O.s have to report back to camp twelve hours before the others at the end of our seventy-two?'

I was referring to the three days' leave which we were to get at the end of our basic training, and to which we looked forward with an eagerness that is difficult to describe. Booth-Henderson seemed somewhat taken aback by my question.

'Yes, I believe that's the form. Why do you ask?'

'Well, I think it's rather unfair, sir. It means leaving home on Sunday morning. It cuts your leave down to a forty-eight.'

He paused portentously before delivering his reply.

'Browne, I must say I don't think you're approaching this thing in the right spirit at all. Surely the loss of a few hours' leave is a small thing compared to the honour of becoming an officer?'

I was silent, and as he could not apparently think of anything else to say, he dismissed me. In the corridor outside his room, Mike who had already been interviewed was waiting for me.

'Well, how did you make out with the White Hope of the British Army?'

'Pretty badly, I should think. I asked him about having our leave cut short. I think he took a dim view of it.'

'The man's a cretin. I could scarcely keep a straight face.'

We walked towards the huts to collect our eating-irons for tea. A fine drizzle was falling, and we slithered on the muddy paths. Groups of tired soldiers moved like shadows through the rain towards the cookhouse. Mike said:

'Jon, d'you really want to be an officer?'

'I suppose not.'

'Neither do I. All along I've felt in a false position, being a P.O. I detest the Army – the discipline, the snobbery, the idea of doing what you're told and asking no questions. The rest of it doesn't worry *me* so much, but some of the other lads, – I don't mean the tough nuts, they're all right; but the slightly dumb ones, the married ones, the nervous ones, the ones like Percy – they look so bloody miserable, as if they don't know what's hit them. It seems so unjust to me. And I feel that if I became an officer I'd be participating in that injustice. D'you know what I mean?'

'Yes. I feel exactly the same.'

'We'd have to pretend to be like that cretin Booth-Henderson. We'd have to cultivate a whole new set of attitudes: other ranks are animals; officers are gentlemen. Other ranks are dirty; officers have batmen. Other ranks must only have beer in the canteen, or they get drunk; officers can pig themselves with whisky. Other ranks are issued with French letters at the guard-room; officers pride themselves on getting an exclusive form of pox from Madame Marie's.'

I laughed. Madame Marie, according to Mike, who had a curious fund of anecdote, was a lady who ran a select call-girl agency for officers on leave in London. A young R.A.S.C. officer of Mike's acquaintance had telephoned the establishment and had been informed by a shocked voice: 'We only cater for the *best* regiments.'

'It's all true, Trooper.'

'Well I've decided to withdraw my application for a commission. How about you?'

'Mmm. It's a bit drastic.'

I thought it over as we approached the hut. Mike's altruistic scruples scarcely touched me. It came down to this as far as I was concerned: did I want a commission badly enough to take the considerable risk of failing to get it? Outside the hut we met Fallowfield.

'Well?' he said abruptly.

'Well?' Mike returned.

'How did you two get on?'

'Not very well. I pulled his hat over his eyes and beat him over the head with his swagger stick,' replied Mike with a straight face. 'How about you, Jon?'

'Oh I just told him to stop picking at his pimples.'

Fallowfield turned away with an irritable shrug. He threw back over his shoulder: 'Full kit lay-out tomorrow.'

'We know,' retorted Mike, though we didn't. 'Why do people

like Fallowfield take such a pleasure in spreading bad news?' he muttered.

As we plodded over to the cookhouse, it occurred to me that if Mike withdrew his application for a commission, and I didn't, we would be separated.

'I've decided, Mike,' I said. 'I'll withdraw my application, too. How do we set about it?'

With typical perversity the Army, having consistently impressed upon us the unlikelihood of our obtaining commissions, made it almost impossible for us to withdraw our applications. We were reluctantly obliged to approach Baker first.

'Frightened you off have I?' he said with a sneer. 'Thought you had more guts in you, Brady.'

'It's got nothing to do with guts,' replied Mike, reddening. 'It's just that we don't want to be officers. What do we do?'

'You'll have to see Lieutenant Henderson,' said Baker. He always deliberately shortened Booth-Henderson's name.

'Will you arrange an interview then?' I asked.

He turned his head slowly towards me with exaggerated astonishment.

'You've got a fugging nerve, Trooper. I've got more important things to do than run around arranging interviews for the likes of you. And another thing, I'm "*Corporal*" to you.'

'Sorry, Corporal,' I mumbled. I'd swallowed so much pride by then, another mouthful wouldn't make any difference. But Baker didn't help us any further.

When we caught Booth-Henderson a couple of days later he looked troubled. 'I don't advise you to do anything rash,' he said. 'Think it over.'

'We've thought about it and we're quite certain, sir,' I said.

'Well, I'll look into it.' He hurried off.

A few days later our names appeared, with those of the other P.O.s, on Squadron Orders, for the C.O.'s interview. I asked Baker what we should do.

'You can read, can't you?'

'Yes, Corporal.'

'Well, what does it say?'

'It says that we're to parade for interview on Friday afternoon outside the C.O.'s office.'

'Well then, you fugging well parade. Jesus Christ! It couldn't be any clearer.'

'But we told you last week that we didn't want to be P.O.s any longer,' I explained patiently.

'Did you see Lieutenant Henderson?'

'Yes.'

'What did he say?'

'He said he'd see about it.'

'Well I don't know anything about it, and what's more I don't give a monkey's fugg. You'll have to explain it all to the C.O.'

The explanation of Baker's and Booth-Henderson's strangely evasive behaviour suddenly dawned on me. From their point of view it would not look good if two P.O.s in their charge withdrew their applications. Many are called but few are chosen, was the official attitude to a commission. Awkward questions might be asked if anyone proved indifferent to the call. Baker and Booth-Henderson were no doubt hoping that we would not have the nerve to announce our decision to the C.O. himself. In this they were wrong. We hadn't been in the Army long enough to acquire that awe-struck reverence which is the usual attitude towards a Commanding Officer.

Our determination gave great pleasure to Percy who, not long before, had been demoted from the status of P.O. on Baker's recommendation. At one point, indeed, it had seemed not impossible that he might be discharged from the Army altogether. This was not unknown. A mentally deficient in 'B' Squad, who had inexplicably been called up, was discharged after a couple of weeks. Mike and I met him one afternoon shambling down the road towards the camp entrance, dressed in civilian clothes and carrying a suitcase.

'Compassionate leave?' I asked.

'Naw. Got m' discharge. No more fugging Army for me.'

We tactfully refrained from asking him why he had been discharged, though I doubt if he understood himself. I doubt if he had understood anything that had happened to him in the Army, except that for two long weeks he had been harassed and bullied and laughed at and shouted at through some dreadful mistake which had now happily been rectified. We watched him depart with an ironical envy of his feeble, stunted mind.

Percy, however, despite his eccentricities and lack of co-ordination, was not mentally deficient. There were no grounds on which he could be discharged from the Army. After a second interview with the Personnel Officer he ceased to be a P.O., and this was obviously a pathetic disappointment to him. 'Something to do with his family,' Mike explained to me. He was therefore pleased when Mike (particularly) and I told him that we were going to withdraw our applications.

By this time, however, Percy had already degenerated. A furtive, haunted look had come to fill the vacuum of innocent wonder in his eyes. The ribbing of the other soldiers was much milder than in his first days, but he was much more sensitive to it, often flying into childish fits of rage or lapsing into deep sulks. This of course only re-awakened in the others a desire to tease which might otherwise have remained dormant. I have a picture of Percy, white-faced and writhing with impotent anger, while Norman held him effortlessly at arm's length by his lapel. Sometimes Mike would intervene, but even he seemed to appreciate that Percy must not be too much protected if he were to survive. Sooner or later they would be separated.

Once Percy broke down and cried on the square. We had been sweating hard all the morning under a strong sun, striving to master the turn on the march, Baker was in a vile temper, and his venomous tongue flickered over the squad, leaving its poison to linger and bite under the skin. But, as usual, Percy came in for most of the abuse. Finally, at a particularly grotesque display on Percy's part, in which he tripped himself up and actually fell to the ground, Baker clapped his hand dramatically to his forehead and swore loud and long.

'Fugging Christ, Higgins,' he concluded. 'You march like a WRAC walking through these barracks – with her legs crossed!'

The rest of the squad guffawed mechanically. But when Percy slowly picked himself off the ground, he was crying. The squad looked at him with curiosity or pity.

'Eyes front!' snapped Baker.

We stared ahead listening to Percy's muffled sobs. Mike was directly in front of me, and I saw his neck glowing red.

'Higgins, I always knew you were a fool,' said Baker. 'But I didn't know you were a coward. Crying like a big baby, because the rude man shouted at you! Or did you hurt your tootsies when you fell over?'

Gasping for breath Percy replied:

'It's not – that at all. It's – because you – keep saying fugging – Christ.'

Even Baker was momentarily disconcerted. There was a breathless silence, abruptly and incongruously punctured by the chimes of a mobile ice-cream van which drove up to the side of the square.

'Smoke-break,' said Baker.

We broke up gratefully. Some drifted over to the van to buy ice-lollies. Mike and I loosened our webbing, and threw ourselves on to the grass which bordered the square. Mike tossed me a cigarette, and we smoked in silence for a while, inhaling hungrily. I was smoking quite heavily now. Mike glanced over at Percy, sitting alone and at some distance from everyone else. Guessing his thoughts I said:

'Perhaps we shouldn't have told him.'

'Perhaps not.'

We were both remembering the previous evening. The three of us had been sitting round a table in the Y.M.C.A. Canteen, delaying the moment when we would have to return to the hut and get on with our bulling. The canteen was a small, poorly furnished shack, but we preferred it to the institutional hygiene of the Naafi; and besides, the coffee was better. I was working on a poem – it was more of a gesture, a cultural nose-snook at the Army, than a serious attempt to write anything, – Mike was smoking and reading a tattered newspaper and Percy was brooding with his hands cupped round his beaker of coffee. Suddenly he broke the silence.

'What does "fugg" mean?'

The question startled us. I tittered nervously and looked round to see if anyone had heard. The word which had become as common to our ears as the definite article, sounded suddenly shocking on Percy's lips. Mike told him.

'And "c——t"?'

He went methodically through the list of Army obscenities, with Mike explaining as tactfully as possible. Then he said:

'How disgusting. How absolutely damnable.'

I believe 'damnable' was the strongest word I ever heard Percy use.

'Don't let it worry you, Percy,' said Mike gently. 'They don't really mean what they say.'

'Oh yes they do,' Percy replied quickly. 'They've got filthy, filthy minds.'

I felt relaxed, and almost light-hearted as I lined up with the other P.O.s on the veranda outside the C.O.'s office. The others fiddled nervously with their uniforms, rubbing their belt-brasses with handkerchiefs, and polishing their toe-caps on the inside of their trouser-legs. Fallowfield asked Mike if his cap-badge was in the middle of his forehead. 'Like Cyclops' eye,' he assured him. Fallowfield seemed dubious, and checked his appearance in a nearby window-pane.

'I wish they'd hurry up,' he said.

'Why?' I asked. 'The longer it takes, the less drill we have this afternoon.'

'I don't mind drill,' he replied. 'But waiting makes me nervous.'

Our conversation was cut short by the appearance of the R.S.M., who brought us to attention and treated us to his professional, ill-tempered glare. We were marched in, one by one, to the usual accompaniment of rapidly-shouted orders, the Army's technique for instilling a sense of inferiority and insecurity in the private soldier when he appears before his commanding officer.

Eventually my turn came – before Mike's. I marched into the

room, turned and saluted. Lieutenant-Colonel Lancing sat behind his desk, flanked by Captain James from the P.O. Wing, the Personnel Officer, and the Second-in-Command, reclining in chairs in indolent attitudes.

'Good afternoon, Browne,' said the C.O. civilly. 'Take a seat there.' I sat down on the seat he indicated.

'Uncross your legs, Browne,' said James. I did so. The C.O. grinned at James.

'Just a small point, Browne,' he said to me. 'But small points are important if you want to be an officer. Now I want you to tell me *why* you want to be an officer.' He smiled encouragingly.

'I feel in rather a false position at the moment, sir,' I replied. 'Because the fact is I don't want to be an officer.' The C.O.'s smile vanished abruptly. I continued: 'I told Lieutenant Booth-Henderson last week, but my name appeared on Orders for this interview, and Corporal Baker told me I should attend it.'

The C.O. turned to James.

'Did you know anything about this, Ronny?' he asked.

'No, sir,' said James, – and, to me: 'Why didn't you come and see me about this, Browne?'

'No one told me I should, sir.'

The C.O. turned to the Personnel Officer: 'This man *is* a P.O. I take it?'

'Yes, sir. He asked me to put him down as a P.O. when I interviewed him.'

This little exchange amused me. Confronted with the unexpected and possibly embarrassing situation, Lancing instinctively tried to detach himself from it, and to put the onus on his subordinates. However he recovered his self-possession quickly. I suppose he thought he would demonstrate the absurdity of my attitude.

'Well now, Browne, suppose you tell me why you have changed your mind?'

I thought I might as well enjoy myself while I was there.

'Well, sir, I'll be quite frank with you. I don't like the Army. I know I'm stuck with it for two years, but I'm sure I shall continue to dislike it. I don't see how I could possibly be an officer with that point of view. Don't you agree, sir?'

'What don't you like about the Army?'

'Almost everything, sir.'

The 2 IC smiled slightly, and looked at his shoes. The C.O. began to look rather angry.

'Now look here, I've been in the Army for twenty-five years. You've been in it for four weeks. I think you've got a lot of nerve to sit there and say the Army's all wrong.'

'I'm sorry, sir, I didn't mean to be impertinent. I quite understand that my position must seem inexplicable to you.' I began to get into my stride. 'I suppose it's my education. I've been encouraged to question everything, to form an independent judgment. In the Army one has to accept orders without questioning them. I feel that if I were to hope to become an officer I would have to give up too many principles.'

'When you're older, Browne, you'll discover that there must be some sort of authority which is obeyed without question. But this is all beside the point. The point is that whether you like it or not you have been called up to serve your country for two years. I don't think you've got any reason to grumble about that. Your country has been pretty good to you up till now. It's given you a damn' fine education for one thing. Now are you, or are you not, going to make the best of it?'

'I don't think I've been given the opportunity of making the best of it,' I replied. 'I applied to go in the Education Corps, where I think I might have been of some use to the Army and to myself. In the R.A.C. I feel I'm wasting my time and the Army's.'

'Is there any chance of getting this man transferred to the Education Corps?' the 2 IC asked the Personnel Officer.

'None at all. I told you that before, Browne.'

'Well, Browne,' resumed the C.O., 'there's obviously no point in arguing with you, though I think you're making a great mistake. What do you want to do now. Train as a Signaller/Gunner? If you work hard you might become a tank-commander in time.'

He obviously hadn't understood a word I'd said.

'No, sir, I think I'd rather be a clerk.'

'Is that all right, Harold?'

The Personnel Officer nodded sourly.

'All right then. That's all, Browne.'

'Go over to the P.O. Wing and wait for me,' said Captain James. 'You'll have to sign a non-desirous statement.'

I saluted and left the room. Outside Mike was still waiting for his turn. I winked at him, and strolled over to the P.O. Wing. A little later he joined me.

'You were lucky to go in first,' he said. 'They were hopping mad. The C.O. said: "What is this, a conspiracy?" '

I laughed elatedly.

'We've got them worried, boy!' Then, 'Did you say you wanted to be a clerk?' I asked anxiously.

'Yes. No alternative,' he replied glumly.

The prospect of a warm, easy, sedentary occupation appealed to me, but filled Mike with dismay, Fortunately for me, he had no alternative. For Mike suffered from claustrophobia. On the afternoon when we had been taken to the tank park and allowed to clamber over the muddy monsters, he had emerged pale and trembling from the cabin. Therefore the tank trades were out of the question for him. I was never tempted by them. Tanks seemed to me to be ugly, noisy, dangerous, and quite absurdly obsolete in terms of modern war. Anyway, I was delighted by his news.

'Good. That means we'll do our Clerks' training together,' I said.

At this moment Captain James stalked past us into his office. We heard the clatter of a typewriter.

'This must be a rare case,' I murmured to Mike. 'He's having to type out a pro-forma.'

We were called in to sign the statements.

'I think you're a couple of insolent young fools,' he said. 'I hope you're satisfied. That's all.'

After the dramatic little scene on the barrack square, Baker perceptibly restrained his language. But unlike most N.C.O.s he did not rely exclusively on blasphemy or obscenity for his invective, and Percy's life was still a misery. Baker frequently threatened to back-squad him. I believe now that this was never a real possibility, for Baker prided himself on his ability to make a soldier of the most unpromising material. But with an Inquisitor's subtle cruelty he kept the threat dangling over Percy's head. Percy's dread of being back-squadded did not seem exaggerated to us. We were in a more or less permanent state of physical exhaustion and mental depression, and we longed for the end of Basic Training with an indescribable longing. We did not know what our Trade Training or our regimental life would be like, but we felt that it could not possibly be worse than Basic Training. To forfeit the precious seventy-two after the passing-out parade, and to begin Basic Training all over again, was unthinkable.

Two images rose persistently to the surface of one's mind during Basic Training at Catterick: one was prison, and the other was hell. The sense of being in prison was created by an accumulation of factors: the confinement to barracks, the bad food, the warder-like attitude of the N.C.O.s, the ugly denims, the shaved heads, the pervasive dreariness and discomfort of daily life. The photograph on my identity card, the haggard face and the cropped hair, with my Army number across my chest, irresistibly recalled a convict's dossier. The evening bull-sessions seemed as pointless and soul-destroying as sewing mailbags. Our weekly pay of one pound always seemed curiously unwarranted and unexpected when it was issued: one had no sense of earning money by service, only of being punished.

The feeling of being in prison was perhaps the dominant one, but there were times when life was touched by a quality of surrealism, of nightmarish unreason, and the prison-image gave way to one of hell. Not a real hell of course, but a kind of *opéra bouffe* hell, a macabre farce, one's response to which oscillated between hysterical laughter and a metaphysical despair.

An occasion when this impression was most forcefully made was when we were first ordered to prepare a full kit lay-out. With practice this becomes a relatively simple, though always tiresome operation. But to us the task seemed gigantic. Every single item of equipment had to be cleaned, polished or blancoed. All clothing had to be pressed to regulation measurements until it was no longer recognizable as clothing, but only as a number of flat, oblong shapes. There was one iron between fifteen of us. The official lights-out time was ignored by the N.C.O.s for, as they well knew, the task took us long into the night, and the early hours of the morning. I did not get to sleep until 3 a.m., and several others did not go to bed at all. When my travelling alarum clock woke me at five, they were still bent, red-eyed, over their boots as the grey light of dawn competed with the feeble electric light bulbs. I woke myself at five because to arrange the kit according to the complex regulation lay-out was itself a lengthy process. Little Barnes in fact laid out his kit at 2.45 a.m., and, wrapping himself in a blanket, lay down to sleep on the cold stone floor beside his bed. No one else adopted quite such a Spartan expedient, but several slept on the bare wire mesh of their bed-frames, their kit laid out on the mattress beside them, to be lifted on to the bed in the morning.

Everyone grumbled and swore, of course, but still we did it. And I can't really understand why we drove ourselves to such lengths. Fear of punishment? Perhaps, in some cases, but I doubt it. The punishment would only be abuse, and that would come however hard one worked. In any case, no punishment could be worse than the task itself. Pride in the work? There are a few chronic bullshitters in every squad, but this certainly didn't apply to most of us. Perhaps one has to admit, however grudgingly, that the Army's despotic authority does make itself felt on the most rebellious temperament, that very quickly one does become conditioned to respond automatically to any order, however absurd. Once you acknowledge this, it is very difficult to forgive the Army for it, and even more difficult to forgive yourself. It was with some half-conscious realization of this that Mike and I, while we flogged ourselves as remorselessly as the rest of the squad through that seemingly interminable night, tried to maintain an attitude of ironic detachment from the whole absurd affair. But it was not easy.

The rhythm of activity varied in tempo as the night dragged

on. At about 10.30 a general melancholy fell upon the occupants of the hut. Someone began to hum *Unchained Melody*, a pop-song much in favour at that time, and the rest took it up, humming and singing. The tune was a plangent, melancholy series of cadences in a curiously repetitive form which, I suppose, accounted for its title. The words went something like this:

> *Oh, my love*
> *My darling,*
> *I've hungered for your kiss*
> *A long,*
> *Lonely*
> *Time.*
> *Time*
> *Goes by*
> *So slowly*
> *And time can do so much,*
> *Though you're*
> *Still mine.*
> *I need your love,*
> *God speed your love,*
> *To me.*

It is difficult, and embarrassing, to believe that one was ever moved by words so trite and meaningless. But at certain moments life out-manœuvres the defences of sophistication, lays one open to a shrewd flanking attack of cheap and vulgar sentiment.

It was not long before this mood of quiet melancholy was dispersed by Norman, starting up a rousing bawdy ballad, in his hoarse, dissonant voice:

> *Mary the maid of the mountain glen,*
> *Shagged herself with a fountain pen,*
> *They called the bastard Stephen,*
> *They called the bastard Stephen,*
> *They called the bastard Stephen,*
> *For that was the name of the ink!*

Percy looked at us reproachfully, as Mike and I chuckled. I was constantly surprised by the wit and intelligence which obscenity seemed to reveal in the lower ranks of the Army who otherwise seemed scarcely literate. In the course of my service I was often handed a grubby piece of paper on which was typed some scurrilous doggerel, of stomach-turning obscenity, yet possessing an ingenuity and wit which Rochester would not have been ashamed to own.

As the night wore on, and p.m. changed unbelievably to a.m., weariness and desperation combined to produce a mood of hysteria in the hut. Instead of finishing off the task as quickly as possible, we snatched eagerly at every distraction and interruption. Brief, spontaneous fights broke out. Norman and his friends indulged in several 'riding' sorties against each other. One lad, who had abandoned his kit and was trying to sleep, cursed them for the noise they were making, and they retaliated by lifting the bed with its occupant into the air and carrying it round the hut shoulder high, finally tipping the unfortunate youth on to the ground in a heap of blankets.

At about 2 a.m. Norman decided to sweep his end of the hut. The floor was made of stone flags. Several were cracked and pieces were missing, leaving open cavities. Norman swept the refuse into the largest cavity to save the trouble of dumping it outside.

'Yer can't leave all that shit there, Norman,' protested someone. 'Pox and Faker'll 'ave somethink to say about that.' (Sergeant Box and Corporal Baker were known familiarly as 'Pox and Faker', 'Faker' lending itself to a further, obvious distortion.)

'Fuggit, I'll burn it then,' retorted Norman, and applied a match to the rubbish. There was quite a lot of newspaper and brown paper in the cavity, and the flames leapt up alarmingly, igniting a gleam of wicked, infantile pleasure in the eyes of the spectators. A few ran to feed the fire with more paper and rags.

Little Barnes sniffed the smell of burning in his sleep, and sat up bolt upright in his bed screaming 'Fire!' We howled with laughter at his panic, eyes running with tears, tears of laughter, tears provoked by the stinging smoke, tears that were at the same time *lachrymae rerum*.

Norman and two of his cronies commenced a grotesque ritual dance around the fire, roaring and whooping at the tops of their voices. Others drummed on their lockers with knives and forks. A demonic frenzy seemed to have seized everyone, and though I was only a spectator, I was completely absorbed in the spectacle, until I caught sight of Percy, crouched on his bed, his hands over his ears, white-faced and shivering as if in the grip of an ague.

'What's the matter, Percy?' I yelled to him; but he just looked at me and shook his head.

The flames quickly died away, but the density of the smoke increased. Someone shouted: 'For fugg's sake, Norman, put the fire out.'

'Give us some water then,' he growled hoarsely, lurching towards the ironing table where Joe Matthews, a sharp little Cockney, had a mug of water for pressing. Joe snatched up his mug.

'Get your own bleeding water, Norman.'

'Come on youth,' said Norman. 'Ah haven't got time to get any water. The whole bloody hut'll go up in flames in a minute.'

'Then piss on it.'

The suggestion appealed to Norman, and ripping open his flies, he emptied his capacious bladder on to the smouldering remnants of the fire.

'*Gulliver's Travels*,' I said to Mike, and he grinned in acknowledgement of the reference. His grin faded as he inhaled the foul-smelling steam which now mingled with the acrid smoke. Laughing and cursing, the others struggled to open the windows, or stampeded to the door, which parted from its one remaining hinge and fell outwards on to the ground. They stood on it, hooting and shouting into the hut, where Norman was trying to stamp out the fire.

'You vile bastard, Norman!'

'You silly c——t, Norman!'

'Wrap up or I'll ride ya!' he retorted.

Eventually the smoke cleared, the temporary exaltation faded, and we returned to our tasks, more exhausted than ever. Percy came over and sat at the end of my bed, prodding ineffectually at a boot.

'I can't get this toe-cap to shine,' he said hopelessly.

I inspected the boot. The toe-cap was marked by hundreds of minute scratches.

'The first thing you want is a new duster,' I said. 'That one must have some grit in it which is scratching the surface.'

'Here, borrow mine,' said Mike, tossing over his duster from the next bed. 'I've had enough for tonight.' He took off his boots and, without undressing further, got between the blankets, where he smoked his customary nicotine night-cap.

'Well,' he said, 'it won't be long before we've finished square-bashing.'

'It's all right for you,' said Percy. 'But I'll probably be back-squadded.'

'Baker won't back-squad you, Percy,' I said.

'Oh yes he will. He'll wait till the day before passing out, and then he'll tell me.'

'Well, if the worst comes to the worst,' I argued, trying to console him. 'At least you won't have Baker in charge of your new squad.'

'It's not just Baker,' he replied vehemently. 'Do you think I could bear to go through this again?' He swept out his arm, embracing the whole scene, the bleak, badly-lit hut, the glum soldiers hunched over their boots or groaning in their sleep, the lingering fumes of the fire and of Norman's urine. 'I'd rather die,' said Percy.

In fact Percy died on the Tuesday of the last week of Basic Training. That day we went out to the rifle range. It was raining, a fine, persistent drizzle, but there was a holiday atmosphere in the coach that took us out to the moors. We were tired, because the day before we had been doing various physical fitness tests. The standards required were not exacting, but since all the tests were held on one afternoon – the mile, the hundred yards, the high jump, the long jump, rope-climbing and several other items –

the total expenditure of energy was pretty considerable. However, all that was behind us; passing-out and the seventy-two were before us; and the present, the expedition to the moors, was at least a novelty. The inside of the coach was warm and smoky; the radio was playing 'Housewives' Choice'; even Baker, sitting with the driver, seemed in a better humour than usual, and did not check the exuberance of the passengers, except to say 'Pipe down, c———t-struck,' when Norman bellowed like a bull in June at a couple of girls we passed.

We quickly left the camp behind, and drove through a lunar landscape of rugged moorland, torn and rutted by the tanks which crawled over it night and day like sluggish prehistoric monsters. Eventually we reached the rifle range, which was situated across a valley: on one side were the butts, on the other the firing points. There was no shelter, apart from an open-sided structure of corrugated iron, and a ramshackle latrine with no plumbing. The rain fell softly but unremittingly, and the prospect of spending a day in this bleak, inhospitable place began to look distinctly unattractive.

The party was divided into two parts: 'C' squad was detailed to man the butts, while the other two squads fired; later, we would have our turn. We wrapped ourselves in our groundsheets and trudged across the squelching grass to the butts. The butts consisted of a wide concrete trench, partially flooded with rain-water, which protected us from the rifle fire. Each target was manned by two men. It was raised by a pulley to be fired at. Between each round we signalled a bull, 'inner', 'magpie', 'outer', or miss, with various flags. After five rounds had been fired we lowered the targets and pasted over the holes with appropriately coloured pieces of paper. It was a slow, tedious business. Each man's score was being recorded by frowning, pencil-licking N.C.O.s across the valley. Queries had to be answered by the antiquated field telephone. The novelty of the first few minutes, the temporary sense of danger as the bullets whined over our heads, soon gave way to damp boredom. Baker's good humour melted away in the rain with his trouser creases, to be replaced by one of his wickedest tempers. It was rarely profitable to seek an explanation of Baker's black moods, but I caught him stroking his cheek a few times, and a slight swelling there made me suspect toothache.

'I think Baker's got toothache,' I said to Mike, as we hoisted our target above the trench.

'Stop, you're breaking my heart,' he replied.

At half past twelve we ate our corned beef sandwiches with the hot sweet tea brought out by the Naafi van. At about half past two it was our turn to fire.

'Have you ever fired a rifle before?' Percy asked me, as we struggled across the valley, our sodden capes flapping round our knees.

'Apart from the ·202 the other day, no.' We should have had a practice at firing ·303s a few days before coming out to the range, but at the last moment there had proved to be a shortage of ammunition. So for the majority of us this was our first experience of firing a proper weapon. Yet we were supposed to attain a certain standard of accuracy before passing out.

'I hope I manage all right,' said Percy. 'I hope Baker doesn't watch me. It's just what he will do, of course. He'll put me off completely.'

'You'll be all right, Percy. But watch your right shoulder. I believe the recoil can give you a nasty bruise.'

'I'm left-handed,' he said.

'Well then, your left. What about you, Mike?' I asked, turning to him. 'You did pretty well at the small-bore range.'

'I've done a bit of shooting in Ireland,' he replied. 'But not with these clumsy great things. I thought they went out with the Boer War.'

'Higgins! Browne! Brady! not so much gab,' called Baker from behind. 'Get a bloody move on. We don't want to be here all night.' I glanced briefly over my shoulder. Baker was holding a khaki handkerchief to his jaw, and appeared to be in some pain.

When we reached the firing point, Baker curtly explained the procedure:

'When it's your turn to fire your name will be called. You go to Sergeant Box and he will give you a clip of five rounds. You will then take up your position ten paces behind one of those already preparing to fire. When he has finished you step forward and lie on the ground. On the command "Load!" you insert the clip into the magazine. On the command "Release Safety Catch!" you release your safety catch. At the command "Aim!" you aim your rifle at the bull of your target, taking care to align both sights. At the command "Fire!" you will fire one round and operate the bolt to eject the empty case. You will fire five rounds in this manner. Do *not* fire before the order is given. Do *not* fire more than one round at a time. When you have fired five rounds you will pick up the empty cases and return them immediately to Sergeant Box. Anyone who attempts to take away a live shell is liable to be court-martialled. Is that understood? Right. Let's get the fugging thing over as quickly as possible.'

The drizzle did not make for accurate shooting, and the general standard was low. Baker fretted and swore at the recumbent marksmen. We stood around on the wet hillside, awaiting our turn, fiddling apprehensively with the heavy rifles.

Mike and I were firing immediately after Percy, and we stood behind him, suffering with him. He was trembling with nerves as he lowered himself to the ground. Immediately, he had trouble getting the ammunition into the magazine. He tried to force it, his hand slipped, and a red gash appeared on the back of his hand.

'For Christ's sake, Higgins, can't you even load the fugging thing?' yapped Baker; and snatching the rifle from Percy's nerveless fingers, he effortlessly pushed home the clip with the palm of his hand. He stood over Percy while the latter fumbled awkwardly with the safety catch which, as he was left-handed, was on the 'wrong' side for him.

'Is the target moving, Higgins?' Baker inquired sarcastically, as Percy took aim.

'No, Corporal.'

'Then what's your bloody barrel waving about for?'

Percy steadied his arm, and one could sense the determination and concentration in his rigid figure.

'Fire!'

The shots rattled out. After a pause the butts began to signal. Percy's target indicated a miss. A spasm of pain crossed Baker's face, and his hand went up to his jaw.

'Get your finger out, Higgins,' he said in a low, dangerous voice. 'I'm warning you.'

Percy went on firing. Each time the red and white flag waved sadly over his target. Baker grew more and more insensed. For the last time he ordered 'Fire!' As the shots began to rattle out a Regular came up to Baker with a message.

'Sergeant Box says the butts have rung up to say there are seven holes in number two target and what the fugginell are we playing at,' he said with a grin. Baker went white with anger. With his boot he rolled Percy on to his back.

'You stupid c——t, Higgins! You've been firing at the wrong target! That does it. I don't want to see you again, you horrible man. You're back-squadded. Some other poor fugger can try and make a soldier of you. I've had enough. Get out of my sight. Go on! Get out.'

Percy stumbled miserably between Mike and me, and we watched him dragging himself blindly up the hill through the rain. We couldn't follow him, because Baker called us forward to take up our firing positions.

'Jones!' Baker called to the Regular who had brought the message. 'Pick up that c——t's empty cases.'

Sprawling on my damp groundsheet, I tried to put Percy out of my mind and concentrate on shooting accurately. I didn't want to get back-squadded too. Jones, rooting in the grass at my side, was an irritating distraction.

'Come on, Jones,' called Baker.

'There's only four cases, Corporal,' the soldier replied.

'Oh Jesus! Go and get the——'

His words were cut short by a muffled explosion from behind us, followed by an anguished moan, terrifying because it seemed to come from a distance, and yet was clearly audible. There was a paralysed silence. Then Mike scrambled to his feet and, throwing down his rifle, began running like a stag up the hill.

'Brady! What the——' began Baker. But then he was running too, and we were all running.

We found Percy behind the foetid latrine, lying on his rifle, a horrible stain creeping swiftly through the turf around his body. Mike, with tears streaming down his cheeks, was lifting Percy's face from the wet grass.

'Act of Contrition, Percy,' he was saying urgently. 'Your Act of Contrition. "O my God, I am heartily sorry for all my sins . . ." '

I knew what Mike was afraid of: suicide. The unforgivable sin. And it seemed as if Percy understood too, for he tried to shake his head. He made no sound, but his eyes bulged from their sockets, as if he were astonished by so much pain. Mike looked up at Baker.

'You swine,' he said softly.

Baker had suddenly become old and yellow and crumpled.

'It was an accident,' he said dully.

Mike opened his mouth to reply, but suddenly Percy murmured:

'Accident.'

Baker straightened perceptibly. 'You heard that, – it was an accident,' he said in a dry, eager voice to the little group of terrified soldiers. 'Higgins said it was an accident. You're all witnesses to that.'

Percy opened his mouth to speak again, but all that came out was a gush of blood. I turned aside and, leaning against the latrine wall, my fingers digging into the rusting corrugated iron, I was violently sick. When I turned back Sergeant Box was ordering the soldiers away from the scene; two soldiers who had fainted were being slapped into consciousness; Baker was nursing his jaw; Mike was crossing himself; and Percy was dead.

Percy performed one last, ironic service for us by his death, for our Basic Training ended with it.

The firing, of course, was abandoned immediately, but no one seemed to know what to do. Harassed N.C.O.s flapped about like startled poultry. We saw Booth-Henderson, summoned by the field telephone from the butts, running clumsily up the hill towards us. Eventually he drove off in a jeep to find a call-box. Soldiers loitered in the drizzle, sucking on damp cigarettes, casting scared, surreptitious glances at Percy's body, covered with a wet groundsheet.

'A soldier's death,' said Mike bitterly. 'A soldier's bloody death.' He didn't say anything more.

Booth-Henderson returned after about twenty minutes, and said that we were ordered back to camp. We were herded into the coaches, and jogged back to Catterick in a stunned silence. In the warmth of the bus a strange, sickly smell of rotting vegetation emanated from our damp khaki. We passed an ambulance and two police cars going in the opposite direction.

'There's an ambulance,' cried someone, as it passed. 'They're taking him to a hospital. Perhaps he's not dead after all.'

'Don't be so bloody daft, man,' retorted another. 'There has to be a post-mortem. He's dead all right, the poor bugger.'

The cleaning of rifles had been forgotten. We handed them back, still dirty and fouled, to the resentful armoury staff. Then we dispersed to our huts. Quietly, almost guiltily, the soldiers took their eating irons from their lockers and moved off to the cookhouse. I threw myself on my bed. The bout of vomiting had left me feeling weak and dizzy, and, callously, I was more concerned with my trivial distemper than with Percy's death. Every time the image returned of the blood bubbling up in Percy's throat like a hot spring, I retched. It was painful retching on an empty stomach, but I could not face the evening meal. I tried not to think about Percy's death, standing like a stone-faced guard between my stomach and compassion. But, inevitably, Mike, who was lying beside me, broke his silence when we were left alone in the hut.

'Well, what do you think about it?'

'I don't know. It's a terrible thing. I've never seen death before. I feel sort of numb.'

'Oh I've seen death before. It runs in our family,' he replied, with grim, cracked humour. 'But I don't want to see a death like this again. It was like a murder. Baker killed Percy. He did everything but pull the trigger.'

'You think it was suicide?'

'No I don't. It was an accident. But it wouldn't have happened if Baker hadn't got Percy into such a state of nerves and misery that he didn't know what he was doing.'

'What makes you so sure it wasn't suicide?'

'Percy said it was an accident, for one thing.'

I pondered for a while, and then observed:

'But don't suicides often say that? – try to make their deaths appear to be accidental?'

Mike frowned. 'Yes, I know. My reasons for believing it was an accident probably won't mean much to you. It's simply that Percy was a Catholic. A convinced, practising Catholic. He knew that suicide is the ultimate sin of despair, that he would be risking his immortal soul. But I don't expect you to understand that.'

'I understand,' I replied, slightly nettled. Why did Catholics always assume that their theology was beyond anyone else's comprehension? Mike sat up and swung his legs to the floor.

'Look, Jon,' he said. 'In one sense I would be pleased if it *were* suicide. There might be some chance of getting Baker to answer for his crimes then. But it wasn't suicide. I'm convinced of that. And the only thing we can do for Percy now, is to make sure that the Coroner's Court doesn't bring in a verdict of suicide.'

'What on earth can we do about it?' I asked, surprised.

'We're key witnesses. Tomorrow probably, very soon anyway, the police or someone will be asking us questions and taking evidence. We mustn't give any evidence that would suggest suicide.'

'You're not suggesting that we perjure ourselves?'

'Of course not. It's just a question of emphasis. We mustn't emphasize Baker's persecution of Percy. We must play down any possible motives for suicide. It goes against the grain, I know; I'd like to see Baker rot in Hell. But we must do it.'

'I don't know . . .' I muttered doubtfully. Mike's motives, as far as I could follow them, seemed to derive from a curious mixture of materialism and eschatology. 'I mean, I don't see how whatever we do is going to affect Percy——'

'Of course not, from your point of view,' Mike cut in angrily. 'To you he's just dead.'

'No, I mean from *your* point of view. Surely, theologically, whatever *we* decide happened won't affect his destiny in the next world, if there is one.'

Mike fumbled impatiently with a packet of cigarettes. He omitted to offer me one.

'The trouble with you Agnostics is that you regard theology as a kind of cold mathematical science like economics. It's not like that at all. First of all let me make it quite clear that I'm not attempting to disguise a suicide. I don't believe Percy committed suicide, though I think there's a considerable risk that the law will reach that opinion. You say that wouldn't affect Percy's eternal destiny. Well, in a way you're right. He'll have to answer for his actions whatever we make of them. But it isn't quite as simple as all that. Our Church is made up of the Church militant, the Church suffering, and the Church triumphant, – that is the faithful on earth, the faithful in purgatory, and the faithful . . .'

'In Heaven. Yes. I do know a little about Christianity you know.' Mike grinned, and relaxed a little. He tossed me a cigarette.

'Well, all these three parts of the Church are very closely connected by prayer and mutual help. We invoke the saints to intercede for us; we offer up masses for the repose of the souls of the faithful; and when *they* get to Heaven they intercede for us. Now if a soul slips out of this system of prayer and mutual help it's a great pity. If Percy is stigmatized as a suicide, there'll be no requiem mass, no masses for the repose of his soul. He'll be buried in unconsecrated ground, without a prayer said over his body. He'll be regarded as a shameful chapter in the history of a very old and devout Catholic family. We have a great affection for our dead. It would be tragic if Percy were denied that affection.' He paused.

'Well,' I said, anxious to placate him. 'I don't really understand you, but I'll do what I can, short of lying.'

'Good man!' He got to his feet, and reached for his sodden cape.

'Where are you going?'

'To church.'

'Won't you need a pass?'

'Fugg the pass.'

It was the first, and the last time I heard him use the word. I recalled him explaining it to Percy. Throwing his cape round his shoulders he went out into the rain. I heard him squelching past the window.

The other occupants of the hut began to drift back from tea. Someone came round giving back the beer-money that had been collected for an eve-of-passing-out booze-up planned for the next evening. I decided to go over to the Y.M.C.A. Canteen for a cup of coffee. When I returned there were only a couple of incorrigible bullers at work. No one felt like sitting there polishing brass in the presence of Percy's empty bed, and already there was a rumour that the passing-out parade was cancelled. I was asleep before Mike came in.

The next morning's parade was later than usual. We hung about in the hut until 8.30, when Sergeant Box appeared, and hurried us on to the square. But there was no inspection. A number of names were called out, Mike and mine among them, and we were ordered to fall out and line up at the side of the square. We were marched off to the Orderly Room, while the rest of the squad were taken on a cross-country run by one of the P.T. instructors.

Baker was waiting outside the Orderly Room, looking tense and pale. From the veranda the Adjutant explained to us that we were to be interviewed by the Coroner's Clerk in connection with the death of Trooper Higgins. Baker went in first, and was inside for a long time. We stood at ease on the veranda, the object of curious glances from passing soldiers. A small, bullet-headed lad under detention was picking up leaves by hand from the lawns and flower beds which, bordered with whitewashed stones, encircled the Orderly Room. He edged his way up to the veranda.

'Got a fag, mate?' he whispered.

As Mike's hand went to his pocket the regimental policeman

overseeing the prisoner rapped a command, and the prisoner shuffled off with a rueful grin.

Through the window on my right I saw two pretty shorthand typists making their mid-morning tea. Women look maddeningly desirable in an Army camp. Perhaps that is why they choose to work in such places: it must be exhilarating to know that you are being mentally raped a hundred times a day. It looked cosy in their office. The electric fire was glowing. One of the girls smoothed her skirt over her haunches as she sat down, like a cat licking itself contentedly. Standing on that narrow peninsula between the soft, well-cared-for typists, and the unfortunate soldier grubbing about in the dirt, I was struck by a sense of the injustices, the inequalities of life.

A few minutes later the prisoner was marched off, the policeman striding behind him rapping out the time at an absurd pace: 'Leftrightleftrightleftrightleft,' with the poor fellow straining grotesquely to keep in step. I found the whole business of Army discipline deeply shocking. Like the bad old penal code, it seemed to create crime in order to punish it. Crime and punishment, which were purely abstract ideas in civilian life, seemed to nudge me on every side in the Army. A small slip, a thoughtless action, the neglect of some trivial regulation, and you were suddenly a criminal, incarcerated, bullied, stigmatized. With sub-intelligent soldiers the thing tended to snowball. One night at the end of their leave they didn't want to go back to camp, and so they sat by the fire until the last train had gone. The next morning, they were scared to return, they hid themselves. Soon they were deserters, hunted, there were footsteps in the street at night, loud knocks on the door, they were arrested, brought back to camp under escort, thrust into a cell.

Not only did the system degrade the prisoner; it degraded the policeman too. The regimental police at Amiens camp, in their black webbing, with the diagonal strap that distinguished them from ordinary soldiers, had an air of the Gestapo about them. Shouting and bullying was their trade, and yet most of them were National Servicemen like myself. The Army gave too many people too many opportunities of cultivating sadism.

At last Baker emerged, and walked away without a glance at us. The Coroner's Clerk dealt more rapidly with the next three soldiers, but Mike was in quite a long time. Then it was my turn.

The Coroner's Clerk had been loaned the 2 IC's office. He was a heavily-built, middle-aged man, with greying hair and a relaxed manner. When I entered he was plugging his pipe with tobacco.

'Close the door, will you? Thanks. Now you're Trooper Browne, aren't you? Sit down and make yourself comfortable. My name's Adams. You know who I am, I suppose? And what this is all about?'

'Yes, sir.'

He administered the oath, and asked me a few routine questions, – name, age, etc. Then:

'Were you a friend of Trooper Higgins?'

'In a way I suppose. I mean I saw quite a bit of him, but I wouldn't describe him as a friend exactly.'

'You didn't like him particularly?'

'Oh I liked him all right. It depends what you mean by "friend". We hadn't very much in common.'

'I see.' He exhaled a mouthful of smoke. 'Now, suppose you tell me in your own words what happened yesterday afternoon, from the time Trooper Higgins prepared to fire. I may have to ask you to go slowly, because I shall be taking down your evidence in longhand.'

I gave him a brief, factual account of the incident. From time to time he interrupted me to ask a question.

'Could you describe more exactly the position of the rifle, in relation to Higgins's body?'

'Yes, he was lying on the rifle, face downwards. Perhaps I could draw you a sketch?'

'That would be very helpful. Thank you.' He passed a pencil and paper over the desk. He studied my sketch and turned his mild, grey eyes on me.

'The butt of the rifle then, projected from his right side?'

'Yes. And as I said, his thumb seemed to be caught in the trigger guard.'

110

He nodded. 'Just a few more questions: did Higgins appear to be in an unusual frame of mind on Tuesday?'

'No, nothing that struck me.'

'Not nervous or tense?'

'He was always nervous and tense.'

'Why was that d'you think?'

'Well, he found life in the Army pretty unpleasant.' I searched my mind for more explanations: we were approaching the ground I had agreed with Mike to avoid. 'As you probably know he was going to be a priest before he came into the Army.'

'Yes, so I believe. Tell me, how do you account for his possession of the bullet that killed him?'

I thought for a moment. 'I suppose he didn't fire his last round. As I said, Trooper Jones came up with the message just as they started to fire. Possibly Percy – Trooper Higgins – was slow to fire because he was specially anxious to get his last shot in the target. Presumably Corporal Baker thought he had fired and missed again, when he ordered him away.'

'This "back-squadding" Corporal Baker threatened Higgins with. What does it mean exactly?'

I explained.

'Is it a very serious thing?'

'No . . . but it doesn't happen very often I think.'

'Did Higgins ever say or write anything about suicide to your knowledge?'

'No. He certainly didn't say anything. I didn't see anything he wrote. In fact I don't remember ever seeing him writing.'

'Not even letters?'

'Once or twice perhaps.'

'Did he receive many letters?'

'No, not many.'

'Did he have a girl-friend.'

I almost smiled. 'Percy? I should be very surprised if he had.'

Adams grunted, and tapped out the charred contents of his pipe.

'What was the first explanation of Higgins's death that occurred to you, Browne?'

'That it was an accident,' I replied. This was true. It was only when I realized what was in Mike's mind as he muttered the Act of Contrition that suicide entered my mind, and proved difficult to dislodge. And yet Mike claimed that he had never thought it was suicide: the Act of Contrition was what he would urge on any dying Catholic.

'Why did you think it was an accident?'

'I don't know exactly. I think it must have been because Percy was so clumsy, accident-prone I suppose you might say, – though it sounds rather flippant. He was always hurting himself unnecessarily. Why, he cut his hand just in trying to load his rifle.'

'Ah yes, there *was* a cut on his hand I believe. Now I'd just like you to read through this summary of your evidence . . .'

In the afternoon the whole intake was addressed by the C.O. As his comrades, he said, we must all be deeply shocked by the tragic misadventure of Trooper Higgins. We would be glad to know that a telegram had been dispatched to his relatives on behalf of the regiment, expressing profound regret and sympathy for them in their bereavement. A Coroner's inquest would be held in due course, and also a regimental inquiry, at both of which some of us would be required as witnesses. Meanwhile the incident should impress upon our minds for the rest of our service the great importance of exercising the utmost care when handling fire-arms and live ammunition. In the circumstances the passing-out parade scheduled for the following afternoon had been cancelled. He realized that this would come as a great disappointment to us and to our instructors after the hard work of the previous weeks, but he was afraid that it was unavoidable. We would therefore proceed on leave that afternoon, as soon as bedding and equipment had been handed in to the stores. A number of those soldiers who had been interviewed by the Coroner's Clerk that morning, however, would be required as witnesses at the inquest, and would be confined to the Garrison until the inquest had been held, after which they would get their leave. Their names were . . .

But I knew before my name was called that I was among the unlucky ones. To be disappointed, at the last moment, of the long-awaited leave, and of the extra day (for I was sure we would not get the extra day afforded to the others by the cancellation of the passing-out parade), – it completely overwhelmed any genuine grief I felt at Percy's death. Mike was kept back too, of course, but part of the bitterness of my disappointment was in the knowledge that I would have to conceal my feelings from him out of piety to Percy's memory. I could scarcely bring myself to speak to Mike, as we walked back to the hut, for fear of losing that status as Percy's friend which was now inextricably involved with my claims on Mike's friendship.

'I should have thought the C.O.'s speech was out of order,' he commented. 'That bit about handling fire-arms for instance: it suggested that it was an open and shut case of death by misadventure. It's pretty clear how *they* want the verdict to go. No nasty scandal in the Press, and questions asked in the House.'

'Well, that suits you doesn't it,' I replied irritably.

He shrugged his shoulders. 'I suppose so.'

'It's a nuisance about this leave,' I said, unable to hold my tongue any longer. But Mike appeared not to have heard.

There was a subdued elation in the hut. Mike and I sat on our beds and watched the other lads thrusting clothing into kitbags, to be deposited in the stores. I could just imagine how delighted I would be in the same position. Percy was more popular in his death than in his life. Someone began to whistle. Scouse Miller, a good-humoured and popular lad, called across to his mate.

'Hey, Albert!'

'Yeah?'

'Bit of luck i'n it eh? I'll be 'ome in time to take me tart to the pictures.'

'Yeah. Where will you go? Regal? Me mum wrote there's a good film on this week.'

'Dunno. It's no odds. I don't take 'er to the pictures to watch the bloody film.'

There was a general laugh.

'*Shut up!*'

Mike was on his feet, his face white and strained. 'Don't you know *why* you're going home tonight? Because a boy died. Yesterday. One of us. A boy you've all been so very kind to, from the first night he arrived. The least you can do is to keep a decent silence, instead of rubbing your hands over the women you're going to . . . Oh you make me *sick*.'

Miller flushed, and bridled.

'I know Percy was a mate of yours, Ginger. I'm sorry for the poor bloke. But *I* didn't kill 'im. There's no need to bite *my* 'ead off.'

Just as Mike began to relax, someone said:

'It's all right, Scouse. Didn't you know? Ginger's 'ad 'is leave cancelled. Fuggin' 'ard luck, i'n it?'

A premonitory shudder passed through me as I located the voice. It was Hardcastle, the Regular with whom Mike had clashed over Percy's kneeling figure that first evening. Ever since then he had maintained an attitude of sneering indifference to Percy and Mike. What devil, what stupidity, had prompted him to make his move *now*?

He was a big, rugged fellow, a formidable brawler, one would have said. But Mike carried into the fight a crusader's righteous indignation, and a ruthless intention to punish rather than conquer. He dominated the encounter, refusing to wrestle, and forcing Hardcastle to box, circling his victim, dodging the latter's clumsy blows and methodically battering at his face. The fight took place in a curious, shamefaced silence. Shamefaced because everyone else present realized that they were being punished in the person of Hardcastle, punished for not loving Percy. Eventually a number of the spectators intervened, and Hardcastle sank down on the nearest bed, dazed and speechless with pain. Mike stalked out of the hut in an embarrassed silence.

It was just as well that Mike had the opportunity of releasing his pent-up feelings of rage and pity on Hardcastle, because it probably permitted him to bear stoically the undisguised jubilation of the rest of the intake. Each squad had little or no contact with the others, and Percy's death touched 'A' and 'B' squads very little, except insofar as it had caused the passing-out parade to be cancelled, and the seventy-two to be extended. There was therefore much hilarity and joy in and around the huts as their occupants prepared to go on leave, and I was apprehensive that Mike would start another mêlée, in which I might feel obliged to go to his defence. But he appeared to ignore further provocations.

The others did not get away as quickly as they had expected. When we went to tea we saw them lining up outside the Squadron office to collect their leave passes, and it was a small satisfaction to know that Scouse Miller would not be taking his tart to the pictures that evening after all. But when we returned to the hut it was bleak and deserted: beds stripped of blankets and mattresses, doors hanging open on vacant lockers, dust and shreds of paper on the floor. We sat down on our beds and lit up.

'Well, it's nice to have a bit of privacy,' I remarked, with hollow cheerfulness. My voice rang in the empty room. At the same moment Sergeant Box poked his head round the door.

'Oh, 'ere you are. I've been chasing you two for the last hour. Where've you been?'

'Only to tea.'

'Well you've been a fuggin' long time about it. Anyway, get your kit packed up and your bedding. You're moving.'

'Where to, Sarge?'

'All witnesses are being moved to Waiting Wing until the inquest is over.'

'What will we do there?'

He gave a sadistic grin. 'Fatigues, I should think.'

Waiting Wing was a kind of Limbo, where soldiers who had finished their training were billeted while awaiting posting. As Sergeant Box had prophesied, we were kept occupied by fatigues, shovelling coal and coke. It was a dreary, depressing existence, – only slightly less disagreeable than Basic Training in that there was no bulling, and morning inspections were perfunctory.

On the Saturday we went into Richmond and tasted the heady pleasures of the two cinemas, the '& chips' cafés, and the Naafi Club, where a dance was being held. The revolving doors spun round, feeding in a steady stream of unappetizing female flesh from Richmond and Darlington, to be snapped up by the soldiers who stooped like vultures along the walls of the vestibule. With a five-to-one majority of men, the women swiftly began to look like badly-mauled carrion.

The Naafi Club was scarcely a relaxing place. Women were not the only commodity in short supply. The TV Room overflowed. There was a queue for table tennis. There was a queue in the canteen. If you vacated a chair in the Quiet Room, somebody else was in it before you had straightened up; and a discarded newspaper scarcely reached the table before it was whisked away by another hand. But the Club was probably the warmest place in Catterick as an autumnal chill spread through the region, and we spent most evenings there. We discovered that there were baths (again only two between the thousands of troops), and from then onwards I ceased to use the draughty and erratic showers at Amiens camp.

The days passed slowly. The cancellation of our leave seemed totally unnecessary, as we were not interviewed again until after the rest of the intake had returned. This second interview was very brief. We were simply asked whether Percy was left-handed or right-handed. Even then we didn't catch on.

The Coroner cleared his throat and began his summing-up.

'Gentlemen of the jury: the death into which we are inquiring today presents many problems. The evidence you have heard is extremely complex, and it is my duty to try and reduce this evidence to order, and to help you to reach your verdict.

'First of all, I think you can rule out the possibility of homicide. The bullet that killed Higgins was fired from his own rifle at point-blank range. There is no evidence that anyone else was near him at the time. Neither, I think, need you consider for very long a verdict of manslaughter. There is no doubt that, whatever the reason for Higgins's death, it would not have occurred if he had not been allowed to leave the firing point with a live bullet. There are strict military regulations, which have been described to you, to prevent such an eventuality. Clearly Corporal Baker, who was in charge of the firing at the time, was seriously negligent here;

and you may feel that in other ways his conduct was not beyond reproach. He seems to have lost his temper with Higgins, though there was the extenuating circumstance that on this particular day Corporal Baker was suffering from toothache. However, the important point I wish to make is that in order to reach a verdict of manslaughter you must be convinced that the death was caused by someone's *criminal* negligence, wanton, deliberate disregard for human life; and if you did reach such a verdict the person concerned would face a very serious charge indeed. There has been negligence in this case, gentlemen, and no doubt the military authorities will conduct their own inquiries into the matter, and take appropriate disciplinary measures. But I do not think you can say there has been *criminal* negligence.

'The alternative explanations which suggest themselves in this case are that Higgins's rifle went off accidentally, or that he took his own life deliberately.

'Some of the evidence that you have heard would seem to support the first explanation, – that the rifle went off accidentally. The deceased himself is reported to have uttered the word "Accident" just before he died. Higgins has also been described as a person of poor physical co-ordination, – "accident-prone" is how one witness described him. On the other hand, it would be dangerous to place too much weight on the last words of the deceased. He might have a motive for wishing his death to appear accidental, – to conceal the fact that he had tried to kill himself, for instance. And you have heard Inspector Jordan explain and demonstrate that it would be extremely difficult to inflict this kind of wound on oneself accidentally while carrying a rifle in the way Higgins was last seen carrying it, or, indeed, while carrying it in any normal way.

'You must consider, then, the possibility of suicide. Higgins was a shy, sensitive boy, thrown into the rough-and-tumble of Army life, after a sheltered life at home and at school. The hardships of a raw recruit's training, which more robust young men take in their stride, might have acted on such a temperament in such a way as to drive him to suicide. But in this case you may feel that there is not very much concrete evidence to support such a conclusion, nothing but the general impressions, partly conflicting, of his comrades, N.C.O.s and officers. Second Lieutenant Booth-Henderson has said that he did not detect signs of undue stress in Higgins at any time. But recruits are rarely open with their officers, and Higgins's comrades have left me, at least, with little doubt that he was deeply depressed and unhappy in the Army. There is however, no concrete evidence that this depression and unhappiness had reached the point where he would seek escape in this terrible and tragic way. He left no note, no reference in any letter to such an idea, nor did he speak of it to anyone. The most weighty piece of evidence which suggests suicide is the fact that he was found with his thumb in the trigger-guard of his rifle; for a person aiming a rifle at his own body would find it easier to operate the trigger with his thumb than with his finger. Against the supposition of suicide you must weigh two further pieces of evidence. Firstly, Higgins was a devout Roman Catholic, to whom suicide would be a serious sin, perhaps the most serious of all. This in itself is not conclusive, but it deserves to be considered. You may be inclined to give more weight to the second piece of evidence: Higgins, as I said, was found with his thumb caught in the trigger-guard of the rifle – but it was the thumb of his *right* hand. And Higgins was *left*-handed. You may think that a left-handed person, about to shoot himself, would naturally use his left hand. What possible reason could Higgins have for pulling the trigger with the thumb of his right hand? The only explanation that I can think of is one that has no doubt occurred to you as you listened to the evidence: that Higgins intended to shoot his left hand, to shoot off his trigger finger.

'This kind of self-mutilation is of course not unknown in times of war. Soldiers on active service have been known to take this drastic step in order to be invalided out of the Army. Of course in actual combat it is possible to claim that the mutilation was in fact a wound, for self-mutilation is a serious military offence. Higgins may not have known this, or not thought about it; or perhaps he hoped to pass off the mutilation as an accident. Anyway, supposing that this was Higgins's intention, you have heard Inspector Jordon explain what might have happened. The rifle, which you have seen, is a long, heavy weapon. Higgins may have rested the butt on the ground, and stooped, or perhaps knelt, to get his thumb on the trigger, while holding his left hand outstretched in front of the barrel, or against the mouth of the barrel. Then, through nervousness, clumsiness, any one of a dozen causes, he may have slipped, overbalanced, or the rifle may have skidded on the wet grass so that when the weapon exploded, the barrel was pointing not at his finger, but at his body. This, perhaps, was the 'accident' to which Higgins referred with his dying breath.

'How does such a hypothesis fit in with the rest of the evidence? We have a young man, deeply unhappy in the Army, and no doubt desperately anxious to escape from it. Not sufficiently desperate to contemplate suicide, perhaps, against which he would have religious, and ordinary human scruples. But still capable of seizing on any other expedient, however drastic. On the day of the rifle-practice his unhappiness reaches a climax. He fails humiliatingly at the rifle-firing. He is roughly reprimanded by his N.C.O. He is told that he will be "back-squadded" – that is, he will have to begin all over again the training he has hated so much. But at the same time he is left alone in possession of a weapon with a live round in it. It is unlikely, I think, that the idea of mutilating himself should have occurred to him out of the blue at that moment. But you have heard his friend, Trooper Brady, recall that he had casually mentioned self-mutilation in Higgins's presence. The reference was clearly made in jest: Brady and some other soldiers were joking about ways of getting out of the Army. But the suggestion may have lodged in Higgins's mind, with the tragic result that we know. If so, it is scarcely necessary to say that Trooper Brady has no cause to feel in any way responsible. Only a somewhat unbalanced mind could have taken his joke seriously.

'Well gentlemen, I have put to you the alternative explanations of Higgins's death as clearly as I can. You may feel that none of the explanations can be proved beyond reasonable doubt. In that case you would have to return an open verdict. . . .'

After retiring for three-quarters of an hour, the jury returned an open verdict. But neither Mike nor I had any doubt that Percy had met his death by trying to shoot off his trigger finger and, characteristically, had bungled the operation.

It was a shock to Mike, but to me merely a surprise. I was mildly piqued at not having perceived the significance of the fact that Percy was left-handed. The shrewd and careful investigation of the Coroner's Court drew from me a half-grudging respect for 'our British Institutions'. It had been an interesting experience, but I was glad that Percy's death, with all its attendant inconveniences, was over and done with. Or was it? I wondered, looking at Mike huddled in the corner of the truck that was taking us back to camp. In defiance of regulations he was smoking, frowning as he drew deeply on the cigarette. In the presence of the other soldiers who had been witnesses at the inquest, conversation was imprudent, but I guessed what he was brooding about: the probability, revealed to him for the first time as he stood in public view in the witness box, that his casual joke about shooting off one's trigger finger had suggested to Percy an escape route from his private military hell that led to his death. It was a remark that anyone might have made, and had I done so, my conscience would not have been troubled. But Mike's mind did not work like mine, and I had a feeling that behind that frown a guilt-complex was already in gestation.

But I was wrong; or at least Mike said I was wrong. We didn't have the opportunity to speak openly until we were in the train that took us from Richmond to Darlington, on our way to London for the long-delayed seventy-two. As it was a Thursday evening there were few passengers in the train, and we had a compartment to ourselves. I said as casually as I could:

'You're not worrying about what you said to Percy, are you?'

'What I said to Percy?'

I couldn't decide whether he genuinely hadn't caught my meaning, but his answer when I was more specific was reassuring.

'Oh no. I'm not "blaming myself", if that's what you mean. If Percy was that desperate . . . it doesn't really matter where he got the idea from.'

'What's on your mind then? You don't look too happy. After all, they didn't come to a verdict of suicide. Isn't that what you wanted?'

'But don't you *see*?' he burst out, dragging off his beret, and running his fingers through his coarse red hair. 'Don't you see? Don't you see what fools we've been? By trying to protect Percy from a verdict of suicide, we had to protect Baker. But it was totally unnecessary. Baker was responsible for Percy's death; without him Percy would never have tried to mutilate himself. Now he's going to get off scot-free.'

'I wouldn't be so sure. Remember what the Coroner said. And there's the regimental inquiry.'

Mike merely said: 'We'll see,' and relapsed into a moody silence. Then he said:

'The young fool.'

'Who?'

'Percy. What did he think he could gain by shooting off his finger? He'd have been court-martialled straight away. How was he going to explain it?'

I began to take an academic interest in the problem. 'Yes, he'd have been better advised to shoot off his big toe. I believe they used to do that in the War. It's easier to explain as an accident.'

Mike regarded me suspiciously, as if he thought I was being too detached. I continued hastily:

'The whole thing's full of tragic irony. After all, if there were seven holes in the other target, at least three of them must have been Percy's. He couldn't have been such a bad shot after all.'

Mike nodded gloomily. 'You'd think,' he said, 'that some of the other witnesses would have had the guts to tell the Coroner how beastly Baker was to Percy all along.'

This seemed so irrational, that I made no reply. The train trundled sluggishly through the dark, misty countryside. I was suddenly filled with impatience to get home.

'Will you get to Hastings tonight?' I asked.

'I'm not going home this week-end,' he replied. 'I couldn't face it.'

'But won't your family expect you?'

'I didn't tell them about the leave. I'm staying with some friends in London.'

'Oh,' I said, surprised. Then I added: 'What about meeting somewhere in London on Sunday, and coming back together?'

'Good idea.'

'Where then? And what time?'

'Have a drink with me on Sunday. Could you manage two o'clock?'

'Maybe,' I said doubtfully. I wanted very much to meet Mike, but I knew it would upset my parents if I missed the ritual of Sunday dinner.

'I'll be at O'Connell's Club. It's just off the Tottenham Court Road. Ask the doorman for me.'

'O.K., I'll try and make it. I might be a bit late.'

'I'll be there till about three.'

Darlington Station seemed more than ever like a frontier post: on the broad, busy platform where the London expresses pulled in, one inhaled liberty with the sulphurous air. It was a relief to see, for the first time in weeks, people who had no connection at all with the Army. But in another way this made one more keenly aware of one's exclusion from the free world. In our coarse, ill-fitting uniforms and clumsy boots, we lost the right to be considered as individuals; we were marked out as 'soldiers', an inferior species of humanity. The middle-aged woman in our compartment of the London train eyed us over her *Harper's Bazaar* with vague alarm, as if she expected to be raped at any moment. Her presence inhibited conversation, and in a way I was glad. Matching Mike's concern over Percy's death was becoming rather a strain. Lapped around by the warm upholstery and the fug, I surrendered to sleep.

I was surprised by my own excitement as we approached London. The northern suburbs flashed past, and then, more slowly, the dingy, sooty environs of King's Cross. I went into the corridor and put my head out of the window, watching the great engine picking its way delicately over the points. It seemed impossible that I had been away for only two months.

'Cor, ain't it bleeding marvellous to be back in the dear old Smoke,' said a Cockney soldier behind me.

It was.

FOUR

After lunch I sat on my bed polishing brasses for the guard-duty. It was a hot day, and the other occupants of the hut lay prone on their beds, held back on the brink of sleep by the dance music from somebody's portable radio. At 1.45 the programme changed to 'Listen With Mother'. We listened solemnly to the nursery rhymes and tales of anthropomorphous railway engines.

In the afternoon I went round the camp with Roy Ludlow, checking the P.R.I. inventory. Panes of glass in the carpenters' shop; mowing machines in the gardeners' shed; vacuum cleaners in the technical museum; armchairs in the unit Quiet Room; heaps of broken electrical equipment in a deserted Nissen hut. . . . It was the busiest day I had had at Badmore for a long time.

When we got back to the 'A' Squadron Offices, Henry the barber was in action. He toured the camp every week, visiting a different section each day.

He was a sleek, dapper little man, with a neat, black moustache, and thin, black, oiled hair combed straight back from his widow's peak. The usual Army barber is a kind of half-tamed sheep-shearer, but Henry was a true representative of his ancient trade: I felt sure that somewhere in the case where he kept his scissors and combs, there was a razor and cupping-bowl. He really belonged to some marbled emporium, applying the mysterious arts of hot towels and vibro-massage, discreetly urging the beneficial effects of brightly-coloured and exotically-named hair lotions. His various working-places at Badmore could scarcely have been more different. He cut 'A' Squadron's hair, for instance, in the unit Sports Store, which adjoined the Squadron Offices, surrounded by piles of mud-encrusted football jerseys, taking his equipment as he needed it from his battered case. His customers did not pay him personally: each man had sixpence per week stopped from his pay for one haircut per week, whether he wanted it or not. There was thus no incentive to Henry to give individual attention, and yet he did. Poised on the balls of his feet, he snipped deftly at our hair, delicately adjusting personal tastes to the exigencies of Army regulations; while from the corner of his mouth dribbled a constant stream of banter, gossip, innuendo and – to anyone above a lance-corporal – servile flattery. Since Henry was paid by the P.R.I. he was particularly deferential to me.

I deliberately left it late before going to get a haircut: I wanted to be Henry's last client. When I entered the Sports Store there were only two customers: Roy Ludlow was in the chair, and his pal Connolly was waiting. Henry was in the middle of one of his salacious anecdotes.

'. . . he was up and down, up and down, faster than a barmaid's knickers——'

Connolly, who hadn't heard the expression before, guffawed.

'Good afternoon, Corporal!' Henry greeted me. 'I didn't expect to see you again.'

'Neither did I, Henry. The bastards have put me on guard tonight.'

Henry clucked sympathetically. 'That's hard, that is; and you being released on Wednesday.'

'Go on, Henry,' said Ludlow, anxious to hear the rest of the story.

'No, I'm sorry,' said Henry firmly. 'Corporal Browne is a pure-minded young man. I wouldn't want to scandalize him.'

'Fugg off,' protested Connolly derisively.

'How old are you?' Henry asked him.

'Eighteen. Why?'

'Eighteen, and using language like that,' sighed Henry, shaking his head with every appearance of real concern. 'What would your mother say?'

'She don't know anythink about it. I don't swear when I'm at 'ome. 'Sa funny thing that,' he continued reflectively. 'In camp

128

I'm fugging and blinding all day long, and when I'm at 'ome I don't say nothink except maybe "soddit", and me ma says that 'erself when she's burnt the joint or somethink.'

'Thanks, Henry.'

Ludlow got up from the chair, running a finger round the inside of his collar. 'See you,' he added to Connolly. As his heavy footsteps receded I pondered the truth of Connolly's observation. For us soldier-commuters 'home' and 'camp' were two disparate, self-contained worlds, with their own laws and customs; every week we passed from one to the other and back again, changing like chameleons to melt into the new environment. At home I drank tea without sugar; in camp I drank the common, intensely sweetened brew. They seemed like totally different drinks. The particular instance Connolly had stumbled on had more serious implications. I had been swearing more and more steadily as my military service lengthened and approached its end. At Catterick Mike and I had, by tacit agreement, abstained from using obscene language, as a kind of gesture, a way of signalling our resistance to the brutalizing forces of the Army. My present free use of obscenity was a measure of how far I had moved from those days of stubborn non-conformity.

'Now, Corporal,' said Henry, shaking Connolly's glossy curls from his cape.

I seated myself on the hard wooden chair, and Henry tucked the cape round my neck with his cool, moist fingers.

'Not too much off, Henry.'

'I know. Just enough to get past the inspection tonight. Who's Orderly Officer?'

'The Adjutant.'

'Hmm. I'd better take a bit off the sides then. He's a great one for having the sideboards level with the ears, is the Adjutant.'

'O.K., Henry, you know best. But remember, I'm released on Wednesday.'

'Trust me, Corporal. Nobody will know you've been in the Army.'

'I don't know about that. I shall feel like shouting it to everyone I meet.'

'Glad to get out eh? Well, it's not surprising. I won't say I didn't enjoy my time in the Army. But that was different. France and Belgium at the end of the war.'

'I shouldn't have thought that was very enjoyable. There were some pretty tough campaigns then, weren't there?'

'Oh I kept well out of that. I was batman to a captain on the general staff. We were in Paris after the liberation; then Brussels. Lovely. Those French women, they were so grateful they were fighting to sleep with you. Exhausting it was, in the end.'

'That reminds me, Henry,' I said, grasping the opportunity. 'I want some French letters off you.'

The snip-snap of the scissors behind my ears faltered momentarily. I was grateful that there was no mirror in which I would have to brazen out his surprise.

'Certainly, Corporal, certainly,' he murmured obsequiously, after a pause.

'Could you give them to me now?' I asked, alert for the sound of another customer approaching. Henry laid down his scissors and took a cardboard box from his case.

'How many, Corporal?'

'Oh, I don't know. Two? No, make it half a dozen.' How many times could you use them? I wondered vaguely.

'Plain or teat end?'

'Plain.'

I didn't stop to ask what the difference was. I was sweating slightly under the strain of appearing unconcerned. Henry gave me the packets, and I slipped them into the map pocket on my thigh, as it was the most accessible. It occurred to me that I had never used it before, for maps or anything else.

'How much do I owe you, Henry?'

'Forget it, Corporal.'

'No, Henry——'

'You've done me a few favours in the past, Corporal. Getting me my money early last Christmas. Have them on me. A little parting gift.'

There was no humour in his voice: rather an almost sentimental gravity. He continued to cut my hair in silence, while I gradually relaxed.

I trusted that the things were as easy to use as they seemed to be in theory. And that Pauline would have no objection. But my mind was fairly easy on that score. Hadn't she said once that Catholic teaching on marriage was 'squalid'? No doubt that had been one of the knottiest problems in her tangled relationship with Mike. When had she said that? It was a long time back. It must have been a time when Mike was still very much the link between us, when we anxiously talked and corresponded about him, like two watchers conferring at the bedside of someone gravely ill, our fingers straying imperceptibly towards each other in the darkness of the sick-room. One of those strangely tormented, bitter-sweet week-ends wrested from the serfdom of Catterick.

My first leave was inevitably a disappointment. Three short days in London could not fulfil the expectations that had been built on them in the preceding weeks. The more unfruitfully the priceless hours passed, the more exasperated I became, with myself and with others. It was, of course, foolish to have imagined that things would be different. The three days were not particularly important to my family or acquaintances. They did not realize that those three days constituted for me a precious parole, that I needed their co-operation to squeeze from that short time the essence of the free life, so that I could carry it back with me like a cordial, to warm myself with it in captivity. Somewhere in the back of my mind I had nourished the absurd expectation that everyone would greet me like a returned veteran, overflowing with sympathy and admiration, exerting themselves to give me a good time, and (girls) throwing themselves generously into my arms. Nothing of the sort happened of course. I knew no girls, and had few friends. I had left a dull, uneventful life to go into the Army, and I returned to find the same dull, uneventful life. It was not surprising that no one felt particularly sorry for me, because my pride prevented me from revealing how deeply miserable the Army had made me. Nevertheless, at the time, I was disappointed by what seemed to me the selfishness and callousness of other people.

The first evening, Thursday, was agreeable enough. I shed my uniform as soon as I got home, although it was late. The silky caress of my worsted trousers and poplin shirt, the savour of home cooking, and the resilience of my Dunlopillo mattress, made the evening and night pass in a trance of sensuous euphoria.

The next morning I visited my college: a mistake. Term was only a few weeks old. The anxious, excited faces of the freshers, the self-absorbed assurance of the older students, the atmosphere of easy, casual self-indulgence, excited a mixture of aggravating emotions in me: envy, regret, nostalgia, impatience, loneliness. Once again I felt keenly my lack of friends. I dearly wanted to meet someone who would know me, who would come up and clap me on the back, congratulate me on my degree, and take me off for a coffee. But my own generation had left with me, and I knew few people outside that group. I tried smiling at a few people I recognized, but their acknowledgements were faint or puzzled, and I gave it up in embarrassment. I went over to the English Department: there were few people there as it was a Friday, when there weren't many lectures. My professor, with whom I had hoped to discuss a research project, was away. I had a few desultory conversations with some members of the staff. They all thought I looked well, which infuriated me. The Senior Tutor, who had been asked for a testimonial by the War Office, asked me if I had got my commission yet, and seemed disgruntled when I told him I had withdrawn my application. I climbed the stairs to find Philip Meakin's room.

Meakin had been, I suppose, my closest friend at college. Our mutual lack of personal charm, and exclusive interest in study, had drawn us into a lukewarm friendship of the kind that exists between 'swots' at school, in which the strongest element was one of jealous rivalry. I had been very pleased when he had obtained an Upper Second instead of his expected First in Finals. Since then, however, his fortunes had improved. He had been exempted from military service on medical grounds, and the Prof. had offered him a Research Assistantship. This meant that he earned a small salary by doing a little tutoring in the department, while working for a higher degree.

There were a couple of female freshers giggling nervously outside Meakin's room. I gathered that he was their tutor, and that they were waiting to see him. The awe with which they appeared to regard him seemed absurd to me, and I was tempted to inform them of his total lack of qualifications to teach them anything useful. Instead I raised my fist to knock on the door.

'Mr Meakin's engaged,' said one of the girls reprovingly. I believe she thought I was another of Meakin's consultants. The idea of my consulting Meakin on anything made me smile. I knocked on the door, but at the same moment Meakin opened it to usher out another, very pretty girl.

'Thank you, Mr Meakin,' she said, fluttering her eyelashes.

'That's all right, Miss——' He goggled through his spectacles at me. 'Jonathan! What are *you* doing here? I thought you were in the Army.'

'Even the Army gives one a few days off from time to time,' I replied sourly. 'Can I come in?'

'Of course. No, just a minute. Would you mind if I saw these two students first? I've just got to give them a book-list.'

He kept me waiting for about ten minutes before the two girls emerged, their eyes lowered reverently as if they had just received an audience from T. S. Eliot. I barely restrained an urge to bawl 'Pity about your Upper Second' to Meakin while they were still in earshot.

'Well,' he said, when we had seated ourselves. 'How's life in the Army?'

'The expense of spirit in a waste of time.' I had been polishing this epigram for some time, but it was wasted on Meakin. 'You don't know how lucky you are,' I added.

'I expect you feel pretty peeved about chaps like me?'

'Oh no,' I lied. 'I've every respect for anyone who manages to wangle out of National Service.'

'I didn't wangle,' he protested. 'I've always been asthmatic.'

If my words were malicious, they were nothing to my thoughts. Tarring and feathering was too good for Meakin as far as I was concerned. I was seized by an overwhelming self-pity. It was *I* who should be occupying this book-lined study, soaking up the admiration of pretty freshers, not Meakin. I looked past him, through the window. It was damp and foggy outside, but warm and snug in the room. Meakin would go on being warm and snug, physically and spiritually insulated against the cruel outside world by his books, his status, and the old-fashioned central-heating which bubbled and clanked in the pipes. While *I* saw ahead of me nothing but a bleak prospect of windswept barracks, cold water in the early morning, the harsh cries of stupid authority, the dreary monotony of the slow-moving days. I wept dry, invisible tears of chagrin.

The shadow of Catterick lay over the rest of my leave. On Friday evening I saw a play, and on Saturday a film. But in the middle of a dramatic scene my mind would wander off into a brooding anticipation of the return to camp. Without a companion to talk to I was defenceless against these gloomy thoughts. By Sunday I was longing to see Mike. So, callously ignoring my parents' disappointment, I bolted down my roast beef, bade them a hurried farewell, and rushed, belching, out of the house at a quarter to two. Unfortunately I was obliged to wear my uniform, as I did not intend to return home again. I was hoping to hang on to Mike until we caught the 11.15 train from King's Cross.

O'Connell's was an Irish drinking club occupying a dingy basement in a narrow passage off the Tottenham Court Road. A man in shirt-sleeves and braces looked up from a newspaper called *The United Irishman* as I entered.

'Michael Brady? Aye, he's expecting you. Go on down.'

I descended the rickety staircase and peered into the saloon. The air was thick with cigarette smoke and the brogue. I saw Mike's crew-cut glowing like a red coal at a table near the bar. I shuffled through the crowd, rather self-conscious in my uniform, boots and gaiters, which attracted many curious looks. Mike was wearing an expensive-looking suède jacket, and the cleanest shirt I had ever seen him in. He was sitting with a couple of young men, one plump, curly-haired, with twinkling eyes, the other tall, thin and saturnine, with a cow-lick of straight black hair across his forehead.

'Jon! It's good to see you,' Mike greeted me, standing up. 'Come and sit down. What will you have?'

'Could I have a coffee?' I asked.

'Ssh. Coffee's a dirty word round here,' said the plump one. 'Have a glass of porter.'

'What's porter?' I asked.

'*What's porter?*' He turned to Mike. 'What kind of a barbarian is this man of yours then?' Mike grinned, and the speaker continued: 'What's porter? What's nectar? I'll tell you what porter is. It's a particularly glorious form of Guinness, and it's specially imported from Ireland by O'Connell himself, and if you ask me what Guinness is I'll leave immediately.'

I laughed, and agreed to a porter, though I had never liked Guinness. Mike interrupted:

'Jon, let me introduce you: Jonathan Browne, Brendan Mahoney, Peter Nolan. They know who you are.'

Mike pushed his way to the bar, and I noticed with surprise that his resplendent dress terminated in army boots. While he was away, Brendan Mahoney, the tubby one, treated me to a disquisition on the properties and ingredients of Guinness. He seemed to be an expert on the subject, and laid special emphasis on the fact that the water used to make the drink came from one special well. Mike returned with, to my dismay, a pint tankard of the black, unappetizing fluid. He seemed to be in good spirits.

'Have a good leave?' I asked.

'Great,' he replied. 'And you?'

'Not bad. Quiet. Don't feel like going back to camp, do you?'

He grimaced, and swigged his drink. 'Don't talk about it.'

'I don't know how you stick it, Mike,' said Nolan, the tall one, speaking for the first time. 'They'd never get me in their bloody Army.'

'Knowing you, Peter, I don't think they would,' Mike agreed with a grin. He turned to me: 'You remember that Lane Bequest picture that was stolen from the Tate not so long ago?'

I did. An Irish student had coolly walked out of the Tate Gallery with the picture under his arm, in full view of the public and the gallery staff. His confederates had even tipped off a Press cameraman in advance, who photographed the student walking nonchalantly down the steps with the picture under his arm. The bare-faced cheek of the theft had caused a minor sensation in the Press, until the picture was traced to Ireland, and handed back.

'Well, tell it not in Gath, but Peter here was one of the brains behind the operation,' said Mike. Nolan permitted himself a thin smile.

'I never really understood what it was all about,' I admitted; and immediately Nolan and Mahoney launched into an involved explanation of the legal history of the Lane Bequest, and the perfidy of the English interpreting the law to their own advantage.

'Why did you give the picture back then?' I asked finally.

'It wasn't my idea,' said Nolan darkly. 'I——'

'It was no use to us,' interposed Mahoney. 'There's only one place where it belongs: the Municipal Gallery in Dublin. It's all ready for the pictures. There's a room with "The Lane Bequest" written over the door. You go in, and there's nothing there except for Lane's portrait. The room is waiting for the pictures; and one day they'll come. We made people think by pinching that picture from the Tate.'

I sipped my porter slowly, and with distaste. I was beginning to find the noise, the smoke, and the Celtic fanaticism of Mike's companions rather wearing. I was glad when Mike got up to leave. We all shook hands. Nolan did not release Mike's hand at once.

'Remember, Mike, you can always count on us.'

'Sure, Peter,' said Mike. 'See you.'

'Where to now?' I asked, as we emerged into the fresh air, deliberately assuming that we were going to stay together.

'Would you like to come and have tea with a friend of mine?'

'Delighted. But do they expect me?'

'No, she doesn't. But it'll be all right.'

'She! It wouldn't be the one who's been sending you all those long, mauve envelopes by any chance?'

'The same.'

I looked forward to the meeting with interest.

'I didn't know you had a girl-friend, Mike,' I observed, as we walked towards the tube station.

'Why should you? I never told you. We've known each other for about a year.'

'What's her name?'

'Pauline Vickers. Ghastly, isn't it?'

'What is she, – a student?'

'Was. She's a librarian now. I met her at some hop. Have you got a girl-friend, Jon?'

'No one specially,' I said, unwilling for some reason to reveal my total lack of female acquaintance. 'You look smart,' I added, to change the subject.

'All borrowed,' he explained, 'Except the boots. Couldn't find a pair of shoes to fit me. I don't like this suède much though. It creaks.'

'I wish I weren't wearing this uniform,' I said. I was anxious to make a favourable impression on Mike's girl, – otherwise she might resent my presence. And khaki did not become me.

We took the Piccadilly line from Holborn, northbound, and got out at Turnpike Lane. As we left the station a group of young children turned to follow us along the pavement, chanting:

> *Ginger, you're barmy,*
> *You'll never join the Army.*

They scattered, shrieking, as Mike rounded on them. 'If only it were true,' he observed with a rueful grin. As we walked on, the children began again, from a safe distance.

> *Ginger, you're barmy,*
> *You'll never join the Army,*
> *You'll never be a scout,*
> *With your shirt hanging out,*
> *Ginger, you're barmy.*

Pauline occupied a bedsitter on the first floor of a large Victorian house honeycombed with small apartments. The first feeling I registered as she opened the door was one of surprise. She seemed too conventionally pretty and normal to attract or be attracted by Mike. She seemed a little put out to see me, but recovered herself quickly and put me at my ease. She appeared pleased to discover that I had been at college with Mike.

'It's a pleasure to meet a friend of Michael's who isn't from that dreadful Irish drinking club,' she said.

'Another word from you against the Irish, and I'll put you across my knee and spank you,' he replied. I glanced involuntarily at Pauline's neat round bottom. She stroked it as she sat down. It reminded me of the typist in the Orderly Room.

'Can I take my boots off?' demanded Mike.

'If you wash your feet first.'

'A good idea. I think I'll have a bath while I'm about it.'

'I'll get you a towel,' said Pauline. 'And don't make a mess in the bathroom, or Mrs Partridge will be after me. Do make yourself comfortable,' she added to me. 'Take your boots off. I'm sure *your* feet are clean.' She giggled and blushed.

'Oh it's quite all right,' I replied hurriedly.

While Mike was having his bath I had the chance to size up Pauline, and fill in her background with a few well-chosen questions. She is rather difficult to describe physically, for none of her features is particularly striking. She just makes a kind of blurred impression of well-distributed prettiness: softly-waved, light brown hair; a round, slightly asymmetrical face, unobtrusive nose and mouth; a modestly curved figure; unexceptional, unexceptionable legs, size five feet. Her dress that afternoon was attractive but not chic, the hem at least two inches below the fashionable length. She made a pleasant, eye-resting picture as she sat opposite me in one of the two armchairs that flanked the gas-fire. One thing I noticed, and liked, at once, was that she took full advantage of an armchair, instead of sitting perched on the edge like most women.

I learned that she had taken a Lower Second History degree at Westfield, a girl's college of London University, and subsequently a diploma in librarianship. Her people lived in Essex, but she preferred to live on her own in London. Her parents hadn't liked the idea at first, but she had talked them into accepting it.

The conversation turned to the Army.

'Michael never tells me anything, so you must.'

The invitation could not have been more welcome. This was the audience I had been seeking all the week-end. I described the miseries and inanities of army life, affecting a humorous and detached tone, but drawing exquisite sighs of dismay, incredulity and sympathy from my listener.

'Has Mike told you about Percy, – the young chap who was killed?'

She looked grave. 'Yes. It was terrible, wasn't it? But he didn't tell me much.'

A muffled gurgle of water from across the landing indicated that Mike had almost finished his ablutions.

'I think it would be best if we kept off the subject,' I said quietly. 'Mike is very upset about the whole thing. He was very attached to Percy. Percy was a Catholic, you see. Are you a Catholic?'

She frowned slightly. 'No. Are you?'

'No.'

Mike came into the room, red and glowing, with little beads of perspiration on his forehead. 'Phew! I'm limp,' he said, prostrating himself on Pauline's divan bed.

'You had it much too hot, Michael; you always do. Did you open the window?'

'I think I did.'

Pauline clucked her tongue, and went out to inspect the bathroom. Mike grinned at me.

'You look a bit more comfortable now.'

I was. Relaxing under Pauline's easy friendliness I had taken off my battledress blouse and loosened my collar. I now put myself finally at ease by taking off my boots.

The evening passed lazily and agreeably. We had tea, washed up, and listened to gramophone records. Pauline collected mainly L.P.s of musicals and Spanish folk-music. She had been to Spain that summer with her parents.

'I'd like to go again,' she said, 'But not on one of those ghastly coach tours.'

'We'll go together when I'm released from the Army,' said Mike.

'I don't know what Mummy and Daddy will have to say about that.'

'Oh you'll talk them into it.'

'Anyway, that won't be for two years. What am I going to do until then? I feel like a nun already.'

'A very good way to feel,' said Mike.

'Oh you just don't care,' pouted Pauline.

As far as I was concerned, there was only one fly in the soothing ointment of that evening: the nagging suspicion that Mike and Pauline would naturally prefer to be alone together. I selfishly suppressed this thought until about ten o'clock, when Pauline was in the tiny kitchenette making some coffee.

'Look, Mike,' I said, 'I hope I haven't spoilt your last evening by staying on. I mean, two's company and all that. . . .'

'It's all right, Jon. I invited you on purpose. It's stopped her getting all upset before I go back. But perhaps if you could manage to nip off a few minutes before me. . . .'

So at about ten past ten I explained to Pauline that I had to phone my mother before leaving London, and that I would meet Mike at the tube station. She smiled gratefully; and when I saw the phone in the hall I realized that she had seen through the manœuvre. I was curiously pleased that she had done so. As I clumped down the empty Sunday-night street, the metal studs of my boots grating on the pavement, I cast a covetous glance back at the window of Pauline's room. The main light went off, leaving just the faint red glow of the gas-fire.

The tube station was quite busy, and among the travellers I noticed many of my own kind, – dispirited youths in ill-fitting uniforms, and soldiers of longer service who were permitted to wear civilian clothes on leave. The latter were chiefly distinguished by the small, cheap canvas grips which they carried, probably containing shaving kit, sandwiches against the journey, and a pair of socks which Mum had washed and darned over the week-end. Mike was a long time coming, and I was beginning to look anxiously at the clock and to contemplate leaving him behind,

141

when he appeared, dressed in his uniform. This meant that he had kept it at Pauline's, and I wondered in a vaguely troubled way whether he had spent the last three nights there. But his religion, and Pauline's undemonstrative air of virginity, allowed me to dismiss the idea. Mike's mouth was set in a grim line, and he only grunted when I rallied him for being late. I had to urge him to run for a train, and we only just made it. Everything indicated that his parting from Pauline had been painful, and I maintained a tactful silence.

With each successive stop, the proportion of soldiers among the passengers on the tube train became greater. King's Cross, that Sunday night, seemed to be swarming with them. They stood or sat about the platforms, waiting for their trains, clad in creased uniforms or rumpled suits, smoking, or playing the automatic vendors, or just shuffling their feet amongst the litter, staring out of numbed, hopeless eyes: disconsolate shades on the banks of the Styx waiting to be ferried across to Hades. Many were being seen off by their girl-friends, and for once I was glad that I was unattached, so wretched did the couples seem: joking unhappily, or holding hands in dumb misery, or striving to lose consciousness in a joyless kiss of parting. I watched one couple writhing in a passionate embrace up against the wall of the Gentlemen's lavatory; they separated abruptly, and the girl walked away without a word or a flicker of expression. With a slight shock I saw that they were both chewing gum. All over the station people were demonstrating their inability to say good-bye.

I had time to observe all this because we discovered that the train left at 11.30 instead of 11.15. Our miscalculation was advantageous; we secured an empty compartment at the front of the train, and pulled down the blinds on the corridor side. Our hearts sank as someone ruthlessly pulled back the door, but a shout from one of his mates drew him away. So we had the unusual good fortune of a compartment to ourselves. We were able to extinguish all the lights, except for the blue bulb which glowed dimly in the ceiling, imparting a weird purplish tinge to Mike's hair. As soon as the train was in motion we stretched out on the seats, munching a couple of apples from the food-bag my mother had thoughtfully slipped into my small pack.

The dim light, the metallic syncopation of the train wheels, and a mutual melancholy at being carried back to Catterick, encouraged me to risk an intimate question.

'Are you and Pauline engaged?'

He shook his head. 'Too many problems. Family, religion' – he bit deeply into his apple, munched, and swallowed, – 'Me . . .'

'Pauline isn't a Catholic,' I said, poising my intonation half-way between a question and a statement.

'No. I wanted her to receive instruction, but she's scared of it for some reason.'

I lapsed into meditation as Mike fell effortlessly asleep. I thought about the evening I had just spent. It had been both soothing and disturbing. Soothing because it had assuaged a hunger which had been a dull pain in my bowels for so long that I had come to live with it, almost ignoring it: woman starvation. It was not just sex, – though that too of course, – it was *femininity* that had wanted in my life.

I had gone up to college, young, pimply, diffident, but with my mind full of erotic poetry and my desires aimed at beautiful, shameless young women. There were plenty of those, both in college and on the streets around, but I was too callow to make any impression on the former, and too scared to approach the latter. This had such a humiliating effect on my ego that, rather than console myself with the normal, friendly, unsensational type of girl who could always be found with patience, I retired into an eremitical existence and devoted my energies to study. Although I lived at home, I found no compensation in my mother: the Oedipus complex seems to have missed me out somehow. My relationship with my mother since the 11-plus has been rather like that between a bachelor of fastidious tastes and the woman who 'does for' him.

So what soothed me that evening was not Pauline herself, but her femininity, which she exuded like an essence in which her whole environment had become steeped. The mingled perfumes from her dressing-table, the teddy-bear in which she kept her night-clothes (Mike had unzipped its belly to demonstrate), the prints of Degas's ballet dancers on the wall, the stockings and petticoats hung out to dry on the line in the kitchen, – all this was indescribably novel and delightful to me.

It was Pauline herself who was the disturbing element in the evening. I coveted her. I had not yet arrived at the stage of consciously desiring her; but I wanted very much to own her. I wanted to have her on my arm, to have her write me letters, to enjoy that easy familiarity and almost wifely solicitude which I had seen Mike enjoy. I am not an envious person in the ordinary sense. I am, I think, as conscious of my limitations as I am of my merits, and I do not waste time and energy coveting what is manifestly beyond my reach, whether it be an expensive car or an expensive woman. My envy is really an impatient sense of unfitness in the world around me, of some dislocation of the natural order of things. Thus, for instance, it seemed to me that it was not merely unfortunate, but *unjust* that Meakin should have the comfortable berth in the English Department, and not me. Mike's relationship with Pauline afflicted me with no emotions of erotic jealousy or envy. I simply recognized in it another example of inefficiency in the cosmic administrative machinery which had allowed them to become intimate before I had had a chance to intervene. For they were manifestly unsuited to each other, the neat, sensible Pauline and the wild, unconventional Mike; whereas she fitted *me* like a long-lost glove. I whiled away some of the long hours of that journey back to Catterick trying her on in my imagination. She fitted beautifully.

I woke from a troubled sleep at 6 a.m. The train had stopped. I lifted the corner of the blind and peered out. We were at York. I went out to the w.c., where a notice reminded me not to use the lavatory while the train was standing in a station. Waiting for it to move I leaned against the door, surveying the dismal furniture of the cramped room. Another notice said: '*Gentlemen lift the seat*'. Statement or imperative? I wondered. With a pencil I scrawled '*Officers &*' before the word '*Gentlemen*'.

When I returned to our compartment there was another soldier in it. Mike and I did not speak to the newcomer, nor to each other until we reached Darlington. The second train was full, and dawdled slowly through the damp countryside, stopping at every small station to deliver milk and mail. At the terminus lorries waited to cart us off to our respective units. We paid a penny for the transport. Although this was preferable to paying for a taxi or walking, the Army's thoughtfulness in providing the transport seemed slightly sinister, as if we were being rounded up into captivity as efficiently as possible. Standing in the back of the truck, swaying and stumbling as it swung round corners, the high-pitched whine of the four-wheel drive seemed the most melancholy sound in the world.

The personnel undergoing training in the Clerks' Training Wing at Amiens Camp were a curious collection. We were a concentration of misfits; all of us, for some reason, were unfitted for the normal pursuits of the R.A.C., and had either chosen to become clerks, or had been press-ganged into doing so, for there was always an alleged shortage of clerks in the R.A.C. The average IQ was startlingly high, because we included several ex-P.O.s who had failed Uzbee or Wozbee, some of whom were graduates. Of course the majority were only just literate, but there were better brains to be found among us than anywhere else in the unit, including the Officers' Mess. It was as if the authorities had determined to seed out from the intakes of new recruits anyone with a spark of intelligence or individuality, together with the odd moron or psychopath, and to subject us all to the most farcical and futile form of training they could devise, just to teach us our place.

The training course lasted for a month. The first fortnight was devoted to learning a few simple facts about Army procedure which a bright schoolboy could have mastered in ten minutes. The second fortnight was occupied mainly by learning to type at the hair-raising speed of fifteen words a minute.

There were only three instructors: Sergeant Hamilton, Corporal Wilkinson, and Corporal Mason. Hamilton was a rather pathetic little man, with the ugliest countenance I had ever seen. His mouth was obscenely crowded with teeth, – when he drew back his melon-slice mouth to smile you could count hundreds of them, – and their luxuriant growth had given him a deformed jaw which projected into space like some craggy promontory. His words tended to lose themselves in this dental jungle, and to emerge in a strangely primitive guttural splutter, raining saliva on anyone within ten feet. Few people could resist grinning when he spoke, and that I managed to avoid doing so was the only explanation I could produce for his strangely benevolent attitude to me.

Hamilton, wisely, left most of the instructing to the two Corporals. Wilkinson was a spoilt, baby-faced sibling of the *petit-bourgeois*, who owed his two stripes to his ability as an opening batsman in the Brigade XI. Far more interesting was Corporal Mason, a Regular. I later had the opportunity to check on his age, and was astonished to find that he was only nineteen. He looked at least twenty-nine. He had a white, depraved face, with pale, bloodless lips, and cold, almost colourless eyes. I think he enjoyed his job. He liked the sense of power, and was of a speculative turn of mind. His first action when we clattered into the Nissen hut which served as our classroom, was to order someone to stoke up the stove. (The room was always kept at a stifling temperature, with the windows tightly shut and streaming with condensation.) Then he would write something on the blackboard, which we copied into our exercise books. We spent the rest of the day 'learning' this, while Mason conducted a kind of Socratic dialogue with various members of the class. He would ask us personal questions with a calm presumption that his right to do so was unquestionable. The first thing he ever said to us, on our first morning in the classroom, was:

'How many of you are virgins? Come on, put your 'ands up.' He counted the hands, and observed to Wilkinson 'Three more than last time.' I think he was conducting a kind of amateur Kinsey report. He proceeded to interrogate everyone more closely concerning their sexual experience. I had noticed that Mike had not raised his hand, a fact of no small interest to me; but when Mason commented on this Mike replied angrily that he had refused to answer the question. I then wished I had not put my own hand up.

On another occasion Mason asked everyone what they had been doing before their call-up. Several of us said that we had been at a university. It was just the time of year when graduates were being drafted. Mason looked at Wilkinson.

'Fugg me, we've got a right lot 'ere. Shower of bleeding long-'airs.'

'What did you study?' he asked me.

'English, Corporal.'

'English? What you wanner study that for? It's your native fuggin language i'n it? What about you?'

The man now interrogated confessed to having read psychology at Manchester.

'Psychologist eh? I've always wanted to meet one of those queers. Reckon you know what everyone's thinking, don't you?' He brushed aside the psychologist's disclaimer. 'Know what I'm thinking now?'

'No, Corporal.'

'I'm thinking you're a fuggin lot of use if you don't know what I'm thinking.' He guffawed.

'I'm a psychologist, not a thought-reader,' said the other testily. But Mason was unperturbed.

''Ere, I bet when you're lying on a woman, you're working out why she's lying there. You never wonder why the fugg *you're* lying there.'

The kind of one-sided debate which Mason conducted could be irritating, and occasionally embarrassing, but we all co-oper-ated out of sheer boredom with the paltry 'work' we were given. All, that is, except Mike, who remained sullen and resentful. I knew he loathed the whole set-up of the Clerks' Course, and observed him with some anxiety. I was afraid that he might do something desperate to escape, like changing his trade or volunteering for the paratroops. For myself, I counted the tedium and the humiliation a small price for the relief from the rigours of Basic Training.

Mason and Wilkinson occasionally enlivened proceedings by

147

deliberately provoking one of the class to insolence, and then punishing him. Their favourite punishment consisted in making the victim stand at the end of the room, against the door, and throwing a tennis ball at him. Wilkinson, who was a good thrower, took a sadistic delight in this sport.

We had occasional 'evening classes'. These were imposed upon us with the object of bringing the Clerks' Course more into line with the Wireless and Driving Courses, which entailed night exercises. Our evening classes were of course absurdly unnecessary: no more teaching or learning was done than in the day classes. But Mason and Wilkinson rarely kept us for the full hour, and on Thursdays, pay day, there was no evening class at all if enough volunteers could be found to risk the Queen's pound in a poker-session with the two instructors.

A few days after we had commenced the course, we were astonished to find Norman in our midst. He had been thrown out of the Driving Course after having rammed a telephone kiosk with a Centurion tank, and the authorities, with inspired lunacy, had thought to make a clerk of him. At least he provided a diversion: to watch him entering notes in his exercise book, tightly grasping the pen-holder in his great fist as if it were a chisel, ink seeping slowly over his hands, wrists, uniform and face, was a memorable experience. He quickly adapted himself to the whimsical despotism of Mason and Wilkinson, and justified Mike's original description of him by playing Caliban to their Prospero and Ariel, by turns slave, clown and victim. It was Norman who laid and stoked the fire in the classroom, Norman who offered Mason and Wilkinson the most outrageous cheek, and Norman who usually ended the morning crucified against the door, roaring and bellowing with simulated pain as the tennis balls thudded into his thick torso.

If Basic Training invited traditional images of hell, the Clerks' Course suggested more sophisticated versions, such as Sartre's in *Huis Clos*, its pains compounded of *ennui*, futility and a sense of time passing with unbearable slowness. This, multiplied by two years! I could never bring myself to do the sum.

It was perhaps because of the low state of my morale that Pauline took such a hold of my imagination. Loyalty to Mike should have made me put her out of my mind, and common sense too, for I could not persuade myself that I was likely to win her from him, even if I were prepared to forfeit his friendship in the attempt. But I could not force the memory of her vague prettiness, her insidious femininity, from my mind. Sleep, as I say, is the opium of the soldier, but I looked forward to bed for a special reason. Between the blankets, warm and comfortable at last, eyes shut against the squalid realities of my existence, I could indulge in weaving fantasies about myself and Pauline, fantasies which are embarrassing to recall. I can understand why the pure of heart are generally religious people. If you believed that there was a fanlight in your mind, through which an old man with a beard was perpetually peering, taking down notes, you would think twice about throwing orgies in there.

I had to discipline severely my constant desire to talk about Pauline with Mike, forcing myself always to let him introduce the subject. But he rarely did, even when he received one of those tantalizing, long mauve envelopes.

'Letter from Pauline?' I would say, as we walked away from the office where the post was distributed.

'Mm,' he would grunt, thrusting the letter into his breast pocket.

'Read it if you want to. Don't mind me.'

'It'll keep.'

I rejected the cheap comfort of supposing that their relationship wasn't proceeding smoothly (though such a hypothesis was useful when the curtain went up on my nightly fantasies); I thought it was more likely that Mike was still brooding on Percy.

During the first week of the Clerks' Course we were both called to give evidence at the regimental inquiry into Percy's death. Mike suggested that we should try now to shift attention to Baker's responsibility, but, although I vaguely agreed, I stuck to the same story I had given the Coroner's Court. It seemed to me that it would be dangerous to do otherwise. Mike emerged baffled and irritable from his session with the inquiry; I gathered that all his attempts to steer the discussion away from the particular circumstances of Percy's death, and on to Baker's general behaviour towards Percy, had been sharply checked as irrelevant. He regarded the whole inquiry as a put-up job aimed at saving the Army's face. No doubt this was true, but only, I think, on a subconscious level. No doubt the officers concerned were predisposed in Baker's favour, but only because of sheer ignorance of the possible effects of Basic Training on a sensibility like Percy's. At any rate, Baker was charged as a result of the inquiry.

'They couldn't avoid it,' commented Mike. 'After what the Coroner said. The point is, what has he been charged with. It ought to be a court-martial.'

We never found out precisely what Baker was charged with, but he did not appear before a court-martial. He appeared before the C.O. and lost one stripe as a result. To Mike this was disgustingly inadequate, an insult to the dead.

That evening he sat at the table in the middle of the hut, writing a letter, tearing up several drafts in the process. We were having a kit inspection the next morning, and all except Mike were busy mopping floors, polishing windows, and dusting lampshades. Sergeant Hamilton had told us that our next forty-eight depended on the appearance of the hut, and this was an incentive we all respected, however grudgingly. Mike's refusal to do his share was vocally resented, but he appeared oblivious to the taunts and complaints. I thought perhaps he was releasing his feelings in a letter to Pauline, but when he finished I noted he had sealed two envelopes. Then he went out.

He returned about ten minutes later, and threw himself zestfully, if belatedly, into cleaning operations. My hands were chapped and sore from mopping the floor, and I gladly resigned my rag to him. I sat down on a bed and lit a cigarette.

'I've just posted two letters,' he observed. The platitudinous remark reverberated with a certain elation.

'What's the hurry? They won't be collected till tomorrow morning.'

'I didn't want to have time for second thoughts. I've written to Percy's guardian and the *Times*.'

I gaped at him. 'What about, for God's sake?'

'Percy, of course. And this squalid regimental inquiry.'

I whistled. 'You've done it now. God knows how many regulations you've broken. Writing to the Press for a start.'

'I didn't sign that one,' said Mike with rather pathetic slyness.

I felt a certain relief. Almost certainly the *Times* wouldn't print it, and with luck Percy's guardian would ignore the other letter. I managed to laugh.

'Why the *Times* anyway? It's practically run by ex-Guards officers. You'd have had a better chance with the *Mirror*. It's right up their street.'

'D'you think so?' he said seriously. 'Perhaps I'll write another——'

'For God's sake don't,' I interrupted hastily. 'You'll spend the rest of your service in the glasshouse if you go on like this. If I were you I'd be at the post-box when it's emptied tomorrow morning, and try and get those letters back.'

'No, I won't,' he replied obstinately. 'Anyway, we'll be on parade then.' He wrung the water out of the rag and began wiping the floor furiously.

Our hut passed the inspection, and we got our forty-eight. My hopes of seeing Pauline again were dashed when Mike declared his intention of taking her to stay with his parents at Hastings. I spent a moody week-end devoid of all pleasure except a fleeting sense of escape at the beginning. On the Saturday evening I went to see the sexiest Continental film I could find, but the images of lust, always fading exasperatingly just before the act, only aggravated my frustration. Afterwards I wandered through Soho eyeing the prostitutes, but when one accosted me I fled to the bright lights of Shaftesbury Avenue, which was thronged with Scotsmen, maudlin drunk because their football team had lost. At home that night, I sat up late reading the last chapter of *Ulysses* for the dirt, which, in my morality, is a kind of mortal sin.

Sunday passed like a stifled scream. I realized with horror that I was almost impatient to get back to Catterick. When parole affords no pleasure there is nothing to distract one's mind from the misery of returning to prison, and one wants to get the painful business over as quickly as possible.

I was forty-five minutes early at King's Cross, and decided to secure a carriage for Mike and myself. To my surprise and some annoyance Gordon Kemp walked up to the window from which I was leaning, looking out for Mike. I had to invite him into the compartment. When I returned to the corridor, and leaned out of the window again, I saw Mike coming up the platform, holding Pauline's hand. I waved vigorously, and Mike acknowledged the signal with a listless gesture. They both looked unhappy. I saw Mike say something to Pauline, and she smiled vaguely in my direction. They threaded their way through heaps of parcels and mail-bags, and came abreast of the window. I surveyed Pauline hungrily. She seemed more desirable than ever, but less composed than when I had seen her before.

'Hallo, Jonathan,' she said. I liked her refusal to abbreviate names. We exchanged a few meaningless remarks, Mike oddly silent throughout. Then, reluctantly, I retired into the compartment to let them say goodbye.

Gordon was wearing a white flash on his shoulder-tab which indicated that he had passed Wozbee. He was still very thin, but looked less haggard than when I had seen him on that first evening in Catterick. 'Congratulations,' I said, dimly recognizing an echo of that same evening.

'Thanks,' he said, with a ready grin. He was understandably full of Wozbee, and seemed undiscouraged by my lack of interest in the subject.

'Mike'll miss the train if he doesn't hurry up,' I said, glancing at my watch, and making this an excuse to peer through the window. They were standing by one of those machines which imprint your name on a strip of metal for the modest sum of one penny. Mike was operating the lever with a kind of wilful violence and concentration, while Pauline looked sadly and silently on. Something is wrong, I thought, with guilty pleasure. Then Mike extracted the metal slip and gave it to Pauline. She read the inscription and smiled. The guard's whistle bleated. They kissed.

Mike boarded the train as it began to move, and turned to lean out of the window. Pauline raised the metal strip to her mouth and kissed it to him. Then the train left her behind. Mike came in the compartment and lit a cigarette.

'Well, Gordon?' he said. 'I see you know how to use your knife and fork.' He nodded towards the white flash. Gordon grinned, unruffled. We soon gave up teasing him about his prospective commission. He was a decent, harmless sort of chap. He plainly regarded the commission as just another test in the long series he had been presented with since the primary school, and to all of which he had applied himself with the same dogged, unquestioning perseverance. The conversation became desultory. We all said we had enjoyed our leaves, but only Gordon, I suspected, was being truthful. I was eager to probe Mike about the week-end at Hastings, but Gordon's presence made it impossible. I occupied my mind with trying to analyse the kiss I had just witnessed, trying to distil from it the nature of Mike's relationship with Pauline. I could best define it by negatives: it had not been passionate, nor cool. It had not been a prolonged kiss, nor a brief one. It had not been awkward – they had kissed before; but it had not been characterized by that conscious display of technique which one observes in lovers of real physical intimacy. It had been, I decided, a tender, gentle kiss, between two people for whom a kiss had not yet been devalued by habit or excess. I wasn't sure whether this conclusion was consoling or not. But I reminded myself that no amount of cogitation was going to allay my tormented sense of hopeless attraction to Pauline, nothing except perhaps time and distance. I decided that I would try and get posted to the Far East, and fell into an uneasy sleep, dreaming of delicate, charming and unspeakably licentious geisha girls.

The farce of the Clerks' Course took a new direction that morning: we began the typing classes. These were presided over by a gentle, grey-haired elderly spinster, Miss Hargreaves, in an old house converted into classrooms. Both she and her teaching methods had a charming antique quality, reminiscent of Miss

Beale and Miss Buss. Had I given any thought, before being called up, to my possible experiences in the Army, I could never have envisaged that one day I would be sitting in a stuffy classroom, with a motley collection of oafs, morons, and university graduates, clad in the uniform of a soldier, hunched over a typewriter, tapping out a series of letters in time to the wheezing tune from an old gramophone, obedient to Miss Hargreaves's tirelessly gay 'Carriage return', after every twelve bars. The novelty of the situation, however, soon evaporated, and most of the students were quickly bored, restraining their irritation only out of politeness to Miss Hargreaves. She was wonderfully patient and enthusiastic, but Norman nearly broke her spirit. He wrecked three typewriters in as many days, and on the fourth day managed to inflict a ghastly wound on his hand by thrusting it into the bowels of his machine and pressing the tabulator key. He swore vividly, and then put his bleeding hand to his mouth in clumsy, but somehow touching repentance for having offended Miss Hargreaves's ears. She looked at the blood, blenched, and hurriedly sat down.

'Trooper Norman,' she said, in a faint voice (when she had first asked Norman his name he had cheekily given her his Christian name, and had not disillusioned her when she took it to be his surname), 'Trooper Norman, I'm afraid you will have to go.'

So once again Norman was without a trade, and it was a question of some theoretical interest to us how the Army would contrive to employ him.

The Clerks' Course had at least one virtue, – it was shorter in duration by half than the other trade training courses. The days passed very slowly, but they passed, and sooner than I expected the end of the course, and separation from Mike when we were posted, hove in view. The prospect of parting with Mike (for it was unlikely that we would be posted to the same regiment), aroused ambiguous feelings in me. I could not deceive myself that our friendship had been deep and instinctive: it had been almost artificially forced by our mutual distaste for the Army. On the other hand I viewed with little enthusiasm life in the Army

154

without Mike's moral support. I mean 'moral' literally. Mike's hostility to the Army seemed to have an essentially moral basis, which somehow sanctioned my more self-centred grievances. But it was becoming increasingly clear to me that Mike's 'morality' was an unreliable guide to conduct, and I did not wish to become involved in some wild, quixotic crusade against the Army. The deciding factor was Pauline: it would surely be better for me if I could disengage myself from both of them. In the last week of the course I went to see the officer responsible for postings, and put in a request for the Far East. He said that there were only two R.A.C. regiments in the Far East, and that he didn't think there were any vacancies for clerks, but he would see what he could do.

I was coming back from this interview when I saw Mike turning away from the notice board where Squadron Orders were displayed. He came up to me and announced:

'We're on guard on Thursday.'

I groaned. We had done one guard, and I had hoped that we would complete the Clerks' Course without doing another.

'Well, at least we're on together,' I said.

'Yes, and guess who's the N.C.O.?'

'Who?'

'Lance-Corporal Baker.'

I grimaced. 'Should be a jolly little party.'

We went over to the cookhouse for tea, and discovered that the meal was Shepherd's Pie. We had rashly eaten this before. Mike swore it was made from real shepherds. 'After all, this is Yorkshire, – sheep country,' he said. I lent Mike some money, and we went to the Y.M.C.A. instead. I had frequent cause for self-congratulation on having saved a useful sum from my State Scholarship, which enabled me to buy myself a certain amount of comfort in the way of food and cigarettes. I often lent money to Mike, but usually got it back promptly. I was certain that Pauline paid for his fares to London, and kept him in pocket money. This thought angered me intensely.

We were due for another forty-eight at the coming week-end, after taking our trade test on the Thursday. The number of forty-eights enjoyed by the clerks was a cause of considerable jealousy among the other trainees, but as Mason and Wilkinson were partial to forty-eights, they had to wangle them for us too. The only soldiers more favoured were the professional footballers, perhaps the most privileged group in the Service. They were pounced on by the training regiment as soon as they were called up, and their lives were only slightly affected by National Service: they played football for the Army all the week, and had a forty-eight every week-end to play for their clubs.

'Going to Hastings again this week-end?' I asked Mike, as we bit into our hot dogs.

'No,' he replied. 'It wasn't exactly a success the other week.'

'Why was that?'

'Mother doesn't approve of Pauline.'

'I should have thought she was a very presentable girl-friend,' I said carefully.

'The term "girl-friend" is meaningless to my mother,' he said wryly. 'There are no such things as girl-friends. Only potential wives.' He changed the subject abruptly by inviting me to go out with himself and Pauline at the week-end on the coming Saturday. I accepted with mixed feelings.

'What were you thinking of doing?' I inquired.

'Oh, I don't know . . . a dance or something.'

This didn't appeal to me for several reasons. I produced the most cogent:

'I can't dance.'

'Oh. Well, what d'you suggest?'

I suggested a play and a meal afterwards, and Mike agreed. I said I would get the tickets on Saturday morning. What plays had they seen? I asked him; and was surprised to learn that they rarely went to the theatre.

'I'm too lazy to organize it,' he explained. 'So we usually end up at a dance, or a cinema.'

On the way back from the canteen Mike dropped in at the unit Reading Room, run by the Education Corps, to check the correspondence columns of the *Times*; but his letter had not appeared of course. Nor had he heard from Percy's guardian.

156

Since it was a training regiment, guard duty at Amiens Camp was attended with considerable pomp and circumstance, deliberately designed to impress the raw recruit with a sense of awe and terror. The inspection was lengthy and meticulous, and the guard was called out for a second inspection at midnight. The possibility of being charged for an ill-polished button was never remote, and was particularly near on that Thursday evening when Mike and I presented ourselves at the guard-room. For the Orderly Officer was our old friend Second Lieutenant Booth-Henderson. Rumour had it that he had been caught entertaining a Darlington tart in his quarters; at any rate he had committed some delinquency, and the C.O. had punished him by making him Orderly Officer for ten consecutive nights. This was his seventh, and already he had acquired a considerable reputation for irascibility and the liberal preferment of charges.

I tugged nervously at my uniform and webbing, fearing that our forty-eight was in jeopardy. I glanced over my shoulder and looked straight into the eyes of Baker, who was watching my efforts to improve my appearance with a sardonic leer. I plunged my hands into the pockets of my great-coat, tingling with humiliation and rage.

'Baker's over there,' I muttered to Mike, who was flicking his boots with a handkerchief. He straightened up and looked across to Baker. The latter had quite recovered his poise. He stood effortlessly erect, spick as a recruiting poster. His single stripe, neatly painted with white blanco, stood out on his arm like a fresh scar. For a few moments it seemed that he and Mike were trying to stare each other out. Then the Orderly Sergeant summoned us to fall in. Baker spat with deliberation, and turned on his heel.

It was the first time I had seen him since the inquest, except for occasional glimpses. He was a very different man from the yellow-faced, swollen-jawed Baker shaking with fear and shock over Percy's corpse. His malevolence seemed to have returned: there had been something unmistakably hostile in the way he had looked at us. It occurred to me for the first time that perhaps he considered the loss of his stripe, which seemed to us a mere

157

token punishment, to have been unduly severe, and that we, as chief witnesses, had been the cause of it. I did not look forward to the night's guard.

Booth-Henderson's inspection went according to expectation: it was full of malicious tricks. He made one soldier take off his belt, and charged him because the brass on the inside of his belt was not highly polished. Another soldier was charged because the back of his cap-badge was dirty. He nagged everyone petulantly, – everyone except Baker, that is.

Booth-Henderson drew level with me. I came to attention and gabbled off my name and number, hoping that he had forgotten me and our absurd interview during the Basic Training. He regarded me with a frown; drew back two paces and squinted at me with his head on one side; prowled round behind me; and suddenly tugged at the shoulders of my great-coat. I jumped.

''Shun!' yelped the Orderly Sergeant, to whom Booth-Henderson had communicated a nervous irascibility.

'Your great-coat doesn't fit,' said Booth-Henderson.

'No, sir.'

'Get it changed tomorrow.'

'I've tried to before, sir. Stores say they won't change it.'

'Sergeant!'

'Sir!'

'See this man gets a new great-coat tomorrow.'

'Sir.'

The Orderly Sergeant entered my name and number in his note-book, while I cursed inwardly. A new great-coat meant tarnished buttons to polish, and pleats to be pressed. Booth-Henderson passed on to Mike, who escaped with a lecture on the buckles of his gaiter straps.

Baker's job was to post the sentries, and ensure that they were performing their duty. He read the orders, issued us with bicycle lamps, whistles and pick-axe handles, and allocated the 'stags'. Guard duty was from 6.30 p.m. to 6.30 a.m. – two hours on, four hours off for each man. Mike and I were put on second stag, generally regarded as the least pleasant. Our duty was from 8.30–10.30 p.m., and from 2.30–4.30 a.m.

Time passed with indescribable slowness. When we came off our first stag I already felt exhausted. The supper which had been brought to the guard-room at nine was cooling and congealing in aluminium canisters. I forced down a few mouthfuls, lubricated with lukewarm tea, and then dropped on to the hard bunk. Baker, beside the stove, was reading *Tit-bits* with sober concentration, – somehow he made it last all night, – while the Sergeant was snoring under his great-coat. I found it difficult to sleep under the bright lights, wearing boots and gaiters, my high-waisted trousers uncomfortably tight about the crutch. When I did manage to fall asleep I was woken – immediately it seemed – by the order to fall in on the guard-room veranda, where Booth-Henderson inspected us again. After that it was impossible to sleep until 2.30 when Mike and I commenced our second stag.

2.30 a.m., on guard, was a physical and spiritual nadir. At no other time was one more overwhelmed by the meaninglessness of National Service. There we were, guarding nothing against nobody; or, if anyone had been insane enough to covet the Nissen huts full of mouldering blanco and damp mattresses that we guarded, we were ludicrously ill-equipped to defend them. Soldiers of the modern Army, armed with wooden clubs a cave-man would have disdained.

It was November now, and bitterly cold, but we were too tired to restore our circulation by walking briskly. We moved slowly between the dark buildings, swaying slightly with weariness, dragging our pick-shafts along the ground. Painfully we climbed the hill that overlooked the camp, where some stores were situated, to check the padlocks. They were locked, though the moorings were rusty, and could have been pulled away with a sharp tug. Nearby was a derelict hut, its doors and windows missing. Inside we found two old chairs, one minus a leg, the other with its back wrenched off. We were both seized by an overwhelming desire to sit down. The hut smelled of sheep dirt, so we dragged the chairs to the doorway, and seated ourselves precariously. Mike took out a packet of cigarettes and offered me one.

'Suppose Baker or someone comes snooping round?' I said.

'It's all right. This is a good position. We can see anyone

coming before they see us. First principle of military strategy: take the high ground.'

I accepted the cigarette, and we smoked in silence for a while, keeping the cigarettes in our lips so that we could warm our gloved hands in our pockets. The camp sprawled out beneath us, asleep. In the huts, smelling sourly of sweat and boot-polish, bodies groaned and stirred restlessly in their sticky dreams, while consciousness and the grey reality of another day in the Army stole noiselessly up on them from beneath the eastern horizon. In the cookhouse, where soon pasty-faced cooks would be warming up yesterday's sausages for breakfast, only the cockroaches disturbed the silence, scuttling across the greasy floors. I said aloud:

> '*I should have been a pair of ragged claws*
> *Scuttling across the floors of silent seas.*'

'What's that?' said Mike. 'Eliot, isn't it.'
'*The Swan-song of Trooper J. Alfred Prufrock,*' I confirmed. Mike repeated the lines meditatively.
'What does it mean?' he asked.
'I've no idea.'
'It's good. D'you ever feel that suddenly you don't know who you are or why you're here?'
'In the Army you mean? Frequently.'
'One day you're marching along to the typing class, or some such stupid nonsense, and suddenly you don't know why on earth you're putting one foot in front of the other. There seems no reason why you shouldn't just stop, let the others cannon into you, or walk past.'
'The reason is you'd be put on a charge.'
'But that shouldn't make any difference. That's giving in. The fact that you'd be punished for not doing something you regard as purposeless is the very worst reason for doing it. I mean, I know I wasn't put on this earth to wear army boots and put one foot in front of the other just because somebody tells me to, and to stop because he tells me to.'

160

'What *were* you put on this earth for then?'

He paused before saying, in the curiously pedantic tone he reserved for such statements: 'To exercise my free will, and to save my soul.' After another pause he added, more conversationally: 'Now I've no free will, and my soul is drying up like a prune. The Army's evil, Jon. It's intolerable, isn't it, that pacifism is considered the only ground for conscientious objection. I don't object to war, – a just war. I object to conscription, to being forced into uniform and being made into an automaton so that I can be pushed into the front line when some politician decides that he's going to embark on a war which he may consider just but I may not.'

I vaguely murmured my agreement. I objected to conscription too, but not on these grounds. I objected to having my studies interrupted, my liberty curtailed, my comforts removed. I objected to being woken up at 5.30, being offered revolting food, being made to do menial tasks. The theoretical questions of war and conscience which Mike raised scarcely touched me. The possibility of having actually to *fight* in the Army seemed infinitely remote.

'We'd better move,' I said, getting stiffly to my feet, 'or we'll get frost-bite.'

We made our way down the hill, and resumed our futile perambulations. It was still dark. I looked at my watch. Only 3.25. More than an hour to go.

We were looking up the road towards the guard-room, when the door opened, and a man was silhouetted against the light from within. The door closed again.

'It's Baker,' I said. 'Coming to snoop. Lucky we saw him in time. We'd better separate.' (Guards were not supposed to patrol together.)

'Who's going to challenge him?' said Mike.

'You can,' I said. I could not trust myself to pronounce the challenge with proper seriousness. 'Who goes there, friend or foe?' sounded so archaic. And my voice might crack with nervousness, for I didn't like the idea of Baker stalking us in the shadows.

'What about laying a little trap for him?' said Mike. 'Giving him a little shock.'

'What do you mean?' I said apprehensively.

'Well, you walk up the road under the lamps so that he can see you, and then sidle off round the bedding store as if you're going for a smoke or a pee. He'll follow you, hoping to catch you napping. I'll wait in these shadows, and as he goes by I'll roar out a challenge that'll make him jump out of his boots.'

'I don't know,' I said doubtfully, 'isn't it a bit risky?'

There was a just perceptible curl to Mike's smile. Had he penetrated my mask of sardonic self-assurance, and perceived the timid, cautious soul beneath?

'*You* haven't got anything to worry about. All you've got to do is——'

'All right,' I agreed hastily. 'I'll go.'

I stepped out into the road and walked slowly down the middle of it. I restrained myself with difficulty from glancing over my shoulder, fearing that Baker, having eluded Mike, might at any moment hiss some sarcastic remark into my ear, or even grip me in a half-nelson. I turned the corner of the bedding store without any pretended furtiveness such as Mike had suggested. Then I wheeled round, and took up a stance facing the corner of the store, clenching my bicycle lamp and pick-shaft, my heart thudding absurdly. I could see nothing of course, and I could hear nothing. It suddenly occurred to me that Baker might have made a detour to come round behind me on the other side of the hut. I turned again and peered round the back of the store. It was like hide-and-seek, a game I had always detested in childhood. By this time my head was almost revolving on my shoulders, as I tried to look in two directions at once. I cursed Mike and his crazy schemes. Suddenly the silence was broken. I heard a faint crack, and a thud. I stumbled to the corner of the stores and looked up the road. About fifty yards from me Mike was standing astride Baker's prostrate form, leaning on his pick-shaft like some primitive warrior surveying his vanquished enemy. He lifted his face towards me, white under the lamps. Then, deliberately, he shouted into the silence: 'Who goes there? Friend or foe?' After a brief pause he raised his whistle to his lips and blew three short blasts on it. I ran up the road towards him.

'Christ. What have you done?' I gasped.

'He didn't answer my challenge,' said Mike slowly.

'But you challenged him after you hit him!'

A light went on in the nearest store, and further up the road the door of the guard-room opened, spilling light on to the road. There was a noise of boots thudding on the boards of the veranda.'

'No, Jon, you heard me give the challenge quite clearly, and *then* I hit him. Because he didn't answer.'

I lost my temper. 'Look, Mike, if you want to get yourself court-martialled, that's your business. I think you're a bloody fool, but I'm not getting myself dragged into it.'

Mike's lips curled openly now. 'I may not have the virtue of Christian prudence,' he said with deliberation, 'but God help me from the unchristian sort.'

We glared at each other in silence, in declared conflict at last. There was a shout of inquiry from the direction of the guard-room.

'Look, Mike,' I appealed desperately. 'What do you expect me to do? Be reasonable. . . .'

He gave a swift look over his shoulder. 'All right. All you need do is say that you saw nothing. Just that you heard me give the challenge. It'll be up to them to prove——'

He stopped as the door of the store opened, and the security man came out rubbing his eyes, a great-coat over his pyjamas and boots on his sockless feet.

'Wha's a' this?' he mumbled; and then, as he saw Baker's recumbent form, 'Christ!'

It was raining as I came out of Turnpike Lane station, and I pulled up the hood of my duffle coat. I looked down the toggles of the coat to my fawn Bedford cord trousers with satisfaction, and with satisfaction reminded myself that under the coat I was wearing my slate-blue corduroy jacket. I was glad that this time

I would not be presenting myself to Pauline in the dung-coloured garb of a soldier.

As I left the main road, busy with Saturday-morning shoppers, and stepped, strangely light-footed in shoes, down the grey, gaunt street in which Pauline lived, I told myself severely that mine was not a mission of pleasure. To Pauline I would be either a bearer or a confirmer of bad news, depending on whether or not she had heard from Mike. Yet I could not suppress a certain feeling of exhilaration and excitement at the prospect of seeing her alone. However, I adjusted my face to an expression of suitable gravity as I pushed open the sagging gate, and walked up the tiled path. It was as well I did so, for, as I approached the porch, I glanced involuntarily up at Pauline's window, and met her startled eyes staring down at me, as she stood pressing a duster against the window, arrested in the act of cleaning it. I lifted my hand and smiled wanly. She disappeared from the window, and I waited for her to open the door.

When she did so I saw that she was dressed in trousers and an old, hand-knitted jumper, – both garments agreeably tight, as women's old clothes tend to be.

'Jonathan! What a surprise. Michael said in his letter that we were meeting you this evening . . .'

'What letter was this?' I asked.

'I got it on Wednesday. Why? Anyway, come in. You must excuse these awful clothes, but I'm doing some housework.'

I stepped into the hall and wiped my feet. 'Oh, I see. He's probably written again, but you haven't received it yet.' I was perversely pleased to be the one to break the news. As she led me up the stairs I said: 'I'm afraid Mike won't be coming this week-end.'

'Not coming. Why?' She stopped and turned on the staircase. Her face was suddenly pouchy with disappointment, making me feel simultaneously jealous and ashamed.

'Shall we go up first?' I said gently.

As soon as she had closed the door of the bed-sitting-room she asked anxiously:

'Michael is all right, isn't he? There hasn't been an accident or anything?'

'No, there hasn't been an accident. But Mike's not all right, I'm afraid. He's in trouble.'

'What sort of trouble?'

'He's under arrest for assaulting an N.C.O.,' I said, suddenly struggling to keep a straight face. For the first time, at the most inopportune time, I was struck by the essentially comic quality of Mike's action in clubbing Baker with a pick-shaft. Pauline cupped her face in her hands and sank down on the nearest chair.

'Oh *no*,' she murmured.

I told her briefly the events of Thursday night. I had considered very carefully what version I should give her of what I knew about the incident, and had decided to tell her what I should say when Mike was charged. My motives were, firstly, to rehearse the story properly, and secondly, to position myself as favourably as possible in relation to Pauline. This latter problem was by no means simple. If I told her the truth, – that I knew Mike had struck Baker first, and challenged him afterwards, but that I was going to say, for his sake, that I had only heard the challenge, and could not say whether it preceded or followed the blow, – I would certainly ingratiate myself with Pauline as Mike's defendant. But if I was willing to lie to that extent, she might argue, might I not as well go the whole hog and testify that I had definitely heard or seen the challenge precede the blow? The short answer to that was that if, as was highly probable, Mike was found guilty, I would, in such a case, lie under suspicion of perjury: but it was an answer that I could not give to Pauline without indicating some lack of real loyalty and concern for Mike. So I cut my losses, and told Pauline that I had only heard the challenge, and had no means of judging the sequence of events. I gained no glory from this, but I was in a strong position when Pauline later hinted that I might support Mike's claim that he had not recognized Baker, that he had challenged him and, as he had not answered, had struck him.

'I'm sorry, Pauline,' I said gravely. 'I'd do anything to help Mike . . . except perjury.'

165

She lowered her eyes and blushed charmingly.

'I'm sorry, Jonathan, I shouldn't have——'

'Forget it. I understand how you must feel.'

She got wearily to her feet, shaking her head. 'Oh dear, oh dear . . . what a fool that boy is . . . just a wild Irish boy that never grew up . . . not a scrap of common sense . . . I'm sorry, Jonathan, I haven't even asked you to take off your coat. It must be wet. Do take it off, and I'll make a cup of coffee.'

'Let me make it,' I said solicitously, rising from my chair.

'No, I'll do it, – oh darn, the gas is going. Have you a shilling by any chance? I've run out.'

I rooted in my pocket. 'Yes, here's one. Where's the meter?'

'You'd better let me do it. It's terribly tricky unless you know how.'

She squatted down by the sideboard, and fumbled with the meter, which was awkwardly situated underneath. The broken zip at the side of her trousers gaped, displaying a segment of blue nylon pants. I felt that somehow it was not playing the game to enjoy this in the circumstances, and looked away. Then I thought, what the hell, I might as well look my fill while I've got the chance. But as I turned back the coin fell noisily into the meter, the gas-fire flared, and Pauline stood up. When she came back from the kitchenette with the coffee she said:

'What do *you* think, Jonathan? Do you think Michael hit this man deliberately? Why should he?'

'The man was Baker. I don't know if you remember hearing about him before.'

'Baker. Wasn't he the Corporal who was so beastly to both of you in Basic Training?'

'He was beastly to Percy Higgins. I think that was what Mike's motives might have been. Sort of revenge I suppose. Some crazy idea like that. Mike thought Baker had got off too lightly, I do know that.'

'So you think he did hit him deliberately?'

I paused cautiously before replying.

'Yes, Pauline, I'm afraid I do. I shan't say so to the Army of course, but from his manner immediately afterwards, I would say

166

he did. God knows what good he thought it would do.' Or when the idea came to him. Had he been waiting all along for an opportunity to avenge Percy, or did the temptation to split Baker's head open seize him irresistibly as he stood in the shadows and Baker passed him, falling neatly into our trap in his eagerness to catch us out? A thought struck me:

'Has Mike ever had a nervous breakdown, or anything like that?'

'No. Why?'

'I just thought it might be a possible defence.'

'No. He's always been a wild, wayward boy. Never did any work, – well you know that. Never had any money. Never any thought for the future. But no nervous breakdown, or anything like that.'

We sipped our coffee in silence for a few minutes. Pauline, untypically, sat hunched on the edge of her chair; but whether this was because of her perturbed state of mind, or because she felt self-conscious in her trousers, I couldn't decide. Her eyes fell on a heap of dirty linen; she scooped it up with an apology and took it out to the kitchenette. When she sat down again she asked me what would happen now.

'Well, Mike's under close arrest on suspicion of having assaulted Baker. I suppose they can't bring a charge until Baker recovers.

'*Recovers!*'

'Yes, he's got concussion.'

Suddenly Pauline began to cry, mumbling between sobs:

'He might have killed . . . what will they do to him? They'll put him in prison . . . for years. . . .'

I rejected the comforting arm around the shoulder as too corny a gambit. Instead I leaned forward towards her as far as I could without actually getting off my chair.

'Don't get upset, Pauline. It's not as bad as all that. Maybe I'm wrong. Maybe Baker didn't respond to the challenge. I didn't mean to upset you. I just thought you ought to be prepared for the worst. But in any case Mike stands a good chance of getting off. After all, it's only Baker's word against Mike's.'

'But they'll never believe Mike's word against a corporal's.'

'That's not necessarily true.' I spoke without conviction, but Pauline looked up hopefully at me. She took a wrinkled paper tissue from her pocket and blew her nose delicately. Then she treated me to an embarrassed half-smile.

'I'm terribly sorry to have made such a fool of myself.'

I murmured my dissent.

'I'm very fond of Michael you see.'

I said nothing. There was a long silence. I swallowed the cold dregs of my coffee and said I ought to be going. I didn't want to go, but I couldn't think of any pretext for staying.

'Yes, I'm sure you must be very busy. It was awfully kind of you to come and tell me everything.'

'I'm not busy,' I said hopefully, 'but I'm sure you are.'

'Well I've got to go to the launderette. If you can wait a moment, I'll walk down to the station with you. The launderette's just near there.'

It was still raining as we left the house. I carried the washing, and Pauline put up an umbrella. She held it awkwardly, trying to shelter us both without coming too close to me. I said that I didn't need the umbrella, and raised the hood of my duffle coat.

'Should Mike's parents be told about this?' I asked her. She looked suddenly cross.

'*You* can tell them if you like. I shan't.' Observing my surprise, she added: 'They'll probably blame me for it.'

I said:

'I gathered from Mike that you didn't quite hit it off with his parents. I must say I was surprised.'

She smiled. 'Why?'

'Well, as I said to Mike at the time, I should have thought you were a very presentable girl-friend.'

She laughed shyly, but I could see she was pleased.

'What are they like?' I asked

'Who? Mike's parents? Well they're both Irish of course. They've both got broad Irish accents, though none of the children have.'

'Mike has brothers and sisters then?'

'Oh yes, two brothers and three sisters. And two others died. I've only met Sean, – he's a medical student, – and Dympna, she lives at home and works as her father's receptionist. He's a doctor, as you probably know. The other girls are married, and the eldest son's a teacher in Africa.'

'Mike is the youngest?'

'Yes, unfortunately.'

'Why "unfortunately"?'

'Oh, you know what mothers are like with their youngest sons. She worries about him all the time. Not without reason I must admit. Michael said to me once: "You know that deep furrow in my mother's forehead, just over her nose? Well that's my furrow." And it's true. He showed me the family album once. She never had it till he was born.'

We were now approaching the station. Pauline glanced up at a clock.

'Good heavens! It's ten to one. I had no idea . . . I'm terribly sorry. You'll probably be terribly late for your lunch.'

'It's all right. I'm not going home for lunch. I was thinking of going to Charing Cross Road this afternoon to browse in the bookshops. I'll get something to eat at a snack bar.'

Pauline had come to a halt in the middle of the pavement, frowning slightly, and obviously pondering whether to invite me back to lunch. I studiously avoided an expression of expectancy; looked away from her to the trolley-buses hissing on the wet tarmac; transferred the bag of washing to my other hand.

'Look, would you like to have lunch with me, Jonathan? I was expecting Michael, and I bought a big steak and kidney pie. I shan't be able to eat it all.'

After a token show of hesitation, I accepted. We entered the launderette, had the clothes weighed, and collected a little beaker of soap-powder. Pauline opened a machine, and began to stack the clothes neatly around the inside of the drum. I watched her deft, efficient movements admiringly. She pulled out a soiled brassière from the bag and put it back again.

'Jonathan, would you mind terribly getting me some frozen vegetables while I'm doing this? It will save time.'

When I returned from the errand she was sitting before the machine, staring into the little window behind which the clothes were revolving, as if it were a crystal ball that could tell her something about her future, or Mike's.

I ate Mike's portion of steak and kidney pie with relish. Pauline picked listlessly at her meal. There was only one topic of conversation. To talk about Mike seemed essential if my protracted visit was to be respectable. But I kept trying to nudge the conversation on to Pauline herself.

'So Mike's mother is the problem,' I said, as we were washing up.

'Yes. Mr Brady's all right. I get on with him quite well. A bit too well. He pinched me once.'

'Where?'

She blushed and said: 'The usual place.'

Laughing, I explained: 'I mean whereabouts. I mean, did Mrs Brady see him? It might explain her hostility.'

'No, she didn't see, thank goodness. It was on the landing. No, the trouble with Mrs Brady is that she's so pious. She goes to mass every morning before anyone's awake, and makes everyone else feel guilty at breakfast. Even *I* felt guilty.'

'And Mr Brady isn't religious?'

'Oh he's religious in a way. He goes to church on Sundays – the last mass always. But he doesn't make a show of it like Mrs Brady. In some ways he seems to dislike his religion. He's always making cracks against the parish priest over Sunday dinner, and Mrs Brady gets quite angry because she thinks he shouldn't say such things in the presence of a non-Catholic.'

'Meaning you?'

'Meaning me.'

'Do you feel any attraction towards Catholicism yourself?'

'No, that's the trouble. If I did, everything would be all right. Mrs Brady would be pacified; and Michael would be delighted. He's always trying to convert me. And he got me to agree to have lessons, – instruction, they call it, – once.'

'What was it like?'

'I don't know. I got cold feet outside the priest's house, and refused to go in. We had an awful row.'

She hung up the wet dish-cloths, and we went back into the sitting-room. I offered her a cigarette, and for the first time she accepted one. She handled the cigarette without familiarity, closing her eyes as she blew out the smoke.

'Are you a Christian, Pauline?' I asked.

'No. Well, not really. My parents are C. of E. They go to church occasionally. I used to when I was younger. I still do at Christmas, just to please them, and because I like the carols. But I don't really *believe*. If I did, I think I'd go back to the Church of England. It's sort of sane and reasonable. It leaves you alone; it doesn't go prying into your mind like Catholicism. And it's so much simpler. I mean, Catholicism is so *complicated*. I mean, it's difficult enough to believe in God, – why make it more complicated with Transubstantiation and the Immaculate Conception and indulgences and all that? It's like algebra. And it eats into them, you know. They can't stop talking about it, Michael's family. And it's all mixed up with Irish politics, which makes it even more confusing. They keep teasing me because I'm English, and because the English were so beastly to the Irish, and really, sometimes I feel like asking them why they're all living in England if they despise us so much.'

I laughed sympathetically, recalling my experience at O'Connell's Club. We had a cup of tea, and then I had to go. I could think of no further excuse for staying, and Pauline made no attempt to keep me. She said she would write a letter to Mike that evening.

'But Jonathan,' she added, 'I don't suppose Michael will tell me anything in his letters, in case it would upset me. He never writes much anyway. So I rely on you to let me know if anything serious happens. Otherwise I'll only worry all the more. Would you mind?'

I promised to keep in touch.

'You wanted to see me, Sergeant?'

I had been told when I handed in my pass that Hamilton

wanted to see me, and I stood now in his 'office', a stone-flagged annexe to the Clerks' classroom, containing only a wooden trestle table and a chair. The stove in the middle of the floor had only just been lit, and gave little warmth. Wisps of smoke escaped from the cracked chimney. Sergeant Hamilton sat with his overcoat on, and wore fingerless mittens. He looked up.

'Thank Christ you're back, Browne. I nearly lost a stripe over you.'

'Why was that, Sergeant?'

'You weren't supposed to go on your forty-eight because of this Brady business. You're a witness.'

'I didn't see anything, Sergeant.'

Hamilton displayed his multitudinous teeth in a sly grin. 'That's you're story and you're sticking to it, eh?' I shuffled back half a pace, out of range of the fine spray of saliva which issued from his mouth. 'Well anyway, Brady's going to be charged. Baker came round in hospital on Saturday.'

'Is he all right?'

'Yes; lucky he had his beret on. Your friend might have killed him otherwise. As it is he'll get two years for this.'

Two years! It sent a shiver through me.

'Does it count towards your National Service, Sarge, the time you spend in the glasshouse?'

'Does it fugg. It's added on. When he comes out he'll start all over again.'

I was too numbed by this revelation to reply. Hamilton leafed through some papers on his desk. 'He was a rum character that Brady,' he continued. 'I could see he was heading for trouble. He even messed up his trade test.'

'He passed didn't he?' I asked. Surely not even Mike could have failed the trade test.

'Yes he passed,' replied Hamilton grudgingly, 'but only just. He spoilt his paper with a lot of silly jokes.' Hamilton pulled Mike's script from the pile of papers. 'Like the specimen charge sheet. He made it out for the C.O. and charged him with conduct to the prejudice of good order and military discipline in that his fly-buttons were undone on parade.'

I laughed.

'Of course he covered himself. He didn't write down Lieuten-ant-Colonel Algernon Lancing. He put Trooper A. Lancing. But it's obvious, isn't it?'

I agreed that it was. Hamilton drew out my own script, and smoothed it out on the desk.

'Well, Browne, you didn't mess *your* paper up. You came top with 100 per cent.

I mimicked an expression of mingled pride and modesty appro-priate to a Nobel prize-winner. Hamilton seemed to expect it. 'Thank you, Sergeant,' I said.

'The Army needs more clerks, Browne, needs them very badly. With a little experience you should make a very good clerk.'

'Thank you, Sergeant,' I said again. What was this leading up to? I wondered: conferment of a degree? letters after my name? Trooper Jonathan Browne, B.A. Hons (Lond.), Clerk B III (Catt.)?

'How would you like an opportunity to gain some experience before you're posted?'

'What do you mean, Sergeant?'

'The Orderly Room is a bit over-worked at the moment. They've asked me if I can find a man who could help out temporarily. What do you say?'

There was something touching in Hamilton's naïveté. He really thought that I was keen on being a clerk in the Army. The incentive he offered was quite ridiculous, but I didn't hesitate to accept the offer. It would mean that I would avoid the boredom and fatigues of Waiting Wing. Instead of shovelling coal in the raw November air, I would be comfortably installed in a warm office.

My expectations were not disappointed. The Orderly Room was probably the most comfortable berth in Amiens Camp. Para-doxically, the nearer one gets to the hub of authority in the Army, the easier and idler is one's existence. Discipline was lax, nobody bothered about parades, one could wear shoes instead of boots, there were frequent cups of tea, and mild flirting with the short-hand typists. I was excluded from this last diversion, since the

173

girls in question were uninterested in anyone with less than two stripes. But I was content to make myself as inconspicuous as possible, and to ride out my last weeks at Catterick in relative comfort.

I was placed in the Records Office to assist Lance-Corporal Gordon, a volatile Scot jubilantly in sight of his release date, the 15th of January. I bore patiently his gloating over our relative positions, and he soon tired of it. Why I had been co-opted into the Orderly Room remained something of a mystery, for Gordon did not seem over-worked. In fact there were many hours when we just sat about chatting, or reading the newspapers with an eye cocked on the door. I amused myself sometimes by looking up the record cards of various people in the unit and finding out their past histories. It was there that I discovered Mason's age, and read the Personnel Officer's comments on my first interview with him. I also discovered that I had failed at pistol shooting in my Basic Training, which seemed rather unfair, as I had never fired a pistol either before or since being called up.

I saw Mike again when he went before the C.O. It was bitterly cold. We were all on the veranda outside the C.O.'s office, – Mike, Baker and I, standing at ease in a curious, artificial silence. Baker had a thick white plaster round his head. I did not see him and Mike look at each other once. I caught Mike's eye and he smiled, but the Provost Sergeant who was escorting him told him to keep his eyes to the front. Mike's smile was produced with an effort, it seemed to me. He looked worried, scared even.

I was reminded of an incident at College, more than a year before. We had met by chance outside the room of one of the lecturers, where we had come to collect our sessional papers from the pile heaped on a chair in the corridor. We exchanged a nod and a muttered greeting. I flipped through my script, and noted the mark with satisfaction. I had narrowly beaten Meakin. As I made to move off Mike said to me: 'What did you get?' I felt a momentary embarrassment as I said 'Alpha minus'. He was bound to have done badly, and I felt obscurely that it was slightly improper for him to compare marks with me. I refrained from the customary return of the question, but he volunteered the information that he had got a Gamma minus. He stood turning over his paper with a puzzled, hurt expression, as if he had been hard done by. I was sorry for him, but I thought to myself: 'What did you expect, for God's sake? You told me yourself as we went into the examination hall that you hadn't done a stroke of work.' I made an excuse and hurried away, but somehow the incident had blunted the pleasure of my Alpha minus.

And now, as we stood on the veranda, eyes watering in the cold wind, our breath clouding the air, that feeling returned. Mike had got himself into this mess, it was nothing to do with me, and yet his misfortune gnawed at my sense of relative comfort and security like a worm of conscience. Two years in the glass-house! And then two years of National Service to do! A kind of vicarious desolation swept through me every time I thought about it.

Of course I could no longer fend off the implications of Mike's possible imprisonment. It would, as they said, give me a clear field with Pauline. But would it? Best-friend-of-imprisoned-man-makes-love-to-his-girl cast me too melodramatically as the cad. And I suspected that persecution would only endear Mike to Pauline.

The C.O.'s car drew up, and he stalked past us as if we were invisible.

'Take your cap and belt off,' said the Provost Sergeant to Mike. For some reason accused soldiers had to remove their belts and berets when they appeared before an officer. Whether this was intended, with the rest of the ritual of shouting and stamping, to unnerve the accused, or whether it was, as some said, a precaution against the accused assaulting the C.O. with his belt, or his beret, using the badge as a cutting edge, I never established. It certainly made Mike look already a condemned convict. His hair was so short that one could see the bumps on his scalp.

Mike was remanded for Court Martial. I wrote to Pauline and told her that this was inevitable in the circumstances, and not necessarily a cause for despair. The more formal and public the proceedings, I argued, the better Mike's chances of getting off lightly (for I could not see him getting off completely). It was still Baker's word against Mike's, and although the court might be more disposed to believe Baker than Mike, there would still be, as far as the court was concerned, the puzzling absence of a motive, on Mike's part, for assault, unless someone in the old 'C' Squad leaked to an officer the truth about the triangular relationship between Baker, Mike and Percy. It was clearly not in Baker's interest to do this himself, since it would revive the whole question of Percy's death.

A frequent visitor to the Records Office of the Orderly Room was Corporal Weston, the C.O.'s driver. He was a tall, handsome man, with a dashing moustache. His battle-dress blouse was garnished with the medals of many campaigns, and he wore a paratrooper's wings on his sleeve, although he was now, of course, in the R.T.R. His battle-dress was tailor-made, and he was the only man I ever encountered who looked smart in that curious garment. He was popular with the shorthand typists, who perceptibly protruded their buttocks as they passed him, unnecessarily inviting a pinch or slap. He spent long periods waiting for the C.O. in the offices of the Orderly Room, and mainly in ours. When he had finished the *Mirror*, he would regale us with anecdotes of his military service. These were exclusively of a sexual nature. He told us of the field-brothels set up in North Africa during the Second World War, and painted a vivid picture of soldiers stumbling out of their tents in the early morning for a 'blow-through' before breakfast, at sixpence a time. He told us of the curious habits of Korean prostitutes. He told us of the street in Hamburg with gates at each end, where female flesh was displayed in the windows of every house like butcher's meat. All this with a wealth of detail that put Lance-Corporal Gorman, who had spent his two years in England, beside himself with envy and frustration, and almost made him sign on for another year in the hope of going abroad. Only once did Weston go a little too far, even for Gorman: when he described how, in North Africa an Arab woman came up to him and offered him her ten-year-old daughter for a bar of chocolate.

'About this high she was,' he said, holding his hand about three and a half feet off the ground.

'You didn't, did you?' said Gorman.

'It didn't mean anything to her,' said Weston defensively. 'She wasn't even a virgin.'

'You vile bastard,' said Gorman. Then, curiosity winning over disgust: 'What was it like?'

For me Weston epitomized the paradox of military courage. This was the man we had decorated for valour; the man to whom we owed our freedom. And yet what had carried him through innumerable bloody campaigns was a fundamental barbarism, an utter disregard for human life and human decencies. He was not even proud of his military achievements. He was just a fighting, rutting animal in uniform, a true descendant of the mercenaries of the ancient world. He was rather a rare type in the modern Army, and I found him perversely fascinating.

As the C.O.'s driver, Weston had considerable opportunities for overhearing conversations between the C.O. and other senior officers, and he was a mine of information on regimental matters. On the Friday morning of my first week in the Orderly Room he came into the office and, instead of taking out his *Mirror*, addressed himself to me.

'Did you say this bloke Brady was a mate of yours?'

'Yes,' I said. 'Why?'

'Only that you won't be seeing much of him for a few years,' replied Weston, with a cruel grin.

'Why?'

'Up for court-martial, isn't he? For assaulting Baker?'

'Yes. But he may get off.'

'Not now, he won't.'

'Why's that?' I asked, more calmly than I felt. To show curiosity or anxiety would only incite Weston to delay giving me the information he obviously possessed.

'Not that I blame him for belting Baker. He's a big-headed bastard, that one. And he's got fuggall to be proud of. Never seen any service. Any *real* service. I don't call chasing a lot of bloody wogs in Kenya service.'

I remained silent. Weston spoke to Gorman, indicating me with a jerk of his head.

'Not very worried about his mate, is he?'

'I'm just waiting to hear something new,' I said patiently.

'O.K., here it is: you remember that silly c——t who shot himself a few weeks back – what was his name?'

'Higgins.'

'That's right, Higgins. Well, it seems your mate wrote a letter to Higgins's old man.'

'Guardian,' I corrected mechanically. I knew what was coming. 'His father's dead.'

'Well guardian then. Well Brady wrote a letter to this guardian bloke saying that Baker was responsible for Higgins's shooting himself. And the old geezer has just sent it to the C.O.'

'How do you know?'

'Heard the C.O. say it himself this morning to the Adjutant. In the car.'

I turned away and looked out of the window. A squad trotted past at the double on their way to the gym, cold and wretched in their thin P.T. clothes. There was no hope for Mike now.

Weston was saying to Gorman: 'Brady picked the wrong bloke to write to. The old geezer was a captain in the cavalry in the First World War!' They laughed. I rounded on them.

'It's bloody funny isn't it?' I said with heavy sarcasm. 'I can't think of anything funnier than a bloke getting two years in the glasshouse.'

They seemed to agree, for they laughed more loudly than ever.

'You stupid, selfish bastards!' I shouted against their mounting laughter. ' "Fugg you Jack, I'm all right" – that's it isn't it? Well——'

At that moment the door opened, and the R.S.M. poked his flushed, irritable face round the door.

'What's all this bloody racket? Weston!'

'Sir?'

'You're wanted by the C.O. Look lively.'

'Sir.' Weston went out quickly, straightening his tie. The R.S.M. came into the room. Glaring at me he said:

'Who are you?'

'Trooper Browne, sir.'

'What are you doing here?'

'Sergeant Hamilton sent me here to help out, sir, while I'm waiting to be posted.'

'Well, you're not doing much helping by the look of it. And who said you could wear shoes?'

'I thought all clerks could wear shoes, sir.'

'You can when you're on the permanent staff. Until then you wear boots. Understand?'

'Yes, sir.'

He made to go out, then stopped.

'Done a guard this week?'

'No, sir.' My heart sank.

'Well you're doing one tomorrow. We're one man short. Main Guard Room, 2 p.m.'

'Yes, sir.'

The R.S.M. went out. A twenty-four-hour guard. And I had hoped to slip off for another forty-eight, with Sergeant Hamilton's assistance.

'Fugg the Army,' I said. Gorman laughed heartlessly.

It was not until the following morning, when I was bulling my boots in preparation for the guard, that it occurred to me that the duty might give me an opportunity of seeing Mike, even perhaps of talking to him. I did not hesitate long before deciding to tell him Weston's gloomy news: he might as well be prepared to face the new evidence.

There were only two other soldiers in the hut; everyone else was in the Naafi or on week-end leave. One, like me, was bulling his boots, spitting into the polish and rubbing the toe-cap in small circles, and the other was writing to his girl-friend, biting the end of his Biro and staining his lips with ink.

'I can never think of a fuggin' thing to say to my bird,' he grunted at last.

'Tell her if she's going to chuck you up to do it when you're on leave,' said the other sombrely. 'It's fuggin' awful when they tell you in a letter.' It quickly came out that *his* girl had lately written such a letter to him. He took it out and read it aloud:

' "Dear Alan, Thank you for your last letter which I received yesterday. I'm afraid what is in this letter is going to come as a shock to you Alan, but I have to say it. You have taken an awful lot for granted, Alan . . ." '

She repeated this last remark several times, without explaining what she meant. Her overt reason for breaking off the relationship was: ' "I don't think we should be tied to each other for two years while you are in the Army".' But she twice suggested that they should continue to write as friends, and concluded by begging him to reply to her letter.

'Are you going to?' I asked.

'No. But when I get my next forty-eight I'll find out who she's knocking about with, and then I'll get my mates together and we'll do 'im.'

The other soldier told an anecdote about his elder brother who was in Malaya when his fiancée wrote to break off the engagement. He had handed the letter round to his mates and they had all (there were about thirty of them) written to the girl simultaneously and told her what they thought of her. Knowing the soldier's capacity for abuse, I shuddered sympathetically.

'Wasn't that a bit hard on the girl?' I asked. They looked at me uncomprehendingly.

'If a girl can't wait for you while you're in the Army,' said the one who had read the letter, spitting into his polish, 'she's no good. Nothing's too hard.'

I saw Mike as soon as I entered the guard-room. He was sweeping the floor and looked up and smiled at me. But the Provost Sergeant locked him into his cell at once, and so I had no opportunity to speak to him. There was only one other prisoner, a haggard-looking N.C.O. who, I learned, was awaiting court-martial on a charge of buggery, committed with a young recruit in his squad. Quite apart from my personal relationship with Mike, I found the proximity of these prisoners disturbing. A few of the younger soldiers on guard observed them with a sort of awed fascination, but the officer and N.C.O.s seemed to fall easily into the impersonal attitude of professional warders.

I found my first twenty-four-hour guard even worse than I had anticipated. Time crawled with painful slowness through the Saturday afternoon and evening. The food was revolting, but one had to eat it: I couldn't get the taste of slippery fried eggs, baked beans and sweet tea out of my mouth for days afterwards. As the guard wore on I became increasingly tired, and increasingly incapable of relieving my tiredness. I found it impossible to sleep in the four-hour breaks between stags.

The bunks were hard and uncomfortable, the lights always blazing, the corporal's portable radio always tuned relentlessly to Radio Luxemburg.

I came off my third stag at 4 a.m. on Sunday, almost faint with exhaustion. Mercifully the guard-room was peaceful. The sergeant was snoring, and the rest of the guards asleep. The corporal was out, posting another guard. I went over to the stove and poured myself a cup of well-stewed tea. I heard a whisper from Mike's cell.

'Jon.'

I walked over to the cell, keeping a nervous eye on the sergeant. It seemed impossible to prevent my hob-nailed boots from making a tremendous noise on the wooden floor. Mike's pale face appeared at the bars of his cell. He clasped them in his hands, as all prisoners seem to do. We spoke in whispers.

'Hallo, Jon. Got any cigarettes?'

I gave him half of my packet.

'Thanks. They only allow us three a day.'

In the adjacent cell Mike's neighbour groaned and muttered in his sleep. Mike's use of the first person plural struck me. He seemed to have already acquired the convict's sense of solidarity.

'How's life?' I asked.

'Pretty bloody. I'll be glad when the court-martial's over.'

'Mike. I've got some bad news for you.' His grip tightened on the bars.

'What?'

'That letter you sent to Percy's guardian. The old man sent it back to the C.O.' Mike bit his lip.

'Hell, that's bad.'

After a pause I said: 'I thought I ought to tell you.'

'Yes. Thanks.'

'I'm very sorry.'

'Yes.'

'But don't give up hope.'

'No.'

I heard the boots of the returning corporal and guard scrunching on the gravel path.

'They're coming back, Mike. I'll have to go.'

I got back to the stove just as they came in. I lay down on my bunk and closed my eyes, but could not sleep. I heard the rasp of a match from Mike's cell. Then, to my surprise I felt a tug on my shoulder and a voice said:

'Your stag, mate.'

When I returned at ten, everyone was awake and it seemed that I would not have another opportunity to speak to Mike. But as I was filling my mug from the tea-pot on the stove I heard Mike's voice say:

'Can I have a cup of tea, Sarge?'

'Give 'im a cup of tea,' said the sergeant from behind his *News of the World.*

I went over to Mike's cell, and he handed me his mug.

'Wash it out for me, mate,' he said.

I looked into the mug and saw at the bottom a folded envelope.

'What d'you think this is, a bleeding 'otel?' said the sergeant.

'Don't be like that, Sarge,' said Mike. I sensed the anxiety beneath the humorous, placatory phrase. I carried the mug into the lavatory and took out the envelope, stuffing it at once into my pocket. Then I rinsed the mug in the wash-basin, although it was already clean. As I gave Mike his tea he said:

'Thanks, mate.'

I didn't look at the envelope until long after the guard was dismissed at two. I was sure it contained some message for me, and I wanted to read it in private. I took a bus into the Camp Centre and went to the Naafi Club for a bath. While the water was running I took the envelope from my pocket and unfolded it. It was not addressed to me but, mysteriously, to 'Gordiano Bruno' at an address in Camden Town. It puzzled me. I had never heard Mike mention an Italian friend. And why had he been at such pains to smuggle it out? As far as I knew he was allowed to write letters. After my bath I stamped and posted the letter. Then I went to the Quiet Room and wrote a letter to Pauline.

Later I was eating in the canteen when Fallowfield, Peterson and Gordon Kemp came in. They were wearing civilian clothes, a privilege for Potential Officers who had passed Wozbee. Their clothes seemed curiously significant and revealing after the anonymity of khaki in which one had become accustomed to seeing them. Peterson wore a superbly tailored hacking-jacket and tapered cavalry-twill trousers, Fallowfield a navy-blue blazer and charcoal-grey trousers, and Gordon a Burton tweed sports-jacket and shiny light-grey flannels. I didn't particularly want to talk to them, but Gordon, in his friendly way, led them, bearing trays of food, to my table.

'Hallo,' I said. 'Wearing "mufti" I see?'

'Yes,' replied Fallowfield, oblivious to my sarcastic emphasis on the word, 'It's a jolly useful concession. Means you don't mess up your best B.D. at week-ends. Particularly on leave.'

'You don't mean to say,' I asked, 'that you had any scruples about wearing civvies on leave before? Did you two?'

Gordon, who was eating voraciously, shook his head. 'Not me, old boy,' said Peterson, 'I can't stand battle-dress. Makes me want to scratch all the time.'

'Well, it won't be long before you can wear that nice, smooth officers' gaberdine,' I observed.

'It's not a question of scruples,' said Fallowfield, slightly net-tled. 'It's a question of obeying an order when there's no one to check up on you, just as you would if there were someone to check up on you.'

'That's what I call a scruple,' I replied.

After a pause, Fallowfield started a conversation with Peterson about a recent map-reading exercise. Gordon said to me:

'How's Mike, Jon? Have you seen him lately?'

'I saw him last night as a matter of fact. On guard. It's obviously a strain.'

'It must be. I was very sorry when I heard about it. What are his chances, d'you think?'

'Not too bright.'

'What really happened that night, Jon? You were on guard with him weren't you?'

Fallowfield and Peterson stopped talking and pricked up their ears.

'I'd rather not go into it now, Gordon, if you don't mind. After all, it is *sub judice* and so on.'

'Who's having scruples now?' said Fallowfield.

'All right. Put it another way. I don't particularly want to give other people an opportunity of gloating over Mike's troubles.'

'I wouldn't gloat,' said Gordon.

'I know you wouldn't, Gordon,' I replied, pushing back my chair. 'Well I must be going. I'd hate to interrupt a fascinating conversation about map-reading. So long.'

At the door Gordon caught up with me.

'Jon . . . I was wondering whether there was anything we could do for Mike.'

'What *can* we do?'

'I was wondering . . . perhaps the Prof. would write a letter on his behalf. . . .'

'My dear Gordon, you know Mike wasn't exactly the Prof.'s blue-eyed boy. This will only confirm his opinion.'

'Yes . . . well . . . I suppose we must just hope for the best.'

'Yes.'

There was a brief, awkward silence between us. Then Gordon said:

'You know, Jon, I reckon you made the right choice. I mean about refusing a commission.'

'It wasn't quite as grand as that, Gordon. I refused to *go in* for a commission.'

'Yes . . . well . . . anyway, I'm getting pretty sick of it in the P.O. Wing. They're a frightfully snobbish lot. And half of them are queer. When I came in late the other night, two of them were in bed together.'

'Not Fallowfield!' I exclaimed. 'Surely nobody of either sex would get into bed with Fallowfield.'

'No, not Fallowfield,' said Gordon grinning. 'He's all right really, you know.'

'Yes, he's all right; he's just a pig-headed, pompous idiot, that's all. If it's all so ghastly, why don't you chuck it?'

'Oh I don't know. Now I've got this far . . . and my parents wouldn't understand. Though I'll probably be thrown out of Mons anyway.'

I patted him on the arm. 'You'll be all right, Gordon. They won't chuck you out. When do you go?'

'Next week.'

'Well, the best of luck.'

'Yes. Same to you.'

We parted. I was beginning to feel the effects of the guard, and looked forward to an early night. Outside the Club I saw the red M.G. in which Peterson had brought Fallowfield and Gordon. Gordon was a decent chap. Why had he gone out of his way to tell me that I had 'made the right choice'? Did he think I envied him?

On the following Thursday morning Weston came into the Records Office with that smug expression on his face which denoted that he had another morsel of news. As he opened his mouth to speak I forestalled him.

'Yes, we know. He escaped last night.'

That evening I made a trunk call to Pauline. A woman, probably the landlady, answered the phone, and went to fetch Pauline. There was a long pause. Then, very faintly, I heard Pauline's voice. It broke in the middle of 'Hallo', and she repeated the word.

'Hallo, Pauline?'

'Yes?'

'This is Jonathan.'

'Who?'

'Jonathan. Jonathan Browne.'

'Oh.' A nervous, almost hysterical laugh followed. The receiver clattered on to a table. I caught a mutter of voices. Men's voices. What the hell was going on? Then a gruff voice spoke to me.

'Hallo, this is the Military Police here. Who is speaking please.'

'My name's Browne. I——'

'I understand you are a soldier. Rank and number please.'

'53174979 Trooper Jonathan Browne. With an "e".'

'Five three . . .?'

'Five three, one seven——'

'One seven . . .'

'Four nine, seven nine. Look——'

'Four nine seven nine. Trooper Browne. With an "e". Regiment?'

'Twenty-first R.T.R. Look this call is costing me money. I want to speak to Miss Vickers.'

At that moment the pips sounded.

'All right. Just a minute. Operator!'

After a long wrangle the M.P. managed to get the operator to extend the call, and charge it to the Army. Then he came back to me.

'Are you acquainted with Trooper Michael Brady?'

'Yes I am. That's what I want to speak to Miss Vickers about.'

'You know where he is?'

'No, I don't.'

After some more questions I was put on to Pauline.

'Hallo, Pauline. It seems you know all about Mike already.'

'Yes. I thought it was him when you phoned. . . . It's terrible . . . what . . .'

'Sorry, I didn't catch that.'

'What will happen to him?'

'I don't know. I should think they'll pick him up pretty soon. The sooner the better. He's only making things worse for himself.'

'What will happen to him?' she repeated, as if she had not

186

heard me. I caught sight of my face in the mirror of the call-box, contorted with the effort to hear and communicate.

'I thought it was him,' she went on. 'They made me promise to try and find out where he was.'

'The swine. Why don't you chuck them out?'

'Pardon?'

'It doesn't matter. Look, we can't talk properly over the telephone. Shall I come and see you this week-end?'

'Yes please, Jonathan.'

'Saturday? I'll give *you* lunch this time.'

'Yes, that would be nice.'

'Well, good-bye till Saturday then.'

'Yes, good-bye, Jonathan.'

I waited for her to put the receiver down, but she didn't. So I said 'Good-bye, and don't worry,' and put down my receiver.

The next morning I went to see Sergeant Hamilton to get a leave pass for a forty-eight. As I was filling it in he said:

'So your mate has scarpered.'

'Yes.'

'Silly man. Assaulting an N.C.O. Desertion while under arrest. He's up to his eyes in trouble. They'll pick him up of course.'

'I suppose so.'

'Where d'you think he'll make for?'

'I haven't the faintest idea.'

'He made a neat getaway, I'll say that for him. Taking the roof of the guard-room to pieces. Nobody thought of that before.'

'Perhaps they won't find him so easy to catch then.'

'Oh they'll catch him. Some time.'

I completed the leave form and handed it to him.

'You'll have to get it initialled by the Chief Clerk first.'

'O.K., Sarge, I'll do that now.' As I was moving towards the door he said:

'How do you like it in the Orderly Room?'

'Oh, it's all right.' I added, with an effort: 'It's quite interesting really.'

'Your posting hasn't come through yet, has it?'

'No.'

'Any preferences?'

'I've put in for the Far East.'

He sighed. 'Why is it all you blokes want to go to the Far East? Bet you think it's all beer and brothels, don't you. Well, it is – for about two weeks of the year, on your annual leave. The rest of the time it's flies and heat and patrols and dysentery.'

'Well, I don't suppose I'll get there anyway. Some God-forsaken hole in Germany most likely.'

Hamilton searched amongst the papers on his desk. 'I've just had a letter from an old friend of mine,' he said. 'The Chief Clerk at Badmore, – the R.A.C. Special Training Establishment. He needs a new clerk, and he's asked me to send him a good one. Would you be interested in going there?'

'Where is this place?'

'Hampshire, Dorset, – somewhere round there.' He paused before adding slyly: 'About a hundred miles from London.'

About a hundred miles from London. That was a comfortable distance for forty-eights, and not too bad for thirty-sixes, if the travel was reasonable.

'You'd probably be put in the R.T.R., unattached to any particular battalion. Well, anyway, think it over.'

'There's no need, Sergeant. I'd like to go, if you can fix it.'

'I can fix it,' he replied. 'Let's go round to the Posting office now. You won't regret this.'

Walking to the Posting office we passed Baker. His eyes met mine for a second, glittering with hate. I was sure that all along he had hated me more than Percy or Mike, and yet it was them, and not me, that he had driven out into the wilderness.

FIVE

By the end of the afternoon the sky had clouded, curving like a dull, metallic lid over the camp. It became hotter rather than cooler, prophesying a storm. Reluctantly I exchanged my working trousers, worn smooth and threadbare, for my best trousers, thick and itchy with their pristine nap intact. When I rolled down my shirt-sleeves and buttoned up the battle-dress blouse I began to sweat. I transferred Henry's parting gift from the map-pocket of the discarded trousers to my wallet.

I stepped out of my cubicle to inspect my appearance in the long mirror, and glanced enviously at a group playing cards round someone's bed: they were coolly dressed in jeans and light cotton shirts. A little shower of chaff was tossed casually in my direction.

'All bulled up, Corp?'

'Don't wake us too early tomorrow.'

'That's a shit-hot pair of boots you've got there.'

'Jock Gordonstone does 'em for 'im. Never bulls 'is own boots, the lazy sod.'

'Watch your language, Trooper,' I said, stamping my feet to get my trousers to fall neatly over the gaiters.

'Want some weights, Corp?' It was a common, though illegal practice, to put lead weights, or lengths of bicycle chain in one's trouser legs, which pulled the latter over the gaiters and kept the creases taut.

'No thanks.'

''Ere, Corporal. What size are them boots?'

'Eights.'

'That's my size. What about swapping them before you go?'

'Not likely. Stores wouldn't accept your boots. They look as if a Centurion ran over them.'

'No, me *best* boots, Corporal.'

'I *mean* your best boots.' The rest of the group cackled.

I had become accustomed to the image that confronted me in the mirror, but it still bothered me with a sense of the ridiculous. I never wore the uniform – it seemed to wear me, with a sheepish sense of failure. The khaki imparted a sallow, unhealthy hue to my skin, and the over-large beret sat uneasily on my forehead, making the face beneath look pinched and wizened. Pauline said that when she first saw me I looked like a refugee who had been hastily clothed by a liberating army in whatever came to hand. I never presented myself to her in uniform if I could possibly help it. I was turning away from the mirror when I realized that I had forgotten to transfer my shoulder flashes from my second-best battle-dress. I got them from the cubicle, and slipped them on to my shoulder-tabs. Brown, red and green stripes. 'Through mud and blood to green fields beyond,' as the regimental motto had it. Through boredom and discontent to blessed civvy street beyond. The thought of release was reviving.

'Well, this is the last guard I shall push,' I observed to the card-players, as I picked up my grip containing blanket, thermos flask, book, and cigarettes.

Chalky White was waiting outside the Montgomery guard-room when I arrived.

'What are you doing here, Chalky?'

'Same as you. I'm doing a guard for Nobby Clarke, and he's doing mine on Friday. I want a forty-eight next week-end,' he explained. 'The group's got a job on Saturday, starts early.' He added: 'Put me on first stag tonight, Jon, will you?'

'O.K., Chalky.'

Other soldiers began to appear, moving slowly and unwillingly toward the guard-room.

'There's a bullshitting bastard,' muttered Chalky, as an immaculately turned-out R.E.M.E. craftsman approached us. 'Bet he gets stick.'

Chalky was referring to the quaint ritual of the 'Commanding

Officer's Stick', a non-existent object which was symbolically awarded to the best-turned out trooper at the inspection of the guard. The recipient was then excused the guard duty.

'I wouldn't mind getting stick myself tonight,' Chalky added, yawning. 'I always feel shagged on Mondays, after the week-end.'

I yawned also, and murmured my agreement. The short sleep of the previous night would soon begin to tell, and the next day I would feel dead. Fortunately a corporal's lot on guard was easier than a trooper's. And by 6 a.m. I should be a happy man, my last irksome duty completed, only one full day between me and liberty.

Suddenly I saw Sergeant-Major Fotherby approaching us from the direction of the Sergeants' Mess, wearing a sash.

'Good God! Don't tell me Fotherby's Orderly N.C.O. tonight?'

'Don't you ever read orders?' Chalky inquired.

'I didn't bother. Everybody else was so bloody eager to tell me what was on them.'

I made an effort to retain my self-possession as Fotherby drew nearer; in retrospect, my appeal to him that morning must have seemed to him more impertinent than ever.

Fotherby was accompanied by Sergeant Earnshaw and Sergeant Mayhew, the N.C.O.s in charge of Montgomery and Vehicle Park guard-rooms respectively. Earnshaw was a stupid, lazy, but not ill-willed man who could be relied on to steer us through the duty with the minimum of effort by all concerned. Fotherby glanced at his wrist-watch and told us to fall in. We spread out across the square, and formed up facing the guard-room. The Vehicle Park guard was the largest, since three men were required on each stag to patrol the hangars and tank parks. Montgomery Guard only required one man at a time to patrol the camp entrance. Therefore, besides myself, there were only three troopers in Earnshaw's file: Chalky, the resplendent R.E.M.E. craftsman, and an unhappy-looking little trooper from 'B' Squadron, whose name I did not know.

Behind us were the Armed Picket, supposed to be able to defend the camp from attack by the I.R.A., who had brought the Army into derision about a year before by a series of successful raids on regimental armouries in the North. This scare had long since passed, but the Armed Picket continued in existence, following a familiar military law by which measures designed to meet emergencies are never revoked, but absorbed into the ritual of the unit, more and more rules accumulating about them as their original significance fades into the past. The Armed Picket slept, fully clothed and with its boots on, in a hut near the Montgomery guard-room, from which it could be alerted by means of an electric bell. After the guard had been inspected the picket loaded its rifles, which were then locked into a wall-rack. On hearing the bell the N.C.O. in charge unlocked the rack, distributed the rifles, and led his men out to combat. That, at least, was the theory. In fact, the picket was a more real menace to itself and to the rest of us, than to any potential aggressor. The soldiers of Badmore were not used to handling fire-arms, and were easily flustered when they were alerted for practice purposes. Such occasions rarely passed without a rifle going off by accident, and one man had already been shot in the foot and invalided out of the Army, to his great delight.

As we stood at ease, waiting for Fotherby to make his preliminary inspection, Sergeant Earnshaw said to me:

'Aren't we one short, Corporal? There are usually four on this guard for inspection.'

He was correct. The fourth man would replace whoever got stick, unless he got it himself.

'You're right, Sergeant. But I don't know who's missing.'

'Sounds like him now.'

There was a sound of heavy footfalls, and round the corner of the bedding store lumbered a familiar uncouth shape: Norman.

'Get your finger out, Trooper,' cried Fotherby. He looked regretfully at his watch. 'Another ten seconds and you'd have been on a charge.'

Norman panted up, winked at me, and took his place at the end of the file. Fotherby began his inspection.

Since Badmore was the R.A.C.'s waste-paper basket, where troublesome or defective personnel could be conveniently disposed of, it had been no surprise to me when Norman had turned up there about a year before. At Badmore he realized himself at last. 'There's a place for you in the Regular Army,' the recruiting posters had told him when he enlisted; and at last, at Badmore, he had found that place. He was in charge of the unit piggery. Tanks and typewriters were things that went suddenly, disastrously wrong in Norman's hands; but pigs, – not even Norman could damage pigs. Indeed there was a certain *rapport* between them. There was a real gleam of affection in Norman's eyes as he heaved a bucket of swill into a trough and watched his charges guzzling an obscene cold stew of cabbage, potatoes, mince, suet pudding, gravy and custard, the left-overs from the troops' dinner. Norman, the product of an industrial slum, had become quite agricultural. He was to be seen occasionally with a straw in his mouth, and talked of 'going into pigs' when his three years were up.

· Fotherby took longer than was customary over his inspection. In his own regiment he had probably been used to the Orderly Officer's duty, but there was a plethora of officers at Badmore, and most of the Warrant Officers had to be content with being Orderly N.C.O. He returned to the guard-room veranda, and we stood at ease under the dull, stifling sky, waiting for the Adjutant. A trooper in a red singlet and jeans, with a towel round his neck, emerged from a hut and made his way to the wash-house, whistling shrilly. His whistling faltered and died away as his glance met the silent, expressionless ranks facing him. A faint odour of pigs was wafted from my left where Norman stood, still breathing heavily.

The muffled growl of a powerful engine announced the approach of the Adjutant's Jaguar, changing down as it entered the camp. A touch on the throttle brought the low, green car to the steps of the guard-room in a single pounce. The driver stopped the car, and ostentatiously revved the engine before switching off the ignition. Captain Gresley emerged from his car, and stood erect in all the bizarre glory of his dress uniform: dark green hat, with a gold band and a glossy peak, deep maroon jacket, dark green trousers narrower than any Teddy-boy ever dreamt of in the wildest excesses of his sartorial imagination, with a broad gold stripe down the sides. Silver chain-mail had settled like snow on his shoulders, and silver spurs were screwed to the heels of his boots. He jingled faintly as he walked towards Fotherby, whom he greeted with a smile, for they were both in the same cavalry regiment.

'Ain't he gorgeous?' whispered Chalky.

'What must they all look like on mess-nights?' I replied. 'A commissionaires' conference.'

As Chalky had prophesied, the R.E.M.E. craftsman got stick. The unhappy-looking little trooper from 'B' Squadron, whose name proved to be Hobson, received a thorough grilling from Gresley and Fotherby, from which he emerged looking unhappier than ever. It was his misfortune to belong to the same regiment as them. He had never been with the regiment, knew nothing about it, and I imagine he fervently hoped that he would never have the opportunity to extend his knowledge. The inspection passed without further incident; we marched off the square; the duty truck bore the V.P. guard away to the other guard-room. I took the soiled mill-board on which the guard's orders were pasted, and intoned them to my oddly-assorted trio. I gave Chalky the first stag, Hobson the second, and Norman the third.

The guard-room was hot and stuffy. Gresley stalked about the room, elaborately checking that everything was in order. There were no prisoners in the cells. He pressed the alarm bell button, and we heard the bell ringing shrilly in the Armed Picket hut. Then he and Fotherby left. We began to settle down for the night.

Sergeant Earnshaw seated himself at the high desk, and began laboriously to fill in the guard report. Norman produced a tattered paper-backed novel entitled *Hell Beach*. A snarling Marine leapt from the cover, with a sub-machine-gun blazing from his hip. It was a not insignificant irony, I reflected, that the favourite form of escape literature among soldiers of the modern Army was not pornography, not Westerns, but war-books. I took out of my grip Empson's *Seven Types of Ambiguity*. Hobson sat on his bunk staring vacantly before him. He had not provided himself with reading matter. Or perhaps he couldn't read. Suddenly he said to me:

'Eh, Corporal: will it be dark on second stag?'

'Dark? I suppose so. It's pretty dark already. I should think there'll be a storm. Why?'

After a brooding silence he said:

'I don't like this bloody guard.'

'Neither do I as a matter of fact. But it's the last one I'll be pushing.'

'Getting released soon?' asked Norman.

'Wednesday.'

'Chuffed eh?'

'What do you think?'

We resumed reading.

'It's that bloody *tank*,' said Hobson suddenly.

'Eh?'

'That tank. That German tank. I don't like being near that tank when it's dark.'

'Oh I get you. The ghost. Norman, this lad's frightened of the ghost. Will you hold his hand on second stag?'

'I'm not so bloody keen on that tank myself,' he muttered darkly.

'What's all this about a tank?' inquired Earnshaw from his desk.

'Haven't you heard about it, Sarge? It's supposed to be haunted by the ghost of a German soldier.'

'All burned, his face is,' said Hobson, in a half-frightened, half-gloating voice.

'Ghost!' spat out Earnshaw scornfully. 'Never heard such a load of crap. Nervous as a lot of virgins, you nigs are.'

Silence returned, disturbed only by the ticking of the clock, and the tread of Chalky's boots as he paced his beat round the guard-room, the bedding stores, the armoury, the Armed Picket hut, the garage for the C.O.'s car. Round and round he went, like a satellite circling a dying planet. I read on into Empson, admiring the way he delicately dismantled a metaphysical lyric, laying out the components for inspection; then deftly reassembled them, shaking the mechanism into motion, holding it up triumphantly to your ear. The intellectual exercise of following him was flattering, and brought with it a comfortable premonition of the life that awaited me: the warm library at nightfall, the feel of new books, the smell of old ones, the pleasantries and vanities of footnotes and acknowledgments. I sniggered as Empson flicked the last remnants of his bard's robe off another eminent nineteenth-century poet.

'What yer reading?' said Earnshaw, who had left his desk. To avoid the labour of an explanation, I passed him the book. He glanced at the title on the spine, and began to read where I had left the book open, his brows knitted.

'What's it about then?'

'Literature.'

'Yer, but what's it about. Anything 'ot in it, like?'

'It's not a story. It's literary criticism. It's——'

'Wodjer wanner read that sort of crap for?' he interrupted, handing back the book.

'I happen to be interested in it.'

'Won't do you any good, will it?'

'As a matter of fact it will, though that's not why I'm reading it.'

'Why, what good will it do yer?'

'I hope to make the study of literature my career.'

'Gerna be a teacher I s'pose. But what *good* will it do yer? Or the kids yer teach. What *use* is lit'rature?'

I opened my mouth to launch into a defence of the study of literature . . . *getting to know, on all the matters which most concern us, the best which has been thought and said* . . . and then closed my mouth. I was not eager to return to the university because I thought my research would be of any use, to myself, or to others. All human activity was useless, but some kinds were more pleasant than others. The Army had taught me that much philosophy. There was no such thing as communication operating over the whole of society. In fact, there was no such thing as society: just a collection of little self-contained boxes, roped untidily together and set adrift to float aimlessly on the waters of time,

198

the occupants of each box convinced that theirs was the most important box, heedless of the claims of the rest. Success did not consist in getting into the box where most power was exercised: there were many people who were powerful and unhappy. Success consisted in determining which box would be most pleasant for you, and getting into it. If you were forced to inhabit an unpleasant box for a time, then you could make it as comfortable as possible until you could get out. Luck or cunning were the most effective attributes in this world, and cunning, though it worked more slowly, was the more reliable.

'What's it mean, anyhow, the name?' asked Earnshaw from the desk to which he had returned.

'What name?'

'That book. Seven types of whatever it is.'

'Oh, "ambiguity". It means a word or statement which can have more than one meaning.'

Earnshaw laughed incredulously.

'You're a queer bugger and no mistake,' he said.

Luck or cunning. And if you didn't have either, you were like Mike, at home in no box, vainly trying to ignore the existence of boxes, tossed and buffeted by the pitiless winds that blew outside them. For it was better to be in the most uncomfortable box than outside, in the confusion of the elements.

''Ere, if you're so clever,' said Earnshaw, coming back to my bunk. 'See if you can do this.' He spread out six pennies in a triangle and challenged me to put them in a straight line in two moves. His conviction that my education had been useless seemed to be confirmed by my inability to solve the puzzle. There was a low rumble in the distance.

'Thunder. There'll be a storm soon,' said Earnshaw, sweeping the pennies into his palm. But the storm receded, or was circling. The hours passed without relief from the close, oppressive atmosphere.

At ten Earnshaw said he would have a sleep for a few hours.

'Wake me at two, then you can have a kip. And keep your ears pricked for the Adjutant. He's a keen bastard, – and so is Fotherby. They're likely to try and catch us napping.'

'O.K., Sergeant.'

I seated myself at the desk, and poured a cup of coffee from the flask I had brought with me. The darkness outside was lit occasionally by a flicker of sheet lightning on the horizon. Hobson's boots shuffled on the path outside. He was not moving very far from the guard-room. I went to the window and called out unkindly: 'You're supposed to patrol this whole block, you know. Don't stay up this end all the time.' He gave me a scared, reproachful look, and moved off in the direction of the tank.

Chalky was telling Norman about a Scotsman in his hut who talked in his sleep about his sexual adventures. I strained my ears to catch his words.

' "Are ye cold," he says – he must have had this tart in a ditch or something – "Are ye cold, Jenny? Och, your poor wee tits are cold, Jenny, let me warm them for ye," – no, I'm not kidding, just like that, you can ask anyone in the hut. "Keep your head down, Jenny, there's someone coming," he says. We were all round the bed, pissing ourselves trying not to laugh out loud and wake him up. Then Nobby Clarke put his helmet in Jock's hands, and he ran his hands over it, smooth like, and "Och, you've a lovely arse on you, Jenny," he says . . .'

It was the hour for lubricious dreams. I wondered idly in what circumstances I would learn the last secrets of Pauline's clean-smelling body, and find that mental anaesthesia which I looked for between her smooth white thighs. In the hotel bedroom at siesta time perhaps, the strong Mediterranean sunlight broken up by the venetian blinds into golden bars that burned into her naked torso. Or as we rubbed each other dry and glowing with rough towels after a midnight swim; her skin would taste of salt . . .

There was a noise of someone running towards the guard-room, and a frenzied knocking on the door. Sergeant Earnshaw threw off his blanket and leapt to his feet, cursing under his breath.

'Go and see who it is,' he said to me, buckling on his belt.

When I opened the door Hobson almost fell across the

threshold, pale and quivering with fright. His mouth opened, but nothing came out.

'Well?' said Earnshaw.

'I've seen the ghost!' blurted out Hobson.

Earnshaw flung down his belt in disgust.

'For fuggsake, is that what you woke me up for. I've a good mind to put you on a charge.'

Hobson turned pleadingly to me. 'It's true, Corporal. I saw 'im, by the tank. There was a flash of lightning, and I saw 'im. 'E 'ad one of them long German coats on, like you see in the pictures.'

'Why didn't you challenge him?' demanded Earnshaw.

Hobson stared blankly: 'Because 'e was a ghost, Sarge.'

Earnshaw stepped over to Hobson, grasped the lapels of his battle-dress, and lifted the unfortunate youth on to his toes. 'Now listen to me,' he bellowed. 'There is no bleeding ghost. Get back to your post in ten seconds from now, or I'll have you in the guard-room so fast your feet won't touch.' The formula came out before the speaker realized that he was already in the guard-room, but the words had their effect. Hobson stumbled miserably out into the dark. Earnshaw turned to me.

'You'd better go out and have a look. Someone may be snooping around.'

I picked up a flashlight, and stepped out on to the veranda. The heavy warm air seemed to part in front of me, and close behind, like water.

'Let's go and have a look,' I said to Hobson, who was cowering against a wall.

He kept close to me as we approached the tank, and his pace faltered as another flash of lightning on the horizon silhouetted the antique outline of the vehicle. Never having been troubled by fears of the supernatural, I enjoyed a sense of superiority over the terrified trooper as we came up to the tank. It was just a shell, the disembowelled carcass of a prehistoric animal. The back had been removed so that one could climb into it. I did so, and flashed my torch round, illuminating nothing but a few cigarette stubs and a small heap of dog's excrement. It was difficult to believe that this narrow evil-smelling room had ever churned through the mud of Flanders field, crunching the bones of dying men, bullets rattling like hail on its thin plate. Tanks, 'mobile coffins' as Mike had described them once. It was easier to imagine that this had been the fiery grave of a German soldier. It had the look, and the smell, of a vacated tomb.

The ground outside was hard, and yielded no clues.

'You must have been dreaming,' I said to Hobson as we walked away.

'I wasn't, Corporal, honest.' Then, abandoning the attempt to convince me, he added with more urgency: 'Don't make me stay out here any longer.'

I glanced at my watch. 'It's nearly half past ten anyway. Stay near the guard-room for a few minutes, and I'll send the next man out to relieve you.'

Ten to one. 'The still point of the turning world.' I sat perched on a high stool behind the high desk, under the glare of the electric light. Chalky's footsteps slowly approached, passed, receded, beginning another circle. Earnshaw and Norman snored, irritatingly at different tempos. For a time they would snore alternately, then Norman would slowly begin to overtake Earnshaw, draw level with him, then pass him. Hobson, his blanket drawn over his head to keep out the light, or the ghost, sighed and whimpered in his sleep. Empson's words danced before my blood-shot eyes. I pushed the book aside, and picked up a newspaper which Earnshaw had brought with him. I flipped idly through the crumpled pages: gossip column, woman's page, film starlet stooping to reveal her breasts, competitions. *Win a new Aston Martin or £3000, cash.* Whoever chose the cars in these competitions, I wondered. And if nobody, why not just offer the cash? *Suddenly! A new way of life.* An advertisement showed a young couple in a luxurious bed, watching a television set placed on a shelf at their feet. 'George! Take your hand away. It's *Wagon Train* next.' Well, what odds, if they found it pleasant? An editorial drew my attention.

The Minister for Defence announced in the Commons yesterday that the Government hopes to bring conscription to an end within four years.

The nation is proud of its National Servicemen. They have fought bravely, shoulder to shoulder, with their Regular comrades in Korea, Malaya, Cyprus, Suez. Industry in booming Britain will welcome the labour released by the ending of conscription. Mothers will sleep easier at night.

But this last thought prompts another. National Service has done much to teach the younger generation independence, initiative, responsibility, – qualities which have stood this country in good stead in two World Wars. We must not send the youth of Britain from the barrack-square to the street-corner. Some substitute must be found which will have the same beneficial effects of character-training as National Service . . .

Mentally I phrased a reply: 'I think it will be difficult to find a substitute which will inculcate bad habits, bad language, idleness, slothfulness, drunkenness, and the amiable philosophy of "I'm all right Jack" half so successfully as National Service . . .' But the ignorance of newspapers was invincible. Journalism was another useless, self-compensating activity, like literary research, like soldiering itself.

The leader-writer went on to suggest that an extension of the Outward Bound schools would be the answer. I had nothing against the Outward Bound schools. If people enjoyed impressing the Duke of Edinburgh by scrambling over mountains and sleeping in the open, I would not wish to stop them. Evidently they found it pleasant. But the suggestion that such activities bore any resemblance to National Service struck me as ludicrous. I had never slept in the open, or under canvas, in the whole of my two years; nor, for that matter, had I taken part in any tactical exercise, nor fired a rifle more than twice, not indeed done or learned anything that might have made me the slightest bit more use in time of war than I had been when I first caught the train from King's Cross to Catterick. I had long ceased to feel any resentment about this, but I did rather resent suggestions that anything else was the case.

Yes, I had long since ceased to feel any resentment about National Service. Once one had accepted the fact that the whole thing was pointless and futile, it was easy enough to accommodate oneself to its trivial demands, and to make oneself reasonably comfortable. And yet, if it *was* quite meaningless, why in these last few days did my thoughts revert so insistently to my first weeks at Catterick, as if from them, and their contrast with my existence at Badmore, I hoped to tease out a meaning?

Perhaps it was just the insidious flattery of time, which persuades us that what is about to come to an end must have meant something, must have been significant. Who has left a hospital, in which he has suffered misery, pain and embarrassment, without a sudden, treacherous pang of regret, an irrational surge of affection for the fellow patients who kept him awake with their selfish groans, for the nurses who only got the hypo in properly at the third attempt, for the surgeon who let his wound get infected? I suppose even released convicts feel the same as the prison doors close behind them; and perhaps, too, even the souls winging their way through the gates of purgatory when their time is up.

National Service was like a very long, very tedious journey on the Inner Circle. You boarded the train with a lot of others, and for a while it was very crowded, very uncomfortable; but after a while the crowd thinned, you got a seat, new faces got in, old faces got out; the slogans on the advertisements got tiresomely familiar, but you sat on, until, after a very long time, you got out yourself, at the station where you had originally boarded the train, and were borne by the escalator back into the light and air. It was natural, then, that as you approached your destination, you should try to connect the end of your journey with the beginning, try to recall all the shapes and forms of humanity that had shoved and jostled and brawled and snored in the narrow, swaying compartment. Fallowfield, more like a seminarian than a cadet, Peterson with his Old Etonian smile, Gordon Kemp, good-humoured and generous; Hardcastle squaring up to Mike's bare white torso over Percy's kneeling form; little Barnes recommending

The Lady Of The Lake; Baker, his face contorted by a rictus of anger; Mason, conducting his sexual seminars in the overheated classroom. Many were nameless: the mentally deficient shambling happily out of Amiens Camp in civilian clothes, the youth reading out the letter from the girl who had jilted him, the soldier – Jones, was it? – searching fruitlessly in the sodden grass at my side for the fifth shell-case. An endless succession of figures, many blurred by time, rose up and passed across my mind like the ghosts in *Macbeth*. Where were they all now? One of them was snoring only ten feet away. But Norman, oddly enough, provided no link between my first and last days in the Army. Norman at Badmore was a different creature from Norman at Catterick – like a strange, sinister shape in a child's darkened bedroom, which the morning light reveals as a harmless, if ugly piece of furniture. Where were the rest now? All, like me, awaiting release, polishing their boots for the last time, pushing their last guard, gloating over their comrades?

No, not all. Some would not be released. Percy would not be released. Gordon Kemp, shot in the back as he walked down a sun–lit street in Cyprus, would not be released. And Fallowfield had already been released: the strain of the officer cadet course had been too much for him; he had taken an over-dose of aspirin, but they had found him in time, and he had been medically discharged. Ironic, that he, of all people, should have gained his freedom, the freedom he did not want. As for the rest, where were they now?

I did not really care. They had no importance for me, except that at one time they had formed fragments of a mosaic in which a particular experience of my own had been delineated. Now I stooped to wipe away the dust of two years, and reveal the forgotten faces; but as the years passed I would tread over them again, more and more indifferent to the picture that was slowly disappearing beneath my feet. There was only one visage that would take some time and effort to efface, that stared up at me like a gaunt Byzantine saint, and would continue to stare. It would be difficult to lay that ghost.

The telephone rang. A routine call from V.P. guard-room. I walked slowly across the room to answer it.

'Montgomery guard-room. Corporal Browne speaking.'

The voice that replied was breathless and excited. 'This is Sergeant Mayhew, V.P. guard-room. Someone's just got away with a truck.'

'What?'

'A truck. Somebody's just stolen a bloody truck. They got into the hangars, and drove it past the guards.'

'Who did?'

'How do I know for Christ's sake. You'd better send up the Armed Picket.'

'Hold on a minute.' I went over to Earnshaw and shook his shoulder. He surfaced grudgingly from sleep.

'Whatisit?'

'V.P. is on the phone. Someone's stolen a truck. They want us to send up the Armed Picket.' He stared at me for a moment, then leapt to his feet.

'Well, don't just stand there. Press the bloody bell.'

He ran across the room to press the bell himself. We listened, but heard nothing.

'Bloody thing must have broken. Go and wake them up. And be quick about it.' He seized the phone and began talking excitedly to Mayhew. I ran out of the guard-room to the Armed Picket hut. I switched on the light and hammered on a tin locker with my fist.

'Wake up, wake up!'

Some of them sat up in their beds, blinking in the light and rubbing their eyes. I located the N.C.O. with some difficulty, and woke him up.

'This is a fine bloody game,' he grumbled, pulling on his boots.

'It's no game. Somebody's stolen a truck from V.P.'

'What are we supposed to do about it? They may be half way to Salisbury by now.'

'I don't know, but you'd better get cracking.'

For fifteen minutes confusion reigned. Most of the soldiers had taken their boots off, and fumbled awkwardly with bootlaces.

The N.C.O. couldn't find the key to the rack in which the rifles were locked, and in the end we had to break it open. At last the rifles were distributed, and the Armed Picket drove off in the duty truck. Lightning flickered, and there was a loud thunderclap. Running back to the guard-room I bumped into Chalky.

'What's up?'

'Truck pinched from V.P.'

'Blimey! Somebody's gernna be in trouble. 'Ere, 'ave you got a groundsheet? It's gernna rain.'

'Haven't time.' I ran on.

Earnshaw was still on the phone when I re-entered the guard-room. 'I'm trying to get the Adjutant,' he said. 'But he doesn't seem to be at the Mess.'

'The Armed Picket's gone off.'

'Took enough bloody time didn't they?' Still holding the phone to his ear, he turned towards Norman and Hobson, who, strangely, were still asleep.

'Wake those lazy sods up.'

As I moved towards them there was a knock on the door.

'That's probably the Adjutant. Let him in.'

I opened the door. There was nothing there except my shadow, thrown forward across the veranda. I stepped over the threshold, and an arm hit me in the throat like an iron bar, throttling me and dragging me sideways. A gag was wound round my face, and the voice of the Adjutant whispered in my ear, 'Relax, Corporal.'

The Adjutant and Fotherby stood together in the middle of the guard-room, wearing sweaters and plimsolls. They were breathing heavily, and their blackened faces were runnelled with sweat, but they radiated cocky triumph. The Adjutant was trying to look stern, but he kept grinning at Fotherby. Chalky and I stood together nursing our throats and mouths. Norman and Hobson were trying to button up their uniforms as unobtrusively as possible. Sergeant Earnshaw was sitting on the end of a bed, looking sick.

'Feel all right, Sergeant?' asked the Adjutant.

Earnshaw muttered something about his heart.

'You put up a good fight, anyway, Sergeant. Not like some of the other so-called soldiers in this unit.' He swept the rest of us with a contemptuous glance. 'You, Corporal, for instance,' he said to me. 'Do you usually open the guard-room door without finding out who's outside?'

I could not trust myself to reply.

'Anyone would think you were playing Postman's Knock.' Fotherby sniggered. The Adjutant turned to Chalky. 'And you, Trooper. We watched you for several minutes, and you didn't look to your right or your left. As for you two——' Norman hung his head and Hobson quaked – 'We might have taken over the whole bloody camp without waking *you* up.' He began to strut up and down the guard-room. 'Well, I'm twenty pounds richer now. I bet the C.O. that with one man, – from my own regiment of course' (he grinned at Fotherby), 'I could steal a truck from V.P. and capture the Montgomery guard-room; and I have. I shouldn't think he'll be in a very good mood when you all see him tomorrow morning.'

There was a vivid flash of lightning, followed by a resounding thunderclap; then the sky burst over our heads like a swollen paper bag. The rain dinned on the roof, and hissed on the concrete outside the guard-room. Almost at once it searched out a leak in the roof, and water began to drip on to the floor. For some moments we were all struck dumb by the deluge. Then, as the intensity of the torrent diminished slightly, Earnshaw said anxiously:

'You're not charging us, sir?'

'I shan't charge *you*, Sergeant, since you put up such a good show. But the guards who let us get away with the truck, you Trooper' – he nodded to Chalky, and I froze as he turned to me – 'and you, Corporal: you were all negligent, and you'll have to answer for it. The security in this unit is disgraceful, and I shouldn't be surprised if there were a regimental inquiry into this business.'

I struggled to control the questions, expostulations and protests which seethed within me. Exasperation at the humiliation and absurdity of the whole affair struggled with anxiety, rapidly turning to dread, about the effects it might have on my release. My timetable was tight. If I did not get away on Wednesday Pauline and I would miss the charter flight early on Thursday morning, and there was no other flight. My mind wandered off into calculations of possible alternatives, whether the airline would rebate the fares, if so, at what notice. Angrily I recalled my thoughts to the main issue. What would be the result of this stupid prank of the Adjutant's? Probably I would lose a stripe. That wouldn't worry me, and shouldn't delay me unduly. It might be all over tomorrow. But it might not. And there was that ominous reference to a regimental inquiry. Would they keep me back for it? Could they keep me back for it? In any event they might easily keep me back till Thursday, which was the statutory day for release. I could not keep silent any longer. The Adjutant was on the phone, trying to get the operator.

'Excuse me, sir,' I said.

'Well?'

'I'm due for release on Wednesday, sir. Will this affect it? You see, I've booked——'

'I really couldn't say, Corporal.' He turned back to the phone, tapping the receiver-rest impatiently. Fotherby was looking at me with undisguised delight. The Adjutant said:

'This phone seems to be dead, Sergeant Earnshaw.'

'It was all right a few minutes ago, sir.'

'Must be the storm. Corporal, will you cut along to the Orderly Room and use the phone there, if it's working. Ring up V.P. guard-room, and explain the situation. Tell Sergeant Mayhew to round up the Armed Picket, and send them back here. I want to see the N.C.O. in charge.' He turned to Fotherby. 'How long did they take to get out, Sergeant-Major?'

'Well, we were down here a good ten minutes before they left, sir. So I should say about twenty minutes altogether.'

'Disgraceful.'

'The alarm bell wasn't working, sir,' put in Earnshaw. 'Corporal Browne had to go and wake them up.'

'It was working earlier this evening. Anyway, that's no excuse.

It could only have made a couple of minutes' difference. All right, Corporal, that's all.'

A curtain of water confronted me as I closed the guard-room door. I had no cape, but I stepped heedlessly into the deluge. The rain was as warm as blood. The great blunt drops bruised my face, ran down my neck, soaked into my khaki as if it were blotting-paper, boiled and bubbled at my feet. I splashed my way mechanically towards the Orderly Room, brooding on the sudden blow to my plans. It was not, however, the particular problems which had arisen which chafed me most: it was the general sense that the machinery which had been silkily responsive to my touch for so long had suddenly run amok. I had looked forward with pleasurable expectation to my last days at Badmore: I would leave the Army in a mood of relaxed enjoyment, my finger-tips on the controls until the last moment. It would be a ceremony, a ritual, trivial in its forms perhaps, but highly significant in its import, for its climax would be the transubstantiation of the soldier into the free man. But now I knew that whatever happened, even if I did contrive to get away in time to catch the plane, my last hours at Badmore would not be spent in the serene enjoyment of this ceremony. They would be spent in anxiety, and doubt, and helplessness, – emotions I had thought I had left behind me at Catterick.

I had to knock several times on the Orderly Room door: the duty clerk, incredibly, seemed to have slept through the storm. Eventually he opened the door. Yawning and rubbing his eyes he asked me foolishly:

'Is it raining?'

I stood in the doorway in my sodden uniform, a puddle spreading rapidly at my feet.

'No, someone's pissing off the roof,' I replied. 'I want to use your phone. The guard-room one's packed up.'

I squeezed past the camp-bed which was set up in the middle of the office.

''Ere, mind me sheets.'

Ignoring his protests, I sat down on the end of the bed to make the phone-call. V.P. guard-room was still in a state of considerable perturbation, increased by their inability to communicate with the Montgomery guard-room. It took me some time to explain the situation to Sergeant Mayhew, to answer his questions, and to listen to his oaths.

'The Armed Picket's out on the moors,' he said. 'It'll take me some time to round them up.'

'O.K. I'll tell the Adjutant.'

'I'm going to get fuggin' soaked looking for them.'

'You won't be the only one.'

''Ere, you've left a bloody great wet patch on my bed,' said the duty clerk, as I put down the phone, and rose to my feet. Then, curiosity winning over his sense of grievance, he pestered me about the night's events. I gave him a few short, surly answers, and left.

As I approached the guard-room my scepticism about supernatural phenomena received a severe jolt. A flash of lightning revealed through the sheeting rain a figure in a long, belted coat, that answered disconcertingly to Hobson's description of the ghost. I halted, my heart pounding as loudly as the thunder. I stood peering through the darkness. Lightning flickered again, but the figure had vanished. A few more steps, however, took me in sight of the guard-room, and I saw through its windows a tableau that taxed my credulity more than any ghost. The Adjutant and Fotherby had their backs to me, and their hands up. Between them I could see a masked man by the door, holding a Sten gun.

I was congratulated for the coolness with which I acted subsequently, but no one knows how much that coolness was due to the simple desire to understand what was happening. The events of that one night had been more bizarre and dramatic than all my nights at Badmore put together. I was too numbed to act impulsively.

Cautiously I skirted the guard-room, and reached the veranda of the Q.M.'s offices, which faced one side of it. Hidden in the shadows, I stared into the guard-room. The rain, drumming on the veranda roof, prevented any sound which might have carried through the windows of the guard-room from reaching me. It

211

was rather like watching a film when the sound-track has broken down: violence enacted and emotions registered in a comical silence. They were all there as I had left them in the guard-room, with one addition, a figure in pyjamas whom I identified as the security man from the armoury. A raid was in progress, in earnest this time; and the raiders had struck a most lucky moment, with the Armed Picket dispersed over the water-logged moors a mile away, and the telephone out of action, – but this last must be their doing, I realized, and the failure of the alarm bell. The ghost too, he must have been one of them.

Another man, also with a scarf round his face, came into the guard-room and seemed to say something to the man with the Sten gun. The latter nodded, and motioned the Adjutant and the rest towards the cells. His companion took the keys, neatly labelled for his convenience, from the rack on the wall, and proceeded to lock the captives in the cells.

I deliberated as to what I should do. (It was only much later that I wondered why I had assumed that I ought to do something.) There were soldiers sleeping within fifty yards of me, but what use would they be, unarmed and fuddled with sleep, even if I managed to wake them in time? There was a phone in the Q.M.'s office, but the door was locked. The nearest accessible phone was the one in the Orderly Room, but by the time I got there they would be gone.

I slipped off my gaiters and boots, and padded along the veranda until I was out of sight of the interior of the guard-room. Then I scuttled quickly across the space between the Q.M.'s offices and the armoury. Between the armoury and the bedding store there was a narrow, noisome passage. I squeezed my way to the end, lowered myself reluctantly into the mud, and peered round. I saw the dim shapes of a Bedford van and, beside it, a Ford Consul. Noises of heavy objects being loaded came from the rear of the van. The light outside the armoury had been turned off, but a flash of lightning illuminated the vehicles. I shrank back into the passage. The Bedford van was grey, the Consul black. I protruded my head again like a tortoise. The thunder rumbled. I waited impatiently for another flash of lightning, and when it came glimpsed the number plate of the Bedford: MUP 5 – I had not seen any more. I waited for another flash, but the door of the van was slammed, and I heard voices and hurried footsteps. I withdrew into the passage, and slithered backwards until I judged it safe to stand up and turn round. The engines started, and the vehicles moved off. I ran back to the Q.M.'s veranda from the end of which I could see the camp entrance. The Bedford turned left, the Ford right, and both accelerated out of sight.

I ran back to the Orderly Room in my socks, muttering to myself: 'MUP 5, MUP 5 . . .'

'For fuggsake, you again?' protested the clerk. 'Where are your boots?' he added in astonishment, as I squelched past him and seized the phone.

'Get me the C.O.'s home telephone number,' I said.

First I phoned the police, then Brigade, then the C.O. The C.O. said he would be round right away.

I padded slowly back to the guard-room. The rain was easing. My mind, which had been suspended through the time of action, began to function reflectively again. The agreeable thought came to me that I might gain some credit for what I had done, sufficient to gloss over the unfortunate incident earlier in the night, and to facilitate my prompt release from the Army. In any case the minor matter would be submerged in the major, and the Adjutant was unlikely to proceed with his threatened charge. He would have quite a lot of explaining to do himself, in fact, when the C.O. arrived and found him locked in a cell with Norman and Hobson, his face blackened, and dressed in civilian clothes.

I went first to the Q.M.'s veranda, where I took off my socks, wrung them out, put them on again, and donned my boots. I heard the C.O.'s car approaching.

'Well, Corporal Browne, you did a fine job of work for the Army in your last week. The police had no difficulty in tracing those cars with the description you gave them. And you did well to observe the directions they took. In fact you acted with remarkable initiative if I may say so, remarkable initiative.'

I smiled modestly back at the C.O., and murmured something deprecatory. The writers of the schoolboys' stories I had read in childhood had done their work well; I could think of no other reason why I should experience such pleasure at being the hero of the hour. It satisfied an appetite I had not known I possessed. The morning sun shone brightly into the C.O.'s office, bleaching the carpet and the drawn face of the Adjutant. It had been a trying night for him. The raiders had taken away the keys to the cells and it had been two hours before the duplicates had been found.

'When are you due for release, Corporal?'

'Tomorrow, sir.'

'Hmm. Trouble is you'll probably be required by the police in connection with this business.'

I started worrying again.

'I hope not, sir. I've arranged to go on holiday to Majorca on Thursday. My plane leaves early on Thursday morning.'

'Oh. Well, we can't let this interfere with your holiday, can we. How long will you be away?'

'A fortnight, sir.'

'Hmm. Just a minute.'

He picked up the phone and asked the operator to get him the Chief Constable of the county, whom he addressed as 'Fred'. I began to relax as the conversation proceeded, and the C.O. put down the receiver with a triumphant smile.

'Well that's fixed, Corporal. You won't be needed in person until after you come back. In the meantime I've arranged for you to make a statement to the police this afternoon in the town. My driver will run you down there this afternoon. You'll be able to get off in good time tomorrow morning.'

'Thank you, sir. I'm most grateful.'

'It's a pleasure, Corporal. Badmore would have been the laughing stock of the Army if those I.R.A. blighters had got away. Isn't that right, Geoffrey?'

The Adjutant nodded sourly. I saluted, and turned. As I crossed the room to the door the C.O. said:

'I think this is your line of country, Geoffrey. One of the

blighters was a deserter apparently. The police want to know what——'

I turned slowly back to face them.

'Excuse me, sir.'

'Yes, Corporal?'

'The deserter you mentioned. . . . Do you know his name by any chance?'

'Er, Brady I think. Yes, that's right, Brady.'

'Not Michael Brady?'

'Yes that's right, Michael Brady. Why what's the matter man? You're white as a sheet!'

'I'm all right, sir. It's just that I knew him once.'

'Who, Brady? I hope he's no friend of yours. He's in a lot of trouble.'

'No, not what you might call a friend, sir. I'm sorry, sir. Excuse me.'

I saluted weakly and left the room under their curious gaze. As I negotiated the corridors leading to the 'A' Squadron offices, a hand touched me on the shoulder. I jumped.

'Take it easy! Got a guilty conscience or somethink?' The Post Corporal was grinning at me. 'Letter for you. Blimey, you do look queer.'

'I'm all right.'

He held the long mauve envelope under his nose before passing it to me.

'Smells nice. Some people 'ave all the luck.'

Instead of returning to my office I went to the lavatory, and sat in a cool, smelly closet to think. Already my mind had instinctively connected certain facts to form a picture of Mike's progress since he had deserted. Somehow he had got to Ireland, no doubt with the aid of that mysterious Italian to whom I had posted Mike's letter. At this moment it flashed upon me that 'Gordiano Bruno' was a pseudonym for Peter Nolan, the Irishman at O'Connell's. Bruno of Nola! It was a favourite pun of Joyce's. And Nolan was just the type to be associated with the I.R.A., probably a member of it. Mike had been smuggled across to Ireland, and there had become involved with the I.R.A. Why? There was his family background of militant nationalism. But surely anyone of Mike's intelligence could see that nowadays the I.R.A. was nothing but a bad joke, – and a criminally dangerous one at that? Was he still, then, bent on revenging Percy's death, accepting the I.R.A. as a convenient tool, as the Jacobean revenger employed the trivial squabbles of the rest of society to encompass his own obsessive ends?

These queries were forced to the perimeter of my mind by the increasing pressure of another thought. I stared with horrified fascination at the fact that I, of all people, had unwittingly betrayed Mike, in the one act of my military career that had exceeded the minimal performance of duty. Some malicious providence had thrust me, with a powerful hand in the small of the back, into a double treachery: to Mike himself, and to that code of contempt for the Army which we had once shared. Or was it merely the working-out of a treachery I had practised ever since Mike had deserted, in my subtle conquest of Pauline, and my easy self-adjustment to Badmore?

I still held Pauline's letter in my hand. I opened the envelope, and read the neat, round handwriting.

My Dearest Jonathan,

I thought I had to write, although I shall be seeing you so soon, just to tell you that you really mustn't be jealous about Mike, because honestly I never think of him at all. He was my first boy-friend, and if I'd been more experienced I'd have known that we could never get on together, and I'd have stopped the thing before it got started. In fact it never got very far, although it dragged on a long time. As far as I'm concerned, he's gone out of my life, and I don't particularly want to see him again. I thought I would write and get this off my chest because I think that there's been a certain strain between us about him. I've noticed that once or twice when the conversation seemed to be moving in that direction, you suddenly stopped talking. So it's perhaps a good job that we've had it out, and it can be forgotten. Don't let's talk about it any more.

I'm so looking forward to Wednesday, and of course I'm terribly excited about our holiday. I never thought Mummy and Daddy would agree, but they trust you! What do you think? I've bought a bikini! Well it's not really a bikini, but it's a two-piece, and rather daring for me. I hope you like it. Anyway, I'll try it on for you on Wednesday night and you can tell me if you think it's decent, I believe the Spaniards are a bit prudish . . .

I crumpled the letter in my fist and dropped it absently between my legs into the w.c. bowl.

After a long wrangle the Inspector said:

'Well, all right, Corporal. It's all against regulations, but I'll give you five minutes. Sergeant, take him down will you?'

'Yes, sir.'

'I will be alone with him, won't I?'

'Absolutely out of the question, Corporal. I'm permitting more than I should already.'

'Yes, I know. I'm very grateful. All right then.'

The Visitors' Room was a cross between a confessional and a Post Office. I sat facing the wire grille and waited for Mike. After all my efforts to see him, now I could not think what I would say. I heard footsteps approaching the door behind the grille.

I had asked the Sergeant to give Mike my name, so that time would not be wasted while he recovered from the surprise. But his face still wore an expression of astonishment as he entered the room.

'Jon! What are you doing here? I——'

The sergeant broke in with some formula about speaking clearly and other regulations, but I scarcely heard him. I too was taken by surprise, – by Mike's appearance. His hair was black, and he wore a heavy black moustache, like a French workman's, which obscured his upper lip. It made him look much older. Foolishly, the first question I asked him was:

'What happened to your hair?'

'Dyed. But what on earth are you doing here, Jon? How did you know . . .?'

'I was at the camp you raided last night. I was on guard.'

He whistled softly.

'We knew there should have been another N.C.O. I was prowling round looking for him. My God, Jon, I might have coshed you.'

'It would have been better for you if you had. I was watching all the time. I contacted the police at once. But I didn't know you were one of them.'

There was a pause while Mike took it in.

'It's all right, Jon. You were only doing your duty.'

'Oh fugg my duty.'

The sergeant stirred restively on his seat a few yards away.

'I see you've got a couple of stripes,' said Mike. 'You must be getting near the end of your time mustn't you?'

'Yes. Tomorrow.'

'Tomorrow?' He was silent. What was going on behind those pale blue eyes? It was too painful to speculate.

'Mike, I must know, if you can tell me,' – I shot a glance at the sergeant. 'Why did you get mixed up with that lot?'

'The Irish Republican Army?' He rolled the syllables with ironic unction. 'It's a long story. They got me out of England, as you probably realized. They hid me in a convent for some time, – that's another long story. I was sort of automatically enlisted. There wasn't much else I could do. Funny really: out of one Army and into another. There's not much to choose between them, I can tell you. Mind you, as long as it was just a matter of breaking into armouries, and making the Army look silly, I didn't mind. But a few weeks ago some fools blew up a telephone booth in Armagh, and some people were hurt. That was enough for me. We made a deal, that if I helped them with this raid, they'd get me to South America. The rest you know.'

'Your time's up,' said the sergeant. Mike stood up.

'Jon.'

'Yes?'

'You haven't seen Pauline lately, have you?'

218

'Yes. I see her quite a lot actually.'

'How is she?'

'She's fine.'

'Give her my . . . best wishes. I'm sorry I haven't been able to write. It was too risky. Perhaps I'll write now.'

'Come along,' said the sergeant.

'I shouldn't do that, Mike. It might upset her.'

He looked at me for a moment, then said gently:

'All right, Jon. You know best.'

'I'll write and explain,' I exclaimed desperately, as the sergeant took him away. 'I'll come and see you again.'

As the door closed he lifted his hand in a gesture of . . .

. . . of what? Reassurance? Dismissal? Benediction? Would I ever know?

I leaned from the corridor window, and took my last look at Badmore. The guard's whistle blew, and the wooden platform of the halt began to slide backwards. A mile away the huts of the camp clung to the side of a hill. Behind them, tanks crawled like sleepy bugs over the moors.

A train had carried me into the Army, and a train was bearing me away. In the compartments behind me tweedy middle-aged travellers listlessly turned the pages of their magazines, yawned, nibbled chocolate, checked the progress of the train by their watches. For them it was a dull, unimportant journey to London. How could they know how momentous it was to me, how strange it felt to be travelling at all on a Wednesday morning, wearing civilian clothes . . .

But I had no enthusiasm to pursue these ideas. I had looked forward to this journey for two years, but I could not conceal from myself that I was not enjoying it; and the reason was not hard to seek. Reassurance? Dismissal? Benediction?

The train gathered speed. I thrust my head into the blast, and looked back along the foreshortened line of carriages. The camp was still visible, low, black and ugly in the August sunshine. Beyond, the spires of the county town came into view. Beneath them my friend was immured.

'Ginger, you're barmy,' I murmured into the slipstream, which tore the syllables from my lips, carried them away with a paper bag that fluttered from a distant window. The train had reached a bend, and the curving carriages elbowed Badmore and the town out of sight. I withdrew my head into the corridor.

My friend. 'No, not what you might call a friend, sir.' For what friendship could exist between two people whose temperaments and destinies were so opposed? My temperament was prudence and my destiny success, as surely as Mike's were foolhardiness and failure. The Army had revealed our disparity with the precision of litmus.

'Excuse me, sir,' said an obsequious voice.

I pressed back to allow the restaurant-car attendant to pass. 'Morning coffee now being served!' he called out.

Mike still retained the knack of draining the sap of my own self-satisfaction: I had no zest for the journey, and the successful life that awaited me at the terminus seemed as heavy a sentence as that which awaited Mike. But I checked myself: was that not a mere sentimental hyperbole? For success was bound to be more *pleasant* than detention in a military prison. My own philosophy barred me from expiation. Even the wild idea of renouncing Pauline had to be rejected as soon as it occurred; for Pauline wanted *me*, not Mike. And one could not blame her. Mike was no hero, he was barmy, and there was no place for him. The most that could be said for him was that he was 'innocent', as they called barmy people once; and if the supernatural paraphernalia of his faith turned out to be true, and we found ourselves standing together at the bar of judgment, I knew who would blink and squint most in that dazzling light. If that happened, would Mike feel the same discomfort on my account as I did on his? Was Lazarus distressed because he could not moisten the parched tongue of Dives with a single drop of water?

Questions, questions . . . one could not forbear to ask them, tossing the pennies in the air, crying 'Heads' or 'Tails'; but they all fell behind a wall that could only be climbed in one direction. Meanwhile there was the coffee to be sipped in the quaint Edwardian comfort of the Pullman car, the cigarette to be savoured as the familiar landmarks between London and Badmore flashed past in the preferred order, Pauline to be greeted with an easy kiss at Waterloo, the mild dissipations of a Mediterranean holiday to be enjoyed, another degree to be acquired, a middle-class wedding to be arranged, a semi-detached house to be purchased, a carefully-planned family to be raised . . .

Before taking a seat in the restaurant car, I went to the w.c. and flushed Henry's parting gift down the plug.

Epilogue

I remember revising that penultimate paragraph, that vision of my future with its curious mixture of smugness and guilt, a few hours before Pauline shattered it beyond repair with the news that she was pregnant. That was about two months after our return from Majorca, two months spent in absorbed contemplation and revision of my story. Curious, how intricately that story is woven into the texture of my life, – not only in the experiences it records, but in itself. Michael, for instance, sitting on his pot beside me as I write, owes his existence to it in a way.

Almost as soon as we arrived in Majorca, Pauline was stricken with severe food poisoning, and confined to bed for several days. Three times a day I visited her darkened room, where she lay beneath a single sheet, looking wan and grey, her hair streaky with perspiration. She confided, with a feeble attempt at coquetry, that she had nothing on beneath the sheet, but I found myself unmoved by the information. Between these visits to the sickroom I was left to my own devices. I did not enjoy myself very much. The diversions of the beach soon palled: I am not a good swimmer, and a rash exposure of my white body to the sun resulted in a painful sun-burn. It was too hot to walk for long, and in order to sit down in the shade it seemed necessary to buy an unwanted drink at a café. Pauline spoke a little Spanish, but I had none; and I found my inability to communicate a constant embarrassment and irritation.

I tried to will myself into enjoying the long-awaited holiday by reminding myself that I was free; but I felt less at ease in the glaring gaudy, hedonistic resort than I had been in the Army.

The dusty offices of Badmore, the gloomy huts of Catterick, tugged at my thoughts with a strength like nostalgia. And at the core of my uneasiness was of course Mike, silently reproaching me from his cell in the county gaol.

I had postponed telling Pauline about Mike, fearing that it might spoil our holiday. It became more and more difficult to tell her as the days passed, though the pressure of my unshared thoughts on the subject increased at a swifter rate. On the fourth day I bought a notebook and began to write. I covered fifty pages and completely forgot to visit Pauline at the usual hour.

She emerged from her sick-room to find a very different escort from the one who had brought her to Majorca; or rather, no escort at all. I told her vaguely that I was writing a novel about National Service, and at first she was impressed and intrigued. But when I declined to answer her inquiries, and more particularly when she realized that the book took precedence over her and her entertainment, she displayed a natural resentment. She was panting to make up for the lost days of her holiday, and though I obediently followed her from *pension* to beach, and from beach to café, the soiled, dog-eared notebook always accompanied us, arousing as much venomous jealousy in Pauline as if it had been another woman.

'I don't know why you bothered to come on holiday with me,' she would complain sulkily. 'Why didn't you stay at home with your old book?'

On such occasions I would relent, put aside my manuscript, and cajole her back into a good humour by taking a boat trip or fooling around in the tepid water. But before long I would relapse into abstracted silence, as some detail I had been searching for came welling up from the memory, and my fingers would be itching to curl themselves round a pen again. Poor Pauline! What a rotten holiday she had, – and the last Continental holiday she'll have for a long time too. On our last evening in Majorca she burst into tears and said it was the worst holiday she had ever had, and I don't think she was exaggerating.

It happened that I had just brought the book to a tentative conclusion that very afternoon, and was experiencing that euphoric state of relaxation and relief which follows literary creation: the intelligence and imagination are exhausted, but the other faculties and senses awaken, and one feels benevolent to the rest of the world. I took Pauline to a sort of night-club and blued the remainder of my pesetas on the best dinner and champagne that the place could provide. I even shuffled round the floor in a tipsy imitation of the other couples, and became demonstratively amorous as we walked back to the *pension* along the beach, where palm-trees, moonlight and gentle waves belatedly exerted the romantic charm about which I had heard and read so much. Pauline, demoralized and disarmed by my erratic behaviour, responded with starved eagerness, and I ended the night in her bed. There, after much effort and with little pleasure, I succeeded in rupturing her hymen, and planted in her the sperm which became the small boy now emitting such an offensive odour at my feet. Afterwards as we lay together, sticky, limp and dissatisfied, I chain-smoked and told her all about Mike. I left her silently weeping; but whether this was because of Mike, or the loss of her maidenhead, or just physical pain, I did not discover.

The next morning she had rallied, and I was the unhappy one, brooding on the possible consequences of the previous night, and cursing the impulse that had deprived me of the security of Henry's parting gift. But Pauline said that the date was all right; and once back in England I became immersed in the revision of my book, an occupation which pushed Pauline, and all thoughts of the future, to the rim of my mind.

Pauline's announcement that she was pregnant induced in me what most people would call a nervous breakdown, and some perhaps a spiritual crisis. The neurotic symptoms I developed were, I realize now, merely defensive mechanisms designed to postpone action. The only possible course of action was to abandon my postgraduate research, marry Pauline, and get a job. I did not want to do any of these things. Then Mike's long-delayed trial came up.

My relationship with Mike had been a fuse laid in the bedrock of my self-complacency, which had been smouldering for two years, occasionally disturbing me as I sniffed its acrid smoke. Now it detonated, and with explosive force the possibility presented itself to me, for the first time in my life, of doing something positive and unselfish. Looking at Mike in the dock, gaunt and wild-eyed, as he listened to the judge's ominous summing-up, I wondered despairingly what would become of him. Whatever sentence he received, it would no doubt be lengthened by many insubordinations. Perhaps he would even try to escape again. He would never find rest or peace. Because he was barmy. Then my idea came to me, and I smiled broadly at him. He must have thought *I* was barmy at that moment.

I married Pauline hastily – a quiet, off-white wedding at her parish church, – and as soon as I discovered which prison Mike had been sent to, we moved down here and rented this narrow cottage. The local secondary modern was glad to take me on, since teachers are not attracted to this damp, isolated place, where the local industry is a prison. On the first Sunday of every month for the past three years, I have visited Mike – except for one or two occasions recently, when I managed to persuade Mrs Brady to resume relations with her black-sheep son. Mr Brady, who is secretly rather proud of his son's criminal record, had made the long journey from Hastings a few times before, to visit Mike with me; but when he brought his wife I had to yield up my place, as only two visitors are allowed. I was strangely miserable on those two Sundays when I missed seeing Mike.

Crash! Another plate has bit the stone flags in the scullery. Being pregnant again makes Pauline clumsy, but she's nervous too at the prospect of entertaining Mike to lunch. For she has not seen him for nearly five years. She always made the baby the excuse for not accompanying me to the prison; but her reasons must surely lie deeper. Perhaps she thinks Mike is still in love with her. But I cannot very well tell her that he is not, still less that he is unlikely to fall in love again when he sees her as she is now. Another crash! But then I'm nervous too. I began and abandoned three books this morning before I unearthed this manuscript from a drawer. In only twenty minutes Mike will be standing outside the prison gates in his cheap new suit, inhaling the sweet smell of freedom. He didn't want me to meet him.

I hope Mike will agree to stay with us for a while. He has been the focal point of my life for so long that I am curiously jealous of the rest of the world with whom he will shortly resume contact. Also I feel a certain panic when I reflect that he will no longer need my support. It is not a question of what he will do without me, but of what I will do without him. Now he is free, and I am shackled, – by a wife and family I do not greatly love, and by a career that I find no more than tolerable.

I had always assumed that we would move back to London when my 'mission' was completed, and that I would pick up my research on the justly neglected eighteenth-century antiquarian and bibliographer whom I chose as my thesis topic. But now I am not so sure. It seems to me that the decision which I must make now is at least as important as the one that brought me here three years ago. The effort of combining a full-time teaching job with part-time research would be merely another excuse (Mike's welfare is the current one) for fulfilling no more than the statutory requirements of a husband and father. Pauline, absorbed and distracted by maternity, does not seem aware of any lack in our marriage, but she will be eventually. I must forestall her. Somehow I must learn to love her. And it seems to me that it will be easier to do so here, than in London.

And besides, I have become strangely attached to this place, where the fogs come down in October, and scarcely disperse until Spring. In this remote community, besieged by nature for half the year, I feel I could build a life of modest usefulness. The lectures I gave at the prison have aroused my interest in remedial work. Since Mike began to study externally for his degree the idea has caught on, and several of the prisoners are preparing to sit for the G.C.E. Mike was fortunate to be tried by the civil authorities, and to be sent to a prison with so enlightened a governor.

It will be difficult to explain to Pauline why I want to stay here; but if, as seems likely, they offer me the deputy headship of the school next year, we might be able to afford a house with a bathroom and indoor lavatory, two amenities that would bribe Pauline to do almost anything.

Twelve o'clock striking. I must put a clean nappy on Michael, lay the table, and get out the cider. And the Guinness.

The British Museum is
Falling Down

To
Derek Todd
(in affectionate memory of B.M. days)
and to
Malcolm Bradbury
(whose fault it mostly is that I
have tried to write
a comic novel)

Life imitates art.

OSCAR WILDE

I would be a Papist if I could.
I have fear enough, but an
obstinate rationality prevents me.

DR JOHNSON

ONE

There were moments of happiness in the British Museum reading-room, but the body called him back.
GRAHAM GREENE

It was Adam Appleby's misfortune that at the moment of awakening from sleep his consciousness was immediately flooded with everything he least wanted to think about. Other men, he gathered, met each new dawn with a refreshed mind and heart, full of optimism and resolution; or else they moved sluggishly through the first hour of the day in a state of blessed numbedness, incapable of any thought at all, pleasant or unpleasant. But, crouched like harpies round his bed, unpleasant thoughts waited to pounce the moment Adam's eyelids flickered apart. At that moment he was forced, like a drowning man, to review his entire life instantaneously, divided between regrets for the past and fears for the future.

Thus it was that as he opened his eyes one November morning, and focused them blearily on the sick rose, three down and six across, on the wallpaper opposite his bed, Adam was simultaneously reminded that he was twenty-five years of age, and would soon be twenty-six, that he was a post-graduate student preparing a thesis which he was unlikely to complete in this the third and final year of his scholarship, that the latter was hugely overdrawn, that he was married with three very young children, that one of them had manifested an alarming rash the previous evening, that his name was ridiculous, that his leg hurt, that his decrepit scooter had failed to start the previous morning and would no doubt fail to start this morning, that he had just missed a first-class degree because of a bad Middle English paper, that his leg hurt, that at his primary school he had proved so proficient in the game of who-can-pee-highest-up-the-wall of the boys' outside lavatory that he had wetted the biretta of the parish priest who happened to be visiting the playground on the other side of the wall at the time, that he had forgotten to reserve any books at the British Museum for this morning's reading, that his leg hurt, that his wife's period was three days overdue, and that his leg hurt.

But wait a minute . . . One of these mental events was unfamiliar. He could not recall any sensation of pain in his leg on retiring the previous night. And it was not, he reflected bitterly, as if he had enjoyed any strenuous physical activity *after* retiring. When Barbara's period was overdue, neither of them felt much inclination for sex. The thought of another pregnancy had a dampening effect on desire, even though they knew the issue must be already settled, one way or another, in Barbara's womb. At the thought of that womb plumping with another life, a spasm of cold terror coursed through Adam's bowels. In a year's time he should, with luck, have completed his Ph.D. and obtained some kind of job. It was essential that they should avoid conceiving another child at least until then. And if possible for ever.

How different it must be, he thought, the life of an ordinary, non-Catholic parent, free to decide – actually to *decide*, in calm confidence – whether to have or not to have a child. How different from his own married state, which Adam symbolised as a small, over-populated, low-lying island ringed by a crumbling dyke which he and his wife struggled hopelessly to repair as they kept anxious watch on the surging sea of fertility that surrounded them. It was not that, having produced the three children, he and Barbara would now, given the opportunity, actually will them back into non-existence; but this acceptance of new life was not infinitely elastic. Its extension had limits, and Adam thought they had now been reached, at least for the foreseeable future.

His mind turned, as it not infrequently did, to the circumstances which had brought them to this pass. Their marriage more than four years ago had been a hurried affair, precipitated by the announcement that Adam, who was doing his National Service after graduation, was to be posted to Singapore. Shortly afterwards he had proved to be suffering from an ear condition which had restricted him to home postings. This had been a source of joy to them at the time, but in gloomy moments Adam wondered retrospectively whether it had been altogether fortunate. In spite of, or perhaps because of being widely separated – he in Yorkshire and Barbara with her parents in Birmingham – and coming together only on weekend leaves, they had managed to produce two children during his army service.

They had embarked on marriage with vague notions about the Safe Period and a hopeful trust in Providence that Adam now found difficult to credit. Clare had been born nine months after the wedding. Barbara had then consulted a Catholic doctor who gave her a simple mathematical formula for calculating the Safe Period – so simple that Dominic was born one year after Clare. Shortly afterwards Adam was released from the Army, and returned to London to do research. Someone gave Barbara a booklet explaining how she could determine the time of her ovulation by recording her temperature each morning, and they followed this procedure until Barbara became pregnant again.

After Edward's birth they had simply abstained from intercourse for six months of mounting neurosis. Having managed, with some difficulty, to enter the married state as virgins after three years' courtship, they found it hard that they should have to revert to this condition while sharing the same bed. A few months ago they had applied for help to a Catholic Marriage counselling organisation, whose doctors had poured a kindly scorn on their amateurish attempts to operate the basal temperature method. They had been given sheets of graph paper and little pieces of cardboard with transparent windows of cellophane to place over the graphs, and recommended, for maximum security, to keep to the post-ovulatory period.

For three anxious months they had survived. Unfortunately, Barbara's ovulation seemed to occur late in her monthly cycle, and their sexual relations were forced into a curious pattern: three weeks of patient graph-plotting, followed by a few nights of frantic love-making, which rapidly petered out in exhaustion and renewed suspense. This behaviour was known as Rhythm and was in accordance with the Natural Law.

From the next room came a muffled thump and a sharp cry, which modulated into a low whining that Adam attributed hesitantly to his youngest child, Edward. He glanced sideways at his wife. She lay on her stomach, sucking a thermometer. A small peak in the bedclothes further down indicated the presence of a second thermometer. Unable to decide on the relative accuracy of the oral and rectal methods of taking her temperature, Barbara had decided to employ both. Which would be all right as long as she could be relied upon not to confuse the two readings. Which Adam doubted.

Catching his eye, Barbara muttered something rendered unrecognisable as a human utterance by the presence of the thermometer, but which Adam interpreted as, 'Make a cup of tea.' An interesting example of the function of predictability in casual speech, he mentally observed, as he pulled back the bedclothes. The lino greeted his feet with an icy chill, and he pranced awkwardly round the room on tip-toe, looking for his slippers. It was difficult, he found, to limp and walk on tip-toe at the same time. He discovered his slippers at last in his shirt-drawer, a minute plastic doll made in Hong Kong nestling in the toe of each. He hurriedly donned his dressing-gown. There was a distinct nip in the air: winter was contending with autumn. It made him think of electricity bills. So, when he looked out of the window, did Battersea Power Station, looming vaguely through the morning fog.

After filling and switching on the electric kettle in the kitchen, Adam made his way to the bathroom. But his eldest child had forestalled him.

'I'm passing a motion,' Clare announced.

'Who else is voting?' he cracked uneasily. In theory, Adam fully supported his wife's determination to teach the children an adult vocabulary for their physical functions. But it still disconcerted him – perhaps because it was not a vocabulary he had ever used himself, even as an adult. And it seemed to him positively dangerous to encourage the articulacy of a child so precociously fascinated by physiology as Clare. When Barbara had been in labour with Edward, and a kindly neighbour had hinted archly,

238

'I think you're going to have a baby brother or sister,' Clare had replied: 'I think so too – the contractions are coming every two minutes.' Such feats were the source of a certain pride in Adam, but he couldn't help thinking that Clare was missing something of the magic and mystery of childhood.

'What's voting?' asked his daughter.

'Will you be long?' he countered.

'I don't know. You just can't tell with these things.'

'Well, don't be long, please. Daddy wants to use the lavatory.'

'Why don't you use Dominic's pot?'

'Daddies don't use pots.'

'Why don't they?'

At a loss for an answer, Adam retreated to the kitchen. Where he had gone wrong, of course, was in categorically denying that Daddies used pots. Daddies often used pots. Eighty per cent of the rural dwellings in Ireland had no sanitation of any kind, for example. The correct gambit would have been: '*I* don't use pots.' Or, better still: '*You* don't use pots any more, do you, Clare?'

The kettle began to boil. Adam suddenly wondered whether he had over-estimated the function of predictability in casual speech. Supposing Barbara had not said, 'Make a cup of tea', but 'Edward has fallen out of his cot', or 'My rectal thermometer is stuck'? He hastened back to the bedroom, pausing only to peep into the children's room to assure himself of Edward's safety. He was quite all right – placidly eating strips of wallpaper which Dominic was tearing off the wall. Adam made Edward spit them out and, holding the moist pulp in his outstretched hand, proceeded to the bedroom.

'You *did* want me to make a cup of tea?' he enquired, putting his head round the door.

Barbara took the thermometer from her mouth and squinted at it. 'Yes,' she said, and replaced the thermometer.

Adam returned to the kitchen, disposed of the pulp and made the tea. While waiting for it to draw he mentally composed a short article, '*Catholicism, Roman*', for a Martian encyclopaedia compiled after life on earth had been destroyed by atomic warfare.

ROMAN CATHOLICISM was, according to archaeological evidence, distributed fairly widely over the planet Earth in the twentieth century. As far as the Western Hemisphere is concerned, it appears to have been characterised by a complex system of sexual taboos and rituals. Intercourse between married partners was restricted to certain limited periods determined by the calendar and the body-temperature of the female. Martian archaeologists have learned to identify the domiciles of Roman Catholics by the presence of large numbers of complicated graphs, calendars, small booklets full of figures, and quantities of broken thermometers, evidence of the great importance attached to this code. Some scholars have argued that it was merely a method of limiting the number of offspring; but as it has been conclusively proved that the Roman Catholics produced more children on average than any other section of the community, this seems untenable. Other doctrines of the Roman Catholics included a belief in a Divine Redeemer and in a life after death.

Adam put the tray on the floor outside the bathroom, and entered purposefully. 'Come on, you're finished,' he said, lifting Clare from the seat.

'Wipe my bottom, please.'

He obliged, washing his hands afterwards to set a good example. Then he guided Clare firmly to the door.

'Can I stay and watch?'

'No. There's a biscuit for you on the kitchen table, and one each for Dominic and Edward.'

Adam micturated, and considered whether to wash his hands a second time. He decided against it. On re-entering the bedroom, he found Dominic urging his mother to rise.

'Up, up!' screamed the child. 'Dominic, leave your mother alone. She's busy,' said Adam. Burdened with the tray, he was too slow to prevent Dominic from pulling off the bedclothes. Barbara was the Callipygian type, but the thermometer spoiled the effect. Adam interposed himself between Dominic and the bed. 'Dominic, go away,' he said, and thoughtlessly remarked to

Barbara: 'You look like a glass porcupine with all those things sticking out of you.'

Barbara yanked at the bedclothes and plucked the thermometer from her mouth. 'Don't be rude. Do you think I enjoy this performance every morning?'

'Well, yes, I do, as a matter of fact. It's like Camel and his pipe. You were both weaned too early. But this latest development . . . It strikes me as a bit kinky.'

'If you don't shut up, I'll break these damn things over my knee and – '

'Have a cup of tea' said Adam conciliatingly.

'Just a minute.' Barbara entered the readings of her two thermometers in a small Catholic diary. This was not a conscious irony on her part, but Adam followed the relationship between the liturgical year and his wife's temperature chart with interest. He practised a special devotion to those saints whose feast-days fell within the putative Safe Period, and experienced disquiet when a virgin martyr was so distinguished.

'Up, up!' shouted Dominic, red with anger.

'Dominic,' said Adam, 'Clare has got a bikky for you.'

The child trotted out. They sipped their tea.

'I wish you wouldn't use those silly baby-words, Adam.'

'Sorry. I keep forgetting. What was your temperature?' At this stage of Barbara's cycle, her temperature was of largely academic interest, except that marked changes from day to day might indicate that conception had taken place. Another cold wave of fear rippled through Adam's frame at the thought.

'One said 97.8 and the other 98.2.'

'What does that mean?'

'It's down a bit . . . I don't know.'

'Have you . . . You haven't started your period yet?' he asked wistfully.

'No. I don't think so.'

'Go and find out,' he wheedled.

'Give me a minute.'

How lovely it would be if she came back from the bathroom and said yes. How happy his day would be. How transfigured the

British Museum would appear. With what zest he would collect his books and set to work . . . But he had forgotten to reserve any books. That meant a long delay this morning . . .

'Eh?' he said, conscious that Barbara had asked him a question.

'You haven't listened to a word I've been saying.'

'Yes I have,' he lied.

'What did I ask you, then?'

He groped around in his mind for a likely question. 'You said, why was I limping?'

'There, you see? I said, "Have you looked at Edward's rash?" '

'I didn't exactly look. But I don't remember noticing it.'

'I hope it isn't measles. Why *are* you limping anyway?'

'I don't know. I think I must have pulled a muscle.'

'What?'

'In the night.'

'Don't be ridiculous. How could you pull a muscle when you were asleep?'

'That's what I don't understand. Perhaps I run in my sleep.'

'Perhaps you do other things in your sleep,' said Barbara, getting out of bed and leaving the room.

Her words did not immediately sink into Adam's consciousness. He was fascinated by a mental picture of himself running through the streets of London in his pyjamas, at tremendous speed, chest out, arms pumping, mouth swallowing air, eyes glazed in sleep.

PYJAMA ATHLETE SMASHES RECORD

Early yesterday morning late-night revellers were astonished by the sight of a young man clad in pyjamas speeding through the streets of London. Herman Hopple, the British Olympic coach, spotted the mystery runner when returning to his Bloomsbury hotel, and having a stop-watch in his pocket, timed him at 1 minute 28.5 seconds as he lapped the British Museum before disappearing in the direction of Battersea. An official of the A.A.A. who was fortunately acompanying Mr Hopple at the time later measured the perimeter of the British Museum at exactly 800 metres. The pyjama athlete has thus smashed the world record, and qualifies for the $10,000 prize established by an American millionaire for the first man to cover the distance in less than a minute and a half. 'We are very anxious to trace him,' said Mr Hopple this morning.

Barbara's words suddenly formed up and came resoundingly to attention in his mind. *Perhaps you do others things in your sleep.* Could you, he wondered, and not remember it? That would be the supreme irony: to conceive another child and not even be conscious enough to enjoy it. There was that night not long ago when they had come back from Camel's place drowsy and amorous from drinking Spanish wine . . .

Barbara returned from the bathroom, and shook her head at Adam's hopeful glance. She was carrying Edward under her arm, breech presentation.

'I've been thinking,' said Adam, 'about what you said just now. It's just possible you know. That evening we came back from Camel's. Do you remember, the next morning my pyjama trousers were on the floor and two buttons had come off your nightdress?'

'Don't be ridiculous,' said Barbara, rummaging in a drawer for a nappy. '*You* might not know what you were doing, but I would.'

'It's not ridiculous. What about *incubi* and *succubae?*'

'What about them?'

'They were demons who used to have intercourse with humans while they were asleep.'

'That's all I need,' said Barbara.

'How many days overdue are you?' Adam asked. As if he didn't know.

'Three.'

'Have you been that much before?'

'Yes.'

Barbara was bent over the wriggling torso of Edward, and her replies were muffled by the safety pins in her mouth. Barbara always seemed to have something in her mouth.

'Often?'

'No.'

'How often?'

'Oh, for God's sake, Adam!'

Barbara clicked the second pin shut, and let Edward slide to the floor. She looked up, and Adam saw with dismay that she was crying.

'What's the matter?' he wailed.

'I feel sick.'

Adam felt as if two giant hands had grasped his stomach and intestines, drenched them in cold water, and wrung them out like a dishcloth. 'Oh Jesus,' he murmured, employing the blasphemy he reserved for special occasions.

Barbara stared hopelessly at Edward, crawling across the lino. 'I can't think how we could have made a mistake. My temperature went up at the right time and everything.'

'Oh Jesus,' Adam repeated, aloud. When his own innate pessimism was balanced by Barbara's common sense, he could survive; but when Barbara herself was rattled, as she clearly was this morning, nothing could save him from falling deeper into despair. He could see it was going to be a bad day, of a kind he knew well. He would sit slumped at his desk in the British Museum, a heap of neglected books before him, while his mind reeled with menstrual cycles and temperature charts and financial calculations that never came right. He made a brief mental prayer: 'Please God, let her not be pregnant.' He added: 'And I'm sorry I swore.'

'Don't look at me like that,' said Barbara.

'Like what?'

'As if it was all my fault.'

'Of course it isn't your fault,' said Adam testily. 'Or mine either. But you don't expect to see the Lineaments of Gratified Desire all over my face, do you?'

The entrance of Clare and Dominic put an end to further conversation.

'Dominic says he's hungry,' Clare announced, accusingly.

'Why aren't you having any breakfast, Mummy?' asked Clare.

'Mummy doesn't feel well,' said Adam.

'Why don't you feel well, Mummy?'

'I don't know, Clare. I just feel sick.'

''ick,' said Dominic sociably.

'*I* only feel sick *after* I eat things,' observed Clare. 'So does Dominic, don't you Dominic?'

''ick.'

'Sick, Dominic. Say "Sick".'

''ick.'

'I wish to hell you wouldn't talk so much at breakfast, Clare,' Adam said.

'Don't lose your temper with the children, Adam,' Barbara intervened. 'Clare is only trying to teach Dominic.'

Adam swallowed the last morsel of his bacon without relish, and reached mechanically for the marmalade. Barbara intercepted him. 'Actually,' she said, 'I feel better now. I think I'll have some breakfast after all.'

Songbirds! A ray of sunshine! Bells ringing! Adam's heart lifted. Barbara smiled faintly at him and he raised his newspaper before his face to hide his absurd joy. An advertiser's announcement caught his eye:

'Write the second line of a rhyming couplet beginning:
  I always choose a Brownlong chair
  ....
– and win a new three-piece suite or £100 cash.'

Now that was the kind of competition a literary man ought to be able to win. A modest prize, too, which should cut down the number of competitors to a reasonable size. *I always choose a Brownlong chair* . . . Because . . . because . . . Ah! He had it. He read out the terms of the competition to his family.

' "*I always choose a Brownlong chair.*" What about the next line?'

'*Because it's made for wear and tear*,' suggested Clare.

'That's what I was going to say,' said Adam, resentfully.

When Adam came to dress, he could not find a pair of clean underpants. Barbara came into the room at this point, carrying Edward.

'I don't think he's got measles after all,' she said.

'Good. I can't find a pair of clean pants.'

'No, I washed them all yesterday. They're still damp.'

'Well, I'll just have to wear the pair I had on yesterday.' He moved towards the soiled linen basket.

'I washed those, too. While you were having your bath last night.'

Adam came to a halt, and rounded slowly on his wife. 'What are you telling me? D'you mean I haven't got a single pair of underpants to wear?'

'If you changed them more often, this wouldn't happen.'

'That may be so, but I'm not going to argue about personal hygiene at this point. What I want to know is: what am I going to wear under my trousers today?'

'Do you *have* to wear something? Can't you do without for once?'

'Of course I can't "do without"!'

'I don't know why you're making such a fuss. I've gone without pants before.' She looked meaningfully at Adam, who softened at the memory of a certain day by the sea.

'That was different. You know the trousers of my suit are itchy,' he complained in a quieter tone. 'You don't know what it's like, sitting in the Museum all day.'

'Wear your other trousers, then.'

'I've got to wear the suit today. There's a post-graduate sherry party.'

'You didn't tell me.'

'Don't change the subject.'

Barbara was silent for a minute. 'You could wear a pair of mine,' she offered.

'To hell with that! What d'you take me for – a – transvestite? Where are those damp ones?'

'In the kitchen somewhere. They'll take a long time to dry.'

In the passage he nearly tripped over Clare, who was squatting on the floor, dressing a doll.

'What's a transvestite, Daddy?' she inquired.

'Ask your mother,' Adam snarled.

In the kitchen, Dominic was tearing the morning paper into narrow strips. Adam snatched it away from him, and the child began to scream. Cravenly, Adam returned the newspaper. He looked at the clock and began to get angry at the way time was slipping away. Time when he should be at work, work, work. Ploughing ahead with a thesis that would rock the scholarly world and start a revolution in literary criticism.

He found a pair of underpants in a tangle of sodden washing in the baby's bath. Improvising brilliantly, he pulled out the grill-pan of the electric stove, wiped the grid clean of grease with a handkerchief, and spread out his pants. He slotted home the grill-pan, and turned the switch to High. Fascinated, Dominic stopped tearing up the newspaper and watched the rising steam. Adam stealthily confiscated the remaining portion of the newspaper. The competition again caught his eye.

> *I always choose a Brownlong chair*
> *Whenever I relax* au pair.

Or

> *I always choose a Brownlong chair*
> *For laying girls with long brown hair.*

No, it was worth going in for seriously.

> *I always choose a Brownlong chair*
> *For handsome looks and a price that's fair.*

Didn't scan very well.

'Dadda, 'ire,' said Dominic, tugging gently at his sleeve. Adam smelled burning cloth, and lunged at the grill. Ire was the word. He stuffed the scorched remains of his underpants into the garbage pail, burning his fingers in the process.

'More, Dadda,' said Dominic.

In the passage Adam met Barbara. 'Where did you say your pants were?' he asked casually.

'In the top left-hand drawer.' She sniffed. 'You've burned something.'

'Nothing much,' he said, and hurried on to the bedroom.

Adam, who had hitherto valued women's underwear on its transparency, now found himself applying quite different standards, and deploring the frivolity of his wife's tastes. Eventually he located a pair of panties that were opaque, and a chaste white in hue. Unfortunately they were also trimmed with lace, but that couldn't be helped. As he drew them on, the hairs on his legs crackled with static electricity. The clinging but featherlight touch of the nylon round his haunches was a strange new sensation. He stood thoughtfully before the mirror for a moment, awed by a sudden insight into sexual deviation.

'Mummy says a transvestite is a poor man who likes wearing ladies' clothes because he's silly in the head,' remarked Clare from the door.

Adam grabbed his trousers and pulled them on. 'Clare, how many times have I told you not to come into this room without knocking. You're quite old enough to remember.'

'I didn't come in. I'm standing outside,' she replied, pointing to her feet.

'Don't answer back,' he said dispiritedly. What a mess he was making of his parental role this morning. Oh, it was going to be a bad day, all right.

Adam's family lined up in alphabetical order to be kissed goodbye: Barbara, Clare, Dominic and Edward (seated). When the principle behind this nomenclature dawned on their friends they were likely to ask humorously whether Adam and Barbara intended working through the whole alphabet, a joke that seemed less and less funny to Adam and Barbara as time went on. Adam kissed Barbara last, and scrutinised her for signs of pregnancy: coarse-grained skin, lifeless hair, swelling breasts. He even looked at her waistline. With an immense effort of rationality, he reminded himself that she was only three days overdue.

'How do you feel?'

'Oh, all right. We must try and be sensible.'

'I don't know what we'll do if you're pr—'

'*Pas devant les enfants.*'

'Eh?'

'That means, not in front of us,' Clare explained to Dominic.

'Oh yes,' said Adam, catching on. 'I'll phone you later.'

'Try and do it when Mrs Green is out.'

Dominic began to snivel. 'Where Dadda going?' he demanded.

'He's going to work, like he always does,' said Barbara.

'At the British Museum,' Adam said impressively. As he closed the door of the flat, he heard Clare asking Barbara if there were any other transvestites at the British Museum.

TWO

As I go to my work at the British Museum I see the faces of the people become daily more corrupt.
RUSKIN

When the door of the Applebys' flat was closed, the staircase leading to the ground floor was plunged in total darkness, as the single switch of the hall light was at the bottom, near the telephone, and was always kept in the 'off' position by Mrs Green. Adam groped for the banister, and slowly descended the stairs, impeded by the two canvas holdalls he carried, one containing books and the other papers; having discovered with tiresome frequency that whatever portion of his thesis material he left at home he was bound to need at the British Museum, he had resigned himself to carrying the whole apparatus backwards and forwards every day.

He was making good progress down the stairs when his cautiously-extended foot encountered a soft, yielding, object. He drew back his foot with a gasp of fright. He stared hard, but could distinguish nothing in the gloom.

'Pussy?' he murmured. But if it was Mrs Green's cat, it was asleep – or dead. The foot he inched forward again aroused no life in the mysterious object.

The thing to do, of course, was to step smartly over it, whistling loudly. But somehow the idea was distasteful. He recalled a novel he had read about a man who had been locked up by the Gestapo in total darkness with a sinister, soft, moist, yielding object, which the man in his terror imagined to be all kinds of horrible things, such as a piece of human flesh looking like a lump of raw meat, but which turned out to be nothing more than a wet cloth. Adam placed his bags on the stairs behind him, and struck a match. It was a lump of raw meat.

'Is that you, Mr Appleby?' inquired Mrs Green, as Adam's half-stifled scream lingered in the air. The light came on in the hall.

'Is this yours?' inquired Adam, with cold politeness, indicating the cellophane-wrapped joint at his feet. Mrs Green came to the foot of the stairs and looked up.

'Mrs Appleby asked me to get it for her. I was out shopping early this morning.' She bounced a reproachful look at Adam off the dial of the clock in the hall. Mrs Green considered it little less than criminal for a married man with three children to be leaving the house in the middle of the morning, and not to work either, but just to sit in a library reading books. Her look, however, accused him of more than idleness. Adam knew very well what Mrs Green supposed him to have been up to, while respectable people had been up and about.

To Mrs Green, herself a widow with an only son, Adam's paternity of three young children, whom he could patently not afford to support, indicated an ungovernable sexual appetite of which Barbara was the innocent victim. 'Ooh, isn't Mr Appleby naughty?' had been her first response to Barbara's nervous announcement of her third pregnancy; and subsequently Adam had had to endure from his landlady the kind of half-fascinated, half-fearful appraisal usually reserved for prize bulls. As he calculated that there could be few married men in Metropolitan London who enjoyed their marital rights as seldom as himself, he found this situation particularly trying. But it was difficult to communicate to Mrs Green the true state of affairs. Shortly after Edward had been born she had taken Barbara aside, and hinted that there were Things You Could Use, and that she had heard it rumoured that there were Clinics where they gave you the Things, not that she had any experience of them herself, she had never been troubled that way with poor Mr G., he was more for the fretwork, but she thought she owed it to Mrs Appleby to tell her. Barbara had thanked her and explained that their religious convictions prevented them from profiting by her advice. Undeterred, Mrs Green had consulted a female relative who belonged to some obscure non-conformist sect, and returned with the counsel, 'You'll just have to Pull Away, dear, at the critical moment, if you get my meaning; just Pull Away.' Adam and Barbara tolerated these intrusions into their private lives for the sake of the flat, the rent of which Mrs Green had not raised during their tenancy out of compassion for Barbara.

'I hope you haven't hurt that meat, Mr Appleby,' Mrs Green remarked as Adam reached the hall. 'I see you're limping.'

'No, no, the meat's quite all right,' Adam replied. 'My leg's been hurting since I got up. I think I must have pulled a muscle.'

'You ought to get more exercise,' said Mrs Green, adding meaningfully, 'in the open air. It's not healthy to be reading all day.'

'Well, I won't get much reading done today unless I hurry,' he replied jovially, bustling to the door. 'Goodbye.'

'Oh, Mr Appleby – '

He got the door swinging just in time to pretend that he hadn't heard, but in the instant before it slammed behind him he caught the end of her sentence:

' – a letter for you.'

A letter. Adam experienced a kind of psychic salivation at the thought of a letter waiting for him behind the door. He loved mail, even though his own consisted almost exclusively of bills, rejected scholarly articles and appeals for donations from missionary nuns who obtained his address from letters he wrote to the Catholic press about Birth Control. He had a tantalising mental image of the letter on Mrs Green's hall-stand – he could swear now that he had seen it out of the corner of his eye as he had rushed for the door – not a bill, not an appeal, not a creased brown foolscap envelope addressed in his own handwriting, but a plump letter in a thick, white, expensive envelope, his name and address typed on it in a distinctive typeface, a crest on the flap suggestive of an important, semi-official source, a letter bringing good fortune: *Would you accept . . . We should like to commission . . . It is my pleasure to inform you . . . State your own terms . . .*

He would have to concede that he had heard Mrs Green's parting words, and return ignominiously. With luck, she would already have retreated to the kitchen which, appropriately enough, always reeked with the smell of cooking cabbage. Adam fumbled in his pocket for his keys, only to discover that he had left them in the flat. He agitated the door-knocker gently and apologetically. There was no sound from within. He knocked harder. Stooping, he pushed open the flap of the letter-box, and called coaxingly, 'Mrs Green!' To his surprise an envelope flew out of the aperture and lodged itself between his teeth.

'Thank you, Mrs Green,' he called, spitting out the missive, and glaring at a small boy who was sniggering on the pavement.

The appearance of the letter was as odd as the manner of its delivery. The envelope was a specimen of old-fashioned mourning stationery, with a thick black band round the edges. It appeared to have been formerly used in correspondence with a restaurateur, but wrongly addressed, so that it bore much evidence of the patient efforts of the G.P.O. to deliver it correctly. The envelope was sealed with Elastoplast, and Adam's name and address trailed between the other cancelled addresses in heavy green biro. Exerting all his paleographic skills, Adam made out at the primary level of the palimpsest the name, 'Mrs Amy Rottingdean', who, he deduced, was the probable source of the letter addressed to himself. He was unable to attach the name to anyone he knew. Scrutinising the envelope, Adam quivered slightly with expectancy and curiosity. He found the sensation pleasant, and to prolong it he thrust the letter into his pocket. Then he braced himself to confront his scooter.

Adam kept his scooter under a filthy tarpaulin in Mrs Green's small front garden. He pulled off the tarpaulin, kicked it under the hedge, and regarded the machine with loathing. He had been given the scooter by its former owner, his father-in-law, when the latter's firm had provided him with a small car. At the time, he had regarded the gift as one of astounding generosity, but he was now convinced that it had been an act of the purest malice, designed either to maim him or ruin him, or both. He had accepted the gift on the assumption that the running costs would be more than compensated for by the savings on fares, a prediction that still wrung from him a bitter laugh whenever he recalled it, which was usually when he was paying for repairs. Paying for repairs was, however, one of Adam's smaller worries. *Getting* the damned thing repaired was infinitely more difficult.

Of all the industries in the country, Adam had decided, scooter-maintenance exhibited the most sensational excess of demand over supply. In theory, a fortune awaited the man who set out to meet this demand; but at the bottom of his heart Adam doubted whether scooters were repairable in the ordinary sense of the term: they were the butterflies of the road, fragile organisms which took a long time to make and a short time to die. By now, Adam had located every workshop within a five-mile radius of his flat, and without exception they were crammed to the ceiling with crippled scooters waiting for repair. In a small clearing in the middle of the floor, a few oily youths would be tinkering doubtfully with a dismantled machine or two, while their owners, and the owners of other machines in dock, loitered anxiously outside trying to catch the eyes of the mechanics to bribe them with cigarettes or money. Adam, an innocent in the world of machinery at the best of times, had experienced the most humiliating and desperate moments of his life in scooter-repair workshops.

Adam strapped his heavy bags to the luggage rack, and pushed the scooter into the road. He gave the starting pedal a ritual kick, and was so astonished when the engine fired that he was too slow in twisting the throttle. The engine died, and a dozen further kicks produced not the faintest symptom of internal combustion. Adam resigned himself to adopting his normal procedure for starting the motor. Grasping the handlebars firmly, he selected second gear, disengaged the clutch, and pushed the scooter along the road with increasing momentum. When he had attained the speed of a brisk trot, he abruptly let out the clutch. A juddering shock was transmitted from the engine, via the handlebars, to his arms and shoulders. The engine wheezed and coughed, inexorably reducing Adam's speed. Just as he had abandoned hope, the engine fired and the scooter leapt forward at full throttle, dragging Adam with it. With feet flying and duffle coat flapping, Adam careered past interested housewives and cheering children for some fifty yards before he recovered sufficient balance to scramble on to the seat. His pulled muscle throbbed painfully from the exertion. Reducing speed, he chugged off in the direction of the Albert Bridge.

A notice at the approach to this bridge undermined confidence in its structure by requesting soldiers to break step while marching over it. Adam foresaw the time when he would be the innocent victim of military vanity.

– *The men seem in good spirit this morning, Ponsonby.*

– *Yes, sir.*

– *Keeping step very well.*

– *Yes, sir. Sir, we're approaching the Albert Bridge.*

– *Are we, Ponsonby? Remind me to compliment Sar'nt Major on the men's marching, will you?*

– *Yes, sir. About the Albert Bridge, sir – shall I give the order to break step?*

– *Break step, Ponsonby? What are you talking about?*

– *Well, there's a notice, sir, which requests soldiers to break step while marching over the bridge. I suppose it sets up vibrations . . .*

– *Vibrations, Ponsonby? Never let it be said that the 41st was afraid of vibrations.*

– *Sir, if I might –*

– *No, Ponsonby. I'm afraid this is a blatant example of the civil power's encroachment on military territory.*

– *But sir, we're already on the bridge –*

– *Ponsonby!*

– *Safety of other people, sir!*

– *There's only some long-haired layabout on one of those silly scooter things. March on, Ponsonby, march on!*

And so the column of soldiers would march proudly on over the bridge, feet drumming on the tarmac. The bridge would quiver and shake, wires twang, girders snap, the road subside, and the soldiers step nonchalantly over the brink, as he himself was hurled into the cold Thames, with only a faint plume of steam to mark the spot where he and his scooter had disappeared beneath the surface.

Lost in this reverie, Adam drifted towards a huge limousine

halted at traffic lights, and pulled up just in time. The advertising copy for this model, he recalled, drew particular attention to the fact that the blades of the fan which cooled the radiator were *irregularly set* to reduce noise. It had been news to Adam that the fan caused noise: certainly it was not detectable on his own machine beneath the din of the exhaust and the rattling of various insecurely attached parts of the bodywork.

Inside the limousine, a fat man was smoking a fat cigar and dictating into a portable dictaphone. Adam turned in his saddle to face a melancholy line of people queueing for a bus.

'O tempora, O mores!' he declaimed, his voice rendered safely inaudible by the noise of his machine.

A man stepped forward from the queue and approached Adam, evidently under the impression that he had been personally addressed. Adam recognised him as Father Finbar Flannegan, a curate of his own parish, whom he and Barbara, in a private opinion poll, had voted Priest Most Likely to Prevent the Conversion of England.

'It's very kind of you to offer me a lift, Mr Appleby,' said Father Finbar, climbing on to the pillion. 'Could you drop me off near Westminster Cathedral?'

'Have you ever been a pillion passenger before, Father?' asked Adam, doubtfully.

'I have not, Mr Appleby,' replied the priest. 'But I'm sure you're a very capable driver. Besides, I'm late for my conference.'

'What conference is that, Father?' inquired Adam, moving off with the limousine, as the lights changed.

'Oh, it's some Monsignor or other who's giving a lecture on the Council to the priests of the diocese. One priest was invited from each parish, so we tossed up for it, and I lost.'

Adam heeled over the scooter to turn right, and his passenger tried to compensate by leaning in the opposite direction, yachtsman-style. The machine wobbled perilously, and Adam found himself clasped in a painful embrace by the alarmed priest who, he observed in the wing-mirror, had pulled his black Homburg down over his ears to leave his hands free.

'It's easier if you lean over with me,' observed Adam.

'Don't you worry, Mr Appleby. I have my Saint Christopher medal with me, thanks be to God.'

These, and subsequent remarks, had to be shouted to be audible above the din of the scooter and the background traffic noise.

It did not surprise Adam that Father Finbar lacked enthusiasm for the Second Vatican Council, on which he and Barbara and most of their Catholic friends pinned their hopes for a humane and liberal life in the Church. Father Finbar's ideas about the Catholic Faith were very much formed by his upbringing in Tipperary, and he seemed to regard the London parish in which he worked as a piece of the Old Country which had broken off in a storm and floated across the sea until it lodged itself in the Thames Basin. The parish was indeed at least half-populated by Irish, but this was not, in Adam and Barbara's eyes, an adequate excuse for nostalgic allusions to 'Back Home' in sermons, or the sanctioning of collections in the church porch for the dependants of I.R.A. prisoners. As to the liturgical reform and the education of the laity, Father Finbar's rosary beads rattled indignantly in his pocket at the very mention of such schemes, and he would, Adam suspected, chain up all the missals in the parish at the drop of a biretta.

Indignation rising in his breast at these thoughts, Adam coaxed his scooter above the statutory speed limit, and embarked upon some stylish traffic-weaving. He even managed to overtake the limousine, in which the fat man with the fat cigar was now using a radio telephone. In his right ear, he heard the Litany of Our Lady being recited in a tone of increasing panic.

The wind whistled through the rents in his windshield, and made Adam's eyes water. But he always enjoyed his morning sprint along the embankment. The Thames lay folded in fog; but away from the river the fog cleared, and the orange disc of the sun was clearly visible. A turn in the road brought into view the campanile of Westminster Cathedral, the most blatantly phallic shape on the London skyline.

The spectacle and the association deflected Adam's thoughts into a familiar channel, and he waxed melancholy at the recollection of Barbara's symptoms that morning. He grew convinced that they had had intercourse while sleeping off the effect of Camel's Spanish wine, and he tried unsuccessfully to work out the position of that evening in Barbara's current cycle. He released his grip on the handlebars to count with his fingers, but his passenger, abandoning prayer, shrieked a protest into his ear.

'For the love of God, Mr Appleby, will you take a little care!'

'Sorry, Father,' said Adam. Then, on a sudden impulse, he yelled back over his shoulder, 'Do you think the Council will change the Church's attitude on Birth Control?'

'What was that, Mr Appleby?'

Adam repeated his question at louder volume, and the scooter lurched as his passenger registered its import.

'The Church's teaching never changes, Mr Appleby,' came the stiff reply. 'On that or any other matter.'

A traffic jam blocked the road ahead, and Adam went down through the gears to save his ailing brakes. Father Finbar's teeth chattered under the stress of vibration.

'Well, all right – let's say "develop",' Adam went on. 'Newman's theory of doctrinal development –'

'Newman?' interjected the priest sharply. 'Wasn't he a Protestant?'

'Circumstances have changed, new methods are available – isn't it time we revised our thinking about these matters?'

'Mr Appleby, I don't have to explain to a man of your education the meaning of the Natural Law . . .'

'Oh, but excuse me Father, that's just what you do have to explain. Modern Continental theologians are questioning the whole – '

'Don't talk to me about thim German and French!' exclaimed Father Finbar furiously. 'They're worse than the Protestants thimselves. They're deshtroying the Church, leading the Faithful astray. Why, half the parish is straining at the leash already. One hint from the Pope and they'd be off on a wild debauch.'

'You mean, fulfilling the true purpose of marriage!' protested Adam.

'The true purpose of marriage is to procreate children and

258

bring them up in the fear and love of God!' asserted Father Finbar.

Adam, his scooter locked in traffic, twisted in his saddle. 'Look, Father, the average woman marries at twenty-three and is fertile till forty. Is it her duty to procreate seventeen children?'

'I was the youngest of eighteen children!' cried the priest triumphantly.

'How many survived infancy?' demanded Adam.

'Seven,' the priest admitted. 'God rest the souls of the others.' He crossed himself.

'You see? With modern medical care they might all survive. But how could you house and feed even seven in London today? What are we supposed to do?'

'Practice self-restraint,' retorted the priest. '*I* do.'

'That's different –'

'Pray, go to daily communion, say the rosary together . . .'

'We can't. We're too busy –'

He was going to say: 'changing bloody nappies'; but became aware that a strange silence had fallen upon the traffic, and that his dialogue with Father Finbar was being listened to with interested attention by the bystanders and drivers leaning out of their cars.

'We must talk about it again, Father,' he said wearily. In a curious way, the discussion had made Father Finbar more human, and Adam felt he would not be able to invoke him so easily in future as a symbol of blind ecclesiastical reaction.

The strange silence was explained by the fact that most of the drivers around him, evidently resigned to a long wait, had switched off their engines. Adam now followed suit.

'What's going on?' he wondered aloud.

'I think a policeman is holding up the traffic,' said Father Finbar, dismounting. 'If you don't mind, Mr Appleby, I think I'll walk from here. Perhaps the Queen is driving through.'

'O.K., Father. You'll get there quicker on foot.'

'Thank you for the lift, Mr Appleby. And for the discussion. You should join the Legion of Mary.'

His black Homburg hat still pulled down over his ears, Father

Finbar threaded his way through the stationary vehicles, and pushed through the bystanders lining the pavement.

An expectant hush had fallen on the scene. From nearby Westminster, Mrs Dalloway's clock boomed out the half hour. It partook, he thought, shifting his weight in the saddle, of metempsychosis, the way his humble life fell into moulds prepared by literature. Or was it, he wondered, picking his nose, the result of closely studying the sentence structure of the English novelists? One had resigned oneself to having no private language any more, but one had clung wistfully to the illusion of a personal property of events. A fond and fruitless illusion, it seemed, for here, inevitably, came the limousine, with its Very Important Personage, or Personages, dimly visible in the interior. The policeman saluted, and the crowd pressed forward, murmuring, 'Philip', 'Tony and Margaret', 'Prince Andrew'.

Then a huge plosive shout of 'The Beatles!' went up, and the crowd suddenly became very young and disorderly. Engines revved, horns blared, drivers cursed, and the wedge of traffic inched its way forward through the herds of screaming, weeping teenagers who spilled out into the road and pursued the vanishing car. A familiar figure in black darted in front of Adam, and he braked sharply.

'Did you see them, Mr Appleby? It's the Beatles!' cried Father Finbar, red with excitement. 'One of them's a Catholic, you know.' He lumbered off after the other fans.

Only one figure kept a still repose in the ebb and flow of vehicles and people. At the edge of the pavement an old, old lady, white-haired and wrinkled, dressed in sober black and elastic-sided boots, stood nobly erect, as if she thought someone really important had passed. In her right hand she held a speaking trumpet, which she raised to her ear. Adam, drawing level with her as the traffic surged slowly forward, murmured 'Clarissa!' and the old lady looked at him sharply. Suddenly frightened, Adam accelerated and drove off recklessly in the direction of Bloomsbury. Bloomsbury. *Bloomsbury!*

THREE

I have seen all sorts of domes of Peters and Pauls, Sophia,
Pantheon – what not? – and have been struck by none of them as
much as by that catholic dome in Bloomsbury, under which our
million volumes are housed. What peace, what love, what truth,
what happiness for all, what generous kindness for you and for me
are here spread out! It seems to me one cannot sit down in that
place without a heart full of grateful reverence. I own to have
said my grace at the table, and to have thanked Heaven for this
my English birthright, freely to partake of these bountiful books
and speak the truth I find there.
THACKERAY

Adam drove noisily down Great Russell Street and, bouncing in the saddle, swerved through the gates of the British Museum. He took some minutes finding a space into which he could squeeze his scooter: many businessmen had discovered that by leaving their cars in the South forecourt, walking through the Museum and sneaking out through the North Door, they could enjoy free parking all day in the centre of London.

He limped slowly towards the colossal portico, balancing the weight of his two holdalls. The Museum wore an autumnal aspect, as if built of petrified fog. The gilt statuary reclining above the bulging pillars provided the only gleam of colour. Pigeons stalked grumpily about, ruffling their feathers as if they felt the cold. Tourists were sparse. The British Museum was returning to its winter role – refuge for scholars, post-graduates and other bums and layabouts in search of a warm seat. In particular, Adam regretted the departure of the pretty girls who sat on the steps in summer, eating sandwiches and writing post-cards, their carelessly disposed legs providing an alluring spectacle for men approaching on ground level.

It seemed base, somehow, to come daily to this great temple of learning, history and artistic achievement in the same weary, mechanical spirit as the jaded clerk to his city office. But there it was: not even the British Museum was proof against the seda-

261

tion of routine. Adam pushed listlessly at the revolving doors and crossed the main hall with dogged, unswerving steps. As always, he vowed that one day he would really go and look at the Elgin Marbles, which could be glimpsed to his left, but the vow carried no conviction. The previous year, he and Camel had drawn up an elaborate plan for acquainting themselves with the whole Museum by inspecting one gallery a day in their lunch hour. If he remembered rightly, they had given up after looking at only Japanese armour and Egyptian vases.

There was one feature of his diurnal pilgrimage to the British Museum that afforded Adam a modest but constant gratification, and that was the fact that, as a familiar figure, he was not asked to show his card on entering the Reading Room. When he passed the door-keeper with just a nod of greeting he assumed, he hoped, an air of importance for the group of casual visitors who invariably hung about outside the door, trying to peer into the Reading Room.

'Could I see your card, sir?'

Adam, his hand already on the swing door, halted and looked with astonishment and hurt pride at the door-keeper, who grinned and pointed to a notice requesting all readers to show their cards that day.

'The annual check, sir,' he said, taking Adam's card from his hand. 'Ah, two months out of date. I'm afraid you'll have to go and renew it.'

'Oh look, I'm late as it is this morning. Can't I do it after I've ordered my books?'

'Sorry, sir.'

Adam dropped his bags with an angry thud at the feet of an Easter Island god, and stumped off to renew the ticket. Near the Elgin Marbles was a heavy door, guarded by a stern-looking porter with a huge key. When notified of Adam's errand, this official grudgingly unlocked the door, and ushered him into a long corridor. He then rang a little bell, and went out again, *locking the door behind him.*

Adam, or A as he would now more vaguely have identified himself, had been all through this before, but could not be sure whether he had dreamed it or actually experienced it. He was trapped. Behind him was a locked, guarded door; in front of him a long corridor terminating in a room. He could not go back. He could not stay where he was – the men in the room at the end of the corridor, warned by the bell, were expecting him. He went reluctantly forward, down the long corridor, between the smooth polished wooden cabinets, locked and inscrutable, which formed the walls, stretching high out of reach. Craning his neck to see if they reached the high ceiling, A felt suddenly dizzy, and leaned against the wall for support.

The room at the end of the corridor was an office, with a long, curving counter behind which sat two men, neat, self-possessed, expectant. A approached the nearer man, who immediately began writing on a piece of paper.

'Yes?' he said, after a few minutes had passed, and without looking up.

A, his mouth unaccountably dry, enunciated with difficulty the words, 'Reading Room Ticket.'

'Over there.'

A sidled along the counter to the second man, who immediately began writing in a ledger. A waited patiently.

'Yes?' said the second man, closing his ledger with a snap that made A jump.

'IwanttorenewmyReadingRoomTicket,' gabbled A.

'Over there.'

'But I've just been over there. He sent me to you.' Out of the corner of his eye, A saw the first man watching them intently.

The second man scrutinised him for what seemed a very long time, then spoke. 'One moment.' He went over to the first man, and they held a whispered conference, at the conclusion of which the first man came over to A and sat down in the second man's seat.

'What is it you want, exactly?' he asked.

'I want to renew my Reading Room Ticket,' said A patiently.

'You want to *renew* it? You mean you have a ticket already?'

'Yes.'

'May I see it?'

A presented his ticket.

'It's out of date,' observed the man.

'That's why I want to renew it!' A exclaimed.

'When did you last use the Reading Room?'

'Two months ago,' lied A, cunningly.

'You haven't used it since your ticket expired?'

'No.'

'It wouldn't matter if you had,' said the man. 'As long as you're not lying.' He tore A's ticket neatly into four sections, and deposited them in a waste-paper basket. It distressed A to see his ticket torn up. He experienced a queasy, empty feeling in his stomach.

'So now you want to renew your annual ticket?'

'Please.'

'You see, you didn't make that clear to me just now.'

'I'm sorry.'

'I assumed you were a casual reader wanting a short-term ticket. That's why I sent you to my colleague.' He nodded in the direction of the second man. 'But when he realised you wanted an annual ticket, he directed you back to me. That is the reason for our apparently contradictory behaviour.'

He flashed a sudden smile, displaying a row of gold-filled teeth.

'I see. I'm afraid it was my fault,' A apologised.

'Don't mention it,' said the first man, opening the ledger and beginning to write.

'Could I have my new ticket now?' said A, after some minutes had passed.

'Over there.'

'But you just said you were responsible for renewing annual tickets!' protested A.

'Ah, but that was when I was sitting over there,' said the first man. 'We've changed places now. We do that from time to time. So that if one of us should fall ill,' he continued, 'the other can cover his work.'

A made his way wearily to the second man.

'Good morning. Can I help you?' said the second man, as if greeting him for the first time.

'I want to renew my annual Reading Room ticket,' said A.

'Certainly. May I see your old ticket?'

'No, the other man – gentleman – has just torn it up.'

'It *was* an annual ticket you had?'

'Yes. He just tore it up. Didn't you see him?'

The second man shook his head gravely. 'This is very irregular. You shouldn't have given him the ticket. He's on short-term tickets now.'

'Look, all I want is to have my ticket renewed. What does it matter which of you does it?'

'I'm afraid I can't renew a ticket which, as far as I'm concerned, doesn't exist.'

A gripped the counter tightly and closed his eyes. 'What do you suggest I do then?' he whispered hoarsely.

'I could give you a short-term ticket . . .'

'No that won't do. I'm working here every day. My livelihood depends upon my being here every day.'

'Then I can only suggest that you come back when my colleague and I have changed places again,' said the second man.

'When will that be?'

'Oh there's no telling. You can wait if you like . . . in that room over there . . . you'll find plenty of people to chat to while you're waiting . . . your name will be called . . .'

'Are you all right, sir?'

Adam found himself lying on the floor of the corridor. The door-keeper and some other people were bending over him with looks of concern. Scattered over the floor beside him were fragments of his expired Reading Room ticket. He rose unsteadily to his feet. His head ached.

'What happened? Did I faint?'

'Looks like it, sir. Would you like to lie down somewhere?'

'No thanks. I'm all right. If I could just get my Reading Room ticket renewed . . .'

'This way, sir.'

As he stooped to reclaim his bags, which lay, like votive offerings, at the feet of the pagan god, Adam felt his shoulder clasped in a bony grip.

'And what sort of a time is *this*, Appleby, to get into the Museum?'

Adam straightened up and turned.

'Oh, hallo Camel. I got held up by the Beatles. I think they were on their way to open Parliament.'

'Don't give me any excuses,' continued Camel in his hectoring voice. 'Do you realise that there are droves of eager industrious scholars prowling round the Reading Room in search of a seat, while the one I illegally saved for you – '

'I hope it's a padded one.'

'It is indeed a padded one, which only adds to the offence. . . . Come and have a smoke,' he concluded, losing the thread of his sentence.

Adam had given up smoking when Dominic was born but, always eager for distraction, he usually accompanied Camel during the latter's periodic consumption of nicotine in the Museum colonnade. Conscience pricked him now more sharply than usual.

'Oh look, Camel, not today. I must get on.'

'Nonsense, old boy,' said Camel, in his bland tempter's voice, steering the willing Adam towards the exit. 'You look tired, peaky. A breath of air will do you the world of good. Besides, I've just thought of some new legislation that I want to tell you about.'

'Oh, all right, just for a minute.'

'You may entertain that pretence if you wish,' said Camel sardonically, now sure of Adam's company.

'It's too cold out here,' complained Adam, as they emerged into the raw, damp air. 'Why don't we have a coffee in the cafeteria instead?'

'I detest the cafeteria, as you well know. The Museum has degenerated since the cafeteria was introduced. When *I* started my research, we had no such luxuries. There was nowhere to go for a smoke – nowhere, mark you, in the entire building. You had to go out on to the colonnade, even in the bitterest weather. We had several cases of frostbite, I remember,' he went on, in his

266

old soldier's voice, 'in the winter of '57 . . . Scholars brought back frozen stiff, pipe-stems bitten through. Had to thaw 'em out in the North Library. You youngsters have no idea.'

Camel (whose surname fitted so perfectly his long, stiff-legged stride, humped shoulders and droll, thick-lipped countenance, that it was generally taken to be an inspired nick-name) did not seem to be particularly old, but he had been doing his Ph.D. thesis as long as anyone could remember. Its title – 'Sanitation in Victorian Fiction' – seemed modest enough; but, as Camel would patiently explain, the absence of references to sanitation was as significant as the presence of the same, and his work thus embraced the entire corpus of Victorian fiction. Further, the Victorian period was best understood as a period of transition in which the comic treatment of human excretion in the eighteenth century was suppressed, or sublimated in terms of social reform, until it re-emerged as a source of literary symbolism in the work of Joyce and other moderns. Camel's preparatory reading spread out in wider and wider circles, and it often seemed that he was bent on exhausting the entire resources of the Museum library before commencing composition. Some time ago a wild rumour had swept through Bloomsbury to the effect that Camel had written his first chapter, on the hygiene of Neanderthal Man; but Camel had wistfully denied it. 'I'm the modern Casaubon,' he would say. 'Don't expect progress.' He had no Dorothea to support, however, and earned enough by teaching evening classes in English to foreign students to keep himself.

'Well, what's your new legislation, then?' Adam enquired, as they seated themselves on a grimy wooden bench, flecked with pigeon droppings, at the extremity of one wing of the colonnade. He and Camel had devised a game, now of long standing, entitled, 'When We Are In Power'. This consisted in their imagining themselves to enjoy absolute political power, and thus the freedom to impose any law they liked upon the community – an opportunity which they would exploit not for the purposes of any crude self-advantage, nor to promote a programme of large-scale and idealistic reform, but merely to iron out the smaller inequalities of life, overlooked by the professional legislators, and to score off

267

sections of the populace against whom they had a grudge, such as taxi-drivers, generals and scooter-manufacturers.

'Well, I've been thinking,' said Camel, plugging his pipe with tobacco, 'that it's time we turned our attention to the private motorist. Now what would you say is the greatest injustice in that area?'

'They have cars, and we haven't.'

'Yes, of course. But When We Are In Power, we shall have cars ourselves. But you're on the right track. Has it occurred to you why so many people, of no apparent distinction in life, are able to run cars? And not just old, wheezing, corroding, bald-tyred, unreliable vehicles such as you or I may, with luck, look forward to owning after many years of labour, but shiny, new, powerful models straight out of the showroom?'

Adam thought for a moment, and remembered his father-in-law.

'Because they get them from their firms?'

'Right. Now – '

'You want to abolish firms' cars?'

'No, no. That's much too crude. You're losing your finesse, Appleby. We must keep within the bounds of possibility.'

'You could prohibit the use of business cars for pleasure.'

'Too difficult to enforce, though I did consider it for a while. No, what I hit upon was this: All cars supplied by commercial firms, government authorities, or other institutions, must have painted on them, on both sides, the name of the firm, authority or other institution, together with the appropriate trade mark, symbol, coat-of-arms or iconic representation of the product.'

'Marvellous,' said Adam.

'I thought you'd like it,' said Camel, with shy pride.

'It's a classic. It's founded on a simple desire for truth. No one can object.'

'But how they'll hate it! Just imagine any suburban street after the law is passed,' said Camel, gloatingly. 'All those sleek new cars with "Jeyes Fluid" or "Heinz 57 Varieties" plastered all over them.'

Adam giggled. 'My father-in-law travels in fertiliser.' He added anxiously: 'Shouldn't we specify a minimum size for the lettering?'

'A good point. Six inches, would you say?'

'Nine.'

'Nine.'

They sat, sniggering quietly to themselves, for several minutes.

'You're looking better,' said Camel, at length. 'You did look queer just now.'

'I had a queer experience,' said Adam, deciding to confide in Camel. ' . . . And this morning on my way to the Museum,' he concluded, 'I met Mrs Dalloway grown into an old woman.'

Camel regarded him with concern.

'I say, you want to watch this, you know. Are you overworking?'

Adam uttered a hollow laugh. 'Does it look like it?'

'Something else worrying you, then?'

'Something else is always worrying me.'

'Barbara's not pregnant again?'

'God, I hope not; but she felt sick this morning.'

'Ah,' said Camel.

As they re-entered the Museum, Adam asked Camel casually, 'By the way, what date was it that we came round to you?'

Camel consulted his diary. 'The 13th. Why?'

'Oh, nothing. You must come round to us soon. Look, I'm just going to ring Barbara. Don't wait.'

'You know, Appleby, I don't think you're going to get as far as the Reading Room today.'

'I won't be a moment.'

To Adam's annoyance, Mrs Green answered the phone.

'Oh, hallo Mrs Green. Could I speak to Barbara, please?'

'Is that you, Mr Appleby? Did you get your letter?'

Adam had completely forgotten the letter. He patted his pocket. It was still there.

'Yes, I did, Mrs Green, thank you. Is Barbara there?'

'I'll call up the stairs.'

While he was waiting for Barbara, Adam took out the letter

and inspected it with renewed curiosity. He was trying to open it with one hand, when Barbara picked up the phone.

'Hallo, Adam?'

'Hallo, darling,' said Adam, thrusting the letter back into his pocket. 'How are you feeling?'

'Oh, all right.'

'No queasiness?'

'No. Only a little.'

'You *do* feel queasy, then?'

'Only a little. Look, Adam – '

'Camel says we had those drinks with him on the 13th. Where does that come in the temperature chart?'

'Look, Adam, I can't discuss that now.'

'Why not?'

'I just can't. And it's absurd anyway.'

'You mean Mrs Green is listening?'

'Of course.'

'All right. I'll ring back later. But just check on the 13th, will you?'

'No, I won't.'

'How are the children?' Adam asked, pretending he hadn't heard.

'What do you mean? How are the children? You saw them less than two hours ago.'

'It seems longer than that.'

'Adam, are you feeling all right?'

'I'm fine. I'll ring back. Oh, I had a letter today.'

'Who from?'

'I don't know.'

'Adam, you're not all right.'

'Yes I am. I haven't had time to open it. It's been a terrible morning. I'll ring back.'

'Adam – '

''Bye, darling.' Adam put down the phone, and took the letter out of his pocket. Someone tapped on the window of the telephone kiosk. It was the fat man with the fat cigar he had seen in the limousine. Adam opened the door.

'If you've finished in there,' said the fat man, waving his cigar, 'I have an urgent call to make.' He spoke with an American accent.

'Yes, I've finished,' said Adam, emerging from the kiosk. 'If you don't mind my pointing it out, you're not allowed to smoke inside the Museum.'

'Is that so? Thanks for the tip. Do you have any small change?'

'How much do you want?' said Adam.

'I want to call Denver, Colorado.'

'Not that much,' said Adam. 'You'd need about sixty shillings. Or a hundred and twenty sixpences. Or . . . two hundred and forty threepenny bits. There's a bank round the corner,' he concluded.

'You should be president of it, young man,' said the fat American. 'Take my accountant's adding machine away and he wouldn't know how many fingers he had.'

'Yes, well . . . if you want to use the phone.' Adam gestured politely to the empty booth. 'Perhaps you could reverse the charges.'

'Collect? That's a good idea. You're a great nation,' said the fat man, as he squeezed himself into the booth.

Adam muttered a farewell, and hastened to the Reading Room, brandishing his new ticket in readiness.

He passed through the narrow vaginal passage, and entered the huge womb of the Reading Room. Across the floor, dispersed along the radiating desks, scholars curled, foetus-like, over their books, little buds of intellectual life thrown off by some gigantic act of generation performed upon that nest of knowledge, those inexhaustible ovaries of learning, the concentric inner rings of the catalogue shelves.

The circular wall of the Reading Room wrapped the scholars in a protective layer of books, while above them arched the vast, distended belly of the dome. Little daylight entered through the grimy glass at the top. No sounds of traffic or other human business penetrated to that warm, airless space. The dome looked down on the scholars, and the scholars looked down on their books; and the scholars loved their books, stroking the pages with soft pale fingers. The pages responded to the fingers' touch, and yielded their knowledge gladly to the scholars, who collected it in little boxes of file-cards. When the scholars raised their eyes from their desks they saw nothing to distract them, nothing out of harmony with their books, only the smooth, curved lining of the womb. Wherever the eye travelled, it met no arrest, no angle, no parallel lines receding into infinity, no pointed arch striving towards the unattainable: all was curved, rounded, self-sufficient, complete. And the scholars dropped their eyes to their books again, fortified and consoled. They curled themselves more tightly over their books, for they did not want to leave the warm womb, where they fed upon electric light and inhaled the musty odour of yellowing pages.

But the women who waited outside felt differently. From their dingy flats in Islington and cramped semis in Bexley-heath, they looked out through the windows at the life of the world, at the motor-cars and the advertisements and the clothes in the shops, and they found them good. And they resented the warm womb of the Museum which made them poor and lonely, which swallowed up their men every day and sapped them of their vital spirits and made them silent and abstracted mates even when they were at home. And the women sighed for the day when their men would be expelled from the womb for the last time, and they looked at their children whimpering at their feet, and they clasped their hands, coarsened with detergent, and vowed that these children would never be scholars.

Lawrence, thought Adam. It's time I got on to Lawrence.

He weaved his way to the row of desks where he and Camel usually worked, and noted the familiar figures at whose sides he had worked for two years, without ever exchanging a word with any of them: earnest, efficient Americans, humming away like dynamos, powered by Guggenheim grants; turbanned Sikhs, all called Mr Singh, and all studying Indian influences on English literature; pimply, bespectacled women smiling cruelly to themselves as they noted an error in somebody's footnote; and then the Museum characters – the gentleman whose beard reached to his feet, the lady in shorts, the man wearing odd shoes and a yachting-cap reading a Gaelic newspaper with a one-stringed lute propped up on his desk, the woman who sniffed. Adam recognised Camel's coat and briefcase at one of the desks, but the seat was unoccupied.

Eventually he discovered Camel in the North Library. They did not usually work there: it was overheated, and its low rectangular shape and green furnishings gave one the sense of being in an aquarium for tropical fish. The North Library was used especially for consulting rare and valuable books, and there were also a number of seats reserved for the exclusive use of eminent scholars, who enjoyed the privilege of leaving their books on their desks for indefinite periods. These desks were rarely occupied except by piles of books and cards bearing distinguished names, and they reminded Adam of a waxworks from which all the exhibits had been withdrawn for renovation.

'What are you doing here?' he whispered to Camel.

'I'm reading an allegedly pornographic book,' Camel explained. 'You have to fill out a special application and read it here under the Superintendent's nose. To make sure you don't masturbate, I suppose.'

'Good Lord. D'you think they'll make me do that for *Lady Chatterley's Lover?*'

'Shouldn't think so, now you can buy it and masturbate at home.'

'What seat did you save for me in the Reading Room?'

'Next to mine. Number thirteen, I think.'

'You seem to have an attachment to the number thirteen where I'm concerned,' said Adam, petulantly. 'I'm not superstitious, but there's no point in taking chances.'

'What kind of chances?'

'Never mind,' said Adam.

He returned to the Reading Room and, wielding the huge volumes of the catalogue with practised ease, filled in application slips for *The Rainbow* and several critical studies of Lawrence. Then he returned to the seat Camel had saved for him, to wait. One of the Museum's many throwbacks to a more leisured and gracious age was that books were delivered to one's desk. So vast was the library, however – Adam understood it amounted to six million volumes – and so understaffed, that it was normal for more than an hour to elapse between the lodging of an application and the arrival of a book. He sat down on the large padded seat, ignoring the envious and accusing glances of the readers in his vicinity. For some reason only about one in ten of the Reading Room seats was padded, and there was fierce competition for the possession of them.

The padded seats were magnificently comfortable. Adam wondered whether they were made by Brownlong and Co. If so, he felt he could address himself to the competition with real enthusiasm.

> *I always choose a Brownlong chair*
> *Because I wrote my thesis there.*

The manufacturer's name was usually found on the underside of chairs, wasn't it? Adam wondered whether he might turn his chair upside down for inspection, but decided that it would attract too much attention. He looked round: no one was watching. He deliberately dropped a pencil on the floor, and bent down to recover it, peering under his seat the while. He dimly discerned a small nameplate but could not read the inscription. He put his head right under the seat, lost his balance, and fell heavily to the floor. Startled, annoyed or amused faces were turned upon him from the neighbouring desks. Red with embarrassment and from the blood that had rushed to his head while he hung upside down, Adam recovered his seat and rubbed his head.

Adam was filled with self-pity. It was the second time that morning that he had fallen down. Then there were the hallucinations. Clearly, something was seriously the matter with him. He was approaching a nervous breakdown. He repeated the words to himself with a certain pleasure. Nervous. Breakdown. They evoked a prospect of peace and passivity, of helpless withdrawal from the world, of a huge burden of worry shifted on to someone else's shoulders. He saw himself lying mildly in a darkened room while anxious friends and doctors held whispered conferences round his bed. Perhaps they would make a petition to the Pope and get him and Barbara a special dispensation to practise artificial contraception. Or perhaps he would die, his tragic case be brought to the attention of the Vatican Council, and the doctrine of Natural Law revised as a result. A fat lot of good that would do *him*. Adam decided not to have a nervous breakdown after all.

To work, to work. He began briskly to unpack his bulging holdalls. Soon the broad, blue leather-topped desk was heaped with books, files, folders, index-cards and odd scraps of paper with notes and references scribbled on them. Adam's energy and determination subsided like the mercury of a thermometer plunged in cold water. How would he ever succeed in organising all this into anything coherent?

The subject of Adam's thesis had originally been, 'Language and Ideology in Modern Fiction' but had been whittled down by the Board of Studies until it now stood as, 'The Structure of Long Sentences in Three Modern English Novels.' The whittling down didn't seem to have made his task any easier. He still hadn't decided which three novels he was going to analyse, nor had he decided how long a long sentence was. Lawrence, he thought hopefully, would produce lots of sentences where the issue would not be in doubt.

Adam listlessly turned over pages of notes on minor novelists who were now excluded from his thesis. There was this great wad, for instance, on Egbert Merrymarsh, the Catholic belletrist, younger contemporary of Chesterton and Belloc. Adam had written a whole chapter, tentatively entitled 'The Divine Wisecrack' on Merrymarsh's use of paradox and antithesis to prop up his facile Christian apologetics. All wasted labour.

Adam yawned, and looked at the clock above the entrance to the North Library. There was still a long time to go before his books would arrive. Everyone but himself seemed to be working with quiet concentration: you could almost hear a faint hum of cerebral flywheels and sprockets busily turning. Adam was seized by conflicting emotions of guilt, envy, frustration and revolt. Revolt won: this still repose, this physical restraint, was unnatural.

He fiddled idly with his pencil, trying to make it stand on end. He failed, and the pencil fell to the floor. He stooped cautiously to recover it, meeting, as he straightened up, the frown of a distracted reader. Adam frowned back. Why shouldn't he be distracted? Distraction was as necessary to mental health as exercise to physical. It would be a good idea, in fact, if the Reading Room were cleared twice a day, and all the scholars marched out to do physical jerks in the forecourt. No, that wouldn't do – he hated physical jerks himself. Suppose, instead, the circular floor of the Reading Room were like the revolve on a stage, and that every hour, on the hour, the Superintendent would throw a lever to set the whole thing in motion, sweeping the spokes of the desks round for a few exhilarating revolutions. Yes, and the desks would be mounted so as to go gently up and down like horses on a carousel. It wouldn't necessarily interrupt work – just give relief to the body cramped in the same position. Tone up the system. Encourage the circulation. Yes, he must remember to mention it to Camel. The British Museum Act. He closed his eyes and indulged in a pleasing vision of the gay scene, as the floor rotated, and the scholars smiled with quiet pleasure at each other as their seats rose above the partitions, and gently sank again. Perhaps there might be tinkling music . . .

Adam felt a tap on his shoulder. It was Camel.

'Why are you humming "La Ronde"? You're getting some black looks.'

'I'll tell you later,' said Adam, in some confusion. He fled from the Reading Room to avoid the hostile glances directed at him from all sides.

In the foyer, he decided to ring Barbara again. To his surprise, the booth was still occupied by the fat man. Adam was beginning to make awed calculations of the cost of a thirty-minute call to Colorado, when his attention was caught by various signs of distress the fat man was making. He had somehow managed to close the door of the booth, which folded inwards, but his girth rendered him incapable of opening it again. After some moments of strenuous exertion, Adam was able to extricate him.

'Well,' said the fat man. 'You seem to be my private boy scout today.'

'Did you make your phone call all right?' Adam inquired.

'I experienced some linguistic difficulties.'

'Don't they speak English in Colorado?'

'Sure they do. But your operator kept saying, "You're through" before I'd even started . . . do you smoke cigars?' he suddenly demanded.

'My father-in-law usually gives me one on Christmas Day,' said Adam.

'Well, save these and astonish him in December,' said the fat man, thrusting a fistful of huge cigars into Adam's breast pocket.

'Thank you,' murmured Adam faintly, as the fat man trundled off.

'Thank *you*!'

Adam entered the phone booth, which smelled suspiciously of rich cigar smoke, and made his call. There was a clatter as the receiver was lifted at the other end, and a childish voice intoned:

'Battersea Double Two One – O.'

'Oh hello, Clare darling. What are you doing at the phone?'

'Mummy said I could practise answering.'

'Is Mummy there?'

'She's just coming down the stairs.'

'And how are you, Clare? Have you been a good girl this morning?'

'No.'

'Oh. Why's that?'

'I cut a hole in Dominic's tummy.'

'You *what*?'

'Cut a hole in Dominic's tummy. With the kitchen scissors.'

'But Clare, *why*?' Adam wailed.

'We were playing maternity hospitals and I was giving him a Caesarian.'

'But Clare, you mustn't do that.'

'You mean boys can't have babies? I know.'

'No, I mean cut people with scissors. Look, is Mummy there?'

'Here she is.'

'Hallo, Adam?'

'Darling, what's all this about Clare cutting a hole in Dominic's stomach?'

'It's only a nick. It didn't even bleed.'

'Only a nick! But what was she doing with the scissors in the first place?'

'Are you trying to blame me, Adam?'

'No, darling. I'm just trying to get at the facts.'

'As long as you're not trying to blame me. You've no idea what it's like having to look after Clare all day.'

'I know, I know. But if you could just keep the scissors out of her reach . . .'

'I do. She got the step-ladder out.'

'Did you smack her?'

'You know smacking doesn't have any effect on Clare. She just says, "I hope this is doing *you* good, Mummy." She's heard us discussing Doctor Spock.'

'God help us when she learns to read,' sighed Adam. He decided to drop the subject. 'Have you looked up the 13th in your diary?'

'You'll wish you hadn't asked.'

'Why?' said Adam, his heart sinking.

'According to the chart, ovulation should have taken place about then.'

Adam groaned.

' . . . And the 13th was a Friday,' continued Barbara.

'This is no time for joking,' said Adam, suspiciously.

'Who's joking?'

'I'm certainly not. Can't you remember anything about that night?'

'I remember you were a bit . . . you know.'

'A bit what?'

'You know what you're like when you've had a few drinks.'

'You're just the same,' said Adam, defensively.

'I'm not blaming you.'

'D'you think we could have . . .?'

'No. But I wish my period would start.'

'How do you feel now?'

'About the same.'

'What was that? I've forgotten.'

'Never mind. I'm getting bored with the subject. Shouldn't you be working?'

'I can't work while I'm trying to think what we did that night.'

'Well, I can't help you, Adam. Look, I can't stay any longer. Mary Flynn is bringing her brood round for lunch.'

'How many has she got now?'

'Four.'

'Well, there's always someone else worse off than yourself.'

'Goodbye then, darling. And try not to worry.'

'Goodbye, darling.'

On his way back to the Reading Room, Adam had a thought. He returned to the phone booth and rang Barbara again.

'Hallo, darling.'

'Adam, for heaven's sake – '

'Look, I've had a thought. About that night. Did you happen to notice the sheets the next day . . .?'

Barbara rang off. This is denaturing me, he thought.

He was getting tired with trekking backwards and forwards to the telephone. After the coolness of the foyer, the atmosphere of the Reading Room, when he re-entered it, struck him as oppressively hot. The dome seemed screwed down tightly on the stale air, sealing it in. It hung over the scene like a tropical sky before a storm; and the faint, sour smell of mouldering books and bindings was like the reek of rotting vegetation in some foetid oriental backwater. Appleby cast a gloomy eye on the Indians and Africans working busily in their striped suits and starched collars.

There comes a moment in the life of even the most unimaginative man – and Appleby was not that – when Destiny confronts him with the unexpected and the inexplicable, when the basis of his universe, like a chair which has so habitually offered its comforting support to his limbs that he no longer troubles to assure himself of its presence before entrusting his weight to it, is silently and swiftly withdrawn, and the victim feels himself falling with dismaying velocity into an infinite space of doubt. This was the sensation of Appleby as, mopping away with a soiled handkerchief the perspiration which beaded his forehead like the drops of moisture on the interior of a ship's hull that warn the knowledgeable mariner that he is approaching the equatorial line, he came in sight of the desk where he had left his books and papers. He staggered to a halt.

That *was* his desk, surely? Yes, he recognised on the one next to it his comrade's raincoat and broad-brimmed trilby. His own belongings, however, had vanished: books, papers, index-cards – all had disappeared. But it was not this fact which made Appleby lean against a bookcase for support, and pass his right hand several times across his eyes. Grouped round his desk, and gazing at it with rapt attention, were three Chinese: not the Westernised, Hong Kong Chinese he was familiar with, draped in American-style suits and wielding sophisticated cameras, but authentic Chinese Chinese, dressed in loose, belted uniforms of some drab, coarse-grained material.

It was their attitude, above all, which made the hair on Appleby's nape prickle as at the brush of a passing ghost – an attitude which suggested prayer rather than conspiracy, and was the more frightening because the more unaccountable. If they were waiting for him, why were their backs turned, why were they poring, with bowed heads and hands clasped behind their backs, upon the bare expanse of his desk? It was as if they were engaged in some hypocritical act of mourning for a crime they had already committed.

Appleby perceived that the strangers' presence had not gone unnoticed by the other readers in the vicinity, but it seemed almost as if the latter were trying to pretend otherwise. Without lifting their heads from their books, they were stealing glances, first at the Chinese, and then at himself. An African law student, sitting near him, rolled a white eye and seemed about to speak, but thought the better of it and turned back to his books. If only, Adam felt, he could see the faces of his visitors, he would know what they had come for. He shrank from the encounter, but

280

anything was preferable to the mystery. Or was it . . .? If he were to walk away, go home and think about it, and come back later, tomorrow say, perhaps they would have gone away, and his books would be back on the desk, and he could forget all about it. As he stood wavering at this fork in the road of his moral self-exploration, he was suddenly relieved of the choice by a light tap on his shoulder and a voice which murmured, 'Mr Appleby?'

FOUR

*I believe there are several persons in a state of imbecility who
come to read in the British Museum. I have been informed that
there are several in that state who are sent there by their friends
to pass away their time.*
CARLYLE

'So it appeared,' said Adam, biting into a Scotch egg, 'that
these Chinese were some cultural delegation or something from
Communist China, and that they'd asked if they could look at
Karl Marx's desk – you know, the one he worked at when he was
researching *Das Kapital*. Did you know that, Camel? That you
saved me Karl Marx's seat?'

Camel, whose face was buried in a pint tankard, tried to shake
his head and spilled a few drops of beer on his trousers.

'I should have thought it would have singed your good Catholic
arse,' said Pond.

'It makes you think, doesn't it?' Adam mused. 'All the famous
backsides who have polished those seats: Marx, Ruskin,
Carlyle . . .'

'Colin Wilson,' suggested Pond.

'Who?' Adam asked.

'Before your time, old boy,' said Camel. 'The good old days of
the Museum, when everyone was writing books on the Human
Condition and publishers were fighting under the desks for the
options.'

'You'd think you only had to sit at any of these desks,' Adam
went on, 'and the wisdom would just seep up through your spinal
cord. It just seems to seep out of mine. Look at today, for instance;
lunch time and I haven't done a thing.'

They were in the Museum Tavern, Adam, Camel and Pond.
Pond was a full-time teacher at the School of English where
Camel taught a few evening classes. It was run by a crook, and
Pond was worked very hard, but Adam and Camel found it

282

difficult to commiserate with him because he earned so very much money. He and his pretty wife, Sally, had a Mini-Minor and a centrally-heated semi in Norwood with a four-poster bed draped in pink satin. Pond usually lunched with Adam and Camel one day a week, among other things in order to rid himself of the xenophobia which, as he explained, was both an occupational state of mind and a professional crime. According to Camel, he was the soul of kindness to his foreign pupils while on the job.

'That's because Karl Marx was a Jew,' he now said in reply to Adam's complaint. 'All you have to do is change your seat.'

'That's right,' said Camel, 'find yourself the seat Chesterton used. Or Belloc.'

'Or Egbert Merrymarsh,' said Adam.

'Who?'

'Who?'

'Before your time,' said Adam. 'The good old days of the Museum, when there was a crucifix on every desk. The trouble is,' he went on, 'that Merrymarsh probably chose an unpadded seat, just to mortify himself.'

'So what about the Chinese?' said Camel. 'What did you say to them?'

'Well, I was just summing up courage to go up to them and say . . . say . . . well, say something, I don't know, like, this is my seat, or, what have you done with my books, when this superintendent came up and explained. He'd been looking for me, but I was telephoning Barbara.'

'He's always telephoning his wife,' explained Camel to Pond.

'Well, that's all right; I like to phone Sally myself occasionally,' said Pond.

'Ah, that's just uxoriousness. Appleby is a neurotic case.'

'I'm not neurotic,' said Adam. 'I toyed with the idea this morning, but I decided against it. Though, I must admit, those Chinese had me worried for a minute.'

'Chinks,' said Pond. 'Don't be afraid of good old prejudiced English usage.'

'I must say, whoever it was had a nerve removing your books,' said Camel.

'Oh, I could see their point. Like tidying up a grave or something.'

Pond shuddered, as he always did at the mention of death, and swigged some beer.

'What exactly did the Superintendent say to you?' Camel asked. 'I want to know exactly what he said. Did he say, "I hope you won't mind, but three Chinese gentlemen are looking at your desk"?'

'Yes, he did, actually,' said Adam, surprised. 'That's exactly what he did say.'

'And what did you say?'

'I didn't say anything at first. I tell you, I felt pretty queer.'

'So what happened then?'

'Well, he looked a bit embarrassed, and said, "It was Karl Marx's desk, you see. We often get visitors wanting to see it." '

'So what did you say then?'

'Well, that's what I was going to tell you. I *think* I said: *Mr Marx, he dead!*'

Camel and Pond looked meaningfully at each other. 'I told you,' said Camel. 'Appleby is cracking up.'

'I can see,' said Pond. 'He's going to become one of the Museum eccentrics. Before we know it, he'll be shuffling around in slippers and muttering into a beard.'

'It's a special form of scholarly neurosis,' said Camel. 'He's no longer able to distinguish between life and literature.'

'Oh yes I can,' said Adam. 'Literature is mostly about having sex and not much about having children. Life is the other way round.'

Pond came back from the bar carrying three pints.

'That's funny,' said Adam. 'You're limping.'

'What's funny about that?'

'Well, I'm limping too.'

'Perhaps it's a bug that's going round,' said Camel.

'I don't think, somehow,' said Pond, 'that our symptoms have the same cause.'

'I don't even know the cause of mine,' said Adam. 'I just woke up this morning with a pain in my leg.'

'Why are *you* limping, then?' Camel asked Pond.

Pond made a grimace. 'That damned *Kama Sutra*,' he said, in the tone of a man boasting of his hereditary gout. 'I forget which position it was – the Monkey or the Goose or something. I know I got a terrible cramp. Took Sally an hour's rubbing with Sloane's Liniment to straighten me out.'

'I hope it will teach you a lesson,' said Camel.

'It was worth it,' replied Pond, winking.

'My God!' Adam exclaimed. 'You mean you're so sated with conventional sex . . . Pardon me while my imagination boggles.'

'It's that four-poster bed that does it,' Camel opined. 'The pink drapes.'

'No, as a matter of fact I think it's the central heating,' said Pond. 'You've no idea how central heating extends the possibilities of sex.'

'Be a waste of money for us, then,' said Adam gloomily.

'Well, drink up,' urged Pond. 'Bloody wogs.'

'Bloody wogs,' they murmured. Pond insisted on this toast when he drank with them. It was only a matter of time, Adam thought, before someone heard them and insisted on their expulsion from the Tavern.

'You know,' said Camel to Adam, 'I think you ought to apostatize. You can't go on like this.'

'What d'you mean?'

'Well, leave the Church – temporarily I mean. You can go back to it later.'

'Death-bed repentance, you mean?'

'Well, more of a menopause repentance. It's not such a risk is it? You and Barbara have a good expectation of living past forty or so.'

'It's no good talking to him like that, Camel,' said Pond. 'There's always the bus.'

'Yes, there's always the bus,' Adam agreed.

'Bus? What bus?' asked Camel in bewilderment.

'The bus that runs you down. The death that comes unexpectedly,' explained Pond. 'Catholics are brought up to expect sudden extinction round every corner and to keep their souls highly polished at all times.'

'How do you know all this?' Adam demanded.

'Sally went to a convent,' Pond explained. 'No,' he went on, 'it's no use talking like that to Adam. We've got to convince him intellectually that Catholicism is false.'

'I wouldn't want to do that,' said Camel. 'I believe in religion. I don't have any myself, but I believe in other people having religion.'

'And children,' Adam interpolated.

'Quite so,' Camel agreed. 'I don't have any affection for children myself, but I recognise the need for them to keep the human show on the road.'

'Selfish bastard,' said Adam.

'But if you must have religion,' said Pond, 'why not Hinduism? Then you can have sex as well.'

'I thought you were against things foreign,' said Camel.

'Well, I think we could have a kind of Anglicanised Hinduism . . . get rid of the holy cows and so on.'

'No, it won't do,' said Camel. 'I want Christianity kept up, because otherwise half our literary heritage will disappear. We need people like Appleby to tell us what *The Cloud of Unknowing* is all about.'

'Never heard of it,' said Adam.

'Or the *Ancrene Rewle*.'

'That's what let me down in my Middle English paper,' said Adam.

'You should read it sometime. There's some very interesting cloacal imagery in it.'

'But Camel,' said Pond, 'for your purposes, it's quite enough if people have a Christian education. There's no need for them to practice the darn thing all their lives. We owe it to Adam to free him from the shackles of a superstitious creed.'

'Go ahead, convince me,' Adam invited.

Pond, who fancied himself as a logician, shifted his chair nearer the table, and leaned his elbows upon it, pressing the fingers of each hand lightly together.

286

'Very good,' applauded Camel. 'The fingers is very good. First round to Pond.'

Pond ignored the diversion. 'Let's begin with the Trinity,' he said. 'The fundamental doctrine, as I understand it, of orthodox Christianity.'

'Doesn't give me much trouble,' said Adam, 'but go ahead.'

'It doesn't give you much trouble, if you don't mind my saying so, my dear Adam, because you don't think about it. In fact you don't really believe it, because your assent is never tested. Since it costs you nothing to accept the idea of three in one, you have never bothered to inquire why you *should* accept anything so utterly contrary to logic and experience. Now just remind yourself, for a moment, of the concept of number. See: one' – he placed a salt cellar in the centre of the table – 'two' – he placed a pepper pot beside it – 'three' – he reached for the mustard.

'I should have brought my clover leaf with me,' said Adam. He spooned some mustard on to his plate, and sprinkled it with pepper and salt. 'Three in one.'

'There!' cried Camel. 'It really tastes horrible, but it's true.'

'I think you're being highly irresponsible, Camel,' said Pond testily. 'Encouraging him like this. Especially as you propose remaining sterile yourself. Do you realise that the birth-rate figures show that England will be a predominantly Catholic country in three or four generations? Do you want that?'

'No,' said Adam fervently. 'But it won't happen because of the lapsation rate.'

'Lapsation?' Camel inquired.

'Falling off from the Church,' Adam explained.

'Why do so many fall off?'

'Not because of the doctrine of the Trinity,' said Adam. 'Because of birth control is my guess. Which reminds me: I have to attend a Dollinger meeting on that very subject this lunch hour. I must hurry.'

The Dollinger Society took its name from the celebrated German theologian of the nineteenth century who had been ex-communicated in 1871 for his refusal to accept the doctrine of Papal

Infallibility. Originally founded to press for the posthumous reversal of Dollinger's ex-communication, and eventually his canonisation (in pursuance of which unlikely objectives the founder-members had encouraged themselves by citing the precedent of Joan of Arc) it had since become an informal discussion group of lay Catholics concerned to liberalise the Church's attitude on more urgent and topical issues, such as religious liberty in Spain, nuclear war, and the Index Librorum Prohibitorum. Its only public activity took the form of writing outspoken letters on such subjects to the Catholic Press. The letters were never published, except in *Crypt*, a subscription newsletter edited by the Society's unofficial chaplain, Father Bill Wildfire O.P., who, after a few beers, could be coaxed into questioning the doctrine of the Virgin Mary's Assumption into heaven. Heretical statements like this, particularly when they had a sacerdotal – or, better still, episcopal – origin, were a source of unholy joy to the Society, circulating among the members much like dirty jokes in secular fraternities. It often seemed to Adam that many Dollingerites declined to follow the example of their patron mainly because the liberal conscience had a more thrilling existence within the Church than outside it.

Adam attended the Society's meetings only spasmodically, but today's had a special interest for him. He wished that he had a clearer head for it. He had consumed more beer than he had been aware of. He staggered slightly, crossing the road between the Tavern and the Museum, and this decided him to walk rather than use his scooter. In any case, the distance was so short that it was scarcely worth the trouble of starting the scooter.

With characteristic daring, the Dollinger Society held its meetings in Student Christian Hall, an inter-denominational centre located in one of the tall, narrow houses in Gordon Square. It had a small canteen in the basement where homely young women served cottage pie and a peculiarly vivid form of tomato soup to anyone who offered himself as a student or a Christian. On the first floor was a reading room, and on the second a lounge, where the Dollingerites gathered once a month for coffee and discussion.

The meeting was already in progress when Adam arrived. He

tip-toed across the floor and sank into a vacant armchair. About a dozen people were present. Adam could tell which of them had lunched downstairs by their orange moustaches. The secretary of the Society, Francis Maple, who was submanager of a Catholic bookshop, was evidently reading out the draft of a letter to the Catholic Press.

'... *advances in psychological knowledge and the increasing personalisation of human relations in different aspects of life have also contributed to a new awareness of the positive contribution made by affective and physical elements in the attainment of marital harmony. Ordered human sexuality, within the legitimate framework of married life, undoubtedly contributes to the development of the whole person* ...'

It was a long letter. As it went on, Adam grew more and more impatient. It was not that these were bad arguments. They were good arguments. He had often used them himself. But their style of high-minded generality, their elevated concern with the fulfilment of the married vocation, somehow missed the real rub of the problem as it was felt by the individual: the ache of unsatisfied desire, or the pall of anxiety that the Safe Method draped over the marriage bed. ... Perhaps the new refinements of temperature charts and whatever really did work, but no one who had experienced an unwanted pregnancy could really trust periodic abstinence. *Post coitum, omne animal triste est*, agreed; but not *before* coition, or for *days* afterwards.

The letter came to an end. After a long silence a flat-chested girl with ginger hair said, as she said on every similar occasion: 'Can't we bring the Mystical Body in somewhere?'

'Why?' Adam demanded. He was surprised by his own belligerence: it must be the beers. The ginger-haired girl cringed; her flat chest became concave. Adam felt sorry for her, but heard himself going on, 'It seems to me that we're concerned with the carnal body here.'

'I agree,' said a young man who had recently left a monastery and got engaged before his tonsure had grown over. 'We'll never get anything done until we have compulsory marriage of the clergy. They just don't understand.'

'Robert and I,' said his fiancée, 'think we should adopt Catholic orphans, instead of having children of our own. But with the present teaching on birth control it would be too risky. We might be overrun.'

There were sympathetic murmurs from the rest of the company. The fiancée looked pleased at the effect she had created.

'I'd like to know,' said Adam, 'what it is we want. I mean, do we want to use contraceptives, or the pill, or what? The letter didn't say.'

There was a slightly embarrassed silence. Francis Maple cleared his throat, and said:

'I think the letter was just intended to air the concern of Catholic lay people, and draw the clergy's attention to the subject.'

'Does anyone know,' said a bald-headed lawyer, the father of five, 'whether the pill is really allowed or not? I've heard there's a priest in Camden Town who recommends it in the confessional.'

'What's his name?' said half-a-dozen voices simultaneously.

'I don't know,' confessed the lawyer.

'As I understand it,' said Francis Maple, 'you can use a pill to regulate the female cycle and make the Safe Period Safer, but you're not allowed to use it to induce sterility.'

'I've heard the pill can make a woman grow a beard,' said a post-graduate student from Bedford College. 'Or make her pregnant when she's seventy,' she added, with a shudder.

'I'd like to know,' said the ex-monk, 'what Mr Appleby wants.'

Adam shifted uneasily in his seat, as the eyes of all present turned curiously on him.

'I don't know,' he said at length. 'I don't suppose anyone really *wants* to use contraceptives, even non-Catholics. They're not things you can work up much affection for, are they? Everybody seems to act a bit furtive about the business. Perhaps the pill will be the solution, but we don't know enough about it yet. What we want is emergency measures to deal with the present situation, while the theologians and the scientists thrash out the question of the pill. At the moment the situation is that we Catholics expend most of our moral energy on keeping or breaking the Church's teaching on birth control, when there are a lot of much more important moral issues in life.'

'Hear, hear!' said a lady whose pet cause was protesting against the Irish export of horses for slaughter.

'The trouble with using contraceptives, from the point of view of practical moral theology,' Adam went on, wondering what conclusion he was going to reach, 'is that it's necessarily a premeditated sin. You can biff someone on the head or seduce someone's wife at a party, and go to confession and say, "Father, I was overcome by my passions," and be sincerely sorry, and promise not to do it again, and do the same thing a week later without being a hypocrite. But the other thing is something you commit, in the first place, in cold blood in a chemist's shop; and once you start you have to go on steadily, or there's no point.'

'That's very well put,' said Maple, as Adam recovered his breath. 'But what can we do about it?'

'The only thing I can see is to get contraception classified as a venial sin,' said Adam, with sudden inspiration. 'Then we could all feel slightly guilty about it, like cheating on the buses, without forfeiting the sacraments.'

This proposition seemed to take the group by surprise, and a long silence ensued.

'Well,' said Francis Maple at length, 'that's a novel point of view certainly. I don't know if there's any machinery for classifying sins . . . But there's a general consensus which can be modified, I suppose.'

At this point the door burst open, and Father Wildfire entered.

'Ah!' said Maple, with relief. 'You come at an opportune moment, Father.'

'Why, somebody dying?' said the priest, with a boisterous laugh.

'No, it's just that we're getting into rather deep theological waters. Adam, here, thinks that the birth control problem could be solved if contraception were just considered as a venial sin.'

'Isn't it?' said Father Wildfire, with feigned surprise. The group laughed delightedly, but discreetly, as if they were in church. 'Is there anything to drink?' asked the priest, unbuttoning his coat. This was a rough serge jacket of the kind worn by building labourers. Underneath it he wore a red woollen shirt and brown corduroy trousers. The Dominicans appeared to have very liberal regulations, of which Father Wildfire took full advantage, concerning the wearing of the habit. Adam often thought that if, as seemed likely, he was eventually de-frocked, no one would ever know it.

A cup of coffee was passed to the priest, who extracted a small flask from his pocket, and poured a generous measure into the cup. 'Seriously,' he said, 'this venial sin – mortal sin business is old hat. Something the scholastics thought up to while away the long winter evenings. All sins are mortal sins. Or, to put it another way, all sins are venial sins. What matters is love. The more love, the less sin. I was preaching at a men's retreat the other day, and I told them, better sleep with a prostitute with some kind of love than with your wife out of habit. Seems some of them took me at my word, and the bishop is rather cross.'

Adam wanted to ask if it was better to make love to your wife using a contraceptive, or not to make love to her at all; but somehow it did not seem an appropriate question to ask Father Wildfire. He lived at the frontiers of the spiritual life, where dwelt criminals, prostitutes, murderers and saints, a territory steaming with the fumes of human iniquity, from which souls emerged, if they emerged at all, toughened and purified by a heroic struggle with evil. In contrast, Adam's moral problem seemed trivial and suburban, and to seek Father Wildfire's advice would be like engaging the services of a big-game hunter to catch a mouse.

The circle of Dollingerites had now broken up into small groups, the most numerous of which was clustered round Father Wildfire, who was expatiating on the problems of Irish girls who came to London to have their illegitimate babies. Thinking of his own healthy and tolerably happy family, Adam was stricken with self-reproach. A favourite remark of his mother's, 'There's always someone worse off than yourself,' stirred in his memory. He found the maxim no more efficacious in removing anxiety now than it had been in the past. Healthy and happy his family might be, but only so long as it stood at a manageable number. Already the problem of supporting them was formidable. He really must begin to think seriously about jobs for next year.

It was cold and damp on the pavement outside Student Christian Hall. The leafless trees in Gordon Square stood black and gaunt against the façade of Georgian houses. The sky was cold and grey. It looked like snow.

I hunched my shoulders inside my coat and set off briskly in the direction of the English Department (*Adam Appleby might have written*). I had an appointment with Briggs, my supervisor. He was a punctual man, and appreciated punctuality in others. I mean that he liked people to be on time. Men who have sacrificed a lot of big things to their careers often cling fiercely to small habits.

Access to the English Department was through a small court-yard at the rear of the College. There seemed to be a lot of young people about, and I had to linger some moments before I caught the eye of Jones, the Beadle. I always make a point of catching the eye of beadles, porters and similar servants. Jones did not disappoint me: his face lit up.

'Hallo, sir. Haven't seen you for some time.'

'Come to see Mr Briggs, Jones. There seem to be a lot of people about?'

'Undergraduates, sir,' he explained.

The English Department wasn't the most distinguished build-ing in the College, but it had history. The brick façade, stained with soot and streaked with rain water, was thought to be a good example of its type, which was turn-of-the-century warehousing. When, some thirty years ago, the expanding College had bought the freehold, rather than demolish the building they had skilfully converted the interior into classrooms and narrow, cell-like offices by means of matchboard partitions. It wasn't what you could call a comfortable or elegant building, but it had character. Its small, grimy windows looked on to an identical building twenty feet away, which housed the Department of Civil Engineering. But, schooled by long practice, I turned into the right door and mounted the long stone staircase.

The door of Briggs' room on the second floor was open, and the sound of conversation floated into the corridor. I tapped on the door and extended my head into the room.

'Oh, come in, Appleby,' said Briggs.

He was talking to Bane, who had recently been appointed to a new Chair of Absurdist Drama, endowed by a commercial television company. This, I knew, had been a blow to Briggs, who was the senior man of the two, and who had been looking about for a Chair for some time. His own field was the English Essay. No one was likely to endow a special Chair in the English Essay, and Briggs knew it. His best chance of promotion lay in the retirement of the Head of Department, old Howells, who was always raising Briggs' expectations by retreating at the beginning of term to a Swiss sanatorium, only to dash them again by returning refreshed and reinvigorated at the beginning of the vacations.

The posture of the two men seemed to illustrate their relationship. Bane was sprawled in Briggs' lumpy armchair, his legs stretched out over the brown linoleum. Briggs stood by the window, uneasily fingering the ridges of the radiator. On his desk was an open bottle of British sherry. At my appearance he seemed to straighten up his tired, slack body, and to become his usual efficient, slightly fussy self.

'Come in, come in,' he repeated.

'I don't want to interrupt you . . .'

'No, come in. You know Professor Bane, of course?'

Bane nodded casually, but affably enough. 'How's the research going?' he asked.

'I hope to start writing soon,' I replied.

'Will you take a glass of sherry wine?' said Briggs, who affected such redundancies in his speech.

'Thank you, but I've already lunched,' I explained.

Briggs glanced at his watch. 'I suppose it *is* late. What does your wrist-watch say, Bane?'

'A quarter to two.'

'We've been talking, and forgot the time,' said Briggs. If Briggs was losing his habit of punctuality, I thought, he must be seriously affected by the promotion of Bane.

Bane got up and stretched himself nonchalantly. 'Well, I think we've talked it out now,' he said. 'Perhaps you'll think it over, Briggs, and let me know what you decide.'

Briggs bit his lip, at the same time pulling nervously on the lobes of both ears. It was a little nervous habit of his which you didn't notice at first.

'I must say,' he said, 'it surprises me a little that the Prof hasn't mentioned this to me at all.'

Bane shrugged. 'Of course, you realise that it means nothing to me, and the last thing I want to do is to put you to any inconvenience. But it seems that the Prof wants all the people with Chairs' – he leaned slightly on the word – 'together on one floor. I think you'll find my little room on the fourth floor quite snug. At least one doesn't suffer from interruptions up there. Put it this way: you'll be able to get on with your book,' he concluded maliciously. Briggs had been working for twenty years on a history of the English Essay.

As Briggs opened his mouth to reply, he was forestalled by a frenzied crashing in the radiator pipes, emanating from the boilers far below, but filling the room with such a din as to render speech inaudible. While the racket continued, the three of us stood, motionless and silent, lost in our own thoughts. I felt a certain thrill at being witness to one of those classic struggles for power and prestige which characterise the lives of ambitious men and which, in truth, exhaust most of their time and energy. To the casual observer, it might seem that nothing important was at stake here, but it might well be that the future course of English studies in the University hung upon this conversation.

At length the noise in the radiator pipes diminished, and faded away. Briggs said:

'I'm glad you mentioned my book, Bane. To be honest with you, the thing I have most against a move is my collection here.' Briggs gestured towards the huge, ugly, worm-eaten bookcase that housed his collection of the English essayists: Addison, Steele, Johnson, Lamb, Hazlitt, Belloc, Chesterton . . . even Egbert Merrymarsh was represented here by a slim, white-buckram volume privately printed by Carthusian monks on hand-made paper. 'I just don't see how it will fit into your room,' explained Briggs.

This was Briggs' trump-card. His collection was famous, and no one would dare to suggest that he break it up. Bane lost his nonchalant air, and looked cross: a faint flush coloured his pouchy cheeks. 'I'll get Jones to take some measurements,' he said abruptly, and left the room.

Briggs brightened momentarily at Bane's departure, no doubt consoled by the thought that Jones was in his own pocket. But the hidden pressures of the discussion had taken their toll, and he seemed a tired and defeated man as he sank into his desk-chair.

'Well,' he said at length, 'how's the research going?'

'I hope to start writing soon,' I replied. 'But I fear I won't be able to submit in June. I think I'll have to get an extension to October.'

'That's a pity, Appleby, a great pity. I disapprove of theses running on and on. Look at Camel, for instance.'

'Yes, I know. What worries me is the question of jobs. I really will need a job next academic year.'

'A job? A university post, is it that you want, Appleby?'

'Yes, I – '

I was about to allude delicately to the possibility of a vacancy in the Department, caused by Bane's new Chair, when Briggs went on, with startling emphasis:

'Then I have only one word of advice to you, Appleby. Publish! Publish or perish! That's how it is in the academic world these days. There was a time when appointments were made on a more human basis, but not any more.'

'The snag is, nothing I have is quite ready for publication . . .'

With an effort, Briggs dragged his attention away from his private discontents and brought it to bear on mine. But the energy went out of his voice, and he seemed bored.

'What about that piece you showed me on Merrymarsh?' he said vaguely.

'Do you really think . . . It's my impression there's not much interest in Merrymarsh these days.'

'Interest? Interest doesn't matter, as long as you get it published. Who do you suppose is interested in Absurdist drama?'

I left Briggs staring moodily into his empty sherry-glass. On my way out of the building I met Bane again, and took the opportunity to ask his advice on a trivial bibliographical problem. He seemed flattered by the enquiry, and took me up to his room to look up the reference.

When I finally made my departure, the trees were still there in Gordon Square, bleak and gaunt against the Georgian façade. I walked back to the Museum under a cold grey sky. I wondered idly which man I disliked most, Briggs or Bane.

FIVE

*I spent my days at the British Museum, and must, I think, have
been very delicate, for I remember often putting off hour after
hour consulting some necessary book because I shrank from lifting
the heavy volumes of the catalogue.*
W. B. YEATS

As Adam approached the British Museum, lethargy and despair
oppressed him. By now, a pile of Lawrence books would be on
his desk, but he felt no quickening of his pulse at the prospect.
In Great Russell Street he lingered outside the windows of bookshops, stationers and small publishers. The stationers particularly
fascinated him. He coveted the files, punches, staplers, erasers,
coloured inks, and gadgets whose functions remained a teasing
mystery, thinking that if only he could afford to equip himself
with all this apparatus his thesis would write itself: he would be
automated.

Feeling a faint pang of hunger – the Scotch egg in the Tavern
seemed very distant – Adam entered a small shop near the corner
of Museum Street, and purchased a bar of chocolate. A headline
in the evening paper about the Vatican Council caught his eye,
and he bought a copy. He crossed the road and passed through
the gates of the Museum, which sat massively before him, its
wings like arms extended to sweep him into the yawning, gap-
toothed maw of the portico. As he mounted the steps, Adam
decided not to be swallowed immediately. He sat down on one of
the benches in the colonnade and munched his chocolate, glancing
at the newspaper. Cardinal Suenens, he was glad to see, had called
for a radical re-examination of the Church's teaching on birth
control. Cardinal Ottaviani had countered by asserting that married Catholics should place their trust in Divine Providence. On
no other issue, the paper's correspondent reported, were the
liberal and conservative factions at the Council so clearly defined.
A prolonged and bitter debate was in prospect, which was likely

to be resolved only by the personal intervention of the Pope, who had not as yet indicated the direction of his own thinking on the matter.

A chill breeze blew round Adam's neck. He raised the hood of his duffle coat and muffled his hands in the sleeves. The hood came down over his head like a monk's cowl. He gazed between the massive Ionic pillars at the vacant courtyard, and saw it thronged with cheering crowds under a blue Italian sky . . .

* * * Indeed it was a day of days, *Father Francesco Francescini, humble member of the Papal household, wrote in his diary,* and I bless the Divine Providence which ordained that I, a humble Franciscan friar, should have been privy to its tremendous doings. Not merely the election of a new Pope – but an English Pope, the first for eight centuries – and not merely an English Pope, but an English Pope who has been married! Little did the Fathers of the Council suspect, I wager, when they approved by so narrow a margin the admission of married men to Holy Orders, that they would soon be acclaiming a Supreme Pontiff with four *bambini*. Most mirific! Astonishing are the ways of God.

I would give my rosary beads, carved from the shin-bone of holy St Francis himself, to know what struggles in the Conclave brought about the election of this unknown Padre Appleby, secretary to the English Cardinal and, they say, ordained but lately, to the highest office of Holy Church. Whatever the true history (and the Conclave's vow of secrecy ensures that it will never be known, not for some days anyway) it is accomplished. We have a Pope! *Habemus Papam!* With what a sour face old Scarlettofeverini, despot of the Holy Office, enunciated the longed-for words to the cheering multitude in St Peter's Square, who for days had watched the black smoke of disagreement floating into the sky above the Sistine chapel. Just before the announcement, in the Papal chamber behind the balcony, he had enquired, with a vulpine snarl, what name the new Pope proposed to take.

'We take the name of Alexander,' said the Pope with deliberation. The Sacred College reeled back in dismay. There was a flutter of ringed hands, a squeaking and cawing as of startled birds.

'*Alexander!*' hissed Scarlettofeverini. 'Will you make a mockery of the Papacy that you take the name of the most infamous man who ever disgraced its annals?'

'Alexander the Sixth was the last Pope to be the father of children,' replied the Pope, with marble poise. 'Let us hope that in these more enlightened times Alexander the Seventh may show such a circumstance is not incompatible with the proper government of the Church.'

Alexander the Seventh! Long may he reign!

This evening Sister Maria of the Sacred Heart, housekeeper to the late Pope, came to me in perturbation. It seems the new Pontiff had requested some Scottish delicacy, compounded of egg and sausage, unknown to the kitchen staff. I recommended that the Scottish College be consulted * * *

* * * After only a few days our new Pope has already won the hearts of the Roman people. At first there was a natural suspicion of this unknown Englishman, but the astonishing sight of the Holy Father riding his diminutive scooter through the streets of Rome, skilfully controlling the machine with his left hand while he scatters blessings with his right, his white robes floating in the breeze like the wings of the Holy Ghost, has endeared him to all and sundry. In particular, it is noted with approval that he favours a scooter of Italian design, albeit an antiquated and unreliable model which, with characteristic humility, he declines to exchange for a new one.

Memo: to confess that I broke my fast today to sample the Scottish egg. Tasty. * * *

* * * This morning the Pope summoned the Sacred College to his chamber to read the draft of his first Encyclical. Entitled *De Lecto Conjugale*, it is concerned with the role of sexuality in marriage and related problems of birth control, world population problems *etc etera*. The Pope made moving reference to his own wife, who died in her fourth childbirth, and not a few of Their Eminences were to be observed surreptitiously wiping away a tear with the hems of their glowing robes. Scarlettofeverini, however,

300

waxed more and more indignant as the reading proceeded, and could scarce restrain himself from bursting into protest. The Pope concluded by asserting that, in the present state of theological uncertainty, the practice of birth control by any method was left to the discretion and conscience of the Faithful. At the same time he called for the establishment of clinics in every parish to instruct married Catholics in all available techniques.

'This is paganism!' Scarlettofeverini erupted, when the Pope concluded. 'This is a return to paganism. This is the darkest day in the history of the Church since Luther nailed up his ninety-five theses.'

'On the contrary,' replied the Pope, 'We believe We have fore-stalled a second Reformation.'

'Luther would have been on your side today,' snarled the Cardinal, gathering the skirts of his robes preparatory to a stormy exit.

'Very likely,' said the Pope, with a smile. 'Luther was a married man.'

'I am the thirteenth child of my mother,' cried the angry prelate.

'And the father of none,' returned the Pope dryly.

Tee hee!

Today, after Vespers, Sister Maria asked me what is this birth control. I told her it did not concern her. Still, I suppose I must find out. * * *

* * * The impact of the new encyclical has been prodigious, despite attempts to have it banned in Sicily and Ireland. The Anglican Church has come over to Rome in a body. So many lapsed Catholics are returning to the practice of their Faith that the churches cannot accommodate them. *Gloria in excelsis Deo* * * *

'Hallo, hallo, hallo! Dreaming again, Appleby?'

Adam relinquished his vision with regret, and looked up. 'Oh, hallo Camel,' he said.

Camel seated himself beside Adam, and pulled out his pipe. Adam said: 'Do you like cigars?'

301

'Why? Have you got one?'

Adam offered him one of the cigars the American had given him. Camel whistled.

'Where did you get this?'

'An American I helped out of a phone booth.'

'Sounds as if you've made a useful friend.'

'If I was the hero of one of these comic novels,' said Adam, 'he would be the fairy-godfather who would turn up at the end to offer me a job and a girl. Don't suppose I shall ever see him again, actually.'

'You never know.'

'Anyway, I've already got a girl. That's the whole trouble.'

'Still, you could use a job.'

'In America? It costs about five hundred pounds every time you have a baby, doesn't it?'

'Poor old Adam,' said Camel, drawing appreciatively on his cigar. 'You really are depressed, aren't you?'

'I don't see the point of my life at all,' said Adam. 'The only thing about it that seems really mine is sex – literature has annexed the rest. But sex is my big problem. I don't have enough of it, and when I do I get sick with worry. For two pins I'd buy twin beds and give myself up entirely to literature.'

'Don't do that,' said Camel.

'Then I think of people like Pond at it night after night, with text-books open for reference on the bedside table, and it just doesn't seem fair.'

'George is an awful liar,' said Camel. 'You mustn't believe all he tells you.'

'What d'you mean,'

'Would you like to hear the true story of his limp?'

'How do you know it?'

'Oh, it came out over a few more beers. In the pub, after you'd left.'

'You're a natural confessor, Camel,' said Adam. 'You should have been a priest.'

'Yes, I've often thought I'd enjoy shriving people,' mused

Camel. 'That's why I started in psychology when I first came up to college. But I couldn't do the Maths.'

'So what's the true story of Pond's limp?' insisted Adam, his curiosity whetted.

Camel exhaled a long plume of blue smoke. The cool breeze off the forecourt blew it back in their faces, surrounding them in an aromatic haze and imparting a smoking-room atmosphere to the chilly, cloistral setting.

'Well, you know the Ponds have one child, Amanda?' Camel began.

'Yes.'

'For some time they have been considering having another.'

'Fools.'

'Have you not observed the unacceptability of the only child in the contemporary middle-class ethos? Anyway, George and Sally decided to have a second child. But they don't want more than two.'

'I should think not.'

'It is particularly desirable, therefore, that the new infant should be of the male gender. Sally always wanted a boy. George is more concerned with the neatness of the arrangement. No point in duplicating, he says. Now, this is one problem modern science has so far failed to solve. But George, as we know, is as superstitious in sexual matters as he is rational in religious matters. It appears that when they were on holiday in Italy last summer they picked up a bit of local folk-lore to the effect that boys are conceived when the wife is full of desire and the husband fatigued and indifferent, and girls are conceived when the opposite circumstances prevail.'

'I should have thought it was the other way round,' said Adam.

'Quite. The formula has just enough unexpectedness to make it plausible,' Camel said. 'Apparently when Italian husbands wish to conceive a boy they visit a brothel before repairing to the matrimonial bed. George thought they ought to follow the prescription faithfully, but Sally wasn't having any of that. So they worked out an alternative scheme.

'The day for the experiment was determined by elaborate calculations performed with the aid of a calendar.'

'Good God,' Adam interrupted. 'D'you mean other people go through all that business?'

'On occasion,' Camel replied. 'The fateful day was a Sunday,' he went on. 'The idea was to get Sally feeling as sexy as possible and George feeling as exhausted as possible. George complained that it was a pity they hadn't known about the scheme before Amanda was conceived so that he could have had his turn at the better half of the deal, but he accepted his role manfully.

'All day long, Sally lounged about the house in a new negligée she had bought especially for the occasion, while poor old George sweated away in the garden, digging up flower-beds, mowing the lawn and trimming the hedges. At about six, he said that if they didn't go to bed soon he would fall asleep on his feet; but Sally persuaded him to wait another hour or two, and told him there was a lot of wood in the garden shed which needed chopping. Before she went upstairs to take a leisurely bath, Sally rooted in George's bookshelves for a sexy book to read in bed, and finally selected a Henry Miller, *Tropic of Capricorn* I think it was, which she'd heard was highly inflammatory.

'So, as dusk fell on West Norwood, and the neighbours settled comfortably before their television screens, Sally sat up in bed, bathed, perfumed and powdered, clad in a transparent black nightie, also bought for the occasion, reading Henry Miller; while, in the garden below, George, his hair matted, his shirt soaked with perspiration, furiously chopped wood, swearing occasionally as he nicked his fingers in the poor light.

'Then, curious things began to happen. Exhausted as he was, George found that the unwonted exercise and fresh air of the day had given him a feeling of health and vigour that he had not experienced for years. As he worked with demonic energy in the gathering dusk, the thought of Sally waiting for him upstairs, stretched out languorously on the four-poster bed in the warm, rosily-lit bedroom, excited him. Even the rank odour rising from his own perspiring body gave him a strange feeling of brutal animal joy. He began to think they would have to change their plans. Still grasping his chopper, he entered the house with the intention of consulting Sally.

'Meanwhile, back at the boudoir, Sally had been having trouble with Henry Miller, whom she found emetic rather than erotic. Reading on and on with appalled fascination, she was filled with a deepening disgust for human sexuality. With a shock, she realised what was happening to her: she no longer had any inclination for intercourse that night. She threw down her book and jumped out of bed, determining to seek in George's library something more conducive to the arousal of passion – *Fanny Hill*, perhaps.

'Sally reached the head of the staircase just as George reached the foot. At the sight of her husband, tousled, dirty, breathing hard, wielding a chopper, Sally froze. For George, the spectacle of Sally, prettily discomposed, standing against the light in her black transparent nightie, was too much. Gone were all thoughts of conceiving children, male or female. George lunged up the stairs intent on nothing less than rape. With a faint scream, Sally fled to the bedroom, George hot in pursuit. Whether from exhaustion or excess of passion, however, he stumbled, tripped, and fell to the bottom of the stairs, the chopper inflicting a slight flesh-wound on his thigh.'

'Hence the limp?'

'Hence the limp. Needless to say, no amorous dalliance took place that night. What makes George madder than anything, apparently, is all the wood he chopped. He'd completely forgotten that they had oil-fired central heating.'

Adam had ambivalent feelings about the story of Pond's limp. On the one hand, he was bitterly envious of those who enjoyed such confidence in the control of conception that they had reached the point of wanting to plan *sexes*; on the other, he took a certain heartless pleasure in the fact that those who had reached such refinements in the ordering of their sexual lives were not immune from humiliation and defeat. On balance, he had to acknowledge that Camel had managed to cheer him up, and he followed his friend into the Museum with almost a springy step.

Unfortunately, he made the mistake of phoning Barbara again. She was a long time answering the phone.

'What is it now, Adam?' she asked wearily.

'Nothing, darling. I just thought I'd ring up and ask how you were feeling.'

'I'm feeling lousy.'

'Oh. No developments?'

'No. Mary Flynn has gone, and I'm lying down.'

'How was Mary?'

'She depressed me. First thing she said when she came to the door was, "Don't tell me: you're pregnant." '

'Oh my God. Why did she say that?'

'I don't know. She thinks she's pregnant again herself, so perhaps she was just trying to cheer herself up. Actually, we were both crying most of the time she was here.'

'But she must have had some reason for saying that.'

'There's a certain look in the eyes of women who think they're pregnant. No, two looks: the smug, happy look, and the desperate unhappy look. I have the desperate unhappy look.'

'So you do think you're pregnant, then?' said Adam miserably.

'I don't know, Adam. I don't know any more. I'm sick to death of the whole business.'

'Why don't you have a frog-test? Then at least we'd know where we stood. It's the waiting that gets you down.'

'Dr Johnson said last time he wouldn't prescribe any more tests – not on the National Health, anyway. Besides, by the time the result came through, I'd know anyway.'

Damn! damn! damn! With this unspoken expletive, Adam marked every step he took down the steep and dangerous staircase that led to the Readers' lavatory. Camel had often told him how, some years before, this convenience had been closed for renovation, compelling scholars belatedly aware, as they rose from their desks to consult the catalogue, of full bladders, to walk a painful distance to the public lavatories in the main building. When the Readers' lavatory was open again, nothing seemed changed, except that the urinal had been raised on a marble plinth, thus ensuring the collision of the unwary head with the cisterns fixed to the wall. Camel had discovered, however, that this alteration could be turned to advantage: by resting one's forehead gently against the cistern while relieving oneself, a refreshing coolness was communicated to the aching brow. Adam now followed this procedure as he straddled his legs and unzipped his fly. His head needed soothing. Damn, damn, damn. Another child. It was unthinkable. Not all that again: sleepless nights, wind, sick; more nappies, more bottles, more cornflakes.

He had been fumbling unsuccessfully in his groin for some moments, and was beginning to suspect that he had been drugged and castrated at some earlier point in the day, when he remembered that he was wearing Barbara's pants. Hastily adjusting his dress, he retired to the privacy of a closet. Squatting there, his ankles shackled in nylon and lace, Adam wondered how they would accommodate another baby in the flat. It comprised only two rooms, plus kitchen and bathroom. One of the rooms had originally been a living-room, but this had long ago become Adam's and Barbara's bedroom, while the children occupied the other. This seemed the logical and inevitable design of a good Catholic home: no room for *living* in, only rooms for breeding, sleeping, eating and excreting. As it was, he was compelled to study in his bedroom, his desk squeezed up beside the double bed, constant reminder of birth, copulation and death. But what would happen now, for a new child could not be accommodated in the children's room. They would have to take it into their own room. Where, then, would he study? Perhaps he could sit in the bath, with a board across the top . . . But the taps dripped all the time. Besides, the bathroom was the busiest place in the house. They would have to move. But they couldn't move. Nowhere could they find a bigger flat in London at even double the price. He would have to leave home to make room for the incoming child. Not that he could afford separate accommodation, but perhaps he could live in the Museum, hiding when the closing bell rang and dossing down on one of the broad-topped desks with a pile of books for a pillow.

Damn, damn, damn. Adam plodded up the steep staircase,

and returned to the Reading Room. He met the eye of the man behind the Enquiries desk, who gave him a smile of recognition. Enquiries he would like to make passed through Adam's head: where can I get a three-bedroomed flat at £3 10s 0d per week? What is the definition of a long sentence? Would you like to buy a second-hand scooter? What must I do to be saved? Adam returned the smile wanly and passed on.

He paused beside a shelf of reference books, and took down a rhyming dictionary.

I always choose a Brownlong chair . . .

Air, bare, bear, care, dare, e'er, fair, fare, glare, hair, hare, heir, lair, mare, pair, rare, scare, stair, stare, ware, wear, yare.

It's just like floating in the air
Another chair I couldn't bear
And then I sit and stare and glare
Like a lion in his lair
Or a tortoise crossed with hare
Or a horse without a mare
Or a man who's got no heir
Or an heir who's got no hair
Hypocrite lecteur! mon semblable, mon frère!

Adam replaced the rhyming dictionary, and moved on. Publish, Briggs had said, publish your piece on Merrymarsh. Little did he know it had already been rejected by nine periodicals. It was no use trying to publish criticism, unless you had a name, or friends. Discovering original materials was the only sure way. 'A Recently Discovered Letter of Shelley's'. 'Gerald Manley Hopkins' Laundry Bills'. 'The Baptismal Register at Inverness'. That was the sort of thing. Even unpublished manuscripts of Merrymarsh would do the trick, thought Adam, as he slumped into his seat before a heap of Lawrence.

At that moment he simultaneously remembered the strange-looking letter he had received that morning, and knew what it ghost-town of the Fun Fair, closed for the winter, brooding on her possible pregnancy, and a pang of pity and love transfixed him. If only he could reach her, and assure her that all was well.

He returned to his desk in the Reading Room, but could not convert his good spirits into industry. The laboriously accumulated notes of his thesis filled him with impatience. That was all behind him now. Let the long sentence trail its way through English fiction as it willed – he would pursue it no longer. He took up Mrs Rottingdean's letter again, and began to draft a reply, asking if he could come round and see the papers as soon as possible, proposing the following evening. Yet he could scarcely contemplate the suspense of waiting even that long. Why should he not phone now, and propose calling on Mrs Rottingdean that very day? He looked again at the letter. Yes, a telephone number was given. Adam left his seat, and hurried back to the telephone.

As Adam pushed the door of the phone booth shut with his posterior and, trembling with excitement, dug in his pocket for change, a telephone bell rang, loud and insistent. Adam looked about him in bewilderment, unable to accept at first that the sound emanated from the instrument before him. But it evidently did. He lifted the receiver, and said hesitantly, 'Hallo.'

'Museum Double-O-One-Two?' demanded a female voice.

Adam obediently scrutinised the number at the centre of the dial. 'Yes,' he replied.

'Hold on please. Your call from Colorado.'

'What?' said Adam.

'Sorry it's taken so long, Museum,' said the operator brightly. 'The lines are absolutely haywire today.'

'I think you've got the wrong person,' Adam began. But the operator had gone away. Adam wanted to go away too, but didn't have the courage. Besides, he wanted to make a phone call himself. He opened the door of the kiosk and, still holding the receiver to his ear, leaned out to look into the foyer of the Museum, hoping to catch sight of the fat American.

'Are you there, Museum?'

'Oh. Yes, but look here – ' Withdrawing his head too quickly, Adam banged it on the door and dropped the receiver, which ghost-town of the Fun Fair, closed for the winter, brooding on her possible pregnancy, and a pang of pity and love transfixed him. If only he could reach her, and assure her that all was well.

He returned to his desk in the Reading Room, but could not convert his good spirits into industry. The laboriously accumulated notes of his thesis filled him with impatience. That was all behind him now. Let the long sentence trail its way through English fiction as it willed – he would pursue it no longer. He took up Mrs Rottingdean's letter again, and began to draft a reply, asking if he could come round and see the papers as soon as possible, proposing the following evening. Yet he could scarcely contemplate the suspense of waiting even that long. Why should he not phone now, and propose calling on Mrs Rottingdean that very day? He looked again at the letter. Yes, a telephone number was given. Adam left his seat, and hurried back to the telephone.

As Adam pushed the door of the phone booth shut with his posterior and, trembling with excitement, dug in his pocket for change, a telephone bell rang, loud and insistent. Adam looked about him in bewilderment, unable to accept at first that the sound emanated from the instrument before him. But it evidently did. He lifted the receiver, and said hesitantly, 'Hallo.'

'Museum Double-O-One-Two?' demanded a female voice.

Adam obediently scrutinised the number at the centre of the dial. 'Yes,' he replied.

'Hold on please. Your call from Colorado.'

'What?' said Adam.

'Sorry it's taken so long, Museum,' said the operator brightly. 'The lines are absolutely haywire today.'

'I think you've got the wrong person,' Adam began. But the operator had gone away. Adam wanted to go away too, but didn't have the courage. Besides, he wanted to make a phone call himself. He opened the door of the kiosk and, still holding the receiver to his ear, leaned out to look into the foyer of the Museum, hoping to catch sight of the fat American.

'Are you there, Museum?'

'Oh. Yes, but look here – ' Withdrawing his head too quickly, Adam banged it on the door and dropped the receiver, which swung clattering against the wall. By the time he recaptured it, the operator had gone again, and a faint American voice was saying anxiously:

'Bernie? Is that you, Bernie? Bernie?'

'No, it's not, I'm afraid,' said Adam.

'Ah, Bernie. I thought I'd lost you.'

'No, I'm not Bernie.'

'Who are you then?'

'My name's Appleby. Adam Appleby.'

'Pleased to make your acquaintance, Mr Appleby. Is Bernie there?'

'Well no, I'm afraid he isn't. I'm sorry you've had all this trouble and expense, but – '

'He's out, is he? Well, O.K., you can give him a message. Will you tell him he can have one hundred thousand for books and fifty thousand for manuscripts?'

'One hundred thousand for books,' Adam repeated, mesmerised.

'Right. And fifty grand for manuscripts,' said the man. 'That's great, Adam, thanks a lot. You been working with Bernie for long?'

'Well, no,' said Adam. 'As a matter of fact – '

'Your time's up, Colorado,' said the operator. 'Do you want to pay for another two minutes?'

'No, that's all. 'Bye, Adam. Say hallo to Bernie for me.'

'Goodbye,' said Adam weakly. The line went dead.

Adam replaced the receiver and leaned against the door, wondering what he should do. He might never see the fat man again. He couldn't carry this undelivered message around with him for the rest of his life. It sounded important, too. A hundred thousand for books. Fifty grand for manuscripts. That meant dollars. Perhaps he should report the whole business to the operator.

Adam dialled 'O', and tried to rehearse a coherent explanation of the situation as he listened to the ringing tone.

'Is that the police?' a male voice enquired.

'Eh?' said Adam. He could still hear a ringing tone.

'My car has been stolen,' said the man. 'Would you please send an officer round at once?'

'You'd better dial 999,' said Adam. 'I'm not a policeman.'

'That's what I did dial,' said the man crossly.

'What number do you require?' said a third voice, female, sounding very faint. The ringing tone had stopped.

'I told you, I want the police,' said the man. 'Look here, my car has vanished. I haven't time to wait here while – '

'Are you there, caller?' said the operator.

'Do you mean me?' said Adam.

'Well, you dialled "O" didn't you?' inquired the operator, ironically.

'I keep telling you, I dialled 999,' screamed the man. 'What kind of a fool d'you take me for?'

'Yes, I dialled "O",' said Adam, dimly aware that he was the only member of the trio that enjoyed two-way communication with both the other parties.

'Well, what do you want then?' said the operator.

'I want the police,' sobbed the man.

'He wants the police,' explained Adam.

'You want the police?' asked the operator.

'No, I don't want the police,' said Adam.

'Where are you speaking from?' said the operator.

'Ninety-five Gower Street,' said the man.

'The British Museum,' said Adam. 'But I don't want the police. It's this other man who wants the police.'

'What is the name?'

'I don't know his name,' said Adam. 'What's your name?' he added, trying to throw his voice in the direction of Gower Street.

'Never mind my name,' said the operator, huffily. 'What's yours?'

'Brooks,' said the man.

'His name is Brooks,' Adam passed it on.

'Well, Mr Brooks – '

'No, no! My name is Appleby. Brooks is the man whose car was stolen.'

'You've had some books stolen, from the British Museum, is that it?' said the operator, as if all was clear at last.

'I've had enough of this foolery,' said Brooks angrily. 'But I assure you, I'm going to report it.' He slammed down his receiver. Adam registered his departure with relief.

'Look,' he said to the operator, 'are you the one who put through a call just now from Colorado for a man called Bernie?'

'Burning?' said the operator. 'You don't want the police, you need the fire service.'

Adam quietly replaced the receiver, and crept into the next booth. Essentially, he felt he had had enough of telephones for that day, but his anxiety to contact Mrs Rottingdean overcame his unwillingness to pick up the receiver again. Repeated dialling, however, elicited only a persistent engaged signal. Adam suspected that the line was out of order, but could not summon up the courage to ring the operator again. He tried ringing Barbara, but Mrs Green answered to say she was still out. Adam made one more unsuccessful attempt to ring Mrs Rottingdean, and retired, defeated and disgruntled, from the telephone. His excitement and enthusiasm were quite dissipated. He thought Barbara was probably pregnant after all.

SIX

*Free or open access can hardly be practised in so large a library
as this. As it was once put, the danger would be not merely of
losing the books, but also of losing readers.*
ARUNDELL ESDAILE (former secretary to the British Museum)

When Adam opened the door of the telephone booth, an unfamiliar and sacrilegious hubbub assaulted his ears. After he had
taken a few paces it was the turn of his eyesight to be astonished.
The main entrance hall was thronged with people chatting and
gesticulating with an animation quite untypical of visitors to the
Museum. They were held back on each side by a cordon of
policemen, leaving open a narrow corridor extending from the
revolving doors at the entrance to the Reading Room. Was it
the Beatles again? Adam wondered. He pushed his way towards
the entrance to the Reading Room, and showed his pass.

'Sorry, sir,' said the man. 'No one allowed in.'

'What's the matter?' said Adam.

The crowd raised an ironical cheer, and looking round Adam
saw that the revolving doors were now fanning into the hall a
steady stream of booted and helmeted firemen, who trotted sheepishly along the human corridor and into the Reading Room.
Hosepipes snaked across the floor behind them.

'They say there's a fire,' said the doorman, with relish.

'Not in the Library?' exclaimed Adam, aghast.

'It's like the war all over again,' said the man, rubbing his
hands together. 'Of course, most of the books are irreplaceable,
you know.'

It wasn't, however, (Adam had ashamedly to admit to himself
later) the fate of the Museum's priceless collection which preoccupied him at that moment, but the fate of his own notes and files.
Only a short while ago he had been filled with disgust for that tatty
collection of paper; but now that it was in danger of extinction he

315

realised how closely his sense of personal identity, uncertain as this was, was involved in those fragile, vulnerable sheets, cards and notebooks, which even now might be crinkling and turning brown at the edges under the hot breath of destructive flame. Almost everything he had thought and read for the past two years was recorded there. It wasn't much, but it was all he had.

'Mind your back, sir,' said the doorman, as a fireman lumbered past. The hosepipe he was dragging by its nozzle caught under the door, and Adam sprang forward to disengage it. Clinging to the hosepipe, he trotted after the fireman.

'Hey!' called the doorman.

Adam ducked his head and kept trotting. It was only when he was inside the Reading Room and to his surprise and relief saw no evidence of conflagration, that he connected the presence of the firemen with his recent triangular conversation on the telephone. Then he wished he hadn't been in such a hurry to get into the Reading Room. He backed towards the door, but another official, more determined-looking than the first, told him sternly: 'Nobody allowed out yet, sir. There's no immediate danger.'

Adam believed him. But the other readers were not so confident. Clasping their notebooks to their breasts, as if the former were precious jewels snatched from the cabins of a foundering ship, they milled about the door begging to be let out. One lady tottered forward to the official and pressed a huge pile of typewritten sheets into his unwilling arms. 'I don't care about myself,' she said, weeping, 'but save my doctoral dissertation.'

Beyond the doorway, similar disorder prevailed. Some readers stood on their desks, and gazed about hopefully for rescue. Pushing his way through the crowd, Adam nearly tripped over a prostrate nun, saying her rosary. Nearby, a negro priest, hurriedly collecting his notes on St Thomas Aquinas, was being urged to hear someone's confession. A few courageous and stoical souls continued working calmly at their books, dedicated scholars to the last. One of them betrayed his inner tension by lighting a cigarette, evidently reasoning that normal fire precautions were now redundant. He was immediately drenched with chemical foam by an over-enthusiastic fireman. Shouts and cries violated the hallowed air which had hitherto been disturbed by nothing louder than the murmur of subdued conversation, or the occasional thump of dropped books. The dome seemed to look down with deep disapproval at the anarchic spectacle. Already ugly signs of looting were in evidence. Adam caught sight of a distinguished historian furtively filling the pockets of his raincoat from the open shelves.

Camel was sitting on his desk and surveying the scene with obvious enjoyment.

'Hallo, Appleby. I say, this is entertaining, isn't it?'

'Aren't you alarmed?'

'No, it's only some hoax.'

'A hoax, you think?'

'Bound to be. Shouldn't like to be the hoaxer when they catch him.'

Adam racked his brains to try and remember if he had given his name to that idiot operator. He rather feared that he had, but surely she wouldn't have got it right? He glanced guiltily over his shoulder, and looked straight into the eyes of a member of the Library staff who was standing near the catalogue shelves, supervising the loading of the huge volumes on to trolleys, by which means they were carted off to safety. The man's face registered recognition, and he began pushing his way towards Adam, waving a piece of paper.

'See you later,' said Adam to Camel.

As he shouldered his way through the panic-stricken crowd, tripping over trailing hosepipes, and stumbling over the backs of firemen who, on hands and knees, were searching under the desks for signs of fire, Adam cast fleeting glances over his shoulder. The assistant was talking to Camel, who was pointing in Adam's direction. Camel's idea of entertainment, he thought bitterly, as he reached the short passage which connected the Reading Room and the North Library.

He knew of no other way out of the North Library: if he went in, he would be trapped. He leaned against the wall at his back and pressed the palms of his hands against its surface. A soft, almost human warmth surprised his sense of touch. It wasn't a wall at all, but a door – a green baize door. His fingers found the handle and softly turned it. The door opened. He slipped through, and closed it behind him.

He was in another country: dark, musty, infernal. A maze of iron galleries, lined with books and connected by tortuous iron staircases, webbed his confused vision. He was in the stacks – he knew that – but it was difficult to connect this cramped and gloomy warren with the civilised spaciousness of the Reading Room. It was as if he had dropped suddenly from the even pavement of a quiet residential street into the city's sewers. He had crossed a frontier – there was no doubt of that; and already he felt himself entering into the invisible community of outcasts and malefactors – all those who were hunted through dark ways shunned by the innocent and the respectable. A few steps had brought him here, but it was a long way back. Never again would he be able to take his place beside the scholars in the Reading Room with a conscience as untroubled as theirs. They worked with a quiet confidence that wisdom was at their fingertips – that they had only to scribble on a form and knowledge was delivered promptly to their desks. But what did they know of this dark underworld, heavy with the odour of decaying paper, in which that knowledge was stored? Show me the happy scholar, he thought, and I will show you the bliss of ignorance.

Voices, sharp and authoritative, were raised on the other side of the door. He had a sudden vision of the capture, the indictment and the punishment, and stumbled blindly towards a flight of stairs. He grasped the bannister like salvation. If only I wasn't limping, he thought; but it was the treachery of Camel which stabbed more keenly than the pain in his leg.

The staircase spiralled up into darkness, like a fire escape in hell, fixed there to delude the damned. He dragged himself up four flights, and limped along a narrow gangway between tall shelves of books. He was in Theology. Abelard, Alcuin, Aquinas, Augustine. Augustine, the saint who knew sin from experience. He took down a volume in some vague hope of finding counsel in it, but was distracted by the sight of a cheese sandwich at the

318

back of the shelf. It looked dry, and a little mouldy: the corners were turned up like the feet of a corpse. He thought he heard the scuttle of a mouse somewhere behind the books. It gave him a strange feeling of consolation to think that another human being – perhaps another fugitive – had passed through this cemetery of old controversies, and had left this mark of his passage.

Iron-shod feet rang on the iron grating. He felt the vibrations rise through the thin soles of his shoes, and through his bones and arteries, to knock at his heart. The hunt was on again.

He crept further along the shelving, past Bede and Bernard, Calvin and Chrysostom. A bundle of old tracts caught his eye. *Repent!* the cover of one admonished, *for the Day of Judgment is at Hand*. Another book bore the device of the Jansenist Christ, arms raised above the bowed head in a grim reminder of the exclusiveness of mercy.

Still the feet came on. A low moan broke from his lips as he turned to face his pursuer. Was this how the affair would end, then – trapped like an animal between walls of mouldering theology?

His hand groped instinctively for a weapon, but lighted only upon books: *A Quiverful of Arrows against Popery, Plucked from the Holy Scriptures* and *The Sin Against the Holy Ghost Finally Revealed*. Holding the two dusty volumes limply in his hands, he remembered the oozing wall of the urinal in the school playground, the tough Middle English paper in Finals, the fly-specked oleograph of the Sacred Heart in the Catholic doctor's waiting room, and Barbara crying on the unmade bed; and the will to resist any longer ebbed out of him like water out of a sink, leaving behind only a sour scum of defeat. The footsteps paused, then came nearer. Twisting his head from side to side in the last throes of panic, he seemed to make out a few paces away the shape of a door, etched in thin cracks of light. He lunged towards it.

Adam realised his mistake as soon as he opened the door, but he had no choice but to proceed. He stepped across the threshold and closed the door behind him.

He had struggled through the entrails of the British Museum, only to come back to the womb again; but in an unfamiliar position. He was standing on the uppermost of the book-lined galleries that ran round the circular wall of the reading room beneath the dome. He had often idly watched, from his desk on the floors below, assistants fetching books from these shelves, and had admired the cunning design of the doors, whose inner surfaces were lined with false book spines so that when closed their presence could not be detected.

As a fugitive, he could scarcely have picked a more exposed and conspicuous refuge. Anyone who happened to glance up from the floor below would be sure to see him. Adam took a piece of paper from his pocket and shuffled along the shelves, pretending to be an assistant looking for books. He was painfully conscious of not wearing the regular overall, but it seemed as if there was sufficient commotion on the floor below to render him safe from observation. At length, lulled into a sense of security, and fascinated by the unfamiliar perspective in which he now viewed his place of work, Adam abandoned his pose and leaned on the gallery rail to look down.

Never before had he been so struck by the symmetry of the Reading Room's design. The disposition of the furniture, which at ground level created the effect of an irritating maze, now took on the beauty of an abstract geometrical relief – balanced, but just complicated enough to please and interest the eye. Two long counters extended from the North Library entrance to the centre of the perfectly circular room. These two lines inclined towards each other, but just as they were about to converge they swelled out to form a small circle, the hub of the Reading Room. Around this hub curved the concentric circles of the catalogue shelves, and from these circles the radii of the long desks extended almost to the perimeter of the huge space. A rectangular table was placed in each of the segments. It was like a diagram of something – a brain or a nervous system, and the foreshortened people moving about in irregular clusters were like blood corpuscles or molecules. This huge domed Reading Room was the cortex of the English-speaking races, he thought, with a certain awe. The memory of everything they had thought or imagined was stored here.

It seemed that the fire-alarm had been called off at last. The firemen were rolling up their hoses, or drifting out with wistful glances at the heavy furniture, fingering the hafts of their choppers. Disappointed journalists were being ushered firmly to the exit. A self-conscious group of readers was being interviewed by the BBC. At the counter for returned books there were long queues of people who had decided to call it a day. It was time he moved on, Adam felt.

He looked up, blinked and rubbed his eyes. Diametrically opposite him, and on the same level, the fat American was leaning on the rail of the gallery in the same attitude as himself, contemplating the animated scene below. Was he authorised to be there, Adam wondered; and, if so, was it safe for him to deliver his message? At that moment the American looked up, and seemed to see him. They stared at each other for several moments. Then Adam essayed a timid wave. The American responded with a nervous glance over his shoulder. It looked as though he had no more right to be there than Adam himself.

Adam began to walk round the circumference of the Reading Room anti-clockwise. The American responded by walking in the same direction. Adam halted and turned about. The American followed suit, keeping the same distance between himself and Adam. Adam wondered whether he could risk shouting his message across the intervening space, and decided he couldn't. Perhaps the gallery was a whispering one, he thought, with a certain pride in his resourcefulness; and pressing his cheek to Volumes IV and V of *The Decline and Fall of the Roman Empire*, he breathed the words, 'Colorado phoned.'

When he looked up to see if his message had carried, the American had disappeared. Adam hastened round the gallery to the point where he had last seen him, and explored the bookshelves with his fingertips, searching for the concealed door. He discovered it when it suddenly opened in his face, lightly grazing his nose and bringing tears to his eyes. An overalled assistant stood on the threshold.

'Excuse me,' Adam said, holding his nose to assuage the pain and mask his countenance. The man retired a couple of paces to let him pass, but eyed him suspiciously.

'What department are you in?' he demanded, adding hesitantly – 'sir.' The 'sir' gave Adam courage.

'Book-counting,' he said quickly. 'It's a new department.'

'Book-counting?' the man repeated, with a puzzled frown.

'That's right,' said Adam. 'We're counting the books.' He stepped briskly to the nearest shelf, and commenced running his index finger along the rows of books, muttering under his breath, 'Two million, three hundred thousand, four hundred and sixty-one, two million, three hundred thousand, four hundred and sixty-two, two million, three hundred thousand, four hundred and sixty-three . . .'

'You've got a job there,' said the man.

'Yes,' said Adam. 'And if you make me lose count, I'll have to start all over again from the beginning. Two million, three hundred thousand, four hundred . . .'

'Sorry,' said the man, humbly, and shuffled off towards the open door of the gallery. Adam poised himself to run; but the man hesitated at the door and returned.

'Sorry to disturb you again,' he said. 'But if you happen to find a sausage roll behind one of them books, you might let us know.'

'I found a cheese sandwich just now,' Adam offered. The man clapped a hand to his brow.

''Lord!' he exclaimed. 'I'd forgotten all about that cheese sandwich.'

When the man finally left him, Adam tiptoed away and scuttled down a narrow flight of stairs. He weaved his way through a labyrinth of bookshelves, hoping to stumble upon some way out. When he met anyone, he halted, and started counting books until they passed. At last he came upon a door from behind which he thought he could hear the sounds of ordinary human life. He slowly opened the door, and breathed a sigh of relief. He was at the North Entrance.

Fortunately for Adam, the North Entrance was thronged with a party of schoolgirls, and his furtive exit from the door marked 'Private' escaped the attention of the Museum attendants. On the other hand, when he had pulled the door shut behind him, he found he couldn't easily move. He began pushing his way through the scrum. Satchels poked him in the groin and hair got in his mouth. The girls giggled, or gave cries of indignation. Adam saw a mistress was observing him suspiciously, and his efforts to escape became frantic. All he needed now was to be arrested for indecent assault.

At last he was in the open air. He filled his lungs, and coughed. The fog was coming back. The end of Malet Street was invisible, and so were the top storeys of the Senate House tower. He turned to his right and began to circumnavigate the Museum. The trees of Russell Square loomed to his left like the vague shapes of drowned ships. He shivered and turned up the collar of his suit in a futile gesture of self-protection against the raw, damp air. His duffle coat was in the Reading Room, and he dared not return to recover it.

He had a vivid mental image of the duffle coat draped over the back of his padded chair, its hood drooping forward like the head of a scholar bowed over his books; and he not only coveted it but, in a strange way, almost envied it. It seemed like a ghost of his former self, or, rather, the external shell of the Adam Appleby who had, only a few days ago, been a reasonably contented man, but who now, haunted with the fear of an unwanted addition to his family, divided and distracted about his academic work, and guilty of a hoax he had had no intention of committing, wandered like an outcast through the foggy streets of Bloomsbury.

He turned into Great Russell Street, slippery with the last wet leaves of fall. A convoy of fire-engines roared through the gates of the Museum, and he shrank back against the railings as they passed. The Museum itself was shrouded in fog. Its windows were dim patches of light which shed no illumination on the bleak forecourt, deserted now except for a solitary taxi. Adam grasped the railings with both hands and pressed his cheeks against the chill, damp bars. Was it the fog or self-pity that made his eyes smart? He rubbed them with his knuckles, and immediately, as if the gesture had some magic property, he saw his wife and three children ascending the steps of the Museum. The atmosphere blurred the figures, but he could not mistake Barbara's baggy red coat, or Dominic's slack-limbed refusal to proceed, or the tilt of Clare's head, lifted to her mother in interrogation. As in a dream he watched Barbara, encumbered by the weight of Edward in her arms, stoop to plead with Dominic for co-operation. And it *was* a dream, of course. Although the Museum was notoriously a place where eventually you met everyone you knew, this law did not include dependants. Scholarship and domesticity were opposed worlds, whose common frontier was marked by the Museum railings. This reversal of the natural order, with himself outside the railings, and his family inside, was a vision, pregnant with symbolic significance if only he could penetrate it. He felt moved but helpless, like Scrooge watching the tableaux unfolded by the spirits of Christmas. He longed to run forward and help his wife, but knew that if he stirred a muscle the vision would 'dissolve. Sure enough, as he released his grasp on the railings and moved towards the gates, a puff of wind stirred the fog, and threw an impenetrable screen between himself and the steps. When it cleared partially, the steps were deserted again.

Still puzzled by the vividness and particularity of the apparition, Adam hurried through the gates and up the steps. He peered through the glass doors, but could see no sign of Barbara. Further he dared not go – the man at the entrance to the Reading Room was on the watch. He was distracted by the sound of children chasing pigeons somewhere to his left. The whoops and cries echoing faintly in the colonnade, mingled with the indignant commotion of wings, could be Dominic's. Adam hurried to investigate, but the children were not his own.

He drank some water at the stone fount near the doors of the Museum, pursing his lips and sucking noisily to avoid touching the lip of the battered metal cup. Then he paced up and down the colonnade, wondering what to do. The Reading Room would be open late that evening, he reminded himself. If he sneaked in towards closing time the fire-alarm might have been forgotten, and he might be able to retrieve his belongings without notice. But what could he do in the meantime? There was the sherry party at six – that would take care of the early evening – but it was only three-thirty now.

Adam toyed with the idea of going to a cinema. He had a keen premonition of the guilt he would feel at adding a further act of idleness to a day already characterised by total non-achievement. But, on the other hand, was it any use fighting destiny? He rooted in his pockets to see how much money he had, and pulled out Mrs Rottingdean's letter. That was a thought. Suppose he took a chance – there would be no more telephoning – and went straight to her house? He might yet snatch something useful out of the day . . .

As he prepared to push-start his scooter, Adam quailed inwardly at the prospect before him. He was not experienced in negotiating for unpublished literary remains, but he knew that the relatives of deceased authors were liable to be touchy and obstructive in such matters. In any case he anticipated all new human contacts with fear and reluctance. He glanced wistfully at the Museum, but its dim, forbidding shape only reminded him how irretrievably he was committed to a career of risk. With stoic resolution he turned back to his scooter, and began to push it with increasing momentum between the lines of parked cars. He was going to need both courage and subtlety to succeed in his enterprise.

SEVEN

*During the autumn and winter the delivery of a book is not
infrequently hindered by darkness or fog.*
A Guide to the Use of the Reading Room (1924)

In the late afternoon the Museum was still there, but he was not
going to it any more. It was foggy in London that afternoon and
the dark came very early. Then the shops turned their lights on,
and it was all right riding down Oxford Street looking in the
windows, though you couldn't see much because of the fog. There
was much traffic on the roads and the drivers couldn't see where
they were going. The traffic lights changed from red to amber
to green and back to red again and the traffic didn't move. Then
the drivers sounded their horns and got out of their cars to swear
at each other. It was foggy in London that afternoon and the
dark came very early.

The house in Bayswater looked on to a square. There was a
playground in the square and some big trees. The swings in
the playground squeaked but you couldn't see the children who
were swinging because of the trees and the fog. It was a tall
narrow house and it hadn't been painted for a long time. The
old paint had flaked off in places and underneath you could see
the raw brickwork. There were six steps leading up to the front
door and more steps leading down to a basement area.

Adam knocked on the front door but it was the basement door
which opened. A man wearing a dirty vest and with a lot of thick
black hair on his arms and chest looked up.

'Mrs Rottingdean?' Adam said.

'Out,' the man said.

'Do you know when she'll be back?'

'No,' the man said, and shut the door.

Adam stood on the top step for a while, listening to the squeak of the swings in the square. Then he went down the area steps and knocked on the door of the basement.

'Come in,' the man said. He held the door open with his left hand and Adam saw that two fingers were missing from it.

'I just wanted to leave a message.'

'I said, "Come in".'

Adam went in. It was a large bare kitchen. There were some wooden chairs and a table and a lot of empty beer bottles in one corner. On the walls were some bull-fighting posters. The bulls were painted to look very fierce and the bullfighters to look very handsome. Two men sat at the table drinking beer and talking to each other in a foreign language. They were not very handsome and when they saw Adam they stopped talking. Adam looked at the bull-fighting posters.

'You are *aficionado*?' the hairy man said.

'I beg your pardon?'

'You follow the bulls?'

'I've never been to a bull-fight.'

'Who is he?' one of the men at the table said. The thumb was missing from his left hand.

'Who are you?' the hairy man said to Adam.

'He's from the café,' the third man said. This man's left hand was in a sling.

'There must be some mistake,' Adam said.

'I'll say there is,' the man with the sling said. 'We just called the café.'

'I haven't come from any café,' Adam said. 'I've come from the British Museum.'

'They have a café there?'

'They call it a cafeteria,' Adam said.

'Same thing,' the man with the sling said.

'That is not so,' the man with one thumb missing said. 'A café is a place where a man may drink with his friends and the drinks are brought to him on a tray by a waiter. A cafeteria is a place for people who should have been waiters themselves, for there you carry your own tray. Also in a café you may drink beer or maybe wine. In a cafeteria only coffee or tea.'

327

'In this country you can drink only tea, wherever you go,' said the man with his arm in a sling. He put the neck of a beer bottle between his teeth and pulled off the metal cap. He spat out the cap and it rolled across the floor to Adam's feet. Adam picked up the cap and placed it on the table.

'Keep it,' the man with the sling said.

'Pay no attention to him,' the man with one thumb said. 'His hand hurts and he has no aspirins. You have some aspirins?'

'No,' Adam said.

'It is of no importance. It is only a small pain.'

'What you do in this Museum, then?' the hairy man said.

'He goes to the cafeteria to drink the tea,' the man with the sling said.

'Shuddup,' the hairy man said.

'I read books in the library there,' Adam said.

The man with only one thumb jerked it towards the ceiling. 'She has a lotta books,' he said.

'Mrs Rottingdean?' Adam said. 'It's her I wanted to see.'

'She's out,' the man with the one thumb said.

'I told him that,' the hairy man said.

'I'll come back later,' Adam said.

'You wait here,' the hairy man said. He pulled up a chair for Adam. Adam sat down slowly.

At the other end of the kitchen a door opened and the figure of a young girl appeared. She had a white face and black hair and her dress was black.

'What do you want?' said the hairy man, without looking round.

'Nothing. Who is that?' the girl said, looking at Adam.

'He's from the café,' the man with the sling said. 'You got any aspirins?'

'No, you've used them all,' the girl said.

'Then get outta here.'

The door closed.

'Bad lot,' the man with the sling said.

'I think I'll be going,' Adam said, getting to his feet.

The hairy man pushed him down with a firm pressure on his shoulder. 'You wait here,' he said.

'So you read books?' the man with the sling said to Adam.

'Yes,' Adam said.

'What kind of books? Love stories?'

'Some of them are love stories.'

'I like a good movie myself,' the hairy man said.

'He is in love with Elizabeth Taylor,' the man with one thumb said.

The hairy man blushed and twisted one leg round the other. 'She is a magnificent woman,' he muttered.

'He has seen "Cleopatra" thirty-four times,' the man with one thumb said. 'Do you think that is a record?'

'I'm sure it must be,' Adam said.

'It is not. The girls who show the seat have seen it more often.'

The man with his arm in a sling choked on his beer bottle. The beer streamed down his chin and throat and soaked his vest. 'One day you will kill me, *amigo*,' he said.

'One day I will kill Richard Burton,' the hairy man said.

'Have you any idea when Mrs Rottingdean will be back?' Adam said.

'Richard Burton would not let you,' the man with the sling said. 'I have seen him knock down bigger men than you.'

'He is no bigger than yourself,' the hairy man said.

'I believe it.'

'I have knocked down many men your size,' the hairy man said. 'I would show you but your hand is in a sling.'

'Do you not understand in the movies it is all faked?' the man with one thumb said. 'It is not Richard Burton who knocks down or is knocked down. They are like children,' he said to Adam.

'I still have one good arm,' the man with the sling said. He thumped his elbow on the table and held his forearm vertically in the air. The hairy man sat down on the other side of the table and did the same, entwining the other's fingers in his own.

'Have it your own way,' the man with one thumb said. He opened another bottle of beer.

The two men struggled to force down each other's arms on to

the table. The sinews on their bare forearms stood out in hard relief. Sweat poured from their foreheads, and formed dark patches under their armpits. The third man encouraged their efforts with a low, guttural crooning.

Adam got up from his seat and walked quietly to the door.

'Where are you going?' the man with one thumb said. The two men at the table stopped struggling and looked at him.

'I was looking for the lavatory,' Adam said.

'Through there.' The thumb gestured to the door at the other end of the kitchen.

It was a long walk between the two doors.

Adam opened and banged shut the door of the lavatory without going in. He did not want to use the lavatory. He did not want to wait for Mrs Rottingdean, supposing she existed. He just wanted to get out of the house and ride away into the fog, while he still had all his fingers. He had seen, in a film somewhere, that trial-of-strength game played with knives on the table.

A dark staircase led upwards from the basement. Adam felt his way cautiously up the stairs until his groping hands encountered a door. It yielded to a turn of the handle and Adam stepped into a carpeted hall. His first action was to close the door softly behind him. A hand-written notice on the door said, 'Keep Locked', and Adam was glad to obey: the key was in the lock. No doubt the girl he had seen in the kitchen had omitted to lock the door when she retreated. He blessed her for her forgetfulness.

He stood with his back to the door for a few moments, taking stock of his surroundings. The hall was dark and a little dingy. There was a large, heavy coatstand, and a grandfather clock with a ponderous, doleful tick. The walls were hung with large pictures of martyrs in various forms of agony: he identified St Sebastian transfixed with arrows like a pin-cushion, and St Lawrence broiling patiently on a grid-iron. While these morbid icons were consistent with what he knew of Mrs Rottingdean's religious background, they made him feel uncomfortable. He shrank from them as from something cruel and sinister. This will teach you to go whoring after unpublished manuscripts, he told himself.

Don't you wish you were snug in the British Museum, counting the words in long sentences? Or at home dandling your three lovely children on your knee – knees?

Apart from the ticking of the clock, the house seemed quite silent and deserted. There was nothing to stop him from walking down the narrow strip of threadbare carpet, opening the front door, and leaping down the steps to his scooter. Nothing except the staircase at his right, to which his back would be exposed as he walked down the hall, and the three doors to his left, anyone of which might open as he passed.

Then, suddenly, he heard the sound of music – pop music. It was faint, very distant, and he couldn't be sure whether it was carrying from some remote part of the house, or from outside. But its intimations of cheerful normalcy reassured him, and gave him courage to walk down the hall. He passed the doors to his left, one, two, three, without incident. A glance over his shoulder assured him that the stairs were unoccupied. His fingers reached out eagerly to grasp the latch of the heavy front door, and he pulled it open.

A large, middle-aged woman stood on the threshold, pointing something at his chest. Adam raised his arms in surrender but checked himself as he saw it was only a Yale key.

'Who are you?' said the woman.

'Appleby – Adam Appleby,' he gabbled.

The woman regarded him through narrowed eyes. 'That rings a faint bell.'

'You must be Mrs Rottingdean . . .'

'Yes.'

'I wrote you a letter, and you wrote me one back. About Egbert Merrymarsh.'

'Oh yes,' said Mrs Rottingdean. 'May I come in?'

Adam stepped aside to let her pass. 'You must be wondering what I'm doing in your house . . .'

'I suppose my daughter let you in?'

'No, some men downstairs – '

'It's very bad of her. I've told her never to answer the door when I'm out.'

'No, she didn't, really. These men – '

'Well, you're here anyway,' said Mrs Rottingdean, who seemed to be a little deaf. 'Won't you have some holy water?'

'I'm not thirsty, thanks.'

'I see you're not a co-religionist, Mr Appleby,' said Mrs Rottingdean, dipping her hand into a holy water stoup fixed to the wall, and crossing herself.

'Oh yes, I am,' said Adam. 'I just didn't understand . . .'

'If you'd like to sit down in here,' said Mrs Rottingdean, throwing open the door of a sitting-room, 'I'll make tea.'

The sitting-room was furnished much like the hall, with heavy, antiquated furniture and sombre religious paintings on the walls. There was a quantity of religious bric-à-brac on all the surfaces. Adam sat on the edge of a hard upright chair. He thought he heard someone pass the door which Mrs Rottingdean had closed behind him, and a few moments later he heard voices, faintly from the back of the house, but raised in anger. It sounded like Mrs Rottingdean and her daughter.

He got to his feet and prowled restlessly about the room. A human finger-bone under a glass case on the mantelpiece caused him a momentary twinge of fear: he wondered whether it had been donated by one of the troglodytes below. But a legend on the case read, 'Blessed Oliver Plunkett, Pray for us.' He went to the window and drew back the net curtains. It was quite dark outside and the street lamps glowed dully, each in an aureole of fog. The squat shape of his scooter was just visible at the kerb. That was all right, then. He turned back into the room and investigated a glass-fronted bookcase. It was locked, but he made out the titles of several of Merrymarsh's books, and other Catholic works of yesteryear: Chesterton's *The Napoleon of Notting Hill*, Belloc's *The Path to Rome*, Henry Harland's *The Cardinal's Snuff Box*, Robert Hugh Benson's *Come Rack! Come Rope!*, the *Poems* of John Gray. They looked like first editions, and he wondered whether they were autographed. A faint quiver of curiosity and excitement revived in him. In particular he was intrigued by a black box-file on the lowest shelf of the bookcase. On the faded label he could just make out the word, 'E.M. – Unpublished MS'.

Perhaps it was a good thing he had come after all. He resolved to make an impression on Mrs Rottingdean.

It was with a, for him, unwonted alacrity that our friend, hearing the tinkle of china in the hall, sprang gallantly to the door.

'I've been admiring your "things",' he said, as he assisted her with the tea-trolley.

'They're mostly my uncle's,' she said. 'But one does one's best.' She gestured vaguely to a cabinet where reliquaries statuettes and vials of Lourdes water were ranged on shelves, dim dusty devotional.

She made tea in the old, leisured way, pouring the water into the pot from a hissing brass urn.

'One lump or . . .?' she questioned.

Weighing his reply, he had time to take stock of his new friend. She wore a simple robe of soft dark material, and shoes that, diffident as he was in such matters, he would not have felt altogether out on a limb in describing as 'sensible'. A plain gold cross at her bosom was her only ornament. Her countenance, innocent of paint, was regular, reposed, righteous – the kind of face he had glimpsed a hundred times in the gloom of cathedral side-chapels, pale above pale hands knotted in beads. She met his apprehension of her like the feel of a fine old missal in the palm: clean but well-thumbed, its cover softened by use but the spine still firm and straight.

'Two,' he said boldly.

'You have a sweet tooth,' she passed it off.

But he kept her to it. 'You are very perceptive.'

'Uncle Egbert had a sweet tooth,' she went on. 'He had a weakness for chocolate éclairs after Benediction on Sundays.'

'You lived with your uncle, then?'

For some reason the question seemed to disturb her, and she fumbled with the teaspoons.

'That was a long time ago,' she said.

The memory of Merrymarsh was evidently a tender one, and it seemed as though the question of manuscripts would have to be delicately broached. He fairly rattled the small change of conversation in his pocket without lighting on a single coin that wouldn't, in the circumstances, seem too soiled and worn, too vulgarly confident of being 'hard' currency.

'Won't your daughter be joining us?' he risked at last.

The shrewd grey eyes took it in. 'She has a headache. I hope you may have another opportunity of meeting her.'

'I hope so, too,' his answer was prompt.

'Perhaps you could explain her to me, Mr Appleby. I confess I don't understand the young people of today.'

Well, he had pressed a button of sorts, at all events.

'No doubt your own mother said the same of you, once,' he ventured with a smile.

Mrs Rottingdean put down her teacup. 'Between a Catholic mother and her daughter there should be no distrust.' She seemed to square him up in the vice of this statement before tapping home her next remark: 'Are you a *practising* Catholic, Mr Appleby?'

He was caught off balance, he couldn't disguise it. She dropped her eyes and murmured, 'I apologise. One should not ask such questions.'

'Oh, I don't mind admitting it to *you*,' he reassured her, with a rueful laugh.

'You mean . . .?'

'I mean there are occasions when, coward that one is, one prefers to let people think the worst. It is the homage virtue pays to vice.'

'Ah,' was all she had to say.

He put down his teacup.

'May I give you another?'

'Please. It is delicious.'

She poured expertly, from a height. 'Virginia has had a strict upbringing. Perhaps too strict. But I have old-fashioned ideas about girls' education.'

'Virginia.' He tested the ring of it. 'That is a charming name.'

Mrs Rottingdean looked him straight in the eyes. 'She will have two thousand pounds on marriage,' she said.

That was it, then. They had touched bottom at last; and like most bottoms it was muddy and a shade disillusioning, littered

334

with the pathetic shapes of old broken things – prams, kettles and bicycle wheels. But he had to admire, as he shot back to the surface with bubbles trailing from his mouth in the form of a gay, 'Then I envy the bachelors of your acquaintance,' the brave effort with which, gasping only a little, she quickly rejoined him in the thinner element of polite conversation.

'You are married? And so young?'

'With three young children,' he rubbed it in. 'Which makes me all the more anxious, dear lady,' he went on, 'to make my fame and fortune with your generous assistance.'

'Oh, I am to be generous, am I?' she teased him.

'To a fault.'

'Ah, that is what I am afraid of.'

'How could you blame me for thinking so, after your kind letter?'

'Oh, *letters*!' Her emphasis was expressive.

'Quite. Letters,' he echoed, glancing involuntarily at the bookcase. Her eyes followed his, and they communed in silence. It took on quite a character of its own in the end, this silence, shaped by the consciousness they both had of the manifold things they, all understandingly, were *not* saying to each other.

'And if I hadn't written . . .?' she said at last.

'Oh, in *that* case . . .' His shrug conveyed, he hoped, the direness of such a hypothesis.

'You would have renounced all hopes of fame and fortune?'

'Well, no,' he admitted. 'But one must have materials.'

Mrs Rottingdean poured herself a second cup of tea and slowly stirred the cream into it. 'And what do you do with "materials" when you get them?'

'Read them, first. Then, if, as one always hopes, they turn out to be of interest, write about them. Perhaps even publish them.'

'And what are your criteria of "interest"?'

It was his turn to drop into directness. 'Well, I can't for instance imagine that anything that threw light on Egbert Merrymarsh and his circle would lack that quality.'

He leaned back in his chair and crossed his legs with a casualness that was not altogether unstudied. Mrs Rottingdean scrutinised him for a moment, then rose to her feet. She took a key from the mantelpiece and went to the bookcase. She returned with the black box-file, which she placed on his lap.

'There you are, Mr Appleby,' she said. 'That contains all the unpublished writings of my uncle that I possess. You can have them for two hundred and fifty pounds. I won't take a penny less.'

Adam sat dejectedly in his chair, a thick manuscript open on his lap. He had long since abandoned reading it. From time to time the sum of money Mrs Rottingdean had mentioned returned to his mind and forced an incredulous snort of derision from his nostrils.

The black box-file had proved to contain a single bulky manuscript and a sheaf of letters from publishers explaining, with various degrees of rudeness, that they could not undertake publication. On the bottom of one of these letters, from a respectable Catholic house, was a note in Merrymarsh's sprawling hand: *More evidence of the Jewish-Masonic conspiracy against my work.*

The manuscript itself was a full-length book entitled *Lay Sermons and Private Prayers.* Adam had got as far as the sermon on Purity.

'When I was a lad at school,' it began, 'we were taught religious instruction by a holy old priest called Father Bonaventure. Father Bonaventure wasn't the greatest theologian in Christendom; but he knew his catechism and he had a great devotion to Our Lady, and that was worth a thousand arguments to our young, unformed minds.

He based his moral instruction on the Ten Commandments, which he went through one by one. But when he reached the Sixth, "Thou shalt not commit adultery," he would say, "I'll deal with that when I come to the Ninth Commandment." And when he came to the Ninth, "Thou shalt not covet thy neighbour's wife," he would say, "I'll deal with that when I come back to the Sixth Commandment."

Some of the boys used to laugh at Father Bonaventure on this account; but it seems to me now, looking back gratefully to my schooldays, that old Father Bonaventure gave us the best instruction on purity that was ever given. For what was his artless evasion of the sixth and ninth commandments but *purity in action?* And to speak the truth, there were few boys in that class, even among those who laughed at their old teacher, who were not secretly relieved that purity, the shyest and tenderest of virtues, was not dragged roughly out into the arena of public discussion.

We were, no doubt, a rough and ready set of fellows. Our collars were not always clean, our prep was not always faultless, and we were not over-scrupulous in respecting the rights of private property, particularly where apple orchards were concerned. But on one score we needed no correction; and if a newcomer to the school let a smutty word fall from his lips, or a lewd book from his pocket, he was soundly kicked for his pains, and was all the better for it. Talk about purity, it might be said at the risk of appearing paradoxical, begets impurity. It puts ideas into young heads which they would be better without. And after all, the talk is unnecessary. No one in his right body needs to be told that short skirts and mixed bathing are an offence against purity; not to mention the novels of Mr Lawrence, the plays of Mr Shaw, or the pamphlets of Dr Stopes in which the modern ideal of the Unholy Family is so graphically adumbrated . . .'

At the end of the sermon, as at the end of all the other pieces in the book, was a rhymed prayer:

> *You who made us pure as children*
> *Keep us pure in adulthood.*
> *Let the beauty of creation*
> *Be not a snare but source of good . . .*

It was at this point that Adam had stopped reading. He tried to cheer himself up by entertaining some impure thoughts, but the circumstances were not congenial. He was locked in the room for one thing, and it made him restive. 'You won't mind me taking this precaution, will you?' Mrs Rottingdean had told, rather than asked him when she left him alone with the manuscript. 'I have to go out, and I don't believe in taking risks with valuable literary documents.' Valuable! No one in their senses would give two hundred and fifty pence for this garbage. One or two of Merrymarsh's books had a certain period charm, a vein of puckish whimsy. But this . . .

He looked at his watch: a quarter past five. If Mrs Rottingdean did not return soon he would be late for the sherry party. He went to the window and pushed experimentally at the sash, but it was stuck. In any case it was a long drop down to the area, and he had no desire to leave by that route.

He heard footsteps in the hall and scuttled back to his seat. As the key turned in the lock he picked up the manuscript and rehearsed the polite speech in which he planned to return the manuscript to its owner and excuse himself from lingering any longer in the house. But the person who entered was not Mrs Rottingdean. It was the girl he had glimpsed in the kitchen.

'Hallo,' she said.

'Hallo,' said Adam.

The girl leaned against the door and appraised him with a slow, sensual smile. She looked about nineteen, but was probably younger. She was pretty in a pale, neglected kind of way, and her figure, eloquently revealed by a black vee-necked sweater and tight skirt, was agreeably contoured.

'Do you know who I am?' she said.

'You must be Virginia.'

The girl sat down on a sofa opposite Adam and crossed her legs. 'D'you happen to have a cigarette?'

'Sorry. I don't smoke.' Something made him add, as if in mitigation, 'I gave it up.'

'Scared of cancer?'

'No, I just couldn't afford it.'

'What did Mother tell you about me?'

'Nothing much.'

'She thinks I'm wild and ungovernable. What's your name?'

'Adam.'

'D'you think I have nice breasts, Adam?'

'Yes,' he said truthfully.

'You can touch them if you like.' She patted the sofa invitingly.

Adam swallowed. 'I see what your mother means.'

Virginia giggled. 'What did she lock you up for? She's a great one for locking people up.'

'I don't really know. But since you've so kindly released me . . .' He stood up and glanced at his watch.

'Oh, don't go!'

'I'm afraid I must.'

Virginia danced to the door, locked it on the inside, and slipped the key inside the neck of her sweater. Then she resumed her place on the sofa, tucking up her legs. Adam sat down again.

'What did you do that for?'

'Can't you guess?'

'I'd rather not.'

Virginia uncoiled her legs and stretched out languorously on the sofa. 'I'm determined to seduce you, so you might as well resign yourself.'

'Please open the door,' he begged. 'Your mother may come back at any moment.'

Virginia shot him an eager glance. 'Is that your only objection?'

'Of course it isn't. For one thing, I have a wife and three children.'

'Good,' said Virginia. 'I like experienced men.'

Adam got up and tried the window sash again. 'It doesn't open,' said Virginia. 'Why did you come here?'

'You may well ask,' said Adam. 'Originally it was because I was interested in the writings of your great-uncle.'

Virginia wrinkled her brow. 'Great-uncle?'

'Your mother's Uncle Egbert.'

'Oh, Egbert Merrymarsh! Mother's lover. Did she tell you he was her uncle?'

'Your mother's *what*?'

'Mother's lover. He seduced her when she was twenty. That's why she's been so strict with me.'

Adam laughed.

'No, cross my heart, it's true.'

'And I suppose you're the illegitimate daughter. How romantic!'

''Course not, silly. He died years before I was born.'

Adam stood over the recumbent girl and stared into her eyes. They were like pools of black coffee, dark but transparent, and they did not waver. 'You're a good actress,' he said at last. 'If I hadn't been reading one of Merrymarsh's books for the last half-hour, I might have been taken in.'

'What have you been reading, then?'

He prodded the manuscript, which was lying on the floor, with his toe. 'This. *Lay Sermons and Private Prayers.*'

'Oh, *that* tripe.'

'Have you read it?'

'She tried to make me, once. *I* could show you something really interesting by him.'

'What?'

'Something *really* interesting.' She chuckled and wriggled her bottom in the sofa cushions.

He turned away. 'I've lost all interest in Merrymarsh anyway.' He went to the door and tested the lock. It was firm.

'Does your wife have frequent orgasms?' said Virginia.

'That's none of your business.'

'You're blushing. Don't you believe in the frank discussion of sex?'

'If you must know,' he said in exasperation, 'we don't have frequent intercourse.'

'But that's awful! Don't you love her any more?'

'We happen to be Catholics, that's all.'

'You mean you believe all that nonsense about birth control?'

'I'm not sure I believe it, but I practise it. Look, are you going to let me out, or aren't you?'

'You've only got to take the key.'

Setting his countenance grimly, he strode across the floor to the couch, and, with a gesture as brusque and clinical as he could manage, inserted his hand under Virginia's sweater. She did not flinch, but Adam did when he discovered that she was not wearing a brassière. He withdrew his keyless hand, going hot and cold by turns. 'You've moved it,' he accused her.

'You have nice soft hands, Adam,' she said.

'Please give me the key. Aren't you afraid of what your mother will say when she comes back and finds you locked in here with me?'

'No. I have a hold over her because I know her past.'

Adam paced about the room. If only he could trip her up in some part of this ridiculous story, he felt, he might be able to bully her into letting him out.

'If that's the case, why don't you leave home – since you evidently don't see eye to eye with your mother?'

'She has a hold over *me*. She has some money in trust for me if I marry with her consent.'

'From Egbert Merrymarsh?'

'No, how could it be, silly? From my father. He died about ten years ago.'

Adam sat down. She was beginning to convince him, and a treacherous pulse of excitement and curiosity began to beat again at the back of his mind. He scented a scandal that would send a gratifying shock through certain quarters of the Catholic and literary worlds.

'Supposing all this about your mother's past is true, how did you discover it?'

'I found some letters from Merrymarsh to Mother. They're very passionate. She must have been a different person.'

'How old was Merrymarsh then?'

'I don't know. Quite old – about forty-five, maybe even more. Would you believe it – he was a virgin until then.'

'Are these letters the "something interesting" you mentioned just now?'

'No, I meant the book.'

'The book?'

'Yes, there was a book – in handwriting, you know, not a proper book. One day I saw Mother burning a lot of papers in the cellar, and while her back was turned I managed to salvage the book and a bundle of letters.'

341

'What kind of a book is it?'

'Well, it's a sort of novel, written like a journal. It's really the story of his affair with Mother, with just the names changed. It's hot stuff, as we used to say at school.'

'Hot stuff?'

'It doesn't leave anything to the imagination,' said Virginia, with a leer.

'This is fantastic,' said Adam. 'Can I see the book?'

Virginia pondered, then shook her head. 'Not now, Mother will be back at any minute. Can you come back later tonight?'

'Just a quick glance,' he urged.

She shook her head again. 'No, I've hidden it, and it'll take some time to get out. Besides, I'm not going to all this trouble for nothing, Adam.' She extruded the tip of a pink, kittenish tongue and moistened her lips suggestively.

'Oh,' said Adam.

Simultaneously they became aware of an engine throbbing in the street outside.

'That's Mother's taxi,' said Virginia, jumping up.

'Oh God,' said Adam, following suit.

Virginia slipped a hand down the front of her skirt and produced the key. 'Next time you'll know where to look.' She went to the door and unlocked it. 'I'll have to lock you in again. See you tonight.'

'But how shall I manage it?'

'That's your problem, Adam.'

He tugged at her sleeve. 'Before you go – there's one question I must ask you. Who are those men downstairs?'

'Butchers,' was the cryptic reply. She slipped through the door, and he heard the key turn in the lock.

EIGHT

. . . studious and curious persons . . .
Users of the British Museum, as defined by the act of 1753.

You who made us pure as children,
Keep us pure in adulthood . . .

Adam, driving blind through the fog, twisted the throttle of his
scooter to try and drown the syllables which droned with madden-
ing persistence in his head. The machine shuddered and lurched
forward, adding a generous quota of fumes to the already foul
atmosphere. The noise was satisfactory, but the speed perilous.
He swerved violently to avoid a lorry abandoned by its driver. A
little later a bone-shaking bump informed him that he had been
travelling on the pavement. He overtook a line of cars following
each other's tail lights at a crawl, and exchanged startled glances
with the policeman who was leading the caravan on a motor-
cycle.

Let the beauty of creation
Be not a snare but source of good.

It was no use. He eased back the throttle and chugged at a more
sedate speed down what he hoped was the Edgware Road.

He did not admit for a moment that Merrymarsh's imbecile
prayer had any message for him. It was true that he had arranged
with Mrs Rottingdean to return later that evening on the pretext
that he had not finished reading the manuscript, excusing himself
in the meantime by reference to the sherry party. But that had
been an impulsive action, performed under the pressure of flus-
tering circumstances. Now that he had escaped from that

enchanted house of locked doors and inscrutable behaviour, he would not be fool enough to return. Or if, by any chance, he should return, he would contrive to lay his hands on the evidence of Merrymarsh's hidden life without embarking on a hidden life of his own with Virginia.

Yet, he had to acknowledge, it was a novel and not altogether disagreeable experience to have a nubile young woman throw herself at him with such wanton abandon. Before he had met Barbara, Adam's sexual experience had stopped short at holding the sticky hands of convent girls in the cinema, and perhaps coaxing from them afterwards a single tight-lipped kiss. The physical side of his long courtship of Barbara had been a tortured, intense affair of endless debate and limited action, an extended and nerve-racking exercise in erotic brinkmanship, marked by occasional skirmishes that were never, in the end, allowed to develop into major conflagrations. When they finally married they were clumsy, inexperienced lovers, and by the time they got the hang of it and began to enjoy themselves Barbara was six months pregnant. Ever since, pregnancy, actual or fearfully anticipated, had been a familiar attendant on their love-making. Adam had long resigned himself to this fate. The experience of unbridled sexuality, the casual, unpremeditated copulation unembarrassed by emotional ties or practical consequences – the kind of thing that happened, he understood, between strangers at wild student parties, or to youthful electricians summoned to suburban villas on warm spring afternoons – this was not for him. He knew it only at second hand, passed to him in fragments of overheard conversation in bar or barrack room. *I tell you she had her belt and stockings off before I could close the door . . .! 'What's the matter?' she says. 'Nothing,' I says, 'I'm just looking for me screwdriver.' 'I bet you're good at screwing,' she says . . .*

Now, it seemed, he had only to stretch out his hand to take such a plum for himself.

A precise tactile memory of Virginia's bare breast disturbed him with its sudden force, and he gripped the handle-bars tightly. He tried to drive away temptation by thinking about Barbara; but she rose up in his imagination encumbered by children, a thermometer jutting from her mouth, a distracted frown wrinkling her brow.

You who made us pure as children . . .

He knew now why he couldn't get that wretched doggerel out of his mind: its rhythm exactly synchronised with the new knock that had developed in his engine.

The sherry party was in full swing by the time Adam arrived. Usually, on such occasions, the staff began drifting away just as the first ice began to melt; but tonight everyone seemed to have decided that in view of the fog it was pointless trying to get home in the rush-hour, so one might as well make a night of it. The single, fortunate, exception to this rule had been the bar-steward, who had departed leaving behind him a generous quantity of filled glasses. Adam, who had seldom felt so grievously in need of a drink, made a beeline for this inviting display.

The post-graduate sherry party was a regular feature of the first term of the academic year, designed to introduce students to staff and to each other. For many it was hail and farewell, since the Department did not have the resources to mount a proper graduate programme, and in any case espoused the traditional belief that research was a lonely and eremitic occupation, a test of character rather than learning, which might be vitiated by excessive human contact. As if they sensed this the new post-graduates, particularly those from overseas, roamed the floor eagerly accosting the senior guests, resolved to cram a whole year's sociability into one brief evening, As he left the bar with his first sherry, Adam was snapped up by a cruising Indian.

'Good evening. My name is Alibai.'

'Hallo. Mine's Appleby,' said Adam. Mr Alibai extended his hand and Adam shook it.

'How do you do,' said Mr Alibai.

'How do you do,' said Adam, who knew what was expected of him.

'You are a Professor at the University?'

'No, I'm a post-graduate.'

'I also. I am to write a thesis on Shani Hodder. You are acquainted with her work?'

'No, who is she?'

Mr Alibai looked dejected. 'I have not met a single person who has heard of Shani Hodder.'

'That happens to all of us,' said Adam. 'Have another sherry?'

'No thank you. I do not drink alcohol, and the fruit juices give the diarrhoea.'

'Well, excuse me. I'm terribly thirsty.' Adam pushed his was back to the bar. He drank two more dry sherries very quickly. His stomach, which was empty, made a noise like old plumbing. He looked around for food, but could only find a plate thinly covered with the crumbs of potato chips. These he ate greedily, picking them up on the moistened tips of his fingers. At the other side of the room he saw Camel, who waved. Adam gave him a cold stare and turned his back. He found himself face to face with a bald-headed man in a pale striped suit.

'What do you think of anus?' said the man.

'I beg your pardon?'

'The novelist, Kingsley Anus,' said the man impatiently.

'Oh, yes. I like his work. There are times when I think I belong to him more than to any of the others.'

'Please?' said the man, frowning.

'Well, you see, I have this theory,' Adam, who had just thought of it, said expansively. 'Has it ever occurred to you how novelists are *using up* experience at a dangerous rate? No, I see it hasn't. Well, then, consider that before the novel emerged as the dominant literary form, narrative literature dealt only with the extraordinary or the allegorical – with kings and queens, giants and dragons, sublime virtue and diabolic evil. There was no risk of confusing that sort of thing with life, of course. But as soon as the novel got going, you might pick up a book at any time and read about an ordinary chap called Joe Smith doing just the sort of things you did yourself. Now, I know what you're going to say – you're going to say that the novelist still has to invent a lot. But that's just the point: there've been such a fantastic number

346

of novels written in the last couple of centuries that they've just about exhausted the possibilities of life. So all of us, you see, are really enacting events that have already been written about in some novel or other. Of course, most people don't realise this – they fondly imagine that their little lives are unique . . . Just as well, too, because when you *do* tumble to it, the effect is very disturbing.'

'Bravo!' said Camel, over Adam's shoulder. Adam ignored him, and eagerly searched the face of the bald-headed man for some response to his own remarks.

'Would you say,' said the man at length, 'that Anus is superior or inferior to C. P. Slow?'

'I don't know that you can compare them,' said Adam wearily.

'I have to: they are the only British novelists I have read.'

'Where have you been all the afternoon?' said Camel.

'I'm not talking to you,' said Adam, going to the bar and taking another sherry.

Camel followed him. 'What have I done?'

The dry sherry tasted like medicine. He put it down half-finished and tried a sweet one. 'You betrayed me to that man in the Museum.'

'What are you talking about?'

The sweet sherry tasted better, but he was conscious of two quite different sensations in his stomach. 'When that man was after me, you put him on my track. I *saw* you.'

It took a long time before Camel finally identified the man.

'Oh, *him*! He just had an application slip you'd filled in wrongly.'

Adam tried to look Camel straight in the eyes, but Camel's face kept bobbing about. 'Are you telling the truth?' he demanded.

'Of course I am. What did you think he wanted?'

'I thought he wanted to arrest me for raising the fire alarm.'

'Did you? Raise the fire alarm, I mean?' said Camel with wide eyes.

'Yes. No. I don't know.' He told Camel the whole story.

'I don't think you've anything to worry about,' said Camel in the end. 'No one's been asking questions about you. Except Barbara.'

'Barbara?'

'Yes, she came to the Museum, not long after you shot off.'

'I *thought* I saw her . . . What on earth did she want?'

'It seems they announced on the radio, a bit prematurely, that there was a fire in the Museum, and she wanted to find out if you were all right.'

'Poor Barbara. Was she terribly worried?'

'Well, not when she got there, of course. When she sent in a message for you I went out and took her and the kids for a cup of tea.'

Adam's tear-ducts pricked him. He gulped another sweet sherry. 'Camel, you're a good friend,' he whimpered. 'And Barbara is a good wife. I'm not worthy of either of you.'

'I'm afraid the confessor came out in me again,' said Camel, with a surprising and rather charming blush. 'Barbara told me she was afraid she was pregnant again.'

'What shall I do?' Adam appealed to him. 'How shall I house it? clothe it? feed it?'

'I was telling Barbara, I think you ought to throw yourself on the mercy of the Department – use this to twist their arm over the job situation.'

'D'you think it would do any good?'

'You have nothing to lose. Listen, do you know how Bane got his first promotion? He was telling me the other day: he'd been an assistant lecturer for six years without murmuring when one day his tank burst and he couldn't pay the plumber. He rushed straight into Howells' room and demanded promotion. Howells made him up on the spot and back-dated his pay six months. Seems it had just slipped his mind.'

'Good Lord,' said Adam.

'Incidentally, now Bane has got this new Chair, there should be a vacancy coming up.'

'There's the Prof in the corner,' said Adam, straightening his tie.

'I shouldn't go directly to him,' said Camel. 'Go through Briggs, who knows you better. He has the Prof's ear too.'

'I don't know that he has, any more,' said Adam, remembering the interview at lunch time. 'I think Bane is the coming man now.'

'Well, please yourself,' said Camel.

Adam felt a tug at his sleeve. It was the bald-headed man again.

'I told a lie,' he said. 'I have also read the work of John Bane.'

'Which John Bane?' said Adam carefully. 'The John Bane who wrote *Room at the Top*, or the John Bane who wrote *Hurry on Down?*'

'*The* John Bane,' said the man, frowning.

'Someone taking my name in vain?' boomed the Professor of Absurdist Drama, swooping down on them.

'In bane,' Adam quipped, and laughed immoderately.

The professor ignored him. 'Hallo, Camel,' he said. 'How's the research going?' Bane was Camel's current supervisor, the original one having died in office.

Camel took out his pipe, and began stuffing it with tobacco. 'I'm working on a new interpretation of *The Ambassadors*,' he said.

'Oh?' said Bane, tweaking the wings of his bow tie. He was in full fig this evening, wearing a corduroy jacket with wales so wide and deep that Adam imagined they must have a special purpose, like the indentations of snow-tyres.

'You remember how Strether refuses to tell Maria Gostrey the nature of the manufactured article on which the Newsome fortune is based?'

'I do indeed,' said Bane. Adam could not resist stroking the sleeve of his jacket, but the professor shook his hand off irritably.

'And you recall that James, quite typically, refuses to tell *us* what it is?' Camel went on. Bane nodded, and removed himself from Adam's reach. People nearby pricked up their ears and began to drift towards Camel, who was always a draw. 'Strether describes it as a "small, trivial, rather ridiculous object of the commonest use," but "wanting in dignity." Scholars have argued for years about what it could be.' Camel paused to light his pipe, holding his audience in suspense. 'Well, I'm convinced that it was a chamber pot,' he said at last.

The girls among his listeners giggled and nudged each other. This was what they had come to hear.

'Once you see it, it becomes a symbol as important as the bowl in *The Golden Bowl*,' said Camel.

'Very interesting,' said Bane. 'And what do you think, Mr Appleby?'

'I think it was contraceptives,' said Adam.

There was a little shocked inspiration of breath among the girls. Bane flushed and stalked away. Camel took Adam to one side.

'I think you'd better stick to Briggs,' he said.

'What's wrong?' Adam complained. 'Isn't everyone entitled to his *idée fixe*? Anyway, you can't describe a chamber pot as small.'

'Bane thought you were getting at him,' said Camel. 'He was the one who stopped the College barber selling French letters.'

'Oh well,' said Adam. He took a medium sherry this time, hoping to effect some kind of reconciliation between the two sensations in his stomach.

'Hallo, Appleby.' It was Briggs. 'How are things with you?'

'Terrible,' Adam said. Camel beat a tactful retreat.

'Oh, I'm sorry to hear that. Blocked on the thesis?'

'Blocked on everything,' said Adam. 'Except paternity. My wife's going to have another baby.'

'Oh, congratulations. Your first?'

'No, our fourth.'

Briggs looked grave.

'I'm desperate,' Adam said. 'I can't get on with my work because I'm worrying all the time about my family. Our flat is full of beds already and I have nowhere to study. The children need new shoes and the electricity may be cut off at any moment. Yesterday the youngest child developed a rash: we think it's rickets.'

'Dear me,' said Briggs. 'This is very distressing.' He bit his lips and pulled on the lobes of his ears.

Adam raised his glass and drained it dramatically. 'This is my farewell to the academic life,' he said. 'Tomorrow I shall burn all my notes and take a job on the buses.'

'No, no, you mustn't be so impulsive,' said Briggs. 'I'll see what I can do.'

'What I need is a job,' said Adam firmly.

'I'll see what I can do,' Briggs repeated. 'Don't do anything rash.'

Adam watched him push his way through the throng towards Howells. As was his custom on such occasions, the Head of Department sat in a corner of the room with his back to the company, drinking with his constant companions, the two technicians who operated the professor's pride and joy, a computer for making concordances. Only senior members of staff generally ventured to approach this tiny court. Occasionally they would introduce some exceptionally promising post-graduate, but there were many students present who, when they eventually left the Department with their Ph.D's, would only be able to say, with Moses, that they had seen the back parts of their Professor.

'I have decided to change the subject of my thesis,' said a voice at Adam's right ear. It was Mr Alibai.

'I'm sure you're wise,' said Adam. 'I couldn't see much future in Shani Hodder. Who was she, by the way?'

'She was an Anglo-Indian novelist. I should be most grateful if you would kindly suggest an alternative.'

'What about Egbert Merrymarsh?' said Adam. 'I could put you on to some interesting unpublished stuff of his.' Mr Alibai looked blank. 'He was a minor Catholic novelist and essayist,' Adam explained.

'I would prefer someone with Indian connections,' said Mr Alibai.

'Ah, there you have me,' Adam sighed.

'Or some unquestionably major figure. I thought the symbolism of D. H. Lawrence . . .'

'I have a feeling it's been done,' said Adam.

'Could I have a word with you, Appleby?'

Briggs was back again. He drew Adam aside, conspiratorially.

'There *will* be a vacancy coming up in the Department, as it happens,' he murmured. 'I've spoken to the Prof and he seemed quite favourably disposed.'

'That's wonderful,' said Adam. 'I didn't even know he knew who I was.'

'I put in a strong plea on the grounds of your . . . personal circumstances,' said Briggs. 'But there's no possibility of starting before next October.'

'Well, I can just about hang on till then,' said Adam. 'I can't thank you enough.'

'Don't go away,' said Briggs. 'I'll try to find an opportunity of getting him to speak to you.'

'Well?' said Camel, coming up as Briggs sloped off.

'It's unbelievable,' said Adam. 'Briggs seems to think that he's got me the job.'

'Good,' said Camel. 'I told you it was worth a try.'

Adam took another medium sherry by way of celebration.

'All shall be well and all manner of things shall be well,' he intoned happily. There was no need for him to return to the devious paths of Bayswater. He could forget the whole upsetting episode, settle down comfortably to work on his thesis again, and learn to be a kind and understanding husband. 'I'm going to phone Barbara,' he told Camel.

It took him a long time to get to the door. The sherry glass he held in his extended hand seemed, like a vain and overbearing dancing partner, to lead him through a series of involved looping movements, sudden changes of direction, rapid shuffles and dizzying spins. On all sides a babble of academic conversation dinned in his ears.

'My subject is the long poem in the nineteenth century . . .'

'Once you start looking for Freudian symbols . . .'

'This book on Browning . . .'

'Poe was quite right. It *is* a contradiction in terms . . .'

' . . . the diphthong in East Anglian dialects . . .'

' . . . everything's either round and hollow or long and pointed, when you come to think about it . . .'

'. . . is it called *The Bow and the Lyre* or *The Beau and the Liar* . . .?'

'So that's what *op. cit.* means !'

'. . . sort of *eeeow* . . .'

'. . . hasn't published a thing . . .'

'. . . "eighteenth-century gusto," and it came out "eighteenth-century gas-stove" . . .'

'No, like this: *eeeow* . . .'

'. . . waited three years for something to appear in *Notes and Queries* . . .'

'If it had been "*nineteenth*-century gas-stove" I might have got away with it . . .'

'. . . then the editors changed and they sent it back . . .'

'I thought it was short for "opposite" . . .'

'. . . *eeeow* . . .'

Three of the young men present were writing academic novels of manners. From time to time they detached themselves from the main group of guests and retired to a corner to jot down observations and witty remarks in little notebooks. Adam noticed one of them looking over the shoulders of the other two, and copying. He felt a tug at his sleeve.

'Mormon Nailer – ' the bald-headed man began.

'Sorry,' said Adam. 'I have to make a phone call.'

A public phone was fixed to the wall of the corridor just outside the room in which the party was being held. Its little helmet of sound-proofing scarcely diminished the roar of conversation, and Adam held a finger in his left ear as he waited for Barbara to answer the phone. When she did so, her voice was unexpectedly sprightly.

'Hallo, darling,' she said. 'It's nice to hear your voice. I thought I was a widow this afternoon.'

'So I hear. I'm sorry I missed you.'

'Never mind, Camel was sweet and gave us tea. Where were you all the afternoon, anyway?'

'Oh, er, I was out . . . researching. Listen, I have good news.'

'What kind of research?'

'It's a long story. I'll tell you later. How are you feeling?'

'I'm feeling much better.'

'Better?' he echoed her uneasily.

'Yes, I went over the charts again and I convinced myself we made a mistake. I felt better immediately. Adam, I'm sure I'm not pregnant.'

'Nonsense!' he shouted. 'Of course you're pregnant!' A couple who were leaving the party gave him odd looks as they passed.

'What do you mean, Adam?'

'I mean, you're so long overdue, and felt sick this morning,' he continued, in more controlled tones. 'Sure signs.'

'But I ate my breakfast in the end.'

'Yes, but only marmalade. I distinctly remember it was only marmalade. It was a craving.'

'Adam, you sound as if you *wanted* me to be pregnant.'

'I do, I do,' he moaned. 'I've just talked Briggs into getting me a job in the Department. But he's only doing it because he thinks we're going to have another baby!'

'Oh,' said Barbara.

'That was my good news,' he said bitterly.

Barbara was silent for a few moments. Then she said, 'Well, look, if it's absolutely essential for us to have another baby to get this job, we can easily arrange it.'

He considered the idea for a few moments, and found it repellent. 'No,' he said. 'Falling for another baby and getting a job in consequence is a pleasant surprise. But having to conceive another baby to get a job is quite another matter. No job is worth it.'

'I agree,' said Barbara. 'But what will you do?'

'I'll just have to bluff it out,' said Adam. 'I can always say you had a miscarriage, I suppose.'

When Adam returned to the party he found Camel talking to Pond.

'Hallo, what are you doing here?' he said.

'Camel invited me to drop in,' said Pond. 'Lot of wogs you have here.'

Adam looked round nervously for Mr Alibai and located him

on the other side of the room. The Indian interpreted his look as a summons, and came over.

'You have a subject for me?' he said eagerly.

'No, but I want you to meet Mr Pond,' said Adam. 'He is a great expert on Anglo-Indian relations.'

'I am most honoured,' said Mr Alibai, extending his hand to Pond. 'How do you do?'

Adam drew Camel aside. 'Look, it seems Barbara may not be pregnant after all.'

'Congratulations,' said Camel.

'Yes, but what shall I do about this job?'

'Say nothing, old chap. If you have to show up with four children on occasion, you can always borrow one.'

'Ah, there you are, Appleby,' said Briggs. 'The Prof would like to have a word with you.'

Camel gave Adam an encouraging pat on the shoulder, which Briggs observed suspiciously. 'I hope you haven't been talking about this matter to anyone, Appleby,' he said, as he steered Adam across the floor. 'There are all kinds of forces at play in the academic world, as you will discover for yourself. Discretion is vital. Mum's the word.'

Adam fought back an urge to confess that mum wasn't the word. He stood behind Howells' broad back, drymouthed and trembling, as Briggs stooped to whisper in the professor's ear. Howells turned his big, bloodshot eyes upon Adam.

'It's Appleby I wanted to see,' he said to Briggs.

'This *is* Mr Appleby, Prof.'

'No, Briggs. This is Camel.'

'I assure you – '

'It's Appleby I want, Briggs. The one who's working on sewage in the nineteenth century or some such thing. Bright man – Bane told me about him. You've got them mixed up.' He gave a short, barking laugh, and turned back to his cronies. 'Tell Appleby I want to see him,' he threw over his shoulder.

'I'll tell him,' said Adam, speaking for the first time.

'I'm sorry,' said Briggs, as they walked away. 'There seems to have been a misunderstanding.'

'Forget it,' said Adam.

Briggs bit his lip and pulled violently on the lobes of his ears. 'Someone I could mention has been intriguing behind my back,' he muttered.

Adam went over to Camel. 'Well?' said Camel.

'Congratulations,' said Adam.

Camel raised his eyebrows.

'Howells wants to see you.'

'Me?'

'Your name is Appleby, isn't it?'

'What are you talking about?'

'You're writing a thesis on sanitation in Victorian fiction?'

'You know I am . . .'

'Well, you've got a job. Howells is waiting to bestow it on you.'

Camel lolloped across the room, pausing occasionally to cast a quizzical, distrustful glance at Adam. Adam waved him on impatiently. He turned back to the bar, where Pond was discoursing to Mr Alibai with every sign of friendly animation.

'Well, we've sorted out Mr Alibai's little problem,' Pond said. 'He's going to work on the influence of the *Kama Sutra* on contemporary fiction.'

'I envy you,' said Adam to Mr Alibai, who gave a proud, shy smile.

'I am most indebted . . .' he murmured.

'Nice chap,' said Pond, when final handshakes had been exchanged. 'He's going to enrol in my Advanced English Course.'

'But he doesn't need it.'

'No, he doesn't, but he seems struck on me. It's a fatal gift I have. By the way, Adam, I was pulling your leg about my limp at lunch time.'

'Oh?'

'Yes, you see Sally and I sometimes take a shower together, and – '

'Telephone for you, Adam,' said someone.

'Hallo? Is that you, Adam?'

'Don't tell me, let me guess,' said Adam. 'You feel pregnant again.'

'How did you know?'

'It had to be that. The job has fallen through.'

'Oh, *darling*! And I thought you'd be pleased. Why?'

The party was breaking up at last, and the corridor was full of noisy people putting on hats and coats. Adam turned a stony gaze upon them, holding his finger to his ear in the attitude of a man about to commit suicide.

'Can't tell you now. Later.'

'How much later, Adam? Are you coming home now?'

'I have to go to the Museum to pick up my things.'

'But it's closed by now.'

'No, it's open late tonight.'

'Well, you're not going to stay there, are you?'

'Yes,' he said on a sudden impulse. 'Yes, I think I'll stay and do some work. Don't wait up for me.'

He put down the receiver quickly, before Barbara could bring any pathos or moral suasion to bear on him. He had reached the moment of decision, and he did not wish to be swayed from his purpose. He would return to Bayswater. He would get his hands on Merrymarsh's scandalous confessions, and with them he would deal a swingeing blow at the literary establishment, at academe, at Catholicism, at fate. He would publish his findings to the world, and leap to fame or perdition in a blaze of notoriety.

As he walked unsteadily away from the phone, the people in the corridor falling back before him, he thought of himself as a man set apart by a dangerous quest. For what was that house in Bayswater, dismal of aspect and shrouded in fog, with its mad, key-rattling old queen, raven-haired, honey-tongued daughter, and murderous minions insecurely pent in the dungeon below, but a Castle Perilous from which, mounted on his trusty scooter, he, intrepid Sir Adam, sought to snatch the unholy grail of Egbert Merrymarsh's scrofulous novel? If the success of this quest, contrary to the old story, necessitated his fall from grace in the arms of the seductive maiden, then so much the better. He had had enough of continence.

Adam swaggered through the doorway intent on a final sherry. He had omitted, however, to remove his finger from his ear. His projecting elbow struck the door jamb, and this trivial collision was enough, it seemed, to level him to the floor. Several departing guests trod on him before Camel and Pond came to the rescue.

NINE

Human Fertility, formerly the Journal of Contraception.
Item in the British Museum Catalogue.

There was only one shop open in the section of the Edgware Road where Adam had parked his scooter. The window was brightly lit, but it was invisible from a distance of twelve paces on either side. Adam was quite sure of this figure because he had walked past the shop about twenty-five times so far.

He had sobered up considerably since leaving the sherry party. Camel and Pond had carried him to the Gents and put his head under a cold tap. Then they had taken him to a coffee bar and made him consume a cheese sandwich and three cups of bitter black espresso. Their efforts had been kindly meant, but he rather wished they hadn't done their work so thoroughly; in the process he had mislaid that happy mood of careless confidence in which his resolution to return to Bayswater had been formed. He struggled in vain to recover the image of himself as a swashbuckling adventurer, bent single-mindedly on his purpose, but prepared to accept imperturbably whatever willing female flesh chance threw in his path. All day circumstances had cracked the whip and urged him through a bewildering variety of hoops, but so far he had not been at a loss for a style in which to negotiate them. Now, when he most needed to assume a ready-made role, the knack seemed to have deserted him. He was alone with himself again, the old Adam, a bare forked animal with his own peculiar moral problem.

There were, of course, plenty of unfaithful husbands in literature: modern fiction, in particular, might be described as a compendium of advice on the conduct of adultery. But he couldn't, off-hand, recall one who, distracted and frustrated by the complexities of the married relation, had sought relief in the willing arms of another woman only to find himself trammelled by the very same absurd scruples from which he had fled.

He paused yet again in front of the shop window. The defective neon sign above it flickered dimly in the fog: URGICAL GO DS. He had need of the urgical gods – he longed to be possessed by the spirit of Dionysian abandon; but this shrine did not throw him into a transport of profane joy. On the contrary, he eyed the contents of the window with feelings of disquiet and repugnance. *Sexual Happiness Without Fear* was the title of one of the books for sale. But it was not only the two flanking volumes, *The History of Flagellation* and *Varieties of Venereal Disease*, which gave the cheerfulness of the first title a forced and hollow note. It was also the trusses, elastic stockings and male corsets, displayed on pink plastic limbs that were oddly like the gruesome votive objects, signifying cures, that hung in the side-chapels of Spanish churches. Still more it was the abundance of little boxes, jars and packets, these guaranteeing a spectacular development of the bust, those offering new hope to the older man, others more enigmatically labelled, containing, as he knew, the instruments of carefree pleasure, but bearing trade names suggestive of medicaments. The whole display was decidedly detumescent in effect, projecting a vision of sexuality as a universal illness, its sufferers crippled hypochondriacs, trussed and bandaged, anointed with hormone cream, hipped on rejuvenation pills, who owed their precarious survival entirely to artificial aids and appliances.

He turned away and recommenced his pacing of the pavement. There was no doubt, he thought wryly, that the conditioning of a Catholic upbringing and education entered into the very marrow of a man. It unfitted him for the prosecution of an *affaire* with the proper gaiety and confidence. The taking of 'precautions' which was, no doubt, to the secular philanderer a process as mechanical and thoughtless as blinking, was to him an ordeal imbued with embarrassment, guilt and superstitious fear; and one which, Adam now saw, might easily come to overshadow in moral importance the act of sexual licence itself.

Perhaps, he tried to persuade himself, his anxiety was misplaced. Virginia was surely the kind of girl who felt underdressed if she wasn't wearing a diaphragm. Couldn't he safely leave that side of things to her? But something told him she was not as experienced as she pretended – how could she be, with that old dragon, her mother, breathing down her neck? Besides, after Barbara's proved incompetence to operate the Safe Method successfully, he no longer trusted women in the conduct of such matters. One slip on Virginia's part and nine months from now he might be the unwilling father of not merely one but two new offspring.

The possibility smote him with such appalling force that he all but abandoned the enterprise there and then. But somehow he couldn't contemplate going home with nothing to cheer him in the face of looming domestic problems. The events of the day lay about him like ruins. Though he had selfishly occupied a seat in the Reading Room since the morning, he hadn't opened a single book; furthermore, he had thrown the British Museum into panic and disorganisation, falsely suspected a friend of treachery, lost a job after enjoying it for ten minutes, and disgraced himself in the eyes of the Department. Overshadowing and darkening all these setbacks were the prognostications of another addition to the Appleby family. If he could return home with Merrymarsh's secret manuscript, that at least would be something achieved, something to go to bed on, dreaming of a brighter future.

It wasn't, in other words, simple lust that had driven him thus far towards the house in Bayswater; it was the lure of a literary discovery. Virginia was just a contingency – though not entirely regretted, he had to admit. In fact, to be quite honest, he looked upon her in the light of a bonus: if the question of Merrymarsh's manuscript hadn't arisen, he wouldn't for a moment have entertained the idea of jumping into bed with her; but if jumping into bed was the only way of getting his hands on the manuscript . . . well, he was only human. Either way, of course, it was what Father Bonaventure would have called a grave sin; but he was in no mood to let that deter him – indeed he looked forward to the experience of being a Sinner in full-blooded style with a certain grim satisfaction. The advantage of the present circumstances was that they permitted him to feel the victim of an almost irresistible temptation which was not of his seeking. And a small voice inside him hinted that if he was going to be unfaithful to Barbara, if he was going to have one wild fling at forbidden fruit, then he could scarcely do so with greater ease, secrecy and freedom from remorse than now.

The very elements seemed to have conspired to draw a discreet veil round his moment of decision. The Edgware Road was eerily silent and deserted. Occasionally the hush was dissipated by a bus, crawling by in low gear, its windows becoming palely visible as it drew level, only to fade again almost immediately. At long intervals a pedestrian, coughing and muffled in scarves, stumbled past and was swallowed up in the anonymity of the fog. If he could not find the courage now to embark on an amorous adventure, what chance was there of his ever doing so in more normal meteorological conditions? It was now or never. Adam braced himself and stepped purposefully towards the shop.

As he did so he heard the sound of footsteps on the pavement behind him. He was tempted to stop and skulk against a wall while the pedestrian passed on, but knew that if he hesitated again he would never recover his resolution. He accelerated his pace, but the footsteps followed suit. He broke into a trot, and heard his pursuer coughing and panting as he strove to overtake. The brightly-lit glass door of the shop loomed up suddenly, and Adam reached for the latch. As he did so, a heavy hand caught him by the shoulder, and he froze in the attitude of an arrested thief.

'Excuse me, sir,' said an Irish voice, 'but am I anywhere at all near the Marble Arch?'

'Keep going, and you'll come to it,' Adam replied. He averted his head from his questioner as he spoke, but his attempt to disguise his voice was unsuccessful.

'Glory be to God, is it yourself, Mr Appleby?' said Father Finbar.

'Were you going in here, Mr Appleby? Don't let me stop you.'

'Oh, it's all right, Father – '

'I'll come in with you. I wouldn't mind getting out of this fog myself, for a minute or two.'

'Let me show you where Marble Arch – '

'Tell me inside, Mr Appleby. Mother of God, did you ever see the likes of this weather?'

Father Finbar took Adam firmly by the arm and led him, struggling feebly, into the shop. A small, dapper man with a toothbrush moustache was sitting on a stool behind the counter, reading a newspaper. He got to his feet with a discreet smile of welcome. As Father Finbar unwound his scarf and revealed his dog-collar, the man's smile slowly hardened into an unnatural grin, a rictus of shock behind which feelings of incredulity, curiosity and fear seemed to be struggling for ascendancy. Father Finbar rattled on comfortably.

'Did I never tell you, Mr Appleby, I have a cousin who's at the Oratory up at Brompton there and being up in Town today, and having the afternoon to myself which doesn't happen very often I thought I'd take the opportunity of dropping in on him. But it was a bad move and no mistake. I've been waiting since five for the fog to clear and I'm blessed if I don't think it's worse now than it was then. So I decided to hoof it in the end. Shocking weather, mister,' he concluded, addressing the man behind the counter, who responded by nodding his head several times, his countenance still distorted by the vacant grin. 'I suppose you think I shouldn't be complaining about fog with the brogue on me, but Irish mist is a different proposition entirely. You could stand a broomstick up in this stuff and it wouldn't fall down. Bad for business too, I suppose?'

'Can I do anything for you gentlemen?' said the man.

Father Finbar looked expectantly at Adam, who raked the shelves desperately for some innocuous purchase. His eyes lighted thankfully on a carton of paper tissues.

'Kleenex, please. The small packet.'

'Sixpence,' said the man.

'Aye, the fog gets right up your nose, doesn't it. Filthy stuff,

I'm half choked m'self,' said Father Finbar. 'Could I have a packet of throat lozenges?' he said.

'We don't stock them,' said the man.

'Don't stock them?' Father Finbar repeated, looking round him in surprise. 'This is a chemist's shop, isn't it?'

'No – ' the man began.

'It's only a step to the Marble Arch, Father,' said Adam, cutting in swiftly and loudly. 'Then you can walk down Park Lane to Hyde Park Corner and along Grosvenor Place and that brings you to Victoria, and if I were you – '

'Aye, I'll be on my way in a moment,' said Father Finbar. 'You know Adam – you don't mind if I call you Adam? – you know I'm very glad we bumped into each other, because I've been thinking about that most interesting conversation we had this morning.'

'Oh, it's not worth talking about,' said Adam deprecatingly, edging towards the door.

'Oh, but it is. It was most in-ter-est-ing. I'm thinking you feel the Church is too hard on young married folk – '

'Oh no, no, not at all!' Adam protested. He opened the door, but Father Finbar showed no inclination to budge.

'Don't leave the door open, please,' said the man behind the counter. 'It lets the fog in.'

'That's right, just hold your horses, Adam,' said Father Finbar. He turned to the man. 'You don't mind us taking a breather here for a moment, do you, mister? An empty shop is bad for trade, isn't that right?'

'It's the other way round in my line of business,' said the man, who seemed to be recovering his self-possession. He looked suspiciously at Adam and Father Finbar as if he suspected he was the victim of a hoax.

'Is that so?' said Father Finbar curiously. 'Now, why would that be the case?'

'What were you saying about our conversation this morning, Father?' said Adam, leaping desperately from the frying pan to the fire.

'Ah, yes, now where was I? I was meaning to say, Adam, that

you mustn't think the Church forbids birth control just to make life harder for young couples.'

'Of course not – '

'It's just a matter of teaching God's law. It's a simple question of right and wrong . . .' His voice, which had been so far mild and gentle, suddenly rose to the pitch of a pulpit-thumping tirade. 'CONTRACEPTION IS NOTHING LESS THAN THE MURDER OF GOD-GIVEN LIFE AND THE PEOPLE WHO MAKE AND SELL THE FILTHY THINGS ARE AS GUILTY AS THOSE WHO SUPPLY OPIUM TO DRUG ADDICTS!' he roared.

'Here,' said the man behind the counter. 'You can't say things like that to me.'

'This is a private religious discussion,' Father Finbar retorted with a fierce look, 'and I'll thank you to keep your opinions to yourself.' He turned back to Adam. 'Did you know,' he went on in a vibrant whisper, 'that the manufacture of contraceptives is an industry so vast that no one can even make a guess at the profits? that the whole dirty trade is so covered up with shame and secrecy that these profiteers don't even pay taxes? that the whole affair is actively encouraged and supported by the Communists to sap the vitality of the West.'

'No,' said Adam, keeping his eye on the man behind the counter. He was surreptitiously using the telephone, and Adam had no doubt that he was calling the police. 'Don't you think we'd better be going, Father?' he pleaded.

'Perhaps so,' said the priest, raising his voice. 'Some people in this world don't like to hear unpleasant truths.' When they were outside on the pavement he said to Adam: 'You know, I shouldn't be surprised if our man back there didn't deal in the things himself.'

'No!' said Adam.

'Oh, yes. I shouldn't be surprised at all. Under the counter, you know, under the counter . . . And what are you doing here, Adam?'

'I was just buying some paper handkerchiefs,' said Adam, eagerly brandishing the evidence under the priest's nose. He broke open the packet and blew his nose vigorously.

'No, I mean what are you doing in the Edgware Road? Lost your way?'

'Oh. No, I was on my way to . . . some friends. In Bayswater.'

'They must be very good friends to keep you out on a night like this. I'm off home myself. It's going to be a long walk, but I have my rosary in my pocket so the time won't be wasted. Is this the way to the Marble Arch? Good night then, and God bless you.'

'Good night, Father.'

Adam watched the priest melt into the fog. For some reason his broad-brimmed trilby was the last feature to disappear from sight, and for a second or two Adam had the impression that a disembodied hat was sailing gently down the Edgware Road. Then the hat was gone. Adam tip-toed to his scooter and pushed it softly in the opposite direction.

Adam knocked on the front door, but it was the hairy man who opened it. 'Come in,' he said. In his mutilated left hand he held a long knife.

'I'll come back later,' said Adam.

'No. Mrs said you must come in.'

Adam glanced over the man's shoulder and saw Virginia on the stairs. She nodded vigorously and beckoned. Adam stepped hesitantly over the threshold. 'Where is Mrs Rottingdean?' he asked.

'Out,' said the man. 'She has to collect a wreath.'

'Who for?' said Adam, eyeing the knife.

The hairy man was distracted by Virginia. 'Get back to your room, you,' he said. Virginia pouted and retreated up the stairs, swinging her hips. 'Bad lot,' the man commented. He threw open the door of the sitting-room. The manuscript of *Lay Sermons and Private Prayers* was on the chair where Adam had left it. 'You read – I watch,' said the hairy man. He sat down on the sofa and took out of his pocket a piece of emery paper with which he began to sharpen his knife.

'Where are you from?' said Adam conversationally.

'Argentina. Mrs said I must not talk. You read – I watch.'

Adam opened the manuscript at random and stared at it unseeingly for a few minutes. 'I don't like reading with someone watching me,' he said at length. 'Could you wait outside?'

'No,' said the hairy man, testing the blade of his knife on his thumb.

The door opened and Virginia came in.

'I said, get back to your room,' growled the hairy man. 'Your ma said you stays in your room till she gets back.'

'All right, Edmundo,' said Virginia demurely. 'I just thought I'd tell you there's an Elizabeth Taylor film on the television.'

The hairy man stiffened and regarded Virginia suspiciously. 'I'm not watching telly tonight,' he muttered. 'I'm watching him.'

'All right. I just thought I'd tell you,' said Virginia, making to go out.

'What movie is it, then?' said the hairy man.

'*National Velvet*,' said Virginia. 'Her first big picture – when she was just a girl. Fresh as a flower. Sweet, innocent. You'd love it, Edmundo.'

'I haven't seen it,' said the hairy man, licking his lips.

'You could leave the doors open,' said Virginia. 'Mr Appleby will be quite safe.'

The hairy man was silent for a moment. 'You turn the telly on and go back to your room,' he said at length. 'And I'll see.'

Virginia went out, leaving the door open. After a minute or two the sounds of hoof-beats and girlish cries were wafted faintly to their ears. Virginia passed in the hall and winked at Adam. They heard her go up the stairs, and her door slammed.

Two minutes passed: Adam counted them by the mournful tick of the grandfather clock in the hall. Then the hairy man got to his feet. 'You stay here, right? You want anything, you knock on the wall.' He demonstrated with the knuckle of his good hand.

'All right,' Adam said.

The hairy man thrust the knife into his belt and left the room.

The clock was striking the quarter hour when Virginia came downstairs again. She poked her head into the sitting-room, her eyes bright.

'Come on,' she whispered.

Adam gripped the arms of his chair. 'What about that man?' he hissed.

Virginia beckoned by way of reply. He followed her on tip-toe to the open door of the adjoining room. 'Look,' she said.

Adam peeped in. The hairy man was sound asleep in front of the television set. His mouth was open and he snored gently.

'It never fails,' said Virginia.

'What about the other two men?' whispered Adam, as they crept upstairs.

'They're locked in the basement. Don't worry about them.'

'Who are they?'

'I told you – butchers.'

'He said he was from Argentina.'

'My father had a meat business there – he brought them over. God knows why – they're very careless at their job.'

'You mean . . . the fingers?'

Virginia nodded. 'Mother runs the business now, though she tries to pretend she doesn't. Well, here's my little love nest.'

She opened the door of a bedroom and switched on the light. Panting slightly from the long climb, Adam went in.

The room was a teenage slum. The bed, dressing-table and bookshelves evidently provided insufficient surface space for Virginia's possessions, most of which were strewn over the floor: books, magazines, records, dolls, sweaters, trousers, combs, brushes, cushions, scissors, nail-files, and jars – jars of cold cream, jars of nail polish, jars of bath salts, jars of sweets, even jars of jam. Discarded stockings and underwear had drifted up against one corner of the room. Pinned to the walls were seaside post-cards, travel posters, a life-size portrait of the Beatles and a photograph of Virginia in her First Communion dress. It all made her seem much younger than she looked.

Virginia switched on the bedside lamp and turned off the main light. She locked the door and put her arms round Adam's waist. 'Isn't this fun?' she murmured, nestling up to him.

Adam was still holding the manuscript of *Lay Sermons and Private Prayers*, and he clasped it to his chest as a buffer between himself and Virginia. 'The papers,' he said.

Virginia pouted and disengaged herself. 'I'm not going to let you read them here,' she said. 'You can take them away. Time's too precious.'

'You promised to let me see them,' he said.

'Just a peep then.' She went to a cupboard and took out a hat-box, which she presented to Adam with a curtsy. He opened it, and took out a sheaf of letters rolled up in an elastic band and a thick exercise book. Both letters and book were charred at the edges, and a few flakes of burned paper fell back into the box as he lifted the documents out. He removed the elastic band with great care.

'I can't see properly,' he complained. 'Turn the light on again.'

'Sit on the bed,' said Virginia.

He went over to the bed and sat down near the lamp. Virginia joined him and began taking off her stockings. But he was soon lost in his discovery.

And it was a discovery. The letters were important only as verifying Virginia's story about Merrymarsh and her mother. Some of them were love letters, written in a mawkish sentimental style with a lot of baby-talk; others were brief notes, assignations, cancellations. But the book – the book was quite another matter. Adam riffled the pages with gathering excitement.

Entitled *Robert and Rachel* (pseudonyms for Merrymarsh and Mrs Rottingdean) it told, in the form of Robert's journal, the story of a middle-aged man's first love affair. Robert was a bachelor, a man of letters with a modest reputation, a popular apologist for Catholicism. At the age of forty-eight he had nothing to look forward to but a repetition of his existing routine, a gentle decline into the tranquillity of old age, a pious death, respectful obituaries in the Catholic press. Then, by a train of circumstances which seemed improbable though evidently based on fact, he was left alone in his country cottage for several days with a young girl, the niece of his housekeeper. One day he blundered into a room where she was bathing herself. He had never seen a grown woman naked in his life before, and the sight unleashed in him an overpowering desire of which he had never dreamt he was capable. After prolonged and feverish skirmishing, hampered by inexperience and guilt on both sides, they became lovers. Then the housekeeper returned, the niece had to return to London. He begged her to marry him, but she refused, saying they would never be able to respect each other after what had passed. He followed her back to London, and they resumed the relationship, now as mistress and keeper . . .

At this point the story broke off. There had evidently been another exercise book which had been burned. It was a great pity. *Robert and Rachel* wasn't quite a literary work of art: it was feeling crude and unrefined, turned out clumsily from the rough moulds of real experience. There was a kind of embarrassment, a shamefulness in the confessions, from which no detail was spared, of a man whose sexual desire was ignited for the first time at the very moment when his sexual vigour was declining. It wasn't really art, and of course it hadn't been intended for publication; but it was unquestionably the best thing Egbert Merrymarsh had ever done. That description of the young girl, for instance, standing nude in the tin tub, her hair falling to her waist . . . As Adam turned back to read the passage again, the manuscript was snatched from his hands.

'That's quite enough,' said Virginia.

Adam's protest died in his throat. Virginia was sitting beside him, quite naked.

'You don't really want to go through with this, Virginia?' Adam pleaded, pacing up and down the room.

'You promised.'

'No, I didn't really promise . . . Anyway, your mother may come back at any moment. And that man – '

'She's gone to a wreath maker in Swiss Cottage and she'll be gone hours in this fog.'

'What does she want a wreath for, anyway?'

'For Merrymarsh. I think she has a little wreath-laying ceremony in store for you.'

'Good Lord! Where is he buried?'

'You're deliberately wasting time, Adam,' she accused him. 'I've kept my side of the bargain. Now it's your turn.'

'But why? Why? Why pick on me? I'm not the kind of man you're looking for. I'm no good in bed. I don't have enough practice.'

'You look kind. And gentle.'

Adam looked at her with suspicion.

'Have you . . . that is . . . are you a virgin?'

She flushed. 'Of course not.'

'How old are you?'

'Nineteen.'

'That's a lie.'

'Seventeen.'

'How do I know whether to believe you? You might be a minor for all I know.'

Virginia climbed on to the bed and took down her First Communion picture. She pointed to the record of her age and the date at the bottom.

'All right, so you're seventeen,' Adam said. 'Doesn't that picture make you feel any shame?'

'No,' said Virginia.

'Well, for God's sake put some clothes on,' said Adam. 'You make me feel cold.'

Virginia's response was to light the gas fire. 'Is that all I make you feel?' she said, a little sadly, as she crouched over the fire.

'No,' Adam admitted, watching the reflected glow of the gas fire deepen on her skin.

She came towards him radiantly. 'Take me, Adam,' she whispered. She took his hand and placed it over her breast. Adam groaned and closed his eyes.

'I can't, Virginia. I daren't. I haven't . . . taken precautions.'

'Don't worry about that, darling,' she murmured in his ear. Her breath made his skin tingle. With his free hand he began to stroke her back.

'You mean . . .' he said hoarsely, letting his fingers slide down her spine.

'I don't mind taking a chance.'

He opened his eyes and jumped back. *'Are you mad?'*

She came after him. 'I don't, really I don't.'

'Well, I do,' Adam said. He sat down, feeling faint. He had nearly lost control that time. He racked his brains for some further means of procrastination. 'Have you got a thermometer?' he said.

'Yes, I think so. Why?'

'If you really want to go through with this, you'll have to take your temperature.'

'You are a funny man.' With an air of humouring him, Virginia rummaged in the drawer of her dressing-table and withdrew, from a jumble of broken combs, broken jewellery, broken fountain-pens and broken rosaries, a miraculously unbroken thermometer. He took it from her and, having shaken down the mercury, slid it under her tongue.

'Sit on the bed,' he ordered.

She looked like a naughty child, sitting there naked with the thermometer in her mouth. Adam drew up a chair and took a paper and pencil from his pocket.

'Now, how long was the shortest of your last three periods?' he enquired.

Virginia spat out the thermometer. 'I haven't the foggiest,' she said. 'What is this all about?'

Adam replaced the thermometer. 'I'm trying to determine whether this is a safe time for relations,' he explained.

'Not very romantic,' Virginia seemed indistinctly to say.

'Sex isn't,' he snapped back. He plucked the thermometer out and examined it. '97.6,' he announced, and wrote the figure down. He stood up and began to collect the Merrymarsh papers with the air of a doctor at the end of a consultation. 'Now, if you'll just go on taking your temperature every night and drop me a line when it rises sharply for three consecutive days, we'll see what we can do.' He gave her a bland smile.

Virginia jumped off the bed.

'You beast, you're just teasing me.'

'No, no, really.' He backed away.

'Yes you are. I've lost my patience, Adam.'

'Honestly, Virginia, it would be the height of folly – '

He reversed round the room, with Virginia in hot pursuit.

Stockings entangled themselves round his ankles, and jars rolled under his feet. The back of his knees struck the edge of the bed, and he toppled back on to the counterpane. Virginia gave a little shriek of glee and threw herself upon him. He felt her fingers undoing his belt, and his trousers slowly receding. He struggled to retain them, but, on a sudden inspiration, desisted.

'Oh,' said Virginia. She got up and stepped back. 'Oh,' she said again. She snatched up a dressing-gown and held it in front of her. 'What are you wearing those for?'

Adam stood up, and his trousers fell to his feet. He fingered the lace on Barbara's pants. 'I've been trying to tell you all the evening,' he said in a broken voice. 'I'm . . . funny that way. I told you I wasn't the kind of man you're looking for.'

Virginia put on the dressing-gown and knotted the cord. 'You mean, you're really a woman?' she said, with wide eyes.

'No, no! I've got three children, remember.'

'Then why . . .?'

'Religion has played havoc with my married life,' he explained. 'If sex can't find its normal outlets . . .' He shrugged, and snapped the elastic on Barbara's pants.

The silence that followed this confession was broken by a sudden uproar from downstairs. 'Mother!' said Virginia. She opened the door and hung over the bannister. Holding his trousers up with both hands, Adam followed her.

At the bottom of the stair-well, Mrs Rottingdean could be seen haranguing the hairy man, who was rubbing his eyes stupidly and trying to evade the blows aimed at his head. Mrs Rottingdean was carrying an immense wreath of holly and yew, which she finally pulled over the man's head. She unlocked the door leading to the basement, and the other two men tumbled out, wielding meat-axes. With dramatic gestures Mrs Rottingdean urged them up the stairs.

Adam fled back to the bedroom. Virginia followed and locked the door.

'What shall I do?' said Adam frantically.

'There's a fire escape,' said Virginia, throwing up the sash of her widow. 'I'll say you went hours ago, while Edmundo was asleep.'

'And the papers?'

'You can keep them,' said Virginia dejectedly. 'I don't suppose I'll have another chance to use them.'

Adam scooped up the papers and stepped to the window. 'I'm sorry, Virginia,' he said, and implanted a chaste kiss on her forehead.

Virginia sniffed. 'And I did so want to be the first sixth-former in St Monica's to do it,' she said.

'So you are a virgin after all?'

She nodded, and two tears trickled down her cheeks.

'Never mind,' said Adam consolingly. 'There'll be other opportunities.'

Mrs Rottingdean's myrmidons pounded up the last flight of stairs. 'You'd better go,' said Virginia.

As Adam stepped on to the fire escape, his trousers slipped down again. To save time, he took them off and wound them round the Merrymarsh papers. The fog coiled damply round his bare legs, but he was grateful for its cover. As he cautiously descended the ladder he was conscious of re-enacting one of the oldest roles in literature.

TEN

*Now I find the evenings intolerable after the British Museum
closes; and think you might let me have something to read by
way of change.*
BARON CORVO (Letter to Grant Richards)

Adam crawled wearily into the Reading Room just as the bell
stridently announced that the Library would close in fifteen
minutes. As he sank on to his padded seat everyone around him
began standing up, pushing back their chairs, yawning, stretching,
sorting their papers and arranging their books. Many of them
had been there all day: their countenances were fatigued but
contented, conveying the satisfaction of work well done – so
many books read, so many notes taken. Then there were the
Night People of the Museum – those writing books or theses
while holding down day-time jobs. Hurrying from their offices
to the Museum through the rush-hour, pausing only to snatch a
quick meal at Lyons, they worked through the evening with fierce
and greedy concentration. Now they looked reproachfully at the
clock, and continued reading even as they stood in line to return
their books. Adam felt an imposter in this company, especially
when they stood respectfully aside as he carried his huge, tottering
pile of unread Lawrentiana to the central counter.

'I want to reserve them all,' he said, and returned to his desk
to collect his belongings. A man tapped him on the shoulder and
waved an application slip.

'Mr Appleby, isn't it? I think you've got the press-mark wrong
on this one.'

'Oh, yes,' said Adam, taking the slip. 'Thank you. I'll see to it
tomorrow.'

The desk next to his was vacant. Camel had gone home. But
he had left a note for Adam.

The job I have been offered is a fiendish plot to make me finish my thesis. Bane just told me I shall be on probation until I get my Ph.D. Doubtless I shall be the first university teacher to retire while still on probation. – C.

Adam smiled, and lifted his duffle-coat from the back of the seat. Another note fell out of the hood.

A new proposal for the statute book – *Academic Publications Act*: 'The Government will undertake to subsidise the publication of a monthly periodical, about the size of a telephone directory and printed in columns on Bible paper, which will publish all scholarly articles, notes, correspondence etc. submitted to it, irrespective of merit or interest. All existing journals will be abolished. This will eliminate the element of invidious competition in academic appointments and promotions, which will be offered to candidates in alphabetical order.' (With your initials you shouldn't have any trouble.) – C.

Adam grinned and shrugged on his duffle-coat. He felt in his pockets for his gloves, and pulled out two more missives. One was a clipping of the Brownlong ad., with a message scrawled across it: *Why don't you go in for this?* – C. The other read:
What about:

> *I always choose a Brownlong chair,*
> *Professors use them everywhere.*

Or:

> *I always choose a Brownlong chair:*
> *The answer to a bottom's prayer.*

Seriously, this is a winner:

> *I always choose a Brownlong chair,*
> *The seat that's neat and made with care.*

(flair?)

But Adam had a better idea. He sat down at the desk and took out the sepia postcard of the British Museum which he had purchased that afternoon. He addressed it to Brownlong & Co., and stamped it, ready to be posted on the way home. The Reading Room was almost empty, and an official lingered impatiently near Adam, waiting for him to leave. But Adam refused to be hurried as he penned his couplet in a bold, clear script. He leaned back and regarded it with satisfaction. It had the hard-edged clarity of a good imagist lyric, the subtle reverberations of a fine *haiku*, the economy of a classic epigram.

> *I always choose a Brownlong chair,*
> *Because it's stuffed with pubic hair.*

Adam drove slowly along the Embankment, straining his eyes for the sight of a convenient pillar-box – convenient in this instance meaning one he could reach without getting off his scooter and stalling the engine. The noises coming from the engine were getting increasingly ugly – all this travelling in low gear had taken its toll – and he was not confident that, once stopped, it would ever start again.

Posting his contribution to the Brownlong competition had become a matter of some importance to him, the completion of his one, small achievement of the day. No, that wasn't quite true – he had the manuscript of *Robert and Rachel* snugly tucked away in the tool compartment of his scooter, swaddled tenderly in his college scarf. But, interesting as it was, he was growing increasingly doubtful that he would be able to turn it to his own advantage. Someone – Mrs Rottingdean presumably – held the copyright, and she was clearly not going to let him publish it. Perhaps she could even prevent him from reporting on it – he was uncertain about such legal technicalities. Furthermore, he had inadvertently brought away with him from Bayswater the manuscript of *Lay Sermons and Private Prayers* and he would have to find some way of returning it to Mrs Rottingdean before she put the Metropolitan Police on his trail.

The sudden blast of a fog horn – just behind his left ear, it seemed – made him jump. It was a real pea-souper down here by the river. The atmosphere seemed to be compounded of equal portions of moisture and soot. A faint smell of burning stung his nose and throat – it was as if the whole city were gently smouldering.

He found a pillar-box at last, and drew up beside it. Grasping the throttle of his scooter with his right hand, he leaned out to post the card with his left. But the slit was on the opposite side of the pillar-box and he lost his balance momentarily, dropping the card and losing his grip on the scooter, the engine of which promptly died. Cursing, Adam retrieved the card and posted it. Then he girded himself to push the scooter into life again. It was still a long walk to home, and he was very tired. Please God let it fire, he prayed, as he began to run.

The engine fired all right; in fact, it burst into flames. They licked greedily at Adam's ankles, and he jumped clear, allowing the scooter to proceed alone for several yards, a miniature fire-ship, before it toppled over into the gutter. He ran after it and tore his bags from the luggage grid. Aware of the danger of an explosion, he retreated to a safe distance with his bags, then remembered, with a spasm of horror, the manuscript of *Robert and Rachel*. He hurried back to the scooter and, screening his face from the heat, pried open the lid of the tool compartment. A jet of flame shot up and singed his duffle-coat. He reeled back. Too late! Egbert Merrymarsh's lost masterpiece had perished in its second ordeal by fire.

There was a loud explosion. The scooter arched into the air like a creature in its final agony; it crashed to the ground, a twisted heap of blazing metal, and after two last convulsive jerks and a muted wail from its horn, expired.

There was total silence except for the brisk crackling of flames and the sympathetic lamentation of fog-horns from downstream. Adam stood stunned, waiting for the policemen, the firemen, the bystanders to assemble. But no one came. At last a dog limped out of the fog and lay down before the pyre, licking its chops appreciatively. Adam picked up his bags and prepared to walk. His legs felt weak and he staggered slightly. He heard, rather than saw, a large car draw up at the kerbside. A door opened and shut.

'Hi there,' said a familiar voice. 'Having trouble?'

'Oh, hallo,' said Adam. 'I've got a message for you.'

'Drink?' enquired the American, pulling down a flap behind the driver's partition and revealing a row of bottles.

'I'd love one,' said Adam, sinking into the soft grey upholstery. The limousine was purring slowly along the Embankment, but the blinds were drawn inside and he had no sensation of movement. Soothing music was coming from a speaker concealed somewhere behind his seat.

'Scotch, Bourbon, gin, Cognac?'

'Cognac, please.'

The fat American poured a generous measure of brandy into a huge balloon glass and handed it to Adam. 'That should give you a lift. Tough break, your scooter catching fire. Still, it's insured I guess?'

'I hadn't thought of that,' said Adam, brightening.

'So what was that about a message?' said the fat American, opening a bottle of whisky.

'Oh, yes, someone phoned from Colorado – I got the message by mistake. Something about a hundred thousand for books and fifty thousand for manuscripts. Or was it the other way round . . .'

The American uttered a sigh of impatience. 'Those guys think too small,' he said. He splashed soda in his glass and Adam heard the chink of ice. 'Well, here's to our third meeting today – '

'Fourth,' said Adam.

'How's that?'

'Wasn't it you this afternoon on the gallery in the Reading Room?'

'Geeze, was that you? What were you doing up there?'

'I was running away.'

'Is that right? And I was running away from you . . . Well, here's to our fourth meeting, then. And the Summit College Library.'

'Here's to them,' said Adam. They drank.

'Say, I forgot to ask, where do you live, Adam?'

'Battersea.'

The American slid back the glass partition and spoke to his chauffeur. 'You know where Battersea is?'

'Yes, sir.'

'Well, that's where we're going.'

'Right, sir.'

'That's very kind of you, Mr, er . . .'

'You're welcome. Schnitz is the name, but call me Bernie.'

'I hope the fog – '

'Don't worry about the fog. I think he has radar in the front there. This car's got damn near everything else.'

'It's marvellous,' said Adam, sipping his brandy. Emboldened by the liquor, he put a question:

'What were you doing in the Reading Room, then . . . Bernie?'

'I figured I'd take advantage of the confusion to really examine the structure of the building . . .'

'The structure?'

'Yeah, it's like this, I had this great idea, a vision, you might call it. I was going to buy the British Museum and transport it stone by stone to Colorado, clean it up and re-erect it.'

Adam boggled. 'With all the books?'

'Yeah, you see we have this little College in Colorado, high up in the Rockies – highest school in the world as a matter of fact, we have to have oxygen on tap in every room . . . Well, it's a fine place, but we're not expanding as we should be – you know, we're not getting the good students, the top teachers. So I told the trustees what was needed: a real class library – rare books, original manuscripts, that sort of thing. "O.K. Bernie," they said, "go to Europe and get us a library." So I came to the best library in the world.'

'I don't think it's for sale, somewhow,' Adam said.

'No, I guess you're right. I hadn't figured on it being that big,' said Bernie, sadly. Adam almost shared his regret. It was a thrilling vision he had conjured up, of the B.M. scoured of its soot and pigeon droppings, its tall pillars and great dome gleaming in their pristine glory, starkly outlined against the blue Colorado sky

380

at the summit of some craggy mountain. 'Never mind,' he said consolingly. 'With all that money, you'll be able to buy a good collection.'

'Yeah, but I haven't the time to buy it in bits and pieces. Hunting for manuscripts especially – you've no idea the time it takes.'

'I've got an original manuscript with me, by an odd chance,' said Adam. 'But I don't think it would interest you.'

'Let's have a look at it, Adam.'

Adam took *Lay Sermons and Private Prayers* out of one of his bags and passed it over. 'It's very boring and of no literary merit whatsoever,' he said, as Bernie thumbed through the manuscript.

'Was this ever published?'

'No. Merrymarsh published a number of books, but he couldn't get anyone to take that.'

'Well, we will,' said Bernie. 'How much do you want for it?'

'It's not mine,' said Adam. 'The owner wants £250 for it.'

'Let's say two seventy-five,' said Bernie. 'You're entitled to a commission.' He took out a thick wad of five-pound notes and began counting them into Adam's hand. Adam stopped him at the fifth.

'Would you mind paying the owner direct?' he said. 'You'll find her name and address on the inside of the cover.'

'O.K.' said Bernie. 'Say, Adam, could you use a part-time job?'

'What kind of job?'

'Scouting for books and manuscripts for our library. It's like this: I have to go back to the States soon. You could be our buyer on the spot. Ten per cent commission and expenses. Is it a deal?'

'I think so,' said Adam. 'But I'll have to ask my wife.'

Bernie dropped Adam at the corner of his street. As they shook hands, he pressed a card into Adam's.

'This is my hotel. Call me when you've talked to your wife.'

Adam bounded down the street, indifferent to the bags banging against his knees. He was going to do more than talk to his wife. He was going to make love to her.

He paused at the gate and looked up at the window of their

bedroom. The light was on, so she wasn't asleep yet. Was that a star he could see above the roof . . .? The fog was clearing then. And, yes – he flexed his leg – he had lost his limp. It was absurd to let this pregnancy thing get on top of you. If she was, they might as well make the best of it, and if she wasn't –

His elation subsided as he suddenly thought of something. Supposing . . . supposing, since he had last spoken to her . . . supposing . . .

It was absurd, but he actually hoped her period hadn't started.

EPILOGUE

Perhaps she ought to wake Adam up and tell him it had started, Barbara thought, as she came out of the bathroom. The passage was quite dark but, schooled by many night-time alarms and excursions, she negotiated it with confidence. Their bedroom was dimly lit by the street lamps shining through the curtains, and Adam's face had a bluish tint. He was sound asleep. She wasn't surprised – by the sound of it he'd been tearing all over London all day in the fog; and she wouldn't be surprised if he'd been drunk at the sherry party. That was probably how he lost his job, she speculated. The job he never had. They were going to give it to Camel, apparently. Well, Camel had waited long enough. And this offer by the American sounded all right, if she'd got it straight.

'Adam,' she said softly, as she took off her dressing-gown. But he didn't stir. Let him sleep, then. Tomorrow would be soon enough to tell him. And wouldn't he be pleased. Rush off to the Museum full of beans. He never could work properly when he was worried, which meant once a month at least . . .

As she was getting into bed Barbara heard a muffled cry. Dominic. Resignedly she swung her feet to the floor again and pushed them into her slippers. She shrugged on her dressing-gown and padded into the children's room. Dominic had managed to roll his sheets into ropes and had got them knotted round his legs. She held the whimpering child in one arm while she smoothed the bedclothes with her other hand. As she tucked him up again he fell into a deep and peaceful sleep. Barbara glanced at Edward. From the shadows came Clare's voice: 'Can I have a drink of water, Mummy?'

'Why aren't you asleep, Clare?'

'I'm thirsty.'

'All right.'

Barbara fetched a glass of water from the kitchen. Clare sipped it slowly.

'Is Daddy back?'

'Yes, dear.'

'Where's Daddy's uniform, Mummy?'

'What do you mean?'

'The men who worked at the British Museum had uniforms.'

'Daddy doesn't do that kind of work.'

'What kind of–'

'Shsh. Go to sleep. It's late.'

Well, the children had enjoyed the trip to the Museum, anyway. Still, it had been silly of her to panic like that. What good would it have done, supposing there *had* been a fire? He might have been trying to reach her by telephone. Goodness, he must have spent a fortune in phone calls today. And what had he been doing all the afternoon, anyway? Oh, she hadn't heard the whole story yet, not by a long chalk.

A ruck in the curtains attracted her notice, and she went over to the window to adjust them. Well, he'd nearly burned himself to death anyway, by all accounts, she thought, looking out of the window and catching sight of the crumpled tarpaulin in the garden below. Funny that the scooter had never given any trouble while Dad had it. Perhaps he didn't know how to drive it properly. Who ever heard of a scooter catching fire spontaneously? She wasn't sorry though – he was bound to have killed himself on it one of these days, and the insurance would come in handy. With the money the American had given him, they would be quite rich for a while.

I need a new coat, she thought, as she returned to the kitchen with the half-filled glass. My red one is all out of shape from carrying Dominic and Edward. I'll get a fitted one this time. Act of faith, but I might as well make the most of my figure while

I've still got it. Shoes for Dominic. A blouse for Clare. And underpants for Adam, four pairs at least. Can't have that happening again. I had to laugh when he took off his trousers tonight, I'd forgotten all about it. Supposing you had an accident, as Mum used to say. As if it was all right to have an accident as long as your underwear was respectable.

Barbara emptied the glass at the sink and filled it again to drink herself. This morning he remembered that day in France, she thought, that day we went swimming in our underclothes and afterwards I didn't wear anything under my dress. The sea and the sun and miles from home. That was the nearest we ever came to . . . Good job we didn't. With our luck we'd have had to get married straight away. Have six children now instead of three. Poor Mary Flynn. What will it be? Five all under six. I'd go mad, literally stark staring mad. Damn, I've forgotten to lay the table for breakfast.

With quiet, deft movements Barbara spread a cloth on the table, and began to lay out knives, forks, spoons, cups and saucers, plates, cornflakes and marmalade.

Why I forgot was because he was so keen to get into bed, she thought. But I like it when we make love spontaneously. That's the trouble with the Safe Method, or one of them, it's too mechanical, you're always watching the calendar, it's like launching a rocket – five four three two one, and by the time it's zero you're too tensed up to . . . Not tonight, though. I've not known him so happy for ages, bubbling over with plans for finishing his thesis and finding old books and manuscripts for the American and what was it he said about writing a novel, as if he hadn't got enough on his plate. Probably have forgotten all about it by the morning.

Her eyes were now quite accustomed to the darkness, and it had become in an odd way a point of honour not to switch on the light. She felt delicately in the dark recesses of drawers and cupboards for the things she wanted, taking pleasure in this testing of her sense of touch.

I'll feel awful telling Mary I'm not pregnant after all, she thought. If she hadn't converted her husband they would have been able to use contraceptives. Doesn't seem fair, somehow. Lots of girls marry non-Catholics on purpose. He has to sign a promise, but if he goes back on it and insists the priest will tell you to submit for the sake of saving the marriage. It's the lesser evil, they say, but it only applies if the Catholic partner's a woman. That's typical – as if they never dreamed a woman might want to insist. Perhaps they wouldn't have when they made the rule. The Vatican's always about a hundred years out of date.

Barbara yawned and shivered. She made a last check on the breakfast table, and left the kitchen.

And another thing I've forgotten is to say my prayers, she thought, as she reached the bedroom. Perhaps I'll skip them tonight. But I suppose I've got something to be thankful for. Just a Hail Mary then. There's such a draught across this floor.

Hail Mary, full of grace, the Lord is with thee, blessed art thou amongst women and blessed is the fruit of thy womb perhaps I should tell Adam now. If he wakes before me in the morning he'll lie there all depressed wondering if I'm pregnant. But perhaps he'll see the box on the dressing-table and guess. Wasn't there some French woman who used to change the flower in her bosom from white to red to tip off her lovers? Was it *La Dame aux Camélias*? I don't know. I'm forgetting all my French lit. But they're white and red. The language of flowers. Better than some ways of saying it, like the curse, or what is it they say in Birmingham, 'I haven't seen yet this month.' And that American girl, what was her name, in my last year at college, said falling off a roof. Well, Clare will say period and menstruate if I have anything to do with it. And I'll make sure she knows in good time, not like me up in the bedroom screaming I'm dying, I've never forgiven Mum for that. Or that poor girl, what was her name, Olive in IIIA, Olive Green, couldn't forget a name like that, bad as Adam Appleby. She went up to the teacher in class, 'Please Miss, I've got a terrible headache.' Teacher thought she meant period and gave her a sanitary towel to put on. She came back from the cloakroom half an hour later wearing it round her head, never seen one in her life before. Funny thing was, nobody laughed, though girls are little beasts at that age. Who was that teacher? Miss Bassett, she taught us French and History. It was she who encouraged me to do French at the University. The main attraction was the six months in France, but I'd met Adam by then and I didn't want to go. He was almost out of his mind, wrote to me every day till he couldn't stand it any longer he hitch-hiked right down to the South of France and we decided to get engaged. I'll never forget the day he turned up out of the blue on Madame Gerard's front door step sweating and covered in dust when he took off his rucksack he couldn't straighten up he had to turn sideways and sort of twist his head round to talk to her. I believe she thought he was a tramp his French was incomprehensible a good job I was there or perhaps she would have slammed the door on him not that she was any more pleased when she found out who he was she was a sour old shrew seemed to think my chastity was her personal responsibility chaperoned us all the time except that one day she had to go into Perpignan and we went to the sea . . .

This is no good, I'm falling asleep. Thank you God for not letting me be pregnant. There, that's short and sweet and from the heart. Let's get into bed. Ah. Ooh. My feet are like blocks of ice. I wonder if it will disturb him if I just put my foot just under his knee just there, ah, that's better. Hallo, he's stirring, ow, ouch my leg! Have to make him cut his toenails tomorrow, like having another baby to look after, I must stop Clare getting hold of the scissors, if only he would put a hook in high up somewhere, but if you tell him anything he doesn't listen, comes of having to study in a house full of children. He says if I train myself not to hear the constant racket you can't expect me to hear you and not the children. Perhaps he'll improve if we get a bigger flat or better still a house with a garden, somewhere for the children to let off steam, but I doubt it, he's always in a dream, what was it he said, a novel where life kept taking the shape of literature, did you ever hear anything so cracked, life is life and books are books and if he was a woman he wouldn't need to be told that.

Whoooooo there goes another foghorn, they sound so close, such a melancholy sound, reminds me of when he came to see me off at Dover, standing at the quayside with his hands in his pockets trying to shout something, but every time he opened his mouth the hooter went, and of course it had to be a great handsome French boy who was at the rail beside me I never even spoke to him but he couldn't sleep that night for jealousy he said in his letter funny how jealous he was before we were married well that's one foot thawed out let's try the other ah that's nice he always so warm after we so am I but getting out of bed spoils it perhaps that's what started it off that's happened before our honeymoon was the first time three days early instead of late the last one for about two years too what a honeymoon that was but how was I to know it would be early I suppose that's why they let the girl name the day funny I never thought of that before I didn't have any choice it was his embarkation leave and I thought it would be a safe period anyway it was safe all right after that the sheets looked like a battle had passed over he nearly had a fit the next morning wanted to smuggle them out pretend we'd lost them settle for a new pair as if hotels weren't used to he never could stand the sight of blood nearly has kittens if the children cut themselves I suppose I'll end up putting that hook in myself I seem to lose so much blood since I had Dominic perhaps I could get some pills from the doctor to reduce it but they might upset my cycle that's another thing against the safe method there are so many things that can affect ovulation there was a great list of them in that book what it was change of environment change of diet illness height above sea level emotional disturbance no wonder they called it Vatican Roulette what is love itself but emotional disturbance perhaps this temperature business is the answer this is the third or is it the fourth month it's worked the trouble is though once you've had a failure with any so called safe method Safe method that's a laugh Rhythm isn't much better funny sort of rhythm one week on three weeks off that American girl Jean something was her name Jean Kaufman said once a boy took her to the Rhode Island Rhythm Centre thinking it was a jazz club and taking your temperature every morning that's a bore Mary said she's tried everything including temperature charts she's one of the unlucky ones it won't work for so what is she supposed to do I'd like to know O the Church will have to change its attitude there's no doubt about that and if I was in her place I wouldn't wait there's many in mine who wouldn't come to that they say there's a huge number of Catholics it was in that article he showed me he says the Church is bound to change soon and won't there be an uproar from the older generation you can see it already in the Catholic papers dear sir I have no patience with the moans of young couples today who put a car and washing machine above the responsibilities of parenthood we have been poor but happy all our lives God always provides mother of nine can't blame them really for feeling they've had a rough deal mum told me when she was young even the safe method was frowned on and you were only supposed to use it if you were starving or going to die from another pregnancy the trouble is this myth of the large family what's so marvellous about a large family I'd like to know there was only one child in the Holy Family six in ours and we were at each others throats most of the time who's that Dominic don't say I've got to get out again no he's stopped only a dream I don't want any more three would suit me fine ha some hopes how many years to my menopause could be fifteen years my God and that's when a lot of women have one because they think and I don't suppose the temperature chart's any use then either it's like lactation that's how lactation ovulation basal temperature you get to sound like a doctor after a while that's how Mary had her second funny how many people think you can't conceive while you're breast feeding safe method doesn't work then either so it doesn't encourage you to breast feed but breast feeding's natural so much for the natural law if you ask me nobody gives a damn for the natural law the only reason well perhaps it is the natural law in a way there's something a bit offputting about contraceptives even non-Catholics would prefer not to I don't suppose I'd jump for joy if the Pope said it was all right tomorrow don't like the idea of pushing a bit of rubber and what's that jelly stuff spermicide Moses the name alone is enough to turn you off and they aren't 100 per cent reliable anyway surprising the number of non-Catholics who I bet if we decided to use them now that would happen to us wouldn't that be great perhaps the only way to be perfectly sure would be to combine it with the temperature chart my God you could spend your whole life preparing to get into bed if you let yourself perhaps the pill is the answer but they say it makes you drowsy and other side effects there's always a snag perhaps that's the root of the matter there's something about sex perhaps it's original sin I don't know but we'll never get it neatly tied up you think you've got it under control in one place it pops up in another either it's comic or tragic nobody's immune you see some couple going off to the Continent in their new sports car and envy them like hell next thing you find out they're dying to have a baby those who can't have them want them those who have them don't want them or not so many of them everyone has problems if you only knew Sally Pond was round the other day who'd have guessed she was frigid because of that man when she was nine can't do it unless she's had a couple of stiff drinks got completely stewed the other night she said and bit George in the leg now she's seeing a psychiatrist it makes you wonder if there's such a thing as a normal sexual relationship I don't think there is if you mean by normal no problems embarrassments disappointments there always are not that that entitles the church to sit back and say put up with it can be wonderful too and there are times when married people have to ought to and it isn't always a safe period either like when Adam was in the army that's how we had Dominic well perhaps the church will change and a good thing too there'll be much less misery in the world but it's silly to think that everything in the garden will be lovely it won't it never is I think I always knew that before we were married perhaps every woman does how could we put up with menstruation pregnancy and everything otherwise not like men he has this illusion that it's only the birth control business which stops him from getting sex perfectly under control it's like his thesis he keeps saying if only I could get my notes in the right order the thesis would write itself what was that he said suddenly when I thought he'd fallen asleep I've realised what the longest sentence in English fiction is I wonder what it is he had such an idealistic view of marriage when we were courting I don't think he's recovered from the shock yet though I warned him perhaps he didn't listen to what I said then either even that day at the sea I remember I suppose you could say that was when he proposed though we'd assumed it for some time I wasn't as starry-eyed as he was though I was pretty carried away I admit that beach with not a soul in sight we bicycled for miles to find it because we'd forgotten our costumes and we went swimming in our underwear his pants were inside out I remember that's typical we spread our things on the sand to dry the trees came down to the beach we sat in the shade and ate the sandwiches and drank the wine the footprints in the sand were only ours the sea was empty it was like a desert island we lay down he took me in his arms shall we come back here when we're married he said perhaps I said he held me low down tight against him we'll make love in this same spot he said my dress was so thin I could feel him hard against me perhaps we'll have children with us I said then we'll come down at night he said perhaps we won't be able to afford to come at all I said you're not very optimistic he said perhaps it's better not to be I said I'm going to be famous and earn lots of money he said perhaps you won't love me then I said I'll always love you he said I'll prove it every night he kissed my throat perhaps you think that now I said but I couldn't keep it up perhaps we will be happy I said of course we will he said we'll have a nanny to look after the children perhaps we will I said by the way how many children are we going to have as many as you like he said it'll be wonderful you'll see perhaps it will I said perhaps it will be wonderful perhaps even though it won't be like you think perhaps that won't matter perhaps.

How Far Can You Go?

To Ian Gregor

What can we know? Why is there anything at all?
Why not nothing?

What ought we to do? Why do what we do? Why and to
whom are we finally responsible?

What may we hope? Why are we here? What is it all about?

What will give us courage for life and what courage for
death?

Hans Küng, On being a Christian

ONE

How it was

It is just after eight o'clock in the morning of a dark February day, in this year of grace nineteen hundred and fifty-two. An atmospheric depression has combined with the coal smoke from a million chimneys to cast a pall over London. A cold drizzle is falling on the narrow, nondescript streets north of Soho, south of the Euston Road. Inside the church of Our Lady and St Jude, a greystone, neo-gothic edifice squeezed between a bank and a furniture warehouse, it might still be night. The winter daybreak is too feeble to penetrate the stained-glass windows, doubly and trebly stained by soot and bird droppings, that depict scenes from the life of Our Lady, with St Jude, patron of lost causes, prominent in the foreground of her Coronation in Heaven. In alcoves along the side walls votive candles fitfully illuminate the plaster figures of saints paralysed in attitudes of prayer or exhortation. There are electric lights in here, dangling from the dark roof on immensely long leads, like lamps lowered down a well or pit-shaft; but, for economy's sake, only a few have been switched on, above the altar and over the front central pews where the sparse congregation is gathered. As they murmur their responses (it is a dialogue mass, a recent innovation designed to increase lay participation in the liturgy) their breath condenses on the chill, damp air, as though their prayers were made fleetingly visible before being sucked up into the inscrutable gloom of the raftered vault.

The priest on the altar turns, with a swish of his red vestments (it is a martyr's feast day, St Valentine's) to face the congregation.

'*Dominus vobiscum.*'

There are eight young people present, including one on the altar performing the office of acolyte. They reply, '*Et cum spiritu tuo.*'

A creak of hinges and a booming thud at the back of the church indicates the arrival of a latecomer. As the priest turns back to the altar to read the Offertory prayer, and the rest flutter the pages of their missals to find the English translation in its proper place, all hear the hurried tiptap of high-heeled shoes on the tiled surface of the central aisle. A buxom, jolly-looking girl with a damp head-scarf tied over dark curls makes a hasty genuflection and slides into a pew next to another girl whose blonde head is becomingly draped with a black lace mantilla. The wearer of the mantilla turns her head to give a discreet smile of welcome, incidentally presenting her profile to the thickset youth in the dufflecoat just behind her, who seems to admire it. The dark latecomer wrinkles her nose and arches her eyebrows in comical self-reproach. Now there are nine, plus the priest, and a couple of immobile old ladies who are neither sitting nor kneeling, but wedged into their pew in a position halfway between the two postures, wrapped up like awkward parcels in coats and woollies, and looking as though they were left behind by their families after the last Sunday mass and have been there ever since. We are not, however, concerned with the old ladies, whose time on this earth is almost up, but with the young people, whose adult lives are just beginning.

It is apparent from their long striped scarves and their bags and briefcases stuffed with books that they are students at one of the constituent colleges of the University of London, situated not far away. Every Thursday in term, Father Austin Brierley, the young curate of Our Lady and St Jude's, and a kind of unofficial chaplain to the College Catholic Society (for the official chaplain and chaplaincy, embracing the entire University, have appropriately dignified headquarters elsewhere) says mass at 8 a.m. especially for members of his New Testament Study Group, and for any other Catholic students who wish to attend. They do so at considerable cost in personal discomfort. Rising an hour earlier than usual, in cold bed-sitters far out in the suburbs, they travel fasting on crowded buses and trains, dry-mouthed, weak with hunger, and nauseated by cigarette smoke, to be present at this unexciting ritual in a cold, gloomy church at the grey, indifferent heart of London.

Why?

It is not out of a sense of duty, for Catholics are bound to hear mass only on Sundays and holydays of obligation (of which St Valentine's is not one). Attendance at mass on ordinary weekdays is supererogatory (a useful word in theology, meaning more than is necessary for salvation). So, why? Is it hunger and thirst after righteousness? Is it devotion to the Real Presence of Christ in the Blessed Sacrament? Is it habit, or superstition, or the desire for comradeship? Or all these things, or none of them? Why have they come here, and what do they expect to get out of it?

To begin with the simplest case: Dennis, the burly youth in the dufflecoat, its hood thrown back to expose a neck pitted with boil scars, is here because Angela, the fair beauty in the mantilla, is here. And Angela is here because she is a good Catholic girl, the pride of the Merseyside convent where she was Head Girl and the first pupil ever to win a State Scholarship to University, the eldest daughter of awed parents who run a corner-shop open till all hours and scarcely know what a university is for. Naturally Angela joined the Catholic Society in the first week of her first term and naturally she joined its New Testament Study Group when invited to do so, and naturally she goes along to the Thursday morning masses, for she has been conditioned to do what is good without questioning and it scarcely costs her any effort. Not so with Dennis. He is a Catholic, but not a particularly devout one. His mother, who has shouted herself hoarse from the foot of the stairs, at home in Hastings, on many a Sunday morning to get him up in time for church, would be stunned to see him here of his own volition at an early midweek mass. Dennis is fairly stunned himself, yawning and shivering inside his dufflecoat, yearning for his breakfast and the first fag of the day. This is not his idea of fun, but he has no choice, he cannot bear to let Angela out of his sight a moment longer than is absolutely unavoidable, escorting her up to the very threshold of her lecture rooms in the French Department before hurrying off to his own instruction in Chemistry. As soon as he set eyes on her at the Christmas Hop he knew he must make her his own, she was his dream made flesh in a pink angora jumper and black taffeta skirt. That he was a Catholic gave him an immediate advantage, for Angela trusted him not to be like the other boys she had met at hops who, she complained, held you too close on the dance floor and offered to see you home only in order to be rude. But his faith is a double-edged asset to Dennis, who must act up to the part, not only desisting from rudeness in word and deed, but joining Cath. Soc. and attending its boring study groups and getting up for this early weekday mass in the perishing winter dark for fear that if he does not some other eligible Catholic youth will carry Angela off. Dennis suspects (quite correctly) that Adrian, for instance – the bespectacled youth in the belted gaberdine raincoat, expertly manipulating his thick Roman missal with its four silk markers in liturgical colours, red, green, purple and white – is interested in Angela, and that very probably Michael is too – the boy with the dark slab of greasy hair falling forward across a white snub-nosed face, kneeling some rows behind the others, wearing an extraordinarily shapeless, handed-down tweed overcoat that reaches almost to his ankles when he stands up for the Gospel – but there Dennis is wrong.

Michael is interested not in any particular girl, but in girls generally. He does not want a relationship, he wants sex – though his lust is vague and hypothetical in the extreme. At the Salesian grammar school on the northern outskirts of London which he attended before coming up to the University, a favourite device of the bolder spirits in the sixth form to enliven Religious Instruction was to tease the old priest who took them for this lesson with casuistical questions of sexual morality, especially the question of How Far You Could Go with the opposite sex. '*Please, Father, how far can you go with a girl, Father?*' The answer was always the same, though expressed in different ways: your conscience would tell you, no further than you wouldn't be ashamed to tell your mother, as far as you would let another boy go with your sister. Michael listened to this with lowered eyes and a foolish grin on his face, never having been any distance at all with a real girl. He has not advanced since then. Any reasonably personable female, therefore, will do for his purely mental purposes, as long as she has perceptible breasts. If Angela should happen to take off her coat first in the Lyons cafeteria where they will all have breakfast after mass, he will look at her breasts lasciviously, but if Polly (the latecomer) should be the first he will look at her breasts with equal lasciviousness, though they are of quite a different shape, and the breasts of the women sitting opposite him in the Tube will do just as well, and so will the breasts pictured in the photographic art books displayed in bookshops in the Charing Cross Road – indeed, these will do better because, though not actually present in the flesh, they are uncovered, and thus attest more strikingly to the really amazing, exciting fact of the mere existence of breasts. As for female pudenda, well, Michael isn't (as we say nowadays) into them yet, he doesn't even have a verbal concept for that orifice that he can think with comfortably – cunt being a word that he, and the others present at this St Valentine's mass, have seen only on lavatory walls and wouldn't dream of pronouncing, even silently, to themselves; and though Michael has seen the word vagina in print, he is not sure how to pronounce it, nor is it a word that seems to do justice to what it signifies. He is not at all sure about that, either, never having seen one that was more than three summers old, but anyway breasts are quite enough to keep him in a fever of excitement at the moment. Breasts, and the underclothing that goes with them, are sufficient to be going on with. There is no shortage of reminders of these things, or at least his mind is finely tuned to pick up their vibrations at the slightest opportunity. Give Michael a newspaper double-page spread to scan, with, say, two thousand words on it, and his eye will zoom in on the word *cleavage* or *bra* instantly. American psychologists have since established by experiment that the thoughtstream of the normal healthy male turns to sex every other minute between the ages of sixteen and twenty-six, after which the intervals grow gradually longer (though not all that long), but Michael does not know this; he thinks he is abnormal, that the pollution of his thought-stream is the work of the Devil, and that he is grievously at fault in not only not resisting temptation, but in positively inviting it. For instance, he walks along the Charing Cross Road at every opportunity, even if it involves a considerable detour; and he reads in the Union Lounge, a frowzy basement room filled with damaged furniture and cigarette smoke, the cheap popular papers that are most likely to include the word *cleavage* and pictures of girls displaying that feature, or rather gap – that fascinating *vide*, that absence which signifies the presence of the two glands on either side of it more eloquently than they do themselves (or so the structuralist jargon fashionable in another decade would put it, though to Michael in February 1952 cleavage is just second-best to actual bare tits, which newspapers obviously can't show, something to keep you going until it is time for another saunter down the Charing Cross Road). He does these things knowing that they will give him impure thoughts. An impure thought, he has been told by a boy who had been told by a priest in confession, is any thought that gives you an erection, and it doesn't take much to give Michael one of those. It is almost a permanent condition of his waking hours. (Twenty-one years later he learned from a magazine article about the making of pornographic films in Los Angeles that the producers of such films employed special stand-by studs in case the male lead couldn't manage an erection; you didn't have to act, all they ever filmed was your penis, all you had to do was to get it up, and into the female lead; and he thought, ruefully, that would have been the job for me when I was young – ruefully, because he was having trouble himself getting it up then, and not even reading such an article in a magazine, with pictures of naked girls with their legs apart, would do the trick. He was passing blood with his bowel movements at that particular time, and was more apt to think of death than sex every other minute.) But in 1952 he has erections, which is to say impure thoughts, very frequently. These, he thinks, are probably only venial sins, but he masturbates quite often too, and that is surely a mortal sin.

404

Before we go any further it would probably be a good idea to explain the metaphysic or world-picture these young people had acquired from their Catholic upbringing and education. Up there was Heaven; down there was Hell. The name of the game was Salvation, the object to get to Heaven and avoid Hell. It was like Snakes and Ladders: sin sent you plummeting down towards the Pit; the sacraments, good deeds, acts of self-mortification, enabled you to climb back towards the light. Everything you did or thought was subject to spiritual accounting. It was either good, bad or indifferent. Those who succeeded in the game eliminated the bad and converted as much of the indifferent as possible into the good. For instance, a banal bus journey (indifferent) could be turned to good account by silently reciting the Rosary, unobtrusively fingering the beads in your pocket as you trundled along. To say the Rosary openly and aloud in such a situation was more problematical. If it witnessed to the Faith, even if it excited the derision of non-believers (providing this were borne with patience and forgiveness) it was, of course, Good – indeed heroically virtuous; but if done to impress others, to call attention to your virtue, it was worse than indifferent, it was Bad – spiritual pride, a very slippery snake. Progress towards Heaven was full of such pitfalls. On the whole, a safe rule of thumb was that anything you positively disliked doing was probably Good, and anything you liked doing enormously was probably Bad, or potentially bad – an 'occasion of sin'.

There were two types of sin, venial and mortal. Venial sins were little sins which only slightly retarded your progress across the board. Mortal sins were huge snakes that sent you slithering back to square one, because if you died in a state of mortal sin, you went to Hell. If, however, you confessed your sins and received absolution through the sacrament of Penance, you shot up the ladder of grace to your original position on the board, though carrying a penalty – a certain amount of punishment awaiting you in the next world. For few Catholics expected that they would have reached the heavenly finishing line by the time they died. Only saints would be in that happy position, and to consider yourself a saint was a sure sign that you weren't one: there was a snake called Presumption that was just as fatal as the one called Despair. (It really was a most ingenious game.) No, the vast majority of Catholics expected to spend a certain amount of time in Purgatory first, working off the punishment accruing to sins, venial and mortal, that they had committed in the course of their lives. They would have been *forgiven* these sins, you understand, through the sacrament of Penance, but there would still be some detention to do in Purgatory. Purgatory was a kind of penitential transit camp on the way to the gates of Heaven. Most of your deceased relatives were probably there, which was why you prayed for them (there would be no point, after all, in praying for a soul that was in Heaven or Hell). Praying for them was like sending food parcels to refugees, and all the more welcome if you could enclose a few indulgences. An indulgence was a kind of spiritual voucher, obtained by performing some devotional exercise, promising the bearer so much off the punishment due to his sins, *e.g.* forty days' remission for saying a certain prayer, or two hundred and forty days for making a certain pilgrimage. 'Days' did not refer to time spent in Purgatory (a misconception common in Protestant polemic) for earthly time did not, of course, apply there, but to the canonical penances of the mediaeval Church, when confessed sinners were required to do public penance such as sitting in sackcloth and ashes at the porch of the parish church for a certain period, instead of the purely nominal penances (recitation of prayers) prescribed in modern times. The remission of temporal punishment by indulgences was measured on the ancient scale.

There was also such a thing as plenary indulgence, which was a kind of jackpot, because it wiped out *all* the punishment accruing to your sins up to the time of obtaining the indulgence. You could get one of these by, for instance, going to mass and Holy Communion on the first Friday of nine successive months. In theory, if you managed to obtain one of these plenary indulgences just before dying you would go straight to Heaven no matter how many sins you had committed previously. But there was a catch: you had to have a 'right disposition' for the indulgence to be valid, and a spirit of calculating self-interest was scarcely that. In fact, you could never be quite sure that you had the right disposition, and might spend your entire life collecting invalid indulgences. It was safest, therefore, to dedicate them to the souls in Purgatory, because the generosity of this action would more or less guarantee that you had the right disposition. Of course the indulgences wouldn't then help *you* when you got to Purgatory, but you hoped that others down below might do you the same service, and that the souls you assisted to heaven would intercede there on your behalf. The Church of Christ was divided into three great populations, connected to each other by prayer: the Church Militant (on earth), the Church Suffering (in Purgatory) and the Church Triumphant (in Heaven).

Do the young people gathered together in the church of Our Lady and St Jude on this dark St Valentine's Day believe all this? Well, yes and no. They don't believe it with the same certainty that they believe they will have to sit their Final Examinations within the next three years; and about some of the details in the picture they are becoming a bit doubtful (most of them, for instance, have given up collecting indulgences, as something rather childish and undignified), but in outline, yes, they believe it, or at least they are not sure it is safe not to believe it; and this deeply engrained eschatological consciousness (eschatological, another useful word, meaning pertaining to the four last things – death, judgement, heaven and hell) is probably the chief common factor behind their collective presence here at mass. Only Miles, the tall, sleek figure swaying slightly on his feet during the Credo like a reed in the wind, tilting a handsomely bound old missal to catch the feeble electric light, is positively relishing the service, and he is a convert of fairly recent standing, so it is all delightfully novel to him – the gloomy, grubby ornateness of the church interior, the muttered, secretive liturgy (for only certain parts of the mass are in dialogue, and the Prayer of Consecration to which Father Brierley now turns is his alone), the banks of votive candles flickering amid frozen Niagaras of spent wax, and the sanctuary lamp glowing like an inflamed eye, guaranteeing the presence of God Himself in this place – all

407

deliciously different from the restrained good taste of the chapel at his public school. As to the others, most of them will not be displeased when mass is over and they can hurry off to a day of largely secular concerns and pleasures. They are here not because they positively want to be, but because they believe it is good for their souls to be at mass when they would rather be in bed, and that it will help them in the immortal game of snakes and ladders.

But it is not doing Michael's soul any good at all if, as he thinks, he is in a state of mortal sin. For no matter how many good deeds or acts of devotion you perform, you get no heavenly credit for them if you are not in a state of grace. But is masturbation a mortal sin? There are times when he thinks it can't be. Is it possible that if he should die in the act (an all too vivid picture of himself discovered in bed, frozen by *rigor mortis* like a plaster statue, with his eyes turned up to the ceiling and his swollen member still clasped in his fist) that he would suffer eternal punishment just the same as, say, Hitler? (In fact there is no guarantee that Hitler is in Hell; he might have made an Act of Perfect Contrition a microsecond after squeezing the trigger in his Berlin bunker.) It seems self-evidently absurd. On the other hand, you could argue by the same method that, say, having proper sex with a prostitute isn't a mortal sin, either, and if that isn't, well, what is? Just thinking about it gives him a huge erection under his conveniently baggy coat, at the very moment when Father Brierley elevates the Host at the Consecration, thus heaping iniquity upon iniquity, sacrilege upon impurity. He could, of course, ask a priest's advice on the problem – but that is part of the problem, he can't bring himself to confess his sin for shame and embarrassment. (And is that so surprising – would you, gentle reader? Did you, gentle Catholic reader?) This means that he can't go to Communion either, for one may only receive the Eucharist in a state of grace, otherwise it is a sacrilege. Therefore, when the Communion bell rings at these Thursday masses, Michael is the only one left kneeling in his pew. At first, when this was noticed, he used to hint that he had broken his fast – swallowed water when he brushed his teeth, or thoughtlessly nibbled a biscuit; and when this excuse wore thin he ingeniously pretended to have Doubts about the doctrine of Transubstantiation. He kept coming to mass, he confided to the others, in the hope that one day his faith would be restored. Father Brierley tried to convince him that he was being over-scrupulous, upon which Michael rapidly developed Doubts on other major doctrines, such as the Trinity and Papal Infallibility.

The others are rather impressed by Michael's Doubts, and Polly, catching sight of his pale and mournful visage as she herself returns from the altar rail, is apt to recall the words of Gerard Manley Hopkins (she is reading English):

> O the mind, mind has mountains, cliffs of fall
> Frightful, sheer, no-man-fathomed. Hold them cheap
> May who ne'er hung there!

All go out of their way to be nice to Michael and to encourage his failing powers of belief. In fact, of course, he believes the whole bag of tricks more simply and comprehensively perhaps than anyone else present at this mass, and is more honest in examining his conscience than many. Polly, for instance, frequently comforts herself with a moistened forefinger before dropping off to sleep, but wouldn't dream of mentioning this in Confession or letting it prevent her from taking the Sacrament. After all, she only does it when she is half-asleep and no longer, as it were, responsible for her actions. It is almost as though it belongs to someone else, the hand that slips under the waistband of her Baby Doll pyjamas and sliding between her legs rubs, rubs, gently, exquisitely, the little button of flesh the name and nature of which she does not yet know (though years later she will join a women's gynaecological workshop whose members squint through optical instruments at their own and each other's genitals, looking for signs of cystitis, thrush, polypi and other female afflictions, and will know her way around the uterus as familiarly as she now knows the stations on the Inner Circle line between her digs and College). Of course, she does not bring herself to climax – not the panting, writhing kind of climax demonstrated in films such as those Michael will read about twenty-one years later. Rather, she rocks herself to sleep on wavelets of sensation rippling out from the secret grotto at the centre of her body. When she wakes in the morning she has wiped the act from her memory. It helps her to do this that she has no name for it. 'Masturbation' is not an item in her vocabulary – or Michael's, for that matter, though he does have his own idiomatic phrase for it, which Polly does not. Neither does Angela, who does not need one anyway, because she doesn't indulge in the practice. She has imbibed more deeply than Polly the code of personal modesty impressed upon convent-educated girls. She keeps her body scrupulously clean, she dresses it carefully and attractively, but she does not examine it or caress it in the process. Her movements at toilet are brisk and businesslike. Her complexion gleams with health. She has scarcely ever had an impure thought, whereas Polly has had quite a few. Admittedly, Polly's convent school, a rather posh one in Sussex, for boarders, was a less chaste environment than Angela's in which to grow up. There was inevitably gossiping and giggling and smutty talk between the girls when they were left on their own, whereas Angela went to and fro between school and home every day, with scarcely a moment free, what with studying, games, and helping with housework and the shop, for idle thoughts or words.

As for Ruth, the thickset, bespectacled girl in boots and a school-style navy raincoat, kneeling in the front row, she has put the whole business of sex behind her long ago, *i.e.*, at the age of sixteen. For a while in early adolescence she daily inspected her pimply, pasty complexion, her thick yet flat-chested torso, her lank, colourless hair, wondering if she was merely going through 'a phase', whether she would break through this unpromising chrysalis one day and emerge a beautiful butterfly, as she had seen other girls do. But alas, there was no such metamorphosis, she was stuck with her plainness and resigned herself to it, became a great reader and museum visitor and concert-goer, got interested in religion in the sixth form and, much to the surprise of her frivolous and vaguely agnostic parents, announced one day that she had been taking instructions from the local Catholic priest and was intending to be received into the Church.

All the young people present at this mass (and, of course, the celebrant) are virgins. Apart from Michael and Polly, none of them masturbates habitually and several have never masturbated at all. They have no experience of heavy petting. These facts run directly counter to statistical evidence recently tabulated by members of the Kinsey Institute for Sexual Research in Indiana, but these young people are British, and in any case unrepresentative of their age group. They carry a heavy freight of super-ego. To get to the University they have had to work hard, pass exams and win scholarships, sublimating the erotic energy of adolescence into academic achievement; and if ever a sultry evening or a bold glance took them off-guard and set them yearning for nameless sensual satisfactions, the precepts of their religion taught them to suppress these promptings, these 'irregular motions of the flesh' as the Catechism called them. They are therefore sexually innocent to a degree that they will scarcely be able to credit when looking back on their youth in years to come. They know about the mechanics of basic copulation, but none of them could give an accurate account of the processes of fertilization, gestation and birth, and three of the young men do not even know how babies are born, vaguely supposing that they appear by some natural form of Caesarian section, like ripe chestnuts splitting their husks. As to the refinements and variations of the act of love – fellatio, cunnilingus, buggery, and the many different postures in which copulation may be contrived – they know them not (with the exception of Miles, who attended a public school) and would scarcely credit them were they to be told by Father Austin Brierley himself, who knows all about them in a theoretical way from his moral theology course at the seminary, for it is necessary that a priest should know of every sin that he might have to absolve. Not, he thanks God, that he has ever had to deal in the confessional with any of the more appalling perversions described in the textbooks, veiled in the relative decency of Latin – unspeakable acts between men and women, men and men, men and animals, which seem to someone who has voluntarily renounced ordinary heterosexual love not so much depraved as simply unintelligible.

411

He is not thinking of such matters now, of course, he is thinking of the mass he is celebrating, the sacred privilege he enjoys of changing the bread and wine into the Body and Blood of Jesus Christ, Redeemer. It is very hard to generate an appropriate sense of awe towards something done so often – once a day every day and three times on Sundays. Concentration is so difficult, distraction so easy. When he turned to face the congregation earlier at the Offertory, for instance, he couldn't help checking who was present and feeling a little twinge of disappointment that Polly's dark curls and rosy cheeks were missing; and then, as he turned back and heard the unmistakable tiptap of her high heels, he had to suppress a smile which might have been caught by his server, Edward. Edward is a first-year medical student with a humorous, rubbery countenance, hung between a pair of oversized ears, that stands him in good stead in comic opera and rugby-club concerts, but for liturgical purposes he twists it into an expression of such impressive solemnity that Austin Brierley almost feels nervous when celebrating mass under his scrutiny.

When Father Brierley pauses sometimes like this in the middle of the celebration, he is not, as Edward and the others suppose, rapt in private prayer, but struggling to eliminate from his mind such extraneous thoughts as Polly's late arrival, and to concentrate on the Holy Sacrifice. This is hard precisely because of the rapport he feels with the students. The congregation on an ordinary Sunday, mostly made up of poor Irish and Italians employed in the catering and hotel trades, is just a dense, anonymous mass, coughing and shuffling and shushing their babies behind his back, so that it is easy for him to shut them out from his mind; but these students are different – they are intelligent, well-mannered, articulate, and not very much younger than himself. They have no idea how much he depends upon them for human contact, how the New Testament study circle and the Thursday masses, which for most of them are quasi-penitential exercises, are for him the sweetest hours of the week.

Now the moment of his communion has come. He holds the consecrated host in his left hand while beating his breast with his right fist, as he recites the '*Domine, non sum dignus.*' Lord, I am not worthy that Thou shouldst enter under my roof . . . Behind him, summoned by Edward's bell, the little congregation has gathered at the altar rail, and they join in the prayer: '*sed tantum dic verbo et sanabitur anima mea.*' Say but the word and my soul shall be healed. Having reverently received the host and drunk from the chalice, the priest pauses for a moment in silent thanksgiving before turning to face his little flock. He holds up a host before them. '*Ecce Agnus Dei; ecce qui tolit peccata mundi.*' Behold the Lamb of God; behold Him who taketh away the sins of the world.

Looking, as it were, over his shoulder, at the congregation, you can remind yourselves who they are. Ten characters is a lot to take in all at once, and soon there will be more, because we are going to follow their fortunes, in a manner of speaking, up to the present, and obviously they are not going to pair off with each other, that would be too neat, too implausible, so there will be other characters not yet invented, husbands and wives and lovers, not to mention parents and children, so it is important to get these ten straight now. Each character, for instance, has already been associated with some selected detail of dress or appearance which should help you to distinguish one from another. Such details also carry connotations which symbolize certain qualities or attributes of the character. Thus Angela's very name connotes angel, as in Heaven and cake (she looks good enough to eat in her pink angora sweater) and her blonde hair archetypecasts her as the fair virtuous woman, spouse-sister-mother figure, whereas Polly is a Dark Lady, sexy seductress, though not really sinister because of her healthy cheeks and jolly curls. Miles, you recall, is the ex-public schoolboy, a convert; his handsomely bound old missal bespeaks wealth and taste, his graceful, wandlike figure a certain effeminacy. There is Dennis, Angela's slave, burly in his dufflecoat, the scar tissue on his neck perhaps proleptic of suffering, and Adrian, bespectacled (limited vision), in belted gaberdine raincoat (instinctual repression, authoritarian determination), not to be confused with Ruth's glasses and frumpish schoolgirl's raincoat, signifying unawakened sexuality and indifference to self-display. On the altar is Edward, his rubbery clown's face locked into an expression of exaggerated piety, the first to receive the wafer from Father Brierley's fingers, shooting out a disconcertingly long tongue like a carnival whistle. Back in the pews there is Michael, haggard in his baggy wanker's overcoat and his simulated Doubts, his head weighed down with guilt or the hank of dark hair falling across his eyes, his features slightly flattened as though pressed too often against glass enclosing forbidden goodies; and a girl you have not yet been introduced to, who now comes forward from the shadows of the side aisle, where she has been lurking, to join the others at the altar rail. Let her be called Violet, no, Veronica, no Violet, improbable a name as that is for Catholic girls of Irish extraction, customarily named after saints and figures of Celtic legend, for I like the connotations of Violet – shrinking, penitential, melancholy – a diminutive, dark-haired girl, a pale, pretty face ravaged by eczema, fingernails bitten down to the quick and stained by nicotine, a smartly cut needlecord coat sadly creased and soiled; a girl, you might guess from all this evidence, with problems, guilts, hangups. (She is another regular masturbator, by the way, so make that three, and she is not quite sure whether she is a virgin, having been interfered with at the age of twelve by a tramp whose horny index finger may have ruptured her hymen, or so she confided to Angela, who was shocked, and told Ruth, who was sceptical, having received from Violet an entirely different story of how she had been painfully deflowered by a holy candle wielded by her cousin in the course of an experimental black mass in the attic of his house one day when their parents were out. Really, you didn't know what to believe with Violet, but she was certainly a source of interest.)

Let's just take a roll call. From left to right along the altar rail, then: Polly, Dennis, Angela, Adrian, Ruth, Miles, Violet. Michael kneeling in his pew. Edward and Father Brierley on the altar. And of course the two old ladies, who have somehow levered themselves into the central aisle, and shuffled forward with painful slowness on their swollen feet to stand (for if they should kneel they might never be able to get up again) at the altar rail, their heads nodding gently like toys on the parcel shelf of a moving car, their eyes watery and myopic, their facial skin hanging from their skulls like folds of dingy cloth. No one takes much notice of them. Austin Brierley knows them as regular attenders at early weekday mass and as parishioners whom he occasionally has to visit at home, carrying the Blessed Sacrament into their depressing bedrooms when they are too ill to go out. Good women, pious women, but of no interest. Both are widows, fortunate enough to be looked after by their grown-up children. There is nothing he can do for them except give them the sacraments, listening to their mumbled, rambling confessions of trivial peccadilloes (sometimes they dry up after the opening Act of Contrition, unable to remember a single sin, poor old dears, and sensing their panic, he prompts them with a likely venial sin or two, though it is becoming increasingly difficult as they grow older and feebler, almost as incapable of envy and anger and covetousness as they have been for decades of lust, gluttony, sloth) and administering Communion, fighting back his own distaste at their trembling, discoloured tongues and loosely fitting dentures. He does so now, giving them Communion first so that by the time he comes to the end of the row they will be at least started on the slow journey back to their pew. Edward, holding the paten under their quivering jaws, scans them with professional curiosity, diagnosing arthritis, anaemia, noting a large growth, presumably benign, on the throat of one; but to the rest of the students the two old ladies might be part of the church's furniture, the dark stained oak pews and the dusty plaster statues, for all the notice they take of them. Which is surprising, in a way, when you consider that, as explained above, a principal reason why they are all gathered here is that they believe it will stand them in good stead in the next world. For here are two persons manifestly certain to die in the near future. You might think the young people would be interested to observe the disposition in which the old ladies approach the undiscovered country from whose bourne no traveller returns, would be curious to determine whether a lifetime's practice of the Catholic faith and the regular reception of its sacraments has in any way mitigated the terrors of that journey, imparted serenity and confidence to these travellers, made the imminent parting of the spirit and its fleshly garments any less dreaded. But no, it has not occurred to any of them to scrutinize or interrogate the old ladies in this way. The fact is that none of them actually believes he or she is going to die.

They know it, cognitively, yes; but believe it, intuitively, they do not. In that regard they are no different from other young, healthy human beings. They look forward to life, not death. Their plans include marriage, children, jobs, fame, fulfilment, service – not the grave and the afterlife. The afterlife figures in their thoughts rather like retirement: something to insure against, but not to brood on at the very outset of your career. Religion is their insurance – the Catholic Church offering the very best, the most comprehensive cover – and weekday mass is by way of being an extra premium, enhancing the value of the policy.

But it is also more than that. For their Faith teaches them that God does not only control the afterlife; He also controls this one. Not a sparrow falls without His willing it. As far back as they can remember, the cradle Catholics among them have been encouraged to pray for good fortune in this life as well as in the next: fine weather for the School Sports Day, the recovery of a lost brooch, promotion for Daddy, success at the Eleven Plus. There is a convent somewhere in the south of England which advertises in the Catholic press the services of its nuns, praying in shifts twenty-four hours a day for whatever intentions you care to send them in return for donations to their charitable cause (*'Send no money until your prayer is answered – then give generously'*) and which is heavily in demand around the time that GCE results are expected. You might think that the time to pray was before the examinations were taken, otherwise it was asking God to tamper with the marks, but that was not the way these Catholics looked at it. God was omnipotent, and it would cost Him no effort, should He be so minded, to turn back the clock of history and make the tiny adjustment that would allow you to put the right answer instead of the wrong one and get a Pass instead of a Fail and then set the mechanism ticking again without your marker or the rest of the world or indeed you yourself being

416

any the wiser. If such prayers were not always answered this did not show that the system did not work, but merely that God had decided that it wouldn't be in your interest to gratify your wish or that you didn't deserve it. One way or another, it was obviously prudent to keep on the right side of God, as long as you believed in Him at all, since then, even without your asking, He might reward you by ensuring that the right examination question or the right job or indeed Mr Right turned up when you were most in need.

To be fair to the young people in Our Lady and St Jude's, it must be said that they are not here entirely out of self-interest. To a greater or lesser extent they have all grasped the idea that Christianity is about transcendence of self in love of God and one's neighbour, and they struggle to put this belief into practice according to their lights, trying to be kind, generous and grateful for their blessings. Admittedly, Angela is the only neighbour for whom Dennis has any love to spare at the moment, and Michael feels too hopelessly abandoned to sexual depravity to make much of an effort at being good in other ways, but Angela neglects no opportunity to do a good deed, shopping for an old lady or baby-sitting for her landlady: and Ruth is a more systematic philanthropist, helping in the nursery of a Catholic orphanage on one afternoon a week, sometimes taking Polly along with her – and, although Polly can never be relied upon, when she does turn up she entertains the children more successfully than Ruth, so that Ruth has a struggle not to feel jealous; and Adrian is a cadet in the Catholic Evidence Guild, and spends every Sunday afternoon at Speaker's Corner at the foot of the Guild's rostrum, lending moral support and learning the tricks of the trade against the day when he will take on the atheists and bigots of the metropolis in his own right; and Miles is a tertiary of the order of Carmelites and wears under his beautifully laundered white shirts and silk underwear an exceedingly itchy scapular the discomfort of which he offers up for the souls of all his Protestant forebears who may be languishing in the Purgatory in which they did not believe; and Edward plans to practice medicine for at least two years in the mission fields of Africa when he has qualified; and Violet is liable to sudden, alarming fits of self-mortification and good works, such as fasting for a whole week or descending upon bewildered tramps under the arches of the Charing Cross Embankment, offering them rosaries which they accept in the hope of being able to sell them later for the price of a cup of tea, and, if they have sores, little bottles of Lourdes water, which the tramps drink in the expectation of its being gin and then disrespectfully spit out on to the pavement when they discover it isn't.

Violet is the last to receive Communion. Placing the host on her tongue, Father Brierley murmurs, as he has murmured to each of the communicants, '*Corpus Domini Nostri Jesu Christi custodiat animam tuam in vitam aeternam. Amen.*' May the Body of Our Lord Jesus Christ preserve thy soul to life everlasting. He turns back to the altar to perform the ablutions – purifying his fingers and the chalice with water which he then swallows to ensure that no crumb of the consecrated host, no drop of the consecrated wine, should remain unconsumed and therefore at risk of irreverent or unseemly treatment. Any entire hosts that remain are locked away in the tabernacle above the altar, its door screened by a little gilt curtain. Meanwhile the communicants have returned to their places, where they kneel in silent thanksgiving, their eyes closed, their heads bowed.

This is a difficult business for nearly all of them. For what is it that has happened, for which they are to give thanks? They have received the Body and Blood of Christ. Not literally, of course, but under the appearances of bread and wine – or rather bread alone, for it is not at this date Catholic practice to administer Communion under both kinds to the laity – and not really bread either, for the host bears very little resemblance to an ordinary loaf. A small, round, papery, almost tasteless wafer has been placed on their tongues, and they have swallowed it (without chewing it, an action deemed irreverent by those who prepared them for their First Communions) and thus received Christ into themselves. But what does *that* mean? The consecrated host, they know, has not changed in outward appearance, and if Dennis, say, were, like sacrilegious scientists in Catholic cautionary tales, to take one back to the laboratory on his tongue and analyse it there, he would discover only molecules of wheat. But it would be sacrilege to do so precisely because the host *has* changed into the Body and Blood, Soul and Divinity, of Jesus Christ, Saviour. In the language of scholastic philosophy, the substance has changed but the accidents (empirically observable properties) have not. The doctrine of transubstantiation, as they have been reminded often enough in RI lessons, is a mystery, a truth above reason. That is all very well, but it means that the mind has little to grip on when it comes to making one's thanksgiving after Communion. In fact, the more intently you think about the mystery, the more irreverent and disedifying your thoughts are apt to become. At what point, Dennis cannot help wondering, does the miracle of transubstantiation reverse itself, since it cannot be that Christ submits himself to the indignities of human digestion and excretion? Is it as the host begins to dissolve on the tongue, as it passes the epiglottis, or as it travels down the oesophagus that Christ jumps from His wheaten vehicle and into your soul? Such speculations are not conducive to pious recollection. There are, of course, set prayers which one can say, but they don't mean a lot either.

'*O Lord Jesus*,' Adrian reads from his missal, '*I have received Thee within myself, and from within the sanctuary of my heart into which Thou hast deigned to descend, do Thou give to Almighty God, in my name, all the glory that is His due.*'

Adrian, who has a good logical mind, might well ask by what right he can describe his heart as a sanctuary, and how Christ, being God, can give glory to God, or putting that aside, why He should be bothered to do so in his, Adrian's name, when he, Adrian, is perfectly capable of giving glory to God himself. But Adrian is conditioned not to ask such awkward questions, and while reading these words with a vague feeling of piety, thinks of something else. In fact, within thirty seconds of kneeling down and bowing their heads, most of them are thinking of something other than the Eucharist – of breakfast, or study, or the weather, or sex or just the ache in their knees.

It is easier for them when Father Brierley, having read the Last Gospel, comes to the foot of the altar and kneels to recite the customary prayers to Our Lady.

'*Hail Holy Queen, mother of mercy; hail our life, our sweetness and our hope! To thee do we cry, poor banished children of Eve; to thee do we send up our sighs, mourning and weeping in this vale of tears . . .*' Only the converts actually listen to the words and try to make sense of them – to the rest it is just a familiar pious babble; but all can think, as the baroque rhetoric of the prayer lifts them up on its surging cadences, of Our Lady, a sweet-faced woman in blue and white robes, with her arms and hands lifted slightly and extended forward, as she is depicted in a thousand cheap statues in Lady Chapels up and down the land. Praying to her for help is much easier than puzzling over transubstantiation.

Nevertheless, all feel better for having attended the mass, as they assemble outside the church porch, greeting each other, laughing and chattering, donning scarves and gloves against the cold, damp air. All (all except Michael anyway) feel cheerful, hopeful, cleansed, at peace. Perhaps this is indeed the presence of the Lord Jesus in them, and not just the lift of spirits that naturally comes with the termination of mild boredom and the expectation of breakfast.

Father Brierley has unvested with almost unseemly haste in order to race round the back of the church in time to greet his little flock before they move off to the Lyons cafeteria. 'Good morning, Angela, good morning, Dennis, good morning, Polly – overslept this morning?' He laughs too heartily, showing teeth stained with nicotine, breaks open a packet of Player's and presses cigarettes upon the boys who smoke. The students stamp their feet and shift the weight of their bags and briefcases from one hand to another, impatient to be off, but unwilling to seem discourteous. Violet takes one of Father Brierley's cigarettes, rather to his consternation, for he does not like to see women smoking in public. Some badinage is exchanged about St Valentine's Day, and Father Brierley, desperately aiming at an effect of good-humoured tolerance of harmless fun, doubles up with forced laughter.

'Did you get my Valentine?' Dennis murmurs to Angela.

She smiles. 'Yes. I got two, actually.'

Two! Dennis is immediately stricken with jealous fear. 'Who sent you the other one?'

'I haven't the foggiest.'

Eventually the cigarette ends are stamped into the muddy pavement and the little band begins to shuffle off in the direction of the Tottenham Court Road. 'Goodbye, Father!' they call; and Austin Brierley, thrusting his hands deep into the pockets of his cassock, and rocking backwards and forwards on his heels, calls back, 'Goodbye, goodbye, see you on Monday, at the study group. First Epistle to the Corinthians.'

'Aren't you coming to the St Valentine's Party, Father?' Ruth cries, and then winces as Polly pokes her in the ribs.

'No, no, I think not,' the priest replies. 'There's a meeting of the Legion of Mary . . .'

'What did you do that for?' Ruth mutters, rubbing her side.

'We don't want him there tonight, he's such a wet blanket,' says Polly *sotto voce*, and flashes Father Brierley a brilliant smile over her shoulder.

He blushes, and turns back to the church porch, which the two old ladies have just reached after a laborious arm-in-arm shuffle up the nave, and dutifully pauses to exchange a word with them. Then he makes his way back to the presbytery, where his congealing breakfast awaits him and, behind the *Daily Telegraph* propped on the other side of the table, his parish priest.

'Many there?' enquires the parish priest, without lifting his eyes from the *Daily Telegraph*.

'Nine,' says Austin Brierley. 'Plus Mrs Moody and Mrs O'Dowd, of course.'

The parish priest grunts. Austin Brierley takes the cover off his bacon and egg. It is only eight forty-five and the best of the day is already over.

It begins to drizzle again as the students make their way along the pavements in twos and threes. Rather reluctantly (for the rolling of it is a work of art), Miles unfurls his rapier-thin silk umbrella and gallantly holds it over Violet's head. 'Did you know,

Miles,' she says, 'that Our Lady of Fatima left a message about how the world will end which was sealed up and given to the Pope and mustn't be opened till 1960?'

'My dear, how exciting! He must be awfully tempted to have a peep at it.'

'They say he has, and it was so terrifying, he fainted.'

'You must know,' says Dennis to Angela. 'You must have some idea.'

'Well, I haven't. It wasn't signed, like yours. You're not supposed to sign Valentines, you know,' she says, a little tartly, because she is getting irritated by Dennis's persistent questioning. 'That's the whole point of them.'

'What about the writing on the envelope? Couldn't you recognize that?'

'Oh, for heaven's sake, Dennis, let's drop the subject.'

As they draw nearer the Tottenham Court Road, secular London engulfs them with the hiss and roar of traffic, and crowds of jostling, fretting pedestrians hurrying to work. No Lord Jesus in *them*, anyway, by the look of it; their faces are drawn, their eyes anxious or vacant as they cluster on the pavement's edge, waiting for the traffic lights to change. Flags fly at half-mast on some buildings for the recent death of King George VI, and a newspaper placard announces, THE NEW ELIZABETHANS: SPECIAL FEATURE.

'Did you know you were a New Elizabethan, Michael?' Ruth asks.

Michael, who is gazing lustfully at an unclothed and headless mannequin in a shop window, starts. 'What? eh?' he says, flicking back his lank forelock.

'We're the New Elizabethans, apparently.'

'Gadzooks! Zounds! Marry come up! Buckle your swash!' cries Edward, waving his tattered, broken-winged umbrella in the air. And as the traffic lights change he leads them across the road, crying, 'Once more unto the breach dear friends, once more!' Some of the other pedestrians stare, amused or disapproving. Grinning and giggling, the students straggle after Edward, enjoying the feeling of being young and irresponsible. Their gait has a different rhythm to that of the businessmen and typists hurrying to work. They have no lectures before ten o'clock, or if they have, they will cut them in order to have breakfast. And they *are* dear friends, Ruth thinks to herself; she has never had so many friends before, and it is such a relief to know that the friendship does not depend on one's being pretty or wealthy or smart, but simply on having the same beliefs in common; and she feels blessed, walking along the Tottenham Court Road behind Edward and Polly, who are discussing a sketch to be performed at the St Valentine's party.

It is deliciously warm in the basement of the Lyons cafeteria, a steamy, tropical heat emanating from the kitchens and the hot-water urns. They take off their coats and scarves, heap them with bags and briefcases in a corner, and relieve their hunger and thirst with baked beans and bacon, toast and sticky buns, cups and cups of dark, sweet tea. Ruth stirs two heaped teaspoonfuls of sugar into her cup: it will soon be Lent and she will be giving it up. As indulging a sweet tooth is her only weakness of the flesh, this will be no light penance.

'I hope everyone is coming to the party,' says Polly, who has sat up half the night cutting out paper hearts for decorations. 'Or are you all going to the Union do instead?'

All disown this intention with laughter and mock indignation. Union do's, especially on St Valentine's night, are notoriously dissipated affairs, involving the construction in a corner of the Lounge of a dimly-lit, cushion-lined grotto designed expressly for snogging, if not worse.

'Are you going to the Cath. Soc. party?' Adrian asks, glancing between Angela and Dennis. The 'you' could be singular or plural. Dennis thinks it is meant to be interpreted as singular and addressed to Angela, and that Adrian must be the sender of the second Valentine. 'No,' he says, 'I've got an experiment to write up.'

'Oh, we must go, we must all go,' says Angela. 'Polly will be disappointed if we don't.'

'I think I may drop in for an hour,' says Adrian.

'All right then, if you really want to,' says Dennis grimly to Angela.

Momentous things happen at or around the St Valentine's party. Walking Angela to the prefabricated hut in the College precincts where it is to be held, and unable to bear his jealousy any longer, Dennis stops suddenly under a dripping tree in Russell Square and apologizes abjectly for his boorish behaviour of the morning, recklessly declares his love for her, and asks if she will marry him. Angela is moved, overwhelmed, by this sudden gush of emotion; and feeling her heart knocking, the blood coming and going in her face and, as Dennis takes her in his arms underneath her overcoat, unwonted sensations in her vagina, decides that this must indeed be love, and murmurs into his ear that she loves him too, but she cannot promise to marry him till they know each other better and have their degrees, which is nearly three years away. He says he doesn't mind waiting, and at that moment he doesn't. They move on slowly through the square, with their arms round one another and keep them round one another for the rest of the evening, rotating slowly under Polly's crepe paper hearts to the theme tune of *La Ronde*, a saucy French film still attracting queues in the West End.

'Have you seen *La Ronde*, Adrian?' says Polly.

'I certainly have not,' he replies in his flat Derbyshire accent.

'You should, it's awfully good.'

'It's been banned by the League of Decency in America.'

'Pooh, why should we take any notice of them?'

'Personally, I think we could do with an organization like that in this country.'

'Oh, Adrian, you are the end! Why don't you ask me to dance?'

'I don't dance, as you very well know, Polly. Anyway, I was just going. I have work to do.'

While speaking to Polly, Adrian has been watching Angela and Dennis dancing, and has come to a decision. He will not pursue Angela. To try and win her now would entail too much expense of spirit. To prise her loose from Dennis's possessive embrace, he would have to become as infatuated, as abandoned, as Dennis himself, and Adrian is not prepared to pay that price. No woman is worth it, not even Angela. Looking at her perfectly symmetrical features, slightly flushed and softened by the romantic trance in which she moves about the dance floor, and haloed by the soft waves of her golden hair, he feels a wrenching pang of envy and desire, which he ruthlessly suppresses. Very well, then, if not Angela, then no one – at least until his studies are completed. He tugs tight the belt of his double-breasted gaberdine raincoat and marches out into the cold, dark drizzle. Very well, then, he will work, work and pray. If not Angela, then no one – certainly not Polly, a flighty, frivolous girl who will get herself into trouble one of these days, and not Ruth, either, because too plain, and not Violet, too unstable. He will work hard, he will get a good degree, and he will become a star of the Catholic Evidence Guild. One day Angela will stand beneath his rostrum at Hyde Park Corner, and admire, and regret. Thus Adrian.

Meanwhile Polly, slightly tipsy on the cider cup she prepared, and experimentally tasted rather too often, is dancing with Miles, a quickstep. He dances superbly, beautifully balanced on the pointed toes of his gleaming black shoes, but somehow coldly. There is no warmth in the pressure of his long fingers, splayed out across the small of her back, and when she tries to nestle against him he arches away from her, swings her round in a centrifugal flourish, and breaks into a sequence of rapidly executed fishtails that requires all her concentration to follow. At the conclusion of the record, he spins her like a top at the end of his long arm and bows with mock formality. Polly responds with a theatrical curtsey and nearly overbalances. She is gripped by an almost intolerable desire to be cuddled. Seeing Michael on his own, she goes over to him. Divested of his Artful Dodger's overcoat, wearing a clean white shirt, and having slicked back his quiff with a lavish application of Brylcreem, he looks quite presentable.

Michael watches Polly's approach with alarm. He has been appraising her breasts while she has been dancing with Miles and is afraid that she has noticed. This is not in fact the case, but by coming and speaking to him, she effectively puts a stop to the appraisal. They are in the same Department, English, and talk books for a while. Michael's favourite novel at the moment is *The Heart of the Matter*, and Polly's, *Brideshead Revisited*. 'But Greene's awfully sordid, don't you think?' says Polly.

'But Waugh's so snobbish.'

'Anyway, it said in the *Observer* that they're the two best English novelists going, so that's one in the eye for the Prods.'

After a while the restless Polly moves off to change the records on the gramophone, and leaves Michael free to contemplate her breasts again. He wonders what it is like to live with those twin protuberances, quivering and jouncing in front of you at every moment, like heavy ripe fruit on the bough; what it is like to sponge them at the washbasin every morning, rub them dry with a towel, and fit them carefully into the hollow cups of a brassiere, first the left one, then the right. Extraordinary.

Miles, watching Polly move across the room, recognizes with a certain inner panic that he finds her prominent bust and voluptuous hips repulsive. His spiritual adviser, a Farm Street Jesuit, has assured him that he will come to like girls in due course, given prayer and patience, but so far there are no perceptible signs of it. His erotic fantasies are still of young boys in the showers at school, their high, taut buttocks gleaming under the cascade. Perhaps, he had wondered aloud to the Jesuit, he should renounce sex altogether and try his vocation as a priest; but after a great deal of throat-clearing and tortuously allusive argument he gathered that only guaranteed heterosexuals were eligible for the priesthood. That was manifestly untrue of the Anglican clergy, he had protested. And that's why you get all those scandals in the Sunday papers, was the answer.

Neither Michael nor Miles gives a sexual thought, positive or negative, to Ruth, who is cutting sandwiches in a corner of the room. Yet she is a woman, and particularly conscious of it this evening, for her period has just started and she is bleeding copiously under her limp, dowdy dress of navy blue crepe. Normally Angela would have been helping her, for Angela is that kind of girl, never one to stand idly by when there is work to be done; but tonight Angela is blind to everyone else in the room except

Dennis, and, looking up from her sandwiches and holding her throbbing head, Ruth watches Angela dancing, and Polly flirting (with Edward now) and feels gloomily that the Christian fellowship of the morning has after all been dissolved by sex. A bitter remark scrawled on the wall of a loo at school comes back to her: *'Blessed are the good-looking, for they shall have fun.'* Then, ashamed of these envious thoughts, she bows her head over the sandwiches again. Tomorrow she will put in an extra afternoon at the orphanage, where there is no time – or occasion – for envy. It suddenly comes into Ruth's head that she might herself become a nun. She thrusts this idea away, a little frightened by the plausibility of it, for she doesn't want to give up her freedom, she nourishes dreams of becoming a famous botanist, travelling the world to discover new species, and perhaps marrying another famous botanist who will love her for her mind rather than her looks. And her mother would have kittens. At the thought of her parents' likely reaction to such an idea, Ruth grins to herself, not knowing what a nice smile she has, because no one has ever told her.

Later, there is an entertainment in the form of sketches. In one of these, entitled 'The Return of St Valentine', Edward plays the part of the Roman martyr's ghost, dressed in a toga and holding on to his head with both hands in case (as he explains) it should topple off, for he was beheaded, who returns to earth in modern London and is bewildered and scandalized by the cult being celebrated in his name. Orgies of snogging in the Students' Union are represented by the miming of an extravagant display of passion on a sofa immediately behind the figure of St Valentine, as he recites the woeful story of his martyrdom in stumbling rhyming couplets. This sofa, raised on a dais, has its back facing the audience, so that all they can see are arms and legs appearing in surprising and suggestive positions above and to each side of the sofa, and various garments being discarded on to the floor. It is all done, rather cleverly, by Polly alone, using her four limbs and a collection of male and female attire. She tosses shoes to the right and left, she throws a bare arm languorously backwards over the side of the sofa, she draws on one leg of a pair of man's trousers and lofts it hilariously in the air, she points a stockinged leg, daringly exposed to the very suspender button, at the ceiling and wiggles her toes in a droll signal of alarm or ecstacy.

At this point Father Brierley makes an unexpected and unnoticed appearance at the party. He is not amused. He is appalled. When items of underclothing – panties, brassieres, Y-fronts – begin to fly through the air, he cries, 'Stop, stop, this is too bad!' and turns on the main lights in the room. Edward, startled, freezes in mid-speech, still holding on to his head. The audience blinks, stirs, looks round. Polly, fully dressed, stands up behind the sofa. Austin Brierley is totally disconcerted: first, to find his favourite student responsible for the spectacle, second, that no real indecency has taken place. But he proceeds to do his duty, which is to reproach them for a lapse of moral standards, not to mention taste. Catholic students should set an example to other young people by their purity of mind and body. The Catechism, he reminds them, explicitly forbade attendance at immodest shows and dances as an offence against the sixth commandment. All the more deplorable was it, therefore, actually to perform such degrading entertainments. He was surprised, he was shocked, he was disappointed. He expected an apology, well not an apology, after all it was Almighty God who was offended, Confession would be more appropriate, he would leave it to their consciences, they would talk about it another time, he did not wish to exaggerate, he was not opposed to harmless fun, but there were lines that had to be drawn . . .

He stammers to a halt. There is a long silence. All feel the breath squeezed out of them by embarrassment, and avoid each other's eyes. Then Edward, who has by now lowered his arms to his side, mutters, 'Sorry, Father, it was only meant to be a bit of fun,' and pulls off his toga, his big ears bright red. Ruth offers the priest a cup of coffee. Polly looks very white and angry and says nothing. Father Brierley declines the coffee and leaves. It is only ten o'clock, but the party is clearly over.

'Well, Polly did get rather carried away, I'm afraid,' says Ruth to Edward, as they stack the chairs and tear up the paper hearts. 'You couldn't see what was going on behind your back.'

'Silly girl,' says Edward, 'I believe she was a bit under the influence.'

By now, Polly is weeping in a corner, comforted by Violet. 'You were super, Polly, honestly, you should go on the stage,' says Violet. '*I* couldn't have done it to save my life.'

This isn't, perhaps, the most tactful of remarks, and Polly weeps more violently than ever. 'I'll never go to his stupid study group again,' she vows, 'or his stupid Thursday masses.' Then, shocked herself at what she has just said, she stops crying and, after a while, cheers up.

The incident has broken the spell of romance for Dennis and Angela. On the tube train back to her digs they have a slight disagreement about it. Angela opines that Polly was a fool to make such an exhibition of herself. Dennis, disappointed that Angela did not, like himself, find the sketch erotically exciting, defends it. When they kiss goodnight on the porch of her digs he tries to push his tongue between her lips, but she draws back and says gently but firmly, 'Don't do that, pet.'

'Why not?'

'Because.'

They wrangle for a while about this, the first of many such arguments, until Dennis has to run back to the station for the last train to his own digs on the other side of London. In those days he seemed to have a permanent stitch in his side from running for last trains and buses.

Austin Brierley went home and tossed and turned all night, tormented by the memory of Polly's stockinged leg waving in the air above the back of the sofa. The next morning, on an impulse, he asked his parish priest for counsel.

'You did well to give them a telling-off,' said the PP, when Austin Brierley had told his story. 'What are you worried about?'

'I keep having impure thoughts about the girl, Father,' Austin confessed with a blush. 'I can't seem to get the image of her leg out of my mind.'

'Pooh, pooh! Have you tried ejaculations?'

'Pardon?'

' "*My Jesus, mercy, Mary help*!" That's a good one.'

'Oh, yes, I've tried prayers.'

'Pray especially to Our Lady, she'll help you to forget it. It wasn't your fault, you didn't seek the occasion of sin.' The PP sniffed and blew his nose loudly into a handkerchief. 'Some of these young hussies need their bottoms smacked,' he said indignantly, a careless expression in the circumstances, that didn't do anything at all for Austin Brierley's peace of mind.

TWO

How they lost their virginities

In the fifties, everyone was waiting to get married, some longer than others. Dennis lost track of the weddings he and Angela attended in that decade – weddings in churches and chapels of every size and shape, and receptions of all sorts, from a champagne and smoked salmon buffet on a Thames riverboat to a cheap sit-down lunch of rectilinear sliced ham and limp salad, with tinned peaches and ice cream to follow, in a dismal school hall in Watford. But somehow the weddings were all the same – organ music, hats, speeches, hilarity, indigestion; and they always ended in the same way, with Dennis and Angela standing on the edge of a crowd, waving goodbye to some grinning couple off to the scarcely imaginable pleasures of the marriage bed. Once, they went to two weddings on the same Saturday, one in the morning and one in the afternoon, on opposite sides of London, and the second one was like a nightmare, having to eat cold chicken and sausages on sticks and wedding cake, and drink sweet sparkling wine, all over again, and listen to what sounded like the same speeches and telegrams, and exchange small talk with what looked very much like the same two sets of relatives.

As for themselves, there was Dennis's degree to be got, and Angela's degree to be got and his National Service to be done and her postgraduate certificate of education to be obtained and jobs to be found and money to be saved. Some of these time-consuming operations would overlap, but collectively they would account for at least five years and in fact it turned out to be rather longer before they were married. At a well-wined dinner party in 1974 Dennis was to describe their courtship as the most

431

drawn-out foreplay session in the annals of human sexuality. He was alluding to the infinitely slow extension of licence to touch which Angela granted him over the years, as slow as history itself. By November 1952, when *The Mousetrap* opened in the West End, he was allowed to rest one hand on a breast, outside her blouse. In 1953, Coronation Year, while Hilary and Tenzing were scaling Everest, Dennis was persuading Angela to let him stroke her leg, when she sat on his lap, up to stocking-top height. In 1954 food rationing came to an end, Roger Bannister ran the four-minute mile and Dennis got his hand inside Angela's blouse and on to a brassiere cup. Then there was a setback. One day Angela emerged weeping from the confessional of the parish priest of Our Lady and St Jude's, and for a long time there was no touching of legs or breasts in any circumstances. The Comet was grounded and a link established between smoking and lung cancer.

1954 was the year most of the regular Thursday mass-goers sat their Final examinations. They had stopped going to the New Testament Study Group for lack of time, but to have given up the mass as well would have been inviting bad luck. Adrian, indeed, broke his tight-packed revision schedule to go on Student Cross with Edward (whose medical Finals were some years off) reasoning that the loss of preparation time would be more than compensated for by the spiritual merit earned on the pilgrimage. Student Cross, in case you haven't read about it before, consisted of about fifty young men carrying a large, heavy, wooden cross from London to the shrine of Our Lady at Walsingham in half a dozen stages, reciting prayers and singing hymns from time to time, as an act of penance for the sins of students everywhere (no light undertaking) and for the edification of the general public. The general public stared, looked embarrassed or incredulous, sometimes pretended not to see the pilgrims at all. An old lady on the pavement of Enfield's main shopping street inquired, as they were halted at traffic lights, if they were advertising something. Adrian said, 'Yes, madam, the Crucifixion.' Edward murmured: 'And foot-powder.' All suffered from blisters, especially

Adrian. An experienced walker, he had the misfortune to lose his boots just before the pilgrimage and was obliged to wear new ones, not properly broken in. Soon his feet were covered in blisters, his boots seemed filled with molten fire. Every step was agony, and to ease the pain he tried to walk on the sides of his feet with his legs unnaturally bowed, which gave him cramp. His face was creased with pain, his eyes were glazed. Edward urged him to drop out, but Adrian refused to acknowledge defeat until he keeled over in the middle of the A10 just south of Cambridge and they had to phone for an ambulance. He was sent home in a wheelchair, sitting in the guard's van amid bales of returned newspapers and crates of disgruntled chickens. He tried to console himself with the thought that he had done his best, but it did not seem a good omen for his Finals.

All worked hard in the weeks preceding their examinations, though, as is the habit of students, when they met they pretended otherwise. Violet, however, really wasn't working, or pretending. She found herself incapable of revising, and more incapable the nearer the time of Finals approached. She would go to the Library each morning, open a book and stare at it for hours, turning the pages out of habit, but not taking in a single word; then she would go home to her digs, open another book and stare at that for hours in the same way. She lived mostly on Lucozade and cigarettes, and her hands shook when she lit the cigarettes and poured the Lucozade. She went regularly to the Thursday masses, but when she remarked in the Lyons cafeteria afterwards that she wasn't doing any work the others thought that it was the usual kind of precaution against hubris and paid no attention. They could see that she didn't look very well, but then none of them did. The girls' hair was lank and greasy from neglect, and the boys looked pale and scurfy from lack of exercise and fresh air.

Violet herself came to the conclusion that she was under some kind of spell or curse, that God was punishing her for her sins. She began to go to Confession compulsively, once a day, then more than once, in different churches all over London, hoping to lift the curse. She did not go at the advertised times: there was usually a bellpush somewhere in a Catholic church by which you could summon a priest to hear your confession at any hour of the day or night. She liked to go into some strange, empty church, in the middle of the morning or afternoon, let the door swing shut behind her, muffling the everyday sounds from the street, and walk with echoing footsteps down the aisle to push the bell button for Confession; then kneel beside the confessional wondering what kind of priest her action would pluck from his hiding-place, and whether he would be the one to break the spell. Always she said she wanted to make a general confession for all the sins of her past life. She confessed the same sins to different priests and compared the penances they gave her. Some were lengthier than others, but none of her confessors seemed particularly shocked by what she told them, so she began, at first subtly, then more and more extravagantly, to embellish her sins and to invent totally fictitious ones: she had corrupted her little sister, she had sold herself as a child to an American soldier for chewing gum, she had masturbated with a statuette of the Sacred Heart. These revelations produced a gratifying reaction from the priests – sighs and stunned silences from the other side of the grille, heavy penances and earnest exhortations, until one day a sceptical Franciscan began to question her sharply about details, and reminded her that it was sacrilege to tell anything other than the strict truth in Confession. This threw Violet into a worse state than before, because she was frightened to admit that she had made all the false confessions. She was less able than ever to do any revision and felt certain that she would fail her examinations. She would have tried to kill herself if that hadn't been a surer way than any of going to Hell. When, one Thursday morning at breakfast in Lyons, someone made a flippant remark about Violet's exaggerations, she suddenly burst into uncontrollable hysterics and began throwing crockery at the wall. Edward took her round to the Outpatients Department of the College Hospital, where she was given a sedative and put in a cubicle to rest until her parents could be contacted to take her home to Swindon. Edward explained to the others that it was a nervous breakdown.

Later, Violet wrote to Edward from the West of Ireland, where she was recuperating on her uncle's farm, to thank him for looking after her, and to say that she would not be taking the exams that summer, but was hoping to return to College in due course to do her final year again. The others were very sorry for Violet, but too preoccupied with their own anxieties about Finals to spare much thought for her. Besides, they did not really understand about nervous breakdowns, they did not quite see how a nervous breakdown fitted into the theological framework of sin and grace, spiritual snakes and ladders. Was it your own fault if you had a nervous breakdown, or was it a cross that God had asked you to bear, like TB? They did not know. For most of them Violet's nervous breakdown was the first they had come into contact with, though it would not be the last.

When the examination results were published, Miles got a First in History, Michael got a very good Upper Second and Polly a Third in English, Dennis an Upper Second in Chemistry and Angela a Lower Second in French, Ruth an Upper Second in Botany and Adrian (to his great disappointment, for he had secretly hoped for a First) a Lower Second in Economics. On the whole these results corresponded to the intelligence and/or industry of each of them respectively, rather than to their virtue.

Miles went to Cambridge (where he would have gone as an undergraduate if he hadn't been undergoing a spiritual crisis at the time of the college entrance examinations) to do a PhD, and Ruth went into a convent as a postulant. You are not going to hear much about these two in this chapter because they did not lose their virginities (unless you count mutual masturbation between schoolboys, in which case Miles had lost his already). Ruth did, however, have a kind of wedding when she took her first vows at the end of her novitiate.

She was led into the convent chapel, clothed in a long white dress and veil and carrying a bouquet of white roses, accompanied by two matrons of honour. Angela, who was one of them, thought poor Ruth looked ridiculous in this get-up, and found the whole ceremony faintly morbid. She couldn't get used, either, to Ruth's being called Sister Mary Joseph of the Precious Blood. Together they moved in procession to the altar where the bishop waited.

'What do you ask?'

'The mercy of God and the holy veil.'

'Do you ask it with your whole mind and heart?'

'I do.'

Here the two matrons of honour had to remove Ruth's head-dress, and with a little pair of gold scissors the bishop cut off one lock of her hair.

'Oh Lord, keep thy handmaid, our sister, always modest, sincere and faithful to thy service.'

Then Ruth withdrew into a small room, attended by the Mother Superior and two sisters. The matrons of honour had to wait outside, but they knew what was happening behind the door. So did Ruth's mother, who was sobbing audibly in the congregation. Her father had refused to come.

The two sisters helped Ruth off with her bridal dress, and she put on a plain shift of coarsely woven linen and heavy black shoes and stockings. Then she sat on a stool with a towel round her shoulders, and the Mother Superior ran a pair of electric clippers over her scalp until she was cropped like a convict. Then Ruth put on the black habit, the scapular, the cincture and crown, the coif, the band and the veil, reciting a special prayer with each article of dress. When she returned to the chapel for the rest of the ceremony, she was hardly recognizable as the bride in white – and looked much prettier, Angela thought. All you could see of Ruth now was her face from cheekbone to cheekbone and from forehead to chin, which happened to be by far the most attractive part of her. Everything else was concealed by the graceful folds and starched linen of the habit, which had been modelled on the dress of the *bourgeoises* of Bordeaux in the late seventeenth century, when the Order was founded.

Afterwards there was a kind of wedding breakfast, with an iced cake, but of course no sparkling wine or any other kind of alcoholic beverage, though the sisters seemed to get distinctly tipsy on the cake alone, being unused to such rich ingredients in their food. Later, on the pavement outside the convent gates,

Ruth's mother clutched Angela's arm and declared that if she didn't have a stiff drink in the next five minutes she would die.

'Don't you think it's a shame, a terrible waste?' she said, when they were seated in the corner of a saloon bar (Angela felt strange, never having been in a pub without Dennis before) and she had drained her first gin-and-lime.

'Well, she'll still be able to use her qualifications,' said Angela loyally. 'The Order runs a lot of schools.' But she could not rouse much enthusiasm, having herself steadfastly resisted years of propaganda for the nun's life at school. She fingered Dennis's ring on her left hand, and felt particularly glad at that moment that she was engaged to be married. That was nearly three years after they took Finals.

Immediately after the examinations were over, and before the results were known, Polly and her fiancé of the moment (she had had a different one in each academic year) invited Dennis and Angela to join them for a camping holiday in Brittany. Polly and Rex would provide the car, borrowed from Rex's father, and all the gear. Angela was a little surprised by this invitation, for she had never been a really close friend of Polly's, but she and Dennis accepted readily enough, and not until it was too late to withdraw did they realize that they were being asked along as chaperones – Polly's parents having agreed to the trip only on condition that they took with them a reliable Catholic couple. Rex was not a Catholic, and frankly suggested to Dennis, as they lay in their tent on their first night in France, that as soon as possible they should aim to pair off with the girls in the two tents. He was rather put out by Dennis's uncooperative response, and offered to lend him some French letters if that was the problem. (It was not – *that* problem was still in the future for Dennis.) So Polly preserved her virginity on that holiday, but only just.

They finally pitched their tents in the south of Brittany, on the far side of the Loire estuary. It was too hot to lie out on the beach in the afternoons, so they took their siestas in the tents that were shaded by pine trees, and it seemed absurd not to do that as couples. But those sultry afternoons were occasions of sin if anything was, lolling on air mattresses in their swimsuits, for it was too hot to wear anything else, sensually drowsy from the lunchtime wine, and looking, as they all did, amazingly handsome and beautiful from the sunshine and exercise. Every day Dennis and Angela lay side by side, holding hands across the space that separated them, and listening to the scuffles and giggles and sighs emanating from the neighbouring tent. By the end of the second week, Polly and Rex had reached the stage of petting to climax, as Polly intimated to Angela, asking her if she thought it was possible to get pregnant that way. Angela was shocked and unhappy. She wanted to return home, she told Dennis the next afternoon, or at least stop pairing off in the two tents. When he wheedled out of her the reason in full detail, he became uncontrollably excited. He rolled over on to her mattress and whispered breathlessly in her ear, 'Let's do it, let us do it.'

'What?'

'What they do, what Polly said, oh please let's Ange!'

After a pause, she said: 'Why not do it properly, then?'

Dennis sat up and stared at her. Was she serious?

She was. Angela was suddenly fed up with acting as a moral referee over their endearments, blowing the whistle at every petty infringement and quibbling endlessly over the interpretation of the rules. Besides, she felt erotically excited herself by Dennis's strong, brown body, bathed in the orange light of the tent's interior. She lifted her arms slightly and, half closing her eyes, pushed out her lips in the shape of a kiss. He had never seen her look so seductive, but instead of increasing his desire, it frightened him.

'No,' he said, 'we'd better not.'

By the following day he had changed his mind, but so had Angela, and she was not to be wooed into offering herself a second time. He had plenty of leisure in which to brood on his missed opportunity (if that was what it was), his victory over selfishness or his failure of manhood (whichever it was) in the next two years, most of which he spent in a desolate barracks in northern Germany. His Upper Second was not quite good enough to win him a postgraduate scholarship with further deferment of his National Service, and he was called up into the Royal Signals.

Basic training seemed like some sort of punishment for a crime he hadn't committed: shouts, oaths, farts, bruising drill, nauseating food, monotonous obscenity, fucking this fucking that, from shivering morning to red-eyed, boot-polishing night. I have described it in detail elsewhere. So have others. It is always the same. When the Catholic Chaplain came round to talk to the RCs in Dennis's intake, he had an impulse to cry, '*Help us! Get us out of here!*' and listened with dismay as the priest told them they were soldiers of Christ and should try to set an example to the other lads. He tried for a commission and failed his War Office Selection Board (they told him he lacked enthusiasm). Eventually he was trained as a wireless operator and posted to an artillery regiment stationed near Bremen. On his pre-posting leave he and Angela got engaged. Travelling to Germany after that leave, sitting up through the night in a railway carriage foetid with the breath and perspiration of seven other soldiers, remembering Angela's pale, gold-fringed face held up to the train window for a last kiss, feeling the collar of his battledress blouse chafing his neck, and knowing that he would have to wear it for another fourteen months, he tried to comfort himself with the thought that, whatever happened, life couldn't possibly hold greater misery for him than he felt at that moment. (He was wrong, of course.)

Dennis wrote every other day to Angela and she almost as frequently to him. She refused many invitations to go out with other young men, and he kept himself chaste. To fill the intolerable tedium of his days and nights, and in a determined effort to wrest some material advantage from his servitude, he studied furiously electronics and information theory by correspondence course, passed every trade test for which he was eligible, and rose to the rank of corporal.

Polly broke off her engagement to Rex shortly after they all returned from Brittany – a morose, ill-tempered journey in which everybody quarrelled in turn with all the others. She was dashed to find that she had only got a Third and went to see her tutor about it. She had a little cry in his room, then she cheered up. She met Michael nervously combing his hair in the corridor outside the Head of Department's room, waiting for an interview. He had got a scholarship to do postgraduate research, and was thinking of doing his thesis on the novels of Graham Greene. 'I don't know how you can bear the thought of another year in this place,' said Polly, and made up her mind that instant to go abroad. She went to Italy to be a kind of *au pair* girl with an aristocratic Catholic family in Rome, a connection of one of the nuns at her old school. The head of the family was a count, a handsome, charming man who deflowered Polly quite quickly and skilfully on what was supposed to be her afternoon off. Afterwards she cried a little, but then she cheered up. The count gave her a present of money to buy clothes, telling her not to spend it all at once in case it would be noticed. A couple of months later she had an affair with the young Italian teacher from whom she took language lessons. After she slept with him the first time he said he would have offered to marry her if she had been a virgin, but as she wasn't, he wouldn't. Polly said she didn't want to marry him anyway, upon which he sulked.

She came home to England for Christmas, and at a New Year's party got very drunk and went upstairs with a young man whose name she could not afterwards remember. They found an empty bedroom and thrashed about on the bed by the blue light of streetlamps shining through the windows. When the young man pulled off Polly's knickers she crouched on all fours and presented her broad bottom to him, greatly to his astonishment. Both her Italian lovers had taken her in this position and she had assumed it was the usual one. Either this surprise, or the drink he had taken, unmanned the youth, for he was unable to perform, and Polly went back to Italy with a poor opinion of Englishmen. The trouble with Italians, on the other hand, was that they took no contraceptive precautions, and she had had a bad scare when her period was a week overdue once. However, with the help of a girl-friend who worked in the US Embassy, she got herself fitted with a diaphragm by an American doctor, and was therefore well prepared for her next love affair, this time with a photographer who threatened to kill himself if she didn't yield to his passion. She didn't believe him for a moment, but it was an exciting fiction.

By this time Polly had stopped going to mass except for form's sake. She had come to the conclusion that religion was all form and no content. She had watched the count who had seduced her receive Communion the following Sunday, and even if he had been to Confession in the meantime (which she doubted) he certainly hadn't made a Firm Purpose of Amendment, for he made another pass at her on her very next afternoon off. He was a pillar of the Church, with some important function in the Vatican, yet everyone, even his wife, knew that he had a mistress established in a flat on the other side of the Tiber. At first Polly was shocked by the hypocrisy of Roman life, but gradually she got used to it. The trouble with English Catholics, she decided, was that they took everything so seriously. They tried to keep all the rules really and truly, not just outwardly. Of course that was impossible, it was against human nature, especially where sex was concerned.

Polly explained all this to Michael in a coffee bar near the British Museum after her return to England in the autumn of 1955. Coffee bars, equipped with glittering Italian coffee machines that hissed like locomotives, were all the rage in London at this time. Polly impressed Michael immediately by asking the waiter for '*uno capuccino*' instead of just a white coffee. She had certainly acquired, he thought, a certain worldly wisdom as a result of her year abroad.

'Italians tolerate adultery and brothels because they're not allowed to divorce,' she said. 'English Catholics have the worst of both worlds. No wonder they're so repressed.'

Michael nodded, causing his Brylcreemed forelock to fall forward across his eyes. 'It's the Irish Jansenist tradition,' he said.

'What's that?'

'In penal days, Irish priests used to be trained in France, by the Jansenists, so that over-scrupulous, puritanical kind of

Catholicism got into their bloodstream – and ours too, because, let's face it, English Catholicism is largely Irish Catholicism.'

Michael had long ago overcome his own scruples and resumed the full practice of his religion. A sensible priest, to whom he had unburdened himself, had assured him that his was a common problem, no more than a venial sin, as long as he was sorry for having given way to temptation. Since Michael always felt melancholy after masturbating, this was a satisfactory solution. Anyway, he had shed the habit since falling in love with a student of music called Miriam, whom he met at an NUS farm camp, picking strawberries. She was extremely pretty, with green eyes and copper-coloured hair, though, ironically enough, almost flat-chested. It was in fact because she had no bosom worth looking at that Michael had looked more closely than usual at her face and into her eyes, and discovered there a person whom he very much liked. When Polly rang up out of the blue and proposed a meeting, some instinct had warned him against bringing Miriam along, and he was glad he hadn't when Polly began to hold forth about sex.

'So you've got a girl friend at last, Michael,' she said, when he made some allusion to Miriam. 'Is she a Catholic?'

'She's taking instructions.'

'Goodness, it must be serious.'

'We're thinking of getting engaged, actually.'

'D'you really want to settle down so soon, Michael? Don't you want to have some fun, first?' Polly's expression made it fairly clear what kind of fun she had in mind.

'How can you, if you're a Catholic, Polly? I mean, either you are or you aren't. I am. I often wish I wasn't – life would be more fun, agreed. But I am, and there it is.'

'Oh, Michael! Just like a Graham Greene character.'

'Have you read his new one?'

'No, what's it like?'

'It's about the war in Indo-China. Not like the others, really.' Michael had been impressed by *The Quiet American*, but slightly disturbed too. It seemed morally and theologically confused – there was not the same stark contrast between the Church and the secular world that you got in the earlier novels. Michael's interest was more than academic: in some oblique way the credibility of the Catholic faith was underwritten for him by the existence of distinguished literary converts like Graham Greene and Evelyn Waugh, so any sign of their having Doubts was unsettling. Polly, however, didn't want to talk about Graham Greene, but about her love affairs.

Michael listened, fascinated and appalled. Here was sin incarnate. If Polly were to walk out of the coffee bar now, and under a bus, there was not much hope for her immortal soul. For dissolute agnostics there might be some mercy, but Polly had been instructed in the True Faith. She knew the rules and the penalties for not keeping them, whatever she might say about the instinctive passion of the Italians.

'It's the sun, you see, Michael. It makes everything seem so different.' She drained her transparent Pyrex cup, leaving a large red mouth-shape on the rim. Michael, who was practised in eking out a cup of espresso for an hour and a half, watched her with dismay. 'Would you like another?' he asked.

'Please, and perhaps just a tiny piece of that chocolate gâteau.'

Polly had grown plumper, Michael thought, she looked almost fat, and under the heavy makeup her complexion was not good. By middle age she would be bloated and raddled. He thought of his own lean, lissome sweetheart with complacency.

'Italian men are an awful nuisance,' said Polly, 'pinching you and ogling you all the time on the street and on buses. But at least they notice you.' She looked around the coffee bar at the unnoticing young men, clerks in pin-stripe suits and students in fisherman's knit sweaters and Harris tweed sports jackets. 'God!' she sighed. 'England is so boring.'

That same autumn, Violet went back to College to begin her final year all over again. She had quite recovered from her nervous breakdown, her eczema had cleared up, and she looked very pretty. The Professor in charge of the Department declared that he would personally undertake tutorial responsibility for her work. He was a short man who looked quite tall sitting behind his desk because of his large, handsome head and luxuriant silver-grey beard. He reminded Violet of pictures of God the Father speaking out of clouds. She felt his interest in her progress was a great honour and was determined to prove worthy of it.

The Professor appointed four o'clock on a Tuesday afternoon for her tutorial, which allowed it to overrun the statutory hour. At five o'clock his secretary would knock discreetly and come into the room with letters to be signed. Then, after she had gone, as the corridors of the Department fell gradually silent, and the winter dusk turned to darkness outside the window, he would draw the curtains, and light a single standard lamp for her, shining down on her notebook, leaving him behind his desk in shadow, and bring out a bottle of sherry and two glasses, and then discourse about the classical world to Violet, about things he never alluded to in his lectures, about pagan fertility rites, phallus worship, Dionysian orgies and sacred prostitutes. 'I hope I do not shock you, Violet,' he would murmur, stroking his beard as if soothing a pet, and she would shake her head vigorously, though in truth she often thought she would have been shocked if he had not been her professor and it had not been a tutorial.

Then, one day, as he was holding forth in his melodious cadences, she knocked over her sherry glass and, jumping to her feet in reflex response, saw to her horror and amazement that he had his fly open and was playing with himself under the desk. She stared at him for a moment, then dropped to her knees and began scrubbing furiously at the carpet with a handkerchief. He rose from his place and came round the desk to stand over her. 'Violet,' he said, after several minutes had passed. 'Get up.'

She rose to her feet. 'I've got to go,' she said.

'Violet,' he said. 'Have pity on an old man.' He tugged and gnawed at his beard as he spoke.

'You're not old,' she said, pointlessly.

'I am fifty-five years old and have been impotent for the last fifteen. My wife has left me. Sometimes I can coax a little juice to flow. It does no harm to anyone, does it?'

Violet went home in a trance, twice nearly being run over, and tossed and turned in bed, wondering what to do. The Professor's appeal had not fallen on deaf ears. She did indeed pity this great man, the distinguished scholar of whom the entire Department stood in awe, so starved of love that he was reduced to the ignoble expedient in which she had surprised him. Violet had a strong impulse to sacrifice herself, to become a sacred prostitute, to heal his broken sex. It would be a sin, technically; but also, she thought, a corporal work of mercy.

She went back into College with this purpose vaguely in mind, and was dismayed to discover a note in her pigeonhole stating that she had been transferred to another tutor. With some difficulty, she managed to obtain an interview with the Professor. He looked at her with fear in his eyes, tugging and gnawing at his beard.

'You realize,' he said, 'that if you make a complaint I shall deny everything.'

Violet was unable to speak.

'In any case,' he said, 'my conscience is clear. No genuinely innocent girl would have sat there all these weeks listening to what I told you without a flicker of protest.'

Instead of being outraged by this insinuation, Violet was completely convinced of its justice. It revived and confirmed her old feelings of guilt. There must be something about her, she thought, that brought out the worst in people: there was her cousin in the attic, and the tramp in the shelter, and now the Professor. And she had to admit that she had derived a certain thrill from the Professor's stories of pagan filthiness. She went back to her digs and opened a book and stared at it for several hours without taking in a word. Then she got a letter from her new tutor asking why she hadn't been to see him. He was a young man, recently appointed to the Department. She went into College to tell him that she was going to withdraw from the course, this time for good, for she could feel another nervous breakdown coming on.

'What will you do?' asked the tutor, who invited her to call him by his first name, Robin.

'I don't know,' said Violet. 'I might become a nun.'

Robin laughed, but not unkindly. He was intrigued by Violet, and besides, she was pretty.

'What was the problem with the Old Man?' he asked casually. 'Made a pass at you, did he?'

It was a bold but happy gambit. To Violet it came as a huge relief that this stranger spontaneously assumed that the Professor and not herself might have been responsible for what had happened. She did not tell Robin what that was, but she agreed to carry on with her studies under his supervision. His tutorials also overran the statutory hour, but they were exclusively academic in content. Violet had a lot of work to make up, and he was determined to prove his prowess as a teacher by getting her through Finals.

One day he proposed taking her to see Donald Wolfit in *Oedipus Rex*, as it would help her with her tragedy paper. Robin found her an agreeable companion, deferential but not sycophantic, and full of quaint opinion and anecdote deriving from her Irish Catholic background. (Her parents had emigrated from the West of Ireland to England when she was only three, but for most of the war years she had been educated at a convent boarding school in Ireland, and she returned to the West frequently for holidays.)

'Which of the six sins against the Holy Ghost do you think is the worst?' she said in the Tube, à propos of nothing in particular.

'I don't even know what they are, Violet.'

She rattled them off, parrot-fashion, like a child in school: 'Presumption, Despair, Resisting the Known Truth, Envy of Another's Spiritual Good, Obstinacy in Sin, and Final Impenitence.'

He considered. 'Resisting the Known Truth,' he said at length.

'Isn't that just typical of a university lecturer! *I* think the worst is Final Impenitence. Imagine, at the moment of death, when you've everything to gain and nothing to lose by being sorry for your sins . . . Final Impenitence.' She gave a faint shudder that was not entirely affected. 'I had an uncle in Limerick, they say he died raving against the Holy Ghost. "Get that damned bird out of here!" he kept shouting, on his deathbed. Of course, he was delirious. But it wasn't very nice for Aunty Maeve. It naturally made her wonder about the state of his soul.'

Subsequently Robin took Violet out to other plays and films that had no obvious relevance to her course. When he escorted her home afterwards she did not invite him in because, she said, her landlady would not like it (in fact, because her room was like a pigsty and she was ashamed to let him see it). They said goodbye on the porch and shook hands. On the third such occasion, he leaned forward and kissed her on the cheek, and the time after that on the lips. It seemed to Violet that they must be courting; and though Robin never initiated any discussion of their feelings for each other, he did impress upon her the importance of concealing from the rest of the Department the fact that they were meeting outside tutorials. This threw a romantic aura of the clandestine over their relationship. Violet could hardly believe her good fortune. Robin's slim, dark good looks, his soft, supple clothes of velvet corduroy, suede and cavalry twill, his cool self-assurance and his dry, understated conversation, were to her the quintessence of Englishness, the culture which her family affected to despise but secretly admired.

Violet was very happy that spring, and sailed through her exams in June without stress. After she had sat her last paper, Robin took her to an Italian restaurant in Soho for dinner. Between the chicken *alla cacciatore* and the *zabaglione* he reached across the table and covered her hand with his.

'Violet, darling,' he said, and her heart thumped, because he had never called her darling before, 'you know I care for you very much, don't you?' She nodded. 'And I think you care for me?'

'Oh, Robin,' she said. 'You know I do.'

So this was it. She had often wondered what it would be like to be proposed to, and her imaginings had been surprisingly close to reality: soft lights, a bottle of wine, cosy intimacy. It took her some time to realize that it was not exactly marriage that Robin was proposing, at least not yet. He wanted her to spend a weekend away with him somewhere, 'To see how we suit each other physically.'

'Oh, no,' she said, taking her hand away. 'I couldn't do that,

Robin. Isn't that what they call a trial marriage? Catholics aren't allowed.'

But Robin was a very persuasive young man, and played cannily on Catholic belief in his arguments. Wouldn't it, he asked rhetorically, be madness for two people to contract an indissoluble marriage without knowing whether they were sexually compatible?

'But if they loved each other, wouldn't it be bound to come right in the end?' Violet pleaded.

'Unfortunately there are case histories which prove otherwise.'

After a few bouts of this kind of discussion, Violet gave in. Robin borrowed a friend's car and took her to a hotel in the country for a weekend.

'For heaven's sake, drive carefully,' she said, chain-smoking in the passenger seat. 'I'm in a state of mortal sin, you know.'

He laughed and glanced sideways at her. 'But you haven't done anything yet.'

'No, but I mean to, and that's just as bad. Worse, in a way.'

'Worse?'

'I couldn't say I was carried away by the impulse of the moment, could I?'

'No,' he said gleefully, 'you couldn't say that.' Robin never knew how seriously to take Violet's religious scruples, but overcoming them certainly gave the adventure an extra *frisson* of excitement.

'Suppose I get pregnant?' she said after a while.

'You needn't worry about that. I shall take the necessary precautions.'

'That's another mortal sin on top,' she said gloomily.

After they had checked into the hotel, Violet refused to leave their room because, she claimed, everyone in the lobby had immediately guessed they weren't really married; so Robin had to have dinner sent up at considerable extra cost and trouble. Still, he was willing to indulge her on this occasion. When the waiter had cleared away the dishes, Robin knocked on the door of the bathroom, where Violet was hiding, and said: 'Time for bed.'

'I'm going to have a bath,' she said.

He pushed the door hopefully, but it was locked. When she came from the bathroom half an hour later, Violet was swathed in a dressing-gown from her chin to her feet and insisted on total darkness before she would get into bed. Robin found it difficult to fit his contraceptive sheath in these conditions, particularly as it was not an operation he had performed all that often. Violet also kept his erotic drive in check by her continual chatter.

'You've done this before haven't you Robin how many times I mean how many girls were they not compatible or were you not thinking of marrying them anyway did you just want their bodies for a night?'

'For heaven's sake, Violet, do be quiet.'

'I'm sorry, Robin, it's just that I'm so nervous.'

'Just try and relax.'

In the pitch darkness, impeded by the heavy quilt on the bed, he pushed his index finger in and out of Violet's vagina, hoping that he was stimulating her clitoris. The manual of sexual technique that he had studied rather more frequently than he had actually practised intercourse had laid great stress upon this item of foreplay.

'I'm sorry, darling, but that's hurting,' Violet said after a while.

He pulled his finger away as though it had been burned.

'It doesn't mean that we're incompatible, Robin,' she said anxiously. 'It's just that you were rubbing in the wrong place.'

'I'm sorry,' he said huffily, 'to be so clumsy.'

'Shall I show you the right place?' she whispered.

This was better. She took his long index finger, that had so often pointed out to her the syllabic pattern of Latin verse, and gently guided it on to her favourite spot. As he rubbed, he felt her pelvis heave like a swimmer lifted by a wave, and her legs opened wide and his own member stiffened in response.

They made love four times that weekend, and on each occasion Violet had an orgasm under digital stimulation, but not during the act itself, when Robin had his. This worried him somewhat in the light of the textbook, so that when Violet asked him if he thought they were compatible he said he thought they both needed time to think over the experience of the weekend. She looked crestfallen. 'Let's sleep on it,' he said. 'We've already slept on it,' she said, 'we've done nothing else all weekend.' He kissed her and said, 'You're lovely and I love you, but there's no need to rush into anything.' This was as they were preparing to go home.

'I'm not going away with you for another of these weekends, you know,' she said.

'Do you have to say it like that?' he said, pained by her lack of tact.

'Yes, because I'm going to Confession at the very first church we come to and I must have a firm purpose of amendment or it won't be any good.'

As soon as they returned to London, Robin was buried in examination scripts – not university exams, but 'O' and 'A' level papers which he marked to enhance his meagre salary. Violet helped him check the marks and fill in the mark sheets. One day as they were doing this she said, 'Robin, I think I'm pregnant.'

'What? You can't be.'

'Those things don't always work, do they? I'm three weeks overdue, and this morning I felt sick when I got up.'

'My God.' He stared at her, appalled. It was, he supposed, possible that fumbling with his sheaths in the dark he had nicked one with a fingernail or otherwise mismanaged the business.

'I'm not trying to blackmail you into marrying me,' said Violet. 'But I thought you ought to know.'

'If it's true,' he said heavily, 'you'll just have to get rid of it.'

'You mean, have it adopted?'

'I mean have an operation. It can be arranged, I believe, at a price.' He looked miserably at the pile of scripts.

'I couldn't do that, it would be murder,' said Violet. 'I'll just go away somewhere to a Home for Unmarried Mothers and have it adopted and never trouble you again.'

'Don't be absurd, Violet,' he said irritably. 'It's not that I don't want to marry you, it's just that I don't want to rush into it. And I certainly didn't intend starting a family straight away.'

But in the end he did marry Violet, and in a Catholic church. His doubts about the wisdom of this step were mitigated by her being awarded an Upper Second class degree – a rare achievement by girls doing Classics. The Professor sent them a handsome present, and they went to Sicily for their honeymoon and looked at antiquities. In the fourth month of her pregnancy, late in 1956, Violet had a miscarriage, and fell subsequently into a deep depression.

England was less boring in 1956 than it had seemed to Polly in the coffee bar with Michael the year before. At Easter there was the first CND march. *The Outsider* and *Look Back in Anger* made a great stir and the newspapers were full of articles about Britain's Angry Young Men. In the autumn there was the Suez crisis and the Hungarian uprising.

Only the last of these events touched off an unequivocal response in our young Catholics. They were not, on the whole, a politically conscious group. Their childhood had been dominated by the Second World War, which their religious education had imbued with a mythic simplicity, the forces of good contending with the power of evil, Hitler being identified with Satan, and Churchill, more tentatively, with the Archangel Michael. After that apocalyptic struggle, mere party politics seemed an anticlimax, no doubt – anyway, few of them took an informed interest in such things, or bothered to think how they would cast their votes when they were twenty-one. Their politics in adolescence were international Cold War politics. The betrayal of the glorious Allied cause by Soviet Russia, the enslavement of Eastern Europe with its millions of Catholics, the inexorable advance of atheistic communism in the Far East – all showed that Satan was as active in the world as ever. Their hero was Cardinal Mindszenty, who had been imprisoned by the Communists in Hungary, and was released by the new provisional government in October 1956. When the Russian Army moved in to crush the rising with its tanks, the widespread feelings of outrage and impotence in Britain were felt especially keenly by Catholics.

One Sunday, while the Hungarian patriots were fighting for their lives in Budapest, a huge march and rally in Hyde Park was organized by students of London University, at which Dennis and Angela were present with Michael and Miriam. Dennis had recently been released from the Army, and was camping in Michael's bedsitter while he looked for a job. Angela was teaching in a school in South London. Miriam was just starting her final year in Music. Michael had finished his MA thesis on the novels of Graham Greene, and was just beginning a Postgraduate Certificate of Education course: though he would have preferred to try for a university post, schoolteaching was the only way of avoiding National Service.

They stood on the trampled grass in the middle of a large, excited crowd, the two girls hanging on to the arms of their fiancés, and listened to the speeches. The announcement that a group of students were forming a volunteer force to join the freedom fighters of Hungary was received with great enthusiasm. 'We want volunteers,' declared the speaker, a very young man, pale with sleeplessness and the strain of historic decision, 'but only if you know how to use a gun.'

Of the four of them, only Dennis knew how to use a gun. For a moment or two he contemplated a heroic gesture, for he was genuinely moved by the plight of the Hungarians and the atmosphere of the meeting was heady. He had a brief glimpse of himself, as though through a rift in cloud, manning a barricade, gripping a rifle, hurling a grenade – converting at one stroke all the tedium and futility of his military training into something positive and transcendent. But then he saw himself falling dead across the bodies of Hungarian partisans, or flattened by a Russian tank like a hedgehog on a bypass, and the rift closed. He did not want to die. Especially he did not want to die without having possessed Angela.

Angela, at that moment, was thinking that if Dennis stepped forward to volunteer, she would ask him to make love to her that night without the slightest hesitation or guilt. She saw herself standing before him in the posture of a statue of Our Lady, her arms slightly lifted, her clothes slipping from her like melting snow.

None of them said anything. When somebody came round with a collecting box, Dennis put in more than he could really afford. Later he read in the paper that the volunteers – there were only about twenty of them – had been turned back at the Austrian border.

If Adrian had been present in Hyde Park, he would certainly have volunteered, but at that time he was still doing his military service, as a Second Lieutenant in the Royal Army Service Corps. He had signed on for three years as a Regular in the hope of getting a commission in the prestigious cavalry regiment into which he had been conscripted as a National Serviceman, but he ended up in the despised RASC, in which he could probably have been commissioned anyway. At the time of the Hungarian uprising, which was also the time of the Suez crisis, he was a transport officer in Cyprus, and his frustration and disgust at the turn of events was extreme. His country, instead of flying to the assistance of the gallant Hungarians and Cardinal Mindszenty, was committing itself to a dubious adventure in wog-bashing – that was how Adrian saw it. The actual invasion was so badly organized, however, that he doubted whether the British Army would have been much help to the Hungarians anyway. On the quayside at Limassol, prior to embarkation, one French truck was grouped with every three British trucks, and as the British vehicles had been sprayed with yellow desert camouflage and the French ones had not, this pattern gave away the presence of the trucks to aerial reconnaisance as clearly as could be. When Adrian pointed this out to his CO, he was brusquely told that there was a political reason for it. In Suez, the convoys lost their way, ran out of water, and their wireless equipment broke down. It was a shambles, and an immoral shambles. When Anthony Eden was forced to resign soon afterwards, broken by ill-health, Adrian felt that some kind of justice had been done in Old Testament style. He determined to vote Socialist at the next election. (He had to wait till October 1959 and the Tories won by a hundred seats.)

After his release from the Army, Adrian took a job in Local Government in his home town, Derby. He lived with his parents because they would have been hurt if he had done otherwise, but

453

it was cramped and inconvenient, for they were a large family with several children still at school. It was time, he decided, that he got married. He took dancing lessons and went to parish socials, but the girls he met were afraid of his severe, intense manner. He joined a tennis club, but the girls there found him stiff and priggish. He was not very good, either, at dancing or tennis. In the end he met Dorothy at a weekend conference on Catechetics. Adrian no longer did public speaking for the Catholic Evidence Guild, but he helped with a Sunday School in his parish for children attending non-Catholic schools. Dorothy was doing teacher-training in Religious Education, but she was quite willing to give up her course to marry Adrian, who had a good job and was suddenly very impatient to have sexual intercourse after so many years of continence in the interests of holiness and self-advancement.

Though he knew much more about sex, in a second-hand way, than when he was a student, from barrack and mess-room conversation, from reading the manual of military law, and from censoring the mail of other ranks in the Suez crisis, Adrian was shy of talking about it to Dorothy during their short engagement. She was a virgin, of course – so much so that when, prior to retiring to bed on their wedding night, he kissed her attired only in a dressing-gown, she inquired what hard object he was concealing in his pocket. Under the bedclothes she snuggled up to him happily enough, but when he tried to enter her she went rigid with fear and then grew hysterical. It transpired that she knew almost nothing about how a marriage was consummated. Adrian turned on the bedside lamp, sat up in bed, and lectured her on the facts of life. He was a good lecturer, having benefited by his training in the Army and the Catholic Evidence Guild, though he spoke rather more loudly than was necessary and after a while somebody banged on the wall of the adjoining room (they were spending their honeymoon in a small hotel in the Lake District). Adrian continued his lecture in a lower tone, making three-dimensional diagrams in the air with his fingers. Dorothy watched him wonderingly, with the bedclothes drawn up to her chin.

'Didn't your mother tell you *anything*?' he said.

'Sex was never mentioned at home, Adie.'

'Well, but you must have picked up something from some-where. How did you suppose babies were conceived?'

Dorothy blushed and shifted uneasily beneath the sheets. 'I thought it was enough if the man just touched the woman with his . . . I didn't think he actually had to . . . to . . .'

Adrian sighed. 'Would you like to have another try, now I've explained?'

'If you like, dear.'

Adrian lay on top of his bride and butted at her dry crotch while she winced and gasped faintly beneath him. When at last he succeeded in penetrating her, he ejaculated immediately. 'That wasn't right,' he said. 'With practice I'll be able to last longer than that.'

'It was long enough for me, dear,' said Dorothy, and fell fast asleep.

Adrian lay awake for quite a long while. Undoubtedly it had been a disappointment, the sexual act. But then, so had most things in his life – his degree class, his army career – always falling a little short of his ambition, his ideal. And now marriage. Dorothy was a good, kindhearted girl, utterly devoted to him, but she didn't scintillate, there was no doubt about that, and though she had nice eyes and pretty hair, she was no beauty, her nose was decidedly half-an-inch too long, and her body rather awkward and angular. Adrian had a sudden recall of Angela, whom he not seen for years. Angela in her pink angora jumper – still, it seemed to him, the prettiest girl he had ever met in his life, and he wondered what she was doing now. Married to that chap, no doubt, what was his name, Dennis. Adrian grew gloomier and gloomier. He went through a dark wedding night of the soul. It seemed to him that God had always mocked his efforts. He had always tried to do his best, to do what was right, but always there was this bitter rebuff to his hopes and ambitions. Meanwhile other people, less good, less dutiful, indeed positively mischievous – fornicators, adulterers, unbelievers – prospered and enjoyed themselves. Of course all would get their just deserts in the next

455

world, but he couldn't help feeling some resentment about the lack of justice in this one. He knew for a fact that men who hadn't worked half as hard as himself had got Upper Seconds in Finals, whereas he himself had only got a Lower Second, and sacrificed the chance of winning Angela to boot.

The disloyalty of this train of thought to the young woman sleeping peacefully beside him shocked Adrian out of his melancholy mood. Lying on his back, he made the Sign of the Cross, and said his usual night prayers, which he had omitted in the excitement of going to bed – an Our Father, a Hail Mary and a Glory Be, an Act of Contrition; then he turned over and settled himself to sleep. Tomorrow he would take Dorothy to Great Gable and teach her a few basic rock-climbing skills.

Because he was doing medicine, Edward was still a student of a kind long after his contemporaries had left the University. His main leisure activities were playing rugby and taking part in the College Gilbert and Sullivan Society's productions until, the season before he qualified, someone trampled on him in a loose scrum and damaged a couple of vertebrae, putting an end to his athletic career and bequeathing to him a lifetime of intermittent backache. For recreation that left him with just Gilbert and Sullivan – and girls, for whom he had not previously had much time. The teaching hospital was of course teeming with pretty nurses looking for doctors to marry, and Edward met one of them, Tessa, at the beginning of his houseman's year, when they were on night duty together. Tessa wasn't a Catholic – her family were vaguely C of E – but she was quite happy about getting married in a Catholic church, and bringing their children up as Catholics. This was established long before Edward formally proposed, for after he had taken her out a few times he said, putting on the expression of exaggerated gravity that used to disconcert Father Brierley, that he thought it was only fair to make clear, before they got seriously attached to each other, what the implications were.

'You'd have to take instructions from a priest,' he said. 'Of course, it makes everything much simpler if the non-Catholic partner converts, but it's not essential.'

'Well, I might, you never can tell,' Tessa said brightly, her smooth brown cheeks dimpling, and her dark eyes glancing in all directions. They were in the Brasserie of a Lyons Cornerhouse at the time; Tessa had never been to one before and thought that the gay check tablecloths and the gipsy music and the tangy smells of Continental cooking were heaven. At that moment she would cheerfully have agreed to marry a Hindoo if his name had been Edward.

'And there's another thing,' said Edward, looking more solemn than ever. 'You know about the Catholic teaching on birth control, don't you?' His big ears glowed red with embarrassment, for in spite of his training in anatomy and gynaecology, and the obscene songs that he sang as lustily as anyone else after rugger matches, Edward was remarkably pure-minded and assumed that girls were even more so.

'Well, I believe in large families, anyway,' said Tessa, with a giggle, glancing to right and left.

'It doesn't mean,' he hastened to assure her, 'that the Church is against family planning as such. It's just a question of the method. It's quite all right to use the Rhythm method.'

'Much nicer than the other methods, anyway, I should think,' Tessa said, and then wondered if perhaps she had revealed a little too much knowledge. She was still technically a virgin, but had had a fairly passionate heavy petting affair the previous year with a postgraduate dentistry student who had hopefully explained to her on several occasions the various means of contraception.

Tessa decided to become a Catholic as soon as she discovered that, if she didn't, they wouldn't be able to have a nuptial mass. She liked the idea of being the focus of attention for a full hour in her bridal dress, kneeling up on the altar (it was the only time in her life, Edward explained, that a woman was allowed into the sanctuary, except of course for cleaning and polishing and arranging the flowers) with organ music, choir-singing, Latin prayers and glowing vestments swirling around her. Most weddings she had been to seemed to her to be over far too quickly, and the Catholic service for a mixed marriage was almost as short and bleak as a Registry Office ceremony – no candles, flowers or even music being permitted.

'You do understand what you're doing, darling?' Edward said anxiously the day before she was received. 'You're quite happy about it?'

'Oh yes, darling, quite happy.' In truth Tessa found a lot of the doctrine inherently implausible, but she could see that it all fitted together, and if Edward believed it, who was she to quibble?

Shortly afterwards, Edward took her to a weekend conference for Catholic engaged couples. There would be talks by priests, doctors and counsellors on such subjects as The Sacrament of Marriage, Getting On Together, and The Rhythm Method, plus Mass and Benediction each day and times for private recollection. Edward had the idea that this experience would help Tessa to feel fully assimilated into her new faith. It was held at a retreat house and conference centre run by nuns, on the northern outskirts of London.

They arrived on a Friday night, late because Edward had been delayed by an emergency at the hospital. An aged and irritable nun admitted them and said that they were not expected until the following morning. 'There'll be extra to pay,' she grumbled. 'What's your name?'

'O'Brien,' said Edward.

The nun peered myopically at a list of names pinned to a noticeboard. 'Come with me,' she said, plucking at Tessa's sleeve like a crone in a fairy-tale.

'Shall I wait here?' Edward said.

'You can if you like,' said the nun. 'But you'll get nothing to eat. The kitchen's all shut up.'

'Goodnight then, darling,' said Edward, smiling encouragingly at Tessa, and gave her a peck on the cheek. He could see that she was a bit downcast by this chilly reception. The hall was cold and ill-lit, and smelled faintly of boiled cabbage and carbolic soap. Dark oil paintings depicting martyrdoms and miracles loomed from the walls.

'Goodnight,' Tessa replied in a small voice.

Afterwards they both recalled that the nun had looked puzzled by this exchange.

Edward waited while Tessa was shown to her room. It was deathly quiet. After a couple of minutes the nun slowly descended the stairs and shuffled across the lobby as if he weren't there. Just as she was about to disappear through a green baize door, Edward called out: 'Excuse me, sister, but where is my room, please?'

The old nun looked balefully at him across the black and white flags of the hall. 'Number twenty-nine, up the stairs and turn right,' she said.

Edward located the room and walked in to find Tessa in her slip, brushing her hair. She dropped the brush in fright, and clasped her arms across her bosom.

'Oh, heavens, Teddy, you did scare me, this place is so spooky, what do you want? Have you come to kiss me goodnight? What will the nuns think?'

Edward explained about the nun's mistake, but gave her a goodnight kiss anyway, a proper one which went on for some time. There were two beds in the room and they made some jokes about that, which aroused them both. They had a common feeling of being back at school, riskily breaking the rules. Eventually Edward went back downstairs to try and find out about his room. He checked the noticeboard in the lobby. On a list he found: '*Mr and Mrs O'Brien – room 29.*' All the names on the list were married couples. The sheet was indeed headed, *Conference for Married Couples*, and the programme included talks on The Holy Family, Beating The Seven-Year Itch, and Problems with Teenage Children.

Tessa had locked her door and Edward had to knock for admittance. When he explained that they had come on the wrong weekend, she collapsed on to one of the beds in hysterical giggles. Like many people who are good at stage comedy, Edward did not like to appear ridiculous unintentionally, but after a while he saw the funny side of his mistake too. It was too late to leave and travel back to Town, and although the house was undoubtedly full of empty bedrooms, he didn't want to go prowling around looking for one in case he made another embarrassing mistake. 'You'd better sleep here,' said Tessa. 'And tomorrow morning we'll creep away early.'

'All right, then,' said Edward.

They undressed very decorously with the light off, but then they collided with each other in the dark and one thing led to another and before long they were in, or on, the same bed, and Tessa's nightdress was up round her armpits and she was moaning and writhing with pleasure in his arms. It was a long time since the dentist had petted her and she had missed such comforts in Edward's chaste courtship. Edward himself was quite out of his depth. Feeling the pressure of an imminent and unstoppable orgasm, he was filled with shame and panic at the thought of spilling his seed all over Tessa and the bedclothes. In his perturbation it seemed to him that their sin would be less, certainly his own humiliation would be less, if they performed the act properly. Desperately he rolled on top of Tessa and, with a fluke thrust at the right place and angle, entered her in a single movement. Tessa uttered a loud cry that, if it was heard in that house, was probably not recognized; and Edward, groaning into the pillow, pumped rivers of semen into her willing womb.

Afterwards he was aghast at what he had done, but Tessa covered his face with kisses and told him it had been wonderful, and he was moved with grateful pride. Tessa herself was delighted: she felt finally absolved from guilt on account of the freedoms she had allowed the dentist (which she had confessed in the vaguest terms on her reception into the Church) and finally sure of Edward's love. The next day they rose while it was still dark and let themselves stealthily out of the house. Their feet crunched resoundingly on the gravel of the drive, and looking back over her shoulder Tessa thought she saw the old nun watching them from a high, lighted window. Outside the gates they hitched a lift from a lorry taking vegetables to Covent Garden. 'Not eloping, are you?' quipped the driver, looking at their overnight bags. They often wondered afterwards what the other, the real Mr and Mrs O'Brien thought when they arrived at the convent later that morning to find their bedroom defiled by unmistakable signs of sexual intercourse.

Having made love once, Edward and Tessa were unable to resist further opportunities that came their way, though each time it happened they solemnly vowed it would not recur. Soon Tessa discovered she was pregnant, and they made arrangements to get married rather sooner than they had planned. Edward was excruciatingly embarrassed by all this, guessing (quite correctly) what everyone would be thinking about the reasons for their haste, but Tessa faced it out serenely and did not for one moment contemplate giving up her white wedding and nuptial mass. She had an Empire-line dress made which artfully concealed the very slight swelling of her tummy. Soon afterwards, Edward's training finished and he was called up into the Army Medical Corps. Tessa went to live with her parents in Norfolk and gave birth to a daughter one night when Edward was sleeping out on Salisbury Plain as part of his officer's training. In due course he was posted to a military hospital in Aldershot and Tessa moved into digs there. They waited impatiently for his service to end, so that Edward could start his career as a GP. He had forgotten all about his intention of working for two years in the mission fields of Africa.

Miriam's conversion took longer than Tessa's. Every now and again she dug her heels in and refused to go any further. She had a quick, sharp mind and she was not, like Tessa, theologically illiterate to start with. Her own religious upbringing had been Low Church Evangelical, and she had already reacted against that form of Christianity, its gloomy Sabbatarianism, its narrow-minded insistence on Faith against Works, its charmless liturgy. Since leaving home to attend the University she had ceased to worship, though still considering herself a kind of Christian. Catholicism, to which Michael introduced her, seemed to be just what she was looking for: it was subtle, it was urbane, it had history, learning, art (especially music) on its side. But there was enough of the Protestant left in Miriam to make a lot of Catholic doctrine difficult to swallow, especially in relation to Mary. She was dismayed to discover that 'the Immaculate Conception' did not denote the birth of Christ to a virgin, but the dogma that Mary herself was conceived without the stain of original sin. 'It doesn't say so in Scripture, and how else would anyone know?' she said. Michael, who had been well schooled in apologetics at school, quoted the salutation of the archangel Gabriel, 'Hail, full of grace, the Lord is with thee.' Since Mary hadn't been baptized at that point, she couldn't have been full of grace unless she had been exempted from the stain of original sin inherited from Adam and Eve. Miriam yielded to the logic of this argument (when the Catholic Jerusalem Bible was published ten years later she found that 'full of grace' was translated as 'highly favoured', but the issue no longer seemed important) and shifted her attention to the doctrine of the Assumption of Our Lady into Heaven, which had been defined as an article of faith as recently as 1950 – though, as Michael was quick to emphasize, it had been an important feast of the Church for centuries. 'I still don't see the point of it,' she said. 'Christianity is hard enough to believe in without adding all these unnecessary extras.'

Michael himself was uneasy about the Assumption, for which there didn't seem to be one jot or tittle of Scriptural evidence, and referred Miriam to the College chaplain – no longer Father Brierley, who had been moved to a parish at the end of the Northern Line, but Father Charles Conway, a lively and good-looking young priest with an Oxford degree. He suggested that the doctrine might be looked at as a theological formalization of Mary's special place in the scheme of salvation, and of her presence in heaven as a source of help and encouragement to souls on earth. But Miriam had her reservations about that too. She didn't understand why Catholics prayed so much to Mary to 'intercede' for them with God. 'Do you mean,' she asked, her tulip-cut of glossy copper-coloured hair thrust forward with the urgency of her question, 'that if A prays to Jesus via Mary, and B prays direct to Jesus, A has a better chance of being heard than B, other things being equal? And if not, then why bother going through Mary?' Neither Michael nor Father Conway had a satisfactory answer to that one.

When she had got over these doctrinal hurdles, or bypassed them (for they were, after all, peripheral to the main deposit of faith) Miriam got into a panic about making her first confession. To go into that dark, cupboard-like cubicle and whisper your most shameful secrets to a man on the other side of a wire mesh might be tolerable if you were brought up to it from childhood, but for herself it seemed humiliating, a violation, a hideous ordeal. 'There's nothing to it, really,' Michael reassured her, conveniently suppressing the memory of his own agonizings over masturbation not so very long ago. 'The priest won't know who you are. And you can go to one *you* don't know, if you like.'

'I certainly shan't go to Father Charles, I'd simply die.'

'Anyway, you can't have anything very dreadful to confess,' he said fondly.

'How would *you* know?' she shot at him, with such anger that he was chastened into silence.

They were queueing, at the time, for gallery seats at the Globe theatre to see Graham Greene's new play, *The Potting Shed*. Michael had been looking forward eagerly to seeing the play, which, to judge from the reviews, confirmed that the author's faith was intact, but he found that he was unable to concentrate on the story of vows, miracles, lost and found belief. Later in life all he could remember about the production was a dog barking off-stage and the peculiarly bilious green of John Gielgud's cardigan. (Could it possibly have been, he wondered, a sartorial pun on the author's name?) For most of the performance he was brooding jealously on Miriam's hint of grave sin in her past. Though Michael was no longer so helplessly obsessed with sex as in late adolescence, he still thought about it quite a lot. He looked forward to the night of his wedding (provisionally planned for the coming spring) as a feast that would be rendered all the more delicious by the prolonged abstinence that had preceded it. To lie with his beloved in the same bed, free to explore her body at will, above, below, between, to assuage the long ache of unsatisfied desire in total abandonment, without fear or guilt at last – that would surely be a rapture worth waiting for. The thought that Miriam might not, after all, have waited – that she might already have tasted some of the sweets of sex with another boy, or even boys, tormented him. It did not occur to Michael that she might have been referring to masturbation, for he did not know that girls masturbated (his reading in English fiction had not uncovered this fact). But, as it happened, that was not what Miriam was alluding to. Her most shameful secret was that at school she had joined in the persecution of a girl whom nobody liked and who had eventually been driven to attempt suicide. Miriam and her friends had been in great terror as this event was investigated, but the girl in question had nobly declined to tell on them. The worst thing of all was that when the girl returned to school they all hated her more than ever, and after a while her mother took her away.

After *The Potting Shed*, on the Tube ride back to the little flat in Highbury that Miriam shared with another girl, Michael was silent and morose; and instead of going in for a cup of coffee, as was his custom, he kept Miriam talking in the shadow of a plane tree in the street.

'Did you have any boy friends before me?'

'You know I didn't, I told you.'

'Nobody at all?'

'Nobody serious.'

'You did have some, then?'

Miriam soon got to the source of his mood, and poured scorn on it. 'The trouble with you is that all you think about is sex,' she said. 'You can't imagine people feeling guilty about anything else, can you?'

He admitted it, joyfully. 'It's the Irish Jansenist tradition,' he said.

Soon afterwards, Miriam made her first confession, without telling anybody in advance. She went to Westminster Cathedral, the most anonymous place for the purpose she could think of. Crowds poured in and out of the doors, and sat or kneeled or sauntered about, staring up at the great walls and arches of sooty, unfaced brick. It felt like some huge and holy railway terminus. All along one wall were dozens of confessionals, some offering the facility of a foreign language. Miriam, kneeling in a pew while she got her courage up, considered making her confession in French, a subject in which she had done well at A level, but decided that she would not be able to manage the Act of Contrition. Eventually she plunged into one of the ordinary confessionals at random and gabbled out the formula she had been taught by Father Conway: 'Bless me Father for I have sinned this is my first confession.' She added: 'And I'm terrified.' She was lucky with her priest and came out feeling wonderful, spiritually laundered. She never told Michael about the girl at school who had been on her conscience until long after they were married, by which time he was no longer curious.

The wedding night to which he had looked forward for so long got off to a bad start when they were shown into a room at their hotel with twin beds. Michael, inexperienced in such matters, had omitted to specify a double. When the porter had withdrawn, he expressed his regret.

'Ask them to give us another room,' Miriam suggested.

Michael imagined himself going downstairs and walking up to the receptionist in a crowded, but silent and attentive lobby, and saying: '*Could I have a room with a double bed in it, please?*' 'You ask them,' he said to Miriam.

'No *thanks!*'

They giggled and kissed, but the twin beds were decidedly a disappointment. They were narrow and spaced well apart and the headboards were screwed to the wall.

'Oh, well,' said Miriam, 'never mind.' She opened her suitcase and began to unpack. A cascade of confetti fell to the floor as she shook out a dress. 'That Gwen!' she said, referring to one of her bridesmaids.

'Hold on a minute,' said Michael.

Looking neither to right nor left, he marched out of the room, down the stairs, and up to the reception desk.

'Yes, sir?'

Michael took a deep breath. 'Er . . . what time is dinner?' he said.

'Dinner is served from six-thirty, sir.'

'Ah.' He lingered, squinting at the ceiling as if trying to remember something else.

Michael often recalled that moment of acute embarrassment. He recalled it, for instance, in the summer of 1968, when he was checking into a hotel in Oxford, where he was attending a meeting of GCE examiners, and a young man in a white suit, with blond hair down to his shoulders, came up to the desk and asked the price of a double room. In the background, nonchalantly scanning a newspaper, a girl hovered. 'Do you have your luggage with you, sir?' said the clerk, evidently well used to handling such requests from randy undergraduates. The young man didn't have any luggage and was refused the room; but what struck Michael was that he wasn't in the least embarrassed or disconcerted by the refusal, departing with a peace sign and a broad grin, squeezing his girl friend's waist as they left the lobby. 'Whereas I,' he said one weekend in February 1975, recalling his honeymoon in 1958, 'was legally married. All I wanted was a double bed so that we could consummate it in reasonable comfort. And I was tongue-tied. Beads of perspiration literally stood out on my face.'

'Is there anything else, sir?' said the receptionist in 1958, as Michael stared at the ceiling. Without looking the man in the eye, he mumbled out a request for a room with a double bed, and was given one without fuss. He ran back to Miriam, grasping the key like mythical treasure wrested from a dragon. He felt hugely heroic, masculine, dominant: a true husband. When they got to the new room, he locked the door and carried Miriam across to the double bed. They lay on it and necked, occasionally sitting up to divest themselves of a garment (shades of Polly's St Valentine's striptease) until they were both undressed down to their underwear. Solemnly Michael undid the fastener of Miriam's brassiere and drew it from her shoulders. 'Do you mind that they're so small?' she whispered. 'They're beautiful,' he said, kissing the nipples on her delicate little breasts and feeling them grow hard. 'Let's make love,' he said, scarcely able to draw breath for excitement. 'All right,' said Miriam.

She got up off the bed and put on her nightie. Michael put on his pyjamas and drew the curtains against the slanting sunlight (it was about six o'clock in the evening). Then they got into bed, under the bedclothes. Neither of them saw anything odd in this behaviour. It was how they had always envisaged married love.

But then there was a hitch. There seemed to be no way that Michael could get his penis to go in and stay in. In all his long hours of musing on the moment of consummation, he had never anticipated this particular difficulty. They struggled and heaved and muttered 'Sorry' and 'It's all right,' but after a while the atmosphere became slightly desperate. Had Miriam grasped Michael's penis and guided it to its target, there would have been no problem, but it never occurred to her to do so or to him to suggest it. None of our young brides even touched their husbands' genitals until weeks, months, sometimes years after marriage. All accepted the first nuptial embrace lying on their backs with their arms locked round their spouses' necks like drowning swimmers being rescued; while these spouses, supporting themselves on tensed arms, tried to steer their way blind into a channel the contours of which they had never previously explored by touch or sight. No wonder most of them found the act both difficult and disappointing.

At last Michael admitted defeat, modestly pulled up his pyjama trousers under the blankets, and got out of bed to find a cigarette. Miriam watched him anxiously. 'Perhaps there's something wrong with me,' she said. 'Perhaps I've got a blockage. I'll go and see a doctor.' She was only half joking. They dressed and went down for dinner, silent and sad, smiling wanly at each other across the table. Michael contemplated the prospect of a marriage without sex. After so long a wait, did he love Miriam enough to accept that heavy cross? He reached under the table and squeezed her hand, suffused with a Greeneian gloom, 'the loyalty we all feel to unhappiness, the sense that this is where we really belong,' as a favourite passage in *The Heart of the Matter* put it. When they returned to their room, he proposed one more try.

'I'm awfully sore,' said Miriam doubtfully.

'Haven't you got some ointment, or something?'

She did, as it happened, have some Vaseline with her, which she used for the prevention of chapped lips. Applied to her nether lips it produced almost magical results. Afterwards, Michael put his hands behind his head and smiled beatifically at the ceiling.

'From now on,' he said, 'I'm always going to give Vaseline for wedding presents.'

Angela and Dennis were the last of their College set to get married, and had waited the longest. Dennis had wanted to get married as soon as he was offered his first job, with ICI. When he phoned Angela with the news of his successful interview, late in 1956, he said, 'Let's get married at Christmas.' Angela felt panic choking her and was scarcely able to reply. Dennis thought it was a bad connection and rattled on unconcerned. 'Easter, if you like,' he said. 'Christmas would be short notice for the families.'

When they met the next day, Angela, pale from a sleepless night, told him that she didn't think she was ready for marriage. 'Ready, what d'you mean, ready?' he demanded, bewildered. 'We've waited five years already, how much longer d'you want?'

Angela found it very difficult to explain. She loved Dennis, she appreciated his loyalty and devotion, she wanted to give herself to him. But the prospect of marriage, a lifetime's commitment, frightened her, and the portents in marriages she knew depressed her, especially her own parents' marriage. While she had lived at home she had sentimentalized it, idealized it. The big, warm, happy Catholic family. The house full of noisy bustle and religious zeal. The boys cycling off early in the mornings to serve at mass, priests and nuns dropping in at all hours, family feasts at Christmas and Easter. Now she saw it all differently, aware that her mother's part in all this had been a lifetime of drudgery, her father's a lifetime of worry. The family was like the shop – a tyrant that kept them slaving from morning till night, so that they never had a moment to themselves. Their sexual life was unimaginable, not simply because it embarrassed her to think about it, but because they seemed so exhausted, so drained of tenderness to each other, by the clamorous demands of their offspring. When she went home for weekends now, she threw herself into the domestic front line at her mother's side-washed, ironed, swept and Hoovered – but it seemed to make no difference: the dirty washing accumulated as fast as ever, people tramped through the house leaving mud and dirt everywhere, the fire smoked in the back parlour and the shop bell pinged insistently. Always she was guiltily pleased to be gone, to be back in her snug and neat little bed-sitter in Streatham. She had a teaching job in a girls' grammar school which she found demanding but satisfying, and her career prospects were good. Her eldest brother, Tom, was training to be a priest, and the rest of the children were still at school. She thought it was her duty to work for at least a few years, sending a quarter of her salary home. That was how she put it to Dennis, though the deeper reason was simply that she was frightened of marriage.

'You can go on working after we're married,' Dennis said. 'You can go on giving part of your earnings to your Mum and Dad.'

'For how long? We'll have children, won't we?'

'Not immediately. We'll use the whatdyoucallit, rhythm method.'

'Suppose it doesn't work?'

'Why shouldn't it work? It's scientifically sound.'

'Oh, *scientifically* . . .'

She jeered at his trust in science, uttered wounding remarks about his complacency, his self-centredness. She tried to make herself as unpleasant as possible, to provoke him into breaking their engagement; but he simply sat there, absorbing all her venom, and at last wore her out. All right, he sighed, when she had talked herself out, and was sitting red-faced and dumb, wanting to cry but unable to; all right, he would not press her, they could wait until she was ready. He came over to the divan where she was sitting and put his arm round her shoulders. Why me, she thought, why does it have to be me? Why can't he leave me in peace and find another girl, someone who really wants to get married?

Dennis gave up the post he had been offered with ICI, which would have meant moving to Northumberland, and took a job with an electronics firm in London, on the production side, relying on his Army qualifications for the relevant technical

469

knowledge. This job he saw as a temporary expedient, but in fact it turned out rather well for Dennis, for it was a lively firm in what turned out to be a buoyant market in the sixties. At the time, however, it seemed a waste of his chemistry degree. Dennis's parents were quietly reproachful towards Angela when she visited them in Hastings. They thought Angela was a nice girl, 'a lovely girl', but they couldn't understand her hesitation to marry their son and they couldn't forgive her for keeping him waiting against his wishes. As for her own parents, they were thoroughly in favour of Dennis, a good Catholic, a steady chap with good prospects; and since Angela made it clear that in no circumstances would she allow them to pay for her wedding, they were quite eager to see it come off. Eventually Angela capitulated to all this gentle pressure, and not unwillingly; she felt she had put up a creditable fight for . . . whatever it was that had made her hesitate: independence, conscience, realism. I have made no promises I cannot keep, she told herself, when at last she named the day (it was being matron of honour to Ruth that tipped the balance in favour of marriage), I haved warned him, I have warned them all. And then, she did love Dennis, wanted to make love to him properly after all these years of the tiresome game of How Far Can You Go. When they lay on the divan bed in her bedsitter now, she did not resist the advances of his exploring hands over her body and under her dress, and she felt the quickening excitement of his breathing and the hardness of his male parts pressed against her thigh. He gave her a book to read, written by a doctor, about the facts of sex, and she learned from it many things she had not known before, her cheeks burning as she read, and felt additional impatience to be wed, for it seemed to her indecent to have such knowledge without the experience.

As they were arranging their own wedding, and their families lived so far apart, North and South, Angela and Dennis decided to have it in London, at the University church. This was not the church of Our Lady and St Jude's, of course, but a much more venerable structure in the City. They did, however, ask Father Brierley to officiate as they did not know the current University Chaplain; and Father Brierley, still a curate in the parish at the end of the Northern Line, was touched by the request, and agreed gladly. This gave Dennis and Angela the idea of inviting all the regular members of the group that used to attend the Thursday masses. There was no rational reason for this, really – for though some, like Michael and Miriam, were close friends whom they would have invited anyway, others were not and had been out of touch for years, except for the occasional Christmas card. However, they both agreed that Father Brierley would appreciate a reunion, and in some obscure, inarticulate way they both felt a kind of sentimental nostalgia for those dark, cold, Thursday mornings of their first love, when they trekked in from the suburbs for early mass. 'Imagine,' said Angela, 'travelling all that distance without a cup of tea first. Not even a glass of water. How did we do it?' For by this date, autumn 1958, the Eucharistic fast had been considerably relaxed, and one was permitted to drink any non-alcoholic beverage up to one hour before receiving Communion – a concession particularly appreciated by brides preparing for their nuptial mass.

Everyone agreed that it was a very nice wedding. It took place on a fine October day. Angela looked beautiful and Dennis looked like the cat who was finally certain of getting the cream. Miriam played the organ expertly, and Michael was an efficient best man. Angela's brother Tom, who was a year away from ordination, assisted Father Brierley as deacon, and read the Epistle in a fine clear voice:

'Brethren: let women be subject to their husbands as to the Lord, for the husband is the head of the wife, as Christ is the head of the Church. He is the saviour of his body. Therefore, as the Church is subject to Christ, so also let the wives be to their husbands in all things. Husbands, love your wives as Christ also loved the Church . . .'

Father Brierley's sermon was a little on the heavy side, some thought, but it was sincere, and carefully prepared. This couple, he told the assembled congregation (who scarcely needed to be reminded of the fact) had not rushed into holy matrimony, like so many young people these days. They had tested their feelings for each other over a long period, they had prepared themselves prudently for the great responsibilities of the married state, and now they were calling down God's blessing on their union by this nuptial mass. As St Paul's epistle had reminded them all, the relationship between man and wife was analogous to that between Christ and His Church. ('What's analogous?' Angela's mother whispered to her husband, who shook his head.) Both were founded on Faith, Hope and Love. Dennis and Angela, poised on the threshold of a new life together, did not know exactly what the future held for them: great joys and happiness, certainly, but also trials and tribulations, for such was human life. (Dennis's father stirred restlessly in his pew; it seemed a rather gloomy sermon for a wedding, he thought – more suitable for a funeral.) The Church also at this time stood on the threshold of a new era. A great Pope, Pius XII, had just died, a Pope who had steered the bark of Peter through the stormy seas of the Second World War, who had defended the right of Catholics to practice their faith in the teeth of Communist persecution, a Pope who had never hesitated to stand up for Christian values against the rampant materialism of the modern world. Even as he spoke to them now, the cardinals of all the nations of the world were gathering in Rome to elect a new Pope in secret conclave. No one knew who he would be, or what problems he would have to grapple with. What they did know was that the Holy Spirit would guide the Conclave's choice, that the man who was chosen would be equal to whatever challenge lay before him, because of Christ's promise that he would be with His Church all days, even to the consummation of the world. Likewise, Dennis and Angela knew that Christ would be with them, too, all days, sharing in their joys and supporting them in their sorrows, until death did them part.

Afterwards, at the reception, there were excited reunions between old friends, many of whom had not seen each other for years. Not everyone had been able to come. Sister Mary Joseph of the Precious Blood wrote to Angela to say that the Rule of the Order forbade attendance at weddings, but she wished them both joy and would remember them in her prayers. Adrian wrote excusing himself and Dorothy on the grounds that Dorothy was pregnant and had been ordered to rest. It didn't sound terribly convincing, but Dennis, anyway, was more relieved than sorry at Adrian's absence. All the others, rather to his surprise, turned up. Edward was there, in his Lieutenant's uniform of the RAMC, which made Dennis feel a little queasy, and Tessa, proudly wielding her new baby. Polly came and wept copiously through the wedding service, making the mascara run down her cheeks in black rivulets, so that she had to retire for an interval afterwards to re-do her face. She was twenty-six and was beginning to want very much to be married herself and have babies like Tessa, and like Miriam, who was four months pregnant and looked blooming in a green maternity dress which she scarcely needed yet. Polly now worked for the BBC as a research assistant, and knew lots of young men, but not one of them had asked her to marry him, as she had the reputation of being a bit of a tart. This was hardly fair to Polly, who had had only two affairs in the last two years, but coming back into contact with all these good Catholics, hearing mass for the first time in ages, looking at radiant Angela and proud Dennis, and feeling sure that, incredible as it might seem, they were going to the nuptial bed as genuine virgins, she herself felt distinctly Magdalenish, and began to wonder whether she should start going to mass again, perhaps even to Confession, and try to make a fresh start. But after her second glass of white wine at the reception she cheered up and began to flirt with all the men at the reception, even Father Brierley.

'I don't suppose you remember me, do you, Father? The Salome of Cath. Soc?'

'Of course I do, Polly, yes indeed, how are you after all these years?' said Father Brierley nervously.

'That was a beautiful sermon, Father.'

'Thank you, most kind,' Father Brierley murmured, blushing with pleasure.

'Isn't it exciting about the Conclave! Who d'you think will win?'

' "Win" isn't perhaps the most appropriate – '

'Don't you think it would be fun to have a Yank for a change? Good heavens, there's Miles! Excuse me, Father.'

Polly turned aside and began to push her way through the crush, leaving a heavy smell of perfume lingering on the air in her wake. Austin Brierley was relieved to see her go, for her presence had stirred embarrassing memories and a still-vivid mental image of her silk-stockinged leg.

Polly greeted Miles with a faint shriek, to which he responded with expressions of surprise and rapture. They embraced with a great deal of physical flourish but little actual contact, since Polly did not want to have to repair her make-up again, and Miles did not want her lipstick all over his face and shirt collar. A little circle of the bride's relations watched this performance respectfully, recognizing a code of manners more sophisticated and complex than their own. Michael, observing from further off, realized for the first time that Miles was homosexual, something that had never occurred to him in his innocent undergraduate days. What, he wondered, did a Catholic homosexual do? Sublimate, he supposed. It seemed rather hard. On other the hand it was difficult, not being a homosexual oneself, to believe that what homosexuals did with each other would be difficult to give up. It was always a mystery, other people's experience of sex. Even Miriam, though she enjoyed making love, could not explain to him what it felt like, and became evasive and finally frigid if he questioned her too closely.

A little later, Michael chatted with Miles and learned that he had finished his PhD thesis, which was likely to be published, and had recently been elected to a Fellowship at one of the Cambridge colleges. Miles spoke eloquently of the pleasures of Cambridge, dropped a few great names, and enquired kindly, but a shade patronizingly, about Michael's career.

'I'm schoolteaching to stay out of the Army,' Michael explained. 'How did you get out of it?'

'I failed the medical,' said Miles.

'Lucky sod,' said Michael, unthinkingly. He added hastily, 'I'd like to go into university teaching myself, but I can't afford to be called up, now I'm married and with a baby on the way.'

'Really? My congratulations.'

'Thanks. We didn't really want to start a family right away, but well, you know how it is . . .'

'Not from experience,' Miles smiled suavely.

'I mean for Catholics. Birth control and so on.'

'Oh yes, well, I do sympathize, but on the other hand there is something rather fine about the Church's refusal to compromise on that issue, don't you think? Unlike the Anglicans, poor dears.'

It's all very well for you, Michael thought; but said nothing.

The reception was nearly over, the telegrams had been read, and speeches made, and the wedding cake cut and consumed. Angela was beginning to think of retiring to change into her going-away clothes when Violet made a very late and somewhat disturbing appearance at the feast. She looked very ill and anxious, very much as she had looked just before her nervous breakdown in her Final year. Her clothes were dark and heavy and distinctly unfestive, and she carried a large paper carrier bag. She went up to Angela and apologized for being late, giving some complicated explanation of how she had lost her way on the Tube. 'I've brought you a present,' she said, and produced from the bag a rather untidy parcel tied up in crumpled brown paper. As she seemed to want Angela to open it, Angela did so, and was disconcerted to find inside a complete baby's layette.

'It was for the baby I lost,' Violet said. 'I'm sure you'll have a use for it one day.'

The guests, who had gathered round to see the present, turned away in embarrassment.

'But, Violet,' said Angela gently, 'you mustn't give me this. You may need it yourself another time.'

'No, Robin and I are separated. Anyway, he wouldn't have any more children, he didn't mean us to have that one, it was a mistake, he wanted me to have an abortion, but I wouldn't. He's not a Catholic, you know.'

'Angela,' said Miriam, seeing that Violet had to be stopped from spoiling Angela's day, 'if you don't go and get changed immediately, you're going to miss that train. I'll get Violet something to eat.' And with a slightly worried frown, Angela went off to get changed.

'Well, well, poor old Violet,' said Michael later, when he and Miriam were alone together, walking back to the Tube station arm-in-arm.

'Was she like that as a student?'

'A bit inclined. She had a sort of nervous breakdown in her last year, had to take a year off.'

'It's a shame her losing her baby,' Miriam said, covertly feeling her own tummy, like someone touching wood.

'Mmm. Her husband's a bit of a cold fish, too. I met him once.'

'She said they were separated.'

'A typical Violet overstatement. I gather he's gone to the States for a term. Some kind of exchange.'

'But he didn't take her with him.'

'Expect he wanted to get away from her for a while. Can't say I blame him. Did you see how she got Father Brierley into a corner? He didn't look as if he was enjoying it one bit.'

They walked in silence for a while, thinking their own thoughts.

'Well,' said Michael, 'it all went off very nicely, in spite of Violet. The organ sounded fantastic in that church.'

'And you were a super best man. It was a very funny speech.' She squeezed his hand.

'All the same,' he said, 'I shan't complain if I don't have to go to another wedding for a few years. I've just about had enough.'

'From now on,' said Miriam, 'it's going to be christenings.'

Dennis and Angela's honeymoon was, of course, no freer from awkwardness and disappointment than any of the others, though these feelings were mostly on Angela's side. The book Dennis had lent her had not prepared her for the physical messiness of the act of love, and the orgasms she had read about in its pages eluded her. On the honeymoon Dennis was ravenous for her, begged her to make love twice, three times a night, he groaned and swore in his rapture, said over and over again, I love you, I love you, but always he reached his climax as soon as he entered her, and she felt little except the unpleasant aftertrickle between her legs, staining her new nighties and the hotel sheets. When they got home to their little two-roomed flat, she changed the bedlinen so often that their laundry bill became astronomical (there was nowhere to hang out sheets) and caused their first quarrel; after which she spread towels on the bed when the occasion required it. Then, after a couple of months, she missed her period and felt nauseous in the mornings and knew that she must be pregnant. She told her headmistress that she would be resigning at the following Easter.

THREE

How things began to change

Miriam was quite right. For all of them who married in the nineteen-fifties, except poor Violet, the next decade was dominated by babies. Dennis and Angela, Edward and Tessa, Adrian and Dorothy, Michael and Miriam herself, had produced, by the end of 1966, fourteen children between them, in spite of strenuous efforts not to. That is to say, although each of these couples wanted to have children, the latter arrived more quickly and frequently than their parents had wished for or intended. And the reason for this, of course, was that, obedient to their Church's teaching, they relied upon periodic abstinence as a way of planning their families, a system known as Rhythm or the Safe Method, which was in practice neither rhythmical nor safe. I have written about this before, a novel about a penurious young Catholic couple whose attempts to apply the Safe Method have produced three children in as many years, and whose hopes of avoiding a fourth depend precariously on their plotting a day-by-day graph of the wife's body-temperature to determine the time of her ovulation, and confining their enjoyment of conjugal love to the few days between this putative event and the anxiously awaited onset of her period. It was intended to be a comic novel and most Catholic readers seemed to find it funny, especially priests, who were perhaps pleased to learn that the sex life they had renounced for a higher good wasn't so very marvellous after all. Some of these priests have told me that they lent the book to people dying of terminal diseases and how it cheered them up, which is fine by me – I can't think of a better reason for writing novels – but possibly these readers, too, found it easier to bid

478

farewell to the pleasures of the flesh when they were depicted as so hemmed about with anxiety. Healthy agnostics and atheists among my acquaintance, however, found the novel rather sad. All that self-denial and sacrifice of libido depressed them. I think it would depress me, too, now, if I didn't know that my principal characters would have made a sensible decision long ago to avail themselves of contraceptives.

Why this novel should have been translated into Czech and no other foreign language I cannot explain, for I should have thought that Czech Catholics would have more important things to worry about than problems of conscience over birth control, and I cannot imagine that non-Catholic Czechs would take a great interest in the subject. However, it did elicit, from Mr Cestimir Jerhot of Prague, the nicest request for my autograph I have ever received, or am ever likely to receive. *'Dear Sir,'* he wrote, *'I beg your costly pardon for my extraordinary beg and readings-request, with them I turn at you. I am namely a great reader and books-lover. Among my best friends – books – I have also in my library the Czech copy of your lovely book* 'Den zkazy v Britskem museu'. *I have read it several times and ever I have found it an extraordinary smiling book. I thank you very much for the best readings experiences and nice whiles, that has given your lovely work . . .'*

Thank you again, Mr Jerhot, for your lovely letter. This book is not a comic novel, exactly, but I have tried to make it smile as much as possible.

For Dorothy and Adrian, Tessa and Edward, Miriam and Michael, Angela and Dennis, then, in the early sixties, it was babies, babies, all the way. Nappies, bottles, colic, broken nights, smells of faeces and ammonia, clothes and furniture stained with dribble and sick. Well, that was all right. They were prepared to put up with all that, especially Tessa, who doted on babies, and Dennis, who was thrilled with paternity. The others, too, all had moments of great joy and pride in their infant offspring. Nor were the economic consequences of their fertility an overwhelming concern, though of course the wives had to give up work almost as soon as they were married, and at a time of increasing general affluence they had to be content with cramped, poorly furnished accommodation relative to their peer-group, and acquired cars, TVs and household appliances long after their non-Catholic friends. All this would have been tolerable if they had been erotically fulfilled. But just when they began to get the hang of sex – to learn the arts of foreplay, to lose their inhibitions about nakedness, to match each other's orgasmic rhythms – pregnancy or the fear of pregnancy intervened, and their spontaneity was destroyed by the tedious regime of calendar and temperature chart. For they did not always feel amorous on the permitted days, and if they made the mistake of getting amorous outside the permitted days it was back to the old game of How Far Could You Go. Most galling of all, their efforts to control their fertility always failed anyway, sooner or later. There were times when Angela thought it would be preferable simply to trust to luck and Providence, since it seemed to make little difference in the long run, and the frustration of one's intelligent efforts was almost as bad as the actual consequences – at least it seemed to be so for Dennis, who would pore over their graphs and diaries, trying to pinpoint where they had gone wrong, his scientific self-esteem piqued by failure. More than once they quarrelled over some alleged carelessness or inaccuracy on her part in keeping the record.

During a pregnancy, after the initial vexation and morning-sickness had worn off, and providing there were no gynaecological complications, the couples might enjoy a few months of free and easy sex, but after a new baby was born there would be a long hiatus, for it was not possible to plot the incidence of ovulation with any confidence as long as breast-feeding continued. This circumstance was particularly frustrating for Michael, since Miriam grew the most superb breasts, round and firm as apples, while she was nursing, and he wasn't even allowed to touch them, they were so tender and full of milk. All he could do was sit and watch enviously as his infant sucked and gently kneaded his wife's blindingly beautiful tits – which, by the time he and Miriam could make love again, would have disappeared.

Michael was perhaps the most frustrated of the men at this

time, for his erotic imagination, always sensitive to stimulus, was being fed with more and more hints from the outside world, especially fiction. He followed the trial of *Lady Chatterley's Lover* with intense interest, and was one of the first to buy a copy of the Penguin edition when it was published, travelling into the next town to ensure that no one from the Catholic College of Education where he was now employed as a lecturer in English Literature would observe him making the purchase. He read the pages staring in disbelief at the forbidden words so boldly printed there and marvelling at the acts described. He had never much cared for Lawrence's writing, and one half of his mind sneered at the book's overblown rhetoric and portentous neo-paganism, while the other half felt a deep, envious attraction to the idea of phallic tenderness. When he had finished the novel, he passed it to Miriam, but she stopped reading it halfway through. She thought it was unconvincing and badly written; therefore the sex seemed crude and unnecessarily explicit. Michael could not defend the novel on literary-critical grounds, but he was disappointed, for the knowledge that Miriam was reading it excited him, and he had been hopeful that the passage about Connie Chatterley kissing Mellors' penis, which was the most amazing thing he had ever read in his whole life, might have given Miriam some ideas, but she did not get that far. After the publication of *Lady Chatterley's Lover*, Michael observed, the amount and variety of sexual intercourse in contemporary fiction increased dramatically. Whether this was because Lawrence's novel had encouraged more people to have it off more often, in more different ways, than before, or because it had merely encouraged novelists to admit what had been going on all the time, Michael was in no position to judge. He just felt that he was missing an awful lot.

The others did not envy the growing permissiveness of secular society so candidly. Adrian, for instance, imagined that his intense interest and excitement at the Profumo affair in the spring of 1963 was because it illustrated the general rottenness of the British political Establishment, which he was apt to compare unfavourably with the style and idealism of the American administration led by President Kennedy, the first Roman Catholic ever to be elected to that office. Adrian did not admit, even to himself, that he was deeply fascinated by the shameless self-possession of the call-girls, Christine Keeler and Mandy Rice-Davies, when interviewed about their sex-lives on TV and in the press. They spoke as if there was no such thing as sin in the world. At this time Adrian and Dorothy were abstaining totally and indefinitely from sexual intercourse, since Dorothy's womb was in bad shape following two babies and a miscarriage in quick succession. (At about the same time, President Kennedy was confiding to his friend Ben Bradlee, later editor of the *Washington Post*, that if he didn't have a woman every three days or so, he got a bad headache; and by woman the President didn't mean Mrs Kennedy. But Adrian only read about that many years later in a newspaper excerpt from Mr Bradlee's memoirs.)

Of the four couples, Edward and Tessa probably suffered least under the regime of the Safe Period, for several reasons. They were comparatively well-off, they wanted a large family anyway, and they managed to space their first three children at two-year intervals without too much difficulty. Tessa was a strong healthy girl, with a wonderfully regular menstrual cycle (her graphs, Edward used to say, were a thing of beauty). Edward's problems were more in his professional sphere. A GP in the suburbs of an industrial Midlands city, he had an arrangement with his partners by which he looked after the Catholic patients in the practice requiring family planning advice, and he gave up one evening a week to similar service for the Catholic Marriage Advisory Council. Edward attended seminars arranged by the CMAC and kept up conscientiously with the medical literature on the use of the Safe Period. He instructed his clients in the use of the basal temperature method, and spent many hours beyond the call of duty going over the graphs they submitted to him for interpretation. The failure rate was, however, depressingly high. At first he was inclined to attribute this to lack of care and attention on the part of his patients, many of whom were working-class women unskilled in the use of thermometers and graph paper, but after a few years he began to have graver doubts about the reliability of the method itself, and to dread the faintly reproachful look on the faces of those of his family-planning clients who returned unexpectedly to ask for a pregnancy test.

One night he and Tessa were woken by a frantic banging on the front door. Assuming that he was being summoned to an emergency, Edward grabbed his bag and hurried down the stairs. A stranger with dishevelled clothing and staring eyes exploded into the hall and threw Edward to the ground. *'Safe! Safe! Safe!'* he screamed, banging Edward's head on the floor to emphasize the repetition. Recovering from his surprise, Edward wrestled the man into submission, whereupon he went limp and burst into tears. While Tessa quietened the terrified children, who had been woken by the fracas, Edward took the man into the lounge and gave him a mild sedative. It transpired that Edward had advised his wife on birth control, with the usual result, and that evening she had given birth to a child, their sixth, with some kind of physical malformation which the man could not even bring himself to describe. Tessa came into the room in her dressing-gown in time to hear this story, and scolded the man for relieving his feelings on Edward. 'I'm very sorry for you and your wife, especially your wife,' she said, 'but you really can't blame it on my husband. These things can happen to anybody, at any time.'

Edward nodded agreement, but inwardly he was not so sure. There had been four babies born in the practice with non-hereditary congenital abnormalities since he had joined it, and three of them had been born to his family-planning clients. Somewhere in the medical journals he had come across the hypothesis that genetic defects were more likely to occur when the ovum was fertilized towards the end of its brief life-span, and this was obviously more likely to occur with couples who were deliberately restricting their intercourse to the post-ovulatory period. The theory had not been tested by controlled experiment, and his own experience had no statistical significance whatsoever, but still, it was . . . unsettling. Edward did not mention these disquieting thoughts to Tessa, and was very glad he hadn't when shortly afterwards she became pregnant for the fourth time, unintentionally. Tessa took it very well, joked about Vatican Roulette and said you couldn't win them all; but Edward watched her swelling belly with barely disguised feelings of anxiety and dread. He terminated his voluntary work for the Catholic Marriage Advisory Council, and recommended the basal temperature method to Catholic patients in the practice with more caution than previously.

You may wonder why they all persevered with this frustrating, undignified, ineffective, anxiety-creating system of family planning. They wondered themselves, years later, when they had all given it up. 'It was conditioning,' said Adrian, 'it was the projection of the celibate clergy's own repressions on to the laity.' 'It was guilt,' said Dorothy, 'guilt about sex. Sex was dirty enough without going into birth control, that was the general feeling.' 'I think it was innocence,' said Edward. 'The idea of natural birth control, without sheaths or pills or anything, was very appealing to people with no sexual experience; it took some time to discover that unfortunately it didn't work.' 'It was fear, the fear of Hell,' said Michael. Well, yes, that was at the bottom of it, they all admitted. (They were gathered together in 1969 for the AGM of a pressure group called Catholics for an Open Church, to which they all belonged, and were chatting together afterwards in a pub.)

They had been indoctrinated since adolescence with the idea, underlined by several Papal pronouncements, that contraception was a grave sin, and a sin that occupied a unique place in the spiritual game of Snakes and Ladders. For unlike other sins of the flesh, it had to be committed continuously and with premeditation if it was to have any point at all. It was not, therefore, something that could be confessed and absolved again and again in good faith, like losing one's temper, or getting drunk, or, for that matter, fornicating. (A nice question for casuists: was fornication more or less culpable if committed using contraceptives?) It excluded you from the sacraments, therefore; and according to Catholic teaching of the same vintage, if you failed to make your Easter Duty (confession and communion at least once a year, at Easter or thereabouts) you effectively excommunicated yourself. So, either you struggled on as best you could without reliable contraception, or you got out of the Church; these seemed to be the only logical alternatives. Some people, of course, had left precisely because they could no longer believe in the authority of a Church that taught such mischievous nonsense. More often, those who lapsed over this issue retained a residual belief in the rest of Catholic doctrine and thus lived uncomfortably in a state of suppressed guilt and spiritual deprivation. One way or another, Catholics who used contraceptives were likely to be committing a sin against the Holy Ghost – either Resisting the Known Truth or Obstinacy in Sin – and thus putting themselves at risk of final damnation. So Michael was in that sense right – it all came down to fear of Hell.

'Where we went wrong, of course,' said Adrian, 'was in accepting the theology of mortal sin.'

'No,' said Miriam, who had been listening quietly to their comments. 'Where you went wrong was in supposing that the Church belonged to the Pope or the priests instead of to the People of God.'

They nodded agreement. 'The People of God' was a phrase the Catholics for an Open Church approved of. It made them sound invincible.

In the early nineteen-sixties, however, their main hope was that the official Church would change its mind on birth control; that they would wake up one morning and read in the papers that the Pope had said it was all right for them to use contraceptives after all. What a rush there would have been to the chemists' and barbers' shops, and the Family Planning Clinics! In hindsight it is clear that this was a fairly preposterous expectation, for such a reversal of traditional teaching would have dealt a blow to the credibility of papal authority so shattering that no Pope, not even Pope John, could reasonably have been expected to perpetrate it. Miriam was right: instead of waiting for the Pope to contradict his predecessors, they should have made up their own minds. This in fact they did, in due course, but it took a lot of misery and stress to screw them up to the point of disobedience. In the early nineteen-sixties they were still hoping for a change of heart at the top, at least in favour of the Pill, to which, some progressive theologians claimed, the traditional natural law arguments against artificial contraception did not apply.

In other respects the Church undoubtedly was changing. Pope John, against all expectations (CARETAKER PONTIFF ELECTED, Angela and Dennis had read on newspaper placards when they returned from their honeymoon) had electrified the Catholic world by the radical style of his pontificate. 'We are going,' he declared, 'to shake off the dust that has collected on the throne of St Peter since the time of Constantine and let in some fresh air.' The Second Vatican Council which he convened brought out into the light a thousand unsuspected shoots of innovation and experiment, in theology, liturgy and pastoral practice, that had been buried for decades out of timidity or misplaced loyalty. In 1962, Pope John actually set up a Pontifical Commission to study problems connected with the Family, Population and Birth Control. This was encouraging news in one sense, since it seemed to admit the possibility of change, but disappointing in that it effectively removed the issue from debate at the Vatican Council, which began its deliberations in the same year. Pope John died in 1963, to be succeeded by Pope Paul VI, who enlarged the Commission and instructed its members specifically to examine the Church's traditional teaching with particular reference to the progesterone pill. Catholics, especially young married ones, waited impatiently for the result of this inquiry.

Meanwhile, other changes proceeded at a dizzying pace. The mass was revised and translated into the vernacular. The priest now faced the congregation across a plain table-style altar, which made the origins of the Mass in the Last Supper more comprehensible, and allowed many of the laity to see for the first time what the celebrant actually did. All masses were now dialogue masses, the whole congregation joining in the responses. The Eucharistic fast was reduced to a negligible one hour, before which any kind of food and drink might be consumed, and the laity were urged to receive communion at every mass – a practice previously deemed appropriate only to people of great personal holiness and entailing frequent confession. Typical devotions of Counter-Reformation Catholicism such as Benediction and the Stations of the Cross dwindled in popularity. Rosaries gathered dust at the backs of drawers. The liturgy of Holy Week, previously of a length and tedium only to be borne by the most devout, was streamlined, reconstructed, vernacularized, and offensive references to the 'perfidious Jews' were removed from the prayers on Good Friday. Ecumenism, the active pursuit of Christian Unity through 'dialogue' with other Churches, became a recommended activity. The change of posture from the days when the Catholic Church had seen itself as essentially in competition with other, upstart Christian denominations, and set their total submission to its own authority as the price of unity, was astonishingly swift. Adrian, looking through his combative apologetics textbooks from Catholic Evidence Guild days, before sending them off to a parish jumble sale, could hardly believe how swift it had been. And from the Continent, from Latin America, through the religious press, came rumours of still more startling innovations being mooted – married priests, even women priests, Communion in the hand and under both kinds, intercommunion with other denominations, 'Liberation Theology', and 'Catholic Marxism'. A group of young intellectuals of the latter persuasion, based in Cambridge, founded a journal called *Slant* in which they provocatively identified the Kingdom of God heralded in the New Testament with the Revolution, and characterized the service of Benediction as a capitalist-imperialist liturgical perversion which turned the shared bread of the authentic Eucharist into a reified commodity.

These developments were not, of course, universally welcomed. Evelyn Waugh, for instance, did not welcome them, and wrote furious letters to the *Tablet* saying so. Malcolm Muggeridge did not welcome them, and wrote a polemical piece in the *New Statesman* in 1965 urging 'Backward, Christian Soldiers!' But it was none of his business, anyway, Michael thought, reading the article in the College library. What people needed from the Catholic Church, according to Muggeridge, was its 'powerful pessimism about human life, miraculously preserved through the long false dawn of science.' Reading this, Michael recognized a version of Catholicism he had once espoused. He no longer espoused it. Neither, it seemed, did Graham Greene, whose most recent novel, *A Burnt-out Case*, reflected the evolutionary Utopianism of Teilhard de Chardin's *The Phenomenon of Man*, a book published in 1959 to international acclaim, after having been long suppressed by Rome as heretical.

Miles, on the other hand, considered Chardin a wet and muddled thinker, and reading the same article of Malcolm Muggeridge in the Combination Room of his Cambridge college, nodded gleeful agreement. The *Aggiornamento* or Renewal of the Catholic Church instigated by Pope John looked to Miles more and more like a Protestantization of it, and as he said to Michael and Miriam at the christening of their third child (rather to his surprise he had been invited to be its godfather, and rather to their surprise he had accepted), if you liked that sort of thing the Protestants did it much better, and it was not what he, personally, had joined the Catholic Church for. Michael, at the time something of a fellow-traveller with the *Slant* group, was dismayed by this reactionary declaration, but wishing, ignobly, to avoid a row with Miles, his closest personal link with the great academic world, retired to the kitchen to help his mother-in-law prepare tea.

Miriam did not agree with Miles either – as a convert from Evangelical Protestantism she felt quite at home in the new-style Catholic Church – but she was unable to put her point of view with any force because she was tired from lack of sleep and preoccupied with the needs of her three-week old baby and the jealous demands of the two older children and worried about whether there would be enough cups with handles still on them for their guests. So Miles held forth uninterruptedly, which he was used to doing, being a Cambridge don, while Miriam listened with one ear and cocked the other for sounds of crisis in the kitchen and surreptitiously sniffed the baby to ascertain whether she had soiled her nappy and scanned the crowded living-room for other signs of trouble.

'The trouble with Catholics, my dear Miriam,' said Miles, 'in this country, at least, is that they have absolutely no taste, no aesthetic sense whatsoever, so that as soon as they begin to meddle with the styles of architecture and worship that they inherited from the Counter-Reformation, as soon as they try and go "modern", God help us, they make the most terrible dog's breakfast of it, a hideous jumble of old and new, incompatible styles and idioms, that positively sets one's teeth on edge. Do you remember that little church, Our Lady and St Jude's – no, of course you wouldn't, you didn't know Michael in those days . . . Well, anyway, it was a terribly dingy, dilapidated neo-gothic place without a single feature of interest or beauty in it, but at least it had a certain character, a certain consistency, a kind of gloomy *ambiance* which was quite devotional in its way. You know, banks of votive candles simply dripping with congealed wax, hanging down like *stalactites*, and shadows flickering over painted statues . . . Well, I happened to be in London on Ascension Day, so I dropped in for an evening mass, and, oh dear, what a transformation! No, not a transformation, that was the trouble, it hadn't been transformed, just meddled with. The candles had gone, and most of the statues, and the oil paintings of the Stations of the Cross, which were admittedly fairly hideous but so heavily varnished that you could scarcely see them, had been replaced with ghastly modern bas-reliefs in some kind of aluminium more appropriate to saucepans than to sacred art, and the altar rails had been removed and at the top of the steps there was a plain wooden altar, quite nice in its way but utterly incompatible with the old high altar behind it – all marble and gold inlay, turreted and crenellated in the gothic style . . . and quite honestly the mass itself seemed to me to be the same sort of muddle, bits of the old liturgy and bits of the new flung together, and nobody quite knowing what to do or what to expect.'

'These things take time,' said Miriam. 'Catholics aren't used to participating in the liturgy. They're used to watching the priest and saying their own prayers privately.'

'Well, I must say that some of the things I'm supposed to say publicly nowadays make me cringe with embarrassment. The Responsorial Psalm on Ascension Day, for instance, what was it? *"God goes up with shouts of joy; the Lord goes up with trumpet blast."*

I mean, *really*! It sounds like a rocket lifting off at Cape Canaveral. Or something even more vulgar.'

Miles tittered, and glanced covertly at the clock on the mantelpiece, wondering when he could decently make his departure. He had been invited to stay the night, but had no intention of trying to sleep on the Put-U-Up sofa in the living room which, he had established by a discreet survey of the premises, was the only accommodation for guests. The tiny, semi-detached house, overcrowded with people and cheap furniture so that it was scarcely possible to take a step without bumping into something or somebody, depressed him and made him restless to return to the cool, quiet spaces of Cambridge. It had been a mistake to come. Every now and then he succumbed to a feeling that there was something hollow and empty about his privileged existence, and then he would seize any opportunity to plunge into the ordinary world of domesticity, children, simple living and honest toil. But invariably it was disillusioning. He could see nothing to envy in Michael's existence. How could the spirit develop in such an environment? How right the Church was to insist on a celibate clergy!

That, of course, was the obvious way in which he could make his life less selfish; and he often allowed his mind to play over the possibility, weighing the pros and cons of the various orders – not the Dominicans, certainly, far too left-wing and anarchic, and the Carmelites were not quite learned enough, but both the Benedictines and the Jesuits had distinctive attractions, the former having by far the nicer habit . . . But it would be tricky, taking Orders at the present time, compelled to implement liturgical changes with which one had little sympathy, and wrestle with the squalid intricacies of the birth-control controversy . . . Besides, he would have to give up the elegancies of college life, the good food and wine, the servants and comfortable rooms, and most important, the mildly flirtatious relationships he enjoyed with young men of the same temperament. Not that Miles ever indulged in anything grossly physical, but he moved on the circumference of circles where such things were indulged in, and derived a certain frisson of excitement from the contiguity.

Aggiornamento came very slowly to Father Austin Brierley's parish at the end of the Northern Line, where the Parish Priest regarded Vatican II and the whole movement for Catholic Renewal as an irritating distraction from the serious business of raising money. Fund-raising, mainly to pay off the debt on his church and to meet the Diocesan levy for Catholic education, was Father McGahern's all-consuming passion. Parochial life was one long round of bingo, raffles, whist-drives, dances, football pools, spot-the-ball competitions, sweepstakes, bazaars, jumble sales, outdoor collections, covenant schemes and planned giving. His addresses from the pulpit consisted of one part homily to three parts accountancy. The church porch was papered with graphs and diagrams in several colours, especially red, illustrating the slow progress of the parish towards solvency. The pastoral side of things he left pretty well entirely to Austin Brierley, who could scarcely cope with all the work. There was nothing selfishly materialistic about the PP's single-minded pursuit of lucre – on the contrary, he denied himself (and incidentally his curate) many home comforts in order to swell the parish funds. Heating in the presbytery was turned down to a barely tolerable minimum in the winter, and the electric light bulbs were of a wattage so low that Austin Brierley was sometimes obliged to read his breviary with the aid of a bicycle lamp.

It was a continual source of surprise to Austin Brierley that the parishioners did not seem to object to this constant harping on the theme of money. Indeed, the more active laymen threw themselves into the various fund-raising campaigns with enormous enthusiasm, competing eagerly with each other to bring in the largest amounts, while the apathetic majority paid up regularly and uncomplainingly. Austin Brierley very much feared that they confused this activity with the business of salvation, and measured their spiritual health on the same scale as Father McGahern's graphs, reassured to see that each week they had crept a little nearer to heaven.

Father McGahern had been in charge of the parish for a long time – ever since it had been a raw, unfinished housing estate, with a prefabricated hut for a church – and he rarely left it except to go home to County Cork for his annual holiday. His parish was a little kingdom, which he ruled despotically, and somewhat idiosyncratically. For example, it was his practice occasionally to interrupt the celebration of mass, and step down to the altar rails to deliver himself of some *ex tempore* exhortation or reproach that seemed to him timely. Thus, if there were an especially large number of latecomers he would take a break between the Epistle and Gospel to remind the congregation of the importance of punctuality in God's house; or if it occurred to him that he had not adequately emphasized some point in his sermon, he would interrupt the Eucharistic prayer to add a postscript. Having to say the mass facing the people seemed to make him especially prone to this kind of digression – the expressions he perceived on their faces perhaps put ideas into his head – and it became a special feature of the new liturgy in this parish. Visitors found it strange and indecorous, or engagingly informal, according to their temperaments. The regular congregation, however, grew quite accustomed to it, and did not manifest any surprise or restiveness when these interruptions became increasingly profane in content, reflecting the priest's preoccupation with money, and bearing much the same relation to the mass as commercial breaks to a television broadcast of a Shakespeare play. 'You may not realize it, my good people,' he would say, putting down the chalice in the middle of the Offertory, and ambling to the altar rail, 'but the cost of heating this church is something shocking these days. I have just paid a bill for one quarter to the North Thames Gas Board for one hundred and twenty-seven pounds. One hundred and twenty-seven pounds for one quarter! Now, the reason it's so high, my dear people, is quite simple. During mass the heaters are warming the space inside the church, but as soon as the doors are opened after mass, whoosh, all the hot air flies out and the cold air flies in. So it would be greatly appreciated if you would leave the church as smartly as possible at the end of mass, and not be hanging about talking in the porch, holding everybody up and keeping the doors open longer than necessary.' And back he would go to the altar to carry on with the celebration.

When, one Sunday, he took time out twice in one mass, first to draw the congregation's attention to an increase in fire-insurance premiums, and secondly to say that if any more hymn books disappeared he would have to consider charging a deposit on them, Austin Brierley felt he could be silent no longer. After lunch he made his protest, excited and indignant at first, but gradually petering out, like his outburst at the St Valentine's party years ago. The old priest listened without interrupting him and, when Austin Brierley had finished, remained silent for some minutes, as if stunned by the reproaches levelled at him. At last he spoke.

'Tell me, Father,' he said abstractedly, 'what do you think of Premium Bonds?'

'Premium Bonds?' repeated Austin Brierley blankly.

'Yes. Why shouldn't we keep the money earmarked for the Diocesan Education Fund in Premium Bonds until it's due to be handed over? Then there'd always be the chance of increasing the money with no risk. What d'you say to that?'

A few days later, Father Brierley went to Archbishop's House. He wasn't able to see the Cardinal himself, but he saw a Monsignor who was quite high up in the secretariat. The Monsignor was sympathetic, but not surprised – Father McGahern's eccentricities were well known to his superiors, it seemed. However, as the Monsignor explained, Father McGahern was an old man, and had not a great many years left to serve as parish priest. It would be difficult to persuade him to change his ways now, and harsh treatment to uproot him.

'Well, uproot me, then,' said Father Brierley impulsively. 'I can't face another week in that madhouse. Counting-house, I should say.' He sat hunched in despair before the Monsignor's desk, his knees together and his joined hands thrust down between his thighs. He was conscious of the Monsignor's shrewd eyes appraising him.

'How would you like to go on a course?'

·'What kind of course?'

'Whatever you like. Ecumenical studies, pastoral studies, biblical studies, you name it. You know about this new theological college we've just opened? One of the ideas is that it will provide refresher courses for the secular clergy.'

It was on the tip of Austin Brierley's tongue to suggest that it was Father McGahern who stood in most urgent need of a refresher course, but he was not foolish enough to waste such an opportunity. 'I used to run a New Testament study group, once,' he said reminiscently, 'for university students. I shouldn't at all mind picking up that sort of thing again.'

The Monsignor looked slightly disappointed at his choice. 'You don't think something like Pastoral Studies would be more relevant to your work, Father? Or catechetics?'

'No, Biblical Studies would be just the ticket. I'm terribly rusty. I don't suppose I've read a book on the subject since I left the seminary.' He suddenly had a vision, flooding his mind like a sunburst, of himself sitting in a quiet room, slowly turning the pages of a thick, heavy book with nothing to do except finish it. 'When can I start?' he said eagerly.

Austin Brierley found that things had changed a lot since his seminary days, especially in the field of biblical commentary. When he was of student, the methods of modern demythologizing historical scholarship had been regarded as permissible only in application to the Old Testament. The New Testament was taught as a historically reliable text, directly inspired by God and endorsed as such by the infallible authority of the Church. It came as something of a shock to discover that views mentioned formerly only to be dismissed as the irresponsible speculations of German Protestants and Anglican divines who could hardly be considered seriously as Christians at all, were now accepted as commonplace by many Catholic scholars in the field. The infancy stories about Jesus, for instance, were almost certainly legendary, it seemed, late literary accretions to the earliest and most reliable account of Jesus's life in Mark. The baby in the stable at Bethlehem, the angels and the shepherds, the star in the sky and the three kings, the massacre of the Innocents by Herod, the flight into Egypt – all fiction. Not meaningless, the books and articles and lectures hastened to add, for these fictions symbolized profound truths about the Christian faith; but certainly not factual, like the events one read about in the newspaper, or for that matter in Livy and Tacitus. And the Virgin Birth itself, then – was that a fiction? Well, opinion differed, but there were certainly many authorities who did not see that the literal, physical virginity of Mary (which was nowhere mentioned in Mark, Paul and John) was an essential part of the Gospel message. If this was accepted, then the doctrines of the Immaculate Conception and the Assumption also ceased to signify, they became dead letters, not worth arguing about. What was important was the figure of Jesus, the adult Jesus, himself. But here, too, a startling amount of sceptical sifting appeared to have taken place. The story of his baptism by John the Baptist was probably historical, but hardly the temptation in the desert, a narrative with obvious folktale characteristics deriving from the Jewish Babylonian exile, like the more spectacular miracle stories, the walking on the water and the draught of fishes. And the Resurrection . . .? Well, here even the most adventurous demythologizers hesitated (it was another kind of How Far Could You Go?) but a few were certainly prepared to say that the Resurrection story was a symbolization of the faith found by the disciples through Jesus's death, that death itself was not to be feared, that death was not the end. *That* was the essential meaning of the Resurrection, not the literal reanimation of Jesus's corpse, an idea that could not possibly be as meaningful to an intelligent Christian of the twentieth century as it was to the inhabitants of a pre-scientific world.

Austin Brierley almost rubbed his eyes in disbelief sometimes. He read the professional theological journals with much the same mixed feelings of shock and liberation as Michael read *Lady Chatterley's Lover* and the sexually explicit fiction that was published in its wake. Of course the theologians and exegetes were generally more discreet than the novelists. They expressed themselves with elaborate caution in learned journals of tiny circulation, or exchanged ideas with likeminded scholars in private. It was understood that one did not flaunt the new ideas before the laity, or for that matter before the ordinary clergy, most of whom were deplorably ill-educated and still virtually fundamentalists when it came to the interpretation of the New Testament. The main thing was to get on quietly with the work of updating Catholic biblical scholarship while Rome was too preoccupied with pastoral and liturgical experiment to bother checking up on them. Austin Brierley, however was unable to take this view of the matter. It seemed to him that a dangerous gap was opening up between the sophisticated, progressive theologians and exegetes on the one hand, and ordinary parochial Catholics on the other. The latter still went on believing in the nativity story and the miracles of Our Lord and all the rest of it as literally, historically true. If they woke up one day to discover that their own 'experts' hadn't believed these things for years, they would feel cheated, and might understandably give up the practice of their religion in disgust. It was therefore, he concluded, the clear duty of priests like himself to try and educate the laity in the new, modern way of reading Scripture.

When his course was over, Father Brierley returned to his parish at the end of the Northern Line fired with this sense of mission. His first sermon was given on Ascension Day. He expounded the Gospel reading as a dramatic way of expressing the idea that Jesus was united with the Father in eternal life after his death on the cross, and thus promised all men of faith the same union and the same eternal life. To the disciples, to the first Christians, to the authors of the New Testament (especially the authors of Luke and the Acts, in which the Ascension was most elaborately described) it was natural to express this idea as a physical movement upwards in space, for they inhabited a flat world in which 'Heaven' was identified with the sky above. Today, of course, we knew that the world was round, that space was curved, that there was neither up nor down in the cosmos, that Heaven was not a place that would ever be discovered by a space probe. To understand the Gospel story, we had to interpret it metaphorically.

After a few more sermons like this, the parishioners complained to Father McGahern, and Father McGahern to Archbishop's House, and Austin Brierley was seconded to another diocese in the Midlands that was allegedly short of priests. Before he left, the

Monsignor gave him a sympathetic interview, shook his hand and advised him to go easy on the new biblical scholarship in his new job.

It was a small satisfaction to Austin Brierley that one year later Father McGahern had to be hurriedly retired from his parish, when it came out that he had put the entire proceeds of a special collection for the African missions on a horse in the St Leger. Had the horse lost, the matter could have been hushed up, but as it won at 11–2, the priest was unable to resist boasting from the pulpit about his coup, and the popular press got hold of the story.

Sister Mary Joseph of the Precious Blood took her final vows in 1960. The evening before this solemn ritual, there was a ceremony (borrowed from the Benedictines) that in some ways remained even more vivid to her memory. In front of the assembled community, she had to signify her determination to embrace the life of poverty, chastity and obedience. Two tables were set out before her. On one, neatly folded, were the clothes she had worn on the day she entered the convent as a postulant; on the other, the habit of the Order and, in a little dish, the silver ring which would be placed on her finger the next morning to confirm her as a Bride of Christ. She had to bow to the Mother Superior, and place her hand irrevocably on one table or another. If she chose the secular clothes, she was free to leave the convent without reproach. It made it easier to turn to the other table that those clothes looked so dowdy and insubstantial.

Soon afterwards she was sent to a girls' grammar school run by the Order in the North of England, to teach biology and botany. Her qualifications were particularly valued by the convent, which was usually obliged to hand over these subjects, so sensitive and potentially dangerous to faith and morals, to lay teachers. Shortly before Sister Mary Joseph's arrival, there had been an unfortunate episode involving a young married teacher who had taken it upon herself to give her fourth-formers a lesson on human reproduction in the General Science course. The policy of the school, as Mother Superior told Sister Mary Joseph at her

497

first interview, was that there should be no class discussion of such matters before the Sixth Form, and then only within carefully defined limits. 'What about menstruation?' Sister Mary Joseph enquired. 'We assume that the girls' mothers will attend to that,' was the reply. 'But of course, we are always available to see the girls on an individual basis. You will find that they come to you when they need help.'

Sister Mary Joseph found, however, that they very rarely came to her for that kind of help. Help with preparation for exams, or advice on applying to universities, yes. But everything to do with their sexual development they kept discreetly hidden from the nuns, though even from her own cloistered perspective it was obvious that society at large was becoming increasingly permissive and thus creating acute problems for adolescent girls. Every now and then there would be a sexual scandal of some kind, major or minor, in the school – a girl obliged to leave hurriedly because she was pregnant, a fourth-former caught with a copy of *Lady Chatterley's Lover* in her satchel: glimpses, as through chinks in a fence, of appalling temptations in the world outside. With some of her pupils, especially the brighter and more ambitious ones, Sister Mary Joseph enjoyed close friendship – for a time. But always there came a point of withdrawal on the part of the girl – silent, unexplained, unacknowledged, yet as sensible as the sudden disappearance of the sun behind a cloud, signifying (she was morally certain) that the girl in question had discovered Boys, or possibly, a boy. It was not, at first, a physical withdrawal – the girl might come to her just as often for extra coaching, for walks in the lunch hour – but it would not be the same, a deepening reserve separated them, a no-man's-land of unmentionable experience. It pained Sister Mary Joseph that this should be so, that the girls felt they could not share the crucial problems and anxieties of adolescence with her (nor, she was fairly certain, with any of the other nuns) and she came to the conclusion that the habit and rule of life which the Order had adopted as a sign of its dedication had become an impediment.

When, therefore, in 1965, the call went out from the Vatican Council to all religious orders of women to reappraise their statutes, rules and regulations, to consider what changes might be appropriate to make their vocations more effective in the circumstances of modern life, and Mother Superior convened a series of meetings of all the sisters in the community to discuss these momentous questions, Sister Mary Joseph came out strongly for reform. By the power of her intellect and the force of her eloquence, she carried the day. A television set was introduced into the recreation room. *The Times* was subscribed to. Sugar in tea and coffee was no longer restricted to Sundays and feast days. Permission was no longer required from Mother Superior to take a bath, make a telephone call, or go into town on errands, and sisters were allowed to go out alone, not always in pairs. The 6 p.m. curfew was extended to 10 p.m. For sisters with a full teaching load, meditation and recitation of the Office of Our Lady in Chapel at 5 a.m. was made optional, and the day began normally with mass at six.

The mood in the convent in those days was comparable to that of the French National Assembly in '89. The older generation was fearful and sometimes appalled at the rate of change; the younger and more progressive nuns were drunk on liberty, equality and sorority. They had been schooled in the novitiate to believe that the rules and restrictions of the Order were essential to the pursuit of holiness, necessary ways of subduing pride and crucifying the flesh. When word came from Rome that these rules might in many cases be the fossilized remains of obsolete manners and customs, the accumulated frustration of years exploded like a sudden release of compressed air. Mother Superior escaped, by a narrow margin of votes, having her office abolished and replaced by a committee re-elected monthly. A proposal to allow smoking was defeated only on health grounds, and another to allow attendance at theatres and cinemas was approved. But, without doubt, the subject of the greatest contention, and of the most drawn-out debate, was the question of dress.

Even Ruth (as she now thought of herself again, for the Jacobin nuns in the community began to call each other by their baptismal names rather than their names in religion, which they had not chosen for themselves and had never much liked) – even Ruth, progressive as she was, acknowledged the problems and pitfalls in modernizing dress. The disadvantages of the habit were obvious: it was expensive to make and to maintain (two lay sisters were almost constantly employed sewing, laundering, starching and ironing), it was impractical (particularly in the labs), it was excessively warm in summer, and (though this was disputed) it prevented the wearer from having a normal, relaxed relationship with ordinary people. How to modernize this dress was, however, a difficult and delicate question. When the Order had been founded, its habit differed only in detail from what most women wore at the time in provincial France; but that could hardly be a guideline for them now in the mid-nineteen-sixties, the era of the mini-skirt. As one middle-aged sister, otherwise inclined to liberal opinions, remarked: 'After all, a nun does take a vow of chastity and I really don't think you should be able to see the tops of her stockings when she sits down.'

'Most women wear tights, nowadays, I understand,' said Ruth. But she took the point.

In the end it was agreed that a certain number of the sisters should experiment with various kinds of modernized dress, and that after a trial period the matter should be discussed again. As leader of the progressive party, Ruth felt morally obliged to volunteer, though she did so with misgivings. After the meeting, she went to her cell, took off her headdress and habit, and stood in her shift before the mirror on the inside of her cupboard door. It was something she had not done for many years – ever since being taught 'custody of the eyes' as a novice (the mirror was supposed to be used only for checking one's appearance when fully dressed). Now it was almost physically painful to scrutinize herself. Her hair was thin and lifeless from years of confinement under the headdress, and a deep red weal ran across her forehead where the headband habitually pressed against the brow. Her bosom had grown fuller with the years, but her brassieres had been silently removed from her laundry shortly after she became a novice, to be replaced by a stiff bodice that flattened and spread the breasts into a kind of unitary mound. Her hips were as broad and clumsy as ever and (she stood on a chair and hitched up the skirt of her shift) her legs of almost uniform thickness from thigh to ankle. Walk through the gates with that lot dressed up in a tee-shirt and mini-skirt, she reflected wryly, and the populace would flee screaming in terror.

Eventually she settled for a navy tailored costume consisting of jacket and mid-calf skirt, worn with a high-necked blouse and a little cap and short veil, like a nursing sister's headdress. She had her hair cut and permed, and every night put it in curlers, obedient to the injunction of the hairdresser's assistant ('You must do it religiously,' the girl had said, without apparent irony). When she and the other guinea-pigs first appeared in school in their new get-up, the effect on the girls was, of course, sensational. There were gasps and titters in Assembly, and a crescendo of whispered comment like bees swarming, before Mother Superior was able to restore order and silence. The volunteers were prepared for that, prepared to be the target for curious stares until the novelty wore off. Still, it was rather discouraging to overhear two girls in the cloakroom saying didn't Sister Mary Joseph look a fright in her new clothes, like a cross between a Meter Maid and a Home Help; and it took all Ruth's self-control not to rush back to her cell and put on the habit again. Nor did the new costume have any perceptible effect of breaking down the emotional reserve between Ruth and her pupils. That, she now began to feel, was caused by something much more fundamental than clothing. One of the married teachers, a woman with whom she got on well, put it to her bluntly when they were discussing the catastrophic fall in new vocations to the order: 'Frankly, Sister, girls these days aren't very keen on the idea of perpetual virginity.'

Sister Mary Joseph sighed, and supposed she was right.

'It's hardly surprising,' the teacher went on, 'when you see what they're being fed all the time by the mass media. Just look at this.'

She took from her bag a popular women's magazine. 'I confiscated it from a girl in 5C this morning – she was reading it in a Library session, cheeky devil. Just look at these letters, and the answers.'

Ruth glanced at the page folded back for her perusal. It was an agony column of a familiar type, entitled, *Ask Ann Field*. '*Dear Ann Field*,' the first letter began, '*I am seventeen and have been going out with a boy who I love very much for about six months . . .*' And underneath, in bold type, was Ann Field's answer:

> *Many people today believe that if the couple concerned have a loving and stable relationship, sex before marriage is not necessarily wrong and may be a way of putting a future marriage on a firm foundation. Only you and your boy friend can decide whether this, for you, would be an expression of genuine love or merely selfish exploitation. But if you do decide to commit yourself to such a relationship, for heaven's sake get advice about contraception first. There is, incidentally, no reason why you should not have a white wedding when the time comes.*

'If that isn't encouraging young people to jump into bed with each other, what is?' said the teacher. 'How are a couple of teenagers supposed to know the difference between selfish pleasure and true love, I'd like to know?'

Ruth sighed again. 'It must be a great responsibility to receive such letters,' she said. 'I suppose this, whatshername, Ann Field, I suppose she tries to help according to her lights.'

The teacher looked surprised at this mild response, and reclaimed the magazine with a slightly aggrieved air, as though confiscating it for a second time. 'Well, ten years ago, even five, you'd never have found a magazine like this approving sex before marriage,' she said. '*I* don't know what things are coming to.'

Polly would have been gratified by Ruth's remark, had she overheard it, for as it happened she was Ann Field at this particular time. She was also married, to a successful television producer, to whom she had borne, precisely two years apart, a handsome son and pretty daughter; and she lived in a converted oast-house near Canterbury, with an *au pair* to help with the children and a milk-white Mini of her own to run about in. She led a busy, enjoyable life, only slightly marred by occasional twinges of anxiety about Jeremy's fidelity and perpetual worry about putting on weight, the two being connected.

They had met in 1960, when she was assigned to work on a programme with him. Jeremy's first marriage, to a well-known actress, was breaking up, and when the unit went on location in Scotland (it was a documentary about the depopulation of the Highlands, a somewhat lugubrious subject rendered all the more so by Jeremy's mood of the moment) they inevitably had an affair. The affair required more mothering than eroticism on Polly's part – long, introspective monologues from Jeremy in the huge, high-ceilinged bedrooms of Scottish three-star hotels, his head pillowed on her lap while she gently massaged his scalp – but the erotic moments were satisfactory too; and before his divorce proceedings were completed, Jeremy had asked Polly to marry him and had been accepted with alacrity.

It was necessarily a Registry Office wedding, a circumstance that caused Polly's parents some pain. Though well aware that she had not practiced her religion for years, they pretended to be ignorant of her way of life. Now her marriage to Jeremy (whom her mother insisted on referring to as *divorcé*, with a French accent, as if the English word were somehow indelicate) made it all public and irrevocable.

'I don't know where we went wrong, I'm sure,' her mother said, snuffling into a dainty handkerchief, while Polly nibbled the end of a Biro and tried to draw up a list of the wedding presents she wanted.

'It's nothing to do with you, Mummy,' said Polly. 'It's the way things are. Most of the girls I was at school with are divorced and remarried or living with people. D'you remember the name of that stainless-steel tableware we saw in Harrods?'

'Well, I think it's shocking. The money your father paid that convent in fees . . .'

'Why don't you sue them?' said Polly, trying to tease her mother out of her mood. But she was not amused.

'He's left one wife, how can you be sure he won't leave you?'

'He didn't leave her, she left him,' Polly snapped back. But the barbed remark stung and was not easily forgotten.

They started a family immediately (Jeremy had had no children by his first wife) and to this end Polly gave up her job at the BBC, without much regret. However, they agreed that it would be socially irresponsible to have more than two children, and once Abigail was out of nappies and Jason had started playschool, Polly began to feel a certain return of surplus energy, the need for a more than merely domestic interest in life. 'Something to keep me occupied while you're away filming,' she explained to Jeremy, and added, taking care to smile as she did so: 'To stop me worrying about what you might be getting up to with those pretty research assistants.'

Jeremy pulled a face. 'The last one they gave me had such powerful BO, I could hardly bear to go near her . . . But seriously, darling, I'll keep my eyes open for an opportunity. Something you could do at home.'

'You mean, like addressing envelopes?'

'Yes, sewing mailbags, threading beads, that sort of thing.'

What Jeremy came up with, through a friend of a friend, the editor of a woman's magazine met at a party and invited down to the oast-house for a weekend, was Ann Field. The regular contributor, who had done the column for years, was retiring, and they wanted to experiment with a new, more up-to-date approach. Polly wrote some dummy replies to sample letters and was given a three months trial. She had to travel up to Town once a week, but otherwise worked at home with the help of a dictaphone and a secretary who came out from Canterbury two days a week. The change of tone in Ann Field's column under Polly's tenure provoked an enormous postbag of comment, but when they totted up the pros and cons in the office it came out at 72% in Polly's favour, so she kept the job. She found it fascinating, demanding (she replied to all the letters, not just the ones that were published) and rewarding.

'I think of it as a kind of social work,' she would say to her friends. 'I know I'm not trained or anything, but most of the women who write know what they want to do anyway. You just have to reassure them. Of course, sometimes they're in absolutely tragic situations, and then there's not much one can do except sympathize and refer them to the social services.'

Sometimes she read letters aloud to Jeremy, especially poignant ones from wives with unfaithful husbands, hoping in this way to keep his conscience well-tuned. Some of the most harrowing letters were from Catholic women (and here she had to tread carefully, because the magazine would not allow her to disturb readers' religious beliefs, even in private correspondence) whose problems invariably derived from the lack of effective birth control: frigidity caused by fear of pregnancy, hideous gynaecological complications caused by excessive childbearing, and desertion by husbands unable to tolerate the consequences of their own feckless fucking, the teeming babies and the haggard spouse. 'My God, the Church has an awful lot to answer for,' she would mutter to herself, trying to find some comforting word for these pathetic women that was not false or hypocritical. Yet, deep down, Polly still believed in God, and, willy nilly, He was the Catholic God.

She and Jeremy had agreed that the children should make their own decision about religion when they were old enough to decide for themselves. But when Jason was ill one night, with an alarmingly high temperature, and Jeremy was away from home (he was in the States making a programme about the latest theory of how President Kennedy was assassinated) she was deeply troubled by the knowledge that the child hadn't been baptized and therefore, according to the Catechism, if he should die wouldn't go to heaven, but to Limbo. She tried to tell herself that it was all nonsense, that no God worth believing in was going to penalize the souls of innocent children, but it was no use, she couldn't sleep for worrying about it; and in the middle of the night she got up and baptized her son while he was asleep, pouring a trickle of tepid water from a plastic beaker on to his flushed forehead and whispering, 'I baptize thee in the name of the Father and of the Son and of the Holy Ghost,' as every Catholic was allowed to do in an emergency. Then, thinking that she might as well go the whole hog, Polly went along to Abigail's room and did her too. (She never told Jeremy or the children about what she had done, and when many years later Jason was converted to

Catholicism while a student at Oxford, he was baptized all over again without knowing.)

'Here's a juicy one,' Polly said to Jeremy one evening as they sat in the living-room after dinner around the open (and essentially decorative) fire, Jeremy going through the weeklies and Polly sifting her Ann Field mail. 'I wonder if I dare print it. Listen, darling:

'Dear Ann Field,

I am a Catholic, married to a non-Catholic. Throughout our marriage my husband has used condoms as a method of family planning. Although this is against Catholic teaching, various priests have told me that it is alright for me to submit to it under protest. But now my husband wants me to go on the pill because, he says, condoms are primitive and spoil the act for him. Also, I have never had a proper vaginal orgasm and my husband says that it is because of the condoms too. He attaches great importance to my having a vaginal orgasm. Sometimes I think it means more to him than his own orgasms – '

Jeremy guffawed.

'Quite droll, isn't she?' said Polly, turning to the second page.

'I have asked two priests about taking the pill. The first one said I mustn't and recommended the safe method. But my periods are very irregular, and I have been advised not to conceive again (I have had one baby and several miscarriages). The other priest said it would be all right to take the pill for the sake of a higher good (that is, to preserve the marriage). Before I make up my mind, I would like to know if what my husband says is true, namely – '

'It's frightfully long,' said Polly, turning over another page. Then, as her eye fell on the signature at the end of the letter, she let her hands fall limply into her lap. 'My God,' she said, 'it's Violet.'

'Violet?'

'Violet Casey. Meadowes, she is now. A girl I knew at College. She married her tutor in Classics. They seem to have moved up north.'

'She sounds a rather screwed-up sort of person.'

'She was.'

'What are you going to do with the letter?'

'Answer it, of course.'

'In your own name?'

'Certainly not. She wrote to Ann Field. Ann Field will reply.'

'You know, you're getting a bit schizoid about this Ann Field business. Like Jekyll and Hyde.'

'Which is which?' Without waiting for an answer, Polly went into her study and dictated a letter to Violet. Afterwards she reversed the tape and played it back:

'Dear Violet comma thank you for your letter full stop as to your main question comma two American researchers in this field have recently established by laboratory experiment that there is no such thing as a vaginal orgasm comma i e underline one that is indepen- dent of clitoral stimulation parenthesis Masters and Johnson comma Human Sexual Response underline Boston 1966 close parenthesis full stop however I am sure you and your husband would enjoy more relaxed and satisfying lovemaking if you used the pill full stop your second priest sounds like a sensible man stop yours sincerely Ann Field'

Polly pressed another button on her tape recorder and added a postscript:

'Why not experiment with different positions question mark for instance comma sitting astride your husband comma or kneeling so that he enters from behind question mark'

Polly believed fervently in every woman's right to frequent orgasms, and tried out conscientiously most of the things she read about in the sex manuals and magazines that Jeremy brought back with him from his travels. Jeremy, who had been rather repressed in youth, was making up for lost time. The rediscovery of sex, he was fond of saying, was what the sixties were all about. Every now and then, they sent the children out with the *au pair*, drew the curtains, and chased each other naked around the house, having it off in various unorthodox places, on the stairs, or under the dining-room table, even in the kitchen, where Polly would spread jam or chocolate syrup on her nipples and Jeremy would lick them clean. Their private code-word for sex was 'research'.

When Robin returned from America, not long after Violet's appearance at Angela and Dennis's wedding, they got together again; for Robin found that although Violet was pretty impossible to live with, he missed her when she wasn't there. Violet, he decided, was an addiction, like smoking: it made you feel terrible most of the time, but you couldn't do without it. To cement their reunion he agreed to start a family, but Violet had several miscarriages (which she regarded as a Divine judgement on them for previously using contraceptives) before she managed, after an anxious pregnancy and painfully difficult labour, to produce a daughter. Robin was pleased with his little girl, whom they called Felicity, but said enough is enough, no more pregnancies, no more miscarriages, and was supported in this resolve by their doctor. Hence Violet's letter to Ann Field some years later, though there was another motive for writing it which Violet had not mentioned. She was afraid that Robin might have an affair with one of his students if he felt sexually dissatisfied at home.

By this time they had moved to a new university in the North of England for the sake of a big jump in salary for Robin. It was a place that was setting out to pioneer new developments in curriculum and teaching methods – Robin was in charge of a special programme teaching the classics in translation to all humanities students in their first year – and it attracted a lively, rather anarchic type of student, whose morals were a source of considerable scandal to the local community. The students lived in mixed, unsupervised accommodation, freely supplied with contraceptives by the Student Health Service. Robin, who rather regretted his move, sometimes described the University as 'the only knocking-shop in the country that also gives degrees.' This sardonic stance towards campus permissiveness was reassuring to Violet, but she was well aware that if Robin should take a fancy to one of his students it wouldn't require a weekend in the country and the prospect of marriage to coax her into bed.

When Ann Field's reply came back, Violet showed it to Robin and saw immediately from the expression on his face that she had done the wrong thing. He was furiously angry.

'You must be out of your mind, Violet!' he shouted. 'Suppose they print it? I'll be the laughing-stock of the campus.'

'They won't print it. Anyway, they never give names.'

'What in God's name possessed you, an intelligent woman with an Upper Second, to write to a trashy woman's magazine for advice on such a subject?'

'I just thought it would be interesting to get an outsider's opinion. Have you heard of this book?'

'I think I read about it somewhere,' said Robin. (To be precise, his source was *Playboy*, which he read regularly at his barber's while waiting to get his hair cut, but he did not care to acknowledge this.) 'They got a lot of people to copulate in a laboratory, all wired up to machines and computers and things.'

'Lord, it's a wonder they had any orgasms at all, in the circumstances,' said Violet.

In the same year that Masters and Johnson published the results of their sex research, England won the World Cup at football, which millions saw as the bestowal of a special grace on the nation; John Lennon boasted that the Beatles were more popular than Jesus Christ and, to the disappointment of many, was not struck dead by a thunderbolt; Evelyn Waugh died, shortly after attending a Latin mass celebrated in private by an old Jesuit friend; Friday abstinence was officially abolished in the Roman Catholic Church, and the American Sisters of Loretto at the Foot of the Cross became the first order of nuns to abandon the habit completely. The narrator of Graham Greene's new novel observed: 'When I was a boy I had faith in the Christian God.

Life under his shadow was a very serious affair ... Now that I approached the end of life it was only my sense of humour that enabled me sometimes to believe in Him.' In the spring of that year, 1966, at Duquesne University, Pennsylvania, and a little later at Notre Dame University, Indiana, small groups of Catholics began to experiment with 'Pentecostal' prayer meetings, praying for each other that they might be filled with the gifts of the Holy Ghost as described in the New Testament – the gift of faith, the gift of tongues, the gifts of prophecy, healing, discernment of spirits, interpretation and exorcism. The results were, to the participants, exciting, but passed unremarked by the world at large. Public interest in the Catholic Church was still focused on the cliff-hanging saga of contraception.

In April it was leaked to the press that four conservative theologians on the Pontifical Commission had admitted that they could not show the intrinsic evil of contraception from Natural Law arguments alone. In other words, they still thought it was wrong, but only because the Church had always said it was, and could not have been teaching error for centuries. However, as a letter in the *Tablet* pointed out, the Church had once taught that owning slaves was permissible and lending money at interest was a grave sin.

Miriam read the letter out to Michael.

'Who's it from?' he asked.

'Someone called Adrian Walsh.'

'Good Lord! I was at college with him. Shows how things have changed. He used to be a real hardliner.'

The Catholic press, and even the secular press, was full of correspondence and articles about Catholics and birth control. After reading a good deal of this material, Miriam said to Michael one day: 'I've had enough. I'm going on the pill. It's obvious that there's going to be change sooner or later. I don't see the point of risking getting pregnant again.' Their third child was then a few months old.

Michael was glad to agree, though he probably wouldn't have had the gumption to take the initiative himself. They continued going to Communion, but not to Confession. People went to

510

Confession less and less frequently, anyway, even the idea of making one's Easter Duty seemed to have been quietly dropped, and that made it easier. Their sex life improved dramatically. From time to time Michael checked his conscience for symptoms of guilt. Nothing.

That summer, they shared a holiday cottage in Devon with Angela and Dennis. In the evenings, when the children had been fed, bathed, anointed with sunburn cream, read to, prayed with, put to bed, put *back* to bed, and had finally gone off to sleep, the four adults lolled, exhausted but content, in the little chintzy parlour and chatted. Dennis and Angela, who had found the cottage and were paying rather more than half of the rent, occupied two wing armchairs on either side of the fireplace, while Michael and Miriam sat between them on a small chesterfield. Each husband and wife had come to look more and more like their partners. Dennis and Angela were fair and well-fleshed, red from exposure to sun and wind. Michael and Miriam were both lean and tanned. Michael's hair still fell boyishly down across his forehead, but he wore it dry, now, not steeped in Brylcreem, while Dennis was beginning to lose his. Miriam, who could never bear to be still, however tired, embroidered, while Angela, six months pregnant with her fourth child, dozed with her hands clasped on her belly. Michael and Miriam, who made most of the conversational running, confided the decision they had made about birth control.

'We may do the same after this one,' said Dennis, glancing speculatively at Angela. 'She's asleep,' he observed.

'I really think you should,' said Miriam. 'I know I couldn't stand the thought of having another one.'

'Don't tempt Providence, darling,' said Michael, glancing at the ceiling. 'Himself might put a dud pill in the packet.'

'Shut up,' said Miriam, aiming a slap at him.

'Well, we'll have to see,' said Dennis, rubbing the back of his neck where sunburned skin was flaking. 'It's really up to Ange.' As they hadn't had to worry about safe periods for the last few months, the question had lost some of its urgency for him, and, unlike Michael, he had no financial anxiety about the rapid growth of his family. Dennis had just landed a very good new job with an electronics firm in the Midlands.

'There's a proposal to install contraceptive machines in the students' cloakrooms at college,' said Michael.

'You never told me!' Miriam exclaimed.

'In a Catholic Training College? I don't believe it,' said Dennis.

'It's a very special machine, designed for Catholics,' said Michael. 'You put contraceptives in and get money out.'

Their laughter woke Angela. 'What are you talking about?' she yawned. When they told her, she said, 'I don't know. I'm afraid I'd feel guilty even if I was rationally convinced there was nothing wrong with it.'

'But *why*, Angela?' Miriam thrust her head forward in the way she had when arguing.

'I don't know – upbringing, I suppose. I'd feel I was cheating, somehow. Take my Mam and Dad. All those children, I don't suppose they wanted half that number. Why should we be able to please ourselves, and be much better off too?'

'But you've got four, Angela, or soon will have. Four is enough in all conscience.'

'Yes,' Angela admitted. 'Perhaps four will be enough.'

'According to the population experts,' said Michael, 'it's two too many. If Catholics don't stop breeding soon, we'll all be standing shoulder to shoulder eating recycled sewage.'

'Anyway,' said Angela, 'I'm determined to have this one at home, so that Dennis can stay with me right through.' She practiced natural childbirth, and had had fair success with it, in spite of uncooperative maternity wards which (to his secret relief) had not allowed Dennis into the delivery room.

'Will the new house be ready in time?' Miriam asked.

'I think we'll just make it,' said Dennis. 'You must come and see us when we're settled in. You wouldn't like to be godparents again, I suppose?'

'Why don't you ask Edward and Tessa?' Michael suggested. 'They don't live far from where you're going.'

'That's a thought.'

Upstairs, a child began to cry. Angela and Miriam looked at each other, listening.

'One of ours,' Miriam said, and rose to attend to it. 'I shan't bother to come down again, so I'll say goodnight.' She winked covertly at Michael.

'I'll be up soon, darling,' he said.

In October of that year, perhaps disturbed by evidence that increasing numbers of Catholics around the world were, like Michael and Miriam, anticipating a change in the Church's attitude to birth control, Pope Paul declared that there would be no pronouncement on the issue in the immediate future, and that meanwhile the traditional teaching must be rigidly adhered to. Monsignor Vallainc, head of the Vatican Press Office, when asked by journalists how the Pope could say that there was no doubt about the traditional teaching when his own commission had been appointed to investigate it, replied that the Church was in a state of certainty, but when the Pope had made his decision, whatever it was, the Church would pass from one state of certainty to another. This pronouncement was, according to Father Charles Davis, a leading theologian much admired by Austin Brierley, the last straw that broke the back of his faith in Catholicism, and shortly after it was made he left the priesthood, and the Church, and married, amid great publicity. His claims in the press that he had not left *in order* to get married were naturally greeted with some scepticism by his co-religionists, especially those of conservative views. Even Father Brierley preferred to believe that Charles Davis might have been unconsciously motivated by the wish to marry, rather than by intellectual doubts about the truth of the Catholic faith.

At about the same time as the Pope's postponement of a decision on birth control, another event occurred which for many people placed a much greater strain on religious belief of any variety.

It was a wet autumn, and the rain fell heavily and unremittingly, especially in the valleys of South Wales. At Aberfan, a small mining village near Merthyr Tydfil, a large coal-tip, a man-made mountain of mining waste, became waterlogged, honeycombed and sodden like a gigantic sponge. Springs and rivulets oozed from its sides and ran down into the valley below. No one took much notice. On Friday, 21 October, at 9.15 in the morning, just after morning prayers at the village Infants and Junior School, the tip became critically unstable, and with a thunderous, terrifying roar, as though the constipated bowels of the Industrial Revolution had suddenly opened, a colossal, obscene, evil-smelling mass of mud and stones avalanched into the valley, sweeping aside everything in its path, and burying the school, with some hundred and fifty children and their teachers.

The school was due to break up at midday that Friday to begin the half-term holiday, and had the landslide occurred a few hours later, and destroyed an empty building, it would have been called a miracle in the popular press; but as it did not, it was called a tragedy, the part, if any, played in it by God being passed over in tactful silence. On the following Sunday, prayers were offered throughout the land for the bereaved, for the rescue-workers and (in Catholic Churches) for the departed souls of the victims, but few ministers of religion took up the theological challenge of the event itself. One of them was Father Brierley, preaching at the 9.30 mass in his new parish, a dull market town in a flat landscape that seemed almost scandalously safe that weekend.

The traditional response of Christians to catastrophes such as Aberfan, he said, was to regard it as some kind of punishment for man's sinfulness, or to accept it unquestioningly as the will of God. Both reactions were unsatisfactory. For if it was mankind's sinfulness that was being punished, it was totally unjust that the punishment should fall on these particular children and their families. And if it was the will of God, why should we not question it? If God, as Christians believed, was everywhere in the Universe, then He must be prepared to take responsibility for everything in it, and accept the anger and bitterness he aroused in the hearts of men at times like this.

The Biblical text that was most relevant was the Book of Job, the story of the virtuous man who was suddenly visited by the most appalling afflictions – his sons and daughters killed, his

514

prosperity taken away, and his own body afflicted with loathesome sores. Why did God allow this to happen? Job himself could not understand it, and was unconvinced by the arguments of the pious who tried to reconcile him to his fate. He felt utter despair and alienation from God, and while never denying God's existence, had the courage to challenge God to justify himself:

> 'Yes, I am a man, and he is not; and so no argument,
>   no suit between us is possible.
> There is no arbiter between us,
>   to lay his hand on both,
>   to stay his rod from me
>   or keep away his daunting terrors.
> Nonetheless, I shall speak, not fearing him:
>   I do not see myself like that at all.
> Since I have lost all taste for life,
>   I will give free rein to my complaints.
> I shall let my embittered soul speak out.
> I shall say to God, 'Do not condemn me,
>   but tell me the reason for your assault.
> Is it right for you to injure me,
>   cheapening the work of your own hands?''

When he had finished reading this passage, Austin Brierley looked up from his notes and surveyed the congregation. He saw the usual blank, bored faces, a few with their eyes closed, some perhaps actually asleep, mothers with babies in arms anxiously watching their fidgeting older offspring, a man going surreptitiously through his pockets for change to be ready for the Offertory collection. He didn't know quite what he had expected. Tears? Shocked expressions? Heads eagerly nodding agreement? Not really, but he felt disappointed that the response was as flat as on any other Sunday. He hurried to his conclusion.

Eventually, God had spoken to Job, and Job submitted to his superior wisdom and power. The words that convinced him would not, perhaps, convince a modern Job. They would certainly not convince the parents of Aberfan. But that was not the point. The

515

point of the story – which was, of course, a myth, a poem – was that God only spoke to Job because Job complained to God, gave free rein to his complaint and let his embittered soul speak out. We should be less than human if we did not, this dark weekend, do the same on behalf of the victims of Aberfan.

At lunch, the Parish Priest asked him casually if he planned to repeat his sermon at the evening mass.

'Yes, why? Did anyone object to it?'

'Well, I did hear one or two comments passed after the nine-thirty. It seems to have upset a few people.'

'Good,' said Austin Brierley. 'Someone was listening, then.'

'You're a queer fellow, Father,' said the PP, digging into his apple crumble. 'What good does it do, making people doubt the goodness of God?'

'What are we, then, his priests or his public relations officers?' said Austin Brierley fiercely, and immediately apologised.

'You're looking overtired, Father,' said the PP kindly. 'You could probably do with a holiday.'

'I had a holiday a couple of months ago.'

'A retreat, then. Or perhaps you'd like to go on a course of some kind.'

At about the same time that Sunday, Edward and Tessa were driving along the M1 on their way to the baptism of Dennis and Angela's fourth baby, which had arrived safely, if a little early, at the beginning of October. The rain fell heavily, and cars that passed them threw up great fountains of spray which lashed the windscreen and temporarily overwhelmed the wipers. It had stopped raining at Aberfan, their car radio informed them, which was some small blessing for the rescue workers, still shovelling wearily at the millions of tons of mud. (Adrian was not among them, though on hearing the first news of the catastrophe he had thrown tools into the boot of his car and driven nonstop to South Wales, only to be turned back by the police at Abergavenny; there were more than enough volunteer diggers from the local mining communities, better qualified for the job than himself, the police gave him to understand in the kindest possible way, and only vital traffic was being admitted into the disaster area. So the heroic gesture eluded him once again.) So far, the car radio informed Edward and Tessa, one hundred and forty bodies had been recovered.

'Please turn it off, Teddy,' said Tessa, 'I can't bear to listen. And do slow down.'

'I'm only doing fifty,' said Edward, turning off the radio.

'I know, but these conditions are so treacherous.' Tessa was not normally a nervous passenger, but she felt there was malice in the elements today. Her three children, strapped to the back seat, and the fourth in her womb, seemed terribly vulnerable. She feared for some cruel accident, a skid or collision that would overwhelm them all like Aberfan. 'What a day!' she exclaimed, for the sixth time. 'I wish I hadn't decided to come. I should have stayed at home with the children and let you go on your own. It will be too much for Angela, so many people.'

'Dennis said she was in great form. Apparently the delivery went very smoothly. He was boasting terrifically about having watched the whole thing. Seemed to forget I might have witnessed one or two births myself.'

Dennis and Angela's new house was part of a middle-class housing estate still under construction on the outskirts of a small Warwickshire village. The houses, detached and semi-detached, in four basic designs, stuck up rawly from unturfed, rubble-strewn garden lots separated by wire-mesh fences. There were puddles and mud everywhere. It seemed impossible to get away from the physical ambience of Aberfan. And inside the house, in the lounge, a television screen flickered with monochrome pictures of the wall of sludge, the weary, mudstained figures of the workers, the numbed, grief-stricken faces of the watching mothers. Tessa's two oldest children immediately seated themselves in front of the set, which was being watched by Dennis's parents.

'I think it's terrible,' said Dennis's mother. 'The way they show everything on television these days. It's not right, interrogating people who've just lost their children.'

'There've been a lot of complaints about it,' observed her husband.

But neither of them seemed to think of turning the television off – as though the transmission of harrowing pictures were a natural force, like the landslide itself, which had to be borne as long as it lasted.

Dennis offered Tessa and Edward a cup of tea before they all set off for the church. 'Ange is upstairs, getting the baby ready,' he said. 'Go up if you like.'

'Becky, come and see the new baby,' said Tessa, anxious to get her away from the TV and its morbid pictures. Edward, sipping his tea and nibbling a biscuit, took her place, his attention irresistibly drawn to the screen.

'Ghastly, isn't it?' said Dennis. But there was no real horror in his voice: he was still high on the experience of the birth, which he had found extraordinarily moving, and the pride of his own part in it, for which he had been commended by the midwife. The tragedy of Aberfan could not penetrate this private euphoria. He was also childishly delighted with his new house, and couldn't rest until Edward had been shown round it – the modern, fully-fitted kitchen, the separate utility room for washing machine and deepfreeze, the big garage with his workbench and power tools already installed, the downstairs cloakroom and second loo, the upstairs bathroom with shower and four good-sized bedrooms, in the largest of which they found Angela and Tessa sitting on the edge of the divan bed, chatting, with the new baby lolling between them on a clean nappy.

'So this is our godchild,' said Edward, stooping over the baby. 'How is she?'

'An absolute angel,' said Angela. 'Never cries. I have to wake her up to give her her feeds.'

Edward's hands lightly caressed the child from her cranium to her feet. He took the tiny hands in his and turned them this way and that, tickled the infant's toes and offered her the knuckle of his little finger to suck. Tessa could tell that something was worrying Edward, that he was spinning out the conversation with the fondly smiling Angela while his fingers and eyes probed.

When they got back to their car to drive to the church she said, quietly so that the children in the back would not hear, 'There's nothing wrong, is there?'

Edward turned on the car radio. Music flooded the car. A familiar voice with the accent of Liverpool sang:

Father McKenzie, writing the words of a sermon that no one will hear, No one came near . . .

'Ooh! Beatles!' cried Becky, already hooked on pop music at seven. She clapped her hands in delight.

'Downs' Syndrome,' said Edward.

'Oh, my God. Are you sure? She doesn't look like a mongol. The eyes – '

'You can't always tell from the eyes. I'm ninety-nine per cent sure. There are more reliable indications – markings on the hands, for instance.'

'And they have no idea?'

'Evidently not. The doctor must have spotted it, even if the midwife didn't. Too scared to break it to them, I suppose. Sometimes the parents don't find out for months. Years, even.'

'Oh, my God, how awful for Angela.' Tessa clutched her own swollen belly. 'What causes it?'

'An extra chromosome, it occurs at conception, nobody knows why. Older women are more at risk, but that wouldn't apply to Angela.' He took her hand and squeezed it. 'Or to you.'

She smiled wanly, acknowledging that he had read her thoughts correctly. Edward did not mention the theory that the Safe Method might be responsible for such congenital defects, and was able to conceal his own alarm at this extra piece of confirming evidence. In fact, both of them were queerly and horribly relieved that the affliction had fallen upon Dennis and Angela, for it somehow made it seem more likely that they themselves would escape unscathed. All day, Tessa had felt that there was some malice in the air, still unsated by Aberfan. Now that it had struck, had shown itself, she felt less threatened.

But the baptism was an ordeal, and she could not forbear to

weep as she held the infant's head over the font, and the water splashed on to it, and the child gazed back into Tessa's eyes without uttering a single cry. She was named Nicole, after a French pen friend Angela had kept in touch with since childhood. 'Wasn't she good?' said the grandmother afterwards. 'Not a murmur!'

'Are you going to say anything?' Tessa asked Edward in the car going back to the house.

'I must. I'll suggest a paediatrician should have a look at the child. I'll have a word with Dennis before we leave.'

'Dennis will take it harder than Angela,' said Tessa.

'You may be right, but I must tell him first.'

After the tea and cakes, while Tessa was getting their children ready for the return journey, Edward asked Dennis to show him how the sander attachment worked on his power tool, and Dennis led the way to the garage. Edward followed, feeling like an assassin with a loaded gun in his pocket.

I did say this wasn't a comic novel, exactly.

FOUR

How they lost the fear of Hell

At some point in the nineteen-sixties, Hell disappeared. No one could say for certain when this happened. First it was there, then it wasn't. Different people became aware of the disappearance of Hell at different times. Some realized that they had been living for years as though Hell did not exist, without having consciously registered its disappearance. Others realized that they had been behaving, out of habit, as though Hell were still there, though in fact they had ceased to believe in its existence long ago. By Hell we mean, of course, the traditional Hell of Roman Catholics, a place where you would burn for all eternity if you were unlucky enough to die in a state of mortal sin.

On the whole, the disappearance of Hell was a great relief, though it brought new problems.

In 1968, the campuses of the world rose in chain-reaction revolt, Russia invaded Czechoslovakia, Robert Kennedy was assassinated, and the civil rights movement started campaigning in Ulster. For Roman Catholics, however, even in Ulster, the event of the year was undoubtedly the publication, on 29 July, of the Pope's long-awaited encyclical letter on birth control, *Humanae Vitae*. Its message was: no change.

The omniscience of novelists has its limits, and we shall not attempt to trace here the process of cogitation, debate, intrigue, fear, anxious prayer and unconscious motivation which finally produced that document. It is as difficult to enter into the mind of a Pope as it must be for a Pope to enter into the mind of, say, a young mother of three, in a double bed, who feels her husband's

521

caressing touch and is divided between the desire to turn to him and the fear of an unwanted pregnancy. It is said that Pope Paul was astonished and dismayed by the storm of criticism and dissent which his encyclical aroused within the Church. It was certainly not the sort of reception Popes had come to expect for their pronouncements. But in the democratic atmosphere recently created by Vatican II, Catholics convinced of the morality of contraception were no longer disposed to swallow meekly a rehash of discredited doctrine just because the Pope was wielding the spoon. Of course, if the Pope had come down on the other side of the argument, there would no doubt have been an equally loud chorus of protest and complaint from the millions of Catholics who had loyally followed the traditional teaching at the cost of having many more children and much less sex than they would have liked, and were now too old, or too worn-out by parenthood, to benefit from a change in the rules – not to mention the priests who had sternly kept them toeing the line by threats of eternal punishment if they didn't. The Pope, in short, was in a no-win situation. With hindsight, it is clear that his best course would have been to procrastinate and equivocate indefinitely so that the ban on contraception was never explicitly disowned, but quietly allowed to lapse, like earlier papal anathemas against co-education, gaslighting and railways. However, by setting up in the glare of modern publicity a commission to investigate and report on the matter, first Pope John and then Pope Paul had manoeuvred the Papacy into a dogmatic cul-de-sac from which there was no escape. The only saving grace in the situation (suggesting that the Holy Spirit might, after all, have been playing some part in the proceedings) was that it was made clear on its publication that the encyclical was not an 'infallible' pronouncement. This left open the theoretical possibility, however narrowly defined, of conscientious dissent from its conclusions, and of some future reconsideration of the issue.

Thus it came about that the first important test of the unity of the Catholic Church after Vatican II, of the relative power and influence of conservatives and progressives, laity and clergy, priests and bishops, national Churches and the Holy See, was a great debate about – not, say, the nature of Christ and the meaning of his teaching in the light of modern knowledge – but about the precise conditions under which a man was permitted to introduce his penis and ejaculate his semen into the vagina of his lawfully wedded wife, a question on which Jesus Christ himself had left no recorded opinion.

This was not, however, quite such a daft development as it seems on first consideration, for the issue of contraception was in fact one which drew in its train a host of more profound questions and implications, especially about the pleasure principle and its place in the Christian scheme of salvation. It may seem bizarre that Catholics should have been solemnly debating whether it was right for married couples to use reliable methods of contraception at a time when society at large was calling into question the value of monogamy itself – when schoolgirls still in gym-slips were being put on the Pill by their mothers, when young couples were living together in what used to be called sin as a matter of course, adultery was being institutionalized as a party game, and the arts and mass media were abandoning all restraints in the depiction and celebration of sexuality. But in fact there was a more than merely ironic connection between these developments inside and outside the Church. The availability of effective contraception was the thin end of a wedge of modern hedonism that had already turned Protestantism into a parody of itself and was now challenging the Roman Catholic ethos. Conservatives in the Church who predicted that approval of contraception for married couples would inevitably lead sooner or later to a general relaxation of traditional moral standards and indirectly encourage promiscuity, marital infidelity, sexual experiment and deviation of every kind, were essentially correct, and it was disingenuous of liberal Catholics to deny it. On the other hand, the conservatives had unknowingly conceded defeat long before by approving, however grudgingly, the use of the Rhythm or Safe Method. Let me explain. (Patience, the story will resume shortly.)

It has always been recognized that the sexual act has two aspects or functions: I, procreation and II, the reciprocal giving and receiving of sensual pleasure. In traditional Catholic theology, Sex II was only legitimate as an incentive to, or spin-off from, Sex I – which of course was restricted to married couples; and some of the early Fathers thought that even for married couples, Sex II was probably a venial sin. With the development of a more humane theology of marriage, Sex II was dignified as the expression of mutual love between spouses, but it was still forbidden to separate this from Sex I, until the twentieth century, when, at first cautiously, and then more and more explicitly, the Church began to teach that married couples might deliberately confine their sexual intercourse to the infertile period of the woman's monthly cycle in order to regulate their families. This permission was still hedged about with qualifications – the method was only to be used with 'serious reasons' – but the vital principle had been conceded: Sex II was a Good Thing In Itself. Catholic pastoral and theological literature on the subject of marriage took up the topic with enthusiasm; the bad old days of repression, of shame and fear about human sexuality, were denounced – it was all the fault of St Paul, or Augustine, or Plato – anyway, it was all a regrettable mistake; and married couples were joyfully urged to make love with, metaphorically speaking (and literally too if they liked), the lights on.

This was all very well, but certain consequences followed. If Sex II is recognized as a Good Thing In Itself, it is difficult to set limits, other than the general humanistic rule that nobody should be hurt, on how it may be enjoyed. For example, the traditional Christian disapproval of extramarital sex had an obvious social justification as a means of ensuring responsible parenthood and avoiding inbreeding, but with the development of efficient contraception these arguments lost most of their force, as secular society had already discovered by the mid-twentieth century. Why, therefore, should responsible adults have to be married to share with each other something Good In Itself? Or to take a more extreme example, anal intercourse, whether homosexual or heterosexual, had always been condemned in terms of the deepest loathing by traditional Christian moralists, sodomy being listed in the Penny Catechism as one of the Four Sins

Crying to Heaven for Vengeance (the others, you may be curious to know, being Wilful Murder, Oppression of the Poor, and Defrauding Labourers of Their Wages). But if the sharing of sexual pleasure is a Good Thing In Itself, irrespective of the procreative function, it is difficult to see any objections, other than hygienic and aesthetic ones, to anal intercourse between consenting adults, for who is harmed by it? The same applies to masturbation, whether solitary or mutual, and oral-genital sex. As long as non-procreative orgasms are permitted, what does it matter how they are achieved?

Thus it can be seen that the ban on artificial birth control, the insistence that every sexual act must remain, at least theoretically, open to the possibility of conception, was the last fragile barrier holding back the Catholic community from joining the great collective pursuit of erotic fulfilment increasingly obsessing the rest of Western society in the sixth decade of the twentieth century; but the case for the ban had been fatally weakened by the admission that marital sex might be confined to the 'safe period' with the deliberate intention of avoiding conception. In practice, the Safe Method was so unreliable that many couples wondered if it hadn't been approved only because it wasn't safe, thus ensuring that Catholics were restrained by the consciousness that they might after all have to pay the traditional price for their pleasure. Clerical and medical apologists for the method, however, never admitted as much; on the contrary, they encouraged the faithful with assurances that Science would soon make the Safe Method as reliable as artificial contraception. (Father Brierley's Parish Priest, in the course of a heated argument, assured him that 'the Yanks were working on a little gadget like a wrist-watch that would make it as simple as telling the time.') But the greater the efforts made to achieve this goal, the more difficult it became to distinguish between the permitted and forbidden methods. There was nothing, for instance, noticeably 'natural' about sticking a thermometer up your rectum every morning compared to slipping a diaphragm into your vagina at night. And if the happy day *did* ever dawn when the Safe Method was pronounced as reliable as the Pill, what possible reason, apart from medical or economic considerations, could there be for choosing one method rather than the other? And in that case, why wait till then to make up your mind?

Following such a train of thought to its logical conclusion, millions of married Catholics had, like Michael and Miriam, come to a decision to use artificial contraception without dropping out of the Church. Some couples needed the impetus of a special hardship or particular crisis to take this step (Angela went on the Pill immediately after the birth of her mentally handicapped child; and Tessa, though happily her new baby was born sound and healthy, followed suit, with Edward's full support, neither of them being inclined to take any further risks) but once they had done so it seemed such an obviously sensible step to take that they could hardly understand why they had hesitated so long. It helped, of course – indeed, it was absolutely vital – that, as explained above, they had lost the fear of Hell, since the whole system of religious authority and obedience in which they had been brought up, binding the Church together in a pyramid of which the base was the laity and the apex the Pope, depended on the fear of Hell as its ultimate sanction. If a Catholic couple decided, privately and with a clear conscience, to use contraceptives, there was nothing that priest, bishop or Pope could do to stop them (except, in some countries, making the wherewithal difficult to obtain). Thus contraception was the issue on which many lay Catholics first attained moral autonomy, rid themselves of superstition, and ceased to regard their religion as, in the moral sphere, an encyclopaedic rule-book in which a clear answer was to be found to every possible question of conduct. They were not likely to be persuaded to reverse their decision by the tired arguments of *Humanae Vitae*, and some previously loyal souls were actually provoked by it into joining the rebels (Adrian, who had been teetering on the contraceptive brink for years, was so exasperated by the first reports of the encyclical that he rushed out of the house and startled the local chemist's shop by strident demands for 'a gross of sheaths prophylactic' – a phrase he dimly remembered from Army invoices, but which smote strangely on the ears of the girl behind the counter). Of course, there were many Catholics who with more or less resignation continued to believe that the Pope's word was law, and many who disobeyed it with a residual sense of guilt that they were never able to lose completely, and yet others who finally left the Church in despair or disgust; but on the whole the most remarkable aspect of the whole affair was the newfound moral independence of the laity which it gradually revealed. Indeed, it could be said that those who suffered most from *Humanae Vitae* were not married layfolk at all, but the liberal and progressive clergy.

Conservative bishops and priests had the satisfaction of seeing their beliefs and pastoral practice endorsed by the Pope, but those who had, in the period of uncertainty immediately preceding the publication of *HV*, interpreted the rules flexibly, or actually argued the case for their revision, were now awkwardly placed. What was for the laity a question of conduct which they might settle privately according to their own consciences, was for the clergy a question of doctrine and obedience that was necessarily public. The Holy Father had spoken, and bishops and priests, whatever their own opinions about the matter, were required to promulgate and enforce his message from the pulpit and in the confessional. Some were only too pleased to do so; but many were not, and feared massive disillusionment and disaffection among the laity if the Church simply reverted to the old hard-line teaching. Bishops were in a particularly difficult position, because they could not reject *Humanae Vitae* without the risk of provoking schism. What the more liberal hierarchies did was to make a minimalist interpretation of the encyclical – to say that, while contraception was, as the Pope affirmed, objectively wrong, there might be subjective circumstances which made it so venial a sin as scarcely to be worth worrying about, and certainly not a reason for ceasing to go to mass and Holy Communion. By this casuistry they accepted *HV* in principle while encouraging a tolerant and flexible approach to its enforcement in pastoral practice. Most of the priests who had been dismayed by the encyclical accepted this compromise, but some were unwilling or unable to do so, and if their bishop or religious superior happened to be conservative and authoritarian, the consequences could be serious.

Such priests were apt to become acutely conscious of internal contradictions in their own vocations. For the more deeply they were driven, by the pressure of debate and the threats of ecclesiastical discipline, to analyse the grounds of their dissent from *HV*, the further they were carried towards an endorsement of sexual pleasure as a Good Thing In Itself. And the further they were carried in *that* direction, the more problematical their own vows of celibacy appeared. As long as sexual pleasure had been viewed with suspicion by Christian divines, as something hostile to spirituality, lawful only as part of man's procreative function in God's scheme, the vow of celibacy had obvious point. Unmarried and chaste, the priest was materially free to serve his flock, and spiritually free from the distractions of fleshly indulgence. But when the new theology of marriage began to emerge, in which sexual love was redeemed from the repression and reticence of the past, and celebrated as (in the words of the Catholic Theological Society of America) 'self-liberating, other-enriching, honest, faithful, socially responsible, life-giving and joyous,' the value of celibacy no longer seemed self-evident, and a progressive priest might find himself in the paradoxical position of defending the right of the laity to enjoy pleasures he himself had renounced long ago, on grounds he no longer believed in. A similar collapse of confidence in the value of vowed virginity affected nuns.

Of course, it could still be argued that, without families of their own to care for, priests and nuns were free to dedicate themselves to the service of others; but this argument, too, only holds good as long as reliable contraception is forbidden. Otherwise, why should not priests and nuns marry each other, and take vows of sterility rather than chastity, forgoing the satisfactions of having offspring in order to serve the community at large, but still enjoying the consolations of that interpersonal genital communion which, the orthodox wisdom of the modern age insists, is essential to mental and physical health? For that matter, why, given new control over their own biology, should not women themselves be priests? For the prejudice against the ordination of women is demonstrably rooted in traditional sexual attitudes rather than in theology or logic.

The crisis in the Church over birth control was not, therefore, the absurd diversion from more important matters that it first appeared to many observers, for it compelled thoughtful Catholics to re-examine and redefine their views on fundamental issues: the relationship between authority and conscience, between the religious and lay vocations, between flesh and spirit. The process of questioning and revision it triggered off continues, although *Humanae Vitae* itself is a dead letter to most of the laity and merely an embarrassing nuisance to most of the clergy. It is clear that the liberal, hedonistic spirit has achieved irresistible momentum within the Church as without, that young Catholics now reaching adulthood have much the same views about the importance of sexual fulfilment and the control of fertility as their non-Catholic peers, and that it is only a matter of time before priests are allowed to marry and women are ordained. There is, however, no cause for progressives to gloat or for conservatives to sulk. Let copulation thrive, by all means; but man cannot live by orgasms alone, and he certainly cannot die by them, except, very occasionally, in the clinical sense. The good news about sexual satisfaction has little to offer those who are crippled, chronically sick, mad, ugly, impotent – or old, which all of us will be in due course, unless we are dead already. Death, after all, is the overwhelming question to which sex provides no answer, only an occasional brief respite from thinking about it. But enough of this philosophizing.

Early in 1969, nearly everyone who used to attend the Thursday morning masses in the old days at Our Lady and St Jude's received long-distance phone calls from Adrian. Most of them had been out of touch with him for many years, but he spoke to them as if it was only yesterday that they had breakfasted at Lyons in the Tottenham Court Road. He had traced Michael's phone number through a Catholic periodical for which Michael occasionally wrote book reviews, and from Michael he got Dennis's number, and so on. Adrian sat at his desk in the Town Hall where he worked and dialled them all on STD, robbing the ratepayers without qualms because it was in a good cause, and the cause was short of funds. He was chairman of a lay pressure group calling itself Catholics for an Open Church, COC for short, which had recently been formed, in Adrian's words, 'to fight *HV* and help priests who are in trouble over it'. One of these priests was Father Brierley.

'That meek little man who married Angela and Dennis?' said Miriam. 'I'd never have thought he had it in him.'

'Seems he read out his bishop's pastoral letter about *Humanae Vitae*, which was pretty hard-line, and then told the congregation it was still a matter of conscience.'

'Is that all?'

'Well, then a reporter on the local paper interviewed him and he said that personally he thought the Pope was up the creek, or words to that effect, and some mean-minded parishioner sent a cutting to the bishop.'

'And what does Adrian Whatsisname want us to do about it?'

'He wants us to join this Catholics for an Open Church thing, and sign an open letter to the Cardinal about Father Brierley and the other suspended priests.'

'Sounds like a good idea.'

'The College Governors won't like it,' said Michael, somewhat sheepishly.

'To hell with them,' said Miriam.

'You know I'll be up for promotion soon?'

'To hell with that.'

'OK,' said Michael. 'I'll tell Adrian we'll join.'

As always, he admired Miriam's moral certitude. Breathing it in as if she had handed him an oxygen mask, he felt suddenly strong and reckless, excited by the possibilities of Catholics for an Open Church. The spirit of protest was abroad, but Michael had not yet been able to find a cause he could plausibly identify with. He was too old for the student movement, too apolitical for the New Left (*Slant* had finally bored him), too moral (or too timid) for the Counter Culture of drugs, rock and casual sex. He was finding himself pushed to the margins of the decade, forced into a posture of conservatism and conventionality which made him feel as if his youth were disappearing at an ever-increasing speed, like the earth beneath an astronaut. The idea of challenging ecclesiastical authority in the cause of sexual fulfilment for married couples and freedom of speech for priests seemed an opportunity to hitch his wagon to the *Zeitgeist* in good faith. Michael did not, of course, analyse his motives as explicitly as this, and did not understand (he accounted for it purely as impulse buying) why, shortly after sending off his subscription to Catholics for an Open Church, he bought a pair of the new-style trousers with flared bottoms and a copy of the Beatles 'white' double album, his first non-classical record. He had joined the sixties, in the nick of time.

Michael wore his new trousers to the first annual general meeting of Catholics for an Open Church, held in London that summer, but it proved to be a sadly unfashionable gathering on the whole. Adrian, in the chair, set the sartorial keynote in his business suit, shiny with wear and bulging at the breast pocket with a quiverful of ballpoint pens, flashes of colour against the dark blue serge like the silk markers of his missal in the gloom of Our Lady and St Jude's. He was going bald but did not seem otherwise noticeably different from those days – still stiff, impatient and dogmatic, though he had moved across the ideological spectrum from Right to Left in the meantime. A cursory glance around the hall, hired for the day from the Quakers, told Michael that he had not joined the equivalent of Californian Flower Power or the Paris student communes. Most of the occupants of the rows of bentwood chairs were ordinary, plain-featured, drably dressed, middle-class couples in their late thirties or early forties, with a sprinkling of older people whose concern about *HV* must, he assumed, be entirely academic. Indeed, some of the younger members seemed anxious to claim a similar disinterestedness. 'We find that the Safe Method works perfectly well for us,' said one man to Michael and Miriam over coffee, his wife, with her mouth full of biscuit, nodding eager agreement, 'but we sympathize with others less fortunate.' Another man, with a bushy beard and huge, horny-toed feet in sandals, said, 'Have you ever tried *coitus reservatus?*

It's highly recommended by Eastern mystics. Of course, you have to learn the meditative techniques that go with it.' 'A bit risky while you're learning, isn't it?' said Michael. Behind him a woman was saying, 'I wouldn't care about the population explosion if only it wasn't happening in our house.'

Adrian read out some letters of support, mostly anonymous, for the group's aims, which included some poignant case histories and memorable *cris de coeur* ('What is love? What is conjugal love? Why did God make it so nice?' wrote one correspondent with five children and a wife suffering from high blood pressure). Then a somewhat embarrassed-looking Father Brierley was paraded for their edification, rather like an Iron Curtain defector at a press conference. His sports jacket, trousers and roll-neck shirt were ill-co-ordinated in colour and glinted with the sheen of cheap synthetic fabric. He stammered out a speech of thanks for the group's support – financial as well as moral, for he was not receiving any stipend while under suspension. Catholics for an Open Church had received only a curt acknowledgement of its original letter to the Cardinal, and now Adrian read out the draft of a second, follow-up letter for the meeting's approval. The membership quickly split into two factions, one anxious to be respectful and conciliatory, the other determined to be bold and challenging. Amendments and counter-amendments flew backwards and forwards. The man in sandals made a determined effort to get *coitus reservatus* into the text somehow or other. Tempers rose. It was hard to tell whether the speakers were more hostile to *HV* or to each other. Adrian grew hoarse and irritable, he glared contemptuously at the members like the captain of a mutinous crew, and Dorothy, who was taking the minutes, put down her pen with a theatrical flourish, folded her arms and lifted her eyes to the ceiling. Then Edward – Edward, who had slipped into the back of the hall unnoticed by Michael and Miriam – stood up and took some of the tension out of the atmosphere with a self-deprecating joke and moved that Adrian and Father Brierley should be left to revise the letter in the light of the comments expressed. Michael seconded the motion and it was carried by a large majority. The meeting was closed, and

Adrian announced that Father Brierley would say mass for the members before they dispersed. Strictly speaking, he wasn't supposed to do this while under suspension, but as a jovial African supporter said, mixing his proverbs a little, 'Hang my lambs, hang my sheep.'

At the mass, real wholemeal bread was consecrated and broken, and handed round in baskets, and the congregation also shared the chalice. At the words, 'Let us give each other the sign of peace,' several couples embraced instead of giving each other the customary handshake. Michael and Miriam spontaneously followed suit and, because of the novelty of the circumstances, Michael experienced a perceptible erection as their lips touched. He was not abashed, as at a similar occurrence at the St Valentine's Day mass long ago; after all, that was what they were all gathered together here for, to assert the compatibility of *eros* and *agape*, to answer positively the questions, what was love, what was conjugal love, why did God make it so nice? Both agreed that the mass was the most meaningful liturgical event they had ever participated in.

Afterwards, they sought out Edward. 'Hello, you two,' he said. 'What do you mean by joining this seditious rabble?'

'What about you, then?'

'I'm an infiltrator, paid by the Vatican in indulgences. And why are you wearing those extraordinary trousers, old man?'

In spite of his quips, Edward looked tired and drawn, and was evidently in some pain from his old back injury. 'There is an operation, but I don't fancy it,' he said. 'I know too much about surgeons. And hospitals. Forty per cent of my patients who have surgery pick up secondary infections in hospital. Take my advice, stay out of hospital if you possibly can.'

'I intend to,' said Michael.

'I should knock off that stuff, then,' said Edward, with a nod at Michael's cigarette.

'I only smoke ten a day,' said Michael.

'Fifteen,' said Miriam. 'Twenty, some days.'

'Each one,' said Edward, 'takes five minutes off your life expectancy.'

'You're a cheerful bugger, I must say,' said Michael, stubbing out a rather longer dog-end than usual.

They exchanged news about their families and mutual friends. Adrian and Dorothy joined them.

'I thought Angela and Dennis might have come,' said Adrian, with a slight tone of grievance. 'They did join.'

'Angela rang me, she sent her apologies, but she's tied up organizing some bazaar today. And Dennis isn't much interested in the Church these days. Ever since Anne . . .' Miriam's explanation tailed away.

'Yes,' said Edward, shaking his head, and looking at his toecaps. 'That was too bad.'

Adrian and Dorothy had not followed this and had to have it explained to them, as will you, gentle reader. Two years after Nicole was born, Dennis and Angela's next youngest child, Anne, was knocked down by a van outside their house and died in hospital a few hours later. I have avoided a direct presentation of this incident because frankly I find it too painful to contemplate. Of course, Dennis and Angela and Anne are fictional characters, they cannot bleed or weep, but they stand here for all the real people to whom such disasters happen with no apparent reason or justice. One does not kill off characters lightly, I assure you, even ones like Anne, evoked solely for that purpose.

'Of course, they blame themselves for the accident, one always does,' said Miriam. 'Though it could happen to anyone.'

They were silent for a moment, trying to imagine what it would be like if it happened to them, and failing.

'Well,' sighed Adrian, 'I'm not surprised they didn't come. They must have enough on their plate.' The last vestige of his romantic interest in Angela dissolved with this news. Before the meeting he had been conscious, against his own reason, of a quiver of expectation at the prospect of seeing her again, a foolish wish to shine in her eyes by his conduct of the meeting. Now the thread of sentimental reminiscence that linked them was finally broken, and he recognized her as irrevocably separated from him, robed in her own tragedy, burdened with a grief that he could neither share nor alleviate.

'Have you been in touch with any others of the old crowd?' Edward asked him.

'Eh? Oh, yes. I got on to quite a few. I spoke to Miles, but he didn't sound very keen to get involved. As a matter of fact, he seemed distinctly hostile. Let me see, who else . . .? Polly I didn't bother to trace, I gather she left the Church years ago. Ruth was sympathetic, but she was just off to America.'

'Good Lord, what for?'

'Visiting various convents, I gather, to see what they've been up to over there since Vatican II.'

'She's still a nun, then? And Violet?'

Adrian grimaced and Dorothy rolled her eyes heavenwards. 'Ever since Adie got in touch with her,' said Dorothy, 'she's been ringing him up at all hours.'

'To discuss her personal problems,' said Adrian.

'She's still married to Robin?'

'Just about.'

At Edward's suggestion they adjourned to a nearby pub to continue the conversation, which came round inevitably to the great debate about *Humanae Vitae* and the Safe Method and the question of why they had themselves for so many years persevered with that frustrating, inconvenient, ineffective, anxiety-and-tension-creating régime. 'It was conditioning,' said Edward, who no longer advised patients on the use of the basal temperature method. 'It was the repressive power of the clergy, wielded through the confessional,' said Adrian, a strong supporter of the new rite of Penance being mooted in advanced liturgical circles, with general absolution and no invasions of privacy. 'It was guilt about sex, the way we were brought up not knowing anything,' said Dorothy, who had not yet forgiven her mother for the debacle of her wedding night. 'It was fear,' said Michael. 'Let's face it, it was the fear of Hell.'

Well, yes, they had to agree that had been at the bottom of it: the fear of Hell. And looking at each other, with faintly embarrassed grins as they sipped their drinks, they realized then, if they had not realized before, that Hell, the Hell of their childhood, had disappeared for good.

FIVE

How they broke out, away, down, up, through, etc.

In America, Ruth travelled from city to city, from convent to convent, like a medieval pilgrim, making notes about the changes that were taking place in the lives of nuns. She had been awarded a six-month's travelling scholarship for this project, but when her time was up she felt that she had only scratched the surface of the subject and wrote home for permission to stay longer. She relied on the religious communities she visited for food and accommodation, repaying their hospitality with whatever work was appropriate. She did substitution teaching in schools, auxiliary nursing in hospitals, helped look after senior citizens and mentally handicapped children. Sometimes she donned her habit and gave talks about the Church in England to parochial groups. Afterwards people would come up to her and shake her hand warmly, sometimes pressing into it a large-denomination dollar bill 'to help with your expenses, sister.' At first she was embarrassed by these gifts, but after a while she got used to them, and indeed came to rely on such gratuities for her pocket money.

American nuns, she soon discovered, were in a state of upheaval that made England seem quite tranquil by comparison. In Cleveland, Ohio, she came across a community that had until recently been enclosed, supporting itself precariously by embroidering priests' vestments, and had suddenly decided to train all its members in chiropody and turned itself into a foot clinic. In Detroit, Michigan, a nun in high boots and a mini-skirt ran a free school for juvenile deliquents and led a successful rent-strike against profiteering landlords. In St Louis, Ruth interviewed a sister who was secretary-general of an organization dedicated to opposing male chauvinism in the Church. She wore a trouser suit and scattered words like 'crap' and 'bullshit' in her conversation. On the wall behind her head a poster depicted Moses telling the Israelites: *'And She's black . . .'* In Texas, Ruth visited a community of nuns who came down to breakfast with their hair in huge plastic curlers. After a hasty grace ('Good food, good meat, good God, let's eat') they tucked into hot cakes and bacon; then, immaculately coiffed, and clad in smart clothes, they swept off in huge shiny convertibles to their jobs as personal secretaries in downtown Houston. In the evenings they had dates with priests, who took them out to restaurants and movie shows.

Ruth herself had adventures. Travelling through the night on a Greyhound bus, dressed, as was her custom now, in ordinary clothes, she realized that the man in the next seat had placed his hand on her knee. She froze, wondering what to do. Scream? Cut and run? Stop the bus? After half an hour she dared a look sideways. The man was asleep, his limbs limp, his mouth open. Slowly, carefully, Ruth lifted his hand from her knee and restored it to his own. Eventually she slept herself and woke to find her head on the man's shoulder. 'I didn't like to waken you,' he said with a smile, chafing his numbed arm. Ruth blushed crimson and muttered her apologies. 'You're welcome,' said the man. At the next rest stop he insisted on buying her coffee and doughnuts and telling her the story of his life. He was a shoe salesman, recently retired, going to spend a vacation with his son and daughter-in-law in Denver. 'You'd really like them,' he assured her. 'They made a trip to London a few years back. You'd have a lot in common. Why don't you plan to stay over in Denver a whiles?' When they got back into the bus, Ruth took a seat next to a black woman with a baby on her lap and pretended not to see the hurt and longing looks the shoe salesman sent in her direction across the aisle. At the time, this episode distressed her, but afterwards she was vexed to think how upset she had been, or 'uptight' as the feminist nun in St Louis would have put it. When, some time later, an ugly but genial man tried to pick her up at Dallas airport, she didn't panic, but waited patiently for an opportunity to mention that she was a nun. 'No *kidding!*'

he said, staring. 'Hey, I wouldn't have made a pass at you if I'd known. Jesus – sorry – wow! Hey, I went to a parochial school myself, you know? I mean, I was *taught* by sisters.' He seemed almost afraid that they would rise up out of the past to punish him. He took out his wallet and tried to press a donation on her. Fending off the proffered dollar bills, Ruth glimpsed a woman on a nearby bench observing them with disapproval. 'Put your money away, you're giving scandal,' she said, giggling. She dined off the story more than once.

At last she came to the coast of California, which seemed as far as she could go. Her Mother Superior wrote reluctantly agreeing to a three-month extension of her leave. The letter was fretful and discouraged. One nun had just left the community and another was on the brink. There had been only two new postulants admitted to the mother house that year. By the same post Ruth received a copy of *Crux*, the COC newsletter: Adrian had put her on the mailing list even though she hadn't paid a subscription. It contained articles, news items and book reviews, mostly written by Adrian and Dorothy, correspondence with editorial comments by Adrian, and the text of the third Open Letter to the Cardinal.

Michael had been correct in predicting that the governors of his College, who included several members of the clergy he liked to describe as somewhat to the right of Torquemada in the spectrum of ecclesiastical politics, would disapprove of his membership of Catholics for an Open Church. When the second open letter to the Cardinal, bearing his signature, was published in *The Times* and the *Tablet*, the Principal suggested that it would be in Michael's own interest to resign from the group. His professional association offered to take up the case, but Michael was tired of the place anyway, and applied successfully for a more senior post elsewhere. This was another Catholic College of Education, but only recently established, and known to be progressive in its outlook, dedicated to the spirit of Vatican II, with a lay Principal and a largely lay staff. In preparation for the new life they expected to lead there, Michael and Miriam let their hair grow, he to his shoulders and she to her waist. When Miriam thrust her head forward in the excitement of argument now, a shimmering curtain of copper-coloured hair would fall forward over her green eyes, and she would flick it back with an impatient toss of the head. Michael also grew a moustache, hoping it would distract attention from his snouty nose. He gave up smoking, and Miriam started baking her own bread.

They looked forward to seeing more of some old friends in their new location, for the College was situated on the outskirts of the city where Edward had his practice, and was not far, therefore, from Dennis and Angela's dormitory village. To the same city, in due course, came Father Brierley, to study at the Polytechnic. His dispute with the bishop had been resolved, at least temporarily, like other crises in his priestly life, by sending him on a course – this time for a degree in psychology and sociology.

Father Brierley's bishop was not, in fact, the ogre that Adrian liked to make him out to be. He did not wish to lose Father Brierley, whom he recognized as a sincere, hardworking priest, especially as the diocese was chronically under strength; nor did he personally have very strong feelings about the issue of birth control. The bishop had successfully sublimated his own sexual urges thirty years ago, and didn't understand why Catholic couples couldn't do the same after having a few children. As a young man he would have liked to experience copulation once, just to know what it was like, and to live with that curiosity unsatisfied had been a genuine sacrifice at the time. That people should want to go on doing it, again and again, long after the novelty must have worn off, strained his understanding and sympathy. But he acknowledged that there were a lot of sins worse than spilling the seed, and thought it was very regrettable the way this one issue had come to obsess people.

For the bishop, the controversy was purely a management problem. What Father Brierley said to folk in the confessional was between God and his conscience, but if he was allowed to get away with publicly repudiating *HV*, all the young tearaway curates in the diocese would soon be doing the same, and the older ones baying for a heresy hunt, and then the fat would be in the fire. The bishop put this to Father Brierley, frankly and freely, one man to another, sitting opposite him in the episcopal study in an easy chair, and offering Irish whiskey and cigarettes. Austin Brierley apologized for causing him so much trouble, but stood his ground. The bishop sighed, lit a Senior Service, and asked Father Brierley if he had a girl friend. Austin Brierley flushed and denied the suggestion indignantly.

'Hold your horses, Father,' said the Bishop, 'it was just a shot in the dark. It's only that every priest I've had trouble with in the past few years has turned out to be in love. The poor fools think they've got problems of faith and doctrine but subconsciously they're looking for a way to get out of Holy Orders and into the arms of some woman or other.'

'That isn't my situation,' said Austin Brierley.

'I'm glad to hear it,' said the Bishop. 'But what shall we do with you?'

'Let me go to college,' said Austin Brierley. 'I'd like to take a degree in psychology.'

'What in Heaven's name for?'

'I think it would help me to understand people better. They come to me for advice, but what do I know about ordinary people's problems? All I know about are priests' problems.'

The Bishop grunted sceptically. 'We've managed for nearly two thousand years without degrees in psychology,' he said. But the suggestion had an undeniable appeal. Sending Father Brierley to college would get him out of his parish and out of the limelight for a few years, by which time the controversy over *HV* would have died down. And it would appear a magnanimous gesture on his own part, which would be one in the eye for Mr Adrian Walsh and his society of busybodies. 'You'd have to resign from that Catholics for an Open Church nonsense,' he said. Reluctantly, Austin Brierley agreed to this condition, but he chose his place of study deliberately to be near some of his friends and supporters in COC, and continued to advise them unofficially on matters of theology and ecclesiastical politics.

Michael and Miriam now belonged to a circle of friends, mostly attached to the College in some capacity, who saw themselves as almost a church within the Church. On Sunday mornings they attended mass in the College chapel, where Father Bede Buchanan, a liberal-minded priest who was a lecturer in the Theology Department and chaplain to the student body, tolerated an experimental, avant-garde liturgy that would have lifted the back hairs on the red necks of the local parish priests had they known what was going on in their midst.

Each week the students chose their own readings, bearing on some topical theme, and sometimes these were not taken from Scripture at all, but might be articles from the *Guardian* about racial discrimination or poems by the Liverpool poets about teenage promiscuity or some blank-verse effusion of their own composition. The music at mass was similarly eclectic in style, accompanied by guitar and perhaps flute, violin, Indian bells, bongo drums – whatever instruments and instrumentalists happened to be around. They sang negro spirituals and gospel songs, Sidney Carter's modern folk hymns, the calypso setting of the 'Our Father', Protestant favourites like 'Amazing Grace' and 'Onward Christian Soldiers', and sometimes pop classics like Simon and Garfunkel's 'Mrs Robinson' (*'Jesus loves you more and more each day, hey, hey, hey!'*) or the Beatles' 'All You Need Is Love'. At the bidding prayers anyone was free to chip in with a petition, and the congregation might find itself praying for the success of the Viet Cong, or for the recovery of someone's missing tortoise, as well as for more conventional intentions. At the Offertory, the bread and wine were brought up to the altar by two students, usually a courting couple holding hands and exchanging fond looks, and it wasn't only married couples who warmly embraced at the Kiss of Peace. Throughout the mass the young children of the college lecturers scampered uncontrolled about the room, chattering and fighting and pushing their Dinky cars up and down the altar steps. At Communion, most of the congregation received the Host in their hands rather than on the tongue, and also took the cup, which was brought round by a layman – all practices still forbidden in public worship in England. At the end of mass there was a discussion period in which the congregation was encouraged to pick holes in the homily they had heard earlier.

This liturgy had one indisputable spiritual edge over the old: it was virtually impossible to lapse into some private, secular daydream while it was going on, because you could never be sure from one moment to the next what was going to happen. By suspending their sense of irony, Michael and Miriam derived an agreeable sense of uplift and togetherness from the occasion, while their children positively looked forward to Sunday mornings, and groaned when, during the vacations, the College masses were suspended and they were obliged to attend the parish church, where they were penned in narrow pews and made to sit, stand and kneel, like well-drilled troops, in unison with the rest of the congregation, and obliged to sing the doleful hymns of yesteryear, 'Soul of My Saviour' and 'Sweet Sacrament Divine'. Moving between these two places of worship, and impersonating the two very different styles of deportment that went with them, Michael sometimes felt like a liturgical double agent.

Catholic friends and relatives who came to stay (they now had a large, comfortable old house, with a proper guest room) were taken to the College mass as a kind of treat, or at least novelty. Adrian, who came down with Dorothy one weekend to discuss COC policy (there was a plan afoot to publish a pamphlet demonstrating the fallibility of *Humanae Vitae*) joined enthusiastically in the College mass and offered a bidding prayer inviting the Lord to open the eyes of those clergy who were resisting the spirit of liturgical renewal. This was apparently an allusion to his own parish priest, with whom he was engaged in a long war of attrition. 'You don't know how lucky you are,' he said afterwards. 'Our PP won't even allow women readers.'

'Why not?' said Miriam.

'Menstruation,' said Dorothy, who liked to advertise the distance she had travelled from her inhibited youth by being very outspoken. 'He thinks women are unclean. He probably thinks we bleed all the time.'

'But we'll nail him eventually,' said Adrian. 'Dorothy will read from that pulpit if I have to organize a strike of altar cleaners to do it.'

'Sometimes, at the College mass, we have a woman bring round the cup,' said Miriam.

'Gosh, do you really!' they exclaimed. 'How fantastic!'

But the College liturgy did not always please. One Sunday when Michael's parents were with them, a child taking Communion let the chalice slip and spilled the consecrated wine all over the floor. Michael's father, a retired civil servant, was deeply upset by this occurrence, and muttered audibly that it ought to be reported to the Bishop. 'It's not right,' he said afterwards, over lunch, still agitated and looking quite grey with shock, 'letting the children have the chalice. I don't hold with it, in any case, not even for adults, there's always the risk of an accident. But the way they carry on in that chapel, with any Tom, Dick or Harry taking round the chalice, it's no wonder something like that happens. And all that priest did was mop it up with some old cloth!'

'What did you expect him to do, Dad, eat the carpet?' said Michael. The remark sounded excessively rude when he made it, but his father had irritated and embarrassed him by his public fussing over the incident.

'In my day, the carpet would have been taken up and burned.'

'Burned?' Michael forced a laugh. 'What good would that do?'

'To avoid desecration.'

Michael sighed. 'You still have a very magical idea of the Eucharist, don't you Dad?'

'Respectful, I'd call it. Reverent.'

'Even granted that you still believe in the transubstantiation – '

'Oh, don't you, then?'

'Not in the sense we were taught at school. Substance and accidents and all that.'

Michael's father shook his head.

'But even granted that you still believe it, surely you don't think that Christ is *trapped* in the wine, do you? I mean, you admit that the Real Presence could leave the wine the instant it was spilled, before it hit the carpet?'

'Michael, leave your father alone,' said Miriam.

'Yes, stop it, you two,' said her mother-in-law. 'It's not nice, arguing about religion on a Sunday.'

Michael's father waved these interventions away impatiently. 'Tell me what you do believe, then, son, about Holy Communion, if you don't believe in transubstantiation. What is it, if it isn't the changing of bread and wine into the Body and Blood of Our Lord, Jesus Christ?' He gave a reflex nod of the head at the Holy Name, and his wife followed suit.

'Well . . .' said Michael, more hesitantly, 'it's a commemoration.'

'Pah!' expostulated his father. 'That's what Protestants say.'

'*Do this in memory of me*,' Michael quoted.

'*This is My Body, this is My Blood*,' his father countered.

'That's a metaphor,' said Michael.

'It's a plain statement of fact.'

'How could it be? A plain statement of fact would be, "This bread is bread, this wine is wine." ' He took a slice of Hovis in his fingers and waved it in the air illustratively, exhilarated by the argument, his blood up now, a teacher in full cry. 'In "This is My Body," the verb *is* can only mean "*is like*" or "*is, as it were*" or "*is analogous to*", because any other sense would be a logical contradiction. God can only speak to men in a language that is humanly intelligible.'

His father snorted angrily, baffled but not beaten. 'Are you trying to tell me that what the Church has taught for centuries is wrong, then?'

'Yes. No. Not exactly. Concepts change as knowledge changes. Once everybody believed the earth was flat. Only cranks believe that now.'

'So I'm a crank, am I?'

'I didn't say that, Dad.'

His father grunted, but offered no further resistance. The adrenalin seeped away and Michael was left feeling slightly ashamed of his facile victory.

Miles, who stayed with them one weekend on his way to a conference in Wales, was as dismayed as Michael's father. 'My dear Michael,' he said, emerging from the College chapel with his hand to his brow, like someone with a migraine, 'this is madness. This is anarchy. This is Enthusiasm. Ronnie Knox must be spinning in his grave.' Miles drew an analogy between what he had witnessed and the development of antinomian sects in the seventeenth century. 'It won't be long,' he prophesied, 'before you're dancing naked in front of the altar and sharing your wives and goods in common.'

'Sounds like fun,' said Michael, grinning. 'But seriously, Miles, everyone's antinomian nowadays. Catholics are just catching up with the rest of the world. I mean, the idea of sin is right out. They don't even teach it in Catholic schools any more.' Michael exaggerated somewhat to tease Miles, who awed him less than of old, perhaps because Miles's academic career had not really fulfilled its early promise. His thesis had not, after all, been published, whereas Michael was beginning to publish essays here and there about youth culture, the new liturgy and the mass media, and had hopes of gathering them into a book. When Michael visited Miles at his Cambridge college he was surprised how little envy he felt – his rooms seemed cold and damp and smelled of gas, the furniture was ugly, the conversation at High Table boring and superficial. Apart from the beauty of the external architecture, the ambience reminded him faintly of his father's golf club as it had been in the early fifties. Miles himself, wearing superbly tailored but unfashionably cut three-piece suits, and always carrying his tightly furled umbrella, seemed psychologically arrested in that earlier era.

Miles certainly felt spiritually orphaned by the times. The Catholic Church he had joined was fast disappearing, and he did not like the new one he saw appearing in its place, with its concert-party liturgy, its undiscriminating radicalism, its rather smug air of uxorious sexual liberation. He admitted to himself that there might be an element of envy in his reaction on the last score, for he was himself still hopelessly screwed up over the sexual question. The homosexual subculture of Cambridge was becoming increasingly overt in its behaviour, and beckoning him to join the party, but he held back on the fringe, prim-lipped and buttoned-up. It was at about this time that the word 'gay' became widely current in England in the homosexual sense, but to Miles it had a mockingly ironic ring. One summer he arranged to take a holiday in Morocco with a young colleague of apparently similar temperament, and wondered excitedly whether this would be his first affair, whether the exotic and distant setting would allow him to lose his scruples and his virginity at last, but the young man turned out to be paedophile and spent all his time making assignations with young Arab boys in the marketplace of the town where they were staying. One evening Miles himself cruised the narrow streets diffidently in search of a pick-up, but always drew back when accosted, fearful of being robbed, blackmailed or infected. He flew back to England a week early and settled in tourist-ridden Cambridge to make one more assault on the revision of his thesis for publication. By the end of the vacation he had exactly thirteen pages of uncancelled typescript to show for his pains. 'You're blocked because you're sexually repressed,' said his friend, back from Morocco, bronzed and sated. 'How glib can you get?' Miles sneered, but secretly agreed.

At times when his physical frustration became too much to bear, he took from a locked drawer in his bedroom a small collection of homosexual pornography and masturbated. These acts he coldly confessed at the earliest opportunity to his regular confessor, the now ageing Jesuit. 'Is it really better to live like this than to have a proper loving relationship with someone?' Miles asked.

'You know very well that if you were doing that I wouldn't be able to give you absolution. Pray to Almighty God to give you strength.'

Miles sank into a deep depression. He spent long hours taking hot baths and slept as much as possible, drugging himself with Valium and sleeping pills – anything to reduce the hours of consciousness to a minimum. He cancelled his tutorials frequently because he could not face them, and his students began to complain. Colleagues avoided his company. Cambridge, which he had always thought of as one of the most privileged spots on earth, became hideous to him, a claustrophobic little place, crammed with vain, complacent, ruthless people who were constantly signalling to each other by every word and gesture, '*Envy me, envy me, I'm clever and successful and I'm having it off every night.*'

'Perhaps you should see a psychiatrist,' said his confessor.

'He'll only tell me to have sex,' said Miles. 'That's what they all say, isn't it?'

'I know a Catholic one,' said the priest. 'A very good man.'

After several consultations the psychiatrist said, 'I can do nothing for you. Speaking as a doctor, my advice would be: find yourself a partner. Speaking as a Catholic, I can only say: carry your cross.'

'That's easily said,' Miles observed.

The psychiatrist shrugged. 'I quite agree. With many clients there comes a point when one has to say, your problem is what you are.'

'Like the old joke about the man with an inferiority complex?'

'Precisely. You *are* homosexual.'

'I knew that already,' said Miles, getting up to go. 'But thanks for confirming it.'

Violet also went to a psychiatrist – more than one: she sought them out as she had once sought out confessors, moving restlessly and at random from one to another, hoping to find the one with magic powerful enough to break the spell. She told each one her story and compared their diagnoses. Some said depressive, some schizoid, some prescribed drugs, some group counselling. One prescribed therapeutic sex. When Violet told him about the episode with her professor, he propounded the theory that she had imagined the whole thing. It was clearly a displacement of her desire to have sex with her own father. The guilt generated by this repressed incestuous desire had led her to project it on to other father figures as a violation of her own innocence. She would not be cured until she was able to have a happy, guilt-free relationship with an older man. 'I am an older man,' he pointed out. When Violet broke off the consultation, he said, 'If you make a complaint, I shall deny everything, of course.'

Ruth wrote home for a further extension. It was refused. Come home, her Mother Superior urged, you are needed. Sixth Form science is suffering. Ruth procrastinated, equivocated. She did not want to go home. She felt that she was in the middle of some spiritual quest that could not be abandoned, though she did not know where or when it would end. As for Sixth Form science suffering, that was all rot. The real reason why Mother Superior wanted her back was because two more nuns had left the convent and morale was low. One of the women concerned had written to Ruth. '*I'll make no bones about it*,' she wrote, '*I left to get married, and not to anyone in particular. I woke up one morning and realized that I couldn't face the rest of my life on my own, without a man, without children. I'm going out with a nice fellow now, a widower with two boys, we met through an agency. I'm taking cookery lessons. When I tried to cook a dinner for John and the children he said it was the worst meal he had ever had in his life. I suppose that after a number of years in a convent your taste buds get anaesthetized . . .*'

Ruth herself did not suffer unduly from the pangs of frustrated sexual and maternal longing, but she did feel that there was something missing from her life as a religious, and that she had to find it before she returned home. She wrote back to her Mother Superior: '*I am going through a crisis about my vocation. I must see it through over here.*' Mother Superior wired: 'RETURN IMMEDIATELY.' Ruth ignored the summons. She did not know whether she had been suspended. She did not greatly care.

It was a time of intense political activity in America, and priests and nuns were throwing themselves into the struggle for civil rights, for peace in Vietnam, for the protection of the environment. Ruth marched and demonstrated on behalf of the Berrigan brothers, Jesuit priests jailed for burning draft cards and alleged conspiracy against the State, and was herself arrested and jailed for a night. She hitch-hiked to Southern California to support the strike of exploited Chicano grape-pickers. Her picket line was broken up by thugs hired by the employers. Ruth was hit in the chest and pushed to the ground, screaming 'You cad!' at her attacker. 'Those mothers are mean-looking mothers, ain't they?'

said the worker who picked her up and dusted her down. After that experience, Ruth wore her habit on demos and enjoyed a certain immunity from assault, though an element of risk remained. Thus attired, she stood among a crowd of two thousand on a college campus at the height of the Cambodian crisis, chanting, *'Pigs out! Pigs out!'* and fled from a charge of police dressed like spacemen, her eyes streaming from tear gas. 'Mean-looking mothers, aren't they?' she gasped to a startled fellow-demonstrator. This term of abuse, which she privately interpreted as a contraction of 'Mother Superior', had rather caught her fancy, and she continued to use it freely until enlightened as to its true derivation by an amused Franciscan friar during a sit-in at a napalm factory.

From these experiences Ruth emerged proud and self-reliant. Her life before America, dull and orderly, seemed like an album of monochrome photographs in her memory. But still she hadn't found what she was looking for. The euphoria, the inspiring sense of solidarity with one's brothers and sisters, that was generated by marches and demonstrations, soon evaporated. Eventually the columns dispersed, the marchers went their separate ways. 'This is the darnedest time,' said Josephine, a Paulist sister from Iowa, on one such occasion, just after a big peace rally in San Francisco. The two of them were drinking coffee out of paper cups in a bus-station automat in the middle of the night, waiting for their connections. Blue strip lighting bleakly illuminated the Formica tables and the littered floor. 'While the rally's going on, you feel just great, right?' Josephine went on. 'Like, people are really digging each other, the barriers are down, and when everybody's singing "We Shall Overcome", or "They'll Know We Are Christians By Our Love", you feel it's really true. You think to yourself, gee, this is really great, this is the New Jerusalem, this is what it's all about. But it doesn't last. Soon you're in some lousy automat, zonked out, and the party's over.'

'I suppose it couldn't last, in the nature of things,' said Ruth philosophically. 'You couldn't keep up that intense emotional pitch for long.'

'It's not just that. The others on the demo, ordinary people, have got homes, real homes to go back to. Husbands, wives, families. Folks waiting to welcome them back, wanting to hear all about it. That must be real nice.' Ruth nodded sympathetically, knowing that Josephine's community did not approve of her radical activities and would not want to know anything at all about that weekend's demonstration. 'Whereas, for us, it's just an anticlimax, going back. Anticlimax and loneliness. Gee, I get so depressed after one of these rallies. . . . D'you know what I do, Ruth?' Josephine looked around, and although the automat was empty apart from themselves and a black soldier asleep in the far corner, lowered her voice. 'I buy myself a little miniature bottle of Southern Comfort and then I fill me a big deep tub, very hot, and I have a long, long soak. I lie there for hours, taking a sip of Southern Comfort every now and then, and topping up the hot water in the tub. I usually wind up giving myself another kind of Southern Comfort, you know what I mean?'

'No,' said Ruth, truthfully. Josephine looked at her with a strange expression – quizzical, sceptical, slightly wicked – and suddenly Ruth guessed what she was talking about, and blushed vividly. 'Oh,' she said.

'D'you think I'm going crazy, Ruth?' said Josephine. 'D'you think I should get out before I'm totally screwed up by this life?'

'I don't know,' said Ruth. 'Don't ask me. I don't even know about myself.'

As well as the Sunday masses in the College chapel, Michael and Miriam and their friends held occasional gatherings in their homes on weekday evenings which they called 'agapes', after the common meal or love-feast which accompanied the celebration of the Lord's Supper in the primitive Church. These occasions did indeed make Michael and Miriam and their circle feel a little bit like the early Christians, gathered together in fellowship behind the curtained windows of suburban houses, while all around them people went about their secular pursuits, sat slumped in front of televisions, or drank beer in pubs, or walked their dogs under the streetlamps, quite indifferent to and ignorant of the little cell of religious spirit pulsing in their midst. About a dozen people would be invited and, when everyone had arrived, sat round a table spread with homely and slightly archaic fare – home-baked bread, butter, cheese, dates, nuts and raisins, and wine. The host and hostess would choose some readings, usually from the new Jerusalem Bible, which had 'Yaweh' instead of 'God' in the Old Testament, and then, with some made-up prayer referring to the Last Supper, they would break the bread and pour the wine into a large goblet. These would be passed round the table from person to person, each taking a piece of bread and a swig from the goblet. Then everyone's glass would be filled and the meal would continue with ordinary conversation, serious at first, but getting more lighthearted as the wine flowed.

When Father Brierley came to the city, they naturally invited him to join them at these occasions, and then they would have a Eucharist, but without any vestments or candles, just all sitting round the table as before, with home-made bread and *vin ordinaire*, broken and blessed and handed round, just like at the Last Supper. A certain theological ambiguity hung over these occasions. Was it a real Eucharist, or wasn't it? Outwardly, only the presiding presence of an ordained priest significantly distinguished the event from their improvised agapes. To some, this was a crucial difference, to others it was a relic of the old 'magical' view of the sacraments which they had renounced. In the earliest days of the Church, the commemoration of the Lord's Supper was not restricted to a priesthood, and Austin (as they now called Father Brierley) himself declared that the idea of a special caste exclusively empowered to administer the sacraments was rapidly becoming obsolete. He prophesied a time when the whole elaborate structure of bishops and priests and dioceses and parishes would melt away, house-eucharists would replace the huge anonymous crush of the parochial Sunday mass, and mutual counselling and consciousness-raising groups would replace Confession and Confirmation.

So they stood upon the shores of Faith and felt the old dogmas and certainties ebbing away rapidly under their feet and between their toes, sapping the foundations upon which they stood, a

551

sensation both agreeably stimulating and slightly unnerving. For we all like to believe, do we not, if only in stories? People who find religious belief absurd are often upset if a novelist breaks the illusion of reality he has created. Our friends had started life with too many beliefs – the penalty of a Catholic upbringing. They were weighed down with beliefs, useless answers to non-questions. To work their way back to the fundamental ones – what can we know? why is there anything at all? why not nothing? what may we hope? why are we here? what is it all about? – they had to dismantle all that apparatus of superfluous belief and discard it piece by piece. But in matters of belief (as of literary convention) it is a nice question how far you can go in this process without throwing out something vital.

To the agapes came, on occasion, Edward and Tessa and Angela and Dennis. Tessa found the religious part somewhat embarrassing, especially when the bread was passed round in silence and you could hear the sounds of people munching and swallowing; but that was soon over and then it was quite jolly, with plenty of cheap wine, and perhaps after the food was cleared away some music, even dancing if the spirit moved the group that way – free-form spontaneous dancing to recorded music in the folk-rock idiom, with anyone able to join in and no nonsense about partners. It was almost as good as going out to a real party, which Edward was usually reluctant to do, pleading tiredness and backache. So Tessa always jumped at an invitation to an agape. People dressed informally for these occasions, but since Miriam and her friends favoured long skirts and kaftans to wear about the house anyway, Tessa did not feel overdressed in her long Laura Ashley cotton dresses, which she bought from the original little shop in Shrewsbury. As far as Tessa was concerned, that you didn't have to go to a ball nowadays to wear a long dress, or adjust your dancing style to the limitations of a partner, were the two great social achievements of the nineteen-sixties. (It was by now the nineteen-seventies, but this group of people were having their sixties a little late.)

Though he pretended that Tessa dragged him along to the

agapes, Edward went willingly enough. Since joining Catholics for an Open Church he had been cold-shouldered by his Catholic colleagues in the medical profession – an intensely conservative group in whose collective consciousness the pre-war confrontation between Marie Stopes and Dr Halliday Sutherland still exerted the power of myth. Even if they disagreed privately with *Humanae Vitae*, they saw the pro-contraception lobby as indistinguishable from the pro-abortion and pro-euthanasia lobbies and did not wish to join such undesirable allies in attacking their own religious leaders. Thus Edward found himself pushed, almost involuntarily, into identification with the radical Catholic Underground, though by natural inclination he was far from radical, and at the liturgical gatherings of the Miriam – Michael circle was apt to worry, with a spasm of atavistic superstition, about what happened to the crumbs left over from the bread that Austin had consecrated (or had he?).

And Angela came, as she had come in years gone by to the Thursday masses at Our Lady and St Jude's, because she was invited, because it was obviously a good thing to join with Catholic friends in prayer and fellowship. She had never had much historical sense or any great interest in metaphysical questions; and since the birth of Nicole and the death of Anne she lived more than ever in the present, attending to the tasks immediately to hand. Looking back into the past was too painful, it filled her with a kind of mental nausea. So Angela rarely reflected on the changes that had taken place in the Catholic Church in her lifetime, and was unperturbed by the variety of liturgical practice and doctrinal interpretation that now flourished in it. Whether one prayed in church or in one's living-room seemed unimportant to her, as long as one prayed. It worried her that Dennis no longer seemed to believe in the efficacy of prayer – indeed he seemed to have little faith left at all. She did not discuss the matter with him, partly because they had got out of the habit of discussing serious, abstract questions, and partly because she was afraid of what state of unbelief might be revealed if she pressed him. They had both changed a lot since the birth of Nicole.

When she was told about Nicole's condition, Angela had two quite distinct yet simultaneous reactions, happening, as it were, at different levels of her self. On one level she was shocked and horrified, fought against the truth as long as she could, and, when it could no longer be denied, abandoned herself to grief and self-pity; but on another, deeper level she felt as though she had been waiting all her married life for this, or something like it, to happen. Till now, Dennis had taken all the worries and responsibilities on his shoulders – money, houses, holidays, even the temperature charts – while she had lapsed into a bovine placidity, slowly completing her domestic tasks by day, with a milky-breathed infant invariably in her arms or under her feet, then falling asleep in front of the television in the evenings. It had been a more comfortable and cushioned existence than she had predicted when they were courting, but now Nicole had arrived to confirm her misgivings, and it was almost a relief to know what her cross was to be. When she had cried herself dry, she pulled herself together and resolved to make Nicole the ablest mongol in the land. She read every book on the subject of mental handicap she could lay her hands on, travelled miles to consult specialists, filled the house with educational toys and equipment, joined all the relevant societies, organized playgroups, toy librar-ies, and fund-raising events.

When, two years after Nicole's birth, four-year old Anne ran into the road in pursuit of a runaway doll's pram and was knocked down by a dry-cleaner's van, Angela was sufficiently hardened and tempered psychologically to cope with the crisis. It was Angela who prevented Anne from being moved from the gutter where she had been thrown, who sent for a blanket to keep her warm, and went with her to the hospital in the ambulance, while all Dennis could do was to crouch over his little daughter's crumpled form, swearing frightfully and literally tearing his hair, great tufts of it which blew away from his fingers like thistledown. When Anne died that night in hospital, without regaining con-sciousness, it was Angela who was at her bedside, for Dennis was in shock, under sedation at home. It was Angela who made the necessary arrangements for the funeral and held the family steady through that dreadful time. A great shift of gravity had taken place in the marriage, a transfer of power and will from Dennis to Angela. Anne's death showed it, but Nicole's birth had started it.

To Dennis the diagnosis of Nicole's condition had been a stunning and totally surprising blow. He tried to work out why the possibility of such a thing ever happening had never crossed his mind, and came up with several reasons: Angela's pregnancies had always been quite free from complications, and the first three babies had arrived safe, sound and on time; he had never known anyone who had produced abnormal offspring nor had he had personal contact with any mentally handicapped person in his life. But the more fundamental reason was that he had always subconsciously assumed that he was favoured by Providence, or in secular terms, lucky. There had been setbacks and disappointments in his life, but invariably he had found that if he was patient and industrious the obstacle gave way eventually; and after eight years of marriage he was well pleased with himself and his beautiful wife and bonny children, his new four-bedroomed detached house and company car, his well-paid job as deputy production manager of a prospering electronics firm. As far as he knew, he was earning more than any other man among their college contemporaries, except perhaps Edward, and was fairly confident that before long he would have overtaken him, too. The only significant flaw in his general contentment was the business of birth control, with its attendant frustration and worry, but he was prepared to put up with that – it seemed to be a small price to pay for his other blessings. Because of his upbringing, you see, Dennis could not help crediting his good fortune to God, who was rewarding him for working hard and obeying the rules of the Catholic Church.

The birth of Nicole had rudely upset this simple confidence. Instead of being rewarded, it seemed that he had been punished – but for what? Why me? What have I done to deserve this? was his first thought (it is probably everyone's first thought in misfortune, but those with a religious world-view are especially prone) that wet Sunday afternoon in the garage, as Edward, fiddling with the Black and Decker sander, hesitantly described his misgivings about the child (and for ever after the smell of sawdust was associated in Dennis's mind with bad news, so that when two years later his eldest, Jonathan, rushed into the back garden where he was mowing the lawn and screamed at him to come quickly because Anne had been knocked down in the road, he smelled not grass but sawdust, and felt sick). To Dennis, Nicole's condition was not like the other setbacks in his life, something that might pass away or be overcome; it was fixed and irrevocable, as unalterable as chemistry. People they spoke to about mongolism – Downs' Syndrome, as Angela insisted on referring to it – tried to be encouraging: these children were happy, loveable people, they were often good at music, some had even learned to read. But none of this was any comfort to Dennis. His daughter had been defective from the moment of conception, nothing could undo the effect of that extra chromosome at the primal collision of sperm and egg. Nothing except death. In the early days, Dennis wished very much that the child would die, which naturally increased his sense of guilt – indeed, explained to him why he was being punished, since anyone capable of such murderous feelings obviously deserved to be punished.

Outwardly Dennis seemed to share Angela's determination to make the best of things. He cooperated in the training programme for Nicole – played with her, exercised her, talked to the other children about her, read the literature that Angela brought home and attended some of the public meetings, committees and fundraising events for the mentally handicapped that she was involved in. But it all seemed to him a vain and futile effort to pretend that the tragedy had not happened, that life could resume its former promise. When he came home from work on her first birthday to find her propped up in her high chair, a lopsided paper hat on her head bearing the legend, '*Downs Babies Rule OK*', obviously the work of her older brothers, it seemed to Dennis like a sick joke, an unconscious expression of resentment, not, as Angela obviously felt, a sign of their acceptance of the child, and he had to struggle to raise a smile.

Nicole's birthdays were always bad days, but after that first one things became a little easier. The little girl began to show that she had a distinctive personality of her own, and she was infatuated with her father, exhibiting signs of excitement and delight as soon as Dennis came in sight. It was impossible to resist such utterly innocent affection. Then Dennis began to realize how many handicapped people there were, most of them much more pathetic cases than Nicole. Through personal contact, anecdote, visits to schools and clinics, watching television programmes he would formerly have avoided, Dennis became aware of a whole world of suffering at the extent of which he had never guessed: children horribly afflicted physically and mentally, by brain damage, spina bifida, hydrocephalus, rubella, epilepsy, muscular dystrophy, cerebral palsy, autism and God knew what else; children suffering from multiple handicap, children doubly incontinent, children so hopelessly paralysed that they would live their whole lives on stretchers, children with cleft palates and deformed bodies and scarcely human faces. Dennis began to feel that perhaps he was lucky after all. He no longer automatically compared Nicole with normal children, but with children more crippled and retarded. His child became for him a lens with which to see more clearly the real vulnerability of human life, and also a talisman against further hurt. He began to feel that he did not need the pity and sympathy of his friends with normal children – it was they that deserved pity, for they had not yet felt the blow of fate that opened a man's eyes to the true nature of things. He had nothing more to fear. He had, as the Americans put it, paid his dues.

Then Anne was run over and killed and Dennis gave up. He could see no sense at all in the pattern of his life. The idea of a personal God with an interest in his, Dennis's, personal fortune, became impossible to maintain, unless he was a God who took a personal interest in torturing people. For while Dennis was able to see that there was some meaning, some positive moral gain, in the experience of having Nicole, he could see no point whatsoever in losing Anne, nothing except sterile anguish and futile self-reproach. Perhaps the bitterest, most heart-rending aspect of the whole ghastly business was the impossibility of explaining to Nicole what had happened to Anne. ('Where Anne?' Nicole would say for years afterwards, turning up at their bedside in the middle of the night, tugging gently at Dennis's pyjama sleeve, 'Where Anne?') If one thing was certain it was that Nicole had done nothing to deserve having Anne taken away from her, and would gain nothing from the experience.

Dennis continued going to mass, for the sake of the family, for the sake of a quiet life, but it had no meaning for him. Nothing had, except small, simple pleasures – a glass of beer at the local, a soccer game on TV – handholds by which he kept moving from hour to hour, from day to day. He worked excessively hard at his job to occupy his mind and tire himself out, staying behind at the office long after everyone else had left and often going in on Saturday mornings to the silent, empty factory. Sunday was the worst day of the week because there were so many hours to fill once they had all got back from church.

When Michael and Miriam invited them to an agape, Dennis found an excuse not to go, and Angela went on her own; but intrigued by her account of the proceedings, he accompanied her on subsequent occasions and derived some entertainment, if not spiritual renewal, from these packed, intense gatherings. It amused him to listen to the conversation, to observe the wildly Utopian ideas that blossomed and bloomed recklessly in the hot-house atmosphere, and to interrupt, with a dry question or two, some confident dismissal of, say, industrial capitalism, by a young lecturer in, say, the philosophy of education, who had never put his nose inside a factory, and whose training and salary ultimately derived from wealth generated by industrial capitalism. Dennis posed his questions mildly and without animus, for he had no ideological commitment to industrial capitalism either – he just couldn't see that there was a better alternative available, certainly not the models currently on offer from Russia or China, where most of these innocent Christian radicals would have withered away in labour camps long ago if they had had the misfortune to live there. It was the same with questions of religion: he couldn't understand why they made such a fuss about what they called the authoritarian structure of the Church, why they worked themselves up into furious anger about the conservatism, paternalism, dogmatism of this or that bishop or parish priest. He could see that it would matter to Austin Brierley – after all, it was his job – and with Austin he sympathized; but he couldn't see why the others didn't just leave the Church if they found being in it so irksome.

'But why should *we* leave, Dennis?' they cried. 'It's just as much our Church as theirs.'

'But just as much theirs as yours,' he pointed out. 'Why not live and let live? Everybody do their own thing. Latin masses and novenas for the old-fashioned, and this sort of thing – ' he gestured at the table, the wholemeal crusts, the empty wine-glasses, the big Jerusalem Bible – 'for the avant-garde.'

'Oh, Dennis!' they said, laughing and shaking their heads. 'You're such a cynic. If the Church doesn't renew itself totally, it'll just fall apart in the next fifty years.'

'It seems to be falling apart already, to me,' he said.

So Dennis became a kind of court jester, a licensed cynic, to the group. They recognized that his commonsense was a useful check, or at least foil, to their radicalism, and were apt to glance slyly, almost flirtatiously at him when making some particularly extreme remark. It helped him to play this role that he had aged in appearance more than his contemporaries. His hair was thin and grizzled, his face lined and jowly, and he had a paunch. He smoked thirty cigarettes a day, and when people commented on this said, with a shrug, who wants to live for ever?

Angela was still capable of turning heads when, rarely, she took some trouble over her appearance, but her body had thickened, she suffered from varicose veins and her brows were drawn together in a perpetual frown. When Nicole was four she got her into nursery school and herself began to train as a teacher of the educationally sub-normal, not with any serious intention of getting a job, but in order to learn how best to help Nicole's development. The college was some twenty miles away and their domestic life became one of great logistic complexity, involving the use of two cars and the cooperation of sundry baby-sitters, child-minders and cleaning ladies. They drove fast and rather recklessly along the country lanes around their dormitory village, frequently scraping and denting their vehicles. Angela kept up with her voluntary activities and was frequently going out again when Dennis returned late from work. Once or twice a week, perhaps, if they happened to go to bed at the same time, and Angela was not feeling too tired, they would make love.

It is difficult to do justice to ordinary married sex in a novel. There are too many acts for them all to be described, and usually no particular reason to describe one act rather than another; so the novelist falls back on summary, which sounds dismissive. As a contemporary French critic has pointed out in a treatise on narrative, a novelist can (*a*) narrate once what happened once or (*b*) narrate *n* times what happened once or (*c*) narrate *n* times what happened *n* times or (*d*) narrate once what happened *n* times. Seductions, rapes, the taking of new lovers or the breaking of old taboos, are usually narrated according to (*a*), (*b*) or (*c*). Married love in fiction tends to be narrated according to mode (*d*). *Once or twice a week, perhaps, if they happened to go to bed together at the same time, and Angela was not feeling too tired, they would make love.* Which is not to say that this was an unimportant part of their married life. Without its solace the marriage would probably have broken down under the successive crises of Nicole and Anne. But they themselves could hardly distinguish in memory one occasion of lovemaking from another. Over the years they had composed an almost unvarying ritual of arousal and release which both knew by heart. Their foreplay was a condensed version of their courtship: first Dennis kissed Angela, then he pushed his tongue between her teeth, then he stroked her breasts, then he slid his hand up between her thighs. They usually reached a reasonably satisfying climax, and afterwards fell into a deep sleep, which did them both good. By the next morning they retained only a vague memory of the previous night's pleasure.

It was much the same for most of the other couples. Now that they were using birth control, the sexual act had become a more frequent and, inevitably, more routine activity. For they did not take lovers or have casual copulations with strangers met at parties, or in hotels, or in aeroplanes – the kind of thing they read about in novels (even novels by Catholics) and saw in films and on television. Their sex lives were less dramatic, more habitual, and most of them, especially the men, worried about this occasionally. It was true that there was more sex in their lives than there had been – but was it as much as it ought to be? They had lost the fear of Hell, and staked their claim to erotic fulfilment, but had they left it too late? All of them were nearing the age of forty, they had spent more years on earth after leaving University than before going up, they were approaching – perhaps they had already reached – that hump in man's lifespan after which it is downhill all the way. Death beckoned, however distantly. Their bodies began to exhibit small but unmistakable signs of decay and disrepair: spreading gut, veined legs, failing sight, falling hair, receding gums, missing teeth. The men were aware that their sexual vigour was in decline – indeed it seemed, according to some of the many articles on the subject that began to flood the public prints in the early seventies, that their sexual vigour had begun to decline long before they had ever exercised it, the male's maximum potency occurring in the years from sixteen to twenty-three. Premature ejaculation, which had afflicted most of them in early married life, was no longer a problem; indeed, it could be a matter of some anxiety whether, after a few drinks or several nights' lovemaking on the trot, one could ejaculate at all. As for the women, well, according to the same sources of information, their capacity for sexual pleasure was reaching its peak, but they were all well aware that the capacity of their bodies for arousing desire was rapidly diminishing. Making love with the light on was a calculated risk, unless it was very carefully shaded. Meanwhile, their older children were passing into puberty and adolescence and, stripped for the beach, reminded their parents more forcibly with each passing year of the physical lustre they had themselves lost (or perhaps never had).

The permutations of sex are as finite as those of narrative. You can (a) do one thing with one partner or (b) do n things with one partner or (c) do one thing with n partners or (d) do n things with n partners. For practising Catholics faithful to the marriage

561

bond, there was only the possibility of progressing from (*a*) to (*b*) in search of a richer sex life.

Michael became an addict of sex instruction films, of which there was a spate in the early seventies, mostly produced in Germany and Scandinavia, ostensibly because he was going to write an article about them, in fact because he enjoyed watching even the most clumsily simulated sexual intercourse, and was prepared to sit patiently through long, tedious conversations between white-coated doctors and bashful clients, and voice-over lectures illustrated by coloured diagrams reminiscent of evening class instruction in motor maintenance, for the sake of a few minutes' practical demonstration by a reasonably handsome nude couple in full colour. Michael, with his literary education, was the least willing of all our male characters to admit that sex might become just a comfortable habit. He wanted every act to burn with a lyric intensity, and it was as if he thought that by studying it on the screen he might learn the knack of being simultaneously inside and outside his own orgasms, enjoying and appraising, oblivious and remembering. There was also the opportunity to master through these films the repertoire of postural variation by which married love might, the white coats assured him, be given a new zest, if one's partner were willing to cooperate, which Miriam was not, alas; until one evening when he coaxed her into accompanying him to one of the seedy downtown cinemas that specialized in such films, and she said, afterwards, thoughtfully, as they walked to the bus stop, 'I wouldn't mind trying one or two of those things,' and he leaped ecstatically into the road, shouting 'Taxi! Taxi!' Well, that had been a memorable night, to be sure, and for the next few weeks it was like a second honeymoon between them, and much more satisfying than the first. He went about his work in an erotic trance, hollow-eyed with sexual excess, his mind wandering in seminars and committees as he planned what variations they would experiment with at night. But it was not long before they had to settle between them the old question of how far you could go. In due course their erotic life became as habitual as before, if more subtly textured.

It seemed to Michael that he was no nearer grasping the fundamental mystery of sex, of knowing for certain that he had experienced its ultimate ecstasy, than he had been twenty years before, staring at the nudes in the Charing Cross Road bookshops. Then he began to shit blood and quickly lost interest in sex altogether.

Adrian sent away for an illustrated book on sexual intercourse, delivered under plain cover, which showed forty-seven positions in which coitus could be contrived. He tried to run through them all in one night, but Dorothy fell asleep on number thirteen. When he woke her up to ask which position she had found the most satisfying, she yawned and said, 'I think the first one, Adie.'

'You mean the missionary position?' he said, disappointedly. 'But that's what we always do.'

'Well, I don't really mind. Which do you like best, Adie?'

'Oh, I like the missionary position best, too,' said Adrian. 'It just seems rather unenterprising to do the same thing night after night.'

'Why do they call it that?'

The explanation tickled Dorothy, and afterwards, when Adrian heaved himself on top of her, she would sometimes chuckle and say, 'What are you doing, you dirty old missionary, you?'

Edward and Tessa experimented with positions not so much for the sake of erotic variety as to ease the strain on Edward's back. They found that the most satisfactory arrangement was for Edward to lie supine and for Tessa to squat on top of him, jigging up and down until she brought them both to climax. At first Edward found this very exciting, but the passivity of his own role in the proceedings worried him, and he frightened himself sometimes with the thought that one day he might be incapable of even this style of copulation.

Tessa herself was in a constant fever of vague sexual longing to which she dared not give definition. Her body sent messages which her mind refused to accept. Her body said: you are bored with this clumsy form of intercourse, you want to lie back and close your eyes and be possessed by a strong male force for a change, your body is a garden of unawakened pleasures and time is running out. Her mind said: nonsense, you are a happily married woman with four fine, healthy children and a good, kind, faithful husband. Count your blessings and find something to occupy yourself now that the children are growing up. So Tessa joined keep-fit classes and a tennis club. But the physical well-being that accrued only fuelled the fires of her libido. She exulted in the power and grace of her movements across the court or in the gym. In the changing-rooms afterwards she followed the example of the younger women who walked unconcernedly naked from their lockers to the communal shower heads, while the older and less shapely ones waited timidly for the curtained cubicles to become free. The full-length mirrors on the walls reassured her that her body could stand such exposure. From this exercise she returned home, glowing euphorically, to a jaded and weary spouse. Her body said: it would be nice to fuck. Her mind, deaf to the indelicacy, said: he's tired, he was called out last night, his back is paining him.

Tessa, in short, was classically ripe for having an affair, and in another milieu, or novel, might well have had one. Instead, she bought lots of clothes and changed more times a day than was strictly necessary, collected cookbooks and experimented with complicated recipes, read novels from the library about mature, sensitive women having affairs, and enrolled in the Open University.

In spite of his sardonic remarks about campus permissiveness, Robin was fully conversant with the new polymorphous sexuality from his barbershop reading in *Playboy* and *Penthouse*, and anxious to try a few things himself. In this regard he found Violet suprisingly compliant, though unenthusiastic. In her perverse way she had decided that since she was in a state of mortal sin anyway by taking the Pill, it mattered little what else she did in the sexual line – that her best course of action was to let Robin burn out his lust and then repent everything at one go. Robin, for his part, found the listless, whorish impassivity with which she accommodated herself to his whims disconcerting, and it was as difficult as ever to bring her to a climax by penetration, whatever attitude they assumed. He quickly tired of sexual acrobatics. If he was honest, what he enjoyed most was a slow hand-job performed by Violet while he lay back with his eyes closed and listened to Baroque music on a headset. Violet herself was most readily satisfied by lingual stimulation, and gradually this arrangement became customary, each taking turns to service the other. 'If we're just going to do this,' Robin pointed out one night, 'there's no need for you to take the Pill.' 'If I wasn't on the Pill, I wouldn't be doing it,' she replied. 'You're crazy,' he said. 'Tell me something new,' she said.

When Felicity started school, Violet tried to get herself a teaching job, but without success. She lacked a postgraduate certificate, and there was no great demand for women classics teachers. So to occupy herself, she signed on at the local art college to study sculpture. This increased their circle of friends, though Robin did not care for the art college crowd (or their art). Almost every weekend there was a party invitation deriving either from the University or the College. For Violet was socially in demand. She fascinated people, as she had fascinated Robin, by her behavioural volatility. Party hosts invited her because she brought a whiff of dangerous irresponsibility into their rooms, without which no party was truly successful, not the parties of that time and place anyway. Violet rarely disappointed them. Being more or less permanently on Librium or Valium, she was not supposed to drink alcohol, but when she arrived at the house, wherever it was, thrumming from cellar to attic with the bass notes of heavy rock and thronged with people chatting and eyeing each other in dimly lit rooms, she felt herself shaking with excitement and social terror and was unable to resist the offer of a glass of wine. Before long she would get intoxicated, and make a set at this or that man, dragging him on to the dance floor, where she would either attempt to shake herself to pieces in frenzied jiving or, draped amorously round his neck, twitch negligently to the beat of some languorous soul ballad. Occasionally she would disappear with her partner into the dark recesses of the house or garden and allow him to grope her while they kissed with open mouths – sometimes, if she was feeling very abandoned, groping him back, but never allowing proper sex. The men she led on in this way sometimes turned nasty, but she usually had some ready lie to get herself out of the tightest corner: it was her period, she was pregnant and fearful of a miscarriage, she had cystitis, she had forgotten to take her pill. . . . Then the man, with good or ill grace, would desist, and having adjusted their dress, they would return to the party as nonchalantly as they could manage, and studiously ignore each other for the rest of the evening, commencing new flirtations in due course. At about two o'clock in the morning Violet would nearly, or actually, pass out from drink or exhaustion, and Robin would take her home, stumbling over other supine bodies in the hall and perhaps the front garden, and put her to bed. The next day she would drag herself off to mass with Felicity, speechless with hangover and guilt; but the next time they got an invitation to such a party, and Robin tried to refuse it, she would accuse him of being snobbish and of trying to deprive her of a normal social life. He did not know what to do. Sometimes he even thought of writing to Ann Field.

Polly wasn't Ann Field any more. Now she wrote a weekly column under her own name on the women's page of a quality newspaper, a column in which radical and progressive ideas were put forward in a subtly ironic style that undermined them even as it expressed them, an effect which perfectly suited the paper's readership, mostly middle-class professionals and their wives, with leftish views and bad consciences about their affluent life-styles.

Polly herself, who had been an early apostle of the sexual revolution, was beginning to wonder whether things hadn't gone too far. She had of course been happily doing n things with Jeremy for years, but when he showed signs of wanting to do them with n partners, she jibbed. They received an invitation to a swinging party at a country house owned by a film producer Jeremy knew; he pressed her to go, and sulked when she refused. Anxiously she strove to show more gusto in their lovemaking, proposing games and variations that she knew he liked, though she herself found them a little tedious, bondage and dressing up in kinky clothes and acting out little scenarios – The Massage Parlour, The Call Girl, and Blue Lagoon. These efforts diverted Jeremy for a while, but eventually he began pressing her again about going to swinging parties.

'Why do you want to go?' she said.

'I'm just curious.'

'You want to have another woman.'

He shrugged. 'All right, perhaps I do. But I don't want to do it behind your back.'

'Why do you want to? Don't we have fun in bed?'

'Of course we do, darling. But let's face it, we've been right through the book together, there's nothing new we can do, just the two of us. It's time to introduce another element. You know, sometimes when we're fucking, my mind wanders completely off the subject, I find myself thinking about shooting schedules or audience ratings. That worries me. And you needn't look at me like that. It's nothing personal. It's the nature of the beast.'

'Beast is the word.' Polly felt a cold dread at her heart. Was it possible that the flame of sex could be kept burning only by the breaking of more taboos? After group sex and orgies, what then? Rubber fetishism? Fladge? Child porn? Snuff movies? 'Where does it end?' she said.

'It ends with old age,' said Jeremy. 'Impotence. Death. But I don't intend to give in until I absolutely have to.'

'You don't think there's anything after death?'

'You know I don't.'

'I do.'

'That's just your Catholic upbringing.'

'I don't know what's more frightening, the idea that there's life after death or the idea that there isn't,' said Polly. She thought about death a lot these days – had done so ever since her father died the previous winter. It was a sudden death, a heart attack brought on by shovelling snow. She and Jeremy were skiing in Austria at the time and she was delayed getting back to England by blizzards, arriving barely in time for the funeral. So she never saw her father dead, and in consequence was never quite able to believe that he *was* dead; it was as if he had faded away like the Cheshire Cat, leaving the memory of him, his chuckle, the smell of his pipe tobacco, lingering in the mind, and might rematerialize when one least expected it. Polly decided to make death the subject of her next article, and cheered up immediately. That was in the summer of 1973.

How they dealt with love and death

Michael read Polly's article about death on the train to London, travelling to an appointment with a consultant specializing in disorders of the intestine. After weeks of mute terror contemplating the daily evidence of the toilet bowl, he had confided in Edward, who claimed to have been at college with the best gut man in the business, and fixed up the consultation for him. Michael did not know that the article was written by someone *he* had been at college with, because Polly used her married name for her by-line, and because the fuzzy, minuscule photo of her that appeared beside it, all tousled bubble-cut and outsize spectacles, did not resemble the Polly he remembered, and because it never crossed his mind that the Polly he remembered could have achieved such fame.

Michael usually looked forward to Polly Elton's column every Wednesday, but her choice of topic was unwelcome this particular morning, already sufficiently replete with reminders of mortality. It had begun with his collecting a specimen of his own stool, which he had been instructed to bring with him for analysis, in a small plastic container supplied by Edward. This container, which looked rather like the kind you bought ice-cream in at the cinema, and even came supplied with a little wooden spatula (the whole exercise had had a distinctly Dadaist quality) now reposed, wrapped in a plastic bag, at the bottom of his briefcase on the seat beside him.

Usually, Michael looked forward to one of his occasional trips to London as a little holiday, a day off the leash, a minor feast of misrule. The best kind of errand was a meeting with one's editor (Michael's volume of essays, *Moving the Times: Religion and Culture in the Global Village*, had received respectful, if sparse, reviews, and the publishers had commissioned him to write a textbook on the mass media for the growing 'liberal studies' market) followed by a long expense-account lunch in a Soho restaurant, with plenty of booze before, during and after. Then it was pleasant, stumbling sated and tipsy out of the restaurant in mid-afternoon, and bidding farewell to one's host, to slip into the stream of London pavement life, drift anonymously with the idle, unemployed, sightseeing, windowshopping crowd, eye the goods and the girls, browse in the record shops, buy remaindered books in Charing Cross Road, and then rest one's feet watching the latest sex-instruction film, before catching the early evening train back to the Midlands. But travelling to the metropolis with a lump of your own shit in your briefcase took all the zest out of the excursion; you could hardly look forward to a day of irresponsible self-indulgence while inhaling the reek of your own corruption – for, unless he was very much mistaken, the container was exuding a distinct niff, in spite of its allegedly air-tight lid. What with that, and the prospect of a painful and undignified rectal examination at the hospital, and the constant obsessive fear of being told that he had cancer of the bowel, the last thing he needed that morning was a lay sermon by Polly Elton on the subject of death. '*Is Death The Dirty Little Secret Of The Permissive Society?*' the article was headed. Restively, he let the paper fall to his lap, and observed with some surprise that the seats around him, nearly full when he boarded the train, were now empty. He opened the briefcase experimentally, and hastily closed it again. The dirty little secret of the permissive society was right there.

It was a warm day, and the smell got worse and worse as his journey proceeded. He crossed London feeling like a leper. In the crowded Tube fellow-passengers quickly cleared a *cordon sanitaire* round him. People on the platform where he changed trains began frowningly to inspect the soles of their shoes. Having time to kill before his appointment, he sat for a while in a square in Bloomsbury, with his briefcase on the bench beside him, and it seemed as though the very pigeons strutting on the path veered away from his poisoned ambience. A madman or drunk in a ragged overcoat, hair matted, eyes wild, sat down beside him and thrust under his nose a magazine open on coloured photographs of naked girls with their legs apart. 'Disgusting, that's what I say!' he shouted. 'Filthy cunts, showing off their cunts like that, there should be a law.' He brought his whiskered face confidentially close to Michael's and leered, revealing a few yellow stumps. His breath stank like a lion-house. 'You know what I'd like to do to teach those cunts a lesson?' he said. 'I'd – ' Then the smell from Michael's briefcase hit him, and his head jerked back. He wiped his nose on the back of his sleeve, sniffed incredulously, and shuffled off, muttering to himself.

The man had left the magazine behind, and Michael leafed through it. His professional eye noted the trend towards masturbation poses in the pictures, pseudo-documentary in the stories. He skimmed an article on the pornographic movie industry in California. '*Standby studs are often used for penetration shots*,' he read. Would have been the job for me once, he thought with rueful irony, remembering how he used to walk about London with an almost permanent erection. Now he clung to Miriam in bed more like a child than a lover, nuzzled and caressed her like a baby wanting to crawl back into the womb, his penis limp and discouraged. 'What's the matter?' she would say. 'D'you want to make love?' 'No, I don't feel like it. I'm worried about my guts.' 'See a doctor then.' 'Maybe. I'll see. Just let me hold you. It helps me get to sleep.' But Miriam had got tired of being treated like a dummy or doll and threatened to move into another room if he didn't get some advice from Edward. Which had brought him to this square in Bloomsbury.

He stood up and tossed the magazine into a litter basket, strongly tempted to do the same with the contents of his briefcase. What would it be like to be told you had a terminal illness, he wondered. Not that he expected to get a definite diagnosis this afternoon, but the impending appointment at the hospital concentrated the mind wonderfully on such questions. Would it make the idea of death any more real? Odd how, though one knew one

571

was going to die eventually, one never *quite* believed it. Impossible to believe, for that matter, that all these people in the square (it was the end of the lunch-hour and the paths were crowded) would all be dead sooner or later. If there were ten million people in London, all of them dying sooner or later, how was it you hardly ever noticed them doing so, how was it they weren't falling dead in the streets, jamming the roads with their funerals, darkening the sky with the smoke of their cremations? Holding the briefcase well away from his side, he set out for the hospital.

The people he asked for directions in the labyrinthine corridors of the vast building did not linger to give them with any great detail, and it was some time before Michael found the Pathology Lab and handed over his noisome package to a beautiful blonde laboratory assistant whose courteous smile collapsed into an expression of uncontrollable dismay as she took it between an exquisitely manicured finger and thumb. Sorry, he wanted to say, sorry my shit smells so awful, sorry you've got to have anything to do with it, but I've come a long way and its been fermenting in my briefcase for hours. As he fled, it crossed his mind that perhaps the whole errand was a practical joke by Edward, that no one in his right mind would try and carry a tub of fresh faeces a hundred and thirty miles across England by Inter-City and London Transport, unless it was hermetically sealed. Perhaps the whole thing was a hoax. Perhaps there wasn't even a consultant.

But there was, though Michael had to wait a long time to see him: a plump, cheerful man, very carefully shaven, who was reassuring, diagnosed colitis, was confident of clearing it up with cortisone and a diet. Michael felt life and hope flowing back into him; he left the hospital in a carefree, happy mood, stood on the pavement outside blinking in the sunshine, rejoining the living.

He was in the vicinity of his old college. The buildings had scarcely changed, but the students going in and out of them looked very different: hairy, denimed and with more experienced-looking faces. A girl passed Michael with a teeshirt bearing the legend 'I AM A VIRGO (This is a very old teeshirt)'. Like many of the girls, she was not wearing a brassiere, a new fashion still rarely to be seen in the provinces. Earth has hardly anything to show more fair, Michael reflected, than a fine pair of tits oscillating freely under clinging cotton jersey. With delight, he realized that he was interested in sex again, and began to make plans for a celebration with Miriam that night.

On his way to the Tube, he called in at the bookshop which he had patronized as a student, to check whether they had *Moving the Times* in stock. The shop had vastly expanded its floor space, and he had some difficulty in locating the appropriate section, reluctant to ask for help in case he had to buy a copy of his own book or reveal the narcissistic nature of his interest in it. At last he found two copies on a high shelf in Sociology, and as he took one down a familiar voice behind him said: 'Michael! As I live and breathe.'

With a guilty start, he turned to find Polly smiling at him through outsize spectacles.

'Polly!' he said. 'Good Lord, you're Polly Elton!'

'That's right. Do you read me? How nice! Have I caught you gloating over your own book? Actually, I thought it was awfully good, so did Jeremy, that's my husband, you ought to meet him, he's in television.'

'Jeremy Elton – yes, I know his work. Very good.' (This was not strictly true. Michael did not think Jeremy Elton's programmes were particularly good; but then, neither did Jeremy think much of Michael's book. 'Academic claptrap,' had been his verdict when Polly passed it to him.)

'It's so good to see you after all these years,' said Polly. 'Let me pay for these and then let's have a drink or something.' She was carrying a large pile of books by Kate Millett, Germaine Greer and other feminist writers. 'I decided it was time I really got to grips with the women's movement,' she said, plonking the books down on the table in the wine bar where they ended up. 'I always used to say that I didn't need Women's Lib because I was liberated already, but now I'm not so sure. Does, er, I've forgotten your wife's name. . . .'

'Miriam? She's interested, but the pro-abortion thing puts her off.'

'Ah, yes,' said Polly. 'You're still practising Catholics, then?'

'I suppose,' said Michael. 'What about you?'

'Oh, I'm beyond the pale. Jeremy's divorced, for one thing.'

'Well, that needn't make any difference these days.'

'Really? You mean the Church accepts divorced couples?'

'Well, not officially. But if you don't make an issue of it, the chances are your PP won't either.'

'Goodness, things must have changed a lot in the One, Holy, Catholic and Apostolic Church.'

'They have.'

'I ought to write a piece about it,' Polly mused.

They split a bottle of Liebfraumilch between them before they separated, kissing each other on both cheeks and promising to keep in touch. 'You and Miriam must come and stay one weekend,' said Polly. Michael said that they would love to, if they could find someone to look after the children. 'Bring them, bring them!' cried Polly. 'We have ponies and things to amuse them.' She managed to say this without appearing to show off, but she had obviously made it, Michael reflected, into a world not only of affluence but also of smartness, sophistication, cultural chic. She looked surprisingly good, too: still plump, but shapely, her complexion creamy, her curls lustrous, her clothes smart and new but obviously not 'best'. Her blouse was open at the throat just one button more than was strictly necessary, one button more than Miriam would have left unfastened.

As the effect of the Liebfraumilch evaporated on the journey home, Michael's spirits drooped. Polly had made him feel threadbare and provincial, awakening in him appetites so long and deeply repressed that he was surprised at the fierceness of the pangs: a longing for fame, success, worldly goods. The life he and Miriam had made for themselves seemed suddenly drab and petty: the earnest discussion groups, the cosy liturgies, the food cooperatives and the sponsored walks for Oxfam and its Catholic equivalent, CAFOD. What did it amount to, after all? What trace did it leave on the public consciousness?

Catching sight of his face reflected in the train window, as the sky darkened in the east, blurred and distorted and looking like a disappointed pig, he cut short this sulky stream of consciousness and delivered a self-reprimand: how fickle you are! This morning all you wanted was a clean bill of health, but no sooner do you get it than you're dissatisfied again. You should be celebrating your reprieve, not bemoaning your lot.

For a joke, and also to excite himself, Michael phoned Miriam from the station and told her to have her knickers off when he got home. She did not seem amused. Sounds of riotous children chasing each other up and down the stairs dinned in the background. 'We've got Angela's children for the night,' she explained. 'Her father's been taken ill and she's driving up to Liverpool. Dennis is away on business.' When Michael got home he found Miriam tired and harassed. Angela's Nicole was disturbed by the sudden disappearance of her mother and clung to Miriam. She wouldn't settle to sleep until they took her into their bedroom, so there was no lovemaking after all that night.

Before he retired, Michael phoned Edward to tell him what the consultant had said.

'Jolly good,' said Edward. 'And did you remember to take the specimen?'

'Yes,' said Michael. 'Didn't half make me unpopular on the train, too.'

'Why, how much did you take?'

'Well, I more or less filled the container.' At the other end of the line Edward spluttered and snorted. 'Why, how much should I have taken?'

'Just enough to cover the end of the spatula.'

'Bloody hell,' said Michael. 'Now you tell me.'

Angela's father had been admitted to hospital complaining of pains in his back and chest. The doctors made various tests and X-rays and told him it was bronchitis. They told his wife that it was lung cancer, advanced and inoperable. Hence the distraught phone call which had brought Angela rushing up the M6. She found a melancholy family council gathered in the little parlour behind the shop: her mother, two sisters and two brothers, including Tom, now a curate in a parish on the other side of the city.

Their Dad would be coming home the next day and they would have to look after him until he was too ill to stay out of hospital. The question was, should he be told?

'How long . . .?' somebody wondered. The doctor hadn't been specific. A matter of months rather than weeks. One could never be sure. 'Who would tell him?' 'I couldn't, I just couldn't,' said their mother, and wept. 'I would,' said Angela, 'if we agreed that was the right thing to do.' 'Why tell him?' said the youngest sister. 'It would just be cruel.' 'But if he asks . . .' said another. 'Are you going to lie to your own Dad?'

It seemed to Angela that they weren't getting anywhere. She glanced interrogatively at Tom, whose calling seemed to establish him as the natural decision-maker in the circumstances; though you wouldn't have guessed he was a priest, she thought, sitting there in his corduroy slacks and a sweater. Like most priests these days, he seldom wore the dog-collar and black suit, and it was surprising what a difference it made. He could have been an ordinary man, home from work, tired, discouraged, uncertain what to do in the crisis. 'What do you think, Tom?' she said.

Tom lit a cigarette and blew smoke from his nostrils. A grey haze from previous cigarettes hung in the air. All the men in the family were heavy smokers, perhaps because cigarettes had always been readily available from the shop. No reference was made by anyone to this as the likely cause of their father's disease.

'I see no reason to tell Dad yet,' Tom said at length. 'We should try to keep him as cheerful as possible.'

Their mother looked at Tom gratefully, but fearfully. 'But he must have time to . . . receive the last . . . sacraments and everything,' she faltered.

'Of course, Mam, but there's no need to rush these things. Let's make him as happy as we can for the rest of his days.'

It was their father's habit to walk the dog around the block last thing at night. Tom offered to perform this task, and Angela said she would keep him company. Together they trod the worn, familiar pavements, while ahead of them Spot darted eagerly from lamp-post to lamp-post, adding his mite to the city's pollution.

Every time Angela came home, the district seemed uglier, grimier, more dejected.

'Mam was pleased with your advice, Tom,' she said. 'But I was a bit surprised. I thought you'd say Dad had a right to know.'

'Of course he has – eventually,' said Tom. 'But there's no hurry.'

'As long as we don't leave it too late,' said Angela, 'so that he's too weak and drugged to take it in . . .'

Tom looked at her sharply. 'I do believe you positively want to tell him.'

'Of course I don't, I mean I wish there was nothing to tell, I think it's awful, just when he was thinking of retiring, too . . . but, well, we're supposed to be Christians, aren't we?'

'Certainly,' he said drily.

'Well, doesn't that mean we shouldn't be afraid of, well, death?'

'That's easily said.'

'I know it's not easy at all, but, well, some friends of Miriam's – you remember Miriam and Michael, at our wedding? Some friends of theirs, Catholics, we met them at Miriam's, well, his mother died recently, some kind of cancer, she knew she had it, so did the family, including the grandchildren, they discussed it quite openly, adults and children together. The old lady didn't want to die in hospital so they kept her at home till the end. On the day she died, she said goodbye to them all, she knew she was going. "I'll be glad to go," she said, "I've had a good life, but I'm old and I'm tired. Don't you go getting upset, now." And after she died, the family went downstairs and got out some bottles of wine and had a sort of party. Don't you think that's absolutely fantastic?' Angela found that tears were streaming down her cheeks.

'No, I'm afraid I don't,' said Tom. 'I think it's rather affected, if you really want to know.' Then, seeing that she was hurt, he added, 'I'm sorry, Angela. The news about Dad has upset me.'

Angela blew her nose and acknowledged the apology with a sniff. A little further on, Tom stopped under a wall covered with aerosol graffiti to light a cigarette. Without looking at her, he said: 'I think I'd better tell you something. I've applied to be laicized.'

'What? Why?' Angela was stunned.

'I want to get married.'

'Married? Who to?'

'A girl called Rosemary. I was giving her instructions, and we fell in love.'

'In love?' she repeated stupidly.

'Yes, it does happen, you know. Happened to you, didn't it?'

'A long time ago,' said Angela. 'When I was very young.'

'Yes, well, in those days I was locked up in a seminary, and hadn't the opportunity.' His voice had an edge to it.

'Have you told our Mam? Or Dad?'

'No. And now, I can't, do you see? I'll just have to hang on and keep up appearances until. . . .'

Spot padded back towards them and stopped, legs splayed, ears cocked enquiringly. How nice, Angela thought, to be a dumb unthinking animal. 'Tell me,' she said, 'are you leaving the Church as well as the priesthood?'

'Why should I?'

'You still believe, then?'

'Oh yes, I believe. Not as much as I used to, admittedly. And not as fervently as they do – ' With a smile he indicated the graffiti. Angela read half-comprehendingly: '*Jesus saves – and Keegan Scores on the Rebound*' – '*Steve Heighway Walks On Water.*' Tom said: 'You know they call football "the religion" up here. It's more popular than Christianity, that's for sure.'

'What about your vows, then?' Angela said.

Tom looked annoyed. 'I don't regard them as binding. I was too young and too naive to know what I was doing.'

Angela grunted and resumed walking, her hands thrust into the pockets of her raincoat.

'I assure you, Angela, that if I could continue to be a priest and a married man, I would.'

'Have you slept with this Rosemary?'

He turned upon her fiercely. 'What do you take me for?'

578

'I take you for a great big booby, since you ask. What makes you think sex is so marvellous?'

He gripped her arm, hard enough to hurt. 'I'm not marrying for sex, Angela, difficult as you and everyone else no doubt may find it to believe. I'm marrying for love, for total commitment to another human being. Have you any idea of the intolerable loneliness of a priest's life?'

'Have you any idea of the intolerable things that can happen in married life?'

He relaxed his grip. 'I know you've had a lot to bear.'

They walked on in silence, past the pub, the fish-and-chip shop. Their home came in sight.

'It will break Mam's heart,' said Angela.

'Thanks,' said Tom. 'You're a great help.'

When Angela returned to pick up her children from Michael and Miriam she told them, in confidence, about Tom's plans. 'Mam will take it hard,' she said. 'She'll think it's a disgrace.' No, they assured her, it was so common these days, people scarcely raised an eyebrow. 'You remember Father Conway, who instructed me?' Miriam said. 'He's the latest.' 'There won't be any priests left, soon,' said Angela. She drove off, the frown on her forehead deeper than ever.

'It always seems to happen between the ages of about thirty-five and forty-five,' said Michael, as he and Miriam retired to bed that night. 'It's as if they suddenly realize that they're approaching the point of no return as far as sex is concerned.' He closed the bedroom door and locked it – a coded gesture between them.

Miriam drew off the nightdress she had just put on and got into bed naked. 'How old is Austin, I wonder?' she mused.

'Must be getting on for forty-five, wouldn't you say? D'you think he'll go the same way as all the others?'

'I wouldn't be surprised. If the right woman turned up. He must feel terribly isolated.'

Michael got between the sheets. He no longer wore pyjamas. Miriam slid into his arms. 'Ah!' he sighed. 'Nice. You can't blame them, can you, priests wanting to get married? In the old days, at least they believed they'd get to heaven quicker than other people, have less time in purgatory. Give up pleasures in this world and be rewarded in the next. God pinning a medal on your chest. That was the way they used to promote vocations at school. Now that it's all regarded as mythology, priests must wonder what they've given up sex for.'

So Austin Brierley's friends watched his vocation like a guttering candle, wondering when it would go out. The bishop had discovered that he was still consorting with Catholics for an Open Church and had suspended his allowance and forbidden him to say mass or perform other priestly duties. He looked less and less like the priest they remembered. To save money (he had qualified for a student grant, but was still hard-up) he wore clothes bought from Army surplus stores, thick, hard khaki trousers and parkas with camouflage markings, and a forage cap vaguely suggestive of German prisoners of war in World War II. He grew a beard, wispy and a surprising ginger in colour, and his hair, balding at the crown, fell down lankly on each side of his face, giving him a faint resemblance to Shakespeare. He carried round with him at all times a rucksack stuffed with books, papers, cuttings, and the materials for rolling his own cigarettes.

The cuttings were mainly about *Humanae Vitae* and its repercussions. Sometimes Austin thought vaguely of writing a book on the subject. '*Humanae Vitae*, By a Repercussion.' Meanwhile he collaborated with Adrian on the text of a pamphlet urging Catholics to make their own conscientious decision about birth control, feeling that in this way he was making some amends for all the times he had given contrary advice in the confessional as a young priest. The books in the rucksack were paperbacks on sociology, psychology, philosophy, sexuality, comparative religion. Austin felt that he had a lot of reading to catch up on – too much. His head was a buzzing hive of awakened but directionless ideas. There was Freud who said that we must acknowledge our own repressed desires, and Jung who said that we must recognize our archetypal patterning, and Marx who said we must join the class struggle and Marshall McLuhan who said we must watch more television. There was Sartre who said that man was absurd though free and Skinner who said he was a bundle of conditioned reflexes and Chomsky who said he was a sentence-generating organism and Wilhelm Reich who said he was an orgasm-having organism. Each book that Austin read seemed to him totally persuasive at the time, but they couldn't all be right. And which were most easily reconcilable with faith in God? For that matter, what was God? Kant said he was the essential presupposition of moral action, Bishop Robinson said he was the ground of our being, and Teilhard de Chardin said he was the Omega Point. Wittgenstein said, whereof we cannot speak, thereof we must remain silent – an aphorism in which Austin Brierley found great comfort.

Going to and from Michael and Miriam's house for their liturgical parties, he often saw their eldest son, Martin, a keen amateur astronomer, crouched over his telescope in the dark garden, sometimes actually kneeling on the frosty lawn, immobile, habited like a medieval hermit in balaclava and a long, baggy, cast-off overcoat of his father's. Austin usually stopped to chat with the boy and through these conversations became seriously interested in the Universe. To the rucksack's contents he added popular books on astronomy, from which he learned with astonishment and some dismay that there were about fifty million stars like the Sun in our galaxy, and at least two hundred thousand galaxies in the Universe, each containing a roughly equivalent number of stars, or suns. The whole affair had been going for a very long time, and had spread over a very wide area. Galaxies now being observed for the very first time had started sending, at a speed of 186,000 miles per second, the light that was now being picked up by our telescopes, many thousands of millions of years before the Earth was even formed. If the history of the Universe was conceived of as a single calendar year, the initial Big Bang occurring on 1 January, then the Earth had been formed towards the end of September, and *Homo sapiens* made his appearance at about 10.30 p.m. on 31 December. Christ was born four seconds before midnight.

Austin stored these facts away in his head alongside the theories of Freud, Marx, McLuhan and the rest, and with the opinions of various theologians about God, not finding it any easier to reconcile them all with each other. Indeed, astronomical quantities tended to make all human thought seem both trivial and futile.

'The silence of infinite space terrifies me,' he murmured, squinting one night through Martin's telescope at a faint smear of light that the boy assured him was a galaxy several times bigger than the Milky Way.

'Why?'

Austin straightened up and rubbed the small of his back. 'I was quoting Pascal, a famous French philosopher of the seventeenth century.'

'Interesting he knew that space was silent,' Martin remarked, 'that long ago.'

'You mean, there's no noise at all up there? All those stars exploding and collapsing without making a sound?'

'You can't have sound without resistance, without an atmosphere.'

'So the Big Bang wasn't really a bang at all?'

''Sright.'

'Doesn't it frighten you, though, Martin, the sheer size of the Universe?'

'Nope.'

Austin stared up at the sky. It was a clear, cold night, ideal for observing. The longer he looked, the more stars he could see, and beyond them were billions more that one could never see with the naked eye. It was statistically certain, according to the books, that some of them must have planetary systems capable of supporting life. It certainly seemed unlikely, when you thought about it, that the only life in the entire universe should be situated on this tiny satellite of an insignificant star in a suburb of the Milky Way. But if there was life out there, there must also be death. Had those creatures, like us, myths of creation, fall and redemption? Had other Christs died on other Calvaries in other galaxies at different times in the last twenty billion years? Under the night sky, the questions that preoccupied philosophers and theologians seemed to reduce down to two very simple ones: how did it all start, and where is it all going? The idea that God, sitting on his throne in a timeless heaven, decided one day to create the Universe, and started the human race going on one little bit of it, and watched with interest to see how each human being behaved himself; that when the last day came and God closed down the Universe, gathering in the stars and galaxies like a croupier raking in chips, He would reward the righteous by letting them live with Him for ever in Heaven – that obviously wouldn't do, as modern theologians admitted, and indeed took some satisfaction in demonstrating. On the other hand, it was much easier to dispose of the old mythology than to come up with anything more convincing. When pushed to say what happened after death, the most ruthless demythologizers tended to become suddenly tentative and to waffle on about Mystery and Spirit and Ultimately Personal Love. There was now something called Process Theology which identified God with the history of the Universe itself, but as far as Austin could understand it, the only immortality it offered was that of being stored in a kind of cosmic memory bank.

'I'm going in,' he said to Martin. 'I'm getting cold.'

The same evening, Michael took him aside. 'Austin,' he said, 'I want your advice. Martin's becoming a bit stroppy about coming to mass on Sundays. What do you think we should do about it?'

'I should leave him alone, if I were you,' said Austin.

'You wouldn't like to have a word with him yourself some time? I mean, about religion in general. Even Catholic schools seem to have given up on theology these days. His RE lessons seem to be all about being nice to immigrants and collecting tights for Mother Teresa.'

'Tights for Mother Teresa? I wouldn't have thought she wore them.'

'It seems her nuns use old nylons to make mattresses for the dying. They're having a big campaign at Martin's school to collect them. Well, a jolly good cause, I'm sure, but the syllabus does seem to be avoiding the larger questions of belief.'

Austin did not reply. The reference to tights and nylons had triggered off a faint memory – light years away, it now seemed – of a shapely leg lofted in the air, stockinged to mid-thigh, rising vertically from a lacy foam of petticoats, and he had not attended to the rest of what Michael was saying.

'I thought,' said Michael, patiently, 'that you might find an opportunity to have a chat with Martin.'

'I have already,' said Austin, blinking. 'I'm learning quite a lot.'

Miles decided that he had to get away from Cambridge for a while to think through his problems. In the Easter vacation of 1973 he made a private retreat at a monastery in Nottinghamshire. He slept in an austere cell, rose with the monks at two and six for the singing of Lauds and Prime, ate with them in the refectory while a novice read from Newman's *Apologia*. At other times he read the Bible in the Douai version and, for recreation, Trollope, and took walks in the grounds of the abbey. The setting was less idyllic than he had anticipated. It was mining country and every turn in the paths brought in sight some pithead or sombre slag-heap. The grass and trees were covered with fine black dust, and the morning dew on the grass and shrubs was faintly inky. But this mournful landscape suited his mood. He seriously considered presenting himself as a postulant for admission to the Order. The regularity of the day's routine – office – sleep – wake – office – sleep – wake – office – eat – work – office – work – eat, and so on, around the clock, seemed to take from one's shoulders the terrible responsibility of being happy and successful: it was like some kind of mechanism for keeping in regular motion a body that left to itself would become inert or spastic. He confided this thought to Bernard, a plump, cheerful young monk whom he found a congenial walking companion in the evenings (though the Order observed the Rule of silence, there was a two-hour recreation period after dinner).

'No, sorry, not true at all,' said Bernard. 'You wouldn't be able to stand the life if you weren't at peace with yourself.'

'Then there's no hope for me anywhere,' said Miles.

'Cheer up!' Bernard put his arm round Miles's shoulder. 'Never say die. You're gay, aren't you Miles?'

Miles looked at him, startled both by the statement and the manner of its expression. 'In a miserable, frustrated sort of way, which is why I never use the word, yes, I am.'

'Well, it's nothing to be sad about. Nothing to be ashamed of. God made you that way, didn't He?'

'I suppose so.'

'So accept it. Be proud of it. You have qualities straight people don't have.'

Bernard let his arm drop from Miles's shoulder and put it round his waist, almost hugging him. Miles felt, in quick succession, surprise, panic, then a comforting reassurance. 'That's all very well,' he mumbled, 'but what about . . .'

'What about physical sex? You'll find it easier to do without it once you've accepted yourself for what you are.'

'I wish I could believe that.'

'Anyway, there are worse sins. As long as there's love. It may be imperfect, but it can't really be evil if there's genuine love.'

'Bernard,' said Miles, blinking back tears, 'you're the first person who's ever given me hope.'

Bernard laughed delightedly. 'I've always thought that Hope was the most neglected of the Theological Virtues. There must be a thousand books on Faith and Charity for every one on Hope.'

They had come within sight of the monastery buildings. Bernard disengaged his arm from Miles' waist. 'You'll be all right,' he said, twinkling. And patted Miles lightly but unmistakably on the bottom.

Still Ruth lingered on the coast of California. '*I take it you have severed your connection with the Order,*' her Mother Superior wrote, '*No, still looking for an answer,*' Ruth wrote back. She received no reply.

One day she had a letter from Josephine, the Paulist nun who flashed upon her inward eye every time she saw an advertisement for a certain brand of bourbon. Ruth opened the letter fully expecting that it would announce that the writer had left her Order, probably to get married. To her surprise, Josephine wrote; 'After I got back from San Francisco I nosedived into the usual pits. Then I started to go to a prayer group and it changed my life. I've been baptized in the Holy Spirit, and I've never felt so calm, so happy, so sure of my vocation.'

This was not the first testimony Ruth had heard to the growing prayer group movement, or Charismatic Renewal as it was sometimes called, but it was the most impressive.

At this time, in the early summer of 1973, Ruth was earning her keep helping in a residential institution for mentally handicapped adults near Los Angeles – or perhaps it was *in* Los Angeles – she never quite knew where the sprawling city began and ended. The institution was lavishly furnished and equipped with the conscience money of the families who had dumped their defective dependents there, but the work was demanding and sometimes distressing. The place was run by a diminutive red-haired nun called Charlotte who generally wore training shoes and a track suit. She was a judo black belt and sometimes she needed to be.

Ruth showed her the letter. 'What d'you think about this charismatic business, Charlotte?'

'Me? I couldn't exist without it.'

'You mean you actually go to one of these prayer groups?'

'Sure. Haven't you tried it?'

'I'm afraid it wouldn't be my cup of tea. I'd just be embarrassed.'

'Everybody's embarrassed at first. You soon get over that. You wanna come along with me one evening?'

'I'll think about it.'

Later Charlotte said, 'Hey, Ruth, next weekend there's a Day of Renewal over in Anaheim. A big affair, folks from all over coming to it. There's a plenary session in the morning, then small groups in the afternoon. Wind up with mass. Whaddya say?'

Encouraged by the prospect of a large gathering in which she could be an observer rather than a participant, Ruth agreed to go. The following Sunday Charlotte drove them over to Anaheim, a dull satellite of LA chiefly celebrated as the home of Disneyland. Some two or three hundred people were gathered together in the assembly hall of a Catholic junior high school. There were few seats vacant by the time Ruth and Charlotte arrived, and they had to separate. On the stage, which was festooned with banners declaring 'JESUS LIVES' and 'PRAISE GOD', was a small band of guitar and accordion players dressed in jeans and plaid shirts, and a priest MC at the microphone who led the assembly in hymns and prayers. Ruth was faintly reminded of a concert party at a Girl Guide rally she had attended many years ago: there was the same air of determined joyfulness and good fellowship about the proceedings. When the MC instructed everyone to hold their neighbours' hands as he prayed for the Spirit to descend upon them all, she stiffened in recoil and surrendered her hand reluctantly to the clammy palm of the stout woman sitting next to her. It seemed such an obvious gimmick to create an illusion of togetherness. The MC invited anyone present to pray aloud as if they were in their own homes and to share their thoughts with others. Several people obliged. The accepted mode of prayer was highly informal, personal, intimate, speaking to God as though he were another person present in the room. 'We praise you, Lord, simply because you're alive and with us, and that makes all the difference.' 'Lord, I just have to tell you that I think you're really great.' 'Lord, you make the sun shine and the flowers grow, you made everything. You're so wonderful, Lord, you lift us up when we're down, you comfort us when we're sick, you rejoice with us when we're happy. We really love you, Lord. We really praise you.' Listening to this drivel, Ruth felt herself burning in one big blush.

The MC introduced a speaker evidently well known to the audience, who applauded him vigorously. He was a tall, bony, middle-aged man, with flat hair combed back from a tanned, wrinkled face. He wore a sports jacket and slacks with a collar and tie. He looked as if he might be a salesman for something agricultural. First he relaxed the audience with a few in-jokes. 'Did you know that Bishop Fulton Sheen and Cardinal McIntyre were travelling to the Holy Land for a Charismatic Congress and the Cardinal said to the Bishop, "If you're going to speak in tongues, I'm going to be walking on the water." ' The audience laughed and clapped. Then the speaker asked if there were any Britishers present. Charlotte, seated a few rows ahead of Ruth, looked back at her expectantly, but Ruth kept her hands clasped firmly in her lap. A few hands went up among the audience. Well, said the speaker, they would know that the British had an airline called British European Airways, BEA for short, and it had struck him when he was on vacation in Europe and flying BEA from Amsterdam to London that those letters could also stand for true Christian faith: 'Believe, Expect, Accept. Believe in God. Expect Him to come to you. Accept Him when he comes. . . .' After talking for a while on the power of prayer, and the difference it had made to his own life, he led the congregation in his favourite hymn, *'Oh, the love of my Lord is the essence.'* When they had sung the words of the last verse, he continued to hum the melody into the microphone, and the congregation followed suit, modulating into a variety of strange noises, keening and coaxing and crooning sounds, harmonized like a humming top, punctuated with occasional ejaculations – 'Amen!' 'Hallelujah!' 'Praise Jesus!' Ruth glanced around her. Most of her neighbours had their eyes shut and were swaying in their seats. The stout woman had her fists clenched and was muttering over and over again, 'Praise Jesus, Praise Jesus, Praise Jesus.' Suddenly, from the back of the hall, a voice was raised high in some foreign language, a strange, barbaric-sounding dialect, full of ululating vowels, like a savage chant. So it was true: people really did speak in tongues at these gatherings. How childish it was, just like abracadabra, anyone could pretend to do it. But in spite of herself Ruth felt her skin prickle with the strangeness of it, the high, confident, fluent tone of the utterance. It stopped abruptly. 'Thank you, Jesus,' said the speaker at the microphone casually. 'Thank you, Jesus,' the congregation echoed. 'Could we pray for an interpretation?' said the speaker. There was silence for a moment, then the stout woman beside Ruth stood up and said, 'The Lord says, "If any man is in Christ, he is a new creation; the old has passed away; behold, the new has come." The Charismatic

Renewal is the new creation. It is everyone's chance to be born anew. We can be like newborn babes in the Spirit.' She sat down. 'Thank you, Jesus,' said the speaker. 'Thank you, Jesus,' murmured the rest. 'Could we pray for a healing?' said somebody. 'Could we pray for my sister's little boy who is seriously ill with a suspected brain tumour?' The speaker asked them all to join hands while he prayed with them. At this point Ruth got to her feet and left.

Charlotte hurried out into the lobby behind her. 'What's the matter, Ruth?' she asked anxiously. 'You OK?'

'I just couldn't take any more,' said Ruth. 'I felt faint. Something about the atmosphere.'

'Yeah, it is kinda stuffy.'

'I mean the emotional atmosphere.'

'Take a little walk outside, you'll feel better. This afternoon it'll be the small groups. Quieter. You'll maybe feel more at ease.'

'I really don't think I can take any more today, Charlotte.'

Charlotte eyed her quizzically. 'You're sure you're not fighting something, Ruth?'

'Only nausea. Look, I don't want to spoil your day. I'll meet you back here at four, all right?'

'What will you do till then? Why not join a small group this afternoon, huh? Give the Holy Spirit an even break.'

Ruth shook her head and left the building. For a while she walked aimlessly along the rectilinear streets of one-storey houses, each with its little plot of coarse grass over which the sprinkler hoses plied monotonously, then through a commercial district of shops, gas stations, motels and funeral parlours. Most of the shops were shut, as it was Sunday. Ruth felt hungry and thirsty, but there seemed nowhere suitable to go, only drive-in hamburger places which she felt self-conscious of approaching on foot, or dimly lit bars advertising topless dancers. Eventually she found herself among crowds converging on Disneyland, and thinking that this would be as good a place as any to kill time, passed through the turnstiles. There was certainly no shortage of refreshment inside – the only problem was deciding in what architectural facsimile you wanted to consume it: a Wild West saloon or a

589

wigwam encampment or a space-ship or a Mississippi paddleboat. It was a world of appearances, of pastiche and parody and pretence. Nothing was real except the people who perambulated its broad avenues, fingering their little books of tickets, patiently lining up for the Casey Jr Circus Train, the Peter Pan Flight, the Jungle Cruise, the Monorail Ride. Music filtered from loudspeakers concealed in the trees and fountains played and the Stars and Stripes hung limply from a hundred flagpoles. Huge grinning plaster figures of Disney characters proffered litter baskets at every intersection of paths. Children ran about with balloons, ice-cream, candy-floss and popcorn under the complacent eyes of their parents.

One such couple, overweight, brightly dressed, festooned with cameras, sat down on Ruth's bench to rest their feet, and the wife volunteered the information that they had come all the way from South Dakota. 'Not just to see Disneyland?' said Ruth, with a smile, but they didn't seem to see anything amusing in the idea. 'Well, we're seeing a lot of other places as well,' said the woman, 'but this is the high-spot of the vacation, isn't that right, Al?' Al said it was right. 'He's always been crazy to see Disneyland,' said the woman fondly, 'ever since I started dating him.'

It struck Ruth that Disneyland was indeed a place of pilgrimage. The customers had an air about them of believers who had finally made it to Mecca, to the Holy Places. They had come to celebrate their own myths of origin and salvation – the plantation, the frontier, the technological utopia – and to pay homage to their heroes, gods and fairies: Buffalo Bill, Davey Crockett, Mickey Mouse and Donald Duck. The perception at first pleased and then depressed her. She looked at the crowds ambling along in the smog-veiled sunshine, from one fake sideshow to another, chewing, sucking, drinking, licking, and was seized with a strange nausea and terror. For all their superficial amiability and decency they were *benighted*, glutted with unreality. Ruth began to recite to herself the words of Isaiah: '*For the heart of this nation has grown coarse, their ears are dull of hearing, and they have shut their eyes, for fear they should see with their eyes, hear with their ears, understand with their hearts, and be converted and healed by me.*'

But she must have spoken the words aloud, for the woman from South Dakota turned to her enquiringly. 'I was just thinking,' said Ruth 'that if Jesus really lives, you wouldn't know it in here.' The woman stared. 'Well, I don't go much on religion, myself,' she said, uneasily. 'My husband used to be a Christian Scientist, didn't you, Al?' Al gave a sickly grin and said they ought to be getting along. They left Ruth sitting alone on her bench, staring back at her over their shoulders from a safe distance.

Ruth got to her feet and walked rapidly in the opposite direction, to the Exit turnstiles. She hurried back to the school. In each of the classrooms a small prayer group was in progress. She went from room to room, looking for Charlotte through the little observation windows in the doors. One door had no window, and she opened it. Half a dozen faces turned in her direction. Charlotte's was not one of them. The stout woman who had sat next to her in the assembly hall smiled at her. 'Come and join us. Where have you been?'

'I've been to Disneyland,' Ruth said, closing the door behind her, and joining the circle of chairs. The others laughed uncertainly.

'And what did you think of it?'

'I thought it was like the world must have been before Christ came.'

There was a surprised silence.

'Walt Disney was a good man, a godfearing man,' said someone, a shade reproachfully.

The stout woman said, 'I don't think Ruth is really telling us about Disneyland. I think she's telling us something about herself. Isn't that right, honey?'

To her astonishment and acute embarrassment, tears began to roll down Ruth's cheeks. She nodded and sniffed, groping in her handbag for a Kleenex. 'All my life as a nun there's been one thing missing, the one thing that gives it any point or sense, and that's, well, real faith in God. It sounds ridiculous, but I don't think I ever had it before. I mean, I believed in Him with my head, and I believed with my heart in doing good works, but the two never came together, I never believed in Him with my heart. Do you understand what I mean?'

The stout woman nodded eagerly. 'Would you like us to pray over you, honey?'

Ruth knelt, and the other people present clustered round and put their hands on her head. Even before the woman began to speak, Ruth felt a profound sense of bliss descend upon her.

That night she began to pack her bags for the journey home. She wired her Mother Superior: 'BY THE WATERS OF DISNEY-LAND I SAT DOWN AND WEPT STOP HAVE FOUND WHAT IVE BEEN LOOKING FOR STOP RETURNING IMMEDIATELY'

As part of her Open University course on the Nineteenth-Century Novel, Tessa had to attend a residential summer school, held at one of the new universities in the north of England. 'I believe Robin Whatsisname teaches there,' said Edward. 'You remember, the chap who married Violet, the dotty girl at Angela and Dennis's wedding. You ought to look them up.'

'Oh, I'll be much too busy,' said Tessa. She was excited at the thought of the week ahead, her first trip away from home on her own since she had been married, and she did not want to waste precious time paying courtesy calls, especially not on the notorious Violet.

The student body at the summer school consisted largely of mature men and women like Tessa, who could scarcely believe their luck at having a cast-iron excuse to abandon spouses and children for six whole days and do nothing except talk, read and enjoy themselves. There were lectures and seminars in the mornings and afternoons, and for the faster set, drinking and a disco every night. Tessa retired dutifully to her room to read immediately after dinner on the first two evenings, but on the third, the rhythmic thud of amplified music and the hum of voices drew her downstairs to the bar. She hesitated at the threshold, peering in. There was a general effect of blue denim stretched tightly over buttock and crotch, of empty beer glasses and overflowing ashtrays, of flirtation and pursuit.

'Extraordinary spectacle, isn't it?' said a voice at her shoulder.

It was George, a middle-aged teacher in her seminar group, a dapper, drily amusing man, with a habit of dropping his head and looking over his glasses when he delivered his opinions about *Anna Karenina*, the week's set text. He looked over them now, delivering his opinion on the roaring throng. 'They discuss adultery all day and commit it all night.'

'How do you know?' Tessa laughed.

'Well, I'm reliably informed that all the Durex machines in the men's loos are empty,' he said. 'And it's only Tuesday.'

Tessa blushed and looked away.

'I'm sorry, I've shocked you. My apologies,' said George.

'No, no,' said Tessa, feeling foolish, and to re-establish herself as a mature, sophisticated woman, accepted his offer of a drink. 'Are you married, George?' she asked conversationally, when they had found a table.

'No,' he said with a smile, 'I'm a bachelor. But you're quite safe with me. I don't feel that way about girls. Now I've shocked you again.'

'Oh, no,' said Tessa earnestly, 'how terribly interesting.' This was certainly living.

'Same again, both of you?'

It was another member of their seminar, Roy. A rather vain young man, Tessa had already decided, very conscious of his blond wavy hair and china-blue eyes. He had perfected a lazy film-star's smile that slowly uncovered a row of strong white teeth, and he gave the general impression of being about to burst out of his jeans and cheesecloth shirt. They discussed the foibles of their seminar leader, and whether it was better to read criticism before or after reading the original text. Tessa offered to lend Roy a book on the language of fiction that she had found particularly useful. She insisted on buying another round, which George fetched from the bar. Then Roy asked her if she would like to dance.

'Would you mind?' Tessa asked George.

'Please! Enjoy yourselves.' He waved them away.

When Tessa stood up, she felt the effect of the three vodka-and-tonics she had swallowed. It was a nice effect. She floated through the crowded bar to a darkened annexe where the music throbbed and boomed. Shadowy figures, luridly stained by shifting coloured lights, writhed, ducked and weaved. Occasionally a splash of light illuminated their features and Tessa recognized with surprise some shy fellow-student or awe-inspiring lecturer magically transformed into a creature of mindless sensual abandonment, twitching and shuddering under the invisible lash of the music. She began to twitch and shudder herself. Her limbs, oiled by the vodka, loosened, her head went back, her arms lifted, her torso undulated elastically to the rhythm.

'Hey, you're terrific!' said Roy, as one record faded and another began.

She smiled dreamily. She had forgotten he was there. 'I go to keep-fit classes,' she said. 'We do modern dance sometimes.'

After a while the music changed to a slow, languorous tempo, and the figures in the room began to glue themselves together in couples. Tessa felt Roy's hands low on her hips, his belt buckle pressing into her midriff. Or was it his belt buckle?

'I think we ought to go back to George,' she said. But when they returned to the bar, George had gone.

'Another drink?' Roy suggested.

'No thanks,' said Tessa. 'I must be off to bed. Thanks for the dance.'

'I'll come with you to pick up that book,' said Roy.

Tessa felt panic rising inside her as she led him up staircases and along corridors to her room. Was he going to make a pass at her, or was she being foolish to even think of it, being nearly old enough to be his mother? 'I'll just pop in and get the book,' she said, unlocking the door of her room.

'Do you have any instant coffee in the kitchens on this floor?' he asked.

'Yes, do you need some?'

'Thanks,' he said, 'black with sugar.'

'Oh,' said Tessa, who had not meant that at all. 'All right, just a minute.'

Stupid of me, she thought, as she went to the kitchen at the end of the corridor. Still, coffee was a sobering drink. And if he tried anything funny, she would tip her cup over him. She returned to her room with a steaming cup in each hand, rehearsing the words of some firm but courteous dismissal to be delivered after the coffee had been consumed. Not being able to turn the door handle, she tapped with her foot for admission. The door opened, and closed behind her as she walked in. She turned. Roy smiled lazily. He was stark naked. Tessa screamed and threw coffee. Roy swore and hopped round the room, clutching himself. Tessa ran out of the room and hid in the Ladies. Half an hour later, she crept back to find the room empty, a coffee-stained bedspread in the middle of the floor the only trace of Roy's visit.

The next evening, she did not dance, but drank with George in the bar. Roy, steering a girl with dyed blonde hair through the crush by her denimed rump, studiously ignored Tessa. She and George discussed *Anna Karenina*, compared Tolstoy's technique with George Eliot's, agreed to differ about the heroine of *Mansfield Park*. It was a warm night, and the dancers emerged from the disco glazed with perspiration. George proposed a walk around the artificial lake. At the furthest and darkest part he put his arms round Tessa and started kissing her neck. 'Stop it, George!' she said. 'What are you doing? I thought you didn't feel that way about women?'

'You could cure me, Tessa,' he said breathlessly. 'I have a feeling you could cure me. Come over there by the trees.'

Tessa gave him a push and he staggered backwards, putting one foot into the artificial lake. She ran quickly back to the lights of the hall of residence, laughing, crying.

The next evening, Tessa joined a group of married women of her own age in the bar. They drank shandy or bitter lemon and passed round snaps of their husbands and children. They compared, with affected indifference, the grades they were getting in their courses, and complained about the inconsistencies of the marking system. Tessa was reminded of the ladies who waited for the curtained showers after her keep-fit classes. She left them to make her daily call to Edward.

There was always a queue in the evening for the two pay phones, and as she waited Tessa saw George and Roy weaving unsteadily towards her, their arms round each other shoulders. 'Hello, Tessa darling,' said George. 'We're going for a stroll round the lake. Coming?' He leered at her over the tops of his glasses. Roy smiled lazily.

'I'm phoning my husband,' said Tessa, making it sound like a threat. They went off giggling uncontrollably.

The man and the woman using the phones ahead of Tessa put down their receivers simultaneously, exchanged sly smiles, and walked off hand in hand. Tessa seized the nearest phone.

'Hello,' said Edward. 'How are you, darling? Enjoying it?'

'Yes.'

'Interesting people?'

'Oh, yes. A real mixture. Housewives, teachers, sex-maniacs . . .'

He chuckled. 'I miss you,' he said.

'I miss you, too. What are you doing with yourself in the evenings?'

'Nothing much. I've been to the local once or twice. Michael's invited me round tomorrow night. I thought I'd go. Ruth's staying with them.'

'Ruth?'

'Oh, you never knew her, did you? She was at college with Michael and me. She became a nun.'

'Oh yes. Didn't she go to America?'

'That's right. And she's come back full of this Pentecostal-charismatic caper, apparently. Prayer groups and speaking in tongues and that sort of thing.'

'Doesn't sound very Catholic.'

'Sounds like a lot of tosh, to me. I'm surprised, Ruth was always a sensible sort of girl. But I haven't seen her for donkey's years. Tomorrow's the Assumption, by the way. Will you be able to get to mass?'

'I don't know. I expect so.'

Edward was always scrupulous about mass attendance on Sundays and holydays of obligation, the legacy of being taught as a child that 'missing' was a mortal sin. Tessa, conditioned by the much more casual churchgoing of her Anglican childhood, still found the habits of Catholics in this respect a matter for wonder and occasional irritation. At any mass there would always be a score of people with streaming colds who should obviously have been at home in bed instead of coughing their germs over everybody else, and mothers with yowling babies who couldn't possibly be getting anything spiritual out of the occasion. And if they ever went to a Unity service in one of the neighbouring churches or chapels on Sunday, they had to go to mass as well, because the Unity service, even in these supposedly ecumenical days, didn't 'count'. She was tempted to ignore Edward's reminder, especially as there was no mass on the campus, but the next evening she felt like a change of scene from the bar and disco, so she took the bus into town and heard mass in an ugly little church crowded with tired and bored office workers. Afterwards, she strolled round the city's medieval cathedral, magnificent, peaceful and empty.

As she walked back towards the bus terminus, a street name caught her eye. It was the address Edward had given her for Violet. She found the house, number 83, at the end of a terrace of Georgian town houses, and rang the bell. A slim, dark man with receding hair brushed back over his ears answered the door.

'Mr Meadowes?'

'Yes.'

Tessa went through the rigmarole of introducing herself. He didn't seem very welcoming, and she began to regret her impulse. 'Perhaps I've called at an inconvenient time,' she said.

'I'm afraid Violet's in hospital.'

'Oh, I'm sorry. Nothing serious, I hope?'

'She's in a psychiatric ward.'

'Oh dear.'

A little girl of about nine appeared at the door. 'This is Felicity,' he said. 'Won't you come in?'

'Oh, no, thank you but – '

'Robin! Coffee!' a youthful female voice called from the back of the house.

'Please, come in and have a cup of coffee.' Robin seemed suddenly anxious that Tessa should stay. He led her down a dark hallway and a short flight of stairs into a large basement kitchen, pleasantly decorated and well-equipped, but in a state of squalid disorder. A plump girl of about twenty in a long cotton dress looked up from the stove and pushed a curtain of hair back from her face. She did not seem pleased to see Tessa.

'This is Caroline,' said Robin. 'She's a student at the University, and she babysits Felicity when I'm out. I've just been out,' he said carefully, 'to visit Violet.'

'Hallo,' said Tessa.

Caroline murmured something inaudible and let the curtain of hair fall back.

'It's such a fine evening, why don't we take our coffee into the garden?' said Robin. 'I think we still have one or two unbroken deckchairs.'

'I really mustn't stay long,' said Tessa, more and more convinced that she had made a bad mistake in calling. The garden was an uncultivated rectangle of weeds and long grass with curiously shaped chunks of masonry scattered about here and there. 'Violet's sculptures,' Robin explained, putting his feet up on one of them. Felicity wandered off to a swing at the bottom of the garden. Caroline had remained in the kitchen. 'How well did you know Violet?' he asked.

'Hardly at all. I think I only met her once. It was Edward who knew her really. What is her . . . problem, exactly?'

Robin emitted a harsh, abrupt laugh. 'There have been many theories. Personally, I blame her religious upbringing – you're not a Catholic, are you?'

'I am, actually. A convert.'

'Ah, well, that's different. It's the conditioning in childhood that does the damage.'

'But not all cradle Catholics are . . .'

'Neurotic? No, but it encourages neuroticism. The kind of Catholicism Violet was brought up in, anyway. A convent boarding school in Ireland. Hell-fire sermons, obsession with sin, purity, all that sort of thing.'

'It isn't like that now.'

'Isn't it? I'm glad to hear it, but the change has come too late for poor Violet.' He rocked the sculpture back and forth with his foot. 'She hates herself, you see. I mean, most of us are dissatisfied with ourselves from time to time, but she really hates herself, her body, her mind. She thinks she's no good, so she does something awful to prove to herself that she's no good, then she feels guilty. She isn't happy unless she's feeling guilty. But then she's unhappy *because* she's feeling guilty. Because she's terrified of going to hell.'

'Telephone!' Caroline called from the kitchen window.

'Excuse me,' said Robin. Tessa sipped the dregs of her coffee and wondered how to make her escape. Felicity came up to her, twirling a skipping rope.

'Do you know when my Mummy is coming home?' she said.

'No, I'm sorry, I don't dear,' said Tessa compassionately.

'Is she in a loony bin?'

'No, she's in a hospital, with doctors and nurses taking care of her.'

'Mummy said it was a loony bin,' said Felicity.

'Oh,' said Tessa, nonplussed. 'Well, I expect that was just for a joke.'

With a little smirk, Felicity changed the subject. 'Do you know, Caroline has hair between her legs?'

'So do all women,' said Tessa briskly. 'So will you when you're grown up, Felicity.'

'Do you, then?'

'Of course. Tell me about the school you go to, dear.'

Robin came out of the house. Felicity skipped off to the bottom of the garden, humming a little tune under her breath. Tessa got to her feet. 'I must be going,' she said.

'Oh, really?' said Robin, gazing thoughtfully after his daughter. 'I'll run you back to the University.'

'Oh, please don't bother.'

In the end, she allowed him to drive her back to the bus terminus. 'I hope Violet gets better soon,' she said in the car.

'Yes, I hope so. I'm afraid the whole business is having a bad effect on Felicity. She's getting to the stage where she's curious about sex and so on, and I really can't handle it. On the other hand, God knows what Violet would tell her.'

'I know an awfully good book,' said Tessa. 'Called *Where Do I Come From Anyway?* or something like that. I'll send you the details, if you like.'

'That would be very kind,' said Robin. 'Well, here we are, there's your bus. If you're coming into town again, give me a call. We could continue that interesting conversation about Catholicism. Listen to a little music on my hi-fi, if you like that sort of thing.'

'I'm afraid I'm going home tomorrow,' said Tessa, glad to have this cast-iron excuse.

Back at the University, the bar and disco had reached new heights, or depths, of frenzied hedonism on the last night of the course. Oppressed, and slightly haunted, by the visit she had just paid, Tessa plunged into the throng with a kind of relief. Someone pushed a double vodka and tonic into her fist and she quickly became tipsy. Even the housewives' circle had switched from shandy and bitter lemon to gin for the evening and were tipsy too. They sat, bright-eyed and red-faced, near the entrance to the disco, tapping their feet wistfully to the music. 'Why aren't you dancing?' said Tessa. 'Nobody's asked us,' they said. 'You don't need partners for this kind of dancing,' said Tessa, and chivvied them into the disco room where they flung themselves about with joyous abandon. The bar closed and more people poured into the room. The heavy chords of a record turned up to maximum amplification were greeted with ecstatic cries of 'Stones!' and a wild gyration of limbs. Tessa thought she saw George and Roy dancing in a corner with the dyed blonde in jeans, but, ravished by the brutal power of the music, she no longer cared very much. Her body said: this is almost as good as sex, and without complications.

The mood on campus the next day was melancholy, as the students nursed their hangovers, prepared to terminate their brief love affairs, and braced themselves to return to the bosoms of their families. Tessa, looking in the campus bookshop for something to take home to her children, came across the facts-of-life book she had mentioned to Robin and, on impulse, bought it. She asked the taxi taking her to the station that afternoon to stop at Robin's house and wait. She rang the bell without effect. She scribbled a note of explanation on the wrapping paper and tried to push the book through the letter-box, but it was too big. She went down the side alley to the back of the house, but there was no one in the garden. She peered into the kitchen, but that was empty too, the doors and windows shut. A flight of steps led up from the garden to a small verandah with french windows which seemed to be ajar, though the curtains within were drawn. Pulling these aside just enough to insert the copy of *How Did Get Here Anyway?* Tessa found herself staring at two naked bodies sprawled on floor cushions in a rosy light. She had time to notice before she fled back to the taxi that Caroline was wearing headphones and that Robin's head was clenched between her fat thighs. On her way to the station she stripped the wrapping paper from the book. 'Here,' she said to the driver, 'have you got any children, or d'you know anybody who could use this?'

The man read the title aloud. 'A good question,' he said, 'I've often wondered myself.'

Had the whole world gone sex-mad? Tessa silently posed the question to herself, settling back in the corner seat of her train compartment. She had a sense, exhilarated yet relieved, of having escaped unscathed from a region of danger. The week's experiences had quite appeased her body's hunger for sexual adventure, and she felt happy to be returning to her chaste and blameless married life. She resolved, however, to give Edward a carefully edited account of the summer school, in case he tried to stop her going on another one next year.

When she returned home that evening, Edward was incurious about her experiences, and seemed to have preoccupations of his own. He kissed her warmly and murmured, 'Bed.'

'Goodness, give me a moment to get my breath,' Tessa said, laughing, but pleasantly aroused. She visited the children in their various parts of the house and then went back to the kitchen for a snack. Edward perched on a kitchen stool, with his long legs bent like a grasshopper, sipping whisky while she ate. 'I went over to Michael and Miriam's last night,' he said. 'Ruth was there.'

'Oh yes. What was it like?'

'Well, it turned into a kind of charismatic meeting,' he said. 'Ruth insisted on praying over me.'

'Good heavens! Whatever for?'

'For my back. They go in for healing, you know.'

'And did you let her?'

'Well, I couldn't very well stop her.'

'How very embarrassing.'

'The funny thing is,' said Edward. 'I haven't felt a twinge since. And I did two hours in the garden this morning.'

Tessa stared. 'You're not serious?'

'Well, there's often a psychosomatic dimension to these back troubles you know. I'm keeping my fingers crossed.'

'You mean, your back's *cured?*'

'I don't know,' said Edward. 'But if you'll come to bed, I'll give it a work-out.' He grinned lustfully at her, his big ears glowing.

Edward's lovemaking was more passionate than it had been for a long time. 'I must go away more often,' Tessa purred. She lay back luxuriously and let herself be possessed by his strong male force. But the next day, when Edward woke, his back was paining him again.

'Oh, well,' he said. 'I thought it was too good to be true.'

'Poor darling,' said Tessa, nuzzling against him. Guiltily, she realized that she was relieved as well as sorry. The idea that Ruth might have cured Edward's back had offended her commonsense notion of what the world was like. I shall never be a real Catholic, she thought. I don't really believe in the power of prayer.

When Tessa reported to Edward that Violet was in a psychiatric hospital he was sorry but not really surprised. Half the patients he saw nowadays seemed to be suffering from mental or psychosomatic illnesses, and a large proportion of the prescriptions he wrote were for tranquillizers. Michael and Miriam, who had read R.D. Laing and Ivan Illich, sometimes rallied him about this. 'I can't prescribe happiness, which is what most of my patients want,' he said, 'so I prescribe Valium instead.'

'How do you think the human race managed before Valium was invented?' Miriam demanded.

'That's a good question,' he admitted. 'Of course, there was always alcohol, laudanum, and so on. But I sometimes wonder if there hasn't been a quantum leap, lately, in the average human being's expectation of happiness. I mean, in times past, your average chap was content if he could fill his belly once a day and avoid disease. But now everybody expects to be happy as well as healthy. They want to be successful and admired and loved all the time. Naturally they're disappointed, and so they go round the bend.'

Edward advanced his theory partly in self-defence. He did not seriously believe that it accounted for poor Violet's psychological condition, which seemed more like a hereditary curse or congenital defect, with no reason or justice behind it. He still felt a vestigial interest in and responsibility for Violet, remembering vividly the day he had taken her to the hospital after she started throwing crockery around in Lyons cafeteria. As they were driving north that Christmas, 1973, to stay with his parents, Edward thought they might break their journey to call on Robin and Violet. Tessa wasn't keen. 'There won't be time,' she said. 'Anyway, how d'you know she isn't still in hospital?' So Edward phoned Robin at his University to enquire.

'Violet's out of hospital,' said Robin. 'She's been out for some time.'

'Oh, good,' said Edward. 'She's better then?'

'Well, she is in a way,' said Robin. 'Though as far as I'm concerned she's just exchanged one form of religious mania for another. She's joined the Jehovah's Witnesses.'

'Good God! You're not serious?'

'Someone she met in the hospital converted her.'

'But it's all nonsense, isn't it?'

'Complete nonsense. But then, so is Catholicism as far as I'm concerned. Shall I give her a message?'

'Well, we may be driving through your neck of the woods soon,' said Edward tentatively.

'Well, do drop in, by all means,' said Robin. 'Violet will be glad to see you both.'

But Tessa declined to share the visit. 'You go,' she said, 'while I take the children round the Cathedral. We're too many to descend on someone just out of a mental ward.' So Edward made the visit alone.

It was nearly fifteen years since they had seen each other, but Violet had not changed as much as he had expected. She smiled shyly at Edward when she opened the door to him, and led him into a living-room that was comfortably furnished but seemed oddly bleak. Robin was out. Edward met Caroline, a rather sulky young woman whom Violet introduced as their student lodger but who seemed to comport herself more as a member of the family, and Felicity. Edward asked Felicity what Father Christmas was going to bring her and received the disconcerting reply that Father Christmas wasn't Christian. Felicity looked at her mother for approval as she delivered this rebuff, and was rewarded with a smile. Edward suddenly realized why the room seemed so bleak: there were no cards or decorations in evidence.

Caroline took Felicity off and left Edward and Violet alone. They made small talk for a while, but soon Violet turned the conversation to religion. 'Do you read the Bible, Edward?'

'Not much,' he admitted.

'Oh, you should, it's a great comfort,' she said earnestly. 'I got better, you know, through reading the Bible. I'll give you one before you go.'

'Well, we have got one at home, actually.'

'But this one is different. It's got notes.'

'Well, mine's got notes as well,' said Edward with a smile.

'Ah, yes, but they'd be Catholic notes,' said Violet. 'And the Catholic Church is the whore of Babylon, you know.'

'Violet,' said Edward. 'You don't really believe that.'

'Oh yes,' said Violet. 'It's all in the Bible. That's why the Catholic Church used to try and stop people reading it. The Catholic religion isn't true Bible religion, you know.'

'Isn't it?'

'No. For instance, there's no hell, like they used to tell us at school, only gravedom.'

'Gravedom?'

'That's the meaning of the Hebrew word *Sheol*. And there's no such thing as the soul. When you die, you die, you're just dust, nothing. You can't feel anything, so you can't suffer. You can't be punished. Your spirit goes back to God who created it, until the Coming of the Kingdom.'

'What will happen then?' said Edward.

'Then God will resurrect the dead and reign for a thousand years.'

'And then what?'

'Then there will be a Judgement.'

'Ah,' said Edward.

'But you won't be judged on what you did in this life,' said Violet. 'You'll just have to pass the test.'

'What test?'

'To witness your loyalty to God,' said Violet. 'But after a thousand years of the earthly paradise, with no death or sickness or suffering or violence, a thousand years of happiness and peace for the whole world, who *wouldn't* choose God?'

'And when is this thousand years due to start?' said Edward.

'Quite soon,' said Violet, getting up to fetch a book from a bookcase. 'The Bible says there will be great earthquakes and pestilence and food shortages. Nation will rise against nation and kingdom against kingdom. You only have to read the newspapers. Here.'

She put into Edward's hand a small booklet open on a historical chart headed *Events of History, Past and Present*. It began:

4026 BC — Adam created

and ended:

1975 AD — Man completes 6000 years of history on earth
— UN 'horns' devastate Babylon

> — *Christ destroys nations at Har-Magedon*
> — *1000-year reign starts.*

'Looks as if we'd better make the most of 1974, then,' said Edward.

Angela's father died in the spring of 1974. He had to go back into hospital at the end, and visiting him there in a ward full of coughing old men, shortly before he died, Dennis was deeply shocked. The papers that day were full of a terrible air-crash – a jumbo jet had fallen out of the sky near Paris, killing hundreds instantaneously – but cancer seemed to Dennis an excellent argument for dying in an air-crash as he walked away from the hospital with Angela. She had been up and down the motorway regularly in the past few months to visit her father, so was prepared for his wasted appearance, his slow, shadowy gestures, his tired voice, the eyes that seemed to have retired to the back of his skull, like the eyes of some small animal cornered in a cave. He seemed to know he was dying, and had gratefully accepted the Last Sacraments, but throughout his illness he had been very insistent that his condition was not lung cancer, making the point to all his visitors. As it seemed to give him some kind of comfort to believe this, they naturally humoured him. Perhaps it was a comfort to themselves, too, for at the funeral most of the mourners seemed to be lighting up compulsively every few minutes and then hastily stubbing out their cigarettes for fear of appearing irreverent. The ashtray in one of the cars became jammed with dog-ends and began to smoulder so that the vehicle drew up at the cemetery filled with a nicotine fog, the occupants coughing and weeping and clutching their throats as they fell out on to the gravel drive. Dennis had the odd feeling that he was the only person who saw anything grimly funny about this. The note of disregarded black farce persisted. At the reception after the funeral, held at the house of one of Angela's married sisters, there was a rat-tat on the open front door and a penetrating middle-class female voice trilled, 'Cancer here!' but the murmur of conversation in the living-room scarcely missed a beat. Dennis went to the door and pushed coins into the woman's collection box. 'Thank you *so* much,' she said. 'Having a party, are you? That's nice.' Watching her prance back down the garden path, Dennis pushed a cigarette between his lips; then, on second thoughts, replaced it in the packet. In the car on the way home that evening he told Angela that he was going to give up smoking. She grunted sceptically.

'Did you see that girl of Tom's?' she said. 'That Rosemary.'

The family occasion had brought back a working-class timbre to her voice. It made him think of tight-lipped housewives in headscarves gossiping on doorsteps. 'She seems quite nice,' he said. 'Infant teacher, isn't she? Does your mother guess?'

'No. I don't know. I don't think so. Tom's been very clever, the way he introduced her. She's become quite a family friend. I suppose he thinks it'll take off some of the shock when he tells them he's going to marry her.'

It was late when they got home and Dennis was tired from the drive, but he felt restless and tense. 'Feel like making love?' he said to Angela as they were retiring – diffidently, because she had shown little enthusiasm for sex during her father's illness. Rather to his surprise, she agreed. Why? he wondered, as he went through the ritual of foreplay. Was it some obscure jealousy of Tom's girl that she was appeasing? Or was she pursuing this crazy idea that Christians ought to be cheerful and throw parties when their parents died? It certainly seemed to be on principle rather than for pleasure, for she did not appear to have a climax. But Dennis did, and fell gratefully asleep.

The next day was a Saturday, but Dennis went into his office to see if anything important had cropped up on the previous day. He drove through the gates of the factory with a wave to the security man, and parked in the space that had his car number freshly painted on the tarmac (he was Director of Manufacturing now). He let himself into the empty building with his master key. The air inside smelled stale, slightly tainted with chemical odours, and the benches in the workshops, the shrouded typewriters in the offices, had a dead, abandoned look. But he always liked being alone in the empty factory, soothed by the peace, the silence, the curious sense of freedom.

On his desk, neatly arranged, was Friday's mail, each item clipped to its appropriate file, a record of incoming telephone calls, and a sheaf of freshly typed letters and memoranda which he had dictated on to tape on Thursday evening. Dennis smiled approvingly. Lynn was an excellent secretary, the best he'd ever had. At first he had found her difficult to relate to − a shy, softly-spoken Welsh girl who dropped her head at the slightest discouragement, and screwed up her lips in a sceptical smile when complimented on her work, as if she suspected irony. Dennis certainly never intended it: over the year and a half she had worked for him she had proved efficient, conscientious and fiercely loyal. He lived in perpetual dread that she would tell him one day she was leaving to get married.

As he addressed himself to his papers, Dennis patted his pockets automatically for his cigarettes, then ruefully remembered that he had given up smoking. The need for nicotine stabbed in his veins, but he controlled it and picked up the first of the letters awaiting his signature. One figure needed correction, and he flipped up the top sheet to amend the carbon copy underneath. The carbon was, however, of a different letter. A love letter evidently − or part of one. Dennis detached the sheet, scanned it and turned it over in bewilderment. There was no apostrophe at the beginning or signature at the end. It looked as though Lynn had been doing some private correspondence while he was away and had got it mixed up with the firm's. Amusement at this discovery quickly gave way to disappointment at her lapse and, more surprisingly, jealousy. Then, as Dennis read the letter more carefully, it suddenly struck him that it was addressed to himself. He began to tremble. His hand shook so violently that he had to lay the sheet of paper flat on the desk to read it. He read it over and over again. There was nothing specific in it, no names or other references that would put its meaning beyond doubt, it was all vaguely expressed longing, protestation, self-abasement, like the words of a popular song: but there were hints of problems and difficulties of age and status that fitted the situation of Lynn and himself.

The need for a smoke had become intolerable. Dennis broke into the firm's hospitality room with his master key and found a couple of stale Rothman's in a cabinet drawer. Lighting up with a spill touched to the electric fire in his office, he inhaled hungrily and considered what to do. The most important thing, obviously, was to find out whether the letter really was addressed to himself. That would have to wait till Monday. In the meantime he decided not to tell Angela, in case he was mistaken. And if he wasn't mistaken . . .? Well, he would cross that bridge when he came to it. He folded the letter into his wallet and took it home.

Several times in the course of the weekend Dennis surreptitiously examined the letter. Its ambiguity remained unresolved until five past nine on Monday morning. Then, he had only to glance at Lynn's face as she came into his office with the morning's mail to know. She blushed a deeper red than he had ever seen anybody blush before. Then she went very pale. Then she ran out of the room. Neither of them had spoken. She came back a few minutes later, wearing her outdoor clothes.

'Where are you going, Lynn?' he said.

'To hand in my notice,' she said. 'Save you the trouble.'

'What would you want to do a silly thing like that for? You know I can't manage without you.'

Lynn hung her head and said nothing.

'Take your coat off and come back and take some letters,' he said. 'Oh, and by the way, this one you did on Friday doesn't seem to have a carbon. Be a good girl and see if you can find it, will you?'

Neither of them made any further reference to the love letter. Office life went on much as before – almost. Sometimes Dennis surprised Lynn gazing soulfully at him, sometimes she might have caught his eyes resting on her longer than was strictly necessary. She was not a strikingly beautiful girl, but she was pretty in a quiet way, with delicate features, a small waist and fine brown hair falling straight to her shoulders. It astonished and moved Dennis that this fair young thing should have fixed her affections upon his broken spirit and gone-to-seed body, and he could no more bring himself to rebuff her than he could have stamped on a fledgling that had fallen out of a tree and lay helpless and palpitating at his feet. He had not asked her to fall in love with him, he had not wished or intended that she should do so, but since she evidently had, Dennis bowed his head in resignation, he accepted the gift of her devotion almost as if it were another blow of fate, like the birth of Nicole or the death of Anne. Of course, it was much nicer – indeed it in some ways healed the wounds of those events. The secret knowledge that he was loved restored Dennis's will to live. He whistled in the morning while shaving. The economic recession that had plunged his managerial colleagues into deep gloom merely stimulated him to greater efforts at cutting costs. He succeeded in giving up smoking, and took up golf to keep his waistline under control. As the friends who introduced him to the game played on Sunday mornings, Dennis stopped going to mass. Since his eldest, Jonathan, had mutinied against mass attendance anyway, Dennis no longer felt obliged to set an example, and Angela acquiesced with only a token protest. She for her part would sometimes make the long drive to Michael's college for the student mass because Nicole liked the guitars and folk hymns.

At the College (where Michael was now Head of the English Department) sexual morality was in a fascinating state of flux. Many of the students who had come up as good, obedient Catholics had, in the course of their studies, either lost their religious faith altogether or espoused a radical and highly permissive version of it; and it was well-known to the students and some staff that many couples among the student body were having fully consummated relationships under the very roof of the College. The residential accommodation was segregated only by floor, and supervision was not strict. Little ingenuity was needed to smuggle a girl or boy friend into one's room for the night. The teaching staff found the idea of this nocturnal traffic almost as exciting as did the students who were actually conducting it. They debated anxiously with each other their ethical responsibility in the matter.

To put a stop to it seemed impossible without invoking the full weight of authority, informing the Principal and the Governors; and once the clergy, especially the Bishop, got any wind of it there was no knowing what would happen – the whole place might be closed down, or a highly puritanical regime imposed which would frighten away all the liveliest and cleverest students. Besides, these members of staff were not at all sure in their own minds whether premarital intercourse was necessarily wrong any more. 'I mean,' said Fiona Farrell, a colleague of Michael's, a good-humoured spinster of fifty who had a flat in college and a pastoral responsibility for the girls on her floor, 'with Bede teaching situation ethics in the Theology Department, it's hardly surprising the young people should decide it's all right to sleep with each other – always providing, of course, that it's a serious interpersonal relationship based on genuine trust and a non-exploitative giving of oneself to another. Isn't that the jargon? I daresay I'd do the same in their place. My God, when I think of my own student days! The nuns at College wouldn't even let us lie out on the lawns in summer.'

'You mean with your boy friends?'

'Are you joking? Boys weren't allowed within miles of the place. No, I mean if you took a book into the grounds in summer you had to sit bolt upright on the grass to read it. It was considered immodest to lie on the grass. I don't know whether they were afraid we'd be pollinated by the bees or something. . . .'

Fiona, who had come to terms with her own history of sexual repression by making a running joke of it, was holding forth at a dinner party given by Michael and Miriam for a few friends, including Dennis and Angela. Fiona had got them on to the ever-interesting topic with a spicy anecdote about a cleaner at the college who had that very morning found a contraceptive sheath in the girls' loo on Fiona's floor, and had been restrained with some difficulty from reporting it to the Principal. 'Just think,' she sighed, 'I didn't even know what those things were for until I was thirty-five. I used to think people had been playing about with balloons in the parks.'

'Actually, you know,' said Michael, 'it isn't all cant about serious interpersonal relationships and so on. I reckon most of the students who sleep together while they're here get married eventually.'

'Michael finds it rather amazing,' said Miriam sarcastically, 'that anyone should want to marry a girl *after* he's managed to have sex with her.'

'All right, I admit it. That was our generation, wasn't it? You weren't allowed to have sex outside marriage, so naturally having sex came to seem the main point of getting married.' He opened a third bottle of Sainsbury's Catalonian Red. 'And don't pretend it was a one-sided attitude. Girls hung on to their virginities on the same principle in those days.'

'I hung on to mine too long,' Fiona moaned. 'Now I'd gladly give it away. Or auction it for CAFOD.'

'Those long engagements,' said Michael. 'What were they but institutionalized postponements of consummation? Extended foreplay sessions. What d'you think, Dennis?'

'I think our courtship must have been the longest drawn-out foreplay session in the history of sexuality,' said Dennis.

'You could have slept with me if you'd wanted to,' said Angela, piqued, and a little intoxicated.

'Oh yes, a likely story!' he retorted.

'You could have – once.' Angela challenged and held his gaze, until a long-suppressed memory surfaced, of orange light inside a tent, Angela lying back in a two-piece swim suit, inviting him with her arms, her lips.

'Oh, that,' he muttered, blushing. 'That was just once.'

'Oh! Oh! Tell us, tell us!' they chorused. But Dennis changed the subject, and asked about the Paschal Festival which Catholics for an Open Church were planning for the following Easter. It was to be held at Michael's college and was expected to attract members and fellow-travellers from all over the country.

'Adrian feels the movement needs a bit of a boost,' said Michael. 'Now that *HV*'s no longer such an issue, we need to open up a wider range of areas for Catholic renewal. It should be quite an occasion. We've invited Dan Figuera, you know, the South American liberation theology man. Ruth is going to do her charismatic bit. And Miles has agreed to be on a panel on sexuality. Did you know he's come out, by the way?'

'Come out?' said Angela blankly.

'Admitted he's gay. He lives with an ex-monk called Bernard now.'

'I didn't think Catholics could be practising homosexuals,' said Angela.

'Well, officially they can't, of course,' said Michael. 'But I suppose they can just decide to follow their own consciences, like us with birth control. Or the students who sleep with each other before they get married.'

In the car on the way home, Dennis said musingly, 'I wonder what would have happened if we *had* made love that day in Brittany.'

'With our luck, I'd probably have got pregnant,' said Angela. 'Then we'd have had to get married, with you in the Army, on National Serviceman's pay. A proper mess.' She yawned. 'I hate going out mid-week,' she said. 'I feel so shattered the next day.' Angela had a part-time job now, teaching in the ESN school that Nicole attended. They hardly needed the money, but the work gave her satisfaction, and she was able to keep a close eye on Nicole's development.

'No, but supposing you hadn't got pregnant . . . I wonder if we'd have got married at all.'

'You mean, once you'd got me into bed, you would have lost interest in marriage – like Michael was saying?'

'No, I was wondering if *you'd* have married *me*. You never really liked it, did you, for a long time, sex?'

'We weren't very good at it for a long time,' said Angela.

'That's what I mean. If we'd made love that afternoon, it might have put you off for good.'

'Oh, what's the point of speculating,' she said. 'So many things might have been different. We might never have met at all. I nearly went to Liverpool University instead of London – Dad didn't want me leaving home, God rest him.' She sighed and yawned again.

Dennis drove slowly and deliberately, still feeling a little sluggish from the wine at dinner. He debated inwardly whether to propose sex when they got home, and then reflected how unthinkable it would have been to the young man in the orange tent in Brittany that one day he would be free to possess Angela and would be wondering whether to bother. To lift the oppression of this thought, he urged her to make love when they were getting ready for bed. 'If you like,' she said. But when he came from the bathroom she had fallen asleep with the light on and a towel ready to hand on the bedside cabinet. He could not deceive himself that he was unduly disappointed.

While they were clearing up after the dinner party, Michael and Miriam had a row. She accused him of provoking an embarrassing scene between Angela and Dennis. Nonsense, he said, it was all in fun. We were all a bit merry, except you. That's another thing, said Miriam, you pour out far too much wine, you only think a party's going well if everybody's half-seas over, it's not necessary. I hate dinner parties, anyway, she said, scraping plates angrily into the garbage can, you always tell me to cook too much, and then look at the waste. Yes, said Michael sarcastically, you could feed a whole street in Calcutta for a week on our leftovers. Well, it's true, said Miriam, and while we're on the subject, I want to covenant a tenth of our income to CAFOD. You're insane, said Michael, that's over five hundred pounds a year. If the developed countries are going to help the Third World, said Miriam, they've got to accept a drop in their standard of living. We could do without the car, for instance. I'll give up my car if everyone else will give up theirs, said Michael, but I'm damned if I will otherwise. Is that what you call Christian leadership? said Miriam. It's what I call common sense, said Michael, what use is my five hundred pounds to the Third World, most of it would disappear into the pockets of bureaucrats and middlemen anyway. All right, pay me a proper wage for keeping house, and I'll make my own arrangements, said Miriam. Don't be ridiculous, said Michael. It's not ridiculous, said Miriam, white with anger now. Anyway, I'm fed up with housekeeping, I'll get a job of my own. There aren't any music teaching jobs, said Michael, they've all been cut back in the freeze. I don't want to teach music anyway, said Miriam, I want to be a social worker. A social worker! Michael exclaimed, but you're not trained. I'll train, then, said Miriam, there's a course at the Poly. You're going to train as a social worker, said Michael, at great public expense, and ours too, because you won't get a grant, in order to give half your salary away to the Third World? That's right, said Miriam, any objections? What about the kids, he demanded, you always used to say that you didn't want them to be latch-key children. They're old enough to cope, said Miriam, and if you're so worried about them you can arrange your teaching so that you get home when they do.

Michael snatched up the garbage pail and took it outside to the back garden, where he relieved his feelings by banging the dustbin lids. When he returned to the kitchen with a fully worked out account of why he couldn't reorganize his teaching schedule, Miriam had gone to bed, leaving him the rest of the washing-up. Moodily he made himself a cup of instant coffee. The mild lechery which he had been fuelling throughout the evening with wine and sexy talk had evaporated, and he knew exactly what an unfriendly posture Miriam would have adopted in bed upstairs – her face turned towards the wall, her shoulders hunched, her nightdress pulled down and locked between her ankles. These rows, which had become more frequent of late, frightened him, not so much because of the aggression they released in Miriam but because they made him wonder whether they should ever have married each other. Miriam was a puritan, an ascetic, self-denial was no hardship for her, it was the only way she could be happy, whereas more and more he felt himself to be an epicurean. But it was not clear to him whether they had both changed since they had married, or, brainwashed by the cult of matrimony in their youth, had tacitly conspired to conceal and ignore their real identities. There were times when Miriam seemed like an utter stranger, and their married life like a dream from which he was just beginning to waken. But to what?

Dennis couldn't help wondering whether Lynn was sexually

experienced or not. He presumed she must be, if even Catholic students were sleeping together these days, but he knew almost nothing about her private life, except that she was twenty-five, came from South Wales, and had a flat some miles from the factory. She alluded occasionally to attending evening classes for pottery, but otherwise seemed to have no social life. One day he commented on this enigma to a colleague, who said, 'Didn't you know? I thought it'd been all round the shop. She's got a kid.'

'A kid?'

'What they call a one-parent family, these days, isn't it? In other words, some bloke put her in the family way, and then scarpered.'

'Perhaps she didn't want to marry him,' said Dennis.

'Perhaps. Silly girl should've got it adopted, then. Nice girl like her could get married easy. But who'd take on some other bloke's little accident?'

The discovery gave Lynn a new interest and a new pathos in Dennis's eyes. At the same time it made her crush on him a more worrying responsibility. Sometimes he wondered if it would not be kinder to get Lynn transferred to another job, even another factory, so that she could shake off her infatuation and perhaps meet some decent fellow who would be glad to marry her and give the child a father. But he hesitated and procrastinated, because he was unwilling to seem cruel in order to be kind, and because, in truth, he couldn't bear the prospect of parting from her. Then, at Christmas, their relationship changed decisively.

On Christmas Eve, work stopped on the shopfloor and in the stores and offices at midday, and a kind of serial party began, made up of lots of little parties, stretching round the factory like a paper-chain, with a great deal of drinking and seasonal fraternization between management and workers. Dennis did his bit in this respect, touring the different departments with a pocketful of cigars and taking a drink with each group of merrymakers. An atmosphere of boozy bonhomie and tawdry licence spread through the buildings. In the corridors Dennis crunched crisps and broken glass underfoot, skirted couples kissing greedily, mouth on mouth, still holding unfinished drinks and smouldering cigarettes in their outstretched hands, and heard behind the doors of the women's toilets the sound of young girls unaccustomed to liquor moaning and being sick. In the corner of one of the stores a woman packer, her face a raddled, grinning mask of powder and lipstick, was doing high kicks on a table, urged on by a rhythmically clapping crowd. It was the same every year at this season, one afternoon on which the accumulated repressions and frustrations of the rest of the year were discharged in a squalid orgy, the memory of its excesses being quickly buried in the stupor of a domestic Christmas. Usually Dennis merely tolerated the custom with a skin-deep show of party spirit, but today he felt genuinely excited. A project was forming in his head and would not be removed: under cover of this feast of misrule he could safely give Lynn a kiss, something, he realized, he had been wanting to do for some time. There would be nothing odd or untoward about such a gesture – on the contrary, bosses were kissing their secretaries all over the factory. Lynn could not imagine that he meant by it anything more than a friendly sign of affection, nor would it give scandal if they were observed. The more he thought about this idea, and the more nips of Scotch he took on his tour of the factory, the more excited Dennis became, and as he approached his own department again he was gripped by a hollow, breathless feeling of erotic expectation more intense than anything he had felt in many years.

'Give us a kiss, then, Dennis!'

Doreen Wills, from Personnel, normally the hardbitten career woman incarnate, was ogling him from the door of the hospitality room, a glass in her hand and a paper hat askew on her upswept hairdo. She pointed upwards to a sprig of mistletoe pinned to the door frame. He gave her a perfunctory peck on the cheek, but she twisted her face round to glue her lips to his. 'Happy Christmas, Dennis, darling,' she said, breathing gin and sweet vermouth into his face. He responded absently, looking over her shoulder into the room where an impromptu disco was in progress. 'You know, I could really fancy you, Dennis,' said Doreen. 'Come and have a dance.'

'Sorry, Doreen, I don't go in for that kind of dancing,' he said. 'Have you seen Lynn anywhere?'

'Ah! Want to get her under the mistletoe, eh?'

'No, just got some work to finish off,' he lied, nettled by the shrewdness of her guess.

'For Christ's sake, Dennis, it's Christmas Eve! Anyway, I think she's gone home.'

'Home?' Dismayed, Dennis rushed off to Lynn's office. It was empty, and her coat had gone from its hanger behind the door. Angrily Dennis kicked this door shut, cutting off the sounds of carousing, and strode into his own office by the communicating door. Lynn, dressed in her outdoor clothes, looked up from behind his desk.

'Oh,' she said. 'I was just leaving you a card.' She held out a Christmas card to him like an alibi. He approached her and took it across the desk, in a queer reversal of their usual roles. 'It's very nice,' he said, glancing at it. 'Thank you.'

'I had a job getting a religious one,' she said. Then, leaning forward to peer at him, 'You've got lipstick all over your face.'

'Doreen Wills caught me under the mistletoe.'

'Lucky you,' she said drily. Her back was to the fading light of the December afternoon and he could not discern the expression on her face as she spoke.

'Unlucky, you mean.' He rubbed furiously at his mouth with the back of his hand.

'Don't do that, you'll just make it worse. Here, have a Kleenex.' She rummaged in her handbag.

'Pity we don't have a bit of mistletoe in here,' he said, attempting a light-hearted tone that came out as a strangled croak.

She looked up quickly. 'I'll remember to get some next year, then,' she said, holding out the tissue.

His hand closed over hers and pulled her gently forwards over the desk. 'I can't wait that long,' he said, 'to wish you a happy Christmas.' Supporting herself with her free hand, Lynn turned her cheek to receive his kiss. He had forgotten how soft a young girl's skin could be. 'That wasn't much of a kiss,' he said, keeping hold of her hand. 'Come round here.'

She shook her head.

'Please.'

'You come, if you want to,' she whispered.

Without letting go of her hand, as if performing some stately dance, he stepped round the end of the desk and drew her into his arms.

What followed took Dennis completely by surprise. He had had in mind a single, wistful kiss, a tender but decorous embrace that would convey his appreciation of Lynn and his affection for her, but at the same time confirm their mutual awareness of the circumstances that made any deeper relationship impossible. Lynn, however, clung to him as if she would never be prised loose, she flattened herself against him like a climber marooned on a cliff-face, she shuddered in his arms and sighed and moaned and ran her fingers through his hair and thrust her tongue between his teeth as if she wanted to climb inside his mouth and wriggle down his throat. Dennis's feeble lust was soon swamped by this demonstration. He was appalled by the intensity of the passion he had aroused, and daunted by the task of seeming equal to it. At last Lynn peeled her lips from his, sighed and nestled against his shoulder. Dennis, stroking her back as if comforting a child, stared past her head at the dusk gathering over the company car-park. What now, he thought, what now? What does one do next? What does one say? There was nothing he could say, he realized, after trying out a few phrases in his head, that wouldn't sound either coldly dismissive or recklessly committing. It seemed to Dennis that a stark choice already stared him in the face between being a cowardly prig or an unfaithful husband; that, incredible as it seemed, one kiss had tumbled him irretrievably into a maelstrom of tragic passion and insoluble moral dilemmas.

'Shall I take you home?' he said at last. It was the most neutral thing he could think of, but the way Lynn nodded agreement immediately convinced him that, without intending it, he had sealed some sexual contract with her in the code which governed such matters.

In the car, neither of them spoke, except for her to give, and him to acknowledge, directions. Dennis drove like an automaton. He felt deprived of free will, as if the wheels of his car were locked into grooves carrying him inexorably towards adultery. He felt no excitement or lust, only a sense of doom and a fear that he would fail sexually, humiliating both of them.

He stopped the car outside a semi-detached Victorian villa. 'Will you come in?' Lynn said. It did not seem to Dennis that she meant it as a real question or that he had a real choice. He followed her into the ground-floor flat. There was a pushchair in the hall. 'I suppose you know I've got a little boy?' she said.

'I heard rumours,' he said. 'I didn't like to pry.' The sight of the pushchair had given him hope of a reprieve. 'Where is he now?'

'I've got a friend who collects him from the nursery. She keeps him till I call.'

The main room in the flat was furnished as a bed-sitting room. Lynn lit the gas fire, took off her coat, and flopped down on the divan bed. 'Too much Cyprus sherry,' she said, closing her eyes.

Dennis stooped over her, hopeful again. 'Are you all right?'

She put her arms round his neck and pulled him down beside her. Dennis stroked her breasts through the woollen dress she was wearing, put his hand under her skirt and slid it up over legs glazed in nylon tights. Now that he could see no way of avoiding the sexual act, he was impatient to get it over. 'Why don't you take this off?' he said, plucking at her dress; and sat up himself to take off his jacket, tie, shoes.

This cannot be happening, he thought. Behind him, Lynn said: 'Have you got something?'

'What?'

'You know. . . .'

Dennis stopped in the act of undoing his belt, and turned to face her. She was still fully dressed, her skirt up round her thighs. 'Aren't you on the Pill, then?'

'No. Why should I be?'

'I don't know . . . I just thought. . . .'

'I haven't got a fella, you know. And I don't go in for one-night stands.'

620

'I'm sorry, Lynn.' Red with embarrassment, he began to do up his belt, put on his shoes, his tie, his jacket. When he was dressed, he turned to her. She had not moved. He pulled down the hem of her skirt. 'Can we try and forget this ever happened?' he said.

'No,' she said.

He made a helpless shrugging gesture. 'Can we have a cup of tea, then?'

She laughed, sighed and sat up. Over tea he heard the story of her life, in brief. Brought up in a small town, chapel-going community; trained as a secretary and went to work for a local legal firm. Was seduced by her boss, a married man, and after an extended affair, became pregnant. Refused to have an abortion and left home to avoid disgracing the family. Dennis couldn't help thinking how close they had come to re-enacting the whole sequence. As if reading his thoughts, Lynn said: 'I had to stop you just now – I didn't want it to happen again.'

'It was just as well,' said Dennis. 'I think we were both a bit drunk.'

'You won't ever do it now, will you,' said Lynn, with a wry smile. 'I've missed my chance.'

'What chance, Lynn? I'm nobody's chance – certainly not yours.' Lynn said nothing. 'I should never have started it,' he said. 'It was all my fault, I apologize.' Lynn stirred her tea, smiling enigmatically. Dennis looked at his watch. 'I'd better be going.'

He kissed her again on leaving, trying to make it a chaste and chastened kiss. She clung to him for what seemed like hours, but did not attempt any further show of passion. He let himself out of the house.

When Dennis got home, Angela was in the kitchen, making mince pies. 'What's the matter with your face?' she said.

'It must be lipstick,' he said. 'Doreen Wills trapped me under the mistletoe.'

Angela yelled with laughter. 'Poor you!' She was in good humour, he noted. She liked Christmas, all the bustle and preparation and wrapping of presents, the orgy of spending.

'Where's Nicole?'

'In the lounge. There's a Blue Peter Special I said she could watch, in a few minutes.'

Nicole was sitting cross-legged on a cushion in front of the television. She was addicted to TV and her watching had to be carefully rationed. She scrambled to her feet and came to give Dennis a hug. 'My Daddy!' she sighed, as if he had been away for weeks.

'How are you, love?'

'I'm all right.' She drew him gently to a chair facing the TV and sat on his knee, returning her gaze to the screen.

Nicole, at eight, was doing very well. She could swim like a fish, read quite advanced Ladybird books and write her name legibly on Christmas cards. She was cheerful and friendly and related well to other people. Dennis loved her dearly, yet he could never set eyes on her without a pang. All mongols looked more like each other than like their parents, but beneath the character-istic heavy, curved jaw, the snub nose and stubby unfinished ears, the short thick neck and barrel-shaped torso, he could discern a likeness to Angela when he had first met her – as though an X-ray portrait of Nicole would reveal the ghostly image of the beautiful, gifted girl she might have been but for the rogue chromosome. Nicole! How many times had he regretted the choice of that exotic name, suggestive of French chic and feminine allure!

Some old black-and-white film, a romantic melodrama by the look of it, was coming to an end. Hero and heroine were exchang-ing husky endearments against an obviously painted backdrop of lake and mountains. Violin music swelled in the background. 'Waiting for Blue Peter?' said Dennis conversationally.

Nicole nodded, then pointed at the TV. 'First they kiss,' she explained, 'then it's finished.' She had seen the endings of a lot of old films.

Perhaps, thought Dennis, it would be all right after all. When Lynn sobered up, she would see the afternoon's events as a moment of madness which they could bury, like her letter, and carry on as before. No harm, thankfully, had been done. Perhaps it would even be easier between them, now that the pressure had been relieved. Pressure, safety valves – with these hydraulic images Dennis sought to reassure himself that all was well, that the episode was closed. But the next morning, while most of the family were still in their dressing-gowns after a late breakfast and the opening of presents, there was a ring on the doorbell and Lynn appeared on the step, a small package wrapped in gift paper in her hand. Her face was white and anxious.

'I bought this for your little girl, Nicole,' she said. 'I forgot to give it to you yesterday.'

'Come in, Lynn,' said Dennis, with a sinking heart. 'Come in.'

In Rome that Christmas, Pope Paul, assisted by the Cardinal Penitentiary, chipped with an ornamental tool at the bricked-up Holy Door in the façade of St Peter's and thus inaugurated the Holy Year of 1975. A Holy Year, in case you are wondering, is a year in which the Pope grants a special plenary indulgence to all those who visit Rome and fulfil the usual conditions. The custom dates back to medieval times. In the corridors of the Vatican there was hope that the Holy Year of 1975 would knit the fraying fabric of the Church together by a worldwide demonstration of homage to the Holy See. This expectation, however, was disappointed. The Holy Year was not a success, not even for the Italian tourist trade. Catholics didn't seem to be as interested as they used to be in obtaining plenary indulgences.

Throughout the world, the Church continued to boil with conflict and controversy. Since the Council, this had been chiefly provoked by the ecclesiastical Left, who wanted to identify the Church with socialism, abolish priestly celibacy, ordain women, demythologize the Scriptures, repeal *Humanae Vitae*, and so on. But now a new threat to unity was emerging on the Right, in the person of a French archbishop called Lefebvre, who was right wing enough to think that Pope Paul was a crypto-communist and that the Vatican Council had betrayed the Catholic faith to modernism. This point of view he cleverly associated with a campaign to bring back the old Latin mass – a cause which aroused ready support in the breasts of older Catholics nostalgic for the spiritual certainties of their youth and dismayed by the rapidity of recent change. Tridentine masses, celebrated in defiance of ecclesiastical authority by priests sympathetic to Lefebvre, attracted large congregations and great publicity. The threat of schism loomed. Frantically, Rome tried to steady the rocking boat: Lefebvre was admonished, but so was the modernizing theologian Hans Küng, for questioning the doctrine of papal infallibility.

The Catholics for an Open Church Paschal Festival was going to be a sort of counter-demonstration to Archbishop Lefebvre's movement, and a showcase for the pluralist, progressive, postconciliar Church, as Michael explained to Polly and Jeremy over aperitifs one weekend in February, when his and Miriam's long-mooted visit to the converted oast-house had finally materialized. The Festival programme was settled in outline: the participants would assemble on Holy Saturday morning and throughout the day there would be a continuous programme of lectures, workshops and panels on theology, liturgy, ethics and pastoral practice, leading up to the Easter Vigil and Midnight Mass celebrated by Father Bede, the College chaplain (since Austin was still under suspension), followed by an agape and all-night party, and culminating in a special Easter Dawn Service which had yet to be devised, but would probably involve sacred dancing by nuns.

'Far out,' said Jeremy. 'I want to film it. The whole thing.'

'Really?' said Michael.

'It's perfect for an Elton special. We'll call it "The New Catholics".' Jeremy now worked for a commercial television company and had his own networked documentary every fortnight, called the Elton Special.

'Adrian will be tickled pink,' said Michael.

'So will you, admit it,' said Miriam, squashing Michael since politeness restrained her from squashing Jeremy. She was suspicious of Jeremy, a small but shapely man, with a handsome head and a mischievous, slightly vulpine smile, like a fox in a fable. She couldn't decide whether she positively disliked him, but she certainly didn't trust him – or, for that matter, Polly, who was a charming and efficient hostess, but slightly abstracted in manner, as if she were all the time wondering what use she could put you to in her next column. The affluence of the Elton ménage also made Miriam feel defensive. If their own style of furnishing was Habitat and Handed-down, this was Heals and Harrods: a kitchen straight out of the colour supplements, an Italian dining suite of solid oak and tubular steel, Scandinavian real-hide module furniture in the living room, Japanese hi-fi and video equipment banked up against one wall like a showroom display, hand-woven curtaining fabrics, wall-to-wall Wilton everywhere, a mosaic-topped coffee table covered with the latest weekly and monthly magazines, and a new hardback novel in its pale lemon jacket that had been widely reviewed in the last few days. Miriam could see Michael covertly fingering everything and examining the brand names in barely controlled paroxysms of envy. The Eltons had two Connemara ponies in their stable, and a swimming-pool and a sauna and a sheepdog and a trail-bike and a rowing machine and a table-tennis table and a Victorian rocking horse and a stunning Swedish *au pair* who made Martin's ears glow bright red just by looking at him. Martin and the other two children were as enchanted by this palace of pleasure as Michael. When it had begun to snow heavily at lunchtime and Miriam anxiously wondered aloud whether they would be able to get away on the following day, her youngest, Elizabeth, had burst out, 'Oh, Mummy, I do hope not!' to the great amusement of the Elton children. These, Miriam had to admit, were less spoiled than one might have expected, though infinitely more precocious and sophisticated than her own offspring. Abigail, at thirteen, was already dressing with flair, and had a way of patting her hair with both hands, and of curling up in an armchair, that showed an intuitive sense of her own allure, whereas Miriam's Helen, nearly two years older, was still a tomboy; and Jason, at fifteen, looked as tall and mature as the seventeen-year-old Martin. Miriam watched the interaction of these children with painful interest, scarcely able to restrain herself from intervening to coax from Martin and Helen the qualities she knew they possessed. She wondered fleetingly if she had failed them somehow, they seemed

625

so shy and gauche beside the Eltons; but seeing Michael envying, coveting, flattering, affecting a worldliness that wasn't their true style at all, she braced herself to keep the family's conscience, to resist the blandishments of Mammon.

'Don't you think,' she said now to Michael, as they sipped their pre-dinner drinks around the log fire, with the curtains cosily drawn against the snow, 'that having TV cameras all over the place will inhibit people?'

'No way,' Jeremy intervened. 'After a few hours, they'll forget we're there, believe me. Sometimes I can hardly credit it myself, the things people will do in front of the cameras. We were making this programme the other day about a wedding, a sort of portrait in depth of a typical suburban wedding. . . .' He laughed reminiscently, and Polly took up the story.

'Yes, you see, Jeremy wanted to get the expression on the girl's face when she woke up in the morning and realized it was her wedding day, and would you believe it, they let him park a cameraman in her bedroom all night.'

'Then he overslept, and we had to get the bride to fake it after all,' said Jeremy. 'But honestly I think, if we'd asked, they'd have let us tag along on the honeymoon and film their first fuck.'

'I suppose they were getting paid,' said Miriam frostily. Jeremy admitted that there was usually a fee in such cases. 'And shall we get paid if you film our Festival?'

'Oh, I don't think COC would worry about that, darling,' said Michael.

'Why not? I don't see why the TV people should get us for nothing.'

'Miriam's perfectly right, of course,' said Jeremy. 'There would certainly be some money in it for your organization.' He did not seem in the least discomfited by Miriam's insistence, but rather to respect her for it, 'I'll write to your chairman – what's his name again?'

'Adrian. Adrian Walsh.'

Polly gave a little shriek. 'Not that tall bony boy in Cath. Soc. with glasses and the huge missal?'

'Polly – why don't you come to the Festival with Jeremy?' said Michael. 'There'll be a lot of old friends besides Adrian there.'

'I don't know if I could bear it,' said Polly. 'It's just the sort of thing to make one feel incredibly ancient. Perhaps I will. But supposing I got converted back to the Catholic Church? I'd have to leave you, darling,' she said, with a mock-disconsolate *moue* at Jeremy, 'and make you go back to your horrid bitch of a first wife.'

'No, no,' said Michael. 'If you get converted to our kind of Catholicism you don't have to worry about that kind of thing. You can do whatever you think is right.'

'Really?' said Jeremy, pricking his ears.

'Well, within reason,' said Michael.

After dinner (home-made asparagus soup, a fragrant chicken casserole, chocolate soufflé, Wine Society Beaujolais) they played a tournament of electronic TV tennis with the children; then, when these had retired to bed, or to listen to pop records in Jason's room, or to watch TV in Abigail's, Jeremy distributed whisky and liqueurs and showed some recent Elton Specials on his video cassette equipment. The programmes were all identical in technique. There was no explanatory commentary, just a montage of images and recorded voices. Jeremy explained that his method was to shoot everything in sight, ask people questions, and then make an edited account of the results. The general effect, Miriam felt, was to make the subjects look rather foolish. In the course of this entertainment, Gertrude came into the room to ask if she could take a sauna bath.

'Sure, you know how to turn it on,' said Jeremy.

'Isn't that rather extravagant, darling?' Polly murmured, after the girl had gone. It was the first evidence of the weekend that the concept of extravagance was recognized in this household. Perhaps, Miriam thought, the fact that Gertrude was young and pretty had something to do with it. Jeremy brushed aside the objection. Someone else might like a sauna later.

'I've never had a sauna bath,' said Michael. 'What's it like?'

'There you are!' cried Jeremy. 'We'll all have a sauna together. It can seat four.'

'Together?' said Miriam doubtfully.

'It's all right, Miriam, relax.' Jeremy twinkled. 'We always offer guests the choice: with towels or without.'

'With, then,' said Miriam firmly.

'What d'you have to do?' said Michael, beady-eyed. 'Beating yourself with twigs comes into it, doesn't it?'

'Whisking is optional,' said Jeremy. 'And we don't have the proper birch twigs anyway. Could fix you up with some tomato canes, if that sort of thing turns you on.'

'Basically,' Polly explained, 'it's a wooden cabin, with a stove in the middle, that gets extremely hot, but so dry that it's not uncomfortable. You sit in it for ten minutes or so, and sweat a lot, and then you go and have a cold shower and then you wait a bit and go back into the sauna and then shower again, as many times as you like.'

'I've known Gertrude go through the cycle six times,' said Jeremy. 'She's a real addict.'

'What's the point of it?' said Miriam.

'Well, it's like lying in the sun and then diving into a swimming-pool and then lying in the sun again.'

'And what's the point of *that*?'

Jeremy laughed. 'It's pleasant.'

'It sounds like eating salted peanuts to make yourself thirsty to me,' said Miriam.

'That's a good idea,' said Jeremy. 'Let's all have another drink.'

'Not if we're going to sauna,' said Polly.

'I've had quite enough to drink anyway,' said Miriam. 'And so have you, Michael,' she added as he held out his glass.

'Tell you what,' said Jeremy. 'I'll mull some wine over the fire afterwards.' He bared his sharp-edged teeth. 'And show you some of my special bedtime videotapes.'

'Not *Deep Throat*, for heaven's sake, darling,' said Polly.

'*Deep Throat*? Have you got that here?' said Michael eagerly.

'Friend of mine brought back a pirated tape from the States,' said Jeremy. 'It's hilarious.'

'It's quite disgustingly crude,' said Polly.

'I'd be jolly interested to see it, I must admit,' said Michael.

'What's it about?' said Miriam.

'Oh, you must have read about it, Miriam,' said Polly. 'It's about this girl, Linda Lovelace, who can only come when she's sucking men off. A typical male chauvinist fantasy.'

'But they surely can't show that in a film,' said Miriam.

'Oh yes they can,' said Polly.

'Well, don't let's argue about it now,' said Jeremy, 'let's have our sauna.'

Michael and Miriam went to their room, as instructed, to undress and put on bathrobes. 'You'll find a couple of spare ones in the cupboard,' said Polly, and inevitably these garments were posher than their own dressing-gowns. While Miriam was undressing, Michael came up behind her and ran his hands over her body. 'What fun, eh?' he murmured, nibbling her ear.

'I'm not going to watch that film,' said Miriam.

'Don't be a spoil-sport, Miriam,' he wheedled.

'If he puts that film on,' she said, 'I'm going straight to bed. To sleep.'

'That's blackmail,' said Michael, taking his hands away. 'That's using your body to extort obedience to your will.'

'Well, it's either me or Linda Lovelace,' said Miriam. 'Take your pick.'

'Why d'you want to stop me from watching a blue movie? I mean, why do you feel so threatened by it?'

'That's a phrase you've picked up from Jeremy, isn't it, blue movie? It sounds nicer than pornographic film.'

'Whatever you call them.'

'I think they're sinful,' she said, 'since you ask.'

Michael looked taken aback. Even to her own ear, 'sinful' had a slightly archaic ring. 'I don't see what harm they can do to adults,' he mumbled, 'married people.' Then, with a sly grin he added, 'You might even learn a thing or two.'

'Ah ha!' She pounced on the inference. 'Look, I know how it's done, I just don't want to do it.' She met his eyes and held them, conscious that their talk was wobbling on a perilous edge between badinage and a serious quarrel. Michael opted for badinage.

'It's only a harmless protein,' he said. It was an old joke

between them, a line from the sex instruction film they had watched together long ago.

'I get quite enough protein, thank you,' said Miriam. 'No way.'

'That's a phrase you've picked up from Jeremy,' said Michael.

'Oh, I don't deny that his style is contagious,' said Miriam. 'I just don't believe he has any principles.'

Jeremy and Polly were waiting for them in the hall, draped in matching kimonos and wearing wellington boots. 'There's only one snag about the sauna,' said Jeremy. 'You have to go through the yard to get to it, and there's a fair amount of snow on the ground. So watch your footing. Here are some wellies for you two.'

Shrieking and gasping at the shock of the cold night air, and clutching their bathrobes around them, they galumphed across the yard in their rubber boots, leaving deep footprints in the snow. Jeremy threw open the door of one of the outbuildings, and they tumbled inside. Gertrude looked up, startled, from a slatted pine bench where she was lying, swathed in a hooded dressing gown. There were a couple of other benches, a shower cubicle, and in one corner what looked like a rustic garden shed.

'Is it good and hot, Gertrude?' Jeremy asked.

'Perfect,' she replied. 'One hundred degrees already.'

Jeremy distributed big blue towels, which they exchanged for their bathrobes with varying degrees of decorum.

The heat inside the sauna made Miriam gasp. 'Oh!' she said. 'I shall never be able to stand this. It's burning my nostrils.'

'Breathe through your mouth,' said Polly. 'And sit down low.'

There were two stepped benches on each side of the tiny cabin, with the boxed-in stove on the floor between them. The two couples divided and sat facing each other. Miriam, sitting at the lowest level, found herself staring up between Jeremy's thighs at his surprisingly large genitals. She looked hastily away, then examined his face to see if his self-exposure had been deliberate. His grin, however, was no more mischievous than usual. 'OK, Miriam?' he said.

'Now I know what a leg of lamb feels like inside a Romertopf,' she said.

'It's more comfortable without a towel.'

'Thanks, I'll put up with the discomfort.'

'Jeremy,' said Polly, 'leave Miriam alone.'

'I want to make a hedonist of her,' said Jeremy. 'It's a challenge.'

'You're banging your head against a brick wall,' said Michael. 'I've been trying all our married life.'

'You weren't much of a hedonist yourself, once,' said Polly. 'Remember how I shocked you when I came back from Italy? You must have changed.'

'The world has changed,' said Michael, 'and I've been trying to catch up. But Miriam won't let me.'

'When did the world change?' said Polly.

'The world changed on or about the tenth of June, 1968.'

'Don't you mean May?' said Jeremy. 'Paris? *Les évènements?*'

'No, on the tenth of June, 1968, I was in Oxford, checking into a hotel. . . .' He recounted the story of the undergraduate in the white suit who had asked the price of a double room. 'I realized then that people were no longer ashamed to admit they wanted to fuck. Now on my own honeymoon – that would have made a programme and a half, Jeremy. . . .' Michael told the story of the twin beds. 'I was legally married, dammit. All I wanted was a reasonably comfortable bed to consummate the marriage. God knows, we'd waited long enough. And I was tongue-tied with embarrassment. Beads of perspiration literally stood out on my face.'

'Talking of perspiration,' said Miriam, who had not enjoyed this narrative, 'how much longer do we have to stay in here?'

Jeremy glanced at a clock embedded in the wall. 'You two could go and have your shower now. Polly and I will stay a bit longer.'

Michael and Miriam emerged from the sauna to find that Gertrude had gone. 'Let's shower together,' said Michael.

'I wish you wouldn't use that word,' said Miriam, as they peeled off their towels and donned shower caps.

'What word?'

'You know.'

'Everybody uses it nowadays.'

Miriam stepped into the shower stall and Michael squeezed in beside her. 'I don't,' she said.

'You're not suggesting I picked it up from Jeremy, are you? Actually, I picked it up from D.H. Lawrence. Tha's got a loovely coont, lass,' he said, putting his hand between her legs.

Miriam pulled the lever behind his head. Michael yelled and she herself gasped as the cold water drenched them. But the sensation was not unpleasant. They wrapped themselves in their towels again, and Michael knocked on the door of the sauna, receiving a muffled acknowledgement from within. He said quickly as he sat down beside her, 'Look, do me a favour – just relax and let me enjoy my weekend, eh? Just this once, indulge me. I don't often get the chance to enjoy *la dolce vita.*'

'What good does it do you?'

'I just want to know what it's like. I don't want to die a virgin, *ladolcevita*wise.'

'You're such a baby,' she scoffed. But she allowed herself to be persuaded back into the sauna for a second go. Jeremy filled a ladle with water and sprinkled a few drops on the stove, which hissed and exhaled a puff of steam. As he moved back to his seat, stepping over Polly, his towel slipped from his waist.

'Oops!' he exclaimed. 'Oh, to hell with it, I'm sorry, Miriam, but it just isn't a proper sauna with a towel.' He sat down naked.

'I'm going to take mine off too,' said Michael, suiting the action to the deed.

'Goodness, how shy-making,' said Polly. 'Hadn't we better do the same, Miriam?'

'No,' said Miriam. Polly hesitated, her breasts already half-exposed, but stayed decent. Miriam was angry, but uncertain what to do. To get up and leave would, she felt, be an admission of defeat as well as making an embarrassing scene. But to sit facing Jeremy's blatant nakedness and knowing grin was also an embarrassment, and a kind of defeat. In the circumstances, all she could think of doing was to close her eyes and try to meditate (she had been to evening classes in transcendental meditation.) But what she found herself thinking about was how different Jeremy's penis looked from Michael's – not only bigger, but a different colour and shape, brown and straight like a heavy rope-end, whereas Michael's was pale and curved and slightly pointed, reminding her, when it was flaccid, of a mouse asleep with its head in its paws. It was very hot. She felt perspiration trickling down her breastbone and on to her belly and between her legs. She leaned back and rested her head against Michael's knees. He massaged her head gently with his finger tips, loosening the skin that was tight across the top of her skull. This was an artful move. She was not fooled, of course – she knew that he knew that she liked having her head massaged, and for that matter he knew she knew he knew. But her anger receded. There was certainly something about heat that sapped the will. She wouldn't have greatly cared, now, if her own towel had slipped off, except that she was self-conscious about her almost non-existent breasts; she imagined Jeremy's quick, disappointed appraisal, and Polly's complacent glance. Michael, of course, had always had a thing about big breasts. Well, he was getting an eyeful now, no doubt.

Michael was all enthusiasm for the sauna. He questioned Jeremy about the cost of buying and running the equipment, and talked of installing one himself. 'There must be at least twenty-five things we need more urgently than a sauna,' said Miriam. 'Where would you put it – in the garage? And cool off under the garden hose?'

'Why not?' said Jeremy. 'In Finland they rush outside and roll in the snow.'

'Well, we could do that ourselves tonight,' Polly observed jokingly.

'Great idea!' said Jeremy. 'What about it, folks?'

'Anything you say,' said Michael.

'It *would* be rather a lark,' said Polly.

'You're all mad,' said Miriam, opening her eyes and sitting up. 'You'll catch your deaths.'

Michael begged her with his eyes to join in, and as they were mustering by the door of the outbuilding, murmured, 'Come on, darling, be a sport.' She shook her head, and pulled her bathrobe more tightly around her. The whole prank, she was now convinced, was being staged-managed by Jeremy to get them all naked together. 'I'll watch you make fools of yourselves,' she said.

'Right, strip off, children, and away we go,' said Jeremy. 'Across the yard and into the paddock. Last one to roll in the snow is a cissy.' He dropped his towel from his hips and raced barefoot into the night, followed by Michael. Miriam watched Polly's broad buttocks jouncing in the light that streamed out across the snow from the open door as she waddled after them, squealing and shrieking. In the paddock they raced in circles, yelling and laughing, throwing snowballs, tipping each other up in flurries of powdery snow, rubbing handfuls of it into each other's bare skin. More light was shed on the scene from windows in the house, as curtains were drawn and sashes thrown up. Cries of wonder and encouragement came from the children, hilariously delighted at this untoward behaviour in their parents. It was, Miriam had to admit, a surprisingly innocent and appealing spectacle, a cold pastoral. The wagging breasts and penises, the dark smudges of pubic hair, seemed quite unshocking in that crystal setting. Miriam began to regret that she had not, after all, joined in. It seemed possible, suddenly, that she had been quite mistaken in resisting the momentum of the whole evening, that there was nothing after all to be afraid of, that there might be a kind of pagan salvation, a way back to that state of innocence the poets called the Golden Age, in this shared nakedness, without shame, without erotic intent, this pure, childlike play of naked bodies in the snow. Miriam's hand plucked at the belt of her bathrobe. But it was too late. The others were already running back. Then, as she watched, Michael seemed to stumble and fall, and did not get up. Jeremy and Polly stooped over him, and began dragging and carrying him towards the open door. Miriam ran out to meet them.

'You've killed him!' she screamed.

'He's all right, he's breathing,' gasped Jeremy.

'*Breathing*! I should hope he is breathing,' Miriam shouted. 'Otherwise there'll be a few other people not breathing around here.'

Michael soon recovered when they got him inside, wrapped

him up and chafed his limbs. 'Don't say "I told you so",' were his first words to Miriam.

'I can't understand it,' said Jeremy. 'The Finns do it all the time.'

'Michael doesn't happen to be a Finn,' said Miriam.

'I'll phone Doctor Gordon,' said Polly. 'Just to be on the safe side.'

'I'm perfectly all right,' said Michael. 'Please don't bother.'

'Phone him,' said Miriam.

The doctor came and examined Michael, probed him with a stethoscope and took his pulse.

'You fainted because of the shock to your body,' he said. 'The sudden change of temperature.'

'But the other two didn't faint,' Michael pointed out.

'Well, they've probably got stronger hearts,' said the doctor.

'You mean, I've got a weak heart?'

'Only relatively. But I wouldn't go rolling about in the snow without any clothes on again, especially after getting overheated and putting away a fair amount of drink.'

After the doctor had gone, Michael allowed himself to be taken off to bed, without any further reference to mulled wine or *Deep Throat*. In bed, he clung to Miriam more like a child than a lover, his penis as small and soft as a mouse. 'So I'm not going to die young of cancer, after all,' he said. 'I'm going to die young of a heart attack.'

'Oh, be quiet and go to sleep,' said Miriam. She did not confess that she had been on the point of rushing out into the snow herself. 'By the way,' she said, for it seemed a good moment to make the announcement, 'I've applied to the Poly for admission to the social workers' course.'

Michael gave out a grunt which she interpreted as resigned acceptance.

In the kitchen, where they were tidying up, Jeremy said to Polly, 'Pity about that. I hope he'll be all right.'

'What were you up to, anyway?' said Polly. 'What was your little game?'

'What do you think?'

'You must be mad,' she said, 'to think that you had any chance at all with those two.'

'Oh, I don't know,' said Jeremy. 'Michael was hypnotized by your boobs.'

'He always was,' said Polly.

'And Miriam kept sneaking glances at my prick.'

'So I noticed. But they're still just about the last couple in the world. . . . Apart from the fact that *I'm* not interested in that sort of carry-on, as you very well know.'

'Well, that was it, you see. It struck me that if I could persuade a couple of square RCs to have a go at group sex, you couldn't very well drop out.'

'That was quite clever of you, I must admit,' said Polly.

'Then the silly bugger has to spoil it all by passing out,' said Jeremy.

'Poor Michael,' said Polly. 'How awful if he'd died!'

'Not a bad way to go, actually,' said Jeremy. He got out a bottle of whisky and held it up to the light. 'I can think of worse deaths.'

'Aren't you coming to bed?' said Polly.

'No, I think I'll do some work,' he said. 'Have we got any books on the Catholic Church? I really think that there may be a programme in this Festival thing.'

'I think I've got a biography of John XXIII somewhere,' said Polly. 'Will you read in bed?'

'No, I'll go in the study,' said Jeremy. 'Just tell me where the book is.'

Jeremy read for an hour and a half with total concentration. Then he closed his book and turned out the lights on the ground floor. Quietly he climbed the staircase and entered his bedroom. Polly was asleep, breathing deeply, a glass of water and a bottle of Nembutal tablets on her bedside table. Jeremy touched her shoulder lightly, but she did not stir. He left the bedroom and went softly along to one of the three bathrooms in the house. A few minutes later he emerged, in pyjamas and dressing-gown, but instead of returning to his bedroom he turned in the opposite direction and climbed another flight of stairs to Gertrude's room. He entered quietly, without knocking.

The next morning the snow was beginning to thaw, but Miriam insisted on leaving immediately after breakfast in case the roads got worse, and no one attempted to resist her will. The drive home through the slush was slow and nerve-racking and it was dark by the time they arrived. When Miriam opened the door of the house the phone was ringing. It was Angela.

'Is Dennis there?'

'No, why?'

'We've had a row. He's walked out.'

'What about?'

'He's been having an affair with his secretary.'

'*Dennis*! I don't believe it.'

'I found a letter in his wallet. I was looking for money for mass this morning.'

'Oh, Angela!'

'She came round on Christmas morning with a present for Nicole. I thought she was just being nice. She's not really all that pretty. Young, of course.'

'Listen, I don't understand,' said Miriam. 'Why did she write him a letter if they see each other every day at work?'

'Apparently that's what she does, she slips love letters into his correspondence. This one was to tell him that she'd been on the Pill for over a month.'

'You mean, they haven't actually. . . .'

'According to Dennis, they both got drunk at the Christmas booze-up at the factory and he took her home and he was going to sleep with her because he thought he ought to – '

'Ought to?'

'Because they'd been snogging, he thought it was expected. He thought she'd be hurt if he didn't.'

Miriam couldn't help laughing. 'He would! Just like Dennis.'

'But then he discovered that she wasn't on the Pill, so they didn't.'

'This doesn't sound so bad, after all,' said Miriam. Michael came into the room and cocked an enquiring eyebrow. She gestured him away.

'Yes, but then we had this terrible row and I think he's gone to her,' said Angela.

'Why?'

'Because I told him to.'

'Why did you?'

'Because of this terrible row.' Angela sounded impatient, as if Miriam were being slow on the uptake. 'He said he'd worshipped me with his body and I'd never shown any gratitude. So I told him to try his secretary.'

Miriam was silent, not knowing what to say. It was hard to imagine Dennis moved to the pitch of invoking his marriage vows.

'He said I use Nicole as an excuse for ignoring his needs.'

'That was unkind,' said Miriam loyally. 'And untrue.'

'It was unkind,' said Angela. 'I suppose it might be true. I told him I hadn't got anything out of our sex life for years. That was unkind, but true.' Her voice sounded surprisingly calm and slightly drowsy.

'Are you all right, Angela?' said Miriam. 'Have you taken anything?'

'Just a couple of Valium. Then I had some sherry.'

'That's going to knock you out. You'd better go to bed. I'd come over, but we've only just got back from Kent and the roads are terrible.'

'I'll be all right.'

'I'm sure Dennis will come back tonight.' In the background Miriam could hear Michael and the children arguing peevishly about who should bring something in from the car. She felt a deep anger against Dennis, and a deep compassion for Angela; but how strange it was, and slightly shameful, that the news should make her feel fonder of Michael.

'I never really wanted to marry Dennis, you know,' Angela was saying. 'I tried to get out of it, but he wore me down. Why didn't he leave me alone?' There was a long, choked silence on the line;

then Angela began to cry, like a child, gulping for breath between sobs.

'Angela, listen, hang on, I'm coming over,' said Miriam.

Dennis did not return home that Sunday. He drove about aimlessly for several hours, then he had a number of drinks in a pub, then he called on Lynn. She opened the door to him in her dressing-gown – it was early in the evening, but she had been taking a bath and washing her hair. Perhaps if she hadn't been wearing so little and smelling so fragrant, they wouldn't have made love. Dennis had come to her with no such intention, indeed with no intention at all: he was all at sea, tossed by violent waves of anger, guilt, self-pity, anxiety; sure only that if he slunk back to Angela without seeing Lynn, after Angela had dared him to go to her, then he would be broken, unmanned for ever after. So he went to Lynn, who read in his face what had happened as soon as she opened the door, and drew him inside, and into her arms, and into her bed. They made love, clumsily and urgently at first, then a second time with more rapture, then once more with desperate effort, Lynn licking him erect, and Dennis groaning as he squeezed a few last drops of seed from his aching balls. He woke the next morning to a grey drizzle, the suspicious scrutiny of Lynn's two-year-old, Gareth, and the consciousness that he was well and truly crucified on the cross of adultery. He drove Lynn to work, dropping her on a street corner half a mile from the factory gates so that they would not be observed arriving together. He went through the day in a trance, making no decisions. In the evening he met Lynn at the same corner and drove her home. There was a bedsitter vacant in the house, and Dennis rented it. He ate his evening meal with Lynn, and slept in her bed at night, but before dawn he would creep upstairs to his dreary little room, for he did not like to be discovered in her bed by Gareth in the mornings. He made no attempt to get in touch with Angela. He made no plans, and Lynn, to his relief, did not press him to declare any. She managed to conduct their affair as if it were an extension of their office relationship. She was calm, efficient, self-effacing. It was as if she could only

639

express passion in her letters – and in bed, where she clung and coiled herself about him with a fierce intensity that filled him with wonderment, delight and dread in equal proportions. Only then did she seem to be staking some desperate claim on his future, but if he praised her afterwards she would smile ironically just as when he used to compliment her on her shorthand and typing.

The breach between Dennis and Angela sent shock waves rippling through their circle of friends. For many, it marked the end of an era, the end of illusions. 'We are not immune,' Miriam declared solemnly, and when Michael asked her what she was on about, merely repeated, 'We are not immune.' By 'we' she meant their circle, their peer group of enlightened, educated Christians; and by 'not immune' she meant that there was no magic protection, in their values and beliefs, against failure in personal relationships. If anything had seemed solid and indestructible in that sphere, it had been the marriage of Dennis and Angela, which had been founded on so long and faithful a betrothal, and had withstood such cruel trials and tribulations; yet it had succumbed at last to the most banal of matrimonial accidents.

Dennis, of course, was chiefly blamed, especially by the women; yet they could not, in their heart of hearts, entirely absolve Angela from all responsibility, for they had all noted, ever since the death of Anne, some fundamental absence of tenderness in her character which, however understandable in itself, might well, they agreed, in the course of the many conversations and phone calls which enveloped the affair in a web of words, have driven Dennis to another woman's arms. They also blamed Lynn for throwing herself at Dennis, though the discovery that she had a child complicated their response, for they prided themselves on their compassion for one-parent families, especially young women who had refused the easy options of abortion or adoption and were struggling to bring up their babies alone. It was natural enough that a girl so situated might persuade herself that she was in love with her boss, when what she was really in love with was her idealized picture of his family life. Clearly the attraction of Dennis for Lynn was as a surrogate father for her child rather than as a lover. Yet his response had a reckless gallantry about it that some secretly admired.

Michael, meeting Dennis by appointment at a pub one evening to hand over a suitcase of clothes, found him shy and defensive, but was himself overwhelmed – not with envy, exactly, for no one could envy Dennis the moral and emotional mess he had got himself into – but with a kind of admiration mingled with self-doubt. The unexpected presence of Lynn, sitting beside Dennis in the pub, brought home to Michael the astonishing reality of Dennis's affair, and made him feel himself less real. In the modern literature to which Michael was devoted, adultery was the sign of authenticity in personal life, and marriage the realm of habit, conformity and compromise. By rights, therefore, it was he, Michael, who ought to have been sitting in the corner of this pub, holding the hand of the pretty pale-faced girl with the nicely shaped breasts, and Dennis, dull, dependable old Dennis, who ought to have been pushing his way through the swing door with a suitcase full of shirts and underwear, a nervous envoy from the world of bourgeois morality. It was he, Michael, who ought to have been defying bourgeois morality, and yet he knew that he never would, he would never have the courage, or the wickedness, or indeed the provocation. For ever since the weekend in Kent, he didn't know whether it was because she thought he had died in the snow, or because he had agreed to her doing the social workers' course, but Miriam had stopped being aggressive, had indeed become positively sweet-tempered. They seemed to have renegotiated their marriage and to be bound to each other by some new, more pragmatic and, from Miriam's point of view, more equitable contract. He had been content with his bargain until he saw Dennis in the corner of the pub holding Lynn's hand, a man who had torn up his contract and tossed the pieces in the face of the world. He tried to explain all this to Dennis after Lynn had left, early, to relieve Gareth's babysitter, and several beers had loosened his tongue. 'It's like *Heart of Darkness*,' he said. 'You're Kurtz and I'm Marlow. See?'

Dennis shook his head uncomprehendingly. 'How's Angela?' he said. 'How's Nicole?'

'Fine, fine,' said Michael vaguely, forgetting for the moment, in his absorption in his own fate, that Dennis had deserted them.

So different people reacted differently to the news as it spread. Adrian was alarmed that the episode would bring Catholics for an Open Church into disrepute, and interfere with preparations for the Paschal Festival. Edward was saddened and Tessa intrigued. Violet sent extensive, incoherent letters to all parties from the long-stay psychiatric hospital where she was now confined. Ruth prayed fervently for a reconciliation. Miles was not very interested. Polly felt selfishly relieved that the plague had passed over her own house. Dennis himself, after a couple of weeks, was profoundly miserable, and longed only to be honourably released from his involvement with Lynn. He was exhausted from nightly sex, depressed by the meanness of his surroundings, acutely embarrassed by the gossip at work, and hag-ridden with guilt on account of Angela and the children, especially Nicole.

In the end it was Austin who rescued him – Austin who was urged by Miriam to mediate in the affair and attempt a reconciliation, Austin who had a long interview with Lynn, and somehow persuaded her to tell Dennis to go back to Angela, and persuaded Angela to accept him back without injuring his pride, and persuaded Dennis to let Lynn leave the factory and find a new job. So, after three weeks in which the earth had moved, life returned to normal again. Dennis and Angela picked up the threads of their lives together, a little wary of each other, a little chastened, but both hugely relieved. Their children, who had begun to exhibit alarming symptoms of delinquency and emotional disturbance under the impact of the crisis, swiftly reverted to normal. Their friends tactfully pretended that nothing had happened. For the first few weeks they contrived to go to bed at different times, and slept stretched along the outer edges of their double bed, but one night, by some intuitive mutual agreement, they rolled into each other's arms and sealed their reconciliation.

Austin's part in all this was, of course, highly acclaimed. It seemed to them all that there was something poetic, something positively providential, about the way he had repaired the marriage that he had himself solemnized so many years ago. It was a bit of a surprise, admittedly, when he turned up at the Paschal Festival with Lynn in tow; and since Angela was there too it put rather a strain on Christian fellowship and bonhomie. And it made them all blink to see Austin and Lynn happily holding hands at the party that followed the Midnight Mass. But then, there were plenty of things to make one blink at the Catholics for an Open Church Paschal Festival.

SEVEN

How it is

When Jeremy's programme about the Paschal Festival was transmitted, Michael recorded it on videotape at the College's Audio-Visual Resources Centre. Because of the furore that followed the broadcast, Adrian asked him to write an account of it for reference purposes. Being rather proud of his media know-how, Michael in fact produced quite a polished transcript. It read, he thought, like a kind of coda to everything that had happened to them in matters of belief. He was able to identify all but one of the voices over.

TRANSCRIPT OF THE ELTON SPECIAL, 'EASTER WITH THE NEW CATHOLICS', AS TRANSMITTED 24/4/75.

Opening shot of the College playing fields, just before dawn, looking eastwards. Silhouetted against the horizon, a large boulder with a figure seated on it, back to camera. Silence.

Cut to

Close up AUSTIN
AUSTIN: We can't be sure that the Resurrection actually happened.

Cut to

Playing fields. Dawn. Looking westwards. Long shot of some two hundred people sitting on the grass. Camera moves in, pans over faces in close-up. Faint dawn light reflected in their tired, expectant faces. Sound: birdsong.

Cut to

Close up ADRIAN

ADRIAN: I think we can be pretty sure that no Pope will ever try to make an infallible pronouncement again.

Cut to

Playing fields. Looking eastwards. Two women in flowing robes of saffron and blue approach the figure on the boulder. Sound: arpeggio on flute. The figure turns and extends arms. The skirts of her pleated white robe are attached to her wrists and open out like wings. The other two fall back as if astonished and fearful.

Cut to

Close up MIRIAM

MIRIAM: I can imagine circumstances in which I would consider having an abortion.

Cut to

Playing fields. The tip of the sun's disc now appears on the eastern horizon. The three women begin a dance-mime illustrating the story of the two Marys and the angel at the empty tomb in Matthew. Sound: flute and percussion.

Cut to

Close up RUTH

RUTH: Well, why shouldn't nuns dance? I don't see anything funny in the idea. (Laughs) Unless it was me dancing . . .

Cut to

Playing fields. The sun has risen. It shines through the diaphanous robes of the three dancers. The angel mimes the resurrection of Christ, leaping from the ground. Slow motion.

VOICE OVER (*Ruth*): After all, the psalm says, 'Let them dance in praise of his name, playing to him on strings and drums.'

On the soundtrack the flute and percussion fade out and are replaced by the communal singing of 'The Lord of the Dance':

Dance, then, wherever you may be,
I am the Lord of the dance, said he, etc.

Cut to

College chapel. Night. The end of midnight mass. The packed

congregation is singing 'The Lord of the Dance' enthusiastically. A few people begin to dance in the aisles, up towards the altar. More join in.

AUSTIN (superimposed):

EASTER WITH THE NEW CATHOLICS
THE ELTON SPECIAL

Cut to

Main road, morning. Cars and lorries passing noisily. Zoom in on arrowed AA sign, 'OC PASCHAL FESTIVAL'.

VOICE OVER (*Adrian*): We were rather chuffed to get our own AA sign. It shows we're not just an eccentric fringe group . . .

Cut to

Main entrance hall of the College, crowded with people greeting each other, kissing, shaking hands, etc. Queue at desk marked 'Registration'. Banner on wall: 'Catholics for an Open Church. Paschal Festival 75. Peace and Love in the Lord.' Roar of conversation.

VOICE OVER (*Michael*): Oh, absolutely all sorts of people – teachers, students, civil servants, housewives, priests, nuns . . . no, I don't think we've got any factory workers. I suppose it's essentially a middle-class movement . . .

Cut to

Lecture room, nearly full. ADRIAN on rostrum with DAN FIGUERA.

ADRIAN: I know Dan Figuera doesn't look like a Professor of Theology, but – (Laughter. Close up of DAN FIGUERA in battledress blouse) But I assure you that he is, and one of the foremost figures in the exciting Latin American school of liberation theologians. It's a great pleasure and privilege . . .

Cut to

DAN FIGUERA at the lectern.

DAN FIGUERA: Three questions. One: is Christianity a faith or a religion? I say it is a faith. Two: is its true dimension history or eternity? I say, history. Three: is its aim salvation or liberation? I say salvation *is* liberation . . .

VOICE OVER (*Austin*): What Figuera is saying, basically, is that Christianity took a wrong turning as early as the first century. According to him, Christ came to start a revolution, but instead became the object of a cult.

DAN FIGUERA: It's obvious from the New Testament that Jesus and his disciples thought the revolution, which they called the Kingdom of God, was imminent. Instead of making it happen, the early Christians turned Jesus into a religion, exactly like a hundred other religions in the Mediterranean world at the time, complete with mysteries, metaphysics, and priests.

Cut to

College refectory. Lunch. Pan shot of people at tables eating and discussing. Sound: babble of conversation, clash of cutlery, crockery, etc. Shot of table with AUSTIN, EDWARD, TESSA.

AUSTIN: What did you think of it then?

TESSA: I'm afraid I can't buy the idea of Christ as a freedom fighter.

EDWARD: He seemed to be saying that the Crucifixion was more important than the Resurrection. I always thought it was the other way round.

AUSTIN: Well, of course, there is some independent evidence about the Crucifixion. We can't be sure that the Resurrection actually happened.

Long shot of ADRIAN on his feet, rapping on the table for silence.

ADRIAN: The forum on 'Towards a new theology of sex' will begin at two o'clock, and afterwards we'll split into buzz groups.

Cut to

Lecture room, afternoon. On the rostrum, seated behind a long table, MILES, FIONA FARRELL, BEDE, DOROTHY, and ADRIAN in the chair.

ADRIAN: We've got on our panel a housewife, a priest, a single woman and a . . . bachelor.

Close up on MILES

VOICE OVER (*Miles*): I didn't really want to come here at all. I don't really have a lot in common with Catholics for an Open

Church. I mean, liturgically and theologically, I'm a conservative. I mean, I'd bring back the Latin mass if I had half a
chance, and deport Dan Figuera as an undesirable alien ...
But it is a public forum, and I think one has a duty to bear
witness to one's convictions.

Cut to

MILES on his feet.

MILES: There must be no more distinctions between Jew and
Greek, slave and free, male and female ... (pause) straight
and gay.

Cut to

Close up FIONA

FIONA: I do so agree with what Dorothy was saying about sex
education. The first time I felt sexual desire I thought I must
be sickening for flu ... (Laughter) And of course I agree that
we ought to tell our young people about contraception and so
on, and not be shocked out of our wits if they decide to have
sex before marriage or turn out to be homosexual, as Miles
was saying, but ... But. Where does permissiveness stop, I ask
myself. Is there anything that's definitely not on? Is there
anything we can all agree is wrong in this field? Abortion, I
suppose, but that's not exactly ...

Cut to

A seminar room. A group of about a dozen women.

MIRIAM: I always used to be strongly opposed to abortion, I
signed petitions and marched and so on. I still get angry at
the messianic attitude of some of the extreme women's groups,
as if abortion was the greatest thing since sliced bread. But
now I'm not so sure that it's always and absolutely evil. I can
imagine circumstances in which I would consider having an
abortion. What about you, Angela? I mean, you've got a mentally handicapped ...

ANGELA: (inaudible)

MIRIAM: I mean, supposing you found you were pregnant
again?

ANGELA: I just can't answer hypothetical ... I suppose I'd
have to consider it.

MIRIAM: You see, I'm not sure Bede's right when he said we must completely dissociate the abortion issue from the contraception issue. I mean, if in spite of taking every precaution, I accidentally become pregnant, what am I supposed to think? That God has punished me for using contraceptives? That he's trying to make a fool of me? Obviously I don't believe in such a God. It seems to me that God has given women the freedom to control our own bodies, and we can't avoid the responsibility of using that freedom.

Cut to

The Refectory. Evening. Dinner is nearly over. ADRIAN raps on the table. BEDE stands up.

BEDE: Just to say that there'll be confessions after dinner in the Chapel. Basically, we'll just sit around and talk about our personal failures and hangups, then at the end I'll give general absolution. If anybody here is still into old-style confession, St Peter and Paul's is just around the corner . . . (Laughter)

RUTH stands up.

RUTH: And if anyone is interested in a prayer group, there'll be one in the Quiet Room starting at eight.

Cut to

The Chapel. Evening. About twenty people are sitting round in a circle, looking self-conscious.

BEDE: Look, it might help to break the ice if I set the ball rolling. My own problem is anger. A well-known vice of celibates. (Subdued laughter)

VOICE OVER (*Michael*): I haven't been to old-style confession for years and years. Neither have my children. It's really quite extraordinary. Twenty years ago, if you went into a Catholic church on a Saturday evening, you'd always find a queue of people waiting to go to Confession. And looking as though they were hating every minute of it.

VOICE OVER (*Austin*): Oh yes, I think there's still a place for the sacrament of penance, definitely. But it should be collective as well as individual. Just think of all the misery and repression and suffering the Church has caused in the past. Persecuting heretics, Jews. Torture. Burning at the stake. Terrifying people

649

with the fear of Hell. I think we should do penance for that daily.

Cut to

The Quiet Room. RUTH and some others sitting in armchairs and on the floor in a loosely formed circle.

RUTH: Let's just start with a period of silence, just making space for the Holy Spirit.

VOICE OVER (*Ruth*): There's no set form for a prayer group. It's however the spirit moves you. Sometimes we recite set prayers, like the Our Father or the Gloria, sometimes we sing hymns, sometimes one of the group will witness, tell the others what the Lord has meant to them. Perhaps someone will ask to be baptized in the spirit.

Cut to

The Quiet Room. A woman is kneeling and the others are standing round her with their hands outstretched, fingertips touching just above her head.

VOICE OVER (*Ruth*): It's like a second baptism. It's a gift from God. Not everyone receives it. Very few receive it the first time they ask for it. Some people actually fight against it, which is not so surprising, really. Because it changes your whole life.

VOICE OVER (*Miles*): The growth of Pentecostalism in the Catholic Church is certainly remarkable, because it's a style of religious behaviour that's utterly alien to the Catholic tradition – intensely Protestant, in fact. There's no doubt in my mind that it's a reaction against the demythologizing and politicizing of the Faith that's been going on since Vatican II. The really emotive side of Catholic devotion has withered away – Benediction, Latin plainchant, the rosary, and so on. The magic has gone, the sense of the supernatural, which is what people want from religion, ultimately. So they turn to prayer groups – healing and speaking in tongues and whatnot.

Cut to

Close up of RUTH, eyes shut, speaking in tongues.
RUTH: (unintelligible)

VOICE OVER (*Austin*): I think you could say that the crisis in the Church today is a crisis of language.

Cut to

The College forecourt. Night. No lights visible. A crowd holding unlighted candles are gathered round a brazier. BEDE, dressed in white vestments, strikes a spark to ignite the charcoal bricks in the brazier.

BEDE: Dear friends in Christ, on this most holy night, when Our Lord Jesus Christ passed from death to life, the Church invites her children throughout the world to come together in vigil and prayer . . .

VOICE OVER (*Austin*): That metaphor of the Church as mother is highly misleading. Historically, the Church has been much more like a tyrannical father towards its children.

The Easter candle is brought to BEDE. He inserts five grains of incense in the form of a cross on the side of the candle and lights the candle from the fire.

VOICE OVER (*Adrian*): Undoubtedly the developments of the last fifteen years or so have shattered the old certainties for ever. I think we can be pretty sure that no Pope will ever try to make an infallible pronouncement again, for instance.

BEDE holds the candle aloft.

BEDE (chants): Christ our light.

ALL (chant): Thanks be to God.

BEDE, carrying the candle, and preceded by an incense-bearer, leads the people in procession into the College, along darkened corridors.

VOICE OVER (*Polly*): Certainly Catholics are much more tolerant, much more liberal than they used to be. I was brought up as one and the nuns gave us to understand that unless you were a good Catholic, your chances of getting to heaven were pretty slim. Most of the people at this affair don't seem to think that they're in any way superior to Protestants or Jews, Hindus or Muslims, or for that matter, atheists and agnostics. Which is very decent and humble of them, but it does raise the question, why be a Catholic at all, rather than something else, or just nothing?

651

The College Chapel. Dark. Empty. Camera on open door. Faint glow of approaching light. Incense bearer appears, followed by BEDE. He stops on the threshold and lifts the candle high.

BEDE (chants): Christ our light.

ALL: (chant) Thanks be to God.

ADRIAN, immediately behind BEDE, lights his small candle from the Easter candle.

VOICE OVER (*Adrian*): I think one has to be fairly tough-minded about this. Christianity *is* the best of the world religions – none of the others can touch it for universality of appeal. And, for all its historical sins, Catholicism is the best form of Christianity.

Cut to

The corridor leading to the chapel. The light is passed along the procession from candle to candle.

VOICE OVER (*Angela*): Oh, I'll always be a Catholic, I couldn't imagine being anything else. I suppose it's only chance, yes, the way I was brought up. If I'd been born a Baptist or something I daresay I'd be a Baptist. I think you need a religion to get you through life at all, and mine happens to be the Catholic one.

Cut to

The Chapel. BEDE goes to the altar and fixes the Easter candle in its holder. The congregation file in and take their seats, extinguishing candles.

VOICE OVER (*Tessa*): I really don't bother too much about theology, to be honest. A lot of things I had to subscribe to when I joined the Catholic Church even Catholics don't believe now. I sometimes wonder if it matters whether it's true, as long as it helps people to cope. And if it doesn't help people to cope, would it be any use being true?

DOROTHY goes to the lectern.

DOROTHY (reads): 'In the beginning God created the heavens and the earth. Now the earth was a formless void . . .'

VOICE OVER (*Austin*): Catholics, like most other Christians, have accepted that Genesis is a poem, a myth, not a factual account of the creation. It's rather more difficult for them to accept that a lot of the New Testament may not be literally true either.

Cut to

EDWARD at lectern.

EDWARD (reads): 'And we believe that having died with Christ we shall enter life with him: Christ, as we know, having been raised from the dead will never die again. Death has no power over him any more . . .'

VOICE OVER (*Miles*): I do think it's a pity the way they keep meddling with the Bible. 'Death has no power over him any more.' How feeble it sounds, compared to, 'And death shall have no dominion over him.'

VOICE OVER (*Polly*): I think death is the basis of all religion, don't you? Hearing mass again after all these years, and in English, I was struck by how many references there are to dying and eternal life, almost every other line. I never realized that when I was young. When my father died, a couple of years ago, I found the ritual a great comfort. I shouldn't be surprised if I called for a priest myself if I knew I was dying.

Cut to

The congregation relighting candles for the renewal of Baptismal Promises.

BEDE: Do you reject Satan?

ALL: I do.

BEDE: And all his works?

ALL: I do . . .

VOICE OVER (*Ruth*): Oh, yes, I believe in the existence of the Devil, evil spirits, certainly. I think anyone who has been baptized in the spirit is sensitive to these things. I know people in the Charismatic Renewal who have had very frightening experiences.

VOICE OVER (*Miriam*): No, not as an actual being. The Devil I think is a sort of personification of the evil in all of us, the potential evil.

Cut to

BEDE, celebrating mass, turns to face the congregation.

BEDE: The peace of the Lord be with you always.

ALL: And also with you.

BEDE: Let us offer each other the sign of peace.

BEDE advances smilingly upon a girl at the end of the front row and embraces her warmly. The rest of the congregation smile, kiss, shake hands, etc., as BEDE moves along the front row, greeting each person.

VOICE OVER (*Dorothy*): Catholics, English Catholics, anyway, and Irish, have always been very frightened of the body, of physical contact. In our parish they think it's terribly daring to even shake hands with your neighbour.

Cut to

BEDE, facing the congregation, the host in his hand, raises it over the patten.

BEDE: This is the Lamb of God, who takes away the sins of the world. Happy are those who are called to His supper . . .

VOICE OVER (*Angela*): When my little girl, she's mentally handi-capped, wanted to go to Communion with the rest of the family, I didn't see why not. She's always been very interested in the mass, very reverent. Some busybody, a woman in the parish said, 'But does she really understand what it's about? Could she explain?' I said, 'Could you?' That shut her up.

The people in the congregation begin to come up to the altar to receive communion. BEDE administers the host, which most receive in the hand. DOROTHY and ADRIAN each take round a chalice. VOICE OVER (*Polly*): In my day it would have been sacrilege to touch the host with your hand. And as for drinking the wine! In fact, the mass is hardly recognizable. It's certainly more comprehensible, but rather flat, somehow. Like a room that's too brightly lit. I think you have to have shadows in religion. Bits of mystery and magic.

VOICE OVER (*Michael*): I suppose it all goes back to primitive ritual, like when a tribe would kill their king and eat his flesh and drink his blood to inherit his strength. Then you got a lot of vegetation gods who were identified with the crops and the vine, bread and wine. I don't think it's surprising that Jesus adopted this archetypal symbolism. That's why it's terribly important to have communion under both kinds. Otherwise you completely mess up the symbolism.

VOICE OVER (*Edward*): I suppose I'm very old-fashioned about this. I believe Jesus Christ is really and truly present in the Eucharist. Don't ask me to explain it. Otherwise it would be just a rather empty ritual as far as I'm concerned.

Cut to

BEDE, smiling, arms outspread, faces the congregation.

BEDE: The mass is ended, go in peace.

ALL: Thanks be to God.

An ensemble of guitars, recorders, percussion, etc., strikes up the tune of 'The Lord of the Dance', and the congregation sing:

I danced in the morning
When the world was begun
And I danced in the moon
And the stars and the sun,
And I came down from heaven and
I danced on earth,
At Bethlehem I had my birth.

Dance, then, wherever you may be
I am the Lord of the Dance, said he.
And I'll lead you all
Wherever you may be
And I'll lead you all in the dance, said he, etc.

A few members of the congregation step into the aisles and begin to dance in a free-form, improvised fashion. More join in. They move up towards the altar. BEDE joins in. All around the altar people are dancing.

VOICE OVER (*Who?*): Undoubtedly the Catholic Church has been turned upside down in the last two decades.

Cut to

The Students' Common Room. Night. Party in progress. Disco

655

music. Shots of TESSA dancing with BEDE, MICHAEL with POLLY, and AUSTIN holding hands with LYNN, tapping his feet.
VOICE OVER (*Who?*): Many things have changed – attitudes to authority, sex, worship, other Christians, other religions. But perhaps the most fundamental change is one that the majority of Catholics themselves are scarcely conscious of. It's the fading away of the traditional Catholic metaphysic – that marvellously complex and ingenious synthesis of theology and cosmology and casuistry, which situated individual souls on a kind of spiritual Snakes and Ladders board, motivated them with equal doses of hope and fear, and promised them, if they persevered in the game, an eternal reward. The board was marked out very clearly, decorated with all kinds of picturesque motifs, and governed by intricate rules and provisos. Heaven, hell, purgatory, limbo. Mortal, venial and original sin. Angels, devils, saints, and Our Lady Queen of Heaven. Grace, penance, relics, indulgences and all the rest of it. Millions of Catholics no doubt still believe in all that literally. But belief is gradually fading. That metaphysic is no longer taught in schools and seminaries in the more advanced countries, and Catholic children are growing up knowing little or nothing about it. Within another generation or two it will have disappeared, superseded by something less vivid but more tolerant. Christian unity is now a feasible objective for the first time since the Reformation.

Cut to

The College playing fields. Dawn. The rim of light on the horizon. The tired but expectant faces of the crowd. The nuns begin their dance mime of the Resurrection.
VOICE OVER (*Who?*): But Christian belief will be different from what it used to be, what it used to be for Catholics, anyway. We must not only believe, but know that we believe, live our belief and yet see it from outside, aware that in another time, another place, we would have believed something different (indeed, did ourselves believe differently at different times and places in our lives) without feeling that this invalidates belief. Just as when reading a novel, or writing one for that matter,

we maintain a double consciousness of the characters as both, as it were, real and fictitious, free and determined, and know that however absorbing and convincing we may find it, it is not the only story we shall want to read (or, as the case may be, write) but part of an endless sequence of stories by which man has sought and will always seek to make sense of life. And death.

Freeze frame of dancers leaping from the ground, the sun shining through their robes.

ENDS

The *Catholic Herald* liked the programme, but the *Universe* panned it. The *Telegraph* said it showed that the Catholic Church was now in the same state of confusion as all the other Christian churches. The *Guardian*'s TV critic suggested that the dancing nuns should be signed up for a programme to be called 'Top of the Popes'. There were many resignations from Catholics for an Open Church after the broadcast. Some members resigned because they thought the image it presented of the organization was too radical, others because it was not radical enough. The bishop of the diocese was displeased for a number of reasons, and disciplined Bede for his part in the proceedings. A specially convened meeting of the College Governors deplored the use of College premises for the event, and Michael, as member of staff responsible, was severely reprimanded. His colleagues rallied round him, and wrote a letter to the Governors in his support. When, however, a couple of years later, the Catholic authorities announced plans to close down the College, as part of the nation-wide cutback in teacher training, many thought that the Paschal Festival had contributed to this adverse decision, and Michael became less popular with his colleagues. Offered early retirement or alternative employment as a schoolteacher, he chose the former, and intends to move to London to try his luck as a freelance writer. With his pension and Miriam's salary as a social worker, they should be reasonably secure. Their son Martin is reading physics at Imperial College and Helen, no longer a tomboy, but a

657

rather stunning young woman of Pre-Raphaelite looks, is reading modern languages at Oxford, where she met Polly's Jason again and, to the astonishment of both families, converted him to Catholicism. When she heard about it, Polly commented cynically that she supposed that even in these liberated days a nice Catholic girl wouldn't sleep with non-Catholic boys. In fact the two young people are quite traditionally and chastely engaged.

The Paschal Festival, which Adrian had hoped would inaugurate a new chapter in the annals of Catholics for an Open Church, seemed rather to hasten its demise as a vital force, perhaps by uncovering the irreconcilable variety of aims and assumptions among its members. Adrian survived a vote of no confidence as Chairman, but resigned anyway. The movement continues in a shadowy form, but without his or Dorothy's participation. They are both, these days, heavily involved in the Catholic Marriage Encounter movement, an importation from America which aims to 'make good marriages better' by gathering couples together on residential weekends, lecturing to them about married life, and making them write confessional letters to each other. Edward and Tessa, whom they persuaded to go on such a weekend, found it all rather embarrassing, and not only because the conference centre turned out to be, under a different name, the one where they had first had sexual intercourse. A couple of years ago, Edward decided to risk the operation on his spine, and happily it was a success. He has taken up athletic pursuits again, and he and Tessa go jogging together every evening, cheered derisively by their two younger children slouched in front of the television. The two older ones are at University. It is known to Tessa that Becky is sleeping with her boyfriend, but not to Edward, who would not stand for it, and is sufficiently concerned that she does not go to mass any more. Edward has become an enthusiastic student of the Holy Shroud of Turin, after seeing a film about it a couple of years ago. He will explain in detail to anyone prepared to listen that the image of the man on the Shroud is anatomically perfect, that the wounds shown correspond exactly to those inflicted at the Crucifixion as reported in the Gospels and interpreted by modern historical scholarship and forensic medicine, that pollen tests have proved the fabric has been in Palestine at some point in its history, and that nobody has been able to offer a simple, materialistic explanation of how the image got on to it. Suppose it was scorched into the shroud by radiant energy released at the Resurrection? Edward admits that this is only a theory, but is encouraged by the Shroud in his inclination to ignore the theories of modern theologians and stick to his old-fashioned belief in the Divinity of Christ.

After due consideration, Adrian and Dorothy did not invite Dennis and Angela to a Marriage Encounter weekend, fearing that it might reopen old wounds. In fact, that marriage is in reasonably good shape. Shortly after the affair with Lynn, Dennis decided that it was time to make a move, to a new job, a new place, and Angela did not resist the idea. He is now managing director of a small firm manufacturing electronic ignition systems, on the south coast. He has bought a small boat, and spends most of his spare time pottering about on it. Angela is much involved in raising funds for a sheltered community in which they hope Nicole will eventually find a home. The two boys are both at college. Angela's brother Tom is married and has two young babies. To see him with them makes Angela want to laugh or cry at the way their lives have got so absurdly out of synchronization. Tom and Rosemary run a residential home for kids in care.

Austin left the priesthood shortly after the Paschal Festival and, much to everybody's astonishment, married Lynn. Their friends were scarcely less astonished when, nine months later to the day, Lynn bore him a son. Austin was lucky enough to get a research fellowship at the Poly to do a PhD in the sociology of religion. The Department is Marxist in orientation, but divided ideologically between empiricists of the old New Left and younger Althusserians intoxicated by Continental theory. There are factions, arguments, confrontations, pamphleteering and political manoeuvring. It is all very exciting and exhausting, and, to Austin, reminiscent of goings-on in the Catholic Church since Vatican II. He still regards himself as a kind of Catholic, but, partly in the interests of his research, goes to a different church or chapel each Sunday – Catholic, Anglican, Orthodox, Free Church, Quaker meeting house, in rotation.

Violet is not a Jehovah's Witness any more, but a Sufist. While she was in the long-stay psychiatric hospital she read a book about Sufism, and when she was discharged she went to stay with a Sufist community to learn more about it. Sufism seems to suit her better than Christianity because she has not had a nervous breakdown for two years, nor does she take tranquillizers any more. She lost faith in the Jehovah's Witnesses when none of the things that were supposed to happen in 1975 happened, but her imagination is still markedly apocalyptic. She is convinced that a nuclear catastrophe is imminent, and that Sufists will be the only ones able to cope because they know how to tap the full potential of the human being. She and Robin, whom Caroline eventually deserted for a younger and more virile lecturer at the University, now enjoy a surprisingly tranquil companionate marriage. Violet finds that doing without sex completely is a great relief to the spirit, and Robin, who is himself heavily into yoga and macro-biotic diet, is content with this arrangement, appeasing his lower instincts with occasional clandestine visits to a massage parlour in a neighbouring industrial town. When Polly discovered that Jeremy had been unfaithful to her with Gertrude (and, it emerged, with every other *au pair* girl they had ever had, plus scores of research assistants) she divorced him. The oast-house was sold at a vast profit and Polly invested her share in a feminist publishing house of which she is a director. She lives in a flat in London with her daughter and is deeply involved in the women's movement. Jeremy emigrated to California, where he makes highly profitable pornographic films. Miles is still at Cambridge, but has gone back to the Church of England because, he says, there doesn't seem to be much difference between Anglican and Roman beliefs any more and he prefers the liturgy of the former. An unpleasant scene at the Catholic church where he used to worship, following his appearance on Jeremy's programme, also contributed to this decision. Ruth is headmistress of her school in the North of England, a job which has curtailed her charismatic activities, though she still derives great strength and consolation from a weekly prayer-group attended by interested staff and sixth-formers. I teach English literature at a redbrick university and write novels in my spare time, slowly, and hustled by history.

While I was writing this last chapter, Pope Paul VI died and Pope John Paul I was elected. Before I could type it up, Pope John Paul I had died and been succeeded by John Paul II, the first non-Italian Pope for four hundred and fifty years: a Pole, a poet, a philosopher, a linguist, an athlete, a man of the people, a man of destiny, dramatically chosen, instantly popular – but theologically conservative. A changing Church acclaims a Pope who evidently thinks that change has gone far enough. What will happen now? All bets are void, the future is uncertain, but it will be interesting to watch. Reader, farewell!